I crawled over to the drapes that
concealed the glass doors.

I twitched aside the lower corner to peer out into the night-swamped courtyard.

Shadows marked the glass in blotches and lines. Winged shapes flittered across the sky.

A slender green finger was tapping on the glass. I recoiled. A branch had elongated until it reached the doors, as if trying to find a path inside. A bat perched on the swaying end, staring at me with obsidian eyes. I blinked, and it vanished.

A man pressed against the door. He had Vai's face and he wore a magnificent dash jacket printed with fishes spilling out of gourds.

"We shall find a way in," he said in a low, sweet voice. The scent of guava penetrated the glass separating us. I wanted to kiss him to taste the fruit, but I knew better. "Yee cannot escape us. We know yee killed her."

The latch turned but caught because it was locked. The key shuddered in a gust of wind.

"You can't come in," I whispered.

It was impossible to stare into those dark-lashed brown eyes and not be drawn closer; his lips tempted me; his hands reminded me of the kind of work they could do. But he was not Vai. He was an opia, the spirit of a dead man.

"Open the door," he whispered, "and yee shall have what yee so badly desire."

The hot look in his eyes drowned me. Next thing I knew, my hand was touching the key.

BOOKS BY KATE ELLIOTT

The Spiritwalker Trilogy
Cold Magic
Cold Fire
Cold Steel

Crossroads
Spirit Gate
Shadow Gate
Traitors' Gate

Crown of Stars
King's Dragon
Prince of Dogs
The Burning Stone
Child of Flame
The Gathering Storm
In the Ruins
Crown of Stars

Jaran
Jaran
An Earthly Crown
His Conquering Sword
The Law of Becoming

Writing with Melanie Rawn & Jennifer Roberson
The Golden Key

Writing as Alis A. Rasmussen
The Labyrinth Gate

The Highroad Trilogy
A Passage of Stars
Revolution's Shore
The Price of Ransom

COLD STEEL

THE SPIRITWALKER TRILOGY: BOOK THREE

KATE ELLIOTT

www.orbitbooks.net

Orbit
Hachette Book Group
237 Park Avenue, New York, NY 10017
HachetteBookGroup.com

First Edition: June 2013

Orbit is an imprint of Hachette Book Group, Inc. The Orbit name
and logo are trademarks of Little, Brown Book Group Limited.

The Hachette Speakers Bureau provides a wide range of
authors for speaking events. To find out more, go to
www.hachettespeakersbureau.com or call (866) 376-6591.

The publisher is not responsible for websites (or their content) that are
not owned by the publisher.

Library of Congress Cataloging-in-Publication Data
Elliott, Kate, 1958-
  Cold Steel / Kate Elliott.—First Edition.
    pages cm—(The Spiritwalker Trilogy ; Book Three)
  ISBN 978-0-316-08090-3 (trade pbk.)—ISBN 978-0-316-21515-2
(ebook) 1. Fantasy fiction. 2. Epic fiction. I. Title.
  PS3555.L5917C66 2013
  813'.54—dc23

                                              2012041859

        10 9 8 7 6 5 4 3 2 1

                    RRD-C

        Printed in the United States of America

*To the women who in one way or another supported me
through an immensely difficult drafting process.
This book is dedicated to you, sisters all.*

To quote writer Tricia Sullivan: We have to press on.

Atlantic Ocean

ICE

IVERNIAN
CONFEDERATION

Tara

Deva

BRIGANTIA

Ebora

Lindon

ORDOVICI
CONFEDERATION

Reiacum

Isca

TRINOBANTES

Sulis

Temes R.

Camlun

DUMNONIA

Londun

CANTIACI

Porto
Dumnos

Adurnam

ATREBATES

Audu

Area of detail

Havery

Sicauna R.

Arras

Lutetia

VENETI DUKES

PARISI

Rem

Stampae

Cena

Turo

Senones

GALLIC PRINCES
AND DUKES

Alesia

ARVERNI

Lemovis

Liyonum

ASTURIAS

Xixon

Burdigala

Porto Victoria

Garumna R.

Bracara

CANTABRIA

ZAZPIAK

Iruña

BAT

Tolosa

Rodonus R.

Coimbra

Numantia

Carcaso

OYO

Massilia

Termes

Iberus R.

Porto Lisso

Lisso R.

Okilis

Segeda

New Oyo

Ampurias

Ebora

LUSITANA

IBERIA

Tarraco

Ituci

Saguntum

Oba R.

Carmona

Ebussos

Tartessos

Gadir

Malaca

Nova Carta

Mediterranean Sea

Detail inset:

Reiacum

CATULANIA

TRINOBANTES

Sulis

Temes R.

Camlun

Londun

CANTIACI

Meens

Solent R.

Newfield

Lemanis

Cantiacorum
Four Moons House

TARRANT

Adurnam

ATREBATES

Audui

© 2010 Jeffrey L. Ward

Acknowledgments

Katharine Kerr suffered through more versions, false starts, detours, and backtracks than I really have a right to inflict on anyone. This book could not have been written without her patient encouragement.

Sherwood Smith, Michelle Sagara, Karen Miller, Fragano Ledgister, Shweta Narayan, Nathaniel Smith, Dani McKenzie, Mark Timmony, N. K. Jemisin, Alyssa Louie, Raina Storer, Cora Kaichen, Alexander Rasmussen-Silverstein, and Jennifer Flax all offered comments on early drafts. Laura Kinnaman mentioned woolly rhinos. Elizabeth Bear kindly gave me last-minute climbing advice. I am indebted to Dr. Kurtis Nishimura for his expertise in physics and his skill at brainstorming "alternate physics"; this trilogy became much more interesting because of his contributions over several lunches at my favorite casual restaurant in Honolulu, Kakaʻako Kitchen. I would also like to thank my editor, Devi Pillai, for her wise patience and piercing insight, and Susan Barnes for the details.

As always, my spouse, Jay Silverstein, did his best to support me through a grueling writing process. Thanks also to my children, Rhiannon, Alexander, and David, for sharing the initial inspiration with me and letting me run with it.

Author's Note

The Spiritwalker books take place on a different Earth, with magic. This is a fantasia of an Earth that might have been had conditions included an extended Ice Age, the intelligent descendants of troodons, nested planes of interleaved worlds, and human access to magical forces that can either reverse or accelerate the normal flow of entropy.

Almost all the names and words used are real, not made up. Most of the place-names are, when possible, based on actual names used at one time or another in the history of the various regions. Geographical differences from our own world reflect the extended Ice Age, which would have locked up enough water in the ice sheets to cause the sea levels to drop, as they were in the Late Quaternary and Early Holocene in our time line. Doggerland is the English name for the region that is now beneath the North Sea but was, in our Mesolithic, a land bridge between Britain and the European continent. Naturally, because of these things, history flowed down different tributaries in the Spiritwalker world.

Calendar Notes

The "Roman" days of the week commonly used in this world are Sunday, Moonday, Marsday, Mercuriday, Jovesday, Venerday, and Saturnday. The months are close enough to our own that they don't need translating. From the Celtic tradition, I've used the "cross-quarter days" of Samhain (November 1), Imbolc (February 2), Beltain (May 1), and Lughnasad (August 2), although it's unlikely Samhain was considered the turn of the year.

1

I was serving drinks to the customers at the boardinghouse when a prince came to kill me.

I had my back to the gate and had just set a tray of empty mugs on the bar when the cheerful buzz of conversation abruptly ceased. Behind the counter, Uncle Joe finished drawing a pitcher of ale from a barrel before he turned. His gaze widened as he took in the sight behind me. He reached under the counter and set my sheathed sword next to the tray, in plain view.

I swung around.

As with most family compounds in the city of Expedition, the boardinghouse's rooms and living quarters were laid out around a central courtyard. A wall and gate separated the living area from the street. Soldiers stood in the open gate, surrounding the man who intended to be the next ruler of the Taino kingdom.

Prince Caonabo had a broad, brown face, and his black hair was almost as long as mine, although his fell loose while I confined mine in a braid whose tip brushed my hips. He wore white cotton cloth draped around his body much like a Roman toga, and simple leather sandals. Had I doubted his rank because of the plainness of his dress, I might have guessed his importance from the gold torc and gold armbands he wore, as well as the shell wrist-guards and anklets that ornamented his limbs and the jade-stone piercing the skin just above his chin.

The prince raised a hand, palm up. A flame sparked from the center of his palm, flowering outward as a rose blooms.

"Catherine Bell Barahal, you have been accused in the council hall of Expedition of being responsible for the death of the honorable and most wise *cacica*, what you call a queen, she with the name Anacaona. As Queen Anacaona's only surviving son, and as heir to her brother, the *cacique*, I am required to pursue justice in this matter."

I met his gaze. "I would like to know who made that accusation."

"I made the accusation."

He knew what I had done.

I took a step back, but I could not move faster than magic. Warmth tingled across my skin as the backlash of his fire magic brushed across my skin and stirred heat within my lungs and heart.

Yet as the light of the growing flame shimmered across his face, his features melted quite startlingly, like candle wax. He was as poured into a new mold and began to transform into a different person. I had not known that fire mages were skilled in the art of illusion, able to make themselves appear as someone else! Even the bar and court-yard were cunningly wrought illusions that, like his face and body, dissolved into mist. A gritty smoke filled my lungs, choking me.

Leaping back, I grabbed for my sword, but before I could grasp the hilt, my hand burst into flame. A blast of hot wind dispersed the sting-ing veil of smoke. As my vision cleared, I found myself standing on grand stone steps that led up to the imposing entry of a palatial build-ing. Its walls and roof blazed. Sheets of fire crackled into the air like the vast wings of a molten dragon. Flames clawed searing daggers into my flesh as I groped for my sword. I had no cold magic with which to kill the inferno. Only if I could wield cold steel had I a chance to save myself.

My fingers closed over the smooth hilt. I tugged, but the blade stuck in its sheath. An icy wind poured down in gouts of freezing air that battered against the raging flames, as if fire and ice were at war and I was at the center of the battle. The flames shimmered from gold to white, and in the blink of an eye the fire transmuted to become fall-ing snow. Brushing away the snowflakes icing my eyes and lips, I tried to make sense of what had happened.

Where was I? Why was everything changing so fast? Was I dreaming?

Instead of a burning building, the sheer cliff face of an ice sheet loomed over me. The pressure of its glacial mass slowly advanced, grind-ing and groaning. I pulled on my sword, but the blade was crushed in the ice and my hand had frozen to it. I simply could not move.

Beyond my frozen body lay a hollow cavern that bloomed with the harsh glamour of cold fire. In that lofty cave, the melted form that had first appeared to me as Prince Caonabo glittered as it changed. Frost and crystals shaped themselves into the figure and face of a man I recognized: the Master of the Wild Hunt.

My sire.

His expression was as cold and empty as his heart. "So are you trapped, little cat. You will never be free."

"I will be free! All of us will be free!" I tugged at the sword with all the heart and might I had in me.

Instead, the sword yanked me back the other way so hard that it hauled me right off my feet.

"Cat! Fiery Shemesh! You are talking nonsense in your sleep and besides that trying to drag me off the bed."

My cousin Beatrice loomed over me, her thick black curls framing her familiar and beloved face. Her fingers clutched mine, and I realized I had been holding her hand for quite some time. For fifteen years, since I was orphaned at the age of six, Bee had been my best friend, as close as a loving sister. Just to see her helped me relax enough that I could take stock of where I was and what I was doing.

We had fallen asleep together in the drowsy afternoon heat in an upstairs room of Aunty Djeneba's boardinghouse.

After washing up on the jetty of the city of Expedition, on the island of Kiskeya in the Antilles, I had come to live at the boardinghouse. Here Andevai Diarisso Haranwy, the cold mage I had been forced to marry back in Europa, had courted me and won my heart. Bee and I were napping on the bed Andevai had built for his and my wedding night. I shut my eyes, remembering his kisses. For a few breaths I pretended I could hear his voice downstairs in the courtyard, as if he had just come home from the carpentry yard where he worked. But he was gone.

You will never be free.

I sat up, trying to shake off the memory. "What a frightful nightmare I just had. Pinch me, Bee."

She pinched my arm with the force of iron tongs wielded by a brawny blacksmith.

"Ah! You monster!" I cried.

"You said to do it!"

I shook my arm until the pain subsided, while she laughed. "No, it's all right. I just wanted to make sure I'm finally awake."

Bee tapped my cheek affectionately. "You were talking in your sleep. You've become quite the revolutionary, Cat. You kept mumbling, 'All of us will be free.'"

With a sigh, I leaned against her shoulder. Bee was significantly shorter than I was, but she was sturdy and determined, easily strong enough to hold me up when I needed support. "It's no wonder I mumble such words in my sleep. When I wake up, I remember that my sire threw Vai into his magical coach and drove off with him into the spirit world."

Bee pressed her fingers to my knee, staring at me with brows drawn down as if she could bend the world to her will through her glower, and sometimes I was sure she could. "I know you're worried because your sire is the Master of the Wild Hunt, because he is a powerful magical denizen of the spirit world, and because not even the most powerful cold mage can stand against him. But even though all that is true, it doesn't mean you and I can't defeat him and rescue Andevai."

"I always feel so heartened when you explain things in exactly that cheering way, Bee."

"Do you doubt that we can?" she demanded in the belligerent manner I loved.

"I don't doubt that we must, for certainly no one else can! Anyhow, I'm not going to lie here and cry about it. We will figure out what to do because we have to."

I rose. In the dim and rather stuffy little room, a cloth-covered screen folded out to divide the space into two halves. Vai's younger sister had slept on the other side of the screen, but she had recently married a local man and moved into his family's compound. Two wooden chests held Vai's clothes and other necessaries. His carpentry tools resided in a smaller chest he had built specially to house them. A covered basket held my few possessions, for I had arrived in Expedition with nothing except the clothes on my back, my sword, and my locket. Through the open window floated the sounds of the household waking from their afternoon naps.

A length of brightly printed fabric that depicted green fans was draped over the screen. Tied around my hips, it made a skirt. I pulled a short gauzy blouse over my bodice.

Bee surveyed me critically. "That looks very well on you, Cat. The style would not flatter my figure." She fluffed out her curly hair to get the worst snarls out. "Wouldn't the fastest way to pursue Vai be to enter the spirit world here and follow your sire to Europa through the spirit world?"

"I've been warned off trying to enter the spirit world here in the Antilles. The Taino spirits don't like me. They will do everything they can to stop me entering their territory. Anyway, getting Vai back does not solve our greater problem, does it? The Hunt will still ride every year on Hallows' Night. It will still hunt down powerful cold mages and innocent dream walkers. Nor will rescuing Vai stop my sire from binding me whenever he wishes."

With a frown like the cut of a blade, Bee crossed to the window and set her hands on the sill. "It's true. I can hide from the Wild Hunt in a troll maze, but you can't. And it isn't just about you and me and Andevai. What about other women who walk the dreams of dragons, the ones who don't know that the mirrors of a troll maze will conceal them from the Hunt? I hate to think of what will happen to them when next the Wild Hunt rides. They should be safe, too. Everyone should be safe."

"Yes. I don't see why anyone should have to fear the Wild Hunt just because the spirit courts of Europa demand a sacrifice of mortal blood every year. It's wrong for any person to be torn to pieces and have their head ripped off and thrown down a well." I looked away so Bee would not see my expression, for that was exactly what had happened to Queen Anacaona on Hallows' Night. To speak of how Bee's new husband, Prince Caonabo, had walked in my dream with his threats seemed cruel because it would upset her dreadfully, so I said nothing of it. Bee hadn't been on the ballcourt when the Wild Hunt had descended on the wings of a hurricane, but the prince had seen it all.

Bee did not notice my guarded expression or my pause. She was gazing down on the courtyard, watching the family making ready for the customers who would arrive at dusk to eat Aunty Djeneba's justly famous cooking and to drink the beer and spirits served by Aunty's brother-in-law, Uncle Joe.

"No one should have to live at the mercy of another's cruel whim," she said. "That is the same whether it is the Wild Hunt, or the unjust laws and arbitrary power wielded by princes and mages. It is the toil and sweat and blood of humble folk that feed those who rule us, is it not?"

Her fierce expression made me smile. "A radical sentiment, Bee! And so cogently expressed!"

She tried to smile but sighed instead. "I can't laugh about it. We are caught in an ancient struggle."

I recalled words spoken to me weeks ago. "'At the heart of all lie the vast energies which are the animating spirit of the worlds. The worlds incline toward disorder. Cold battles with heat.' Is that what you mean?"

"You are poetic today, Cat. I mean the struggle between those who rule unjustly merely because they have claimed the privilege to do so, and those who seek freedom to rule themselves."

I studied her from across the room. With only one window for light, the details of her face were obscured, as the future is obscured to every person except the women who walk the dreams of dragons and thus may glimpse snatches of what will come. Over the last two years, since long before she admitted the truth to me, Bee had been having dreams of such clarity and intensity that she felt obliged, upon waking, to sketch the most vivid moments from those dreams. As the months passed, she had discovered that the scenes in these sketches were visions of future meetings.

Naturally, all manner of powerful people wanted to control her gift of dreaming. The mansa of Four Moons House had sent Andevai to claim her for the mage House, but Vai had mistakenly married me instead. General Camjiata had tried to seduce Bee to his cause so he could use her visions to give him an advantage in war, and in a way he had succeeded, for he was the one who had brokered the marriage between Bee and Prince Caonabo; the alliance gave him Taino support for the war he wanted to fight in Europa. Queen Anacaona had wanted her son to become cacique when her brother died, and an alliance with a dragon dreamer like Bee gave Caonabo a prestige other claimants did not possess. But now, the tilt of Bee's head and the tone of her voice worried me. I did not like to think she had sacrificed her happiness believing she had to do it to make us both safe.

"Bee, you told me all about your wedding adventure, but you never really said if you are truly happy, married to Prince Caonabo."

By the way her chin tucked down, I guessed she was blushing. "I do like him. He is levelheaded and thoughtful. I find him interesting to talk to, and he is not at all taken aback that I am knowledgeable about such topics as astronomy or the mechanics of airship design, not as some men are. I must admit, I rather enjoy being a Taino noblewoman, even if my consequence is borrowed. From what I have seen, the Taino court governs in a just manner. But everything that has happened to us, even my marriage, has made me think so much more about what we used to take for granted, the things we thought were inevitable and proper." She leaned out the window and glanced at the sky, then withdrew, looking alarmed. "I must go! I didn't realize we had slept for so long. Usually I dream. How strange that I didn't dream at all."

"Why are you in such a hurry?"

She laced up her sandals and straightened her spotlessly white linen draperies. "Caonabo has diplomatic meetings today with the provisional Assembly here in Expedition. He means to hammer out a new treaty with the new government before we journey to the Taino court in Sharagua. He wants matters with Expedition Territory settled before he presents himself to the Taino court as the rightful cacique." She slipped on enough gold jewelry to purchase a grand house and compound. "I am obliged to be at the palace on the border of Expedition Territory when he returns, to greet him with the proper ceremony."

"Are you?" I asked, then thought better of teasing her about this unexpected display of wifely compliance because she grabbed my hands and squeezed them so tightly I feared my fingers would be crushed.

"Promise me you'll stay out of trouble until tomorrow, Cat. When I come back, we will figure out how to get you to Europa."

"Of course I'll stay out of trouble! When do I ever deliberately court trouble, I should like to ask?"

"When do you *not* court trouble, you should be asking!" Bee snatched her sketchbook from the side table and stuffed it into the knit bag she carried so she could keep it and her pencils next to her at all times. "I am not the one who goes about punching sharks or speaking my mind so caustically to arrogant cold mages that they fall in love with me. Come along."

When Bee set her mind to drag a person along with her to wherever she was set to go, it was impossible to resist, nor did I try. Hand in hand, we descended the stairs to the courtyard. The boarding-house had a wall and gate that separated it from the street, while the living quarters were laid out in a square whose center was a courtyard. Because it was hot year-round in the Antilles, most of the daily life went on in the spacious courtyard. A wide trellis and a canvas awning covered the benches and tables where customers drank and ate and gossiped, but right now, with the heat of the afternoon ebbing, the courtyard was empty except for Uncle Joe and the lads setting up benches and trays while Aunty Djeneba and her granddaughters cooked in the outdoor kitchen.

They were not one bit overawed by Bee's borrowed consequence as she made respectful goodbyes to the women and charming farewells to the menfolk. Outside the gate, Taino attendants handed her into the carriage that had waited there half the day while she visited me. We embraced and kissed, after which she promised ten times to return in the morning.

"Bee, don't fret. How much trouble can I get into overnight?"

"That's what worries me." She squeezed my hands so tightly that I gritted my teeth rather than wince. "Dearest, promise me you'll do nothing rash."

"Ouch! I'll promise whatever you wish, only you're crushing my fingers again!"

She released me at last. I waved as she drove off down the cobblestone street through the quiet neighborhood where lived people whose labor built and sustained the city of Expedition.

The moment I went back inside, one of the lads handed me a broom. I swept between the benches and tables as had been my habit in the weeks I had lived and worked here, for I had come to enjoy the household's routine. When I finished, I went to the shaded outdoor kitchen.

"Aunty," I said to Djeneba as she prepared a big pot of rice and peas, "I don't see Rory and Luce. Did they go to the batey game?"

A wry smile creased her lined face. "So they did, Cat. By that frown, I reckon yee's not so glad to see Luce walking out with yee brother."

My frown deepened. "I am not! He's no better than a tomcat. A pleasant, kind, charming, and well-mannered tomcat, but no better regardless."

"Luce is sixteen now. Old enough to choose for she own self." She handed me a wooden spoon and directed me to stir the pot as she added more salt and pepper. "Is yee determined to wait tables tonight? Yee don' have to work if yee've no mind to do it."

The pot simmered, a luscious flavor wafting up. I licked my lips as I wielded the spoon. "Aunty, you know I can't sit quietly. Waiting tables will keep my mind off Vai."

"It surely did before." Aunty's laugh coaxed a reluctant smile to my lips as I remembered the clever way he had won me over by bringing me delicious fruit to eat and confiding in me about his embrace of radical principles. "Yee never could seem to make up yee mind about Vai. Yee pushed him back with one hand and pulled him close with the other. What settled yee?"

"Really, Aunty, did you think he would give up before he got what he wanted?"

"Yee's a stubborn gal, Cat. I had me doubts."

"You shouldn't have had. I think I was always a little infatuated with him, even back when I disliked him for his high-handed ways. The Blessed Tanit knows he's handsome enough to overwhelm the most heartless gal."

"Good manners and a steady heart matter more than looks, although he have all three in plenty. Still, I reckon yee have the right of it. 'Tis no easy task for a gal to say no to a lad as fine as he. Especially after the patient way he courted yee." She took the spoon. "Yee get that man back."

"I will get him back, I promise you, Aunty." I did not add that I had no idea how I was going to manage it. "Bee will help me. We're going to make our plans tomorrow."

The thought of him trapped in my sire's claws made me burn. Yet not even worrying could dampen my appetite. I ate two bowls of Aunty's excellent rice and peas, by which time the first customers had begun to arrive. They greeted me with genuine pleasure, for even though I was a *maku*—a foreigner—in Expedition, folk here did appreciate my willingness to speak my mind. Better yet, they laughed at my jokes. The easy way people conversed pleased me, and no one thought it at all remarkable that a young woman had opinions about the great matters of the day.

"I certainly hope the new Assembly will not allow the Taino representatives to bully them on this matter of a new treaty," I said to a table of elderly regulars.

"Hard not to feel bullied when a fleet of Taino airships sit on the border chaperoned by an army of soldiers who have already marched once through Expedition's streets," said Uncle Joe from the bar. "Peradventure without yee intervention on Hallows' Night, Cat, we in Expedition would have had to bow before a Taino governor instead of setting up this new Assembly. If yee had not done what report say yee did do."

I dodged past the lad who with pole and ladder was lighting the courtyard's gas lamps. With a shake of my head, I set a tray of empty mugs on the bar as I made a grimace at Uncle Joe. After the dream I had just had, I did not want anyone to begin reflecting on the part I had played in halting the Taino invasion of Expedition Territory. He nodded to show he understood, then turned to draw a pitcher of ale from a barrel to refill the mugs.

Between one breath and the next, the lively rattle of conversation ceased. The courtyard fell silent. I had my back to the gate. As Uncle Joe turned with the full pitcher, glancing past me, his gaze widened. He reached under the counter and set his machete next to my tray.

He had done the same in my dream, only my sword was looped to a cord around my hips. The blade of his machete caught a glimmer of gaslight that carved a shimmering line along its length.

I swung around.

Prince Caonabo stood in the open gate, surrounded by attendants and soldiers.

Just as he had in my dream.

2

All eyes—and it was crowded tonight—shifted from the newcomers to me, and back to the prince's retinue. Aunty Djeneba had been cooking cassava bread on a griddle in the open-air kitchen. She stepped back from the hearth to examine the interlopers. As the thin bread began to crisp, I could not rip my gaze from its blackening edges. The smell of its burning seemed to come right out of the dream I'd had, the way fire had caught in my flesh. Had Prince Caonabo come to kill me?

Was this what it meant to walk the dreams of dragons? Had I dreamed the dream meant for Bee because we were holding hands as we napped and her dreams had bled into mine? Or had I simply been waiting for this meeting, knowing the Taino would not let the death of their queen pass without a response?

Aunty realized the bread was burning, flipped the flat round onto the dirt, and gestured for one of her granddaughters to take over. After wiping her hands on her apron, she walked to the gate. She looked majestic with her hair covered in a vividly orange head wrap. Her height, stout build, and confident manner made her a formidable presence.

"Prince Caonabo," she said, not that she had ever met him before, but there could only be one Taino prince in the city of Expedition. "To see one such as yee here at me gate is truly unexpected."

One of the prince's attendants answered in his stead, for like any lofty nobleman, Caonabo did not need to speak for himself. "His Good Highness has come to this establishment to find a witch."

Most of our customers looked at me. I dressed in the local style so as not to draw attention to myself, but the days when I could hope to be just another maku girl making a living after being washed ashore in Expedition were irrevocably over.

Aunty stiffened. "We shelter no witch in me respectable house, nor have we ever, I shall thank yee to know. Nor need we answer to the prince, however good and high as he may be. Expedition remain a free territory. Yee Taino don' rule us."

The attendant blew a sharp whistle. Taino soldiers swarmed into the courtyard from the street, rifles and ceremonial spears at the ready, but the prince raised a hand to forestall any action.

"This afternoon I have spoken to the provisional Assembly," the prince said with the precision of an intelligent man who has learned through countless hours of intense study to speak a language foreign to him. "We have completed our discussions and renewed the treaty between the Taino kingdom and Expedition Territory. One matter remains before I can leave Expedition."

"What matter might that be, that yee trouble us while we partake of food and drink?"

Aunty still held the paddle she used on the cassava bread, and she had the stance of a woman ready to smack him with it right on his proud, highborn face if he didn't give her a polite answer.

His attendants looked comically startled that a common Expeditioner would speak to a noble prince in such a bold and disrespectful manner, but Prince Caonabo himself appeared neither offended nor taken aback. He seemed like a man who knew his place in the world but didn't need you to know it because it didn't matter if you did. And it didn't matter. In this part of the world, in the Sea of Antilles, he was among the most powerful men alive.

"Catherine Bell Barahal has been accused in the council hall of Expedition of being responsible for the death of the honorable and most wise cacica, what you call a queen, she with the name Anacaona. As Queen Anacaona's only surviving son, and as heir to her brother, the cacique, I am required to pursue justice in this matter."

Because it would be cowardly not to acknowledge him, I met his gaze with my own.

"I would like to know who made that accusation," I said.

"I made the accusation."

Customers got up and, with awkward goodbyes, hurried out the gate.

Uncle Joe muttered under his breath, "Cat, step back here behind the counter. Then yee can make a run out the back."

"No," I whispered. "I'll bring no trouble down on you after everything you've done for me. But please send one of the lads out to make sure Rory does not come back here until the prince is gone. Send him to Kofi's house."

I took in a breath to fortify myself, grabbed a dram of rum, caught Uncle Joe's warning gesture, and set down the rum without drinking. I drained a cup of guava juice instead, for my mouth had gone quite dry. Then I walked to the gate to face my accuser.

"Salve, Your Highness," I said respectfully. I wasn't sure what to make of Prince Caonabo. Despite his accusation, he did not glare at me in a hostile way. Instead, he acknowledged me with a lift of the hand.

"Salve, Perdita," he answered, calling me *lost woman*. That was the name I had been given on the day three months ago when he and other fire mages had discovered me washed up and half-drowned on the shore of Salt Island, a quarantine island I should never have set foot on and hoped never to see again. "You recovered your sword."

"So I did." To all other eyes, my sword appeared as a black cane, but fire mages and the feathered people we called trolls saw it for what it was: a blade of magically forged steel. At night I could draw the blade out of the spirit world, but during the day it was just a cane unless woken by cold magic. "Your Highness, Expedition is a free territory. It is not ruled by the Taino, nor by Taino law."

"Expedition Territory exists as a free territory within the Taino kingdom only because the captains of the first fleet that arrived here from Africa and Europa sealed a treaty with my ancestors. One of the conditions written into the First Treaty was the establishment of quarantine islands against the diseases brought across the ocean. Another condition was the right of accusation. Should a person residing in Expedition Territory commit a criminal act against any Taino, the Taino have the right to demand justice. As the accuser, I am allowed to take you into my custody and deliver you to Expedition's Council

Hall. There you will be taken before a standing inquiry on the charge of murder."

Around us the courtyard lay still and silent. A sound of lively laughter and talk drifted from nearby households. Resonant drumming pulsed from farther afield, signaling a victory dance at the local ballcourt for the batey match that had been completed with the dusk. Three days ago there could have been no batey match, no dance, no drumming, for the entire city had been under occupation by the Taino army.

I lifted my chin. "Queen Anacaona led an invasion of Expedition. An invasion is an act of war."

"The honored cacica's action was not an act of war. Disease hit our people hard when the maku first came across the ocean from the east. Other nations suffered worse than ours because our *behiques* were wise enough to place a fence of quarantine around our islands. So you see, the First Treaty explicitly gives the Taino the legal right to act if any quarantine is broken. As you broke it, by escaping from Salt Island."

"What if I refuse to come with you?" I asked.

He had the look of a man accustomed to gazing at the stars as he attempts to fathom heavenly secrets. He did not look like an enraged kinsman trying to determine if a perfectly well-brought-up and inoffensive young woman has been party to a murder. "I seek justice, not revenge, Maestra Barahal. Duty binds me. I honor my mother as a dutiful son must. Even so, I offer you the protection of the law. If you do not come with me, I cannot answer for what might happen, for it has come to my attention that you have enemies who wish you ill and might use your refusal as an excuse to act against you."

"Who would those enemies be?"

He raised a hand, palm up. A tiny flame rose from the center of his palm. A glow brushed along the skin of the prince's two attendants. Both were acting as catch-fires for his fire magic. The greatest danger to a fire mage was that the backlash of power would consume her, as fire consumes any combustible substance. In Europa there were no catch-fires. Fire mages either became blacksmiths and were inducted into the mysteries of that extended clan, or they died young in sudden and horrible conflagrations. The Taino had learned to protect fire mages with catch-fires.

"I think you know who they are," he replied. "Fire in the wrong hands is a reckless weapon that destroys. In the hands of responsible people, fire heals. It can also offer a means to restrain the hearts of malevolent persons who disrupt the harmonious balance of society. The punishment for murder is that you lose the privilege to walk freely in a peaceful society and must serve it instead. That is why murderers are required to work in the cane fields, or to become catch-fires."

A shiver of doubt crept its icy fingers down my spine. I felt it wisest to say nothing.

The prince curled his hand into a fist, dousing the flame. "Catherine Bell Barahal, upon my authority as heir to the Taino kingdom, and with the permission of the provisional Assembly that rules Expedition Territory, I place you under arrest for the murder of the cacica, Anacaona."

I found a bland smile in my store of weapons, and I brandished it. "I'll go quietly with you, Prince Caonabo, under this condition. Promise on your honor as prince and future cacique of the Taino that you, and any and all of your court and subjects and hirelings, will not harm, persecute, or arrest any person living in this household now or ever. The people living here must never face retaliation for having sheltered me."

He gave my words thoughtful consideration. "On the honor of my ancestors and on the honor of my own person, I give my word that I and all those who are subject to my authority will not now or ever harm, persecute, or arrest any person living in this household."

"Give me a moment, if you please."

I walked over to the kitchen shelter. Aunty had already sent the children into one of the rooms to get them out of the way.

"Aunty, can you quickly put together a satchel of food for me? My skirt and jacket, from my room. And the cloth sleeve for my cane."

Aunty called over her daughter Brenna and gave her instructions, then took hold of my arm. "Do the prince mean to see yee brought to trial even though he is married to yee own cousin?"

"I'm not sure what to think. Please let Bee and Rory know what's happened."

Uncle Joe stepped in under the kitchen roof. His glare was enough to make my eyes water, since I knew he was upset because he cared for me. "Cat, what arseness is this yee's playing at? I reckon the new Assembly ought better protect a gal who cut off the head of the Taino invasion."

"Do the Taino have the legal right to invade, according to the terms of the First Treaty? Because of the broken quarantine?"

"Lawyers might say so. That was a long time ago."

"That it was a long time ago doesn't change the law. I've extracted a promise from the prince that he will never harass or harm anyone who lives here."

Uncle Joe's grip was hard, and yet because it was so, I felt heartened. "Don' forget, gal, that in the eyes of many folk here in Expedition, 'twas the death of the cacica that freed us from the old Council's unjust rule. When she died and the Taino had to withdraw, that was when the Assemblymen had a chance to overthrow the Council and change the government of Expedition."

"Yee shall find people aplenty in Expedition these days who shall fight to keep yee safe, gal," said Aunty. "Don' think otherwise."

"Believe me, I won't let them kill me."

Uncle frowned. "The Taino rule the Sea of Antilles. Don' make the mistake of thinking them weak. Their behiques is the most powerful of all. I reckon yee don' truly understand how far the power of Taino fire mages can reach."

"I have my own secrets. Anyway, I can't die, for if I did, then who would rescue Vai?" Overwhelmed by longing for the home I had so unexpectedly found at the boardinghouse, I kissed her smooth cheek and his rough one. "But I don't know what will happen after."

Uncle Joe sighed. "I shall fetch yee some provision." He went back to the counter and returned with two flasks, one filled with ginger beer and one with rum.

Aunty looked through the satchel prepared for me with flat rounds of cassava bread, unpeeled guava, jerked chicken, and a gourd filled with rice and peas. "Come back to us if yee can."

I slid my ghost-sword into a sleeve of cloth to hide it from trolls and fire mages, made my farewells, and joined the prince at the gate.

Caonabo indicated a low-slung carriage waiting on the street. I climbed to the back bench seat, which was shaded by a hood but open to the air. Prince Caonabo sat on the facing seat.

The carriage rolled down a street illuminated by gaslight. Hooves clopped on cobblestones.

"We Taino did not have horses before the fleet from the Empire of Mali came. They are useful animals, beautiful in form and intriguing in their behavior. Do you not think so, Perdita?"

Two could play that game of batey! "I've not had the opportunity to study the habits of horses. We did not own any at the house where Beatrice and I grew up as devoted as sisters."

"Ah, Beatrice." His expression shaded into a grave smile. "I wondered how soon you would mention her. As you already know, Perdita, when General Camjiata came to Sharagua, he offered Queen Anacaona a trade. In exchange for Taino gold, soldiers, and weapons for his Europan war, he would give her son and heir for bride a young woman who walks the dreams of dragons. Such a woman is precious beyond jewels, for she can see the meeting places and crossing points of the future. With such a bride, my claim to the *duho*—the seat of power— would be strengthened. Naturally, my mother accepted on my behalf."

"Bee won't stand by and let me be condemned. She'll never forgive you if I die."

He sat back against the upholstered seat. "Yet if I am to be accepted as the next cacique, I must see the cacica's murderer brought to justice. Since it was my honored mother's wish that I succeed her brother as ruler of all the Taino, you may comprehend my dilemma."

"I think you should just let me go, Prince Caonabo. My hand did not kill your mother."

"You speak as do the feathered people, disguising your meaning beneath words that hide the truth. I was there the night it happened, on what you call Hallows' Night, on the ballcourt. I saw a sabertoothed cat break my mother's neck. I saw a swarm of creatures with teeth and claws rip my mother apart. I saw a hunting hound run off into the night carrying my mother's head in its jaws. So pray excuse me if I neglect the usual polite talk and cut to the heart."

"Truly, Your Highness, I think we have passed the point where we need concern ourselves with polite words."

His gaze was steady, not angry. "I heard what you said to the maku spirit lord that night. You addressed him as 'Father.' You said, 'Are you going to let that fire weaver destroy me? I guess you can't stop her.' Do you not think those are strange and careless words with which to ask for the death of another person? Because I do."

The cavalcade reached the boulevard that fronted the sea, a long stone-built jetty. Waves sighed against rocks and piers; it was a gentle evening, with a gentle wind and a gentle swell. A wagon drawn by a dwarf mammoth trundling along the boulevard caught the prince's attention. When his gaze flickered that way, it was all the distraction I needed.

Born to a human mother, I had been sired by a creature of the spirit world. That meant I could reach into the interstices that wove together the mortal world and the spirit world and draw those threads around me to hide my body from mortal eyes. With satchel and cloth-covered cane clutched against me, I wrapped myself in shadow. A bounce on the forward seat gave the impression I had leaped out of the carriage.

Prince Caonabo's attendants shouted in alarm. I held my breath and rode the jolt as the driver hauled the horses to a halt. Soldiers scattered to search for me. The prince passed a hand over his face. For no more than a breath, he smiled as if my audacity reminded him of something that amused him greatly. Then a captain ran up, and Caonabo's expression settled back into cool reserve. He beckoned to the soldier. As the captain mounted into the carriage, rocking it, I stepped off.

The shouts of the soldiers covered the thump I made on landing. I dodged away and caught my breath under a hissing gas streetlamp, in full sight but entirely veiled by my shadows. Carters and wagoners on their way home pulled aside. One old carter lit a cigarillo nervously, puffing smoke. Young toughs swaggered into view, as if hoping the Taino would push them into a fight. A young woman with a baby strapped to her back grabbed a ripe papaya out of the basket she was carrying and cocked her arm to fling it at the prince, but an older woman grabbed her elbow to stop her.

A whistle shrilled. As the Taino soldiers resumed formation, I crept away down a side street.

3

The victory drums heard from a distant ballcourt ceased as I hurried down dim streets too unimportant to warrant street lighting. The smoke of cook fires coated the air. Merchants and artisans were closing up shop. The last transport wagons and carts shared the roadways with people making their leisurely way home from work, the market, or the batey game. No volley of shots disturbed the night, so presumably the prince had moved on before trouble started.

Still hidden, I crept into the compound belonging to the household of my husband's trusted friend, Kofi. Vai's sister Kayleigh was busy in the big open-air kitchen, laughing with other young women as they helped with the cooking, supervised by Kofi's mother and aunts. Wheels scraped behind me. I stepped out of the way as the household menfolk entered, pushing empty carts. Kofi was at the end of the line, a tall, broad-shouldered young man with scarred cheeks and his shoulder-length black hair in locks. Falling in beside him, I tweaked the hem of the sleeveless singlet he wore.

"Kofi, it's Cat," I whispered. "I'm in trouble. Meet me in the back."

He startled, eyes going wide, but without a word he helped the other men sweep out the carts and store them for the night. Then he grabbed a lantern and beckoned to Kayleigh. She looked surprised but excused herself to his mother. I walked behind them as they made their way to the back courtyard and entered a shed for broken axles and wheels not yet repaired.

When I unwrapped the shadows, Kofi jumped back in alarm. Kayleigh chuckled. My secret ways did not trouble her, for she had grown up in a hunters' village and with a grandmother who was a wise woman with strong magic.

He frowned, glancing at Kayleigh as his shoulders tensed. "I tell yee, Cat, yee shall not ever do that in front of any but them who know yee well. It don' seem natural."

"My apologies." I kissed Kayleigh on the cheek and Kofi likewise. "I've been accused of the murder of Queen Anacaona by Prince Caonabo. He came to the boardinghouse and arrested me himself. Once we were away from Aunty's, I fled."

"Whsst!" Kofi rubbed his forehead. "Now yee's a fugitive, Cat. It make yee look guilty of the crime."

"How can I be sure the Assembly won't hand me over to the Taino?"

Kofi rested a big hand on my shoulder. "Cat, every Expeditioner shall call the cacica's death an act of war, and yee a soldier fighting against the Taino in defense of Expedition."

"That will scarcely help me if I'm brought to trial and everyone believes I killed her!"

"I don' have the authority to let yee seek refuge here. I must ask permission of the elders of the house." He shifted broken wheels off an overturned wagon bed so we could sit. "Wait here."

As he stepped outside, I said, "I told Uncle Joe to send Rory here. I don't want the Taino to take him into custody. Because he's the one who killed the cacica."

"I don' see it that way." The lamplight made his scars shine, a reminder that he had endured torture in the cells of Expedition's Warden Hall for being a radical and revolutionary agitator. Few things intimidated him now. "'Tis true yee made the suggestion and yee brother struck the blow, but 'twas the maku spirit lord, the one yee call master and sire, who had the power to command it done. Seem to me the spirit lord is therefore the killer."

He walked off, taking the lamp to light his way. In the darkness, Kayleigh took my hand. She was a sturdy, big-boned young woman, not more than seventeen, who looked like her older brother if not nearly as striking. We had not always gotten along, but I was very glad to have her next to me tonight. "What do you mean to do, Cat?"

"I have to get to Europa. I just have to figure out how to get there, for I've no money for a berth on a ship taking passage over the Atlantic. I've already been warned off trying to walk into the spirit world here in the islands. An *opia* came to me looking just like Vai."

She snickered. "That must have startled you."

Heat burned in my cheeks, for I had kissed the opia quite passionately before I realized he was the spirit of a dead ancestor, wearing Vai's face. Being dead, opia could wear any face they wished. "Yes, it was quite disconcerting. He's the one who explained why the Taino spirits are so angry at me."

"Why is that? For it seems to me that here in the Antilles, living people and their dead ancestors are not often hostile toward each other. But perhaps the spirit people here wish to protect the spirit lords of Europa, who might be in some manner their cousins."

"Quite the contrary. Long ago, Taino fire mages wove a protective spirit fence around their islands to keep out the Wild Hunt and any other spirit visitors from other parts of the spirit world."

Kayleigh nodded. This casual talk of the spirit world seemed perfectly normal to her. "I suppose that spirit lords protect their territory just like princes and mages do in the mortal world."

"So it seems. Anyway, I was able to cut a gate in the spirit fence. The Wild Hunt rode through the gap I made. My sire would never have been able to reach the cacica if not for me."

"It's not as if you did it on purpose! You were just trying to save your cousin's life, for it was her the Wild Hunt wanted to kill."

"Yes, but the cacica died regardless."

"You'll need to sail to Europa, then. If we can't get the bank to open Vai's account to you, you shall have the money Vai settled on me when I married."

"I can't take your dowry."

"Of course you can! It's mine to give, because Vai settled the funds on me according to Expedition law, which follows Taino law in giving women title to households and the family purse. Which do you think I would rather have? The money, or my brother? You have to go to Europa. The hunters of our village can help you rescue Vai out of the spirit world. Shh!"

Lantern light shimmered, illuminating carts lined up against the back wall: The family's business was local transport. Kofi shepherded his mother, his aunts, and the eldest men into the dusty shed. I received

21

their blessing, which they gave by each one touching a hand to my hair. His mother offered me a cup of juice. After hearing my tale, they agreed that I might stay for one night. As for my brother, however, they were not so sure, for they had never met him and wished to know more about his character and manners.

One of Kofi's brothers appeared, escorting Rory and Lucretia. I smiled to see them safe, until I noticed the inappropriately intimate manner in which their fingers were intertwined.

"Rory," I murmured, "did I not tell you to stay away from her?"

Rory released Luce's hand. He sauntered right past me to greet the older women, his smile as bright as the lanterns. With his lithe young man's body well clad in one of Vai's fashionable dash jackets and his long black hair pulled back in a braid, he surely delighted the eye. The men watched in astonishment but I knew what was coming. He offered chastely generous kisses to the women's cheeks and tender pats to their work-worn hands.

"My apologies. I mean no offense by charging into your territory without an invitation. But I must obey my sister. You understand how it is with a sister who speaks a bit sharply to one even though she is the younger and ought, I should suppose, to look up to her older brother. Please, let me thank you. Your hospitality honors and humbles me. The food smells so good. I'm sure I've never smelled better." He had routed two already and turned to the remaining skeptic. "That fabric is beautifully dyed, and looks very well with your complexion, Aunty."

A cavalry charge at close quarters could not have demolished their resistance more devastatingly. He turned his charm on the old men, drawing them out with irresistible questions about their proud and memorable youth.

I went over to Luce, grasping her wrist. "Luce. He's a tomcat."

She lifted her chin. Because I treated Luce as a little sister, I often forgot that, at sixteen, she was old enough to marry. "I know me own mind, Cat! I's old enough to do as I wish."

"Be sure that he makes a habit of charming women of all ages and dispositions. And men, too." I glanced over my shoulder. Rory was now seated between two of the women, chatting easily with all six of the elders about how things had been different in the old days. His easy lounging grace made the overturned wagon bed seem like the most gracious reception hall couch.

"He cannot help what he is!" Luce's gaze flashed at me from beneath lowered lashes.

"True words," I agreed. "You're blushing. I want you to go home, Luce." She drew in breath for a retort. "I need your help! Go home and get everything ready. Vai's tool chest. His clothes chests neatly packed, all my things put in. In the morning fetch the winter coats I'm having made on Tailors' Row." I glanced up at Kofi, who had come over to stand beside me. "We might have to leave in a hurry."

"So yee might," he agreed. "I shall be going out to speak to the president of the Assembly and some other folk about the situation." He pinched Luce's cheek with the familiarity of an older brother. "That man is trouble, gal. Mind me words."

"Sweet trouble," retorted Luce. "I's no fool."

"I doubt me that," retorted Kofi in the tone of a man who has seen a girl grow up from a toddling scamp. "Do as Cat ask. Don' forget to pack Vai's mirror and razor. And extra soap."

"I know Vai is vain but surely that is a bit much," I said.

Luce giggled. "I never knew a man could spend so much time in front of a mirror."

Kofi frowned reprovingly at us. "'Tisn't only vanity. 'Tis a shield."

I exchanged a mirthful glance with Luce, but something in Kofi's expression killed any desire I had to laugh. "Wearing fashionable clothes is a shield? From what?"

"Gal, in some ways I reckon yee understand that man well enough, but in another wise yee don' really understand him at all."

Indignation spiked right up into my head, but then I realized Kofi was showing me respect by speaking so plainly. "I suppose not. He was so awful to me when we first met that it took a long time for me to realize it wasn't me he disliked. That most of the things he did, he did to protect himself from the way the other mages treated him so contemptuously. I think he assumed I would treat him the same way. All right, then. Luce, don't neglect any items a man of Vai's high-strung temperament might need. I must say, you're a man of hidden depth, Kofi."

He chuckled. "I know how to get a man talking. Vai was a man who was looking for a friend. I shall walk yee back to Aunty's on my way, Luce. And don' be sneaking back here tonight, for Cat and Rory must share a room."

As they made to go, Rory broke away from the elders to take his leave of Luce. He drew her into the shadows to whisper in her ear so softly that even I had trouble distinguishing words. Then she kissed him in a way that made me suspect the cursed tomcat had kissed her more than once at the batey match, despite my having told him not to do any such thing.

I had no chance to scold him, for we were swept off to eat the evening meal with the entire family in attendance, some thirty people, including elders, adult cousins, all the children, more distant relations who lived and worked in the household, and two lads up from the country to work until they had earned enough to go home and marry.

"Now what do we do, Cat?" Rory asked later when we had retired to a tiny room and its two cots. As I hung a lit lantern from a hook, he dragged a cot over against mine and sprawled out across both. "I don't want to go on the ocean. It scares me."

"Move over! You're hogging all the space."

"I am not a hog!"

"Of course you're not a hog, Rory," I said soothingly, before I pounced for the kill. "But don't make me call you a lecherous seducer. Didn't I tell you not to touch Luce? She's too young and very innocent."

"Not as innocent as you think she is!" He sat up, crossing his arms as he frowned. "I am not like that unpleasant fire mage, James Drake. I would never pet any person without their full and willing consent—"

My throat tightened. "How do you know about my relationship with James Drake?"

"I lived with General Camjiata and his staff for three days before you came to retrieve me. Remember?"

"Did James Drake *say things* to you? About me?"

"Goodness, Cat. Your skin is all blotchy." He patted my flushed cheek. "And warm!"

"I see what you're doing. You're changing the subject. Luce is too young for you."

"Both you and Luce are old enough to breed." He sniffed several times. "You're not pregnant. In fact, you're fertile right now. It's very convenient for me that human women are only fertile part of the time. That makes it easy for me to—"

"Rory! This is not a subject you and I are going to discuss."

"You started the discussion." He ran a hand along his chin and lips like a cat about to start licking its paw in a self-congratulatory fashion. Yet just as quickly, his smirk faded. "As your brother, I ought to warn you. James Drake is a dangerous man."

"I can handle James Drake. It's our sire I'm worried about. What are his weaknesses? How can I defeat him?"

"You can't defeat him. We're bound to him because we are his children."

A tap shifted the door. I grabbed the hilt of my sword.

"Cat?" It was Kofi.

I let him in. Kofi's plain jacket and trousers in the practical Expedition style and his powerful build marked him as a hardworking laborer, but the crisp confidence in his tone revealed him as a successful radical, a member of the new provisional Assembly in Expedition.

"This is a rare commotion, Cat. Now that we Expeditioners have the chance to rule we own selves, we don' like to feel the Taino can tell us what to do. But yee running have made the situation worse. Yee shall have to sail immediately for Europa."

"I haven't money to pay for our passage."

"So Kayleigh told me. Expedition owe yee a favor for saving us from the Taino invasion. I shall escort yee to West Quay at dawn. There yee shall board a Phoenician ship called the *White Horse*, bound for Gadir. The tide turn mid-morning. Then yee shall be out of reach."

"Thank you." My legs gave way as an avalanche of relief crashed over me.

"Don' thank me. Commissioner Sanogo arranged it." He sighed. "I admit I had hoped yee and Vai might settle in Expedition. There is plenty for him to do here. And I reckon the wardens of Expedition should like to hire a gal with the peculiar talents yee possess."

"I would like to try that sort of work."

"Warden's work 'twould suit yee, for I reckon yee's not suited for a quiet life."

"I can live a quiet life!"

25

Kofi laughed. "Yee should last a month, no more, before yee got restless and found some trouble to get into. I reckon Vai love yee for it, and for the knack yee have of getting out of it. If anyone can fetch him back from the spirit world, yee's the one to do it."

We talked a little longer about the logistics of our departure. After Kofi left, Rory and I settled on the cots. I pinched out the wick but could not sleep for fretting about Bee.

"Are you trying not to cry?" Rory whispered.

I sniffled. "I didn't mean to get into trouble before Bee came back tomorrow. What if I never see her again?"

"If it will help calm you, I can comb your hair, or lick your hands and face."

"Lick my hands and face?"

"It's very comforting, I'll have you know!"

I managed a choked laugh. He tucked his back up against mine and began to sing the oddest crooning lullaby in words I could not understand. The melody wound like a nest around my heart, shielding me from the ills of the world.

I slept heavily and woke before dawn, determined to succeed. Luce arrived with the chests. We walked in a trundle of carts through the predawn gloom toward the harbor. Rory pushed a cart among the other men. I walked in the center to be less conspicuous. Luce held my hand. The menfolk bantered in a half-awake, early-morning way. I could not rein in my thoughts, which galloped from the impossibility of rescuing Vai out of the jaws of the Master of the Wild Hunt to the pain of being sundered from my dearest Bee. It was easier not to think at all.

West Quay was the farthest west of the wharves in the main harbor, mostly used by Phoenician ships, and notably marked by a pair of tall wooden posts the locals called Heracles's Pillars for the famous straits at the mouth of the Mediterranean Sea. On the opposite side of the jetty was an inn called Nance's, with a sprawling wooden deck flanked by buildings. The edifice had a grand view of the harbor and of the monumental arch that led into the walled confines of the old city. Almost two months ago, Vai and I had been separated here by an unexpected meeting.

At tables along the railing, men ate with the concentration of sailors savoring their last good meal before shipping out. Barrels were lined up street-side next to the steps. A man leaned against a barrel with an open book in his hands. He met my questing gaze with a polite nod of greeting.

"Blessed Tanit!" I released Luce's hand. "Rory, we've got to run."

The leaning man closed the book with an audible snap. Kofi looked around with a curse. A piercing whistle cut through the hush of dawn. Rory dropped the handles of the cart he was pushing, and the entire line of carts came to a juddering halt. Taino soldiers trotted onto the jetty from where they had been hiding amid stacks of crates. The men who had been eating clattered down the stairs to fan out onto the jetty, brandishing the short swords known as falcatas that were famous as the preferred weapon of Iberian infantrymen. We were surrounded.

The man with the book approached with a measured tread that drew all eyes. He had height and breadth, the look of a man who fought in wars once and means to do so again. Silver streaked his mane of wavy black hair. His face bore the stamp of his father's noble Malian ancestors in having brown skin and his mother's patrician Roman lineage in having a bold nose.

My enemy, General Camjiata.

"I've been waiting for you, Cat," he said with the friendly smile the victor can afford to give the vanquished. "I admire your plan for a bold escape, and your ability to gather allies. But you're going to have to come to the Council Hall to address the charge of murder."

4

"Shall I eat him, Cat?" murmured Rory.

"Rory, don't move. They'll shoot you." I faced the general. "How did you find us?"

"You see, Cat, it isn't that you need to have the dragon dreamer at your side at all times," said General Camjiata as he strolled up to me. "She does not dream the day before of what will come to pass the next morning."

"She doesn't?" I asked, thinking of my dream.

He took no notice because he was too enthralled by the sound of his own voice. "Nor can she walk by purpose into a dream that will tell her what she wishes to know about a crossroads in her future. She may never even recognize what it is she has seen. What you need to make use of a dreamer's gift is a record of her dreams, so you can study this record until you see patterns emerge and weave the pieces together."

He opened the book.

"That's Bee's sketchbook!" I exclaimed. "The one you stole from her!"

The page was a jumble of images drawn in Bee's vivid style: a winged horse galloping across waves; the famous twinned bronze pillars known to stand in the temple of Melqart outside the city of Gadir in Iberia; a black saber-toothed cat; nine half-moons. And a pretty little portrait of me from the back, holding by the hair the decapitated head of Queen Anacaona as I looked over my shoulder as if in flight from a pursuer.

"Gah." I reached across him to turn the page, for the gruesome detail took me aback.

He pulled the book away from me. "The *White Horse* is a ship that will sail to Gadir from the quay known by its pillars of Heracles, which to the Phoenicians are known to be the pillars in the temple of Melqart at Gadir. On the Nones of November, the fifth day of November, which is today, the fugitive accused of the murder of the cacica will arrive at the quay with her brother."

"Why nine moons when November isn't the ninth month? And why the half-moon?"

"In the early Roman calendar, November was the ninth month. Nones refers to the day of the half-moon. If you don't know that, you can't make use of the dream."

"You could just have guessed I might have tried to escape on a Phoenician ship leaving before the tide turns."

Taino soldiers parted ranks to allow a frowning Prince Caonabo to come forward.

The general indicated me. "Your Highness. I told you I would find her. With this one, you really need to use a rope if you want to capture her."

He whistled. In his first war his army had been famed for its Amazon Corps, women who fought with more ferocity than men. My mother, Tara Bell, had been a captain in his Amazon Corps, and she had been condemned to death for the crime of becoming pregnant, with me. A woman dressed in soldier's garb walked forward. Captain Tira sheathed her falcata and unlooped a length of rope. It had a noose, to go around my neck.

"Yee cannot be serious!" said Kofi.

Rory snarled.

Camjiata smiled, as if he hoped I would do something reckless.

Luce, Kofi, and the men of Kofi's household were fenced in. No doubt they would be charged with aiding and abetting a fugitive.

"Your Highness, I'll come quietly," I said to Prince Caonabo, "if you will agree to let these people go free, no questions asked, no grudge held, no charges brought."

"So have I already agreed," the prince replied. "All but your brother may go without prejudice."

"Kofi, just go," I said, for by the gritting of his teeth I could see his frustration building.

His eyes flared as he gestured for his kinfolk to depart, but he went. Luce flung her arms around Rory, who peeled her off and pushed her after the others. The soldiers made an opening for them to push out their carts. A crowd had begun to gather on the jetty, mostly laborers headed for work or women carrying wood or water to their homes.

"An ugly crowd," said Camjiata. "Best we make our way to Council Hall quickly, Your Highness. We need only leash the girl. The young man will follow her."

No longer pretending to smile, he dropped the noose over my neck. The coarse sailor's hemp chafed my skin.

The prince's open carriage rolled out from behind Nance's. I clothed myself in as much dignity as I could gather and stepped up into it. Rory walked behind the carriage to keep an eye on everyone. I wondered if it was his usual position in the hunt when he and his mother, aunt, and sisters prowled the spirit world in search of their next meal.

Prince Caonabo sat facing me. Camjiata sat next to me, holding the rope.

As the driver snapped the reins and the horses moved forward, the Taino soldiers paced in disciplined ranks. The general's Iberian veterans had more of a swagger. Sailors and laborers gathered at slips and quays to stare, and women and wagons moved aside to let us pass. A gaggle of young toughs shadowed us.

"Why have you involved yourself in this inquiry, General?" I asked politely, even if I really wanted to bite and claw.

"Cat, I am not your enemy. Please be assured that Tara Bell's child will always have a home with me if she needs shelter. I want only to protect you." I had never met a man who could speak in such sentimental platitudes and yet have it sound so genuine and unforced. It was one of the most irritating things about him.

"Protect me? You betrayed me!"

"The cacica was required by law to exile you to Salt Island. What you don't understand is that Salt Island was the safest place for you at that time."

"That you can say so with a straight face and such sincerity is almost admirable! Everything I did here in Expedition was machinated by you."

"Perhaps not quite everything. Things are not as simple as you believe they are. But this is not the place to discuss them."

We crossed under the shadow of the gate and into the old city with its encircling stone walls, legacy of an earlier time. For generations, only families with Council ties and wealth were allowed to own property inside the walls, while newer districts were built outside the walls. When the Council still ruled, the gates were locked at dusk and even in the daytime any person entering the old city could be searched. Now the toughs swarmed right in after us, dogging our heels. Their presence heartened me.

I addressed Prince Caonabo. "Your Highness, did you know that the general believes I am to be the instrument of his death? That is why he conspired with your mother the honored cacica to have me permanently quarantined on Salt Island."

"I want the truth," said Caonabo.

We halted at the base of the wide steps that fronted Council Hall. I caught sight of Luce pushing through the crowd. Idiot girl! Rory gestured to warn her off.

The prince's attendants unfolded the carriage steps.

Before any of us could alight from the carriage, a young man descended the steps of Council Hall with a mocking grin that I wanted to punch right off his face. His red-gold hair seemed to blaze like flame and his blue eyes to kindle with heat, or maybe those were sparks from his fire magic. Really, the last person I wanted to see in a situation like this was James Drake. I curled my left hand into a fist as he came up.

"Why, Cat, I've been waiting all night for you to show up." As an afterthought, he acknowledged the prince with a careless wave. "Your Highness, my understanding of Taino law is that murderers are sentenced to labor in the cane fields for life. Or they are assigned as a catch-fire to a fire mage. We all know she's responsible for the Exalted Queen's death. Once she is convicted, I will be happy to take her off Taino hands. I could use a remarkably pretty catch-fire."

Naturally Prince Caonabo had too much dignity to respond to this rude outburst.

But I didn't!

"James Drake! Why are you standing here waiting for me like a lovesick but rejected suitor?"

The general pulled firmly on the rope to keep me on the seat. "Don't be rash, Cat," he murmured. "This is not the place or time for a pissing match."

"I wasn't waiting because I want you!" Drake's gaze flicked around the crowd: the Taino soldiers, the crowd held at a prudent distance by wardens, Camjiata's retinue of veterans, and the guards stationed at the Council Hall doors. He pitched his voice louder. "I hope you finally understand that I slept with you only to show the cold mage he wasn't so high and mighty as he thought he was. Because there's really nothing a man hates more than knowing his wife is a *whore*."

The word stung. "You lied to me and got me drunk."

"The ease with which I got you to have sex ought to give any man pause, knowing how easy it was to tip rum down your throat and coax the clothes off your admittedly attractive body. Still, it scarcely matters now. I'm a magnanimous man. I'd never turn away a pretty girl like you if you offered to warm my bed in exchange for better treatment after the standing inquiry condemns you as a murderer."

My face was burning, and my heart was pounding. "Fortunately, I only had sexual congress with you twice. That's all I needed, to know I needn't bother if I want to take any pleasure from the act."

People in the crowd sniggered.

The prince was literally blinking in astonishment, mouth agape.

Drake laughed derisively, but anyone could see he was furious. "You keep ruining the impression of your pretty face with that crass mouth of yours. Now that you're an accused murderer, I'd be careful about antagonizing the only person in this city who might be persuaded to make your life more pleasant than it will be in the cane fields."

When I shifted forward with fist cocked, the general tugged on the rope to pull me up short.

"I'd have to be dead before I'd let you touch me," I said as the hemp scraped my neck.

"Strange you should phrase it in quite that way." Drake smiled as might a man who is waiting to see your reaction when you realize the trap has closed over your foot.

"James, that is really enough," Camjiata said without raising his voice.

"I will tell you what is enough! *Enough* is that my noble kinfolk stole my birthright and inheritance, and I let them because I was too young and powerless to fight. But I'm not powerless now. I want her as my catch-fire, so I'll cursed well get her as my catch-fire. I'll have the last word after all, won't I?"

"You sound like a man who can't let go of the knowledge that he lost and his rival succeeded. As for you, Cat, this childish bickering insults His Noble Highness the prince and indeed all of us forced to listen to it."

Drake was livid. "I did not lose to him!"

Drake had the power to immolate me, but in doing so, he would burn himself up as well. Unlike Prince Caonabo, he had no catch-fires to spill away the backlash of his magic. I couldn't help myself. I had to keep poking.

"Really? It's never bothered you that you couldn't spoil his love for me because he's a better man than you'll ever be? That the moment I found him I never thought of you again? That he's killed your fire magic more than once and can do it again?"

Light pulsed as the forecourt's gas lamps flared. A mist-like glamour writhed around Drake's body. "When next I meet Andevai Diarisso Haranwy, he will crawl at my feet and admit I am stronger than he is. Fire always defeats ice in the end."

Prince Caonabo spoke sharp words in Taino. Soldiers raised rifles. The murmuring crowd pushed back, for no one wanted to stand close when a fire mage went rogue.

"I said *enough*!" snapped the general. "James, go back to the house."

"Enough is right! I've had enough of this bitch!" His bright blue eyes really did seem to blaze.

Heat flared in my chest, like fire kindling. I lunged, but the general yanked me down so hard I hit my shoulder and banged a knee. In that eyeblink during which I was too stunned to move, I saw what would happen by the stiffening of Rory's shoulders, the tremor in his eyes. Like me he thought with his body. He reacted to danger in an entirely predictable way.

Rory *changed* as thoroughly as if the tide of a dragon's dream washed over him to dissolve him into his true form. His body melted and flowed, clothes ripping at the seams as his shape shifted. A huge black saber-toothed cat leaped.

Reports rang out, guns going off, and the big cat stumbled and went down.

5

Heedless of claws and teeth, Luce threw her body across the thrashing cat. That was the only reason the Taino soldiers did not finish him off.

I ripped the rope out of the general's grasp and jumped from the carriage, brandishing my cane as I ran to Rory's side. "Call them off!"

The instant I pressed my cane against his head to make sure he didn't bite anyone, his body melted away to become a man lying naked and bleeding on the cobblestones. He'd been hit in his right shoulder and left thigh. A liquid pulsed along his skin like blood, although it was clear, not red. His eyes were open, questing back and forth as if trying to fix on a moving target.

I grasped his hand.

"Is this death, Cat?" His voice was a whisper. "I feel my strength draining out of me. Will my spirit pass back to my mother on the other side? Or will I just dissolve into the wind?"

Soldiers blocked us in, facing the angry crowd. Caonabo came up with his catch-fires.

"Don't touch him!" I snarled.

"Make your choice, Perdita. He may bleed out, or I can cauterize his wounds."

His words punched the breath right out of my lungs. I shifted back to let him kneel.

"Rory, this fire mage will stop the bleeding. Allow him to touch you."

Among Rory's people—a pride of saber-toothed cats who roamed in the spirit world—a male trusted his mother and aunts and sisters absolutely. He watched me with eyes as amber as my own, for we had inherited golden eyes and black hair from the creature who had sired us. Luce crept to my side as the prince inspected the wounded leg. He wiped up a dab of the colorless blood, sniffed it, and glanced at me but asked no questions. A man of his education no doubt could draw his own conclusions. After assuring himself the shot had gone clear through flesh, he placed a hand on either side of the thigh.

Caonabo's two catch-fires lit as if they were gas lamps touched to flame.

I gasped. Luce's grip on my arm tightened.

A skin of fire radiated from the prince's hands. Four days ago, on Hallows' Eve, standing under the veil of my sire's terrifying power, I had seen Prince Caonabo's mother casting off the backlash of her magic into a net of catch-fires. The lines drawn between the cacica and her catch-fires had spanned the island of Kiskeya. She had created a woven web through which the backwash of fire magic was drained out of her, through the catch-fires, and into the seemingly bottomless well that was the spirit world. Shimmering threads spun out of Caonabo and into his catch-fires. One catch-fire alone would have burst into flame and died; two could split the backlash between them and pour it harmlessly away.

Rory exhaled sharply. His eyes rolled up, and he passed out.

"Blessed Tanit!" I touched his throat.

His pulse stirred, weak but steady, as pale blood leaked along the curve of his neck. Unthinkingly, I licked his blood off my fingers. It was so sweet, not harsh at all.

Prince Caonabo draped linen over Rory's genitals to give him a scrap of dignity. An elderly woman with feathers and beads woven into her white hair approached, carrying a basket. She produced a pair of tweezers. He probed Rory's shoulder and pulled out a bloody bullet. He then pressed a hand over the wound and cauterized it as well.

Luce sat beside me, clutching my other arm. I scrubbed at my lips but the taste of Rory's blood lingered. I began to shake.

Caonabo rose. "Now we go to Council Hall."

"Yee shall not go with them, Cat!" Luce cried. "They shan't kill yee!"

"Hush, Luce." I grabbed her. "Help Kofi bring our gear. Quickly! Now go!"

She kissed Rory's cheek in a way that brought tears to my eyes. She was free to choose what pleasure and affection she desired. If he died, who was I or anyone to say it would have been better if they had not shared love?

Proudly she rose. At a gesture from Caonabo, the Taino soldiers parted to let her leave. I yanked off the noose over my neck and only then did I think to look for James Drake.

He had vanished. Caonabo was wiping his hands with a cloth, surrounded by concerned attendants.

Camjiata took hold of my elbow. "Don't be a fool, Cat. Drake has guessed the cold mage is still alive, for it is obvious whenever you speak of him. Your plan on Hallows' Night to kill me went badly wrong. Still, I hold no ill will against you. Our lives—yours and mine—are bound by destiny. We are meant to be allies in the struggle for liberation."

I shook off his grip. "I'm not putting that noose back on."

Wardens carried Rory up the steps, through the entryway, and along a corridor. The chamber we entered was furnished with tables and benches. The men settled Rory atop one of the tables and set up guard at both sets of doors. I asked them to bring a basin, water, and cloth, as well as a behique who was a healer.

One door let onto the main corridor. A set of glass-paned doors opened onto a large central courtyard that was completely boxed in by the wings of the Council Hall complex. In the courtyard a monument depicted a buffalo and lion, and a covered cistern provided water. But the most striking object in the courtyard was a majestic ceiba tree, with a wide canopy and ridge-like roots grown out from the trunk.

I paced, one hand on the ghost-sword the Taino believed held my mother's spirit and the other cupped around the locket I wore that contained a portrait of Daniel Hassi Barahal, the man who had called himself my father even though he had not sired me. The locket also held strands of hair from my husband. In the warmth of the locket I felt the pulse of the thread that bound the heart of Andevai Diarisso Haranwy to my own. Somewhere in the spirit world, Vai was alive.

A local healer arrived, an older woman with a fire mage's crackling touch. After helping me wash Rory she coaxed a sweet-smelling syrup down his throat to help him sleep. After she left I sat beside him for the longest time, combing out his hair with my fingers because I had no other way to relieve the churn of my emotions. I'd been a fool to provoke Drake, but it had felt so good! Yet he had wanted me to lose my temper, so I had played into his hands. The fire I'd felt was my anger, not his magic. My rashness had hurt Rory, not me.

I rested my head on my arms on the table. Rory's breathing whispered in my ear. I had to make a plan, but the general's words kept trampling through my thoughts: *"Our lives are bound by destiny."* Chains draped me everywhere I looked.

My night's broken sleep caught up to me. I dozed, then drifted awake to the sound of voices outside. Groggily, I raised my head to look out into the courtyard. Judging by the lack of shadows, it was almost midday. Rory still slept. I jumped to my feet as the door to the main corridor opened.

A troll entered. Prince Caonabo called them *the feathered people*, which was a more respectful and accurate description than the Europan appellation of *trolls*. What they called themselves involved whistling and song, an intricate language whose nuances we rats—as trolls called humans—could not imitate except at the simplest level.

Like all trolls Keer was tall, with the predatorily gracile movement of a creature at home with killing, even though I had never seen her eat anything other than fruit and nuts. She had the snout and teeth of a hunter and big, round eyes like those of a raptor that can see farther and with more detail than any human. Seen from a distance, the tiny brown feathers covering her skin made it look as if she were covered with scales. Close up, the odd shimmer of feathers and the expressive shifting of her feathered crest caused her to seem a blend of lizard and bird and yet, truly, not either one. She was a lawyer, the local representative of the firm of Godwik and Clutch. Her clutch also ran a printing press.

Behind her came Kofi and Luce carrying Vai's chest between them.

Keer approached me in an intimidating manner, but I did not retreat. She passed her cheek alongside mine, and took in an audible sniff. I sucked in a breath myself, for it was always wise to imitate what trolls did as a mark of respect. Her scent reminded me of the perfume of summer in the north, when the sun bakes grass from green to gold.

She bobbed a greeting, then stepped away to pace around the table on which Rory lay. "I have come to represent you at the standing inquiry, and to help you make your defense. Curious, this one. He looks like a rat but he smells like a cat."

I smoothed a hand over Rory's disheveled hair, wondering if Keer was fighting off an urge to taste mancat flesh. "I suppose he does."

She chuffed a trollish laugh. Three trolls accompanied her. Two posted themselves as guards, one at each door. The third sat at the other table, opened a writing case, and prepared to take a written record of the proceedings.

"Cat, have yee eaten?" Luce asked.

"I asked the wardens to bring something, but they never did."

"How like men!" she muttered. "Yee must be famished."

"I am, and really thirsty, too."

"We cannot begin until you are fed," said Keer. "No person can be expected to think properly if she is distracted by hunger." She showed her teeth in an unsettling mimicry of a human smile, which reminded me how easily she could eat me if *she* were distracted by hunger.

"I'll get food," said Luce.

While we waited, Keer, Kofi, and I argued about the latest batey games and gossip. Luce returned with rice porridge, fruit, ginger beer, and enough cassava bread and rice and peas to feed six of me, although I managed to finish almost half of it while the others picked off the rest. When I had done, Keer banished Luce and Kofi.

"I must conduct the interview in privacy, so yee must wait outside." When they had gone, she settled opposite me at the table. She was facile with human language and adjusted her speech to fit her listener. "Tell me everything that happened."

I explained how I had been betrayed by General Camjiata into the custody of Queen Anacaona, and how she had ordered her people to imprison me on Salt Island because I had been bitten by a salter. "But the cacica herself said I was clean. The salt plague is spread by the invisible teeth of the ghouls, eating through flesh and then into the brain. I have no ghoul's teeth in my body. There was nothing to heal."

"Useful to know but not helpful with the case," she said, watching as the clerk scratched markings I could not read. "The First Treaty does give the Taino the right to demand you be turned over to them because of the quarantine. What else can you tell me?"

I explained how, on Hallows' Eve, the Wild Hunt had ridden out of a hurricane and rescued me from Salt Island. At the command of the Master of the Wild Hunt, I had cut a path with my half-mortal blood through the fence of magic that surrounded the Taino kingdom. My sire had told me the Wild Hunt would kill my dear cousin Beatrice if I did not find richer blood to feed the courts who ruled the Hunt. I had meant for the Wild Hunt to kill General Camjiata, the man who had betrayed me. But because Camjiata had no magic, my sire could not see or sense him. Instead, my sire had decided to kill my husband because he was a cold mage of rare and unexpected potency. At the same time, the cacica had been about to kill me together with other fugitives who had escaped Salt Island.

"You did not with your own hands, talons, teeth, or sword kill the cacica," said Keer.

"No, but I convinced the Master of the Wild Hunt to take her instead of Vai."

"You acted in self-defense. The cacica was about to kill you, and you defended yourself."

"What about Rory? Many witnesses saw a black saber-toothed cat break her neck."

She tapped her taloned fingers on the table. "Is a soldier responsible for the deaths he is ordered to inflict in battle? Or is the general who commands the deaths held to be the responsible party? Furthermore, on a night of storm, confused and frightened people may see shadows as giant eagles or as creeping spiders. Perhaps there was such a cat. Certainly in the ancestral territories of my people, what you rats call troll country, such carnivores prowl the land. We have hunted them and been hunted in our turn. But that is not proof that your brother committed the act."

"The prince saw him become a cat and then change back into a man, just now, when he got shot," I said.

"We cannot accuse a man of thieving a hat just because some man was seen to steal a hat and the accused is also a man." She bared her teeth at me in a brilliantly sharp smile, as if she were preparing to eat any lawyers who argued against her. "Very well. I am prepared to make a case."

As the clerk tidied up her notes, we went to the glass-paned doors to look into the deserted courtyard. Afternoon shadows smeared darkness across stone pathways.

Kofi joined us there. "I have set wardens to guard yee so the fire mage can make no mischief before the inquiry. I don' trust him, with the way he went after yee on the steps. As for the general, we shall see who shall come out the winner in this match."

"The general scored a point on you all, didn't he? By catching me at the quay."

His taut smile made him look eager for a fight. "We's not playing batey now. We in the Assembly is playing the game of politics. We don' intend to lose this hard-won freedom. If the Taino can force us to turn yee over to them, then it's as if they rule us. That's why we shall fight so hard to get yee off, despite what the law and the First Treaty say."

Voices were raised outside. We looked around as the door slammed open to reveal stern-faced Taino soldiers, richly dressed attendants, Prince Caonabo, and Beatrice.

6

Some people have the knack of sweeping into any situation as if they were born to be the light of all eyes. Beatrice might be mistaken for a shallow, flighty, and self-absorbed young woman, but I knew her bombastic and flamboyant manner concealed a generous heart, a brooding intellect, and an indignation at the unfairness and injustice in the world. She had had a lot of time to think about the curse of dreaming that would plague her for the rest of her life and had chosen to confront it head-on. Clutching a sketchbook and lead pencil, she sailed into the room.

"Cat! There you are!"

A magnificent white cotton robe in the style of a Taino noble-woman's covered her from shoulders to ankles. A bodice beaded with pearls wrapped her bosom and waist, emphasizing her much admired and voluptuous curves. The lush curls of her black hair cascaded around her shoulders, ornamented with strings of pearls. She embraced me, then looked around my shoulder.

"Rory!" She ran to him and rested her cheek against his. Tears glimmered in her eyes.

"Prince Caonabo healed him," I said, following her. "I thought you should know that."

Prince Caonabo broke his silence. "Assemblyman, how can my people trust those who will not honor the law and our ancient treaties?"

"A heavy accusation, Your Highness," said Kofi, with the stare of a man who feels sure of his ground. I was surprised he spoke so boldly to the Taino prince. "My advice to yee is to be careful in how yee choose yee allies."

The prince indicated the door. "I should prefer to speak to the accused in private."

Kofi looked at me, and I nodded my permission. He, Keer, and all the others left. Bee and I were alone with the prince except, of course, for his catch-fires and Rory.

Bee smiled blindingly at Caonabo for long enough to coax a smile to his grave expression. "I hope you see it is impossible for you to consider hanging my dear Cat."

"Hanging is a barbaric Europan custom," the prince replied as he crossed the chamber.

Reaching her, he extended a hand. To my surprise, Bee meekly handed him her new sketchbook, the one she had started after Camjiata had stolen the other. Bee had started drawing the year my parents died and had never stopped. She often slept with a pencil in her hand. Even now her fingers were smudged with lead. She had been drawing and had come in such haste she hadn't had time to wash.

"So, Beatrice"—he pronounced the name charmingly, like *Bey-a-tree-say*—"we all three know she had a hand in the death of my mother." I would never have dared to thumb through Bee's sketchbook without permission unless I was far enough away from her to avoid objects flung at me. He flipped casually through its mostly blank pages. "Regardless, I have done as you asked."

"What did you ask, Bee?" I demanded.

"I asked nothing." Bee's gaze was fixed on the sketchbook as if she expected spiders to crawl out of it.

"It is true. She asked nothing. A woman like Beatrice does not crudely threaten. She would never remind me in plain words that my claim to the cacique's throne is tenuous and that I need her presence as my bride to give my claim weight. She would never hold over my head how precious a treasure she is. One need only look at her to know that."

She flashed a gaze at him, her chin trembling, then demurely cast her gaze to the floor. "Does the marriage bed not please you, Husband?"

He tensed. "You know it does. But that cannot sway me."

"Sway you from what?" I asked.

"Beatrice went to visit you at your domicile yesterday," said the prince. "She returned to the palace before evening. It was at that time I believe she heard my councillors speak of arresting you for the murder of the cacica. Here is the sketch she drew this morning."

He showed me a sketch. Bee had drawn five people on a wide path. The path was spanned by a huge monumental archway hung with painted gourds in the Taino style. Seen past the arch, lying below the height, spread a splendid city and harbor, almost certainly Taino if one judged by the ballcourt and sprawling palace seen in the distance. Rory loitered at the back of the group with a jaunty grin on his face, as if he'd just gotten away with something he knew he ought not to have done, and certainly ought not to have enjoyed quite so much. A second man was sketched entirely from the back, but I could tell he was Vai. He wore a splendidly fashionable dash jacket printed in an outrageous pattern of flowers like bursting fireworks, and he was holding my hand. In the sketch, I looked as cranky and out of sorts as if I'd been having a discussion I didn't want to have. Fortunately I was wearing a fashionable military-cut riding jacket with a split skirt and a jaunty hat.

In the sketch, Prince Caonabo leaned against the right-hand span of the archway as if he had been waiting a long time for us to reach him. Bee strode out in front looking quite spectacularly...

"Pregnant!" I cried.

"Pregnant," agreed Caonabo. He snapped the sketchbook shut, and Bee flinched. "There you are, Maestra, you and your brother and your husband, alive and well in Sharagua. What man would not be moved by such a pleasing vision of his harmonious future?"

I hadn't had time to examine the sketch closely, for there was one obvious thing that might have caused this puzzling tension between them. "That is you, Your Highness, is it not?"

Bee blushed mightily.

Caonabo did not look at her, only at me. "You wonder if I believe it to be my brother. Haübey and I are twins, shaped to the same mold. Few people can tell us apart. But Beatrice can tell us apart. It is evident to me by certain small signs"—none of which he was going to share with me!—"that the man in the sketch is meant to represent me rather than Haübey. The sketch might be described as a bribe, if you will."

I grasped Bee's hand. Her skin felt like ice. "What do you mean, Your Highness?"

"What man would not wish to make sure such a future came about by protecting all the parts necessary to make this meeting happen? Do you not suppose so, Beatrice? A man's ability to sire children is a mark of potency. Even though it is my sister's sons who will inherit my position as cacique once I pass over, still, a cacique who cannot sire children of his own will be seen as a weak man unworthy of the duho, the seat of power."

Bee's fingers tightened on mine until my hand hurt. Her strength always surprised people, even me as I set my jaw and tried to relax into the pain, for it was clear Bee was truly upset.

He went on in that same level voice, but I could hear an edge. "But one problem remains."

"What is that, Your Highness?"

"Dream walkers are barren."

Bee gasped.

"How can anyone know?" I asked, but my mind was already churning. Camjiata had married a dream walker and she had never borne children. The radical fighter Brennan Touré Du had told Bee and me a story about a young woman from his home village who had seen visions and been killed by the Wild Hunt on Hallows' Night, and Brennan had remarked that although the woman had been married for five years, she had given birth to no child in that time. "I mean, surely even if one or two dreamers never had children, no scholar would claim that means all such women are barren."

"We Taino have studied this matter for many generations. We have our own disciplines of what the Romans name *scientia*. Who first observed the transit of the planet you call Venus? Who invented the steam engine, which was then carried across the sea to Europa? Our scholars have spanned earth and heavens with their investigations. It is known to our scholars through careful investigation that dream walkers are barren. The sketch is a lie, not a dream. Is it not, Beatrice?"

She released my hand. I winced as blood flowed back into my squashed fingers.

"My bride lied to me, deliberately and with forethought. She meant to mislead and manipulate me into doing what she wanted."

From the vivid flush in her cheeks and the tears streaking her face, it was obvious she was both ashamed and defiant. "My other choice was to tell you I would divorce you and not help you gain the throne. I will not stand by and see Cat put on trial and executed."

"Telling me the truth would have been honest." That he did not look at her made his words sound even more hurtful. He stared at me, as if daring me to look away and thus prove my guilt. "Tell me, Catherine Bell Barahal, do you care that you are responsible for the cacica's death? If her exalted rank means nothing, for I believe you once told me that Taino queens and princes mean little enough to you, then do you care that you are responsible for a woman's death?"

"How dare you speak to her like that!" Bee stepped between him and me with such an aggressive movement that both catch-fires turned. "Cat did not murder the cacica! It's unjust of you to blame her just because you need someone to blame!"

I set Bee firmly to one side. "No, he deserves an answer."

Prince Caonabo and I were the same height, so we matched, eye to eye. "I held no animosity toward Queen Anacaona except that she conspired with General Camjiata to exile me to Salt Island. At least her motives seemed disinterested in that regard. But at the ballcourt on Hallows' Night, she was going to kill me. You know it is true."

"I heard her words. She called for the death of salters, as was her right and obligation to protect the kingdom from illness."

"She would have killed your twin brother, too, and other people as well, people whose only crime was to have been bitten by salters and healed by fire mages like yourself. As you once healed your brother. Isn't that right?"

He hesitated, then frowned. "It is true."

"Haübey would have died on Hallows' Night, too?" Bee whispered. "You never told me that!"

A flare of emotion blushed his cheeks.

I leaped into silence, for I wanted him to be angry at me instead of Bee. "I couldn't possibly kill a fire mage as powerful as Queen Anacaona. It seems to me you Taino should direct your anger at the personage who wielded the power to kill the cacica. We Europans call him the Master of the Wild Hunt. I suppose you Taino would call him a spirit lord. But he's beyond your reach, so you cast your spears of revenge at me."

His eyes tightened at the corners as he glanced at Bee, then back at me. "Even with the cacica alive, I would have needed the woman who walks the dreams of dragons to strengthen my position when I travel to Sharagua to claim the cacique's duho. Haübey was the son my mother trained for the duho, not me. But he can never set foot in our land again because, as you say, he was bitten by a salter. That I healed him makes no difference to his exile. He has taken a foreign name, Juba, to show he is dead in Taino country. He has already departed over the sea. Yet I would dishonor my lineage if I allowed a different branch of the family to wrest the duho from me. So you will travel to Sharagua with me, Beatrice. I have the right to ask that of you. And the means to make you do it."

He offered her the sketchbook. She hesitated to take it, for his gesture had an air of finality that made my neck prickle.

He opened his hand. The book fell. Bee grabbed it before it hit the floor.

"When the duho has passed to me and I am proclaimed as cacique, you will leave Taino country and never come back. You didn't just lie. You made use of the pure and sacred vision that is the treasure of dreams you guard, to try and cheat me and my people."

"You forced me to choose between you and my cousin," Bee said. "You accused her unfairly. It looks to me as if you want to sacrifice her in order to gain the throne. I think I am the one who may doubt the purity of your intentions!"

"You have no idea what my intentions are, or how I intended to thread this labyrinth, to find a way to satisfy justice. We Taino do not sacrifice servants forced to obey their master's command. But you treat me as a foreigner who cannot be trusted. Yet you were willing to exchange your body and your dreams for the wealth, security, and knowledge my rank and my people offered you."

She flinched as if his rebuke had been a physical slap. "I have done what my heart told me to do, Your Highness."

"What of your duty?" His calm gaze and measured words fell more harshly than anger would have.

I embraced her, resting my cheek on her hair as I whispered. "Kofi and Keer have a plan for my defense. Kayleigh has money if we need it for berths on a ship. I will support you whatever you choose, Bee. Do what you must."

She took in a shuddering breath. "Hassi Barahals may be mercenaries and spies, but we are never, ever cheats."

"Then go. We can leave messages for each other at any of the law offices of Godwik and Clutch, here or in Adurnam or Havery."

She wiped her cheeks as she released me. Majestic in presence, she faced the man she had agreed to marry believing his exalted position and powerful kingdom could protect us. "I will do my duty toward you, Your Highness. Never think otherwise."

I could not read the book of Caonabo's emotions as I had learned to read Andevai. Despite his vanity and arrogance, or perhaps because of them, Vai had far less restraint. That he believed he had a great deal of self-control while having very little had become one of the things that charmed me about him. Not so with Prince Caonabo. As I watched him watch Bee walk with dignity to the door, I could not tell if he yearned for what they had so quickly lost or if he was simply measuring the odds that he could trust her to do the part he needed her to do.

At the door she glanced back. Her gaze caught mine. We said nothing, for we knew what we needed to know of each other. Our love was our promise and our security. She left, leaving the door open behind her for Caonabo to follow.

The prince paused, turning to give me a last look. "The blood of my mother lies between us, Catherine Bell Barahal. But because I respect the law, I act as the law requires. Do you? Will you take responsibility for your actions, or will you seek the chance to escape what you have brought about without accepting your part in it?"

7

I had to trust in the plan hatched by Kofi and Keer. With Rory wounded, I had few options.

We spent the rest of the afternoon quietly. When Rory woke up, he seemed far better than he had any right to be, but he developed a sulky whine that Luce was better able to tolerate than I was. She demanded that wash water be brought so I could bathe and change my clothes. I sewed buttonholes on the two winter coats because the tailors hadn't had time to finish them. To pass the time, she and I discussed the chamber murals. The paintings depicted the history of the First Fleet: the eruption of the salt plague out of the salt mines of the Sahara Desert; the crossing of the Atlantic Ocean by the multitudes fleeing with the Malian fleet; landfall on the southern shore of the island of Kiskeya in the Sea of Antilles.

Luce traced the adventures of her ancestors with a look of dizzy excitement. "I shall have an adventure, too. I shall come with yee to rescue Vai. I's old enough to leave home. I always wanted to travel, like me father!"

"No, you shall not!" Leaning my forehead against hers, I captured her gaze with mine to bind her to my will. I was implacable; I had to be, because she was a sheltered girl with a sunny good nature from having grown up in a loyal household whose family members cared for each other. "We can't afford your passage to Europa. You can't walk into the spirit world anyway."

Her frown developed a stubborn kick.

"Rory and I can cross into the spirit world because of what we are. People aren't meant to walk there. Hunters apprentice for years to learn the secret lore passed down among them. You will die, or be changed beyond recognition."

Luce glared, trembling. "Everyone say I shall be a great help to me mother to run the boardinghouse. But what if that is not what I want? I don' want to work in them factories neither. And the ships me father sails don' accept women as sailors, for that is the Roman way. I don' have the connections nor the apprentice fee a gal need to get a berth on a ship run by a troll consortium."

"It would just kill your family if you left, Luce. They love you!"

Her dark gaze accused me, as if I had betrayed her.

Rory stirred. "I'm thirsty," he whimpered. She went to him.

At nightfall I went to the doors that looked over the courtyard. Kofi joined me.

"How old is that ceiba tree?" In the night breeze stirring its branches I was sure I felt the breath of the spirit world. Its scent wound through my bones.

Kofi rocked from toe to heel and back. "'Twas a sapling planted here on that very day the Taino caciques and the captains of the fleet met to seal the First Treaty. The story go that they who ruled chose one beautiful gal who did come over with the Malian fleet and one handsome lad who was Taino-born upon this island. They two were sacrificed and their blood and bones set in the earth to feed the tree and bind the treaty."

I pressed a cheek into the glass. I tasted on the air the ancient power of blood to bind the living and the dead.

He put a hand on my forearm. "The Taino believe the ancestors hold them to the right and proper way of living. There was never one thing to stop the Taino all these years from invading Expedition except so far as they held to the law."

"No, I suppose not. The Taino kingdom is so powerful, and Expedition Territory is tiny in comparison. But I must say, Kofi, I really think their greatest strength is their fire mages. If I'm found guilty, will the provisional Assembly allow the prince to take me away into Taino country? Will they hand me over to James Drake? Will they support me or sacrifice me?"

The scars on his cheeks made him seem forbidding until he smiled. "They shall have to find yee guilty first. I tell yee, gal, I have heard yee scold men before, but to watch yee tear into that fire mage Drake made me skin turn cold."

"I know I shouldn't have spoken like that. I'll keep my mouth shut from now on."

He laughed.

I leaned my head against Kofi's shoulder, so broad and solid, but I wished it were Vai I was leaning against. The shock of Caonabo repudiating Bee and her departure with him on a journey sure to be miserable and unpleasant had torn away my shield of determination. All my ugliest fears surfaced like Leviathan breaching the waves.

"Vai's so accustomed to being the most powerful magister, to winning. What if my sire breaks him? What kind of man will he be? And will I still love him?"

"Peradventure Vai shall not survive this. But I reckon I have never met a man with such a high opinion of he own consequence. In such a dark place, a man's vanity and arrogance can be what save him."

I sniveled out something meant to be a chuckle. "If any man's conceit can survive captivity by the Master of the Wild Hunt, it would be his."

"There. Yee have brought yee fear out into the light. I reckon yee have been fretting."

I sniffled, wiping my eyes. "Now Bee's thrown away her future trying to save me."

A windblown branch tapped on one of the glass doors that led out to the courtyard.

"Cat, she done no different a thing than yee did for her. Chance it shall even be for the best. The Taino nobles is a high and mighty people who look down on folk like us. Maybe she would fancy a life in their court, or maybe she would find she own self in a cage that squeeze like a trap. Vai told me one time that the day he was brought up from the village to Four Moons House and taken before the mansa, he reckoned he was the most fortunate lad alive to have such a chance. He came to find they did not want him but dared not turn him away. They treated him like the worst kind of mangy cur. So he decided to become better at being one of them than any of them was at it. Yee said to me one time that the worst thing for Vai shall be if he go back to the mage House and become a cold mage like to what he was when yee two first met. I see now what yee meant. 'Twas no good home for him at the mage House. So why is yee so sure the Taino court would be a good home for yee cousin?"

"Do you think they could crush her?"

He chuckled. "That gal? I reckon not. But that don' mean she shall for a surety live a happy life there. Had she married a Taino man of the common run I reckon she should have as good a chance as any to have a good life, for the Taino live as well and justly as any folk do. But I's not a man to choose a palace of gold and precious shells over a humble room if the first come with a knife in the back and a foot on me heart and the second come with a smile and a kiss. I don' know what yee cousin wish for above all else. She may be glad later to have another choice."

When I thought about it, wondering what Bee would really want, I realized I wasn't sure. If anyone had asked me a year ago if I hoped and dreamed a handsome, wealthy, and well-connected young man would fall in love with me at first sight, I would have laughed and said yes because it was the sort of thing a young woman was supposed to say yes to. But it wouldn't have been true. Bee was the one who dreamed of a romantic story in which she figured as the principal heroine. I had wanted nothing more than to have a chance to follow in my father Daniel's footsteps, to travel the length and breadth of Europa seeing new places and, if I was fortunate, have adventures as he had had. I would have wanted a romantic interlude…at some unspecified later date.

Bee had made her choice. She had chosen to be loyal to me.

I released Kofi's hand and smiled crookedly at him. "Thank you, Kofi."

Rory had fallen back asleep, so Luce took the first watch in a chair and I settled on a bed of blankets on the floor. I shut my eyes, but my mind kept pressing me back into the bitterly sweet memory of lying in Vai's arms the one night we had shared. How he had kissed me! How was a gal meant to sleep if she could not stop thinking of his passionate caresses?

The scratching at the window just would not stop. I sat up. Luce slept, one arm curled against her chest and the other flung out to one side. Kofi was leaning against the interior door, eyes closed, napping on his feet. I crawled over to the drapes that concealed the glass doors. I twitched aside the lower corner to peer out into the night-swamped courtyard.

Shadows marked the glass in blotches and lines. Winged shapes flittered across the sky.

A slender green finger was tapping on the glass. I recoiled. A branch had elongated until it reached the doors, as if trying to find a path inside. A bat perched on the swaying end, staring at me with obsidian eyes. I blinked, and it vanished.

A man pressed against the door. He had Vai's face and he wore a magnificent dash jacket printed with fishes spilling out of gourds.

"We shall find a way in," he said in a low, sweet voice. The scent of guava penetrated the glass separating us. I wanted to kiss him to taste the fruit, but I knew better. "Yee cannot escape us. We know yee killed her."

The latch turned but caught because it was locked. The key shuddered in a gust of wind.

"You can't come in," I whispered.

It was impossible to stare into those brown eyes and not be drawn closer; his lips tempted me; his hands reminded me of the kind of work they could do. But he was not Vai. He was an opia, the spirit of a dead man.

"Open the door," he whispered, "and yee shall have what yee so badly desire."

The hot look in his eyes drowned me. Next thing I knew, my hand was touching the key. I jerked away my hand and fixed it around the hilt of my sword.

"Cat?" The drape rustled away from me.

I jolted back as Kofi joined me. He looked into the courtyard with its dense shadows and a night wind trawling through the branches of the ceiba tree. The nearest branches of the tree waved twenty strides or more from the glass-paned doors. Of branch, bat, or male figure I saw no sign, although a small frog hopped along the paving stones along the side of the building.

"I reckon yee shall step back from there," Kofi said. "That tree have a powerful spirit."

Shapes were climbing in the tree, some grappling up and some slipping down. The movement made me dizzy.

"Do you see them?" I whispered.

Instead of answering, Kofi pulled me back, let the drapes cover the view, and settled me on the blankets beside Luce. I dozed off.

A mosquito buzzed by my ear, and I kept swatting it away and it kept coming back, until I opened my eyes. Both Luce and Kofi slept soundly. But Rory was gone.

One of the glass doors was open, its key fallen to the floor.

With my ghost-sword in hand, I ran out into the courtyard. It was so late I heard not a breath of sound from anyone living.

The soporific aroma of overripe guava drenched the air. As on a gust of wind, a cloud of bats poured down over the roofs that surrounded the courtyard. Their tiny bodies battered me. I drew my sword out of the spirit world where the blade resided and slashed at them, but they darted past into the shadow of the ceiba tree. A hundred ratlike rodents were hauling Rory up the trunk of the ceiba tree, calling to each other with whistling chirps and chortling barks.

I sheathed my sword and ran back into the chamber.

"Kofi! Luce!" No matter how I shook them, they did not wake. They slept the heavy sleep of the enchanted.

I dressed in skirt and sandals and grabbed the two flasks Uncle Joe had given me, as well as trousers, sandals, and a singlet from Vai's chest. Then I raced back out. I could still hear them climbing. The scent of the spirit world breathed down over me. I tasted its dry chaff and a kick of dust, as if I had walked into a mown hayfield baking under a late summer sun. The massive trunk was covered with big blunt thorns. Even had I been able to reach the lowest branch, I would have torn my skin to ribbons and bled all over the tree.

Yet wasn't blood the gate? I surveyed the courtyard: stone sculpture, cistern, tree. In the spirit world, stone, well, and tree set the three points of a triangle to create warded ground. Warded ground had the property of reaching into the mortal world, as if the touch of the mortal world anchored the wards in the ever-changing spirit world. I had crossed into and out of the spirit world through stone. I had crossed into and out of the spirit world through water. Why not through the tree?

The chortles of the thieves faded. I pressed my right arm onto the stinging tip of a thorn. It pierced my flesh with an almost audible groan. My blood trickled down the bark. Beneath my hand the tree smeared to shadow as the trunk became a ladderlike stair leading up into darkness. I tucked up my skirts to keep them out of the way, and I climbed.

8

I climbed up the central pillar of the tree toward a smoky abyss studded with lights. Desperation gave me strength and speed. Perhaps the little creatures were at a disadvantage, them being so many and so small and having to coordinate a large limp weight, for I sensed I was gaining on them.

The canopy of leaves faded into smoke, just as it had in my dream. A sleeting wind cut my face, numbing my lips and then my fingers. With my next step, I kicked out over a gulf of air. Nothingness yawned around me as the tree dissolved. Falling, I flailed desperately.

My sandals caught the rim of a ledge. A bucketing motion beneath and around me made me sway as though I had landed on a moving object. Just before I tumbled off, my hand fastened over a metal door latch. I tried to open it, but it was locked.

"Hsst!" a thin voice whispered. "Quiet! Look through my eyes into those of my sibling inside."

The latch bit me, two pinprick points of pain. Blood slicked the metal. Like a scraping file, its tongue rasped away the moisture.

I shut my eyes. Only then did I realize where I was. A coachman and his coach served the Master of the Wild Hunt. Gremlin spirits inhabited the latches of the coach's doors, one facing in and one facing out. Four days ago, as time passed in the mortal world, my sire had thrown me out of this very coach. Again I pushed on the latch, but it did not budge.

Yet through the latch, linked by my blood, I saw into the interior of the coach.

With a hand open on Vai's chest, the Master of the Wild Hunt pressed him against the opposite seat. Andevai's eyes were open but he seemed paralyzed, both blind and deaf. The gold threads of his red-and-gold dash jacket shimmered under a weirdly glowing light that emanated from my sire. His blue-white mask of ice made my sire seem even more dreadful, for the mask hid his expression and the true color of his eyes.

For all I could tell, my sire had just flung me out a moment ago, as time flowed in the spirit world.

For the longest time—it seemed an eternity and yet maybe I took in only a single shocked breath—he kept himself propped at arm's length, hand splayed open on Vai's chest, while he examined Vai in the considering way an experienced cook examines produce to pick what is best out of the basket. He considered Vai's dark eyes, kissable mouth, very short, trim beard, and shorn-short black hair. His scrutiny had such a disturbingly predatory focus that I opened my mouth to protest, thinking I could be heard through the door. A rough lick from the gremlin's tongue silenced me. My lips went numb.

As if he had seen enough, my sire sat back. The mask of ice melted into the youthful face he had worn on the ballcourt the night he had taken Vai prisoner after the death of the cacica. His was the kind of face that drew the eye even if you could not warm to it. He had long straight black hair like the Taino, eyes with a slight fold like the Cathayans, a thin Celtic nose, and brown skin rather lighter than Vai's deep brown Afric complexion. His golden eyes looked so like mine that anyone would know he and I were related.

Vai sucked in a breath. His gaze swept the confines of the coach, flickering as he noted my sire sitting opposite him. He paused to examine the grubby bundle of clothing and food I'd stolen on Salt Island. The shuttered doors and the rest of the interior had no ornamentation except loops to hold on to, a bracket for a lamp, and a filigree of gold-wire decoration around doors and joinings.

As Vai realized I was gone, his hand tightened on the hilt of his sword, which had been forged of cold steel by the secret mage craft known to Four Moons House. I could almost see his thoughts running. I was pretty sure that much of his exceptional power as a cold mage arose from his patience. He analyzed his situation from all angles before he made a decision, just as he spun illusions out of cold magic and worked them over and over until they were seamless.

Vai's lips pressed into a flat line, and his gaze fell away as if he were looking elsewhere.

The locket I wore at my neck grew warm. Over a year ago a *djeli* had been paid to weave magic to chain our marriage so I could not escape the mansa's command to bind the eldest Hassi Barahal daughter to Four Moons House. The djeli, a bard who was also a shaman, had anchored the magical chain in our bodies, so Vai had told me on the night we consummated the marriage. That night we had pledged in whispers things I dared not think of now because to be able to see but not touch or speak to him, to know he was in danger and cut off from me, made my spirit rage.

His faraway pulse caught in my heart. His mouth twitched.

He knew I lived. Maybe he even knew how close I was.

He glanced cautiously at my sire. The contrast between the two men's clothing could not have been greater. My sire wore a jacket and trousers of unrelieved black, whereas Vai's clothing was a beacon, meant to be noticed and admired. It was one of his best garments, sewn by a master tailor from a tightly woven silk so smooth it was sensual, cut longer than the current fashion but so well built that the length and trim emphasized its flattering fit.

With gaze lowered respectfully, as a younger man addresses an elder, he spoke polite words in an exceedingly polite voice that I was pretty sure disguised a rich vein of sarcasm.

"Where I come from, a man would call his wife's father *Father*. As a courtesy, you understand. To acknowledge the relationship between them. Shall I address you as *Father* then?"

"She's dead."

Contempt flashed in Vai's expression, his chin coming up to allow him to look down his nose at an inferior being. I had seen that look all too often in the first days of our marriage. It was odd to be glad he had it in him when I had disliked him for it before. "We both know she is not dead. I must suppose you will tell me what you did with her when you think it worth your while to reveal the information to me."

"I threw her out the door. She's of no more use to me."

Vai's gaze flickered but he had enough self-control not to glance at either of the doors. "Your own daughter? Able to cross between the

mortal world and the spirit world at any time, of her own will and with a drop of her own blood? Of no more use to you? I don't believe that, and neither do you."

"She accomplished what I commanded her to do. She cut a gate through the spirit fence the creatures of this part of your world have erected to stop my Hunt from entering these lands. Now I have even more fields in which to hunt."

"Let us say that is true. If you truly had no more use for her, you would have no reason to take me. I heard you tell her I was the leash you would use to keep her tied to you. So you do wish to keep her bound to you. If you'd stop pretending otherwise, we might manage a productive conversation."

"I find your arrogance intriguing. I can do what I want to you, and you know it. Yet you speak this way to me."

"I think you cannot kill me. Not until next Hallows' Night. You might be better asking yourself, how can we be allies?"

My sire laughed. "You are entirely delightful. More arrogant than the male who was with Tara Bell, but just as talkative and defiant. The difference is that he had never touched Tara Bell while you have had sex with my daughter. You realize, of course, I will have a claim on any children you sire on her."

Blessed Tanit! I hadn't thought of that!

Judging by Vai's suddenly pinched expression, he hadn't either.

We knew the mansa of Four Moons had a claim on any children we might have until we could find a way to release ourselves from clientage. To condemn our children to the chains my sire had already shackled me with was unthinkable. Yet to gauge by the narrowing of his eyes and the tension in his jaw, the idea of never having children was to Vai unendurable.

"Ah, now I have trapped you," said my sire with a pleased smile. "That wasn't nearly as difficult as I feared it might be."

Horribly, as they had in my dream, his body and face melted, flowing into another face and another body. He became a creature who looked exactly like me, with my thick black hair pulled into a braid. I saw Vai's gaze drawn as by a spell down the length of the braid to the span of her hips. The creature's lips were slightly parted as if she was thinking of eating or speaking, and I couldn't be sure which, but either way she looked as if she was inviting a kiss. She was dressed exactly as I had been when in the coach with him, in a faded length of cloth wrapped to make a skirt and in a damp lawn blouse so thin and threadbare where it clung to the curve of her breasts that the shadow of her nipples showed through the cotton. Was that how I had looked when I had stepped down out of the coach on the ballcourt on Hallows' Night?

Vai inhaled sharply.

Desperately, I tried to open the door, but the numbness in my lips had infested my whole body. All I could do was watch through gremlin eyes.

The creature who looked like me leaned closer to Vai. The neck of her blouse gapped open to reveal no bodice beneath, nothing but bare skin. Vai pressed back against the seat.

Her hands wandered up the front of his dash jacket.

"Sire a child on me," the creature said in a voice like mine but nothing like mine, because its whisper was cruelly seductive, "and I'll leave any children you sire on her alone."

Vai spoke in a hoarse murmur. "You can't bear children. You're a man."

"Do I feel like a man?"

Her lips brushed his. Her knee eased between his thighs and her hands spanned his shoulders to draw him into her kiss. Breasts brushed his chest. Vai became as rigid as if he had turned to ice. I guessed he was angry at himself for being aroused.

I could scarcely blame him. If I hadn't known I was me, I would have thought I was her.

If I'd had a body and an axe, I would have smashed in my sire's head.

"No," Vai said against its lips, his mouth unyielding.

"But you want me," the Master of the Wild Hunt said in my voice, like a purr of desire.

Her voice, her hands on him, were claws digging into my flesh, yet I could do nothing.

"No." Vai's voice was clear and cold. "I want *her*. There is a difference."

"What difference would that be?"

"The shape you wear is an illusion."

"When she comes for you, as you and I both know she is trying to do right now, how will you know if it is she or I who grasps you close and whispers words of hope and love?"

Vai relaxed. My sire did not know the secrets of the djeliw and bards, with their wholly human magic. He did not know about the way our marriage had bound us. He did not know I wore a locket.

"I admit I can tell no difference between you and her," Vai said, a cunning statement that had the advantage of being truth because words can have two meanings. "But right now I know you are not her. I will not do this."

My sire sat back into the other seat, melting back into his young male form, a finger tapping his lips as he considered his captive.

Vai ran a hand down the buttons of his dash jacket, straightening and smoothing, an action that apparently calmed him. I had not been so steadfast in withholding my kiss from the opia.

As this uncomfortable thought chased me, I heard the rumble of wind. The coach rocked and swayed as if caught in the tidal currents of the spirit world. As I clung, barely hanging on, I suddenly remembered why the Master of the Wild Hunt used this coach. In the spirit world, the tides of dragons' dreams altered the landscape and any creatures caught out in it. But the coachman had been made in the mortal world by the cunning artifice of goblins. He, and the coach and four horses that were a part of him, could not be changed. To travel in the coach was to be safe from the altering tidal waves.

"What do you really want?" Vai asked.

"I want what I am required to want. I do the bidding of my masters, just as you no doubt do the bidding of yours."

"The servants of the night court answer questions with questions, and you do not. I would like to know who or what the Master of the Wild Hunt calls master."

"Do not doubt my intentions. If she cannot rescue you, you will be the next sacrifice."

"Not until the next Hallows' Night," said Vai in the clipped tone he used when he was particularly wound up. "So I ask again, if you intend to kill me, what chance is there I would ever agree to sire a child on you if it would gain me nothing? If you do kill me, how can I sire a child on your daughter, if a child born to your daughter is what you require? Neither of these things can be accomplished unless you free me, allow me to return to her, and promise me you'll never hunt me down."

"A well-argued point. Why would I need you at all? I could sire a child on her myself."

The words hit like a punch in the chest. Fingers slipping, I almost lost my grip on the latch.

So fast I didn't see it coming, Vai swung up his sword and stabbed my sire.

He aimed for up under the ribs to the heart, a move he'd no doubt been taught by rote by the mage House's swordmaster. But the close confines of the coach and my sire's astonishingly fast reflexes—an arm flung up—deflected the blow. The tip slid into the meat of my sire's right shoulder.

Pain pierced like steel sliding into my own flesh.

I screamed. A howl rose, shuddering around me and through me: Every creature bound to the Master of the Wild Hunt by blood felt the cut of that blade.

My sire grabbed the blade with his left hand. A clear ichor oozed from his shoulder. The translucent liquid dribbled down the length of the blade. The fingers of my left hand flamed with agony. I was barely holding on with my right, hanging over the abyss.

My sire did not let go of the sword. He raised his right hand to squeeze Vai's sword arm. Eyes flared with fury, he spoke in a terrifying whisper. "What is done to me, I do to her. That was her cry of agony."

Vai froze, struck between horror and disbelief. With a single tug, my sire pulled the sword out of his shoulder and shoved the blade against Vai's throat.

I choked out a wordless cry. The screams and whimpers of the pack echoed me, their pain and my pain churning like so many merging currents until I was almost obliterated. Vai's hand spasmed on the hilt of the sword as he fought uselessly against the paralysis washing through him.

"It would have gone better for you if you'd stayed amusing. I'd have sheltered you then, at least until next Hallows' Night. Now you've made me angry. I'm throwing you into the pit. No mortal can survive there."

I struggled to open the latch, but my limbs had no strength. I was as frozen as I had been in my dream. Frost crackled out from the ichor that seeped from my sire's wounded shoulder, like winter devouring the dying memory of summer. Its lacework beauty ate through the human form my sire had taken. Ice engulfed the interior of the coach, consuming every morsel of space that was not the coach itself. Ice entombed Vai, so cloudy and dense I could see only the line of steel that marked his sword.

Last of all, ice crystals bristled down the length of the latch. With a whimper of fear the outside latch gremlin shut its eyes, leaving me alone in the dark.

9

Yet instead of falling, I held on. Nothing, not even my sire's vile threat, could make me give up. The rocking ceased, and I found myself back on the tree as abruptly as if I had never left it. Clutching the nub of a broken branch, I heaved myself up, gritting past the blaze of pain in my right shoulder and left hand. The pain told me that what I had witnessed was real, not a dream.

As I climbed, the air changed texture, stirred by a guava-scented wind. I emerged into the hollow trunk of a ceiba tree so huge that the buttressing of its aboveground roots rose like the pillars of a house over my head. The chittering of Rory's captors echoed around me, but I could not see them. I sought threads of shadow to conceal myself, but here in the spirit world the shadows were like eels, too slippery to hold. Skulking in the tangle of roots, furious and almost weeping at losing Vai when I had come so close to him, I probed at my shoulder. Just below the collarbone rose a puckered scar, tender to the touch. The fingers of my left hand were scored with whitened scars, cleanly healed. The ache subsided to that of an injury sustained days ago instead of moments. The speed of healing was a brutal reminder of how time passed differently in the spirit world, where an hour might equate to days in the mortal world and a day to months. How much time had passed in the mortal world just while I climbed the tree? How far away was Vai now?

Hidden within the roots, I peered onto open ground, my first glimpse of the spirit world here in Taino country. In the heavens, no sun or moon shone. The sky had a silvery-white sheen like the inside of a conch shell. Straight ahead lay a monumental ballcourt where figures played batey, the game so beloved in Expedition and throughout the Antilles. The players ran up and down the ballcourt bouncing a rubber ball off thighs or forearms or elbows, never letting it touch the ground. They even bounced the ball off stone belts they wore around their hips, although in Expedition no one used the traditional gear.

At the end of the ballcourt closest to me rose a stone platform. A man sat there, cross-legged, watching the game. He wore a headdress ridged with feathers as in imitation of a troll's bright crest, a white cotton loin wrap, and armlets of beaten gold. His septum was pierced by a needle of pale green jade, and he wore dangling earrings carved out of bone. One step below him, a rabbit dressed in a loin wrap was seated at a sloped writing desk with a brush in hand, busily writing in sweeping strokes as its ears twitched.

I crossed the plaza, climbed four steps, and halted below the lord.

"You're the Thunder, the Herald of the storm the people call hurricane."

"Here you are, Cousin," said the Thunder, unsurprised by my arrival. "By what name should I call you?"

"People call me Cat," I replied, for I knew better than to reveal my full name. "Why did you take my brother?"

"You took a life. We took a life."

Dread chilled my heart. "Have you killed my brother?"

"Death is merely the other side of the island."

"I haven't the knowledge to debate questions of natural philosophy with you. I just want my brother back."

"It is time for the match. Batey is the game." He gestured toward the ballcourt. At the motion of his hand, thunder grumbled beneath my feet. "If you score, then we shall give you a chance to stand before the elders and defend yourself against the accusation laid against you. On behalf of the spirit lord you call the Master of the Wild Hunt, you cut a path into our country and allowed him to kill here as if he possessed the right to do so when he possesses no such right. Think how we must look at you, Cousin! We let you walk in our land as a guest, and you betrayed us."

My head was still spinning with the vision of Vai encased in ice. "So if I score a point, I'll be allowed to stand trial before a hostile assembly? That's my chance?"

"If you don't choose to speak in your own defense, it's no skin off my nose."

"It scarcely seems a sporting game if I'm obliged to play a game I only learned a few months ago against spirits and opia who have played for time uncounted."

"I freely offer you a gift, Cousin." A skull inset with beads and gems sat by his right knee, and I was sure it was watching me, for its hollow eyes gleamed. "The gift of the skill you would have achieved had you played the game for as long as these others have."

I had to take the chances I was offered. "That seems fair. I agree only if all responsibility falls to me. If the ancestors find I am not at fault, then my brother and I are both free to go."

"We are agreed."

"I'll need leather cords to tie up my skirt."

The rabbit scribe set down its pen and tossed me a rope of braided cords. I untangled the cords and used them to secure my skirt at knee length. I still wore only my sleeveless bodice.

Thunder himself fitted me with arm guards. There was something not intrusive but intimate in the way he handled my body. He did not loom or leer, but I felt the spark all the same. Loving Vai had opened my eyes to the currents that roil the waters between people who feel attraction one for the other. But while I might have been appreciative, I was not tempted. I smiled to show I understood his game, and I stepped back politely.

He looked me up and down suggestively. "Do you play with the sword attached? Like a man? It will only get in your way."

"I will not give the sword into anyone's hand except my brother's." Although I looked around the central area, I could not see Rory. "If you bring him to me and let him watch, then I will let him hold it for me."

"You do not ask what will happen if you do not score a point."

"I see no need to ask," I said.

He laughed. A second laugh echoed him in a mist of rain. At the other end of the ballcourt rose another platform. There another man sat cross-legged. He had skin the color of waves and hair like long brown seaweed: It was Thunder's brother, Flood, he who had almost drowned me when I had been trapped beneath an overturned boat.

Vai had saved me from the flood.

Resolve steeled my heart. I would not let them intimidate me. "There's no reason for me to play if I don't know my brother is safe."

"I agree," said Thunder with a suspiciously amused smile. I scarcely had time to blink before a bedraggled saber-toothed cat appeared under the ceiba tree's lofty roots. With amber eyes fixed on me, he limped the long painful way to the platform. When he arrived, I examined his shoulder. Like my injuries, the wounds were healing unnaturally fast. I pressed a cheek into the coarse black fur of his head, stroking behind his ears.

"I give my sword into your care until I come back for it. Wait for my signal. We may have to retreat quickly."

I lashed the sword to his body, took a swig of the potent ginger beer, and rubbed my nose against his dry one. At last, I descended onto the ballcourt.

The stone risers, where onlookers sat, swarmed with people and spirits and creatures, some wearing the same form and others shifting through faces as if they had no face of their own. The force of all those gazes made me tremendously uncomfortable, for I preferred the shadows. The players had gathered along the walls of the ballcourt. Most looked as human as I did, but some had the heads of animals or had claws or paws or furled wings. The crowd roared as I looked around to see who would play with me, for alone I could not possibly score. Maybe this was the trick by which Thunder meant to defeat me.

A man strode out to greet me. "Reckon yee don' know me, gal. Yee saved me from under a boat."

I'd only briefly caught a glimpse of the frail old man I'd helped rescue from beneath a boathouse during a hurricane. This man was younger, all sinewy flesh and muscle. He looked like a person who might know how to play batey.

"My thanks."

He grinned in a likable way, then whistled. More men and women trotted out from the shadows to join us. One introduced himself as Aunty Djeneba's deceased husband; others were the deceased relatives of the household or kin of people I had a friendly relationship with in Expedition. They were all the spirits of dead ancestors. I knew it because they had no navels. I thanked them and shook their hands in

65

the radical manner. The more recently dead received the gesture with smiles while the older ones were puzzled, for it was a manner of greeting they'd never before seen.

The opposing team assembled. A man pushed to the front like a captain coming to lead his troops. He looked exactly as my husband would have if he had been stripped down to the short cotton loin-skirt worn for batey by men. I stared, my mouth gone quite dry.

He had no navel. Could he be my sire? Was that the trick?

I whispered into the ear of the dead boatman. "He can't be the opia of my husband, for my husband isn't dead. Is he a maku?"

"He smell of cohoba and tobacco, like a Taino lord might. I know not who he is. Peradventure he have taken a dislike to yee and mean to distract yee."

I could play that game! I took a moment to admire how well the opia had transformed himself into Vai's skin, for his bare shoulders and chest and thighs really were quite admirable, so I admired them with a lift of my eyebrows that made his lovely eyes narrow as if he were bracing for me to cast a spear that he must bat aside.

"You don't frighten me," I said. "Quite the contrary."

He grinned a challenge.

Thunder raised a feathered scepter. A ball dropped into the game. The spirit lord who appeared in the form of Vai tapped it up and down on his knees, never letting it touch the dirt. It was no rubber ball. It was a head with black hair tied into a club. Its waxy features stared.

We were playing batey with the head of the cacica, Queen Anacaona, the mother of the twins Prince Caonabo and the exiled Prince Haübey, called Juba.

But I was the hunter's daughter. I had to admire their ruthless maneuvering.

Let it begin.

I dashed in and caught the head on my elbow, stealing it away from the spirit lord. As I passed the ball to the boatman, I caught the lord's ankle with a sweep of my leg and tripped him. He fell as I dodged past. He grabbed my ankle, yanked me down hard, and rolled us over so I had my back to the dirt and his weight and attractively bare torso pressed on top of me.

"You're not going to play fair, are you?" I demanded.

With his lips a breath away from my own, like Vai about to press a kiss onto my mouth, he spoke. "Where do yee think this shall end?"

"Not with you winning!" The pulse of the game made my heart race and my blood burn.

Voices surged like the sea around us. The footfalls of the running players made a constant tremor, shivering out on all sides through the beaten earth of the court.

I kissed him. His lips were dry; mine were dusty. Surprised by my riposte, he forgot himself, and another face spilled through Vai's features too quickly for me to recognize before it settled back into Vai's form. It was definitely not my sire.

I dug a knee up into his groin and shoved him sideways while he was yelping. As I scrambled up, I scanned the ballcourt. The ball was flying back right at me, the dead face frozen in a grimace. I struck the head with a flip of my hip and angled it toward Aunty Djeneba's husband. Then we ran, never letting the head drop. The ebb and flow of play meant that the head bounced between sides. Here in the spirit world, the players were too good ever to let the ball touch the ground.

You would think they did nothing but play across the ballcourt of eternity, and maybe that was all they did. I wouldn't mind doing that. A gal could play batey all day and lose all track of time if her limbs never grew weak and her throat never croaked with thirst. My cheeks were flushed, and my heart was singing.

I caught sight of the face of the man who wore the features of my husband. He was smiling arrogantly in exactly that triumphant way Vai had when he knew he'd bested you.

Noble Ba'al! They meant to distract me by gifting me with the ability to play well enough to keep up with them. I could lose myself in the play for a hundred years and forget everything but the thrill of my pounding heart and my gaze fixed on the ball, seeking an opening. I had to concentrate.

I ran up beside the boatman. "I need to score a goal," I said.

He nodded. "We shall position yee up to the western eye. Yee must manage the rest, gal."

I raced sideways to the west flank of the ballcourt, marked by carvings of owls, as he worked my teammates down the court with the ball between them. So had I helped him once, risking my life for no benefit except that it was the right thing to do. Every time one of our opponents would catch the ball on knee or elbow or hip, my team would steal it back.

The head spun to me at exactly the right speed and angle. A slap with my elbow sent it flying through the hurricane's eye, a stone circle.

The ballcourt dissolved around me into a swirl of angry mist as the helpful opia fled laughing and my opponents cursed and shrieked.

I stood in a Taino house large enough that it easily sheltered many serious-looking men and women dressed in white cotton and adorned with feather headdresses, beaded collars, and jade bracelets. The roof was lost in shadow far above, sprinkled with lights like stars. Vines grew up the huge wood pillars that held the roof. From the ceiling beams hung painted gourds as vast as ponds and sloshing with fish. A mound of young cassava plants surrounded me. I stood with my sandals in the dirt; leaves tickled my calves. A saber-toothed cat slouched into view behind the seated personages, my sword tied over its back. He turned aside to drink from a pool of water.

"Rory!" I cried. "Never touch food or drink in the spirit world!"

He raised his head to remind me he was a spirit creature. His tail lashed.

A round object hurtled through the air right at me. Reflexively, I caught it as it thumped into my chest.

The head of Queen Anacaona had fallen into my arms.

Her dead gaze met mine in a most disconcerting way. "Speak truth, maku. Speak now before the ancestors. Who is responsible for my death?"

10

After everything I had done and seen, I really thought it was too much that I could still be surprised. However, good manners always bridge an awkward chasm.

"Honored Ones! I stand before you like a daughter, who asks for your blessing." I caught the eye of the man who looked oldest and smiled winningly at him, for the smiles of young women could often soften the hearts of old men. He did not look amused, so I quickly retrenched. "I have arrived unexpectedly here, not knowing what you want of me."

"We want justice," said the head of Queen Anacaona. "You allowed the hunter who rides at the behest of the foreign courts to cross the Great Smoke and raid into our country, resulting in my death. Answer, maku."

I recollected Keer's questions, coming at the debate sideways instead of head-on. "You shouldn't have invaded Expedition Territory."

"Do you scold me, child? The Council of Expedition broke the First Treaty, which their ancestors and ours swore to uphold. That gave the Taino the right and the obligation to invade, to protect our people from diseases like the salt plague."

Here was an opening I could exploit! "It's true that Expedition's Council violated the terms of the First Treaty. But the Council no longer rules Expedition. The people of Expedition replaced the corrupt Council with a new Assembly. It is not justice to punish the Assembly for actions they did not commit." I surveyed the gathered ancestors. They were patient, as the dead can be, but I had an idea they were not going to be patient for long. I had to strike quickly. "Furthermore, you had no right to quarantine me on Salt Island, because I was clean. I was never infested with the salt plague. Isn't that true? Wasn't I clean?"

Queen Anacaona's brown cheeks suffused with natural color, as if blood pumped through them even though she had no heart. "You were clean. And Expedition does indeed have a new government. But both those things are beside the point, as I believe you know. Is it true, or is it not true, that a pack of maku spirit hunters crossed the Great Smoke and raided into our country?"

"What is the Great Smoke?"

"Do they teach the young nothing in your country? The Great Smoke is the ocean of all existence. It embraces all things, just as the ocean of water in the mortal world embraces all lands. It is not easy to cross the Great Smoke, for Leviathan guards it. But it can be done. Long ago, behiques wove a spirit fence around Taino country precisely to keep out the spirit lords from other territories in the spirit world because we did not want them to walk into our lands and disturb us. So let me ask you again. Did the maku spirit hunters cross from your land to ours on a road made of your bone and blood because in your nature and living body you partake both of the spirit world and the mortal world? Was it your presence, your body, that cut a gate in the spirit fence with which we protect ourselves? Did the Hunt enter the land because of you? Speak the truth, maku. Be warned. In this country, lies are knives you wield against your own flesh."

The ancestors' gazes pressed against me as if they were invisible blades waiting to cut my flesh to ribbons. I had to tell the truth, but not because of the knives. I had to tell the truth because this was a court of law. One did not lie in such a place.

"The Hunt did enter your country because I cut a gate in the fence. The Master of the Wild Hunt compelled me to lead him to the dragon dreamer, to my cousin, Beatrice. I never knew there was a spirit fence around your country. I never knew I could cut through it, and that cutting through it would leave your lands vulnerable. For that, I am truly sorry."

Her gaze had a shine that was not like living eyes but more like polished wood beads. I could almost see my reflection in it. "Who turned the eyes and will of the hunter onto me? Who was the instrument of my death?"

I straightened my shoulders. I was not proud, but neither was I ashamed. "I was clean, yet the noble cacica would have killed me as a salter if I had not asked the Master of the Wild Hunt to kill her first. I acted in self-defense."

A gust of rain washed through the hall, dissolving the roof and beams and floor and the ancestors themselves. Wet, I found myself standing ankle-deep in clumps of dirt in a field of young cassava plants. A sandy path snaked away into the forest's canopy, where one tree's crown rose above the others like a tower. Beside me, Rory sank down on his haunches.

The head of Queen Anacaona still rested in my arms. The way she watched me, unblinking, made me shift my feet restlessly, but I could not run away from what I had done.

"What happened to the hall? And the ballcourt?" I asked.

"The lords who sit at the court of justice have released you. You told the truth."

"Does that mean I'm free?"

Her stare bored into me. "My throne is shaken. My sons are scattered and weak because I was torn from the Taino court at an inauspicious time. My brother the cacique was healing in slow measure and would have survived, but instead he took his last breath. My body is dead because of you. Knowing that, do you feel free?"

Even knowing I'd made the only choice I could, and that I had truly acted in self-defense, I did not feel free. I did not want to be the kind of person who would.

"Why are you still with me, Your Highness? Is there some task I may perform for you? Somewhere I may carry you? It seems rude to just...plant you here."

"Take me to my son."

"To Prince Caonabo in Sharagua?" My heart beat faster with excitement, for if we traveled swiftly enough we might reach there in time to spare Bee the ignominy of Caonabo's casting her off.

"I am obliged to lend my power to the one who will become cacique."

"I'm angry about his treatment of Bee, but I know how young men hold their honor high. He seems competent and levelheaded to me otherwise. He certainly honors his relationship to you. So I don't understand why you don't think he's worthy of becoming cacique." 71

"It is the same as tossing me onto the dirt to speak to me with such disrespect."

Prudence dictated retreat. "My apologies, Your Highness. If I am to take you to your son, how do we return to the mortal world and Sharagua?"

"I am always surprised by maku ignorance. This garden is the first garden. That is why the ancestors gather here. As for the worlds, the tree links all."

Of course! *The tree.*

Dried blood matted Rory's thick coat. He circled me once, then sniffed at the cacica's head.

"Yes, this is the head of the noble cacica, Queen Anacaona. She will be traveling with us until we can deliver her to Prince Caonabo."

He gave a low rumble, not quite a snarl. Even injured, he was intimidating, huge, graceful, and deadly. But then he nudged me with his big cat head as if impatient with the sword I'd lashed so awkwardly to his back, and suddenly he was just an annoying older brother whose needs weren't being met quickly enough for his liking. I took back my sword. A slug of rum from the flask Uncle Joe had provided shot right down through my flesh as a brace of courage.

I settled the cacica's head in the crook of my right arm, facing her forward so she could see where we were going. We headed under the shadow of the forest along the path. Birds with bright yellow-and-red plumage flapped away into the foliage. I heard the *toa toa* croaking of frogs.

"Where is the fire bane?" she asked. "I am surprised he is not with you. He possesses something more valuable than power."

"Good looks?"

She actually chuckled, and I was pleased I had made her laugh. "Young people are too easily swayed by sex. Let them dance at *areitos*. It is best for elders to sort out marriages between clans. A shame he was wasted on you."

Her words pricked me like thorns. "Did he turn down an offer to become one of your many husbands?"

Perhaps she did not hear the sarcasm in my tone, because her reply was as considered as if mine had been a perfectly reasonable suggestion. "He is an unusually powerful fire bane. For that reason a challenge I would have savored."

"You told General Camjiata there was no fire bane you could not control."

"Ah! You think I meant to enslave him. That is not what I meant. The people of Expedition call such as me a fire mage."

"Yes, I know that," I retorted, for she had stung me by saying Vai was wasted on me. "I've met other fire mages, like James Drake."

"Fire mages are not like James Drake. He is a criminal, whatever you may have thought of him."

"I didn't like him much, no matter what it may have seemed."

"I could see the nature of your regret developing on Salt Island. You were foolish."

"I was scared."

"You were ignorant."

"All right, then," I replied grudgingly, because it seemed churlish to argue over such a fine point with a woman who was dead because of a choice I had made. "I was ignorant and scared and foolish. Maybe being all those things was also an excuse to do something I was curious about but wasn't honest enough to admit wanting."

Birds fluttered in the trees, plumage flashing through patches of light. My feet crackled on drying leaves. Rory's breath warmed my back.

"All of those things," she agreed, "but it appears you can learn. Yet you are not my kinswoman to be offered to eat from the platter of my knowledge. However, I will not allow you to think I meant to enslave the fire bane who is your husband. This much I will tell you. When we weave, we are not weaving fire, we are weaving what the Hellenes call energy and the Mande call *nyama* and others call the living force. One way it can manifest is as fire. Such dispersal of living force will kill the fire weaver unless she has a way to cast it off."

"That's why you use fire banes as catch-fires. People sell them to you as slaves."

If it hadn't been for the fact that I was holding a severed head in my arms, I could have believed myself talking in an ordinary manner with a woman who found me a little tiresome.

"The fire banes who serve me are not slaves."

"Prince Caonabo said murderers are sometimes punished by being forced to become catch-fires. Anyway, why would anyone volunteer to do something so dangerous?"

"Fire banes can take into their bodies the energy I release. They throw it into Soraya, which is the name we give to what you call the spirit world. Were I to pour the backlash of my magic into a single fire bane, I should kill her. Even if she is only a funnel, she cannot take all without some spilling into her flesh and burning her up. Over many generations, my ancestors taught themselves how to split these wakes into more than one thread and weave them through more than one fire bane. Thus, all are protected."

"So the more powerful a fire mage, the more fire banes she needs? I saw the threads of your magic that night on the ballcourt. You wove them through a dozen fire banes. It seemed your net of magic spanned the entire island of Kiskeya and kept your dying brother alive."

"Interesting. You can see within both worlds, something few can do."

"I never saw anything like what you could do. It was...impressive, and to be honest, Your Highness, it was rather intimidating."

This compliment she let pass without blinking. "It is not that other fire mages do not have access to the lakes of energy which I can tap. Many stand at that shore but cannot or will not wade into the deep. My particular skill lies in the quality and precision of my weaving. There is no fire bane I cannot control, no matter how many threads I weave into the whole. But let me assure you, your husband was at no risk from me. I do not take what is not offered, and he did not offer himself. To be honest, the man talked so much about you that at times he became tedious. I expect you would have found his words gratifying."

A strange, smoky feeling scorched my heart. It was not so easy to wave away responsibility for her death when I was talking to her. It wasn't that I regretted saving my life or Vai's life or Bee's life. It was that I regretted the whole situation we had been forced into. Regret has a way of creeping through flesh and mind the way blood returns to frozen limbs and makes you hurt. If I'd known more or things had fallen out differently, she might have become my ally.

"What the fire bane has is the same way of thinking I have. He is precise. Methodical. Meticulous. Disciplined. I was astounded that he had the means to douse my weaving. I should like to ask him how he did it. Where is he? For I would have thought he would stay with you."

Now that she and I were so closely bound, I saw no reason to hide the truth. "The Master of the Wild Hunt stole him from me."

"The maku spirit lord drank my blood, and then stole the young man. An intriguing strategy. You must ask yourself what the spirit lord wants."

We came to a wide clearing. At its center rose a ceiba tree whose steepled roots flowed like ridges from a massive trunk. Baskets hung from the big thorns that adorned the lower roots. Some were filled with rotting fruit or with animal flesh turned green and putrid with decay. Others gave off a pleasing scent of herbs and flowers. One was filled to the brim with fresh yam pudding that smelled so sweet and tasty that I licked my lips and barely restrained myself from scooping with my fingers and eating it all up. In one, a tiny little creature with a downy coat of feathers slept, curled up all cozy for a long eternity's nap.

I found an empty basket and pulled it off the tree. "With your permission, Your Highness, I'd like to place your head in this basket so I have my hands free to climb."

To my surprise she smiled, not in a friendly way but in the way a rich woman smiles when a servant brings her just the gown she wanted in the morning. "It is a proper place for me to rest."

I wove grasses to make a nest that would keep her face angled up, for it seemed undignified to smash her facedown into the basket. A leather cord laced closed the lips of the basket. I fixed its strap around my body alongside the two flasks. Rory licked his foreleg.

I put a hand on the coarse fur of his neck. "Change into your man form as soon as you can. That's how we'll know we've crossed back into the mortal world."

He looked up the thorn-ridden bole of the tree as if to ask me how we were meant to climb, with the lowest branches out of my reach and him with no hands able to grasp.

"We came in through the roots," I said, "so we go out through the roots."

I smeared the last moist dregs of his drying blood onto my fingers, then pricked my forearm on one of the thorns. Its sting burned into my skin. As we crept into the dark hollows beneath the vast architecture of roots, I wiped our blood on the bark.

Deep in the pit of the tree the shadows melted away into steps ascending. He went first. It quickly grew so dark I had to keep a hand against the curving trunk. My shoulder ached, less sore than before. The grim implication dogged my steps: I could never attack my sire with cold steel if it meant I would harm not just myself but Rory and every other servant of the Hunt.

"Pah!" said Rory, as if he were spitting something out.

"Rory!" My fingers spread across the skin of a muscular back.

"Ouch!" he added. "Don't you think it's strange that it hurts so much when no blade touched us?"

I carefully felt along his shoulder. Where he had been shot a scar had already formed. "At least we're back in the mortal world."

He hissed. "Shh! I smell people. I hear them, too."

We crept through a maze of shallow, stagnant pools, scum slicking our feet. The air was thick with a scent similar to the one I imagined the ancient wrappings of Kemet mummies would have if you were so unfortunate as to be forced to unwrap one in order to clothe yourself. I probed with a foot, my sandal tapping rock.

He whispered, "I hate it when I have no shoes and the ground pokes my feet."

"I brought sandals. Put them on."

"You're such a good sister. Always thinking of my comfort!"

"My comfort, too. Put on these trousers and singlet first!"

"Clothes are so confining. I understand why you wear them when it's cold, but I see no need for them in a warm place like here."

"In human society you are meant to clothe yourself except when you are in private."

"Yes, it would be difficult to pet if one had to wear clothes!" He pressed a hand to my cheek. "Your skin is hot, Cat. Are you feverish?"

"It's called blushing. Is the wound on your leg bleeding? No? Then put your trousers on!"

When he had dressed, we moved on. A salt-sea smell tinged with smoke tickled my nose. Light filtered in, too constant to be torchlight and too bright to be candles. We groped along a rock wall on which figures had been drawn in poses of dancing and eating as at one of the festivals the locals called an areito. It was at such a festival with its dancing and food that Vai had won my heart. I could almost hear the ghost of that night's music in my ears, until I realized I was hearing singing, drums, and the rattle of shaken gourds. A rocky incline dusted with drifting sand gave way to a cave mouth. Its ledge overlooked a massive hollow fitted out with gaslights. From the height of the ledge we gazed across the hollow and through a monumental arch built from massive beams of wood. Through the archway could be seen a magnificent city whose major thoroughfares were illuminated by gas lamps. Right in the center of the city lay the straight lines of a ballcourt and next to it a plaza with high-roofed buildings like administrative offices and palaces. Beyond the city, a full moon glimmered over a flat sea. Masts filled a harbor, and bloated shadows moored to short towers marked airships. The distant jetty was strung with globes, their golden light awash over the dark waters. The entire city seemed to be out celebrating.

It was the view Bee had drawn in her sketchbook, only without us in it.

In the hollow below, an areito let loose in full rhythm. People stamped out a dance in lines of men or of women. Revelers stared as we descended into the hollow. A few offered drink or food as if to see if we were solid. I tested several smiles, trying to seem friendly and harmless. We made our way around the edge beneath the gleam of gas lamps. The hollow had once been a cavern, but its roof had long since collapsed. We struggled through the crowded celebration. I grabbed hold of Rory's jacket and tugged him to a halt as I searched for a route up the other side.

Away across the crowd, I saw the man wearing a terribly dashing dash jacket in a gold-and-orange brick pattern. He smiled in that aggravating way that made my heart melt, the way he'd smiled when he had said, *"How could you not want me, Catherine?"*

My limbs turned to stone as he arrowed toward me. Even when a surge of laughing people cut off my view, freeing me from the chain that linked our gazes, I could not move.

Then there he was, standing right in front of me, looking exactly like Vai except that he was not wearing shoes or even sandals. The bare feet were a dead giveaway.

"Who are you?" I demanded. "What do you want?"

11

"Rory, is that our sire?" I asked.

"Our sire?" Rory took several deep sniffs. All I could smell was the bloom of ripe guava and a whiff of tobacco. "No. That's not his smell. It couldn't be him anyway. Our sire can only cross into the mortal world on Hallows' Night."

The opia's lips quirked up. "Yee's caused a deal of trouble for me, gal. I know what yee carry in that basket. I shall make it worth yee while if yee don' deliver the head of the cacica to the Honored Caonabo, he who is now cacique over all the Taino people."

"Caonabo is cacique already?"

"This is his coronation areito, here and everywhere in Taino land."

"But I promised I would deliver her head to her son."

"So yee shall. Yee shall deliver her head to Haübey, not to Caonabo."

"Haübey was exiled after he was bitten by a salter. He can never return to the Taino kingdom."

"Yee don' know everything." He slid an arm around my waist and pulled me close. Cursedly, he felt exactly like Vai as he murmured in my ear, "Nevertheless, I's willing to make yee a deal. For 'tis certain Haübey is gone over the ocean where I cannot reach him."

"Cat," said Rory.

"How long ago did the general and his army leave?" I cried with alarm. "How long have we been in the spirit world?"

"The reckoning of days and months mean little enough to me."

"Cat," said Rory.

I pulled out of the opia's appealing grasp. "I promised to deliver the head. Then my cousin can help me get back to Expedition. I have to get a ship to Europa."

"What if I could get yee to Europa? Right now? If yee do as I ask and promise to take the cacica's head to Haübey?"

"Cat!"

I was hallucinating Bee's voice.

Rory tugged on my arm. I looked round to see Bee plowing through the crowd. She was hauling the smaller of Vai's wooden travel chests with the aid of a grinning Taino man who was wearing an embroidered loincloth, bronze anklets and bracelets, a beaded necklace, a feathered cap, and nothing more. His friends followed along, dressed in a similarly appealing style. Like me, Bee wore an amply cut Europan skirt, good for striding, but a sleeveless bodice in the Expedition manner because, although it was night, it was plenty warm. She, Rory, and I stuck out like the maku we were, but no one seemed to mind.

"Bee!"

She halted, face flushed and curls in disarray. What I assumed was a pretty "Thank you" in Taino dismissed the young man. After looking over me and Rory, he retreated to his amused friends.

"Here you are, Cat! I was afraid to leave the chest because James Drake saw it and threatened to burn all of Andevai's clothes. If there's one thing you can trust about that man, it's that he hates your husband and he could easily do it."

"That's two things," said Rory.

She skewered him with a black gaze. "You get to haul it all the way back!"

"Where are we?" I had to pitch my voice to be heard above the rattle and song. "Why are you talking to James Drake?"

"We're in Sharagua. I've been divorced and cast off. And here you are, in the middle of the areito on coronation night. I saw our meeting here in a dream. I've made arrangements for us to travel with General Camjiata's army to Iberia."

I looked around. The opia had vanished.

Bee grabbed my wrist, yanking as if she meant to rip my arm out of its socket. "Cat! We have to go! A carriage is waiting outside. The tide waits for no man, and not even for me."

"I'm not going with General Camjiata! Why is he in Sharagua?"

"For the coronation. Anyway, of course he wants me to return with him to Iberia and help him win his war."

"We can't trust him!"

"The situation is not as simple as you think it is. Where did you get this?" With her usual disrespect for my belongings, she pulled the basket around and began unlacing it. "These sort of baskets are only ever used by behiques." She pried open the top of the basket, pulling back her hair with a hand so it didn't fall in her eyes. "Cat," she said in an altered tone, "why do you have a skull?"

Blessed Tanit! Hair, skin, the usual appurtenances of flesh and life had vanished to leave a bone-white skull. "It wasn't a skull before. It was more like the head of the poet Bran Cof, only more commanding and less rude."

"Look!" Rory pointed to the arch.

A dozen foreigners pushed into view. Falcatas swung from their hips, half concealed in the knee-length folds of their dash jackets. I recognized Captain Tira's broad shoulders and short black hair instantly, not to mention the way she swept the crowd with a searching gaze.

"Gracious Melqart!" I said to the air. "Where is that cursed opia?"

"Seem a better offer now, don' it?" he said behind me in a tone I could only describe as gloating.

I spun to face him, clasping the basket shut. "How can I know you'll keep your word?"

"I give yee me word of honor as a Taino man," the opia said. "Besides that, which is truly all yee need, I shall help yee get to Europa because I want the cacica's head to go to Haübey together with a message that he need to come home. So yee see, gal, I's helping me own self. Yee's just the messenger I have at hand."

Such sweet words: *help yee get to Europa*. But I had to rein in my galloping heart. "I promised Queen Anacaona to take her head to Caonabo."

"So yee shall. When yee give the head to Haübey, he shall bring it home to Caonabo."

Blessed Tanit! I shuddered with hope. "What about my cousin? Her blood won't give her passage into the spirit world. She can only cross through water. Anyway, the creatures of the spirit world hate her and want to kill her."

"Peradventure them in Europa do, but our ways are different in this part of the world. As for the dreamer, the pools yee waded through shall give her passage. I shall take yee back that same way."

"Cat, who are you talking to?" demanded Bee.

"Can't you see him?" Rory asked. "Are you *blind*, Bee?"

"Not too blind to kick you. Cat, who are you talking to?"

The opia wearing Vai's face smiled in the smug way Vai had when he knew he was about to be proven right. "Best make up yee mind quick quick, gal. Here they come."

Captain Tira spotted me across the dancing crowd.

"Very well," I said. "In exchange for you delivering us safely to Europa, I will deliver the cacica's head to Haübey with the message that he is free to return from exile."

The opia replied with an impatient smile so unlike any of Vai's expressions that I knew I was seeing a glimpse of the man he had once been. Yet he twined his fingers through mine just as Vai had done and drew me back the way we had come.

"Rory, get the chest," I called over my shoulder. "Bee, are you coming with us, or going with the general? You better come with us. I want you to. Please."

"Of course I'm coming with you!"

We danced and dodged around revelers oblivious to the chase. They smiled and clapped to include us. As we climbed the narrow path toward the cave, a rifle went off, followed by a rousing cheer from the crowd, who evidently thought it part of the celebration.

We had no sooner ducked into the cave mouth than about twenty Iberians ran up in our wake. The opia vanished in a scatter of sand. I drew my sword.

"Stay back," I said to the soldiers. "Rory, take off your clothes and give them to Bee. That will surprise them."

"Blessed Tanit!" cried Bee. "Don't take off...you're not really going to..."

She broke off with an audible gasp as Rory stripped. The soldiers halted in confusion.

"You two go on," I said, keeping my gaze on the soldiers. "Bee,   81 you'll have to haul the chest when he changes. Stop and wait for me once he's a cat. Go!"

They went. The soldiers could have rushed us, but the gleam of my sword and Rory's unexpected disrobing gave them pause.

"I'm reliably informed by the locals that my sword is an object of power known as a *cemi*, inhabited by the spirit of my mother," I said in my most amiable tone. "Tara Bell was an officer in the Amazon Corps. Perhaps you knew her or fought beside her."

Captain Tira pushed through, attended by two men carrying lamps.

"Catherine Bell Barahal, the general wish to speak with yee."

"Then why has he sent soldiers after me, if it's to be a friendly chat?"

"I reckon he thought yee might be a bit recalcitrant." She gestured.

Four of the soldiers broke ranks to approach me.

I thrust at the leftmost, pricking his forearm so he yelped and dropped his rifle. As it clattered down, I pressed in past him to jam the hilt of my sword into the chin of the next man, then swung away before he could counter. The third man clubbed at me with his rifle, but I leaped past him and shoved the fourth man into range of the blow.

The captain shouted a command. Rifles leveled, pointing at me.

"Stand down, gal!" cried Captain Tira.

A gust of wind roared through the cave with a squall of blown sand. The lamps whooshed out. A rifle went off. The sting of its powder lanced up my nostrils. A hand fastened on my shoulder. I twisted away, grabbed the arm, and bit. The man shrieked, reeling away. Men shouted as the lamps crashed to the ground and shattered with a gush of oil that abruptly flamed into bright fire.

The scent of guava flooded the air. A person who looked like me raced past them out the cave mouth. To my left stood a third opia looking just like me. Everyone started shouting at once. In the confusion I dashed for the back of the cave. Another gust of wind doused the burning oil, drenching the cave in darkness. I thudded into a man's body which I knew instantly as Vai's.

"Yee brother and cousin is safe. Follow me."

We splashed through the string of caves up which we had so recently climbed. I stumbled more than once, stubbing my toes on rocks. Blood dribbled down my foot to smear the ground.

When we passed from the mortal world into the spirit world I did not know. But in the dense night of the cave, a big cat's body nudged up beside me. A long incisor grazed my hip as my hand slipped across his moist nose. He licked me with a raspy tongue. I giggled.

"My feet are coated with slime!" exclaimed Bee in the darkness. "It's disgusting."

I laughed.

"Shh!" The opia pulled me close, lips pressed to my ear. "We's not out of danger."

Even knowing I was grasping a stranger—a dead man!—I could not stifle the tremor of arousal I felt at the familiar shape I had my arms around, his strong shoulders, his solid chest. He even had the sawdust-and-sweat scent of Vai as well as the mouthwatering fragrance of guava.

"Then it's best if we hurry," I whispered, my irritation at my body's unwanted reaction making my voice a hiss.

"We can bide a few breaths here, gal, as long as we bide quiet-like. The maku soldiers cannot venture any deeper into the cave. 'Tis a small reward to ask that yee kiss me, don' yee reckon?" he murmured in Vai's coaxing voice. His lips brushed my mouth.

I stiffened my entire body, as Vai had done when my sire had teased him with my form in the coach. "I don't reckon. Not with my brother and cousin right next to me! And the cacica's head in the basket."

"She cannot see with the basket closed up tight, can she?"

"They warned me that opia are dangerous spirits. Why do you appear to me as my husband?"

"Because it vex yee," he whispered, laughter in his tone. "And I like yee when yee is vexed."

A little stab of laughter shook me. "Who are you?"

He rubbed his cheek against mine, the bristle of beard making me shiver. "Just one kiss like that one yee gave me in yee room in Expedition, when yee thought I was him. Don' yee think yee owe me?"

"You haven't gotten us to Europa yet."

"For the chance of it, gal."

"Let me see the face you wore when you were a living man."

He chuckled. "I like the stubborn way yee never give up."

Blessed Tanit, but I took the chance of it. Rory didn't care, the   83 cacica's head was safe in the basket, and it was too dark for Bee to see anything. I pressed my mouth to his. For a single searing kiss, I pretended I was holding Vai. It was a good kiss, strong and sweet.

"Cat, where are you? What is going on?" Bee's hand brushed my shoulder like the flutter of a feather across my skin. Her fingers dug into my upper arm. "*What are you doing?*"

His hand slid down my arm and caught hold of my fingers as he stepped back.

"Cat, there is someone else here with us," Bee said ominously.

"He's an opia. He's helping us so we can do something for him. Help me carry the chest." I hoisted one end of the chest by its rope handle. "It was very clever of you to bring the chest, Bee."

"Cleverness had nothing to do with it. It was pure desperation. I'd already hidden the other two when Drake caught me with this one. The moment he saw Andevai's dash jackets, I saw murder in his eyes. Sartorial murder. I couldn't bear the thought of all that expensive fabric and fine tailoring blazing into ash."

"How came you to have all our gear?"

"I got all three chests from Lucretia before I left for Sharagua. I told her I would deliver them to you. Gracious Melqart, Cat. I must ask, how many fashionable dash jackets can one man own?"

"I haven't yet had the leisure to make an accounting!"

We moved deeper into the night of the spirit world. Vast roots tangled around us.

"By the way, I'm sorry to mention it, but General Camjiata took your father's journals."

This newest betrayal scarcely scratched my already jangling nerves. "Of course he would! At least I know he'll keep them safe."

"We need to go quiet here," murmured the opia as we began to descend. "For I would not want any to hear me who might put a stop to the business we's about."

"Shh," I said to Bee. My breathing grew ragged as we made our way down within the tree, for I both hoped and feared that I would again grasp the latch and see into the coach where Vai was my sire's prisoner. But all we did was descend step by step, me holding the opia's hand as he guided us and Bee linked to me by the chest. Rory padded at the rear.

I smelled the mire of earth and heard the moan of a conch shell being blown. I heard the thump and patter of batey and the cheering shouts of the crowd as one of the players scored. Yet we did not walk into the ceremonial plaza where I had been before.

Down we went and down farther yet, past the charcoal scent of a cook fire and a smell of pepperpot that made me lick my lips with hunger. Rory gave a rumble of displeasure, reminding me that he was hungry, too.

"Don' stop." The opia fastened his fingers tightly to mine. "We shall go deeper, into the realm of the old ones that lie below all."

"What is that voice? Where are we going?" Bee whispered.

I had no words with which to answer her. The black void around us was impenetrable. Warm water tickled over my sandaled feet and streamed off. A salty wind with a bellows' breath hissed against my face like the exhalation of a beast so huge it cannot be seen or touched.

Was this what it meant to crawl into the maw of Leviathan?

I felt as if the gullet of a beast were squeezing around me. Sand filtered into my eyes. I blinked, trying to wet away its scrape.

Beneath my sandals the ground crunched. Glimmers of light shot through the earth like sparks strewn through sand. The walls took on an amber gleam. Rory loped ahead toward a low cave mouth. The shush and sough of a stormy sea sounded from outside. But I did not taste the salt of the ocean. Instead, when I licked my lips, I swallowed smoke.

The opia stopped.

Bee and I set down the chest.

She stared at him. "Blessed Tanit! He looks exactly like Andevai!"

He looked her up and down in a way Vai had never once examined her. A sting of jealousy made my heart flame, for unlike every other man I had ever met, Andevai had never shown the least partiality for Bee, not as all the rest did the moment they laid eyes on her voluptuous beauty.

"'Tis a shame I can go no farther and thereby get to know yee better, dream walker," he said to Bee. "Ask from the old ones that which they owe to yee."

"Where are we?" I whispered, for I was afraid.

"We have reached the Great Smoke, where the old ones bide. In the 85 mortal world, in the language spoken in Expedition, it is called the ocean."

"Have you tricked us? We have no ship on which to sail the ocean."

"'Tis no trick, for here in the spirit world, it have a different substance," he said in another man's voice.

We looked onto the face of a man I had never before met. He was Taino through and through, no mixed-race Expeditioner. He had the long black hair and regular features typical of the Taino. His commanding gaze had a hard measure, but a softness in the line of his mouth suggested that kisses pleased him. He was older than I expected, about the same age as the Europan radical leader and pugilist Brennan Touré Du, whom I would have guessed to be in his midthirties, a man in his prime. He also looked vaguely familiar.

"Have we met before?"

"We have not. Yee killed me before we had that chance."

"I did not kill you! You aren't one of the salters I killed on Salt Island..." I trailed off, watching the promise of his mouth tighten to disapproval.

"I've seen you!" cried Bee. "I met you, the first time I went to Sharagua! But you're dead!"

Had the sun come up at that moment, I would have said that dawn broke upon me. "You're the cacique! Queen Anacaona's brother, the one she was keeping alive. You're Caonabo and Haübey's uncle."

The crow's-feet at his eyes deepened as he smiled. "A smart gal, too."

"No need to mock me. How comes it that you ruled the Taino kingdom and yet speak the language spoken in Expedition Territory, which is but a trifling place compared to the expanse of your noble and mighty empire?"

"Yee's got a mouth on yee, gal, that do grate at times. Yet I reckon that man yee seek have the means to keep yee quiet when he get weary of yee talking. If those kisses was anything to go by."

"A strong man does not need a silent wife," I muttered as my face flamed.

"Kisses!" exclaimed Bee. "When was there kissing? *Cat!*"

His grin had a taunting flavor. "I lived in Expedition as a lad for some years. It happen that me uncle, him who was cacique before me, favored a cousin as heir instead of me. Me sister Anacaona deemed it prudent to keep me out of sight while she played the music she needed to at court. When me cousin died, I was recalled."

"You're younger than Anacaona?"

"By fifteen years. She was the first child born to the honored mother who carried us, and I was the last. I reckon that is why she always thought she could give the orders. Here is what yee don' know. Me sister and me own self never did agree about which of her sons was best suited to be cacique after me. She wanted me to choose Haübey because she always favored him. But I wanted him to serve in the army. Caonabo was my choice for cacique all along because he is the steadier man. But me sister the noble cacica is a stubborn woman. She would never see one single change to the law. I respect the ancestors as much as she do. But there come a time when change must happen. We have contained the salt plague with our behiques, and now we have wars to fight elsewhere. I need Haübey back from his exile."

"He's gone ahead to Europa with a small advance party," said Bee.

"He's a scout gone to Europa, that is certain. Yee shall take the cacica's head to him and he shall make of it a cemi. With the cemi of Anacaona in his possession, he shall be allowed to return to the court of Caonabo. War shall come, from the west or the north, from the Purépecha Empire or the Empire of the Comanche. I's not sure. Caonabo shall administer. Haübey shall fight."

At the cave mouth, the big cat put his ears back. The hair on the back of his neck was all a-bristle. Wind spattered burning sparks of sand all the way up the tunnel, so hot Bee and I had to shield our faces. When we lowered our hands and turned back to the cacique, the opia was gone.

12

"We'd better go." I picked up my end of the chest.

Bee stared at the spot where the cacique had been standing, then grabbed the other handle. With the chest swaying between us, we emerged out of the cave onto a beach.

The sky was as gray as northern slate, and the sea was a churning boil of smoke. Currents and swells roiled the surface, and wind kicked up spills of mist like choppy waves. Whitecaps flicked into existence and vanished. The strand that ought to have been sand was red coals and smoking ash. Only the sandals Vai had gifted me with protected my feet, for although common sense told me the leather ought to be burning, it did not. Bee wore boots. Rory sat in the cave mouth, ears flat, not coming out.

"I can see why it's called the Great Smoke." Bee wiped her eyes. "Do you think that could be the mist I walk through when I dream?"

I smacked my lips. "I hope your dreams don't taste as nasty as this air does. How can we possibly cross that?"

Smoke rushed up from the shoreline exactly like a big wave crashing in. Sulfurous fumes engulfed us. Coughing, I sucked for breath. Surely this was what lungs full of hot tar felt like! Beneath my sandals the ash of the shore hissed. A current like the blast of a furnace dragged at my body. I staggered, boiled off my feet, but the chest anchored me to Bee. She was immovable.

As quickly as it had poured in, the wave of smoke drained away.

I blinked gritty tears out of my eyes. Tufts of mist like the dregs of cigarillos bubbled off my limbs and drifted to the sand. We hadn't moved, but the beach was now smoldering. Fat balls of greasy smoke puffed along its length and rolled downslope into the sea.

"We should have gone with General Camjiata," said Bee.

Gagging, I licked a stink of rotting eggs off my lips. "I'm afraid I made a terrible mistake by listening to the opia." I took a step back, but Bee stayed put, tugging me to a halt.

"No, wait, Cat. Listen! There are voices in the smoke."

Movement chased through the swirl of the Great Smoke. Shapes flashed beneath the surface, but the churning gray fog obscured their features. All I heard was a bass humming like a hoarse man with a very deep voice singing a single tone.

A sweep of color washed through the smoky sea.

"Is it the tide of a dragon's dream?" I croaked, incandescent with terror. I groped for my sword, but it was as inert as lead.

Bee's tone was more breath than voice. "It's a dragon."

Night swept down. Lights like fireflies twinkled against a black sky. The sea surged, lifting like cloth raised from beneath by a hand. A bright shape emerged, smoke spilling off it in streams.

The dragon loomed over us. Its head was crested as with a filigree that reminded me of a troll's crest, if a troll's crest spanned half the sky. Silver eyes spun like wheels. It was not bird or lizard, nor was it a fish. Most of its body remained beneath the smoke. Ripples revealed a dreadful expanse of wings as wide as fields, shimmering pale gold like ripe wheat under a harsh sun. When its mouth gaped open, I knew it could swallow us in one easy gulp.

We had come to a place we ought not to be.

Awe deadened my heart and silenced my voice as I waited for the leviathan to devour us. Because wasn't that what they did? Eat foul little creatures like me?

Bee's voice rang out. "Greetings, Mighty One! I suppose you are one of those whose dreams I am obliged to wander on my restless nights. It's very disconcerting. I must say, I could not appreciate that vision of my dearest Cat embracing a man so enthusiastically. There are some things I really do not care to see, and that is one of them. But be assured! I do as I am told. I'm very obedient! Furthermore, I should like to remind you that my cousin and I at great risk to ourselves unearthed a nest of hatchlings in the spirit world. I must suppose that any hatchlings who survive will grow to become such resplendent creatures as you."

I gaped as the filigree crest flared, tightened, and widened again. Colors flashed through the dragon's skin like spears from a rainbow.

Bee went on as in answer to a reply I had not heard. "So, if you please, Honored One, as a favor, and possibly because we have done you a service beforehand, could you please convey me and my cousin here and that cat over there and everything we carry safely across the Great Smoke to the shores of the land we call Europa?" She dipped a courtesy. "If you would be so kind."

Down its head came like the inexorable fall of fate when the unsuspecting victim's eyes are at last and too late opened to her doom.

"Don't run, Cat," said Bee. "Never run. Stand your ground. Look them in the eye. You were right for us to come here. And now I'm right. *Trust me.*"

I was so scared that I was actually afraid I was going to pee myself. That was the only reason I didn't run, because I knew if I ran I would lose all my dignity and be very sticky afterward.

The dragon rested its head on the burning sands. The head alone was as big as a cottage. Its jaw opened to reveal a pale pink tongue. Instead of teeth, its upper mouth was rimmed with what looked like white, hairy combs as long as I was tall.

"It doesn't have teeth," said Bee. "How interesting! So you see, Cat, it can't eat us."

I found a croak. "It can still swallow us."

"Rory!" she called, ignoring my perfectly rational observation. "We're leaving."

He began to pad away into the darkness of the cave.

"Rory!" I was suddenly more afraid of losing him than of the dragon. "*Come. Here. Right. Now.*"

Head down, he crawled over to us as if I were dragging him on a leash. Maybe I was. Perhaps I had inadvertently leashed him to my service, just as I had been chained by my sire.

When he reached me, I extended a hand. He hissed.

"Don't you dare bite me!" I slapped his nose. "You're coming with us whether you want to or not."

His answering growl was more of a pathetic moan.

"Trust me, Rory." I set a hand on his big head.

The dragon's silver eyes had ceased whirling and now, like mirrors, reflected all that lay before it. I saw myself bedraggled, with the basket over my shoulder and my locket and sword like dull lumps of stone. Rory had fluffed out his fur to make himself look bigger than he already was. Bee shone like a queen, as radiant as a lamp.

I met her gaze in the mirror of the dragon's eyes. I nodded.

She exhaled. "Not every young woman gets to march into the gullet of Leviathan." The crack in her voice betrayed her: She wasn't quite as sure of herself as she meant to sound.

The dragon's breath huffed over us, not rancid but sweet, like the aroma of coconut milk as it bakes through a rice pudding. It pushed out its tongue over the ridge of its lip to make a bridge.

Never let it be said my courage had failed me when put to the test.

I tightened my grip on the loose skin of Rory's neck. Together we walked up the slope. The tongue was oddly firm and dry beneath our tread, not at all slimy. Rory again gave that moaning growl as the tongue shifted beneath us. To keep our balance Bee and I set down the chest and held on to it, and I grabbed Rory, as the creature pulled its tongue back inside.

We slid backward into the smoke. The jaw closed.

Darkness fell as a smothering blanket. Strange noises like drones and squeaks drifted at the edge of my hearing.

Bee and I sat on the chest, clutching each other. Rory leaned against us as if he wanted to climb inside either the chest or us. His trembling shuddered through me. I rubbed his head.

From my oldest, sleepiest memories I scoured out a song. It whispered in my mother's raspy voice, scarred by war and pain. I sang in a low voice.

Sleep, sweet child, as the twilight falls
As the bright day takes its rest.
Let the Wild Hunt search, let the Wild Hunt cry,
I shall hide you at my breast.

"Cat, are you crying?" Bee whispered, pressing her cheek to mine. "What is that lullaby?"

"My mother used to sing it to me."

The creature moved in a gentle undulation. The air stirred with a rhythmic pulse, in time to the slow drum of its heart, like the breath of secrets untold. Atop it floated a sound like a bell's resonant ring drawn out as a thread is spun out of a mass of wool. I trembled, struck by such an upwelling of fear at being trapped inside a living beast that I took a slug from my flask of rum for fortitude. The only way to battle the fear was to talk.

"Bee, how could you think I would go with Camjiata? He probably meant to throw me overboard once we were out of sight of land."

She tensed. "It's not that simple. He told me you've never given him a chance to properly explain. He got you exiled to Salt Island to protect you."

"To protect me?" I snorted. "How can he say these things? And with such sincerity! It's like a disease with him. Protect himself, he means, since he believes I will be the instrument of his death." Rory gave a rumble and nosed against me as I went on. " 'Where the hand of fortune branches, Tara Bell's child must choose, and the road of war will be washed by the tide.' The general thinks my choice will be to kill him. But I already made a choice on Hallows' Night at the ballcourt. I was the instrument of the cacica's death, not his."

"That's not what he thinks." Bee's tone wound like darkness, mellow and soft. The heat made me yawn. "He thinks it's the choice you made between Andevai Diarisso and James Drake, between cold mage and fire mage. James Drake has an ugly, unpredictable temper that might have been soothed by the love of a good woman."

"I hope he did not really say that, and in those nauseating words." I took another slug of rum. "The point is, the general could have entirely misunderstood his wife's words about Tara Bell's child. She wrote down her dreams in garbled poetry. He interprets everything as having some relationship to him. I'm quite sure the dream has nothing to do with me choosing between two men...what a tired story that would be!"

Yet what if it referred to the same choice my mother had been forced to make? What if my sire meant to force me to sleep with him to save Vai's life, as he had forced my mother to have sex with him to save the lives of Daniel and the other men in the Baltic Ice Expedition?

"Cat, why are you shaking? I'm sorry I said anything."

I swallowed a huge gulp of rum. Some things I refused to speak of even to Bee. "The point is, James Drake has stayed alive this long by murdering unwilling people as catch-fires. Beggars, the rootless poor, people no one will miss. Salters and dying men. Meanwhile, the general means to allow Drake to go on killing people as long as it helps him win the war he means to wage in Europa. That's why Drake obeys him, because he knows Camjiata will turn a blind eye to his crimes. Who will miss enemy soldiers who perish in war? So how can we trust Camjiata, knowing he employs a criminal like James Drake?"

"Listen! After Caonabo divorced me, I went to the general. I really didn't have anywhere else to go, as you can imagine. Of course I demanded to know what his intentions are toward you. He promised me that you have nothing to fear from him. Your life is his life. As long as you are alive, he knows he is alive. The general has offered us employment as spies and couriers in his army."

"I'm not spying for the general!"

"How do you plan to eat? In what bed do you plan to sleep with your handsome husband? Do you have any money at all, Cat?"

"No," I admitted sullenly. I groped for the flask, but Bee had hidden it. "Didn't Caonabo give you a dower, some pittance from the Taino treasury?"

"Why, yes, he rewarded me very generously. I was granted the right to collect taxes from two towns on the northern coast of Kiskeya. It's a fine income, but one I have no access to. I received also several thousand cowrie shells, which make me quite wealthy in the Taino kingdom but are worth nothing in Europa. A chest full of exceptionally fine cloth, as well as several crates of excellent tobacco. All of which are on the ship you and I were meant to sail on, together with Vai's other chests. We're destitute, Cat. We haven't a single sestertius to our name. All we have is the gear that is in this chest, which fortunately is the one Luce packed for you."

I crossed my arms fumingly. "I don't even know how I'm going to rescue Vai."

"I do have some gold jewelry I can sell," she mused. "The dash jackets can be sold. We won't starve, not for a while. But those things will run out. At least hold the general's offer in reserve, just in case we need it."

Every road led away into darkness, and while normally I could see unusually well in the dark, my eyes could not penetrate the future. I yawned again, eyelids drooping. The heat made me sleepy. Rory was sprawled out like a big warm comforting purr. He snored in a catlike way with little huffs between times as if he was dreaming of chasing down plump deer. Bee and I leaned against his belly. The rocking motion of the beast had a soporific effect.

I rested my head against hers. "Whatever happens, I love you, Bee. Always."

"Always," she whispered, holding my hand.

My eyes closed. I sank into sleep.

As in a dream, I bucketed through the heavens on the back of a horse whose coat was as black and sticky as tar. I braced the butt of a spear against my booted stirrup. My arms were bare, the skin marked with blue coils like the ink-painting common among the Celts. With a hawk's sight I saw our prey running, a girl with long hair streaming out behind her. Her blood smelled of smoke and dreams, and as we galloped up alongside her, I thrust my spear into her back and brought her down. With my hands gripping the spear, I swung off the horse. She was thrashing, trying to crawl, trying to live. I pressed a foot onto her back to trap her and wiped my fingers through the blood pumping out of the wound. Brought it to my lips.

The blood was redolent with the fragrant bloom of powerful cold magic as mouthwatering as spice. But it was not mine to drink. I owed it to my masters. The chain that bound me to them dragged me back toward their presence.

A voice was murmuring, honey words luring me away from the kill. Vai's kisses sweetened my lips and warmed my flesh. His hands measured the map of my body, fingers tracing each curve as he rolled me over on the bed he had built for us.

I stirred, eyes opening as my hands reached for him.

The basket gaped open and empty across my lap. I blinked, trying to focus, for I was back in the belly of the beast. Its comblike teeth shone with a phosphorescent gleam.

By this light I saw Bee talking to Queen Anacaona. The dead flat shine of the cacica's eyes had deepened to a warm brown.

"I'm not sure I understand, Your Highness. Is the Great Smoke the ocean of dreams through which I walk in my dreams?"

"Yes. The Great Smoke is the ocean of all existence. The currents which we call past, present, and future mingle together in the sea of mist."

I was so hungry and hot. I was not meant to journey through the ocean of dreams. My senses rebelled at the stink and the threat.

The dragon's smoky breath trawled me under, back into sleep. I plunged into the slippery dance of the old ones, the most ancient Taninim. Their intertwining movements created currents that streamed through the smoke like rivers. A ripple caught me, pulling me into a dream so vivid it did not seem like a vision but rather like my body and sight cast into another time and place.

General Camjiata stood with his hand on a door latch. Behind him, the view out an attic window overlooked a town square and a stone castle tower rising above green trees. His hair was tied back with an incongruously bright-green ribbon that matched the old-fashioned bottle-green dash jacket he wore, its cuffs trimmed with lace. He addressed me with a serious look that quite disarmed me. Who would offer such a direct and confiding gaze to an enemy?

"I need you to kill him. You're the only one who can."

Golden spears of late-afternoon sunlight lanced into my eyes, blinding me as he opened the door into a lamplit chamber beyond. Darkness smoked up on all sides.

I did not want to be a killer. If only the Master of the Wild Hunt had not been my sire, I would not have had such dreams. Yet if he had not sired me, I would not be what I was. If I had not been what I was, I would not have escaped the mansa. I would have been dead long before I had been forced to make the choice that had killed the cacica. We are bound to our ancestors and to those who made us, whether we want to be or not. What matters is what we make of what we are.

I opened my eyes, back in the belly of the beast. Bee and the cacica were still conversing.

"Do you wish Caonabo had thrown away his honor merely to please you?" Queen Anacaona spoke not with anger, not with pity, but as if pressing Bee to find the answer to a riddle.

"I didn't say that! But he ought not to have gone after Cat in that way. He shouldn't have cooperated with James Drake and the general."

"Open your eyes, selfish girl. It isn't about you. There are greater battles awakening in the world. Those who have developed a thirst for blood cannot easily be turned aside from their insatiable appetites, no matter whom they harm. The old ones move slowly, but they fight to protect their young."

"You speak in riddles," Bee said. "What does that all mean?"

I slid into the fog of dreams as if in the belly of Leviathan I, too, became a dragon dreamer. Streaming rivers of mist welled up from the deep, currents flowing in vast circles that penetrated close to the gleaming surface before pouring away into darker, smokier depths. Swimming shapes brushed me, hot and cold by turns, rough to the touch and then slickly smooth like eels slithering in coils around and around me.

I startled awake, shuddering, to find myself lying in Vai's arms on the bed he had built for us. His embrace was so strong and comforting that I could have reclined in its orbit forever and not missed the world.

"Catherine," he murmured in a drowsy, contented voice. "You were dreaming and mumbling. It sounded like 'There are greater battles awakening in the world.' What is it, love?"

The feel of his body stretched the length of mine, his skin to my skin, made me want to purr with simple pleasure. "I dreamed I was swallowed by a dragon. And now I have to pee. Do you think those two things are related?"

Chuckling, he kissed me on the lips. After stroking a hand along the length of my torso, he kissed me again, and then longer and with more concentration, until I really did have to get up even though he clearly had other activities on his mind. He rose with me.

"We'll go the washroom," he said, swinging me up into his arms. My hip pressed against his belly. "We both need a wash."

I giggled, for the night was warm and the room stuffy despite an open window, and we were both sweaty. "It's the middle of the night."

"All the better. No one to disturb us." A pinch of light sparked into existence. Cold fire swelled to a fist-size bubble whose light dappled the clothes strewn over the floor beside the bed.

I brushed my cheek against his short-shorn beard, the hair just long enough to tickle instead of scratch. "You must spend hours getting your beard to look just this decorative way."

When he looked at me with a smile of tenderness and mischief mixed so sweetly, I could scarcely breathe, much less think. "Why, Catherine, you *were* watching me all that time, weren't you?"

The currents ripped me away from him just as I realized I was dreaming the night we had consummated our marriage. I flailed and kicked, for I was determined to get back to him, but a whirlpool dragged me down into the crushing abyssal deeps.

Like a gull hovering in the wind, I floated over a rocky path strewn with boulders and pocked with ice. A towering cliff of ice studded with rocks filled the horizon: It was the wall of a vast ice shelf. A gray sea lapped a narrow strand of stony beach. In the shelter of a shallow cave, two longboats had been overturned out of reach of the waves and covered with canvas staked to the earth. Three men with ragged gloves fumbled with stakes and canvas, uncovering one of the beached boats and its treasure of oars and oilcloth. The wind was coarse and unforgivingly cold. They worked frantically as the howls of approaching wolves grew in volume.

On the path that led up a steep incline to the crumbling foot of the glacial shelf stood a hatless woman. She wore a rumpled, dirty uniform and grasped a bloody falcata in her gloved left hand. Her dark red hair was pulled back into a braid and pinned in a coil at the back of her head. Fresh red welts marked a sun-weathered face brushed with freckles. Blood oozed down her cheek and neck. Someone else's blood was splashed across the front of her uniform coat, and drying blood soaked her knees, as if she'd knelt in blood. Her right sleeve was torn to ribbons, exposing a bleeding shoulder and arm. Her ragged breath came in gouts of mist in the freezing air.

Behind her a man with curly black hair as lush and thick as Bee's knelt to crank back the ratchet of a crossbow. He had two bolts remaining in his quiver but no other visible weapon. Four dead dire wolves littered the path, marking the trail of a pursuit. About fifty steps above lay a dead man in a soldier's kit. His corpse was mottled crimson, his belly slashed open and spilling guts. A dying wolf twitched beside him, pink spume riming its muzzle. A falcata had been thrust up to the hilt into its right eye, the tip sticking out through the back of its neck.

High up on the path, three shaggy wolves nosed into view, sniffing the air.

The woman spoke. "More are coming."

The man looked first at her and then higher, up the trail, to the wolves. Both had muzzles smeared with viscera, as if they'd been eating. With the loaded crossbow, he rose to stand beside her. She was tall, big-boned, and confident in her strength even in the face of snarling death. He was a little shorter, with a build meant to be stocky but made lean by privation.

I recognized them. His youthful, smiling face adorned the portrait in my locket: Daniel Hassi Barahal, the man who considered himself my father. I had never seen any likeness of Tara Bell, but despite the dark red hair and blue eyes, she looked so like me that I knew she had to be my mother.

"If it's necessary to hold a last rear guard to get the boat out, you and the others must leave me." She spoke as a shopping woman with many more errands ahead might remark that the family could afford fish for supper but not beef.

"I think it unlikely we shall do so." I admired the warmth of his laugh. He had deep lines at his eyes, the mark of a man who would rather joke than scowl. "Who will mend our clothes if we don't have you to do it for us?"

She actually rolled her eyes, and her lips twitched even as her gaze tracked the wolves. "You must be tired, for that's not your cleverest jest. As if you cared one jot about your clothes, except that they not fall off and expose your shapely arse."

"So you did notice! I thought you were asleep." He added, with a laugh more reckless than amused, "You'll not shake me loose. If you're pregnant, we will face it together."

When she caught his gaze, my child's heart wept. Was that love in her expression? Loyalty? Exasperation? I knew so little about my mother, but right then I knew she trusted him.

"If we escape, I will return to my regiment. I honor my obligations. My oath belongs to my commander. I cannot abandon my comrades. You know you are not the only one I love."

"I do not ask you to abandon anyone, Tara, nor to choose me above any other. I only ask you to remember the oath I make to you now."

He stole a kiss, pressed lightly at the corner of her mouth. Briefly she caught him with an answering kiss, then she pushed him away, and he stepped back with a smile.

Her gaze tracked the wolves. "They will never stop hunting me."

His smiling expression vanished. "My oath is this. If we get out of this, if you need me, then you need only get word to me. I will come for you, and for the child if there is one. No matter who or what hunts you."

The men at the longboat cried out in triumph as they found it seaworthy and its equipment intact. Shouting, they called three names— *Tara! Daniel! Gaius!*—and I realized they did not yet know the man on the path above was dead, for they could see nothing of what had occurred in the rear guard.

With her bloody arm, my mother pulled him against her. She kissed him with the passion of the condemned. When she released him, he was so stricken by astonishment that she had taken several steps away before she realized he wasn't following her.

"Daniel! Don't make me regret that."

Beneath the cruel face of the ice, he laughed, looking like the happiest man in the world.

"You would laugh at a time like this," she said with a smile that made her look like a woman who knew how to jest in a tavern over drinks. "Let's get out of here before those cursed wolves get down the path."

They strode toward their companions and the boats, but she abruptly halted, dragging him to a stop. "Did you hear something?"

He looked up at the face of the ice. "Just the wolves and the wind."

"No," she said. "Something else."

The wolves began to descend.

"Cat! Wake up! You're howling." Bee was shaking me, trying to jostle my head off a cliff.

"Ouch! Let go, you beast!" Then I remembered everything. I sat up just as we jolted on such a bump that I was slammed into the side of a wagon. "Ow!"

Bee and I were crammed into the bed of the wagon with Vai's chest, the Taino basket, and a dozen crates heaped with glistening oysters. The crates jostled with each jounce.

A man looked around from the driver's seat. He was a white-haired, light-skinned elder with a pipe in his mouth and his shirtsleeves rolled up to reveal sun-weathered forearms corded with muscle. "The lass wakes! I thought sure she was drunk as a lord and would sleep it off 'til teatime. Especially with that howling. Thought it was dire wolves, didn't I? Or a pack of women cast off for their unsightly looks and scolding tongues!" He cackled at his own jest.

Fiery Shemesh! What nightmare was this?

"Bee, where are we?" I whispered as I rubbed my bruised shoulder. "Where is the dragon?"

"The dragon cast us out on land," she whispered back.

The road was a cart track, two ruts cutting through damp earth. Mud slopped with each turn of the wheels, but we were high and dry. The two oxen pulling the wagon had the stolid pace of animals who can walk all day without stopping. Around us lay green hills ablaze with spring flowers. I shivered, for although the wagoner was content in his shirtsleeves, it seemed deathly cold.

Rory was sitting up next to the driver, wearing one of Vai's best dash jackets, the fabric red, gold, and orange squares limned by black. He took a puff on the pipe and coughed violently.

The old man chortled again. "You smoke like a woman, lad! No doubt comes of being forced to attend on your sister and cousin all these months, as you say. I'll teach you to be a man."

The sight of Rory wearing the dash jacket distracted me. "Bee! How could you let Rory wear that particular jacket? That's the one Vai wore the morning after we..."

Her foot poked me to silence. "How could I have remembered that!"

"He's already got a smudge on the elbow!"

She gazed past me, steadfastly mute. Back the way we had come rose the roofs of fishermen's shacks next to a small marble temple whose pinnacle was marked with the chariot of a sea god. A sleepy strand gave way to rocky shallows where men raked for oysters. Beyond lay an islet prominently marked by a stone pillar and a tree so large I could tell it was an oak even from this distance. The gray-blue waters of the sea soughed in the brisk wind, chipped with foam. Out on the water it was raining, but up here it was dry and sunny. It looked a cursed lot like the land I had grown up in.

Bee tugged down my skirt, which had gotten ruched up past my knees. "You slept through most of the journey. It's as if you had actually been stunned."

"You were stupefied," added Rory helpfully, turning to address me. "Then you started making smacking noises like you were trying to kiss someone, or had turned into a fish. You didn't start howling until you reached dry land."

"Rory and I had to drag you and the chest out of the Great Smoke and onto warded ground, right there on that little island. An oysterman saw us and brought a rowboat to help us to shore. This kind fellow agreed to convey us."

"That's all very well, Bee, but it doesn't answer my question." My legs were sticky and my skirt was damp. Bee had gotten my wool jacket onto me, although she hadn't buttoned it. I chafed my arms and hands, trying to warm up. I was exceedingly grateful for the sun, however weak its light and heat seemed compared to the blazing sun in Expedition. "Where are we?"

"Why, dearest," she said with a triumphant smile, "we're on the road to Adurnam. We've reached Europa."

13

The rain caught up with us as we reached the outskirts of Adurnam. By the time we reached Westmarket we were soaked through, and the downpour had left Bee's curls plastered to her neck. Vai's dash jacket was creased and sodden and, worst of all, Rory had burned the cuff with ashes from the wagoner's pipe. I had begun shivering so badly I didn't have the energy to scold him.

The wagoner reined up at the edge of the bustling fish market just as the rain ceased. Wagons and carts trundled in from the marshy Sieve, the vast estuary of the Rhenus River.

"This is as far as I come, lasses." He cackled, tapping his hat against the driver's bench to flick water off the brim. "You had me half believing those lively tales you spun about the foreigners over the ocean who allow girls to run about half naked kicking a ball. As if females wouldn't just hurt themselves trying to play such games like men."

Irritation warmed me as I clambered off the wagon. "I was not making it up! The game is called batey. You don't kick the ball, because it's not allowed to touch the ground. Women play it in leagues, just like the men, and people come to watch."

"Folk come to watch, as if they were men! I'd say for another reason, ha ha! Women ruling and men bowing and scraping to stop from being scolded! I'm as likely to believe this tale of an Assembly of representatives voted on by every person in the city. As if a prince would allow that!"

I spoke through gritted teeth. "There is no prince in Expedition."

"No, there's a fancy-dressed queen instead!" He laughed as he wiped rain from his cheeks. "You're killing me, lass!"

Rory pulled me back before I whacked the man with my cane. To soothe me he groomed away tendrils of hair stuck to my forehead. "You're not going to convince him of what is true if he believes it can't be true."

Bee twisted a slender bracelet off one dainty wrist. "Please take this as thanks for your help."

"You don't need to pay me. I'm happy to do a good turn..." The wagoner paused as Bee held up the bracelet. "Is that gold?"

"Gold from the court of the Taino king," she said prettily. "He was so overwhelmed by my beauty that he married me."

"If you want to call that marriage." His gaze hardened. By the way his gaze flicked between us, I guessed he was reconsidering his estimate of what manner of young females we might be and whether Rory was truly my brother or rather our partner in crime.

Bee's diminutive stature led people to think her both mild and harmless, until she shifted her feet to a fighting stance. "We expect to be treated with the respect we have shown you," she said in a voice thick with queenly grandeur. "Do not make me regret I thought you a decent man."

He relaxed. "I see you two girls is having me on. My thanks, then, and I'll take the bauble gladly, as a keepsake of your mischievous ways. Now you get on to your sire, lass. Lest he get tired of waiting for you and come hunting you down. Listen, you can hear him coming now!"

In the distance horns tootled and drums and cymbals clashed.

"What festival parade is that?" I asked as we heaved the chest out of the carriage.

"Tomorrow Mars Camulos has his feast. The mask associations have been practicing for weeks for the festival procession. You Phoenician girls won't be dancing to that Roman horn!"

With a wave and another cackle he drove into the narrow lanes of the market.

"Mars Camulos!" said Bee with a dark frown. "That means tomorrow is the twenty-third day of the month of Martius. The areito to celebrate Caonabo becoming cacique took place on the first of Februarius. Which means we left Sharagua six weeks ago."

"Six weeks! And yet three months before that!" I cried, thinking of Vai, taken from me on Hallows' Night.

Looking toward the stalls of fish, Rory eyed the nearest vendor as if gauging whether he could snatch a fish and run. "No wonder I'm so hungry!"

"Rory, don't do it." Bee grabbed his arm, and he winced. She turned to me. "You've always said that time passes differently in the spirit world. It's still strange to have it happen to us."

Rain started up again in a blowsy mist. My teeth began to chatter. "We need to find shelter and decide what to do."

"I have to speak to the headmaster, Cat. I think we should go there first."

Rory hunched his shoulders. "He's a dragon. You can't trust him. He will eat you."

"He won't eat me, Rory." Bee poked him in the arm. "He might eat you, though, and there are moments when you are so annoying that I must say I expect I would encourage him to do so."

Rory drew himself straight, lips pulled back. "I shall have you know, Beatrice, that I am never annoying. That you find me so is a reflection on your character, not mine."

"We need to scout out our ground first," I temporized, for I sensed Rory trembling at the edge of rebellion. Also, I desperately wanted to dry out and get warm. "Let's go first to the law offices of Godwik and Clutch. It's a long walk across the city, I know. But if there's anyone I trust, it's the trolls...the feathered people, I mean. The Taino always use the more polite phrase."

"We need not imitate the Taino in everything just because they believe themselves to be superior to us!" remarked Bee in a frosty tone. "But I suppose it is wisest to go to the law offices first. Wait here."

She left Rory and me huddled with the chest under the eaves of a decrepit warehouse. Wagons lined up to offload their glistening catch into the baskets and crates of middlemen, merchants, cooks, and men guarding wheelbarrows. No one paid us any mind, for we looked exactly like an impoverished brother and sister who had no home and no means of buying our next meal, but I felt exposed and vulnerable.

"Rory, what did you tell the wagoner about our sire? You ought to have been silent."

"It was while you were howling. I said our sire was the Master of the Wild Hunt. The benefit of telling the truth is that so few people believe you."

I laughed. "When did you get to be so wise?"

"There was this woman I petted in the palace of the prince of Tarrant that time I got trapped there after eating the pug dog and the peahen..."

He regaled me with a story that made me laugh more than once, even if there were particulars I had to command him to skip over because I did not want to hear them. Having no shame, he had no idea there were private things a person did not tell other people. Just as he finished, Bee reappeared carrying three leather peddlers' sacks and a wrapped paper bundle.

Rory took the wrapped paper from her, brushed his cheek against hers, then held the paper to his nose and inhaled. "Fish! You brought me food."

"How did you manage that?" I demanded.

"A noble bride receives a lot of gold jewelry. If she isn't bountifully adorned, it's shameful for her family."

"You had no family in Taino country."

An odd expression creased her mouth from a memory I could not share. "Let's go. We'll transfer the chest's contents to these packs when we have a roof over our heads."

The chest was indeed an unwieldy burden. The coarse rope chafed my fingers as we trudged through the busy streets of Adurnam. The sky was heavy with clouds and gritty with coal smoke from the afternoon cooking. Dreary colors and pinched faces made me feel we walked through a foreign land. To mark the festival of the god who ruled over war, shopkeepers had already adorned their doorways with a red wreath pierced with the short sword known as a gladius or with a wooden mask depicting a ram's head with massive horns. The drinking would begin at sunset, and tomorrow morning there would be a procession through the streets.

We headed east toward the new districts along Enterprise Road. But our steps strayed toward the hills where the ancient Kena'ani settlement had risen long ago and where sanctuaries sacred to Melqart, Tanit, and Ba'al still stood. By unspoken agreement, Bee and I took a roundabout way that led us to the house where we had grown up.

We halted on the edge of Falle Square at dusk. The small four-story town house was shuttered, its front gate padlocked. No thread of smoke rose from the chimney. No festival wreath marked the door, not that any manner of Roman adornment had ever hung there when we lived in the house. The mansa of Four Moons House had purchased the property from the Hassi Barahal clan after my aunt and uncle had fled Adurnam. He had meant to keep Bee and me prisoner there until he sorted out what to do with us, but we had escaped.

Rain spattered as the wind picked up. Bee and Rory waited in the back alley while I wrapped shadows around myself, climbed over the back gate, and scanned the yard with its laundry room, cistern, and outdoor hearth. The old carriage house had been empty for years, for we could not afford horses or carriage, but the new owners had stocked it with hay and bags of feed. Bee and I had long ago hidden a key beneath a pair of loose boards in the carriage house. It was still there, but when I brought it to the door, the locks had been changed.

I tucked up my skirts, shifted the basket to my back, and climbed the tree to the window of Uncle Jonatan's study. A chain of magic still protected the window latch. The whisper of its cold magic woke my sword. I unsheathed my blade and severed the threads. Then I turned the latch and swung into a deserted room.

Uncle Jonatan's desk had been replaced by a table, chairs, and two settees shrouded by heavy covers and the dusty flavor of neglect.

I stepped into the first-floor corridor and listened through the threads that bound the house. Aunt Tilly had spun Kena'ani magic to guard home and property, and its embrace lingered in the walls like a memory of her warm smile. I wiped away a tear, for although I knew she and Uncle had betrayed me to save their own daughter, I still missed the way Aunt Tilly would kiss my forehead at night before we slept. I longed for the plates of sweet biscuits she and Cook had baked when they had extra coin for a treat of honey.

The house lay utterly silent except for the patter of rain. I went down to the ground floor and into the half basement. In the kitchen I opened the shutters and looked around. A new stove with all manner of modern conveniences had been installed in place of the old one where Cook had eked out each last morsel of tough stew meat and mealy turnips to make enough to feed us all. Dust smeared the tabletop, broken by the footprints of mice. Yet the coal bin was full, and the pantry was stocked with sealed pots of oats, barley, and beans.

I found a key hanging beside the back door. By the time the rain really began to pour, we were all safe inside.

I shivered. "No one knows we're in Adurnam, and no one has lived here for weeks. I say we stay here the night, take a bath, and wash our clothes."

Bee nodded. "We can haul water while we're still wet. Now it's coming on dark, no one will notice our chimney smoking. Do you want to haul water or start the fire?"

"I'm cold and wet," said Rory in a tone of offended surprise. "I can't work at hard labor in this condition!"

"You'd be surprised what you could do rather than have me bite you," said Bee.

A grumbling Rory and I filled two copper tubs and the big scullery pot with water while Bee lit lamps, stoked and lit a fire in both the scullery and the fancy kitchen stove, and set oats and beans to soak. She found towels and an entire cake of lavender-scented soap of a kind we had only been able to afford as shavings at the holidays. In the scullery I gave Rory a towel to wrap around his waist and told him to take off his wet clothes.

"If you sit and watch the big pot, the water will boil," I added.

"Really?" He settled on a stool with such a pleased expression that I could not tell whether he simply did not know the old saying, or had a profoundly complex sense of humor.

In the kitchen Bee and I stripped, wrapped ourselves in towels, and hung the wet clothes on a rack by the stove to dry.

"Really, Cat, wasn't that a little mean-spirited? A watched pot never boils!"

"Of course it boils eventually unless there's a cold mage nearby to douse the fire. It will keep him out of trouble." I pulled out Queen Anacaona's skull, with its empty eye sockets and remarkably good teeth. Some peculiar magic was keeping the jaw wired on. "Where shall we set her?"

"You can't mean to set out the skull as if it can see or hear anything!"

"It seems rude to leave her shut up in the basket. I'll set her here on one of the plates so she feels as if she knows what's going on." I placed her on a cupboard shelf, facing out. "There you are, Your Highness. We will be going into and out of this kitchen, but be assured we will not leave the house without you. In fact, if you have any spectral powers, you might warn us if an enemy approaches the house so we can escape. Otherwise you'll fall into their custody and then you'll never reach your son."

I glanced at Bee, sure she was about to make a mocking comment.

Instead, her lips pursed as she considered the skull of the cacica who had briefly been her mother-in-law. She made a courtesy. "My apologies, Your Highness. I regret my rude comment."

We left the cacica to oversee the kitchen while we explored the house. Our bare feet marked trails on the floors. Warmth from the two fires drifted upstairs like the kiss of an opia. The cold mages had repapered the walls, replaced the curtains, and removed all the old furniture. Only two things remained from the house we had grown up in.

One was the big mirror on the first-floor landing, covered by a sheet. I pulled back the sheet and rubbed a finger over the mirror's slick surface, remembering how an elderly djeli had chained the marriage between Vai and me in its dark surface. The light from the lamp Bee held gleamed in the mirror, illuminating us as indistinct figures. Threads of gossamer magic chased around me before receding into the shadows. A faintly gleaming chain spun out of my chest and pierced the surface of the mirror, as an arrow loosed into a pool stabs a path. Although barely visible in the darkness, the thread shot sure and strong into the unseen depths.

Was there movement in the heart of the mirror? I extended a hand to touch it. Its surface was smooth and hard.

"Cat, are you staring at yourself? For you look a sight, with your hair all tangled and that towel draped so fashionably..." She touched her own bedraggled curls with her free hand. "Blessed Tanit! Is that really how I look?"

I pretended to recognize her as if for the first time. "Bee? Is that truly you? I would never have known...I thought perhaps a medusa, with the snakes of her hair all dead and limp—"

She kicked me in the shin.

I let the sheet drop back over the mirror's face. We went upstairs to the bedchamber we had shared for most of our lives. In a secret hiding place in the wall of the chamber we found Bee's first sketchbook with its scrawls, and a scrap of faded calico fabric wrapped around my childhood toys: a red-and-cream polished agate, a little wood play sword, and a tiny carving of a stallion caught in the flow of a gallop.

"You gave me an awful bruise on the head with that thing," said Bee as I brandished the little sword. "You were such a beast, Cat. Always getting into fights."

"I was not! I was always saving you when *you* got in fights! Like the time in the ribbon shop when that Roman girl yanked on your hair until you screamed while her mother pretended nothing was happening."

She grinned as she galloped the toy stallion across the floor. "You had hacked off half her hair before her mother bothered to come look. It's a good thing we can run so fast."

"It's not speed. It's knowing how to distract the enemy."

"Do you remember seeing her again years later when we arrived at the academy?" Bee laughed so hard she had to wipe tears away. "All grown up, and with her hair done in those knots and bows that were fashionable four years ago."

"Thank Tanit that went out of fashion as quickly as it did. Your hair was too curly and mine too heavy and straight."

"How she looked daggers at us! She started a whispering campaign, do you remember? To try to make us feel ashamed of being impoverished Phoenician girls."

We shared a smile, for of course the girl hadn't known we were shameless. We simply didn't care what she and her circle thought of us. Our indifference had demolished her campaign. Not to mention the syrup we had secretly smeared on her knots and bows, which soon attracted ants.

"Let's go down before Rory does something he oughtn't," said Bee, taking my hand.

We gathered our treasures. As we started down the steps I heard splashing.

"Oh, dear," I said. "We'd better hurry."

When we reached the scullery we found Rory happily washing himself as he sang a spectacularly obscene song. Fortunately he was 109 sitting in the tub, and had filled it with hot water. The water was already grimy with his dirt.

"Am I supposed to eat this?" he asked brightly, holding up a sliver he had cut off the cake of soap. Then he laughed as he set back to scrubbing himself. "You should see your expressions!"

"Be careful I don't make you eat it!" muttered Bee. "Where on earth did you learn those crude verses?"

He brushed his lips as if he were grooming up the corners of his grin. "That's a story! Do you remember when you sailed with the general and I was left behind with Brennan Du and Professora Kehinde Nayo Kuti? I discovered they have houses here in Europa where all they do is pet all day and all night!"

"You can tell us another time, Rory," I said quickly.

Bee and I retreated to the kitchen. I prepared a nourishing porridge from oats and pulse while she cleaned the fish and baked it plain, with only salt. Shockingly, we discovered a cache of actual sugar in a glass jar that had been shoved behind a small butter churn in the pantry. When Rory had finished bathing and clothed himself in a towel wrapped around his waist, I set him to watch the porridge while Bee and I bathed. We washed each other's hair in a bucket, as we always used to do, then traded washing in the tub and rinsing with buckets of warm water from the stove. Afterward, we washed our underthings.

"I miss the shower and plumbing at Aunty's boardinghouse," I said. "This seems so awkward now. Think of the faucets in the town house where the general lived!"

"I do think of them," said Bee with a melancholy sigh. "Even that was as nothing compared to the magnificent plumbing in the palace in Sharagua."

With towels wrapped around us, we returned to find the porridge ready to eat and Rory picking slivers off the cooked fish. We dug in.

Bee paused to watch me. "The way you're eating, are you sure you're not pregnant?"

"I am quite sure!"

"She's not pregnant." Rory brushed his face alongside my head. "I have a very sensitive nose. She's not pregnant. Nor is she at the moment fertile."

110   "How can you know that?" demanded Bee.

His affronted expression made her laugh. "Didn't I just say I have a sensitive nose? I know when females are fertile, or not fertile. You human women aren't like the females of my own kind. You are fertile more often, and yet never seem to know it, so it's fortunate *I* can tell."

Bee and I stared at him for so long, mouths dropped open, that his brow wrinkled.

"How can you *not* tell? I would think it would be something you would want to know."

"Goodness," I murmured as heat crawled up my cheeks.

"You look so sweet when you blush, Cat." Bee's smirk made me laugh, although I was still flushed. She crossed to the high basement window with its four expensive panes of glass, cracked the latch, and pushed open the window to let out some of the heat. "What else haven't you told us, Rory? We've asked you more than once to tell us about the spirit world and the Wild Hunt and the spirit courts, but you always say you don't know anything."

A flicker of wildness stirred in his amber eyes. He leaned closer, growing more threatening, like a great cat guarding the succulent deer it has just dragged in. Bee glanced toward the knives hanging by the stove, but I held my spoon and did not retreat.

"You two persist in talking to me as if I am a man. I am not a man. It amuses me to walk in these clothes. I am a cat. I live in the wild, and I hunt. The dragons are my people's enemy. As for the other, I cannot walk in the spirit courts. I know nothing of their kind, except that they rule us."

"How do they rule you?" Bee asked.

He considered the bones of the fish. "How do princes rule here? All creatures in the spirit lands where I grew up bide under the rule of the courts because the courts are stronger."

"But why are the dragons your enemies?" Bee asked.

"If we are caught in the tides of their dreaming, we are changed, and lose both our bodily form and the mind that makes us a self. How can they not be our enemies?"

Bee's smile had the brilliant assurance of the sun flashing out as wind drove off its shield of clouds. "You see! The headmaster must know about dragons, dreaming, and the Great Smoke. Why else

111

would he have tricked us into crossing into the spirit world? Cat, get my sketchbook."

After wiping my hands, I unfastened the lid of Vai's chest. Bee had placed her sketchbook at the top, wrapped in an oilskin pouch. As she flipped through its pages, I went through the contents of the chest.

The top was spanned by the length of canvas, sewn with pockets, in which I kept my sewing things and my other necessaries. Beneath the unrolled canvas lay a pretty pagne I had never before seen, a festive gold-and-orange print with smiling suns and laughing moons. I blinked watering eyes, for it was obviously a special gift from Aunty, one the family had chosen for me with affection. Below this I found trousers and underthings and, beneath them, some of Vai's beautiful dash jackets tucked within clean pagnes for extra protection.

"He can probably describe exactly where and when he got each one," I said, running my hands along the folds.

Bee snapped shut the sketchbook. "What is it like to love someone that much?"

I glanced up at her. "Did you love Caonabo?"

"In that ridiculously infatuated way you love Andevai? No, thank Tanit, I did not love him!"

"How can you say so? At the academy, you were always droning on and on about Amadou Barry's beautiful eyes or whichever young man took your fancy that week. You filled your sketchbook with pictures of handsome young men. And you were always talking—"

"Yes, I was always talking. I enjoyed the attention. Who wouldn't?"

"I wouldn't!"

"Yes, dearest. That's my point. You wouldn't and never did, because you're a different person than I am." She lifted a hand to scrub at her face as if she were tired. "Because I'm beautiful, people expect me to have a romantical disposition. Even you expected it, Cat! But I must say, there is nothing romantical about using cheap ribbons to make an old dress appear newer whenever the family is obliged to appear at a social gathering. Melqart forbid there be any chance we look as poor as we really were, lest people inclined to hire us reject our services due to our wrecked finances! There is nothing romantical about eating tough winter radish or mushy turnips for every meal in chilly Martius and damp April because the root cellar is almost empty, the early-ripening crops aren't yet at market, and there's not enough money for meat."

After a glance at her stormy expression, I pulled a comb out of my sewing canvas and handed it to her. She set down the sketchbook and began to comb out Rory's snarled hair.

I talked to fill in her silence. "Maybe it's not so wise to choose a palace of gold and silk over a humble cottage if the first comes with a knife in the back and a foot on the heart and the second comes with a smile and a kiss."

"Yes, that's very sweet. I am not so sure the smiling and kissing will survive the dreary struggling day in and day out. Or did you not live in the same house I did, watching Mama and Papa with their polite indifference?"

"Bee..." My voice trailed off as she sniffed down angry tears. "It wasn't anyone's fault that we were poor. Especially not Aunt Tilly and Uncle Jonatan."

"You are so loyal, dearest, that even after they sacrificed you to try to save me, you can't bear to speak a word against them. I'm not talking about fault, even if they did take uncounted imprudent financial gambles. I'm talking about bargaining my beauty for wealth and position."

"Was that why you were so angry at Amadou Barry when he merely offered you a position as his mistress? Because it wasn't a more secure contract?"

"No," she said softly. "I was angry at myself. I almost said yes to him just because his kisses dazzled me. What a fool I was! Desire is a foolhardy way for a young woman to secure a livelihood." She glanced at me. "Not that I mean to accuse you of falling into love with Andevai just because of his looks, or his kisses."

"I suppose I was dazzled by his looks from the beginning." I tried to stop myself from smiling and could not. "But he courted me with radical principles. And food."

"This is a new expression for you, Cat. You were always so heartless and sensible before. Now you look absolutely stupefied."

I laughed, but quickly sobered. "Did you really trade yourself and your beauty and your dream walking to the Taino for the security and wealth of the palace and a noble station?"

"Of course I did. Our marriage was arranged for political gain. I didn't go in expecting to love him. But I liked him. He's restful. I didn't realize how pleasant it is to be with a restful person."

"Are you saying I'm not a restful person?" I teased, essaying a joke, for I hated her tears and wanted desperately to make her laugh.

"I think you're a restful person, Cat." Rory brushed the corners of his lips with the back of his hand as if smoothing down quivering whiskers.

"Not that I mean this in a critical way, Cat, but neither you nor your cold mage is restful. Honestly, I can't imagine how you two will get on once you have to manage daily life together."

I pressed a jacket to my cheek. "I will keep his dash jackets in good repair."

"That's a skill he will certainly appreciate!" She wiped a tear from her cheek. "Did you know that in Taino country women can divorce men with the same legal rights as men can divorce women? Now that we're back in Adurnam I can't help but reflect that I would have been left penniless and ostracized if it had happened to me here. Strange to think I should be glad it was a foreign man who divorced me instead of a local one!"

I opened my mouth to make a joke, but no sound came out. My chest felt hollow, for she had sacrificed her grand marriage for me. I could not throw that in her face as a jest.

She kept combing, grip tight. "His relatives wanted him to denounce me in front of the entire Taino court, but he refused to do it. He merely let people assume I was returning with the general to Europa because I was Europan and obligated to serve my people. "

I said nothing, waiting for her to go on.

"He was so angry. Not like Papa gets angry, shouting and stomping, but distant and formal."

Her fiercely vulnerable expression tore my heart in two. "I'm so sorry it ended badly."

"Ouch! Bee! You're pulling my hair." Rory stiffened, teeth gritted.

She released the death grip she had on Rory's locks and began combing with such fixed concentration I knew I was about to hear truth. "I felt so humiliated. Caonabo cutting me off like that when I thought we got on so well, and I know he thought we got on well, too. But he took it so badly. I know it was a lie to draw that sketch. But surely he had to understand I could not just stand by and see you threatened with death! It's as if he holds his honor higher than my love for you or any loyalty to our marriage. Yet why would he not? He's a prince in a powerful nation, and now its ruler. If I did not walk the dreams of dragons he would never have acknowledged I existed. I married him for the security and the position and the wealth, not in a mercenary way, mind you—"

I laughed, and she made to throw the comb at me.

"You know what I mean! I didn't marry him to make use of his rank and riches for my own personal gain, but so you and I would have a rock to stand on in a stormy sea. We have nothing."

"I know," I murmured as I trailed my hand through the silks, damasks, and cottons, and the practical wool challis of my riding jacket. "Nothing but your jewelry, and some expensive clothes with pearl buttons. I suppose we will have to sell them, starting with the buttons."

At the bottom lay winter coats, boots, Vai's carpentry tools, and tiny carved wooden boxes, containers for ornaments and toiletries, including the sheaths made of lamb's intestines Vai had obtained before the night of the areito. I smiled dreamily. He had been so sure I would say yes.

Rory nudged Bee with his shoulder, and she resumed combing.

At the bottom of the chest I found two packets of fine white cotton cloth I had never before seen, wrapped around three heavy bundles, each about the size of my forearm, that had the solidity of metal. I sighed. "I'm glad you escaped with one chest, at least. I suppose the other chests are on the ship with the general, if Drake hasn't burned them. What's wrapped in the cotton?"

"Caonabo asked me to give some items to Haübey, in secret. I hid them with your things so no one would suspect I had them."

"Caonabo divorced you because he was offended that you lied about the sketch. And then asked you to carry out an errand for him?"

"He trusted me to do it."

"I am indignant on your behalf. Of course he trusted you! You're a trustworthy person! Yet he threw you off for what he took as a personal slight. Young men see everything reflected in their own honor."

She chuckled. "Now you're talking about Andevai."

I smiled. "That's better. I like to hear you laugh."

Rory relaxed as Bee's hand lost its death grip on the comb and her strokes grew lighter. "Caonabo intends to change some of the old laws, like the strict one on quarantine. The worst of the old epidemics burned themselves out several generations ago. The behiques can treat illness more effectively now. But people naturally fear bad things will happen if they don't do everything exactly as they always used to do it. Change frightens people."

"Or threatens them," I said. "That's why the mage Houses don't like technology. It threatens their power. That's why they defeated and imprisoned General Camjiata, because his legal code threatens their power, too..."

We took possession of Cook's bedchamber next to the kitchen. Bee and I shared the bed while Rory slept on the floor beside it, resting on the pallet our man-of-all-work Pompey had used in the kitchen at night. "I never sleep alone," he said, "it makes me nervous."

"Hush," said Bee, pinching out the lamp.

In the darkness the memory of Cook's scent settled over me: She had always smelled of flour and onions, but in a comforting way, not an unpleasant one. Home rose around us, although it was dark and abandoned. We could stay the night but never truly return.

Yet the house embraced us. With Bee slumbering beside me in the old familiar way and Rory snoring softly on the floor, I slept soundly.

14

I was awakened in the morning by Bee crawling over me to get to her sketchbook. I slid deeper under the blankets as she perched on the edge of the bed and sketched. Just enough gloomy light leaked through a basement window for her to see the paper. When she had finished, she ran out to use the privy. I followed. Gray clouds promised rain.

She left me to stir the slumbering fire back into a blaze and make the morning porridge while she sat at the kitchen table, studying the sketch. In a modest tailor's shop, two men sat cross-legged on a platform raised off the floor. Glass-paned windows spilled light over half-made garments draped across their laps. A cat sat under the platform, barely visible in the shadows. Bolts of cloth were stacked on a table next to a privacy screen. On the opposite side of the street, buildings housed a row of shops. Seen through the window directly opposite, beneath a sign that read QUEEDLE AND CLUTCH, a troll was being measured for a coat. In the distance, above snow-dusted roofs, rose two slender, square towers, each topped with what looked like a huge golden egg.

"Here we see the problem exactly as General Camjiata described it to me," I remarked, gesticulating with the wooden spoon. "You have to recognize an actual place or piece together the meaning of disparate images to form a message. Then you have to fix a date to it. The cat in the shadows could be me. The most likely person we know who would be in a tailor's shop is Vai. The snow suggests some time between October and April." I allowed myself to hope that I would rescue Vai and thus end up in a tailor's shop waiting for him.

She flipped through the pages, scrutinizing several sketches of the academy. "The general told me the same thing. He is better at interpreting my dreams than I am. The Taino behiques were going to teach me what they know about dream walking after Caonabo became cacique. But of course instead I had to leave. Ah! Look." She displayed a drawing of the headmaster's study, with its mirrors, bookshelves, and chalkboards. The long table was usually piled with books and scrolls, but in the sketch the tabletop was set with five place settings, as for dinner. Seen from the back, I was dressed in a fashionably cut jacket and skirt. Bee pointed to a murky reflection of me in a mirror that also showed a red wreath hanging on the back of a door. "Here is a festival wreath with the sword of Mars, today's festival. There is a lit lamp. Five people will be invited to dinner in the headmaster's study after dark this evening, and you'll be there."

"I don't recognize the clothes I'm wearing. Still, I suppose this will act in the nature of an experiment. We'll have time to go to the law offices first."

Rory strolled into the room wearing nothing but a towel and a smile. "Mmmm. I like porridge! Can we have some more of that sugar on it? Someday I want to pour sugar all over an attractive body and then lick it off—"

"Rory!" cried Bee, clapping her hands over her ears.

"Blessed Tanit!" I muttered as my cheeks flamed, for my thoughts did stray to my husband. I busied myself handing over a sober waistcoat and jacket of an ambivalent but sophisticated gray. "You're not to wear any of Vai's other dash jackets unless you ask me first. You can wear this one and the one you ruined."

He gave me a look as reproachful as if I had called him a dog. "I'm not carrying that cursed chest if I'm not to be allowed to wear any of the extra-fine jackets."

"Hush, you two," Bee said. "While we're gone, we'll hide our things under the floor in the carriage house."

We tidied up, closed down the stoves, and set the pot to soak. After explaining our errand, I returned the head of the cacica to the basket so we could take her with us.

We left the house by the back gate. Mid-morning delivery carts rumbled through the residential district, but otherwise the lanes were quiet. The farther east we walked, the busier the streets got. People hurried past with their faces painted red, headed for the festival procession. Many wore ribbons of the colors of the Tarrant princely clan, while others wore red-and-gold tabards to mark their allegiance to the god. Instead of looking excited and delighted, many appeared grim and even belligerent. Strangest of all, no one in the crowd was wearing the laborer's cap that was the mark of radical sympathies.

Caught in the middle of a clot of people, we found ourselves pushed onto Old High Street. The wide thoroughfare led toward the district called Roman Camp where lay the main temple dedicated to Mars Camulos. With a clash of cymbals and a blast of trumpets, the festival procession marched into view. The sting of fire magic tamped down like buried coals gave spice to the air.

It was traditional for the guild of blacksmiths to lead the way, marching in ranks in their leather aprons and carrying nothing in their hands except the power of a blacksmith's magic, which contained and channeled fire and thus transformed crude metals into the god's weapons of war. Onlookers shifted back with suspicion and fear, for a conflagration might break out at any moment. Few of the blacksmiths were old, and all were male. I studied their stern faces with new eyes. No one talked about fire magic in Europa because it was considered too dangerous and volatile. Blacksmiths guarded their people and their secrets so securely that I had never truly understood what a fire mage could be until I traveled to Expedition.

Had James Drake tried to join a guild of blacksmiths, only to be turned away? Or had his family refused to allow it because as nobles they thought guild work beneath him?

A man in the last rank looked at me, his brow creasing as he dropped a puzzled gaze to my cane.

Blessed Tanit! It hadn't even occurred to me to protect the cane from the sight of blacksmiths, who could see its cold steel with their fire-limned sight. We worked our way down until we found a place where we could dodge across the street. Carts passed, decorated with festival tableaux that included actual people standing in martial poses made famous by the old tales: Caesar's victory at Alesia over the Arverni princes; the death of an Illyrian prince who had rebelled against Rome; the surrender of General Camjiata to a mage, a prince, and a Roman legate after the Battle of Havery. Certainly the festival had taken on an overwhelmingly Roman air! The usual tableau of the Roman legions kneeling in defeat at the battle of Zama before the Dido of Qart Hadast and her general Hannibal Barca was nowhere to be seen!

A line of drummers flew a rhythm along the street. Dancers wearing ram masks and ribbon-festooned ram costumes stepped alongside. Behind drummers and dancers rode a troop of turbaned mage House soldiers. Banners of light woven out of cold magic floated above them. The streaming gold banners were meant to impress the populace, although I thought them shabby compared to what embellishments Vai could manage. The magic whispered my sword awake.

Behind the soldiers rode the Tarrant militia, and behind it marched infantry with a legion's eagle standard held proudly at the front of their ranks. The famous Roman Invictus cavalry in their red-and-gold capes brought up the rear. Fourteen years ago the Invictus had driven General Camjiata's stubborn Old Guard into the river at the Battle of Havery and forced the general to surrender. No wonder we had seen the Havery tableau today.

In the shadows of alleys and under thresholds, folk with sullen expressions watched the parade but did not cheer.

Bee tugged on my sleeve. *"Look!"*

The man riding at the head of the cavalry was a good-looking fellow with a clean-shaven face, hawk's eyes, and gold earrings gleaming against his black skin. Bee's rosebud lips mouthed his name. *Amadou Barry*. A blush rose becomingly in her cheeks, although I could not be sure whether it was pleasure or anger that animated her countenance.

His roving gaze sought trouble in the crowd. Looking our way, he saw her. He rocked back in the saddle. Recovering, he turned to demand the attention of the bluff soldier riding next to him, his brother-in-law Lord Marius.

"Pull your scarf over your head and keep out of sight," I said, wrenching Bee around as I indicated the nearest alley with my chin. "That way. Meet me in Fox Close. Go!"

I wrapped myself in shadow and dodged into the procession. The pounding of drums and blaring of horns washed over me. The masked dancers in their ram costumes spun as if I were a wind blowing through them. The men under the masks were blind except to the drums, but the ram spirits who flowed within the masks saw me. Their eyes were mist and ice, gleaming with power. They scraped the ground in a mocking greeting, and folk clapped and whistled as if the sweep of bows were part of the dance.

Their rumbling spirit voices whispered in the air. "Cousin! What do you hunt here? Why have you come?"

They could cut my concealing threads with their sharp spirit horns, but they let me pass unmolested. I sidled up alongside the horses in time to hear Lord Marius shouting to be heard above the drums.

"You need to give her up, Amadou! It's been over a year since you saw her. You're seeing the ghost of what you wish you'd had, now that you're betrothed. If you'd wanted her that much you should have offered her marriage."

"Against my aunt's wishes and every sensible consideration? To an impoverished Phoenician of disreputable birth? Who turned out to be an agent of General Camjiata all along? I think not!"

"Then be sensible and let it go. You just saw someone who looks like her."

"I'm sure it was her! We know the general means to return to Europa someday. Why not now? Look! There she is! Bring her to me!"

As he pointed toward the alley, I darted to the head of Legate Amadou Barry's fine steed. Two slices ruined the bridle. His grip on the reins went slack. I ducked under his mount's neck to deal the same damage to Lord Marius's tack, although the animal rolled its eyes and pranced away from my scent. I cut my way through the troop, leaving a trail of sheared girths and tack. The drumming beat a pulsing rhythm around us as the dancing line moved on down the street while the beleaguered troop bottled up the road. Soldiers had to dismount to steady their horses.

Lord Marius scanned the trail of my invisible passage through the troops and into the crowd as a man follows the swirl of leaves. With gestures I could see and commands I could not hear, he sent soldiers scrambling after me.

Still wreathed in shadow, I clambered up onto a barrel and shouted, "Have you let yourselves be beaten down by fear? Shame! Shame! Have you already forgotten the words of the Northgate poet? Was it   121 for nothing that he starved himself on the steps of the prince's palace to demand new laws for the common people? A rising light marks the dawn of a new world!"

A gun went off. I escaped along a side street. A clamor of rocks being thrown and glass breaking serenaded me, but the sounds faded as I fled. I was winded by the time I fetched up on Enterprise Road, panting loudly enough that passersby looked around to see who was breathing like a steam engine. I leaned in the stoop of a closed shop until I caught my breath, then made my way to Fox Close. There was something odd about the neighborhood, but I couldn't figure out what it was.

The lane was lined with modern gas lamps, although naturally they were not lit during the day despite the overcast gloom and smoky pallor. The lane lay deserted except for a man loitering at the corner with a hat pulled low over his brow. I did not see Bee and Rory.

I walked right past the law offices. When I retraced my path, no business sign met my eye, only a boarded-up house where the sign of orange letters against a feathery brown backdrop had once proclaimed GODWIK AND CLUTCH. The sign was missing; it had been taken down.

I mounted the steps. The door had been staved in with what appeared to be axe blows, then repaired with planks hammered over the rents. I jiggled the latch and found it unlocked. Cautiously I pressed it down, but remembered before I opened it that it would look awfully strange if anyone caught sight of the door opening by itself. It was quiet along the street, every window shut.

The man at the end of the lane vanished, stepping out of sight onto Enterprise Road. I opened the door and slipped inside. A muted light filtered from streaked mullioned windows above the door, illuminating the stairs that led up to the shadows of the first floor above. A tall mirror had been set on the stairs to catch any movement into or out of the house.

Trolls used mirrors in the complicated mazes they drew around their nests. I could not walk in a troll maze, nor could the Wild Hunt enter one because the confusing tangle of shards and glints woven into a troll maze cut the threads of shadow from the spirit world. I had saved Bee by sending her to troll town in Expedition, where the Wild Hunt could not reach her.

This was no part of a troll maze. This was a djeli's mirror, like the one on the first-floor landing of our old home. In such a mirror, a djeli could see into the spirit world.

My image stared back at me, caught in all my surprise and consternation. Shadows coiled around me like living things leashed to my flesh. I resembled the spinning dancers in their wreaths of flowing ribbons. A silver cord stretched from my heart into the silent depths: the magical chain that bound me to Vai. I had never before seen it so clearly. I took a step forward and brushed fingers over the surface of the mirror where it seemed the glowing cord cut through into the other side. Where my fingers touched, they slid as into water, pulling through a viscous liquid neither cold nor hot but exactly the same temperature as my skin.

"Andevai's bride! This I did not expect." A djeli spoke from within the mirror.

I had walked right into his trap. A crash sounded from upstairs.

I bolted out the door and slammed into Bee.

"We've got to run!" I steadied her before she stumbled down the steps. Rory waited on the street, looking alarmed. "The law offices have been abandoned. Someone has set a djeli to watch the premises with magic. I'm afraid it's the mansa's djeli, Bakary."

In such circumstances Bee never argued or questioned. "Where do we go?"

"We need to find out what happened to the law offices."

At the corner of Enterprise Road and Fox Close, the loitering man had reappeared. He looked our way as he deliberately took off his hat and replaced it with the cap worn by the radicals. He'd seen us, so there was no harm in asking, since he already knew we were there. I strode back to the corner. He touched two fingers to his forehead in a welcoming salute.

I smiled saucily, for I had discovered at the boardinghouse that a flirting smile was likely to get a tip, and right now we needed a tip badly. "May the day bring you peace, Maester. How is it with you and your family? Well, I hope."

The man measured me with a grin. "Better now you've come, lass!"

"Cat, really!" muttered Bee.

"Have you news of what happened to the law office?" I asked.

A pair of mounted men appeared far down Enterprise Road.

The man doffed the cap, tucking it inside his coat. His dusty blond hair hung to his shoulders. "Those with feathers must flee the nest when predators disturb the tree."

"Were the lawyers arrested?"

"Birds cry a warning each to the other."

His cryptic utterances annoyed me. "By which I take it that the prince's militia raided them, but they escaped. How long ago did this happen, Maester?"

"If you want to know more, come in off the street."

We followed him through the public room of a coffeehouse where shabbily dressed men sipped at their brew. They watched us go into a private room furnished with a table and chairs.

"Sit. Will you have food or drink? It's already paid for." The young man had the freckled face of a pale man who has spent a good deal of time in the sun, and a bone-deep weariness made his features melancholy. A woman walked in with a tray of bread and cheese and a pot of hot coffee with four cups. She set it down and went out.

The coffee smelled delicious, and I hadn't eaten decent cheese for months.

"I suppose it can't hurt," said Bee, seating herself next to Rory.

I plopped down next to our new companion and cut off a hunk of cheese to go with my bread. The coffee was rich and sharp.

"To answer your question, the attack on the law offices happened right after the Solstice riots three months ago. A march was held on the first anniversary of the Northgate poet's hunger strike. Why do you want to know, lass?"

"Why would I tell my business to the likes of you, a man loitering on the street like any sort of scoundrel?"

"Whsst! You're a fiery beast, lass. It will take a strong man to harness you."

"It would take a strong man to not speak of harnesses!"

Perhaps I gestured aggressively with the knife, for his laughter ceased. His mouth settled into a grin that twitched with both bravado and an emotion like anger. Men didn't ever like to look as if women frightened them.

"If you want information, lass, you might think a moment about whether you want to antagonize a man who's willing to tell you things. And to feed you most generously, in a city where plenty of folk go to bed hungry and wake up hungry with no hope of even a scrap of bread."

I sighed gustily. "My apologies. We're looking for the troll lawyers."

"Not so difficult, was that? But I'm thinking you don't recognize me. For I surely recognize you two lasses, and the man with you, too. That's why you're in here and not out there."

He had two fingers missing on his right hand. Abruptly, I did recognize him.

"You were the one with the coal cart, Brennan Du's man. You challenged Lord Marius, to catch his attention so he wouldn't find us. He had you arrested. Your name is Eurig."

"That is me in truth, lass." He flashed a more flirtatious smile, perhaps thinking that a woman who remembered him so keenly had been struck by his looks and presence, when in fact I had been trained in a household of spies and messengers to have a good memory. "I remember the day as bright as yesterday even though it was over a year ago."

"We were never able to thank you for the sacrifice you made for us. What happened after you were arrested?"

He glanced at his mutilated hand. "A lot of folk were arrested after the prince got news that General Camjiata had walked into Adurnam and then escaped over the sea. Black-haired Brennan and the professora barely escaped."

"I was with them!" said Rory. "That was fun!"

He rounded on Rory. "*Fun!* One hundred men were executed for treason!"

"I didn't see that," said Rory indignantly. "We were already gone. I would never call executions and arrests fun! I meant that the skulking and running were fun, and Brennan Du taught me how to properly drink whiskey. Did you think I meant I am the kind of person who laughs when people suffer?"

He looked suddenly about twice his normal size, with his chest puffed up and his lips curled back. His braid, like a whip, seemed ready to snap.

Eurig scooted his chair back so fast that it squeaked against the floorboards.

Rory leaned forward. "A person can enjoy fun and be serious at the same time."

"Gracious Melqart, Rory! You're sounding more and more like Cat every day!" Bee pushed him back into his chair and turned her most coaxing smile on Eurig. "What happened to the Northgate poet?"

Eurig's anger broke free. "Why, the Northgate poet died, lass. And our hopes with him. The prince let the poet starve himself to death on the steps of the palace."

I was too shocked to speak, for when we had fallen into the well, the Northgate poet had still been alive.

"Died!" Bee set down her mug. "What of the shame that stained the prince's honor?"

"Tyrants have no honor and therefore no shame. The prince will make merry at his daughter's wedding feast. He serves flesh to a princely Roman legate in exchange for the Invictus Legion to guard his restless lands. Roman boots will walk the roads the empire built in the days of our ancestors, back when we were free men. Every day we wake to see our master the prince of Tarrant walk arm in arm like a brother with the cursed magister who is the mansa of Four Moons House, although they were bitter rivals all the long days before. We live under the law of the sword. They crush us under their boot-heels like the vermin they name us, and so death makes cowards of us all. The prince ordered that every troll must leave the city, and no person raised a voice in protest."

"Every troll?" demanded Bee.

"That's what was strange," I murmured. "There are no feathered people anywhere."

"Every one. And every man in a radical's cap was arrested and his family threatened. Hundreds have been transported to the north. There they must labor with their sweat and their blood in the mines of the Barrens. The salt they haul up in buckets flavors the prince's food while his subjects go hungry. The iron they dig out of the rock forges the swords that kill us."

His poem of grievances so stunned me that I could not help but think of the promises General Camjiata had made. The music of revolution had a more urgent melody when heard in a city where so many voices had been so recently silenced. I wanted to give him hope. "I heard a rumor that the general is returning to Europa. He'll proclaim a legal code that abolishes the ancient privileges of princes and mage Houses."

"Rumor is like a woman's promise that she'll kiss you. Have you a kiss for me, lass?"

"I don't kiss just any man I see! Only the ones I want to kiss! Did I give you reason to think otherwise?"

"A brave man must have taken on the taming of you!" he said with a laugh that made me want to skewer him.

"Our thanks to you for helping us," Bee said as she slipped the cheese knife out of my hand. As if I could not control my temper!

He smiled as easily at her as he had at me a moment before. "My trials were made easier by my knowing such a beautiful young woman was spared thereby." He glanced up as the door opened and the woman appeared.

He rose. "Time for you to move on. I saw with my own eyes when the mansa of Four Moons House came to Fox Close with his djeli to set the mirror in place. An impressive man, the mansa. Rioters had set a barricade in the road and set it afire. He put out the bonfire with a blast of hail and cold wind that shattered windows and made every hearth fire go out. His men will come to see who opened the door. I don't reckon you want to be here when they get here."

"Cat, let's go now." Rory's gaze flickered toward the man, and then toward the woman, and then back to us.

"Of course," I agreed, smiling at the woman, who stared dourly back at me. "Have you any word of where these particular birds might have flown?"

"To another nest east of here by name of Havery."

"My thanks to you for the information, and the food and drink."

"May Bright Venus bring fertility to you and your brave man," he replied. He laughed as I blushed.

We took our leave and stumped along Enterprise Road in a plaguing rain.

"'Bright Venus'! I thought it very rude to wish a person of Kena'ani heritage luck in breeding under the auspices of a Roman goddess. Didn't you, Bee?"

She was chewing over more urgent problems. "The mansa knows you're here, so he'll secure the house."

"We have to get the chest!"

"Ba'al forbid that you lose Andevai's fashionable dash jackets! Some other man might be seen wearing them!"

"If never so well," I muttered mulishly. I missed Vai. How sweet those weeks seemed now, when I had seen him every day.

"Are you saying I don't look well in this fine dash jacket?" Rory straightened his shoulders as a group of two men and two women passed who were laughing in the way of folk out about the business of pleasure. His smile made the women loose their holds on the arms of their beaux as they gave him a closer look over. When the men objected, Rory smiled more deeply, with a hint of dusky corners in his gaze, and one man took a startled step back while the other bit his lip.

Bee's scorching glare drove them off. "Rory! We are skulking and running! We are not lighting a bonfire and ringing bells so people will notice and remember us."

"Cat said I didn't look well in my jacket."

I rapped him on the arm. "It's not your jacket."

"Have we survived the mansa's wrath, the prince's fury, the general's devious plotting, and the Wild Hunt only to have you two squabble over clothes? You look perfectly handsome, Rory, and I am sure many a female would love to pet you, and by that look you just got a few males as well, but none of them will get a chance if I murder you first. Are we done?"

"Yes, Bee, my apologies," he said so contritely I was astonished.

"Cat?" she demanded. "Does Rory look well in that fine dash jacket?"

With a look like that, directed at me, I knew how to answer. "He looks very fine."

"You're only saying it because she told you to," said Rory.

Bee's hand tightened on his arm. "Rory, dearest, did you know that in anatomy class at the academy we learned how the ancient Turanians used to castrate young men so they could no longer engage in petting? I paid careful attention to that part of class but unfortunately there was never a practicum in which we were given an opportunity to see if we could manage the operation ourselves. But I haven't given up hope."

If he could have put his ears down, he would have. Then he laughed, and I did, too.

Yet I could not help but notice how women and men mostly moved in separate groups. Here women never walked anywhere alone, even though in Expedition women had felt free to come and go as they wished. Nor did people laugh and talk with the same friendly clamor with which folk had in Expedition. Voices stayed hushed and dampened. Maybe that was the prince's newly harsh reign, but perhaps it had always been this way and we had just never noticed.

It was strange to think we were only passing through the city where we had grown up, on our way to somewhere else.

"Amadou Barry saw you on the street, and the djeli saw me at the law offices," I said. "Nothing to be done about that now. Since the academy is on the way home, we may as well go there first and hope we find the headmaster before anyone comes looking for us."

15

After a long walk we made our way up Academy Hill past the temple dedicated to the Blessed Tanit. Her gates always stood open. Bee and Rory ducked into the temple to stay out of sight while I wrapped the shadows around me and crept into the academy compound past the servant standing at the gate.

The entry hall lay empty, not a single pupil scurrying late to class under the frieze with its princely white yam, winter wheat, towering maize, and other carvings of plants. Another arch led me into the glass-roofed central courtyard. No one was about. Rain pattered an erratic drumbeat on the glass roof. Although it was early spring, a scent like summer kissed my lips, the smell of the spirit world sensed through the water in the ancient sacrificial well at the center of a paved labyrinth. The blood of sacrifices offered generations ago stung at my nostrils. A year and almost three months ago, Bee and I had fallen through the well into the spirit world. I paused now in the quiet courtyard, looking toward the well, which was covered by an iron grate. My blood would open a path from here into the spirit world, but how would I find Vai in all that vast and changing landscape?

Bee was right: The headmaster knew more than he had ever let on. We had to talk to him.

In a rush of clattering footsteps, a crowd of boys and young men swept into the courtyard, all chattering excitedly. They were dressed in old-fashioned robes cut in the fashion of boubous, a plain drapery of muted colors designed not to excite the eye. I caught snippets of words, and it seemed they had been out to watch the festival procession. Although they had not witnessed the disturbance I had caused, rumor of its occurrence had spread. When an older man with blond hair and the ruddy features of a heavy drinker entered the courtyard at the tail end of the procession, they all hushed so quickly that the voice of the one poor boy who hadn't noticed rang out.

"—They heard a voice say, 'A rising light marks the dawn of a new world.'"

As proctors carrying willow wands converged on the hapless speaker to whip his hands, I looked in vain for a line of girls. I was the only woman in the glass courtyard; no female proctors or servants flocked at the edge of the shuffling horde of youths. The overly talkative boy was biting his lip so as not to cry out under the humiliating punishment as everyone stared.

I could not bear to watch, and anyway, I needed to find the headmaster. A staircase led up to the long corridor and the closed door of his study. The well-oiled latch eased down with a soft click. I slipped inside.

For an instant I thought I had accidentally walked through the wrong door into the wrong room, because nothing in the spacious chamber looked as I remembered it. The chalkboards and desk had vanished, replaced by gilt-embroidered chairs that looked as uncomfortable as they were showy. The bookshelves had been cleared of all their books and scrolls, and they now displayed gold cups, gold bowls, and brass or silver wine flagons. One bookcase held nothing but a grisly collection of skulls, arranged from the largest at the top left to the smallest at the lower right, which horribly seemed to be a baby's actual skull. On the long table lay not a dinner service for five but so many empty wine bottles and empty glasses I did not bother to count them. Only the circulating stove set into the fireplace and the pedestal holding the head of the poet Bran Cof remained from the last time I had entered this room. It surely did not look like the study of a scholar with the many diverse interests and formidable intellect of the headmaster. It took no great acumen to suspect that he had been replaced as master of the academy.

The skulls stared hollow-eyed at me in stubborn silence. The head of the poet Bran Cof sat atop the pedestal in a stony slumber, his brow furrowed with deep thoughts and his lips pinched closed over all the poems and legal knowledge he had hoarded throughout his famous life. With his hair sticking up in stiff spikes and his bushy eyebrows a 131 little raised, he looked noble and magnificent and just a trifle startled, but I knew he was a filthy-minded and staggeringly unpleasant old man who tried to bully young women into kissing him. His body was imprisoned by my sire, who could not only command the poet but also see through his eyes and speak through his mouth. If I woke the head, would my sire reach through him and trap me with the chain of his voice, as he had before?

I had to risk it.

And I knew just the way to wake him up.

Emphatically not with a kiss. I shattered one of the wineglasses on the table and pricked my arm enough to draw blood. This bead I smeared on the head's lips and eyes. The cold grain of his face smeared and smoothed into warm flesh. His eyelids fluttered, then popped open with a look compounded as much of fear as of anger.

"You fool! What do you mean by waking me with blood?"

"I need to ask you some questions." I took a step back, for the transition from stone to flesh disturbed me.

His gaze sharpened to a leer as he recognized me. "The girl whose eyes are amber. Woken with kisses, I see. You have the look of a woman about you now, shaped by a man's caresses. Did you escape the marriage, or embrace its carnal pleasures?" His tone had a greasy unctuousness that made me want to wash myself, but fortunately a new thought struck him before he started quoting obscene poetry as I was sure he was about to. Instead, he glanced around with an expression made comical by its wild exaggeration. "Where is the serpent? Where is she hiding?"

"My cousin? I will bring her to torment you if you do not answer my questions. Have you seen my husband? The Master of the Wild Hunt stole him from me."

A look of cunning creased his features. "I can offer you pleasures the man will surely not have thought of. If you'll just come a little closer..." His tongue moistened his lips.

I lost my patience and my temper. "Do you really think comments like these make me find you attractive? Or are you deliberately trying to put me off? I love him. If you have the least sliver of a human heart left to you, help me find him. Then you can compose a poem about our travails and triumph!"

His face went so still that for several shaky breaths I thought he had fallen back into sleep.

But he blinked, and spoke in an altered tone, like an impatient teacher scolding a student who is slow to learn. "Best hurry, kitten. You should not have woken me with blood, for the masters crave it and will come seeking it the instant its scent reaches their grasping claws. As it will."

"I thought my sire was the only master. You serve him, but surely you don't feed him with your blood."

"The hunter takes souls, not blood. It amuses him to keep me, because of my knowledge of the law. I was not sacrificed to the courts. Instead I was imprisoned in this terrible state, head separated from body."

"Yes, I met your body in my sire's palace." I shuddered, remembering the way Bran Cof's headless body had stumbled to serve his master's bidding. With a gasp, I raised a hand to my mouth. "Blessed Tanit! What terrible thing might my sire do to Vai?"

"You know nothing about the courts and your sire, do you?"

Lowering my hands, I took a threatening step closer. "Tell me what you know!"

His sneer turned mocking as he looked me up and down in a most intrusive way. "For each kiss you give me, kitten, I'll tell you a secret."

I lifted the shard of glass. "Tell me what I want to know, or I'll smear my blood all over your face for the courts to suckle dry!"

His lips pulled back in a horrible grimace, yet he also laughed with a slightly hysterical rasp. "You know not of what you speak, girl. The spirit courts crave mortal blood, for blood gives them protection from the tides and allows them to sustain their power. You cannot challenge them."

"We shall see about that!"

It wasn't until the latch clicked down that I realized I heard voices. It was the work of a moment to hide myself in shadow as a servant showed two men into the room.

Lord Marius and Legate Amadou Barry had come looking, just as Bee and I feared. They did not see me, nor did they notice that Bran Cof's eyes were tracking them, because Amadou Barry walked straight to the tall windows so he could look out over the rose garden, and his brother-in-law followed him without looking around.

"Whenever I enter these halls, I think of her," Amadou Barry said on a heaving sigh as he tapped the glass with the knuckles of one hand. "I know I saw her on the street, Marius!"

Lord Marius laughed. "Be warned! Your balls will wither if you praise her cherry lips and golden hair in my hearing."

"She doesn't have golden hair! It is as black as a crow's wing. Her glorious hair falls like a riot of curls down her back, for a riot is surely how the thought of her affects my heart."

The head of the poet Bran Cof rolled his eyes at this stilted speech in a way that made me want to giggle. Fortunately both men were gazing outside and missed it.

"Bald Teutates! You haven't a Celt's gift of poetry, that is certain, Amadou. You mistook another woman's black curls." Marius wandered over to the table. He picked up several bottles in turn, clearly astounded that they were all empty. "You must give up this unseemly obsession. Your wedding feast will be celebrated the day after tomorrow. Notable men and their retinues have traveled for days to gorge themselves at the table and toast your virility. You will do your duty, as I did mine when I married your sister."

"You can't compare your marriage to mine! You and my sister are well matched in every room except the bedroom. Whereas I am to marry a trembling mouse of a fifteen-year-old who has no conversation, little education, and less personality."

"Her nose twitches, too, have you noticed that? And she has a pointed, rattish chin."

"Stop, Marius! Have pity on me!" the legate said with what I considered a sad lack of generosity. He did not even defend the poor nameless girl from such an unfortunate comparison.

Marius laughed in the hearty way he had, which, I reflected, could start to grate. "You'll be happier with a biddable wife."

"I don't agree." Amadou paced. "My chief pleasure when I was pretending to be a student here was my mathematics seminar. Beatrice sat on the women's side of the room, answering questions with a bold intellect worthy of a man. I could never concentrate. It's just as well your cousin ended the practice of allowing girls to attend the academy when he became headmaster last year. It was too distracting."

Marius examined the skulls and, to my horror, fetched up beside the pedestal. Bran Cof stared at the far wall. Neither of the men seemed to notice the flush of life in the poet's cheeks or the steely glamour of his blue eyes. Their petty self-absorption blinded them to the astonishing magic in the room. "I don't think you truly love her, Amadou. You're just not accustomed to being turned down. That's what has put you in a pique."

"She was too proud."

"You adored her pride until she refused your offer to make her your mistress."

"Too much pride is deadly in a woman. Mine was as good an offer as she will ever get. Yet what can I have expected from a Phoenician woman! They prostitute themselves for their greedy goddess, to gain whatever material wealth and trade advantage they can."

Perhaps his words angered me a trifle, enough that I let slip a thread or two.

"Did you see something?" Lord Marius stepped forward, hand on his sword, as I tugged the shadows tight. He relaxed. "You're not the only one whose heart has been broken."

"That can't have been your heart. I know you found the magister attractive, but there can never have been any hope for you with him. He was fixed on the other girl. You didn't actually proposition him, did you?"

Lord Marius appeared more amused than disappointed. "Nothing so crude. I let my interest be known."

Amadou Barry snorted in a coarse way so unlike the staidly respect-ful student we had believed him to be at the academy that I had to guess I was seeing the legate's true personality. While I had liked the modest, unassuming student named Amadou Barry, I did not like the Roman legate. "Proud Jupiter! The cold mage had the effrontery to turn down a prince's cousin? Still, he is certainly one of the most arro-gant men I've ever met. Did he take offense?"

"Not at all. He fixed me with those beautiful eyes, thanked me for the flattering offer, and told me he didn't sleep on both sides of the bed."

"Prettily done, you must grant."

"Far too prettily done! As polite as if I were an aged uncle asking for another dram of whiskey when he's already had one too many. Gave me nightmares for weeks!"

135

He paused as footsteps sounded in the corridor. The door was opened, and the older man with light hair and ruddy cheeks strode in.

"Cousin Marius! Your Excellency! Legate, to what do I owe this honor? I did not expect you, or I would have sent a deputy to shepherd the students to the Mars procession."

Marius answered. "We have received news that two girls were seen in the city, two fugitives who were students here. They may come to the academy seeking Prince Napata."

"But girls are no longer admitted as students. I made sure of that! It was never appropriate. I cannot interview two young women without a proper chaperone."

"The girls left before Prince Napata resigned and you became headmaster. If they come, you must admit them to your study. Delay them with the promise that Prince Napata will return shortly."

"But the exalted prince left Adurnam over a year ago!"

The head of the poet Bran Cof met my eye, and he glanced at the ceiling as if to share his cutting assessment of this headmaster's sad lack of intellect.

"Yes," agreed Marius patiently, "but they won't know that. Make excuses, have tea brought, and send for us."

"I'll have tea brought now. You must explain your purpose more thoroughly, for I am sure that the prince never mentioned that he intended to return to Adurnam."

I had heard enough, and dared not wait lest my sire discover Bran Cof was awake in the mortal world and talking to me. I escaped when the servants brought the tea service. With a rumble of boys milling outside the children's classrooms and young men trampling around the lecture halls, I sneaked out through the side entry, past the latrines. The door leading up to the balcony of the main lecture hall, where we young women had been allowed to sit, was chained and locked.

Just inside the gates of Tanit's temple, Rory met me with a nervous dip of his head, patting my arm and walking all the way around me. "I smelled the soldiers and the horses. Lord Marius is with them. I liked him, but we can't trust him now, can we?"

"No, we can't. I don't think he's a bad man, I just think he's not on our side. Where is Bee?"

He led me to the withy gate that separated the women's precincts from the rest of the temple compound. "She went in there, but they made me wait outside."

I went in, leaving behind the open ground of the main sanctuary with its monumental stone pillars. The women's precinct had its own garden. Bee's voice floated over the evergreen foliage. A path wound through a maze of cypress and myrtle until I came to an altar set among fig trees, screened by a fence woven of sticks. Under a sheltering roof stood a statue of the goddess in her aspect as Queen of the Heavens. She was dressed in a simple robe in the Hellenic style, and her elaborate ringed coiffure was crowned by a crescent moon. Her arms extended to offer blessing, and serpent bracelets twined up her forearms. The altar was surrounded by urns that held the cremated remains of infants who had died in an untimely fashion, because grieving mothers would dedicate the urns to the temple as an offering after which they would pray for the goddess's blessing and for healthy children to come.

I knelt before the image of the goddess and examined her serene stone face. As Queen of the Heavens she protected sailors and travelers, for so many of the Kena'ani people traveled long distances. As Mother of the Earth she offered comfort to women, and promised fertility to those who desperately desired a child. In Qart Hadast, Tanit was also the lion of war who fought for the city. It was strange to think that General Camjiata's chosen name also meant "lion of war" even though it came from a union of the names of Sunjiata, the first Malian emperor, and fierce Camulos, a god of war among the Celtic people.

"Give me strength, Blessed One," I murmured, "for you have already given me my heart, and for that I am grateful. Protect us, your travelers. Let us rescue those who need help. Let us find a place we can call home."

Adurnam was no longer home. I wasn't the girl who had run to the academy without her coat that day when everything I thought I knew had fallen apart. Hearing Bee's distant laughter, I smiled, for having her gave me all the courage I needed. I pressed my right hand to my locket and my left to the cane as I shut my eyes. For a few breaths, or for hours, or for years, I heard only silence. Then, faint as a whisper, the pulse of Vai's being brushed mine.

He was still alive.

When I opened my eyes the stone statue of Tanit stared at me with the head of a lion, in her aspect as the giver of fierceness and strength. The cat who never gives up.

As I never would.

The path led on to the priestess's quarters. Bee sat on the sleeping-house porch drinking coffee with six humbly garbed priestesses ranging in age from a bent crone to a slight girl seated in a rickety chair with a crutch at her side.

"The cacique is the ruler. The ruler is usually a man, but it may be a woman, like the didos who once ruled in Qart Hadast. The cacique administers the kingdom. But all the women of noble lineage and all the elders have the right to rebuke the cacique if he acts in a way that hurts the kingdom. It is the council of women who approve the choice of heir. And in Expedition, with the new Assembly, women will be allowed both to vote and to serve as representatives, just like men. The trolls insisted on that proviso, because they are citizens of Expedition also."

The bent crone gave a skeptical snort. "I can't imagine the prince of Tarrant, or a Roman legate of patrician birth, or even that old bastard of a high priest in the temple here, allowing a woman to stand over them and give them commands. How can it be so elsewhere?"

"There were once queens in Qart Hadast, and there's no reason there can't be again," said Bee. When she realized I was standing there, she set down the steaming mug she had cupped in her hands. "My dear cousin is come to hasten me on my way. My thanks for the coffee, holy ones."

"You didn't tell us about the architecture," said the chair-bound girl with a yearning sigh.

She kissed them all around, and whispered something in the ear of the girl that made the child blush with the pleasure of having been given a secret treasure to cherish at her frail breast.

The bent crone escorted us to the withy gate.

I faced her. "Holy one, do you know where the headmaster went? Prince Napata?"

"Strange it is that I do. He came here the day he left and he mentioned in particular that should two young Kena'ani women happen by to ask for his direction, I should tell them he is gone to Treverni Noviomagus, where the Rhenus River splits into two channels."

Once we got outside the gate, Bee turned to me and frowned. "Our experiment did not go so well, did it?"

"I did not find Prince Napata in his study on the Feast of Mars Camulos, that is for certain. But if he left a message for us here, that means he wants us to track him down. Perhaps that is what the dream meant, that we would discover where he had gone."

Rory was waiting by the gate, his figure half concealed behind one of the entry pillars. "I saw the other man lurking here, the one called Eurig who fed us."

I chewed on my lower lip. "He must be spying, but for whom? Probably everyone now knows we were at the law offices. Let's see if we can recover our gear before we go."

After making sure no soldiers or spies loitered in sight, we hastened down Academy Hill under glowering clouds. The rain held off until we reached Falle Square. We left Rory in the alley to stand guard. A wind swept in with waves of freezing sleet that drove Bee and me through the back gate with more haste and less caution than we ought to have used. I ran across the courtyard to kneel by the basement window, peering into the dim kitchen to make sure there was no fire and that no skulking visitors were awaiting us. The chamber was empty, just as we had left it. The driving sleet stirred up fallen leaves as it drummed on the cobblestones. Shuddering, I raced back to the carriage house.

Bee had already pried up the boards and opened the chest. "Help me!"

The double doors were cracked open just enough to give light to work. Sleet pattered on the roof and wind rattled the shutters. We set the dash jackets aside, for they would have to go on top, and split the tools and practical clothing into the three packs.

"I had hoped the headmaster might help us get to Haranwy," I said, shivering. "Don't you think it's strange that he quit his post and left Adurnam right after we fell down the well?"

Bee gave me an indignant look. "Of course it's strange. Why bide in Adurnam for so many years and suddenly leave? What do we do, Cat?

I can sell several of my gold bracelets for money for passage on a coach to Noviomagus. It's a long way. It will be so expensive."

"It will take weeks of travel even if the weather improves. I don't dare wait so long. We don't even know if the headmaster can help me. I have to go to Haranwy to ask Vai's brother for help. His people know how to hunt in the spirit world. Once we get to Haranwy, you and Rory can go on to Noviomagus. Anyway, it's better to go to Haranwy first now that the mansa and the legate know we're here. They'll be watching the roads. But we can walk by back lanes and footpaths, where it's easier to hide. We'll need only food, for we can beg shelter in haymows and stables. I remember the route well enough, past Cold Fort and through Lemanis..." I trailed off, remembering Cold Fort.

Never before marrying a cold mage had I had to consider the uses of illusion. In Southbridge Londun, Vai had woven the illusion of a troop of turbaned soldiers riding down a road, a feat that would have impressed me more had I liked him at the time. In Expedition he had done nothing but play with the illusions of small objects, forming light into the shape of lamps or a gleaming necklace with which to adorn me, because in Expedition cold mages had less magic to draw on. Yet he had woven illusions out of cold fire so skillfully they had seemed like solid objects, impossible to know as intangible unless you tried to touch them.

Rory and I had almost been caught near Cold Fort by a troop of mage House soldiers under the command of a cold mage. They had ridden across a field under a mask of illusion that made them invisible to unsuspecting eyes, but not to cold steel.

Too late, I closed my fingers over my cane. The ghost hilt buzzed with the energy of cold magic pouring into it.

"Quiet." I got to my feet. "Abandon everything. Go out through one of the windows. Meet me at the hat shop."

Bee grabbed the little knit bag with her sketchbook. I crept to the carriage house door. The cistern was covered by a plank lid. Unswept leaves from the apple and pear trees littered the ground. The big brick oven was closed tight. Behind, Bee stuffed the flasks and my sewing kit into the knit bag as she eased toward the shuttered windows.

I wrapped shadows around myself and padded under chill daggers of sleet to the basement steps. The hiss of sleet and the whine of the wind drowned all other sounds. I pressed numb fingers against the door. I drove my awareness down the fraying threads of magic that had once protected the house from intruders. A foot scuffed faintly on damp leaves over by the cistern. An exhalation stirred in the passage beyond the door.

There were other people here. I just could not see them, for the courtyard looked exactly as it ought under the cloudy afternoon light.

A slap of wind huffed down over the courtyard with a spray of ice so strong that it hammered me to my knees. As I twisted the hilt to draw cold steel, the basement door was flung open. The wind and ice ceased, to reveal the courtyard walls lined by turbaned mage House soldiers, their crossbows fixed on the carriage house doors. Not yet drawn out of its sheath, my sword withered back into a cane as the cold magic that had been holding the illusion in place vanished and a man spoke.

"Bring them inside."

16

An old man in one of the voluminous robes called a boubou appeared at the open door. The gold earrings he wore marked him as a djeli, a poet who spoke the tales of history and also a person who could handle and chain the energies we called magic. In his right hand he held a mirror, angling it to catch my image. Within the mirror he could see the threads of magic, so he could see me.

"There you are, Catherine Barahal," he said.

I spun, ready to bolt, only to see Bee being marched through the back gate from the alley. Soldiers emerged from the carriage house carrying the three packs and the chest.

"We met before, as you may recall," continued the djeli, in kindly tones.

"Bring them inside, Bakary," repeated the other man, the one I still did not see.

As they brought Bee up, I let the threads of shadow drop. The soldiers exclaimed, swinging their crossbows around. I was relieved when the djeli led us into the house.

The mansa of Four Moons House sat in a chair in the kitchen. The wide sleeves of his indigo robe swept over the arms of his chair. He had concealed himself within a perfect illusion of an empty kitchen. I had thought Vai a master of weaving cold magic into illusions, but obviously I had not properly understood why the mansa ruled the mage House.

He was a physically imposing man of middle age, old enough to be my father but not old. He had the girth of a person who eats well and remains active. His Mande heritage showed in his black complexion, while his tightly curled dark red hair spoke of his Celtic ancestors. His presence made the kitchen seem shabby. We stood before him like suppliants. He examined us, then glanced at our gear, which his soldiers had set on the floor by the unlit stove. Finally he gestured to the djeli.

"Where is Andevai?" asked the djeli.

"He is not in Adurnam, Mansa," I replied, for the djeli was speaking for the mansa, not on his own behalf.

"Yet here are three packs, for three people to carry," said the djeli.

"He is not in Europa, Mansa. You yourself sent him to the Antilles to spy for you."

With the tip of his ebony cane, the mansa fished one of the dash jackets out of the chest. The intricately tailored garment was sewn out of a bold blue-red-and-gold fabric printed with an elaboration of Celtic knots so complex it hurt my eyes. His gaze on me fell as cold as the sleet he had called down. He spoke with his own mouth instead of through the djeli's words.

"Do you think I do not recognize these clothes? Andevai's penchant for fashion started as mockery, so we observed in the House. He wore more and more outrageous clothes to belittle the other young men and their pretentious styles. But of course he always looked good in them."

"We came to enjoy the anticipation of what he would appear in next," added Bakary, amusement making his tone light.

The mansa tossed the expensive dash jacket carelessly over a chair, where it rested in folds and wrinkles. His resonant voice deepened, steeped in disgust. "Do not lie to me regarding his whereabouts. You belong to me because of the marriage chained between you and Andevai. By law, I have power over your life and your death."

"Cat is many things," interposed Bee in a tart voice, "but one thing she is not is a liar. If you wish to know where your spy is, then you must answer to yourself."

"I am puzzled by your impertinence. You are but two girls from an impoverished family of mercenaries. One of you is a bastard. Both of you serve your clan's business by acting as spies for the Iberian Monster. Those cursed Hassi Barahals cheated us twice over. Not only did they give us the wrong girl, but they had already placed her in the service of the general so she could spy on us once she was inside the house. A cunning and unscrupulous plan."

"I am puzzled that you speak of unscrupulous spies as if you are innocent in this regard, since we have already established that you sent the cold mage to spy in Expedition," retorted Bee. I could tell by her flushed cheeks and brilliant gaze that she was just getting warmed up. "Or do you mean to advance the argument that what is wrong for us to do is right for you to do? If we even *were* spies for General Camjiata, which we are not. I do not know what arrangements the Hassi Barahal clan made in the past with the general, but I assure you, Magister, that the day my parents handed Cat over to Four Moons House to spare me from being married off to a cold mage against my will, was the day I considered myself emancipated from their selfish affections."

His eyes narrowed. "A fine and affecting speech, but I must suppose that legally you are still bound to them because you are an unmarried woman and such maidens can never be guardians of themselves."

Bee laughed so sarcastically that everyone in the kitchen jumped as at a gunshot. "By which you mean to say, men like you do not wish such women to be guardians of themselves."

He ignored her in favor of measuring my body. "I must assume you seduced Andevai in the usual way. You have that look about you that may make a young man feel hunger."

At the boardinghouse I had learned to scold any man who ogled me in such an insulting way, and I usually succeeded in getting the other customers to laugh at him.

Bee murmured, "Cat! Don't!"

But I did.

"Rather, I would say that radical principles seduced him. Really, Your Excellency, you have only yourself to blame. Why should he serve an unjust system as if he were a horse placed in harness who has no choice but to pull lest he be whipped if he balks? Even so, Vai made you a vastly generous offer. If you would release the village of Haranwy from the clientage it has labored under for generations, he promised to serve you loyally. He would have sacrificed his own freedom and happiness to assure their liberty. You laughed at him."

"I did nothing so crude as laugh. I gave him his sister's freedom, when in truth she ought to have been bred to see if more cold mages could be produced out of that family. It was far more than I needed to do!"

"Kayleigh is not a brood mare!"

His lack of recognition betrayed that he had no idea that Vai's sister was named Kayleigh. "That I released her shows my appreciation for his value to Four Moons House. We may hope he will sire children on you who have some measure of the strength he has—"

"I'm not a brood mare either!"

"—but the genealogies sung by the djeliw tell us that cold mages with such deep roots rarely breed children who possess as much potency. To think how many advantageous matches the House lost now he is wasted on you! We might have sent him on a successful Grand Tour and afterward prosperously negotiated for three or even four wives for one such as him. Even if he does not sire powerful children, many Houses are willing to make the try for grandchildren out of such a mage. Each marriage creates a rope that binds us and makes us stronger for the coming war."

"Vai is not a stallion to be put out to stud!"

"He is what I choose to make him."

Bee tapped me sharply on the forearm to shush me.

"Are you saying your own children are not as potent cold mages as you so obviously are, Magister?" she asked with a sweet smile that startled the mansa and made the old djeli make a sign to avert disaster. "Have you no lofty sons to inherit your princely seat as mansa of Four Moons House? Are you forced to conceive the awful thought that the young cold mage best suited to become mansa after you is a humble young man born to people who have been enslaved by clientage for so many generations that you cannot think of them as anything except lowborn inferiors whom you may breed like livestock? Yet think! The son of a prince may rule whether he do so wisely or well, and he shall have advisors and kinsmen to steady him. But the son of a magister who has no magic cannot be given magic, can he?"

The temperature in the room dropped precipitously, making my eyes sting and my lips go dry. The mansa strode to the stove. With a look, he drove the soldiers from the kitchen. Accompanied by a horrible groaning strain, the door of the stove buckled.

I kicked over the table and dragged Bee down behind it just as the thick iron door shattered like the hull of a boat shot to splinters. Bee screamed. Shards of metal thunked into the table so hard that a few almost pierced through, their jagged blades the visible threat of his astonishing power. My ears rang. My breathing was all torn to pieces.

"Blessed Tanit shelter us," whispered Bee, her complexion gone a sickly gray-white.

I was shaking. "You couldn't have known. Stay down!"

As I rose, I drew my sword on the shimmering backwash of his magic. The cold steel glittered as if coated with burning oil, making the gloomy kitchen blaze with light.

"I cannot kill you, Your Excellency. Nor do I wish to. You lost Andevai not because I seduced him but because you refused to respect him as a man."

The djeli had survived the mansa's display of power unscathed, for he had his own secrets. He turned on me now. "Maestra, keep silence."

"I won't keep silence! You speak of fruitful alliances and breeding rights, but Andevai and Kayleigh are people the same as you."

The mansa frowned. "Of course they are not the same as me! Their ancestors disgraced themselves and thus put their honor in chains."

"Easy to speak of honor when you get to choose whose honor to champion. Is it the gods who foreordain our birth and position in life, or only chance? What if things had been different, if the history of the world had fallen out in another way? What if your people had been forced into chains? Would it not be wrong that a man of your power be whipped as a common laborer all his life just because of a chance of birth? Would it not be wrong that a man of your dignity be bound to a master who does not respect him and can use or discard or kill him without penalty? What then of your power and majesty? Why do you deny to Andevai what you assume for your own self?"

"You are a fatherless bastard. For you to believe you can lecture one such as me is not just absurd but unnatural. Andevai belongs to Four Moons House. As do you. Understand that I can kill you, and take no legal penalty for doing so."

"Yet you have not done so!"

A spark of cold fire winked into existence, then expanded into a globe of light. "I admit to curiosity about a girl who can vanish and reappear at will. A girl who can walk into the spirit world and return to this one. A girl who can tell me where Andevai is."

Footsteps rapped along the passage. A magister wearing a fine indigo dash jacket under an unbuttoned winter coat stepped into the kitchen. I had seen him before; he was the mage who had unsuccessfully pursued me at Cold Fort, the one whose horse I had stolen.

He made a clipped courtesy to the mansa. "Uncle, we found this man—"

The mansa smiled triumphantly at me. "Ah. My nephew has found him despite your efforts to shield him."

Rory sauntered in, toying with the end of his long braid. "Cat? Do you want me to—?"

"No!" I exclaimed, just as Bee said, "No!"

The mansa stared, startled by Rory's appearance. The djeli tried to catch Rory's image in the mirror's slippery surface, but all he saw was a saber-toothed cat. I studied the young magister, tracing the family resemblance between him and the mansa.

The young man caught me looking. "Caught you this time, haven't we? You'll not escape my uncle now he has taken an interest in you himself."

I offered him a courtesy, to mock him. "My apologies about the horse."

Despite my sword, the fool took a step toward me, a hand raised as if he believed he could slap me.

"Enough, Jata," said the mansa. "Do not touch her."

The young mage turned away from me at once. "The village boy is close by, Uncle, I'm sure of it. He doesn't have the wit to hide, thinking himself so much better than he is."

"Your envy serves you ill, Jata," said the mansa. "Go out and look again. Find him."

The nephew's eyes flared with anger, but he made no retort. Instead, he tramped out.

The mansa gestured toward my sword. "However curious I am about you, Catherine Barahal, I will order my soldiers to kill you and your companions if you cannot bring me Andevai."

Rory's lips curled back. Bee took a step toward me.

I was not a fool. I lowered my blade. "Andevai is in the spirit world. Perhaps with your help, I can get him back."

The mansa laughed, but the djeli did not.

With a frown, the mansa reconsidered. "Bakary, is she telling the truth?"

"A mirror is the water that allows me to look onto the other side, Mansa," said the old man. "It should be possible to discover if she lies or speaks truth. Especially since the mirror in this house is the mirror through which their marriage was chained."

I had been racing down one path, thinking I might convince the mansa to convey us to Haranwy. Like a noose at my throat, the djeli's words yanked me to a halt.

"What do you mean, Honored One, that a mirror is the water?" I asked.

"It is not solid, like stone, and yet not lacking substance, like air. Therefore, it is water, for we djeliw can see through it to the spirit world which lies both beneath and above us."

I caught Bee's gaze with my own, looked down at the packs, and back up to her. Her brow wrinkled as she grasped and considered my unspoken plan. I was playing a very deep game of batey, about to try a hit whose arc would pass right over every person near me with but a small chance of reaching the stone eye that was the goal.

Upstairs, the front door opened and closed. Footsteps approached.

A soldier appeared at the kitchen door. "Mansa! The legate has arrived."

With a sucked-in hiss, Bee closed her hands into fists. We managed to grab the packs before soldiers herded us up the stairs after the mansa. The chest, with most of Vai's dash jackets, had to be left behind, but fortunately no one seemed to notice that my sword was still unsheathed. I wondered if they could see the blade now that the mansa's magic had faded.

In the entry hall the mansa greeted Amadou Barry and Lord Marius, speaking with his own voice to equals. "It is good you came quickly. I have momentous news. I received word this morning that General Camjiata has landed at Gadir."

Bee and I glanced at each other as Lord Marius exclaimed, "At Gadir! He has returned to Iberia! That is the news we feared most!"

Amadou Barry marked us as we climbed into view. His red-and-gold half-cape glistened with raindrops, and made him look quite
dashing. "Beatrice! I knew you would return to me!"

Bee's expression was one of the queenly pride that we of Kena'ani upbringing call the Dido's Fury, a womanly emotion associated with the famous story of the dido and Aeneas, when the queen realized the untrustworthy Roman soldier of fortune had been seeking to rule over her through marriage.

"Legate Amadou Barry! I did not expect to meet you here! Nor, indeed, was any meeting with you a thing I desired, not after our last unfortunate encounter and the condescending insult you offered me. I realize that a man of your exceedingly high position in the world and your exceptional wealth and standing must look at a young woman such as myself with disdain. You may consider my impoverished circumstances and Phoenician connections to be marks against me which you are gracious enough to overlook. But I assure you I am proud of who I am and where I come from. I was sorely mistaken in what manner of man I thought you were. I now understand you are not the sort of man on whom a vulnerable young woman is wise to cast her hopes."

Every man except Rory was staring at Bee with expressions so broad that only actors playing in a farce would have used such gaping mouths to express shocked surprise. I choked down a laugh as I nudged Rory with my hip and indicated he should take the packs to the stairs.

"Indeed, I am done with all of you lordly men!" Bee's gaze flashed sideways to note Rory's movement, then back to her audience. "You believe you have the right to own me merely because you wish to possess me. Some of you desire to control me because I walk the dreams of dragons and others because you consider me beautiful. But I am not your property to be handed about or exchanged according to *your* desire rather than my own. Be sure that I realize you are all far more powerful in this world than I am, for I am only a young woman whose household has neither wealth nor noble status to raise it into the ranks of those who stand on high and look down upon the low. Be sure that I realize you could kill me, or arrest me, or forcibly assault me, or purchase me from the elders of Hassi Barahal house if you offered them a rich enough inducement or a frightening enough threat. We who are not protected by wealth and high station are so vulnerable in the world, are we not?"

"You cannot be Beatrice Hassi Barahal!" Amadou Barry looked as if he had seen a poisonous snake unexpectedly rearing up out of thick grass. "You are some manner of malevolent spirit who has taken the form of an innocent girl."

"Not as innocent as you would wish, Legate!" she said with a smoldering gaze that made his face pinch as she looked him up and down in a frankly sexual way. "Did you not murmur in the greenhouse that you wished to instruct me in the music of sweet pleasure? That I would be an 'apt pupil' if only I let you take command of my heart and my more intimate parts?"

Lord Marius whistled under his breath. "Ripe Venus! No wonder your courtship failed!"

It was all I could do not to burst out laughing at the way her erstwhile suitor's hands crushed into fists and his face tensed with anger at her plain speaking. I was sure Bee felt my shaking, for she swept an axe-blow glance in my direction to warn me to keep my peace.

"How was it you phrased it, Legate?" She tapped a finger against her perfect chin as she glanced at the ceiling for inspiration. "What awkward poetic phrases did you use to describe my—"

"You dare not mock me in this impertinent way."

"I *am* mocking you, Legate. You considered me beneath you, and you meant that in so many different ways. But I am not the woman you wish me to be. I never was."

She dismissed Amadou Barry with a proud lift of her chin and settled her implacable gaze on the mansa of Four Moons House. He was staring at her with an expression of outright astonishment, but I could see the beginnings of a condescending smile pull at his lips. The clock ticked over and rang six bells. No one moved until the last echo of the sixth bell died away.

"You may think me amusing, Mansa," she said, "for I must suppose you are now thinking I am a fiery little lass ripe for plucking by a strong man in his prime. But I do not find you amusing, nor do you awe me, you and your cold magic. You would have murdered my dearest cousin just for the sake of getting hold of my dreams."

"I do what I must," he said, with a frown at her rebuke. "You do not understand the consequences."

"*I* do not understand the consequences? My dearest cousin is the one who would have died, had your command been carried out. I would have been forced to marry a man against my will, and been cast into your House as a prisoner. You couldn't have protected me from the Wild Hunt regardless. I would have been dismembered and my head thrown in a well. So don't tell me that I am the one who does not understand the consequences."

Rory had moved halfway up the stairs, while I stood on the first step. Bee unlaced the basket and pulled out the skull. There was a struggling silence, broken at last by Lord Marius.

"Whose skull is that?"

"This?" she asked with a flutter of eyelashes. "This is the skull of my mother-in-law."

"Did you smite her dead with a scolding lecture?" the soldier asked with a laugh.

"Married!" Amadou Barry's face was cut with a look of sheer jealous rage. He took a step toward her, but Lord Marius fastened a hand on his arm, halting him. "Who married you?"

Bee ignored him. "I did not smite her. I rather liked her, and I believe she rather liked me, although we did not have the leisure to come to know each other well before the unpleasant incident in which she died. I show this to you, Mansa, to let you know that legally you have no grounds to force me to your will. I am a *nitaino*—a noble woman of independent means—in the Taino kingdom. No court and not even my family can use the threat of legal possession over me now. I have standing under Taino law."

"How did your mother-in-law die?" I asked.

"Why, thank you for asking, Cat." She swept them with a combative gaze. "The Wild Hunt killed her on Hallows' Night. They dismembered her and threw her head in a well."

"Bright Jupiter!" muttered Amadou Barry.

When she pressed a hand to her delicate throat, they all flinched.

"Cold mages are themselves at risk of being hunted down on Hallows' Night. I understand it is the reason mage Houses are reluctant to rise to positions of political power in the world. Power draws the Hunt as scent draws hounds."

Amadou Barry and Lord Marius gave each other startled looks. They had clearly never known there might be a hidden reason the 151 mage Houses did not set themselves up as princes and emperors in their own right.

The mansa had not gained control of Four Moons House by being impulsive, thoughtless, crude, or impatient, but even his temper had its limits. "These secrets are not yours to share."

"Who is to stop me from sharing them?" exclaimed Bee. "Will you kill me right now with your magic? Crush me with cold? Shatter me like iron?"

Ice crackled across the tabletop. Bee smiled so gloatingly that had that smile been turned on me, I would have slapped her; it had happened, on one of the rare occasions when we fought.

"I would have you stop and consider one thing before you act, Mansa," she said.

"What we thought was a log has revealed itself as a crocodile," remarked Bakary.

"I expect you mean to tell us, Maestressa, for you have quite the storyteller's gift," said Lord Marius appreciatively.

"My thanks," she said with a pretty courtesy. "Queen Anacaona died because the Wild Hunt must take blood on Hallows' Night. Because I was hidden from the Wild Hunt, Queen Anacaona was taken in my place. Isn't that a thing you would like to know how to do, Magister?"

"Die in your place?" said the mansa.

Bee laughed with genuine amusement at his jest. "Would you willingly die in my place, to spare me?"

His smile flashed. Its easy charm shocked me. One could never look at the mansa and see him as anything except a man of exceptional status and self-confidence, because he lived at the pinnacle of rank and wealth. I had not known the man had a sense of humor, or was able to laugh at himself. The obvious had blinded me: All along Vai had modeled his arrogant behavior on the mansa's, because Vai had been trying to be like the man who commanded his life.

"You intend to trade the secret of how you hid from the Wild Hunt in exchange for your freedom," said the mansa. "How like a Phoenician!"

"I have not relinquished my claim to her!" cried the legate.

152   The mansa looked Amadou Barry up and down in a way that

reminded me of Vai at his most obnoxiously cutting. "Legate, I mean no offense, but to offer to make a woman your mistress is not a claim. I will offer her a legal standing within Four Moons House while you are merely demanding she gratify your sexual desire for her."

"I will marry her! She belongs to me!"

"I do not belong to you, Amadou!" cried Bee so indignantly that a suspicion flowered that she still retained a partiality toward the man. "Perhaps I do not want to marry any man. Perhaps I no longer see marriage as a contract that can benefit me. Look at my poor dear cousin, chained to a man against her will. Is this all I am to be allowed to hope for? I have decided it is not."

"Yes, quite magnificent," Lord Marius said with a shade too much sarcasm for my liking. "You can't marry her, Amadou. The day after tomorrow you are to marry the prince of Tarrant's daughter. I shall have to take charge. You are all dazzled by her fabled beauty, as the Hellenes of old squabbled over a woman and all for her cherry lips and fulsome bosom—"

"In fact," I corrected, "Helen was the heiress to Sparta, a splendidly rich kingdom. They were fighting over her inheritance, not her beauty."

"—but I am not willing to lose the war we are fated to fight because of a squabble over a woman. If we do not use her gift of dreaming, then General Camjiata will. You all know I have no interest in her comely person, so I will take her into my custody until we have sorted out how to best make use of her dreaming to defeat Camjiata."

"Very well, Lord Marius, I surrender most humbly and gratefully, knowing I am to be well kept by such notable personages as yourselves," she said, wielding the blade of sarcasm. "I must say, at least General Camjiata pretended to give me a choice. There is something about the illusion that makes one like a man better for the sake of his wishing to be polite. Yet what can a poor young female do in circumstances such as mine? I will languish in the cage of your making and never learn those things I dream of learning. Meanwhile, naturally, you will find my lips are sealed and my secrets untold. The mansa will never learn how I hid from the Wild Hunt in a way cold mages might also protect themselves."

Lord Marius ran a hand over the lime-whitened spikes of his short 153 hair. "Let me speak clearly. If you try to escape and refuse to cooperate, we will have to kill you rather than risk your falling back into the hands of Camjiata. What baffles me is why the general let you go. He used the dreams of his wife to remain a step ahead of us in his first war. Any good strategist would keep you close and use your dreams to benefit his campaign."

"What makes you think he let us go?" I replied. "We escaped him, too. We do not mean to be owned or manipulated by any man. Not him, and not any of you."

The mansa took hold of my chin. His stare was a command demanding I give up my secrets. I gazed back with all the mulish determination I possessed. He intimidated me. While Vai had edges made of insecurity and youthful pride, the mansa had the surety of a man who has never doubted his worth, his high station, or his honor.

"Maybe it is not to be wondered at that the boy believes himself in love with you. You defied me, and lived to speak of it. He has too much pride. He resented the natural dislike the other boys felt for him, so he refused to acknowledge their higher station. When his magic bloomed to its fullness, he forced them to their knees, just to let them know he could do it. But he never defied me. Never. Not until you did."

"That's very gratifying, Your Excellency."

"Don't mock me, Catherine. Where is Andevai?"

"He is in the spirit world. I need only look into the mirror upstairs to find him."

"Can it be done, Bakary?" the mansa asked. "She is not a *djlelimuso*, a woman of craft and words who can bind the threads of power."

Bakary rubbed his gray beard. "I can see into the spirit world but cannot cross, while you can do neither, Your Excellency. I was taught that only the dead cross into the spirit world." He glanced at Rory as he spoke the words. "Her flesh is living flesh, like ours, yet she has crossed."

Did they not know that the hunters of Vai's village could walk into the spirit world at the cross-quarter days in order to hunt? I kept silence.

The mansa released my chin. "Very well. Show me."

I took the skull and tucked it into the basket. We climbed the stairs. A year and a half ago, I had descended them from the second floor while Andevai had ascended from the entryway. It was strange to return to the place where he and I had first looked on each other, face-to-face. Then, I had wanted nothing more than for him to leave us all alone. Now, I wanted nothing more than to find him.

I dragged the cover off the mirror.

Illuminated by the dregs of fading daylight and a single sphere of cold fire, the mirror reflected the seven people gathered on the landing. I had never realized how my hair writhed as if in a wind blowing off the spirit world. Did my eyes really gleam in that unexpected fashion, like polished amber? A sleek saber-toothed cat watched, waiting for my signal. No whisper of spirit-world magic tangled through Bee, but there was a smoky gleam in her eyes and on her forehead, as if a third eye was about to sprout there.

Lord Marius examined the mirror with the attention of a man trained to strike at the opportune moment. He looked exactly as he seemed. Amadou Barry stared at Beatrice. His visage had an avaricious glint that made him seem less handsome and more selfish.

The mansa's cold magic chased around him like the currents of many streams. One of those currents lashed out into the silvery depths of the mirror as the air around us fell suddenly colder. He was pulling in energy from the other side with which to weave here, although I had no idea how he was doing it.

Of us all, Bakary's was the most solid presence in the mirror: an old man with silver-black hair and a calm gaze.

The glittering chain with which another djeli had bound me to Andevai flowed into the mirror. I brushed my fingers across its gleam. Magic thrummed like a pulse anchored to Vai's heart.

"Catherine? Where are you?" Vai whispered, as if he felt my attention. "Beware, love. Think with your mind, not your body."

The tremor of his beloved voice so shocked me that I yanked on the chain.

It moved. Or I moved. Or the world moved.

Past the surface of the mirror, my gaze spanned the depths as if I were an eagle gliding above and watching the land roll past beneath. Mountains and valleys skimmed by below. Outside a walled town, peaceful eru worked and laughed and gossiped in the same manner as ordinary people did in the mortal world, only the eru were creatures of the spirit world with wings, third eyes in the center of their foreheads, and magic more powerful than that of any cold mage. The fields they farmed were sown in spirals. The beasts they shepherded were antelopes whose triple horns were studded by gemstones and glazed as with silver. A bloated beast like a slothfully blinking airship drifted past above the black line of a road and the warded triangle of a watering hole. A clan of tawny saber-toothed cats had gathered to nose at the pool, lick at a pillar of salt, and lounge in the shade of a tree.

Light flashed on the horizon. Where the land ended in a long straight shoreline, it met not water but the ashy ocean that we had traversed in the belly of a dragon, the Great Smoke. A tide of dark mist washed in, spilling over the land like the sweep of a broom. Beneath the smoke the land vanished. Only the road and warded ground remained unmoved and unchanged. My rope of magic held firm, but when the tide receded back into the smoky churn of the depths, the shoreline had changed.

The once-straight shoreline was now cut by fingerlike bays, as if the Great Smoke had taken bites out of the spirit land. The bloated air beast had vanished, although a large animal lumbered over a field of thorns, crushing all under its hooves. Eru rose in a cloud from the warded walls of their town, but they did not see me. I thought that maybe I wasn't even really there, that the chain acted like a hunter's scent to lead me toward my prey. Was this chain how Vai could always find me?

A white cliff towered above a lake riddled with icebergs. At first I thought it was an ice shelf, but as I swooped closer I realized it was a fortress built of crystal.

I slammed right into its wall.

The impact jolted me out of the vision. I found myself back on the first-floor landing with my right arm halfway into the mirror as if plunged up to the elbow in water, and the rest of me standing in front of the mirror blinking back tears. The heat of summer baked like sun on the arm that was thrust into the spirit world, while the rest of my body shivered in the cold house.

Bakary spoke behind me. "Don't touch her, Your Excellency."

"If Lord Marius stabs her with his sword, will she die?" asked the mansa.

Never let it be said I could not throw caution to the winds and just take the leap.

"Rory, take off your clothes. Bee, the mirror is water. You can cross if you will come."

"Of course I will!" cried Bee.

I cut my skin. Blood streamed from the gloomy spring chill of the mortal world into the hot blaze of the spirit world. When my sword's tip grazed the surface, the mirror peeled back like an eye opening. Was this part of the power I had as a spiritwalker? With my blood to seed it, could cold steel open a gate through which others could cross?

Steel flared at my back, felt on my tongue as the gritty remains of a blacksmith's forge. Lord Marius had drawn his sword.

"She can't be allowed to escape!" cried Amadou Barry.

"Follow me!" I cried.

I fell through, pouring like blood through the gash.

17

My knees thumped onto stony ground. Black night enveloped me, unrelieved by moon or stars. As I lifted my sword arm defensively, fire waxed the blade as a shimmering steel gleam.

"Ah! Something stung me!"

"Bee?"

I held the sword aloft, searching for her in the aura of the blade's light. Just in front of me a wall rose into the darkness, its face too smooth and high to climb. The surrounding land was covered with tall grass as far as the light from my sword reached. I did not see Bee, but I heard a whine like insects swarming.

"Bee!" I called.

Grass crackled. A huge cat with wicked curving canines and eyes as golden as my own sprang up to me. He nudged me with his head, then licked my forearm where a trickle of blood oozed along my skin. The rough trail of his tongue startled me into a laugh.

"Cat?" Bee's voice rose out of the darkness. I still could not see her, but she sounded panicked. "Everything hates me here. This wasn't a good idea! Ouch!"

"Where are you?" I cried.

Rory loped into the darkness. The whining spiked into a shrill buzzing. The big cat returned out of the gloom with Bee pressed to his side. She was waving an arm frantically in the air. I made a few cuts of my sword around her. The buzzing vanished as a cloud of tiny creatures scattered.

She dumped the packs at my feet. "I hope you're happy, Cat. I didn't think I would really cross through. I only meant to pretend to do so, because I was afraid you would refuse to go if you thought I was in danger."

"You *were* in danger!"

"At least there I could have thrown myself into Amadou Barry's arms if I had no other choice. Here I'm going to get eaten, and you're going to have to carry all this alone."

The cat sniffed at Bee, then staggered sideways in a showy manner as if her smell revolted him.

"Stop that!" She smacked him on the nose. "You may find your puerile jokes amusing, Rory, but I don't!"

A cry like that of a rabbit being disemboweled shrieked out of the darkness. Bee leaped backward, only to slam into the wall. Rory pounced in front of her as his tail lashed. Wings fluttered in the grass. The scrape of a sword being drawn shuddered the air, followed by a leaden thump, a squawk of anger, and a battering like a body being beaten to death.

A figure lumbered out of the darkness.

"Bright Jupiter! What is this cursed Tartarus? Where are we?"

Amadou Barry thrashed out of the grass and into the circle of light made by my sword's gleam. He had his military hat in one hand and a drawn sword in the other. The blade was coated with a viscous fluid to which white feathers clung.

"What attacked me?"

Rory opened his jaws to display his teeth. Amadou raised his sword.

"The cat is our ally," I said sharply. I looked up, hearing the flutter of wings. *"Down! Get down!"*

Of course he did not comply. Why would a patrician Roman legate who was also a Fula prince listen to a bastard girl whose mother was a northern barbarian and had been an Amazon soldier in the army of his most hated enemy besides?

A creature with a human body and the head and claws of a harpy struck, claws closing on his shoulder. Hat and sword fell as he shouted in pain and shock. The beast lurched upward, trying to carry him away, but his mortal weight brought it to a crashing halt.

I lunged. My focus narrowed to the beast's emotionless face, for it looked not like a woman but like a creature wearing the mask of a woman. The tip of my blade pierced its golden eye. Its howl shuddered down my blade. I pulled back. My blade slid free as ichor sprayed. In a thunder of wings it sprang into the air and vanished from sight, bleats fading as it flew away.

Bee dropped beside the legate, who lay facedown on trampled grass.

"Bee, is he dead?" I demanded.

"I'm not dead." Amadou sat up with a wince. His fancy cape was shredded. Blood stained his tunic.

Ghastly cries chittered out of the darkness. Huffing heat as of a steam engine chugging stirred the wind. Perhaps my tone was harsh, but I had no patience for ridiculous displays of masculine pride. "Next time you should listen to me, Legate. The spirit world will kill you."

"Legate?" said Bee gently. "May I help you rise—?"

"I do not need your help." He shook her off and rose with a grunt of pain.

"You're just angry that she spoke those truthful words to you which you do not want to hear and aren't accustomed to hearing," I retorted, for I could see Bee's expression twist as she pretended not to be hurt by his curt rejection. "Why were you so stupid as to follow us?"

"To take Beatrice back. You may remain in black Tartarus for all I care."

Bee gasped, but I forestalled her retort.

"How do you intend to take her back, Legate? You have no idea where we are or what to do here. Your steel won't cut the creatures here, although you can beat them with the hilt until they eat you. That creature would have killed you just now if Rory and I hadn't fought it off."

Rory's tail lashed in agreement.

"Rory, if there are more creatures gathering out there to kill us, lick your right paw."

He stared at me with a look I was sure was one of reproach for the inanity of the question. Then he licked his right paw.

"Why are you talking to a monstrous saber-toothed cat as if it can understand you?" asked Amadou Barry. "Where are we? With what magical illusion have you confounded my eyes?"

I ignored him. "Bee, take the head of Queen Anacaona out of the basket."

160   "How can a skull help us?" Amadou picked up his sword from the

ground and brandished it in what I supposed he thought was a manly way. "You two girls need protection. That's why we must return to the house and the mansa."

"In the spirit world, the head of Queen Anacaona is not a skull," I snapped, really exasperated now. "Please be polite."

"My apologies for the rude handling, Your Highness," Bee said in a choked voice as she wrestled open the basket. I could hear how humiliated she was, and how hard she was trying to hide it. "We are hoping your wisdom and experience may aid us."

I was watching Amadou Barry, astounded that the man was too blind to comprehend that he was no longer in a world where his patrician rank or military training meant anything. When Bee lifted the living head of Queen Anacaona out of the basket, he recoiled a step, then pulled himself up short, staring as the cacica blinked to get her bearings.

His mouth creased downward. "What cruel illusion is this?"

Queen Anacaona said, "Turn that way, Beatrice. There are four creatures running toward us. I suggest we move to a safer domicile."

"There is no safer domicile, Your Highness," I replied. "Legate, stay back."

Naturally the legate moved up alongside me, no doubt to impress Bee. Even injured, he looked as if he knew how to handle himself in a fight. He just didn't have any weapons that would work here. Bee dug into one of the packs and hefted a hammer.

Snarling, Rory sprang past me into the night. Two wolves dodged past him into the light shed by my sword. With a crosscut to the head, I sliced one hard across the muzzle and sidestepped with a turn to slash up under the belly of the second. Cold steel hit them like poison. They both collapsed. Snarls and growls punctuated a dirty fight farther out. I ran toward the sound to find Rory with his jaws at the throat of a third wolf, clamping down until the beast stopped thrashing and went limp.

"There's one more," I said.

Bee shouted a warning.

I bolted back in time to see the fourth wolf leap toward Bee as Amadou Barry jumped between them. I grabbed its tail and yanked it sideways with me as I fell. The animal landed square on top of me, punching the air from my lungs. It twisted, shaking up to its feet as its head swung around to bite my face.

Rory slammed into it, and they went rolling away into the darkness in a crash of noise, followed by a yelp. Rory paced back into view. He looked quite dreadfully powerful, muscles rippling beneath his dark flanks and shoulders. Facing into the darkness, he roared. His challenge shook through air and earth like a living thing. When he paused, the night had fallen as silent as if every creature near enough to hear thought it prudent to rethink its strategy.

"Cat?" Bee's voice was remarkably level. "Are you hurt?"

"I'm not touched." I was shaking, not with fear but with fight. I was ready to rip out the throat of the next creature that attacked Bee. "We need to move. Find a gate to get you and the legate back to the mortal world."

"This is a constant nightmare of death!" cried Amadou Barry. "Have we truly crossed into Tartarus, where the ancestors bide? Where skulls are wreathed in the form of living heads? Where every monster seeks to kill?"

Ignoring him, I slung on the pack with Vai's tools and started walking. "I'd call Rory's pride to protect us, but we've no warded ground in sight where they can shelter if a tide rips through."

I led with my sword, keeping my right shoulder next to the wall. Bee followed with the other two packs, slung on before and behind her, and the cacica's head held out in front to guide us. Amadou Barry limped behind her, and Rory brought up the rear. The ground alongside the wall was stony, marked with patches of lichen. Eyes glowed in the night like pairs of fireflies, softly ominous.

"What is a tide?" Amadou Barry demanded. "Why is everything here attacking us?"

I couldn't help but want to rub his nose in his ignorance. "Since you seem to think we do not know what we are about, I should like to inform *you* of what *you* do not know. Now and again young women are born who walk the dreams of dragons in their sleep."

"I know that!" he protested. After a hesitation, he said, "Go on."

"All you powerful men want Bee to make use of her dreams to fulfill your own ambitions."

"We merely wish to keep her out of the hands of the Iberian Monster so he cannot use her dreams to conquer Europa."

I snorted.

"If that was your only purpose, Legate," said Bee in a low voice, "then I am surprised at the insulting offer you made me."

"Bright Venus, but you Phoenicians are too proud!"

I cut in before they could tumble into what would seem too much like a lovers' quarrel. "The tides of those dreams wash the spirit world like great waves of smoke. Where the smoke washes, the land is wiped clean. Every thing and every creature that is touched by the smoke is changed. Except for warded ground, which is what we're looking for now. The creatures who live in the spirit world hate dragon dreamers and want to kill Bee."

"This is the most outrageous tale I have ever heard," he said, but the tremor in his voice made me realize he was actually listening.

"Perhaps my vision deceives me," said the cacica, "but it seems we are not going anywhere."

"These walls are certainly of greater circumference than the walls of Rome," said Amadou, as if relieved to have the conversation change to a subject on which he might account himself an expert.

"Who is this young man?" asked the cacica. "He has not asked to be brought to my notice. Yet he speaks as if I had requested his opinion."

"I do not need anyone's permission to speak!" said Amadou.

I squelched an urge to punch him.

"Your pardon, Your Highness," said Bee. "It was rude of me to forget my manners."

I wasn't sure I liked Bee's simpering expression as she introduced Amadou Barry to the cacica as a young man of high rank like to that of the nobles of the Taino kingdom. The cacica was not impressed by his grudging courtesy. I wasn't either. But I had more urgent concerns. Ahead lay a sprinkle of drying ichor and a mat of white feathers whose pattern I recognized.

"Blessed Tanit! We've come back to where we started. It's not that we're not going anywhere. We're going in a circle around a wall with no entry. The chain that binds me to Andevai can pierce the wall but we can't." I poked at the wall with the tip of my sword. Its substance remained stubbornly hard. "He's inside, but we have no gate."

"No gate?" remarked the cacica, in surprise. "You cut a gate once in the fence the behiques raised around Kiskeya, young woman. As you well recall, since it was through that gate my murderer entered my realm. Why can you not cut a gate here in the same manner?"

Amadou Barry rudely spoke right over her words.

"You just claimed to know what you are about in this place," he said in the tone of a man who has had enough of the pretensions of the lesser folk. "It is time you girls gave up this fruitless quest and returned to Adurnam with me."

Bee turned to look out toward the horizon. "Cat! A light is rising. A dragon is turning in her sleep. I can feel the smoke of her dreams rushing toward us."

A blaze of white fire splintered the darkness, rolling toward us across a flat, grassy landscape.

"Rory! Come here! Bee, get hold of him. Legate, grab Beatrice's hand."

Shuddering with fear, Rory pushed up against Bee as I sheathed my sword and flung one arm around her and with the other grabbed a hank of Rory's pelt. My hip was pressed into Rory's heaving side.

"What are you doing?" demanded Amadou Barry.

"Legate, if you don't grab hold of her now, you will be swept away—"

"Blessed Tanit!" exclaimed Bee.

The tide of the dream, like daylight, illuminated a crowd of animals creeping toward us out of the night. The beasts seemed oblivious to the tide because they were so intent on murdering Bee.

"Brave Jupiter! I shall fight them off!" Amadou advanced like a hero, sword raised to threaten the beasts.

The tide swept down, ripping through them, tearing a gash through the world.

"Amadou!" cried Bee, dropping the hammer. "Grab hold of my hand!"

The light cut through me. The earth fell away as the world tipped to spill me into an abyss through which I would fall for eternity. But

Bee was my rock. She was the pillar that no earthquake or storm could dislodge. She was warded ground.

Amadou Barry did not reach for her. The tide struck him full on. One moment I saw his body clearly, streaked with currents of shining smoke. Then he tumbled into an unseen gash in the fabric of the world. The tide of the dream streamed on, leaving us trembling in its wake as the earth shuddered back into solidity under our feet.

Rory nudged me, and I let go of Bee and knelt to bury my face in his thick black pelt. After I caught my breath, I raised my eyes.

Bee did not move. In one hand she still held the head of Queen Anacaona. Her other arm was extended, but her hand was empty.

She swayed as if caught in a gust of wind, then crumpled to her knees and began weeping.

The tide had taken him.

I was so furious at Amadou Barry for being an idiot who wouldn't listen that I simply could not speak one word.

Those who are caught in the tide of a dragon's dream never come back.

The head of Queen Anacaona stared across a stony plain, now empty of life. The tide had swept away the animals who stalked us. Even the wind had died, leaving flat red earth and a cold gray sky. Behind us the impenetrable wall now appeared as a windowless but modest tower no larger than a watchtower on a Roman wall. The tower was the only object visible in this parched desert. There were not even hills marking the horizon.

"My ancestors built a fence around our kingdom so the tides of the Great Smoke would not trouble our ancestors," the cacica remarked, as if she were accustomed to seeing people vanish in such an abrupt and shocking manner. "All of Soraya, our spirit land, became warded ground. Therefore, our wise and beloved grandparents remain close beside us, to advise us in times of need and to celebrate with us at the festivals."

"Why didn't he hold on to me?" The way Bee's voice cracked broke my heart, or it would have, had I a heart.

"Because he couldn't bring himself to trust us," I said.

Tears streaked her face. "Don't you care?"

"I don't have time to care! Not if I want to save your life and rescue Vai." Feeling helpless made me want to kick something. I kept thinking Amadou Barry was about to step into view from around the tower, but we were alone. "Why did the chain bring me here only to abandon us in this desert?"

"I believe this must be a puzzle," said the cacica. "A piece that fits inside another piece. Just as the behiques of the Taino kingdom built fences to protect our lands, might not the lords of these spirit lands have built fences to close off their places of power? In the palace at Sharagua there are walls inside walls where only some have the privilege and power to enter, and others are forbidden. Could this tower be a gate onto such an inner and more sacred realm?"

"If it is, I don't know how to cut a way through! Bee! That's enough! We can cry later!"

After taking in a breath, she wiped her eyes. Her voice was a slobbery mess, but her words were clear. "The hammer wasn't swept away."

On shaking legs she rose holding the cacica's head in one hand and Vai's hammer in the other. She would have looked comical if she hadn't worn red, puffy eyes and a mask of tragedy.

"Does no one listen to the wisdom of the elders?" asked the cacica. "Are young people taught nothing in these days? Are they all as disrespectful as that unpleasant young man? It is blood the maku spirit lords crave, and blood that feeds them. Life pulses in our blood. They who are without life will drink of the salt of our blood so they can mask themselves in the shape of the living. Blood will cut a gate that they wish to remain closed."

Of course! What was I thinking? *Blood cuts the gate.*

Rory hissed. Wisps of clouds scudded our way. The earth stirred as if hidden carnivores were pushing up from underneath. Out on the plain a pack of lean wolves trotted into view. They would never stop trying to kill Bee.

I nicked my arm and smeared the dribble of blood on the wall. The blood bubbled, eating into the wall until the surface dissolved into a jumbled mass of translucent crystal. When I laid my shoulder into it, the substance crumbled away to form a crude tunnel, something like the gate I had cut in the Taino spirit fence.

"Go! Go!"

Rory and Bee pushed past me and vanished into a blaze of bright light. Salt stung my eyes and made the fresh cuts on my arm burn. Behind me an animal growled, and teeth snapped close by my feet. I flung myself toward the light, and slammed into stone hard enough that the impact momentarily stunned me.

A blowsy breath warmed my cheek. A tongue licked my closed eyes.

"Stop that!" I opened my eyes to find myself embracing a granite pillar about the height of a man. To my left rose a sapling oak. To my right shone a clear pool. We had crossed onto warded ground. Rory nudged me again, and I let go of the pillar.

"Cat! There you are! I thought we'd lost you!" Bee clutched me, her fingers digging into my already-raw cut. Her nose was red from weeping, but her eyes were shining in a belligerent way that boded ill. Yet she spoke in the charming voice she had used at the academy when she wanted to disarm and distract our teachers. "Look who I found, dearest!"

Blessed Tanit. The chain of binding had pulled me right to him.

Vai stood at a prudent remove, his arms crossed on his chest and his mouth set in a crooked line that made him look both annoyed and amused. The sight of him took my breath away.

"I've been telling him all about the lovely wedding journey Prince Caonabo and I took to the amiable Comanche nation," Bee chattered on as I stared.

"Here you are, Cat. I knew you would come for me."

His familiar voice pulled me out of my shock. He was wearing the clothes he had had on in the coach on Hallows' Night. Seeing him so solid and so close hit me as hard as if I had been hammered. His skin crinkled at the corners of his eyes as a smile sharpened his face.

My lips parted. "Vai..."

"I was waiting for you," he added in his silkiest voice.

Bee ground her heel into my instep. "*And* I told him all about the decorative little palace my darling Caonabo and I are building so it will be ready in time for the birth of our long-awaited and much-to-be-cherished child."

Rory hissed, ears flicking back. Bee brandished the cacica's head and the hammer.

I dumped my pack on the ground to leave myself room to maneuver 167 as I confronted the man wearing Vai's face. "You are not my husband. You are my sire. How did you know I was here?"

His laughter had a cruel edge. "I smell and hear and see and taste all. Your voice and your emotions are fingers walking along my skin. I knew you would come after him. Still, you have surprised me, Daughter. You have brought me the dragon dreamer. I did not expect you to hand her over in exchange for the man."

"You are mistaken if you think I intend to let you have her."

"That is what Tara Bell said to me when I told her she would bear a girl child who would grow up to serve me. Why do you bother to resist, when you know how that turned out?" In a melting flash of shadow he changed to become a saber-toothed cat larger and more powerful than Rory. He roared, the threat reverberating through the air.

"Stand behind me, Bee." I raised my sword. There was a great deal I did not know about the spirit world, but what I did know, I could use. I spoke the words the footman who was an eru had taught me the first time I had crossed into the spirit world. "Let those who are kin come to my aid. I call to you, Rory's kinswomen, and I ask respectfully for your protection."

Head down, ears flat, Rory slouched up to join me in confronting our sire. I admired his courage; he was clearly terrified. I was quaking, too, but my sword arm stayed steady.

"You'll have to get through us first," I added. "I do not fear to stab you, even if it means harming myself."

He lashed his tail in warning. I looked past him, for the first time truly taking in our surroundings. We stood on the stone pavement of a monumental plaza. In the distance, to both the right and the left, rose other wards, each with a pillar formed of glass, a glittering crystal tree whose leaves tinkled in a cold wind, and a fountain spilling sleet as an icy breath. In the center of all, far away, stood a white stone palace. Ribbons of silver and gold shimmered along the top of its wall, caught in a wind we could not feel down here. My father had written in his journals of an old folktale that mentioned a palace like this one, with four gates.

In the plaza, shadows and bursts of light coalesced, marking the arrival of the Hunt. Crows flapped down to perch on my sire's back, and what should have looked ridiculous instead heightened the aspect of his power. Lean hounds padded up beside him. A cloud of wasps circled over his head, while a pack of huge gray dire wolves drew muzzles back to show their teeth.

He roared again, the sound so loud the crows took flight, cawing.

A second roar answered.

My sire looked around as if startled.

A pride of tawny saber-toothed cats flowed into view, halting to mill around Rory and me. Not even the Wild Hunt dared rashly charge in against a pride of saber-toothed cats. They dipped heads, rubbed; one of the smaller females nipped at Rory, and he nipped back. The one I recognized as his mother boxed him across the head with a paw. He growled, and she batted him again. His ears twitched, then flattened.

Satisfied, she turned with the others to stare hungrily at Bee.

"Aunt! I pray you, listen to my words. The Master of the Wild Hunt seeks to harm me and mine. Bee is my cousin and will not harm you. Just as your son has been forced to serve his sire, so has she been forced to serve those you call the enemy. Please help me stand against him."

Tentatively I extended a hand so she could sniff my palm. Her beauty dazzled me, as did the sheer force of her physical presence, with its power and majesty and, of course, those teeth.

She reared up to balance her weight on my shoulders. Her gold eyes met mine unblinkingly. She could have ripped off my face with one lazy yawn. Her breath was hot, laced with a carrion scent, and yet it did not disturb me. Predators had these cravings.

She made a sound something like a meow and something like a query.

"The Master of the Wild Hunt mated with my mother as he did with you. He had no affection for my mother. He only wanted to make a child he could command. Now he's stolen my beloved. Please, Aunt, I can only request your help as your stepdaughter, bound to you through my love for your son Rory. Please protect my cousin Bee so the Wild Hunt does not eat her. I will take her away from the spirit world as soon as I can."

She heaved herself down and prowled over to Bee.

Standing as rigid as a statue, her gaze fixed on me to remind me that if she was eaten it would be my fault, Bee endured being sniffed. I wasn't sure I would have had that much courage, but she did.

Last the big cat sniffed delicately at the cacica's head. The two queens eyed each other as might rulers who are not sure whether they are destined to become rivals or allies.

Without warning, my sire sprang.

I spun and thrust.

My blade caught him along the right shoulder, a mere scrape. Pain flamed across my own shoulder, but I knew it was coming so I hardened myself. I heard Rory's mewl, and most importantly the cry of every creature who attended him. Because hurting him hurt them, they were momentarily unable to attack.

I flung myself into him and together we crashed sideways onto the ground. The fur of his shoulder smeared into a new form. I was lying on top of Vai, who had his arms caressingly around me. He was naked, and aroused.

Pain was nothing compared to my disgust.

I shoved off him and scrambled back, keeping my gaze averted as I got to my feet.

"Blessed Tanit!" cried Bee.

"You're a monster. You'll never defeat me, not in this way, not in any way!"

Bee sucked in a harsh breath. The saber-toothed cats had arrayed themselves around her. They faced outward, ears flat, mouths open to show teeth. Every cat had her hair fluffed up to make herself look bigger.

My sire rose to his knees as his body sprouted the wings of an eru. His skin brightened to a sheen like brass. His long black hair stirred as if, like his limbs, it could grasp and strangle his enemies. His wings were feathered with silver. He now wore a kilt woven out of disks. The glittering amulets made me blink from the shine.

He stared at me with eyes the same amber color as mine. But he had also a third eye, a mass of cloudy veins in the center of his forehead. What sights that bloody eye could see I did not know, and I wasn't entirely sure I wanted to find out.

"This is your true form," I said.

"Change is my true form. But the one who gave birth to me had an eru's form when I was disgorged. So it is the form to which I return most naturally."

"No wonder the eru called me *Cousin*," I muttered.

When he opened his wings to their full span, they exhaled an icy mist. He was magnificent. "You must be what you are, little cat. That is why I sired you. Do you not wonder why you can kill without regret, escape certain death, and prowl like a tomcat among males who attract you?"

"I might be able to do those things even were you not my sire." Waves of pain like hot knives still stabbed through my right shoulder. I wondered if I could bring myself to stab him again, even though my first attack had proven successful in forcing the Hunt to retreat.

His stance remained relaxed and confident. "Do you ever ask yourself how it is you can command the loyalty of others? Why they do your bidding at your word? It must be so, because my blood is your blood. Those I command are yours also to command."

"There are better reasons for people to be loyal. People give back to you what you give to them. You may say it is blood or birth that binds servants to masters and plebeians to their patrician lords, but that is only another word for force. The Council in Expedition ruled because they had wealth enough to keep themselves in power. But I watched the people of Expedition speak out in protest. I watched them fight. They took the opportunity to govern themselves. They did not wait for it to be given them. They did not say that their demands for new laws and for justice must cede to the prerogatives of blood and birth."

"Yet blood binds all."

"Does it?" I demanded. "Do you command every creature in the spirit world?"

He said nothing, but he blinked.

I was breathing as hard as if I had been running, or maybe it was just my aching shoulder that made me dizzy. "I think you only command the Wild Hunt, not one creature more."

A smile cut his face. Before I thought to retreat, he folded his wings forward to cage me in their web of ice. His clawed hands pulled me close, not in an amorous way but as if he had decided to dismember me and rip off my head. His voice had the shiver of a bell when a rod is drawn across it to make it vibrate.

"Hear my words, little cat. A prince among slaves is still a slave. The courts bind him with blood in the palace where those without blood cannot walk. You are bound because he is bound."

"I don't care what you say! I will free my husband!"

He let go, opened his wings, and launched himself into the sky. I staggered back. Bee, Rory, and the cats shook free as if chains had been loosened.

"Cat!" Bee grabbed my hand. Rory shoved his head up under my free hand.

My shoulder really hurt. I took in short breaths to get through the sting of pain.

Over the palace the eru caught an updraft and spiraled up until he became too small to see.

The pain ebbed enough for me to think straight. "Bee, how did you know it wasn't Vai?"

"That was easy. First, he met us here. I was here all alone for about ten throbbing heartbeats before you came through after me. When he asked where you were, he referred to you as "Cat." Andevai never calls you Cat. He calls you Catherine. I don't understand why your sire didn't kill me immediately, but I suppose he would want to save me for the next Hallows' Night sacrifice. Did he say something to you when he imprisoned you in his wings?"

I waggled my hand to show I did not mean to answer where my sire might hear, and she nodded, then glanced past me. Her eyes flared as her mouth turned down. Rory's mother coughed a warning. Shapes like fanged butterflies fluttered toward us in a zigzag way that made my skin prickle. The Master and his Hunt had departed, but other denizens of the spirit world had come calling, attracted by Bee's scent.

"You have to leave, Bee."

"Your jacket is wet. What is that?"

I rubbed at my shoulder but I could tell it was a shallow scrape. Rory also had a scratch along his right shoulder, oozing the golden liquid that was his blood.

"Nothing as important as getting you back to the mortal world. Bee, give me all the bottles. And leave the hammer. I'll take Vai's tools."

Her high color suggested she had known this moment would come. "I sorted the packs in Adurnam already. I never thought I'd be able to come into the spirit world with you, Cat. I knew I would just get in your way here."

"Rory will go back with you."

He protested with a coughing grunt.

"Rory, you know perfectly well it's not safe for Bee to travel Europa alone. Don't argue. Queen Anacaona will stay with me. Find a troll maze to hide in if Hallows' Night comes before I return. We'll meet in Havery, at the law offices of Godwik and Clutch."

"Yes," she said. "Havery."

Rory's mother snarled. A swirl of bright leaves swept up as on a blast of icy wind, congealing into a monstrous beast with a lizard's length, a silky coat of pale hair, and a snake's jaws. Two of the cats charged at it, but its claws drove them back. I leaped forward and cut its open mouth with my sword. The beast disintegrated into a thousand shards that clattered to the ground with a noise like chimes.

"Go, Bee! Through water."

"I love you, Cat." Chin lifted, Bee smiled bravely at me.

My look had to speak for me, because I could not produce words. The big cats prowled the perimeter of the warded ground to give Bee time to get away. Shards littering the ground stirred to take on the monstrous shape of a fluttering harpy with teeth like obsidian knives. Four wolves loped up, tongues lolling and breath steaming. More winged creatures appeared in the distance, arrowing our way.

I leaped forward to confront the wolves. "Hurry! Rory, go with her!"

She plunged into the little pool and fell away from us as if running down invisible steps. I smeared a drop of blood from my shoulder onto my boot and stuck the foot in the water to create a gate for Rory. The instant Bee's head vanished beneath the waters, with Rory behind her, the spirit beasts tested the air for a smell that was no longer present. In ones and twos, they trotted away.

18

I had to let go of my unshed tears so I could concentrate on the task that lay before me. By scratching each cat on its big head, I calmed myself. I ought to have been scared of them. Any, except possibly the half-grown littlest, could have ripped me to pieces, but they shouldered their bodies around mine in a way I found so charmingly affectionate that it sucked my tears quite dry. They heartened me.

"My thanks to you. No need to accompany me any farther. Run as far as you can before he comes back."

Yet the cats waited as I retrieved the head of the cacica from the ground where Bee had perforce left her. "Your Highness, you have been generous in aiding us. I feel obliged to confess that I am taking you to Haübey, not to Caonabo."

She regarded me unblinking with a stare I was glad I had never had to face down while she sat on the duho, the seat of power. "Explain yourself."

"Your brother the cacique made a bargain with me. He said he would get me to Europa if I would take you to your exiled son Haübey. I accepted because reaching Europa was the only chance I had to get my husband back. The cacique promised me that Haübey will take you back to Sharagua, and thus to Caonabo."

"I wondered when you would tell me. I can see we do not travel in Taino country. My brother is a persuasive man, and you are young, so I cannot fault you for giving way to his conniving. What is done cannot be changed. In truth, I have seen sights I would not otherwise have witnessed, so my gourd of knowledge becomes weightier. Was that winged creature who attacked us the one who commanded my death?"

"Yes, Your Highness."

"Well, then, you did well to defy him as much as you are able."

I had rarely received a compliment that pleased me more. "My thanks, Your Highness. Since we're here, will you drink?"

"Your manners are improving. Yet is it safe to drink here?"

"Here on warded ground, from this water, it is."

"Then I will do so, for I wish to taste the waters of these springs."

I cradled her in my hands so she could lap, rather like a dog, but it went well enough. I drank to satiety, filled the bottles, and stowed them in my pack. My sire's whispered words nagged at me, but I dared not discuss them aloud with the cacica lest unseen ears overhear. Had he been taunting me, or warning me?

"We must go to the palace," I said.

"In Sharagua, such a central compound would be the cacique's domain. That suggests the palace is the home of the spirit courts of Europa. We can discover what lies within by entering."

Buoyed by this truism, I advanced, with the cacica's hair clutched in my right hand and my sword in my left. We walked at least a mile, if one could measure distance here as in the mortal world, and I was pretty sure one could not. I was pretty sure distances might expand and contract. How else could the cats have reached me so quickly when I called to them? They paced alongside, escorting us. The littlest several times bumped into me on purpose, until I finally swatted her with the flat of my sword.

"Little beast! No wonder Rory finds you annoying!"

She sulked away so like Bee's spoiled little sister Astraea that I laughed. The adult females coughed in what I imagined was shared amusement.

Strange to think that laughter brought us to the walls.

White walls like seamless ceramic rose to the height of ten men, so high I could not hope to climb. A massive sea-green door promised an entry, but it was closed tight. Fortunately, warded ground formed the tongue of the gate, with a smooth pillar, a spring of water rising in a stone basin, and a sapling ash tree. Standing safe between the wards, I examined the huge doors.

The lintel was carved of jade in the form of two eru with hands braced against each other's, their lips about to meet in a kiss that would never be consummated. Did the entrance always look like this, or was it formed this way to taunt me? The doors had neither ring nor latch. When I pushed with a foot, neither budged. The cut on my forearm was still oozing, but a smear of my blood wiped onto the jade did nothing.

Frustrated, I murmured my sire's words. " 'The palace where those without blood cannot walk.' "

"The dead have no blood to offer," said the cacica. "Perhaps the dead cannot cross."

"I could go forward alone. But it seems wrong to leave you behind. I should have sent you with Bee."

"Hers is not the responsibility. You can hang the basket from the tree and return to get me."

"What if someone steals you, Your Highness? What if I can't return this way? Or get out at all?"

"If you are unable to get out, I will be lost regardless." Her clear gaze measured me. "I do not fear you will abandon me. You have proven yourself loyal."

"My thanks, Your Highness." Her praise startled me into an unexpected spike of optimism.

I returned her to the basket, hung the basket from a branch, and from the spring drank my fill of water so cold it numbed my lips.

This time, when I smeared blood onto the jade, the stone parted as easily as curtains. As I pushed through, my first step took me into light so bright it blinded me. My second step brought me to the brink of an impossibly vast chasm. The silence made me wonder if I had gone deaf.

An entire world fell away from my feet like a bowl with tiers. Each of these tiers marked a landscape as wide as continents, and each landscape was surrounded by the Great Smoke. I looked down as might a star, hanging so high that the whole of existence lay exposed as I watched the surge and flow of the spirit world. Tides of smoke swept up from the waterless ocean to engulf swaths of land, then rolled back into the sea. Everything the tide touched was changed, except for the steady gleams that marked warded ground, the straight lines of warded roads, and a few patches that might have been briny salt flats.

According to the story of creation told by the Kena'ani, Noble Ba'al had wrested land out of ocean in his contest with the god of the sea. The sages of my people said that the world was created out of conflict. Was this not similar to what the troll lawyer Keer had told me? *"At the heart of all lie the vast energies which are the animating spirit of the worlds. The worlds incline toward disorder. Cold battles with heat. When ice grows, order increases. Where fire triumphs, energies disperse."*

In the spirit world, land and ocean warred, one rising as the other fell. Where the ocean receded, the span of the land grew. When the ocean swelled, the measure of the land shrank.

How could I see it all, and all at once? For here, on the brink, I was not standing in the spirit world and yet neither was I standing in the mortal world.

The threads of life and spirit stitch together the interleaved worlds. Mages drew their power through these threads, and I used the shadows of the threads to weave concealment and enhance my sight and hearing in the mortal world.

Now it seemed to me that I was standing both inside and outside. I was caught within a single translucent thread that pulsed with the force of life and spirit that some call magic and others call energy. Its span was no greater than the span of my outstretched arms and yet it was also boundless. The contrast so dizzied me that I swayed. The lip of the abyss crumbled away beneath my feet. Flailing, I tipped and fell forward through another flash of blinding light.

My knees smacked onto solid ground. After I sucked down the pain and blinked the afterimages of spots from my vision, I looked around.

I had come to rest on a ledge cut into a cliff side that overlooked a deep bowl of land like a crater. Inside the crater the ground was cut up by narrow ridges and steep prominences in the manner of a maze. A city of bridges and wide balconies wove through this labyrinth of air and wind. Every surface had a crystalline glimmer. The spacious balconies and winding bridges were ornamented with ribbons colored blood-red and melting-butter-yellow and the stark blue those who lived in the north called "the mark of the ice." Rainbows rippled as on invisible currents of water.

I was not alone.

Brightly robed people strolled along arm in arm on these hanging paths, gossiping and laughing with gentle smiles. Others rushed past as on urgent errands. Some wore headdresses of peculiar construction, spiky like quills or curved like crescent moons. The colors they wore made a rainbow of movement. They gathered and split off into new groups at each place where bridges merged and intersections branched. Blues poured in one direction and violets and greens in another, only to meet up at a farther remove, spilling and merging until it seemed their robes changed color as easily as I blinked.

A tiered ziggurat towered above the rest of the city, its highest tiers like an eagle's aerie wreathed with gold and silver wisps. Somehow, from this angle, I could see the entire edifice, even though that should have been impossible. Up the center of each face of the ziggurat ran a staircase. On three of these stairs, figures descended and ascended in constant motion. The fourth stair was riven by a cleft, a gleaming canyon that sliced into a dark interior. The top of the ziggurat lay flat and open like the holy sanctuary in a Kena'ani temple.

The scene on the top of the ziggurat reminded me of a princely hall as described in tales of the olden days told by Celtic bards. A half circle of lordly chairs stood on a dais. Four shone as if beaten out of gold, and four had a texture as black as the depths of a moonless night. No one I could see was sitting in them, yet I felt the whisper of presences ready to materialize. Musicians strolled through, strumming lutes and harps. Drummers played a soft rhythm like the pulse of the hidden earth. A crowd of lordly personages waited at long tables set with platters so bright their glitter made me blink. No one seemed to be eating. I wasn't sure there was food or drink.

The lower levels of the ziggurat lay deserted, empty of life. Four bridges, one on each side, connected the four staircases on the tiered mountain to the rest of the city. A moat ringed the city below the outer cliff wall, filled with a viscous liquid. When I peered down from the ledge, its steamy current gleamed ominously, as if warning me I could not escape, because I was trapped by molten fire. The only way off my ledge was along a narrow bridge that vaulted into the maze.

Where almost everything is in constant movement, that which stands still stands out.

A man waited unmoving on one of the bridges. A swarm of personages in bright robes flowed past, breaking around him as water breaks around a rock.

I memorized a path from my ledge to him through the weave of bridges and balconies. No one tried to stop me as I hurried through the city. Either they did not know I was there, or I was too insignificant to matter. Despite the convoluted path I had to follow, I had no trouble reaching him. He stood facing a gulf of air. A wind rising up from the boiling moat whipped through his dash jacket.

"Catherine!" he called, smiling.

I ran to him, my heart pounding and my lips dry. But as I reached him I slowed. A sword's length from him, I extended my blade instead of my arm.

"Show me your navel," I said.

"Show me yours first, Catherine. How can I know it is truly you?"

"You said you would always know if it was me. What is the first thing you ever said to me?"

He laughed. "That I loved you from the first moment I saw you."

I took a step back, disappointment a pinch in my heart. "That's not the first thing you said."

His laughter deepened into a roar as he changed into a saber-toothed cat.

"Am I a mouse, that you play with me before gulping me down?" I demanded. "If you mean to kill me, then I wish you would just get it over with."

He turned sideways as if to swipe at me but hesitated when he caught sight of something behind me. Like a beaten animal he hissed, head hunched, ears down. I pressed back against the railing as I turned with my blade ready to block.

The personage who approached paid me no notice. I might as well have been invisible.

Such a proud and imposing woman could walk at her ease through any princely court or mage House estate. Her robes shimmered with peacock hues. A headdress and cloak of rustling ornamental feathers made me stare. Her graceful hands had long fingernails painted red, as if she had dipped them in blood.

"There you are, precious." She fastened a gem-studded collar around the neck of the angry cat without the least sign that his size, teeth, and annoyance disturbed her. "It is time for the Hunt."

Unexpectedly she turned, fingers closing like iron around my wrist.

Her eyes had neither iris nor pupil; they looked like shards of ice stabbed into her face. Without so much as asking my leave or apologizing for the discourtesy, she pressed the raw cut to her lips.

Winter leaches warmth from the air. Ice forms into chains that bind quivering souls.

My heart, my thoughts, my very spirit drained into the chasm of winter, crushed under the weight of a glacial shelf. I was the food and the drink; I was the thread of power being tasted and sipped; I was the one bound and chained...

The hand released me. I collapsed to my knees, hacking as if I were coughing out the dregs of my soul. Despair curdled in my gut. I would never find him. He was already dead. Bee and Rory were lost in the mortal world where I could never reunite with them. My tasks undone, my promises unkept...all lost...

"This is weak fare, not the prisoner whose powerful blood you promised us," she said in a cold voice to my sire. "He continues to defy us and has placed himself out of our reach and it seems yours as well. If only he would surrender, as you claimed he would, he would nourish us with that astonishing strength. But since he refuses to feed us, and the time is come for the renewal of the binding, then you, my pet, must hunt in the mortal world for our feast."

With fingers wrapped around the leash, she climbed toward the ziggurat. My sire followed, tail lashing, exactly as might a beast bound into obedient but unwilling servitude.

For the longest time the ice in my veins held me frozen. As they ascended the magnificent stairs, the woman and the cat were joined by elegant personages splendidly garbed in gowns and capes sewn of pearls and silk and shells. Up they climbed to the very crown of the ziggurat. There a cloud of darkness swirled.

Hounds yipped anxiously. Wolves howled and hyenas cackled. Wasps massed in a cloud. My sire changed from cat into a man riding a black horse. He raised a hand, commanding the air.

A churning eye like the center of a hurricane boiled into existence in midair. It reminded me of the goal in batey, a window in the heavens between the spirit world and the mortal world. A smear like a bolt of night surged up from the ziggurat, piercing the air as a deadly lance. Thunder cracked. A gate between the worlds swirled open.

The Wild Hunt had been released.

In a howling, chirping, chortling pack, the Hunt passed through the gate of the hurricane's eye. My sire galloped in their midst with a spear in one hand and fear in the other.

On a second thunderclap, the eye closed and the Hunt vanished.

The dark clouds cleared away. The city fell silent, as if holding its breath. But it was not still. The boiling movement that spun along the bridges and balconies flowed merrily along. Its constantly shifting pattern contracted and expanded like a flock of birds in flight, spinning around and around the center like a whirlpool around an unseen eddy.

My finger twitched. My arms were my own again. I rubbed my eyes to break free from the trance.

Blessed Tanit! If the Wild Hunt rode into the mortal world, then Hallows' Night had come again. Months had passed in what had felt to me like a single day. Bee and I had walked in Adurnam in late March. Now it was the end of October in the mortal world. The Hunt would pursue a person whose blood hummed with the power and energy we humans called magic. It would corner, kill, and dismember the hapless victim, and toss the severed head down a well. Yet looking at the silent personages awaiting their feast atop the ziggurat, I had to wonder: Was my sire the master, or a slave to others' bidding?

This mystery lay beyond my grasp right now. I had to concentrate on what I had come here for. If the crowning feast was the center of the city, then surely my sire would hold his prisoner close to the celebration yet hidden from it. The spirit world did not have shadows but it did have brighter places and places more gray and indistinct. It had places that drew the eye, and places the eye slid away from as water slides off a duck's back.

I found it on the fourth staircase, the broken one. Along the outer rim of the towering crack that split the staircase ran a narrow balcony like an outgrowth on a glassy stone cliff. A figure sat there, unmoving. It was too small for me to see features or even to discern the colors of the clothes it was wearing, although it looked a lot like a dash jacket and he looked like a man. The only way to reach the spot was to be lowered by rope, to climb by ladder, or to fly.

Could I fly? Wasn't I an eru's daughter?

I turned my thoughts inward, searching through my body for a   181 memory of wings, but I remained stubbornly Cat, locked into the mortal flesh my mother had given birth to.

So I did the only thing I could: I plotted out a route and hastened toward the broken stair. Once I reached its jagged steps, I raced up them to the point where the huge gash like a notch made by a giant's knife had cut through the stone into the interior of the ziggurat. A bridge no wider than my hand spanned the gap between the sides of the gash; the balcony lay on the other side of the crevice. I balanced across the gulf of air until I reached a flight of floating steps, some of them missing because they, too, were broken.

After clambering up, I paused to catch my breath on a tiny platform not even wide enough to sit on. Above me rose the sheer face of a cliff, as ominous as a wall of ice. A pretty balcony ornamented by ribbons lay above me, and above it rose more cliff. Below me, the cleft fell away into darkness.

Even from halfway within the ziggurat, my doubled vision could still see the top of the pyramid's flat crown, as if part of me still stood inside one of the threads of power and spirit that weave the worlds. Overhead a churning circle of brilliance swirled in the sky. The eye of the gate opened. Howling and roaring, the Wild Hunt spilled back into the spirit world in a boiling mass of turbulent beasts. The layers and levels of the city emptied as all moving things converged on the height. Human-like presences solidified in the eight chairs: four black as obsidian and four white as snow. They had no faces as I recognized a face. Instead they surged with a force I could only describe and feel as hunger.

The horseman reined his mount to a halt in front of the dais. My sire was glowing, ruddy with a surfeit of blood. Slowly he bowed his head. Every line of his body was tense and tight.

Certainty infused me like a bolt of hot anger through my flesh: He hated the creatures who sat in those thrones. He wanted to slash his spear through every watching, waiting presence but could not because eight chains bound him, one to each chair.

Those chains like whips snapped, bringing the horse to its knees.

A voice like a hammer blow cut through him, turning the mounted horseman into a kneeling eru with wings furled as in pain. He knelt before them. Blood is power because blood binds.

A prince among slaves is still a slave.

He hadn't been talking about Andevai. He had been talking about himself.

"Give us what is ours." The eight personages spoke in one voice. "As you are required to do, because you are bound with the blood of the last feast, and because we bind you with the blood of this feast through the coming year."

The Hunt was merely the conduit. The courts could not walk into the mortal world, so only their servants could bring them the mortal blood they craved.

The blood of the sacrifice poured out of a hundred wounds. Through the chains of binding they sucked the fresh blood of the kill out of his flesh and into theirs.

I licked the air. I tasted the blood of the kill, so rich and sweet, laced with the spice of power, the salt of life. My hunger swelled together with the hunger of all the many presences, the denizens of the spirit courts. The force of their ravenous appetites built like the front of a storm. I took a step, thinking to race back across the bridge that spanned the cleft and regain the staircase, for surely I could rush up to the height and claw in to take my share before they had drained it all.

An unseen person coughed as though waking from a dusty and uneasy doze. The cough startled me back to my own self as I remembered who I was and why I was here.

"Vai? Can you hear me? Is that you?"

"Catherine?" His voice was hoarse.

The ribbon-ornamented balcony above me could only be reached by a skeleton of what had once been a stair-rail as delicate as crystalline branches. Rungs and railings had been shattered by savage blows to make the stairs unusable. I didn't need stairs. I checked my sword to make sure it was secure, found a fingerhold on a jaggedly broken rung, and scrambled up. The weight of the pack threw off my balance, but I was determined. A presence loomed over me.

He said, "Give me your arm. Reach up."

I did so blindly, slipping as I let go. A callused grip caught my wrist. He hauled me over the side and to my feet. His hands on my waist were like fire, I felt them so. His beard was a little unkempt. Streaks of powdery dust smeared his right cheek.

"Catherine." His voice was balm on my yearning heart.

I dislodged his grasp and retreated to the edge of the balcony. The white rock wall behind him was pitted with gouges and holes. A frail ladderlike stair, leading up the cliff face to the next level, had also been smashed. From the far side of the balcony, the cleft cut away deep into the heart of the massive structure, shearing away into the inky depths.

It was strange he was so disheveled and dust-stained when we stood on a spotless white balcony with ribbons streaming off the railing. His trousers were ripped at one knee. A cuff on his dash jacket had torn, and ragged slashes raked through the fabric of its left shoulder, although no blood stained the cloth. The smell of mortal blood lay heavily on him, yet he might be my sire, flown down to confound me with blood still coating his tongue.

"Show me your navel!"

He turned his back on me. "I'll let you find it yourself, if you can tell me how many buttons this jacket has."

"Are you telling me all your jackets are cut to the same pattern? For if they are, then that one has fourteen."

He turned back with a suspicious frown that made him look a little like the mansa. "After all, I am reminded you might have counted them. You've assaulted me before in the guise of my wife."

"Are you saying my sire has tried to seduce you more than that one time in the carriage?"

"How could you know about that?"

"Such secrets are best left unspoken within hearing of they who can see and hear all."

He took a step back, halting beside an object I had mistaken for a boulder but that I now realized was the bundle of stolen clothes, food, and leather bottles from Salt Island. Such a bolt of joy flooded through me that I had to struggle to catch my heart before it crashed right out of my chest. Only Vai would have thought to drag the bundle with him out of the coach. His sword lay sheathed on the ground. I was almost certain my sire could not touch cold steel.

He thought *I* was my sire.

I shrugged off the pack to ease my shoulders. "You claimed you would always know where I was. So I would think you would know this is me, Vai. Who else can carry my sword?"

"There are many things I am no longer quite so sure of." His wary gaze made me cautious, and made me bitter, for I could see my sire's abduction had injured him in an intangible way.

"What was the first thing you said to me, when we first met?"

His lips curled into the scornful sneer I had seen too often in the first days of our acquaintance. "Easy enough to tell. When I saw you that night coming down the stairs, I thought it was the other half of my soul coming to greet me. But I've spoken those words aloud more than once. You might have overheard them."

I raised an eyebrow, trying to mimic his disdain. "Yes, that's lovely and romantical, Vai, but that isn't the first thing you actually said to me."

"Ah. Something about the theater, then." He ran a finger down the line of his beard. "That you're not cut out to be an actress."

"If I'm no actress, then surely you should know I must be me. Yet you stand there with no welcoming embrace! Since you cannot recall your exact words, let me remind you. You said that I might have the looks to be in theater, but not the skill."

"Did I? A truthful statement, you must admit."

I had meant to tease him into recognizing me, but his comment chased all thoughts of teasing from my mind as curiosity burned instead. "Why did you praise my looks? With Bee around, it's a compliment no young man ever threw my way. Bee always dazzled them all."

His rigid posture relaxed. He closed the distance between us and cupped my face in his hands. His fingers had the roughness of a laborer's, but his touch was gentle. He examined my windblown hair and dirt-smudged skin.

"All the better for me that they were blind."

I tried not to look gratified—certainly this was not the place for it—but a blush warmed my cheeks regardless.

"I've always wondered what you thought when you first saw me." His hands slipped down to grasp my hands as he preened just a little with the lift of his chin and the squaring of his shoulders.

I felt obliged to prod him. "I thought you weren't as handsome as you so obviously thought you were."

A laugh crinkled at the corners of his eyes without quite making it to his mouth. "How quickly did you realize you were mistaken?"

"Oh, Vai," I breathed. "I was so afraid I wouldn't find you."

I threw my arms around him just as he crushed my body against his. At first I simply held on, letting my heart beat into the rhythm of his. It felt so good to embrace him. When I tilted back my head to look at him, he pressed kisses on my eyes. I pressed my mouth to his throat. Hot blood pulsed beneath my lips, so close I could have ripped through to it with a single bite and joined in the feast now consuming the thoughts and attention of the spirit courts. I shook myself away, pulling out of his arms.

"We have to go," I said. "The courts will finish feasting and remember you. And what if the tide of a dream washes through and catches us?"

"We're safe from tides here. The walls ward the pit."

"What pit?"

The mocking curve of his lips made me shudder. "Your sire threw me into this pit. The creatures swarmed after me, too many for me to fight off. I climbed up here just ahead of them and smashed both stairs with my cold steel. Since they can't climb, they can't reach me. I would be dead if I had not grabbed that bundle of provisions out of the coach."

"I stole all that when I was imprisoned on Salt Island."

"That's what kept me alive. But I've consumed all the food and drink." He knelt to rummage through my pack. Opening one of the flasks, he took a thirsty swig, then a more measured swallow. After, he offered it to me.

I shook my head. "I drank my fill at the gate."

"No food?"

"None. The mansa found us before we had made all our preparations."

"When did you encounter the mansa? I suppose that is a tale to be told later." He emptied the pack, nodding with approval when he found my sewing kit and some of his carpentry tools. But it was his shaving kit and the little box that held sheaths that made him stare. "Lord of All, Catherine, I must say you are well prepared for adventure of one sort or another."

It is an odd thing to know you stand close to death and yet laugh.

What part of my thoughts he read from my expression I did not know, but his gaze softened. "You never give up, do you, my sweet Catherine?"

"Never. While the courts are busy with their feast, we can go back the way I came, across the bridges and balconies to the ledge, and then back through the jade gate."

"We can't escape by their own paths. Some will scent me and come after me. They are faster than I am. The only reason I'm alive is that they can't climb, and I got up here before they caught me."

"They weren't saving you for Hallows' Night? Maybe after the feast they won't be hungry for a while."

He wiped a hand across his brow, smearing a fine white dust across his skin. "I am scarcely likely to take that chance. It's safer for me to assume they will kill me the moment they get hold of me. But what do you mean by bridges and balconies?" Bands of exhaustion shadowed his eyes, yet he studied me with a look of concern, as if my situation worried him far more than his own dire straits. "Are your eyes veiled by their illusions?"

I rested a hand against his cheek. His skin seemed dry and warm. I hoped he wasn't getting feverish. "Don't you see the city? It's beautiful, just as I thought it would be. All the ribbons and rainbows and bridges and fine white spires and the huge ziggurat with the feasting personages in their elegant robes...however horrible their meal..."

He gathered me against him. "You're seeing an illusion, love. Close your eyes."

I shut my eyes. At first I could not think past the sensation of his arms around me and the whisper of his lips against my hair. There was an odd pressure, like a dense jacket of air tucked tightly against his body, that reminded me of the way air felt just before a storm swept in. I swallowed, and my ears popped. My sword tingled.

I was feeling Vai's cold magic.

"I thought you had no magic in the spirit world," I whispered.

"I thought so, too. But in the spirit world it just lies so tightly against my body that I can't reach with it and thus can't weave magic here. Now keep your eyes shut, love. Here in the pit, your eyes lie to you. See with your heart and your body. They'll never lie to you."

His voice was a coaxing murmur. He could have talked me into any-thing.

He had, hadn't he? In Expedition he had known I was attracted to his handsome face and inviting body, so he had used words and food to persuade me that what I felt for him was love.

"Catherine, you're not paying attention. We're not standing in a city. It's a pit."

"Hush." I pushed my awareness of him down as I listened to the story the wind was telling me. A salty dust tickled my nose. Wind scoured empty slopes, spraying grains of dirt. A weight like hot, dry-ing brine masked my face.

"The cleft is a gate," I whispered. "All the movement in the city eddies around a hidden gate, like water swirling around a submerged and open mouth that's sucking water into it. It's as if we have one foot in the spirit world and one in the mortal world. Dust and salt and sand are blowing in from the mortal world. Gather everything up. I think we can just walk out of here through this hidden gate."

"I see no gate." He released me. "Of course, I didn't dare shed my blood to look for one. Anyway, the hunters of my village only know how to cross through standing stones, and then only on cross-quarter days. I have no means of marking time here."

"I'm a spiritwalker, Vai. I can cut gates between the two worlds and bring you with me whether you've shed blood or not as long as you slip through before the gate closes behind me. I can feel there's a gate already half open, right off this balcony."

Together, we sorted through the gear to divide it between the two of us. He tied the carpentry apron securely around his body, then scooped up a handful of glittering dust.

I shouldered the pack. "Hold my right hand. Keep your sword drawn."

I sliced a shallow cut on my forearm. Where the wall of the cleft cut deeper into the base of the ziggurat, I smeared my blood. Grit stung my eyes as I pushed through, pulling Vai with me right through the rock.

Hot sunlight poured its heat over my face. We stood at the base of a crumbling mine shaft. Sun blazed through the opening above. It was brutally hot. Sweat drenched me just from the effort of standing and breathing. Around lay discarded pickaxes, awls, and baskets, as well as a pair of sleds on runners, heaped with raw salt. Horizontal shafts shot off in different directions, fading into gloom.

"Lord of All," murmured Vai at my back. "We're at the bottom of a salt mine."

By the flavor of the air and the presence of the sun, I knew we had crossed back into the mortal world.

19

"Which way did we come from?" I whispered, trying to get my bearings.

He indicated a trail of scattered salt receding into the darkness of one of the horizontal shafts, then opened a hand to reveal the last bits of the dust he had gathered. "I left a trail to follow. This seems too easy."

"Except for being stuck at the bottom of a mine shaft with no rope or ladder."

He looked up. "I may be able to cut hand- and footholds up the shaft. It's cursed hot. I wonder if this is old Mali. Imagine if we have come to the birthplace of my ancestors..."

"To the very place where the salt plague began," I whispered, shuddering.

A shuffling *slip-slop* echoed out of the darkness.

Slow as molasses, a creature emerged from the gloom of one of the other tunnels. Its steps had the creak of an elder's, but its body was not frail, only stiff. It had the form of a perfectly proportioned person, not ugly or beautiful, neither male nor female, but all white. Not pale-haired and pale-skinned as northern Celts are, but the stark white of a being whose flesh has solidified into salt, like a salter in the final, morbid phase of the disease. Its eyes were salt-white and blind.

I knew what it was although I had never read a description of such a thing in the tales penned by travelers. Who could see such a sight and live to speak of it? No one could.

It was a ghoul.

A tongue licked the air as it tasted the scent of mortal blood.

The lick of its tongue scraped me despite the gap between us. The blood congealing on the cut on my arm began to flow as if it were being suckled out of my body. A drop of my blood struck the ground, its impact shivering a vibration through the soles of my feet. A bell-like clangor echoed through the tunnels, followed by a dead silence as the ghoul halted.

Chiming cries echoed from the tunnels. Unseen tongues licked the air, tasting for blood. Pebbles and dirt spat down on our heads. Far above us ghouls clustered at the mine's mouth, eager to taste blood. One walked right off the cliff. It plunged through the spinning dust motes. Vai yanked me back as it hit with a sickening crunch. The ghoul heaved itself up, unbroken, unmarred.

"We have to go back," said Vai.

I hadn't known they could move so fast. They were on us, me beating at clawing hands and biting mouths. Cold steel stopped them in their tracks but it did not turn them to salt, not as the cut of my blade had dissolved the salters who had blundered into the sea on the beach at Salt Island.

"Vai! Move!"

Bell voices rang down the mines. Too late I heard a scrape behind us.

A ghoul staggered out of the darkness and lunged at Vai. Just as its mouth was about to close on his arm, he thrust his blade between its jaws. The blade caught its teeth a finger's breadth from his sleeve.

I rammed into the ghoul with a shoulder. Fiery Shemesh! It was like shifting rock. It moved just enough for him to jerk back out of reach. It did not claw at me because now the advancing ghouls were all fixed on him, not on me.

"Catherine! I can't see the gate."

More thumped down from above. The breath of the ghouls was like the burrowing tongue of a craving that can never be eased. They would never stop coming. They swarmed toward him, but I had the scent of the spirit world in my lungs, all the gate I needed.

"Vai! Take my hand!" I thrust wildly to give them pause, then dragged Vai backward.

The memory of sun vanished as we crossed the gate. We staggered to a halt, panting, on the balcony where he had taken refuge. The city spread around us in its false beauty. Winds rippled color through ribbons. Bridges vaulted in graceful, intertwined arches, slender spans spun out of gold and silver. I swayed, a hand pressed to my sweaty forehead. A scraping shuffle sounded from the broken staircase as an unseen creature clawed uselessly at the rock.

"No! No! No!" I cried, ready to burst with sheer raging fury. "I'll kill them! *I'll kill them!*"

"Love, love. It's all right." He embraced me. I wasn't sure if he was comforting me, or comforting himself by comforting me. "They can't climb without stairs or ramps. They lack both the agility and the strength. We're safe on this ledge."

"We're not safe! We have enough water for a day, at most. And no food! No way out—"

"Catherine! Enough!"

I broke off, my breath ragged.

His dark gaze met mine. "I saw a salter one time in Expedition, when I went out to the country with Kofi. It was before you came to Aunty's boardinghouse. I saw her beg her brother to kill her. Then I saw her no longer able to speak, dead of mind but still alive in her body, a ravening beast. Worse, for beasts have purpose and their own sort of intelligence. Her family used spears to push her mindless flesh into a pit, but spears did not kill her. They poured salt water over her, and that did kill her, only she shrieked in such agony I have never forgotten the sound."

I would not look away even though I did not want to hear what he was going to say next.

His voice emerged in a harsh whisper. "Promise me, Catherine. Promise me you will kill me cleanly rather than make me suffer that death."

He did not flinch from my answering gaze, nor did his unwavering trust allow me to flinch.

"I promise you," I said, each word a knife in my heart.

He gave a nod so final that my heart squeezed tight with love and terror.

"Now, Catherine, as I was about to say before that unfortunate but understandable venture into the salt mine, I have a plan."

"A plan? What plan?"

"You don't think I've been sitting here with dry maw waiting to die, do you?" He laid out the carpentry apron on the ground. His tools were stowed in pockets, and he removed each one, running his hands over it as if reintroducing himself to its qualities. By the stiffness in his movements and the occasional wince, he was hurting, but I doubted he would ever mention it and I would certainly never dare say a word to him about the shadows under his eyes or the way my sire had effortlessly taken him captive. "I've considered many possible paths, most of which involved your help and some of which involved you being clever enough to bring my carpentry tools."

"They didn't *all* involve me being clever enough to bring your carpentry tools?"

He smiled without looking at me. "Ghouls can't climb, but you and I can."

"There are ghouls on this side, too? I've not seen any."

"They're all ghouls, in their way. What you see as personages in elegant robes, I see as gaunt creatures clawing for my blood. They're not solid on this side, not like the ones we just saw in the mine. Over here they can change their aspect, just as all spirit creatures can do."

The way he set each tool down on the ground precisely in line next to the others told me more than words. He was calming himself through orderly action, methodical, precise, just as the cacica had observed. I could not help but watch his hands, the ones that knew exactly how to do the meticulous work he wanted them to do.

He glanced up as if I had made a noise, then raised an eyebrow in that way that made him look supercilious but that was also, I realized, just a way of showing he was puzzled or concerned. "Catherine?"

My lips parted but no words came out. No words I expected or meant to say.

"I love you so much, Vai."

Had another voice and intelligence spoken through my mouth I would not have been more surprised. His eyes widened, as if I'd blurted out an embarrassing secret he knew he ought not to have heard. Yet the weary slump of his shoulders straightened with new determination as he turned the awl through his fingers and set it down beside the claw hammer. He unrolled the last fold in the heavy leather kit to reveal a set of chisels and a two-bitted hatchet.

"Catherine, can you trust me enough to step blindly off a cliff no matter how it looks to you?"

"Always, Vai. But what is your plan?"

He began to put the tools back. "I've had a lot of time to examine this pit. It is a maze, all connected to this central tower of rock. The maze walls are like low cliffs. If we stay on the walls, they can't get to us."

"They can walk on the bridges and balconies."

"Those are paths within and above the pit. We should be able to climb sideways along the walls all the way to the edge without having to drop to the ground. I've been able to map out a route where it seems there will be plenty of foot- and handholds and a series of ledges where we can rest along the way."

"Are you going to chip out handholds with a chisel and hammer?"

"I likely can't get enough swing on a hammer but we do have them if we need them. We can easily smash stairs, if we need to. We'll stay above and below the ghouls, climb out of the pit, find warded ground, and cross back to the mortal world. We have no money, but we can work our way wherever we need to go with my carpentry and your sewing. So you see, now that we are together, we have everything we need. Are you ready?"

I nodded. He ripped a scrap of cloth from one of the old pagnes and tied it around his neck like a buccaneer's kerchief. Tying the apron back on, he rigged his sword and the hatchet so he could grab them easily. I bound up my skirts, binding my sword and the now-lightened pack across my back. We drained one flask of spring water and, thus fortified, set out.

Handing me a chisel, he said, "Don't look at anything except me."

For once, I had no teasing retort.

We worked our way off the balcony with its decorative ribbons. For the very first part I saw the same thing he did: the uneven face of the cleft. Its manifold protuberances and hand-width shelves were easy to negotiate. But then I had to follow him as onto open air. It was like walking out over a chasm. His shoulders bunching and releasing beneath his jacket became my lodestone. The sweat beading on the back of his neck fascinated me. He had a really beautifully shaped head, brown and lovely.

Watching him helped me not look at my hands groping through

empty air or across illusory vistas that still looked to me like streaming masses of ribbons. Often I shut my eyes and felt along the rugged cliff rather than grow dizzy from the confusion between what I could see and what I could touch.

Hadn't it always been that way with Andevai? When I had first met him, I had seen one man, but I had had to discover the part of himself he kept concealed.

"Catherine, are you paying attention? Don't grab there. Up a little...with your right hand...*there.*"

Often we rested on ledges no wider than my feet, leaning against the rock wall, and I was grateful for each respite because my forearms were beginning to burn and my fingers to get as dry as if they were being sandpapered. But we could not fully relax until we reached what I saw as a polished clamshell of a platform tucked along the curve of an ebony tower. After he smashed the rungs of what looked to me like a glass ladder that led up from below, we sat huddled against the wall and shared half of the water in the second flask. He dozed off, slumped against me. I could not sleep; my hands were smarting and my arms felt numb.

Were the courts still feasting? No movement troubled the bridges and spans and balconies whose complex patterns haunted me. I stared at the beautiful city and I hated it for lying to me. I hated myself for seeing it as beautiful, for believing it must be so because all the tales said it was.

People told so many stories whose fractured truths hid as much as they revealed. What we did not know could hurt us. What we chose to ignore could cause harm, maybe to ourselves and maybe to others.

Vai sighed in his sleep. I rested my head against his. We had come by twists and turns more than halfway to the outer wall. I thought surely I could let him rest for a few more breaths, but then I heard a scuffling and scratching below and above. The rasp of tongues tickled the cut on my arm, and my blood oozed. The cursed creatures were tracking us again.

Vai stiffened, going so tense that I thought he had woken, but he was still asleep. He murmured words in the village dialect he had spoken as a child. Most of the words slipped past, too thickly patois for me to understand. Then he spoke almost desperately. "Don't touch me!"

He jolted awake and shoved me away so roughly that he almost pushed me off the edge.

I grabbed his arms, dragging myself to a stop with his weight. "Vai! It's me. It's Catherine."

He sucked in air. For an instant I was frighteningly certain he did not recognize me. Then all the air went out of him. He pulled an arm out of my grasp and rubbed his eyes.

"What were you dreaming?"

He looked away, jaw clenched. "Nothing."

I pressed a hand on his chest. He flinched.

I sat back, withdrawing my hand. He curled his hands into fists, and I watched him climb the pinnacle of disdain as his expression settled into the scornful arrogance that had so scalded me when we had first been thrown together. One wrong word and he would lash out. Not with his fists—as Auntie Djeneba had once said, "He don' seem like that kind"—but with words meant to cut and intimidate.

"I don't understand how you can see through the illusion," I said soothingly. "I still see the city. The ziggurat is quite splendid if you don't mind knowing you're meant to be the main course at the feast. I'm ready to go on, if you are. You know I trust you, my love."

"We can't get out of this foul pit quickly enough." His voice was harsh, but I understood the anger was not directed at me.

I took a swallow of water and offered him the rest.

He wiped his mouth, his lips so dry they were cracking. "I hear them. They're following us again. There's one gap we have to clear. That gap is the one you described as a moat. But I have a plan for that. If you're sure, Catherine, utterly sure the creatures can't harm you."

"I'm sure," I lied. I could have become an actress in the theater after all, because he did not guess how my heart trembled. "Remember, I was bitten by a salter and not infested. The teeth of the plague can't take hold in my blood."

But even though it was true I could not be harmed by the bite of a human infested with the salt plague, the bite of a ghoul was rumored to be far more potent and virulent. I had to take the chance. Nothing mattered except that we escape, and this was the way we had to do it.

We climbed, sometimes a little up or a little down but always transverse. Once I thought I was moving through a fall of water, only there was no pressure and no current, only grit sifting into my face, the dust and salt of the mortal world. Was this place pitted with gates into salt mines all across the mortal world? Now was not the time to find out.

He had plotted our route well. Had we not had so many narrow ledges on which to take quick rests, I would never have made it, for my arms were beginning to feel they were being squeezed in a vise. Naturally he spoke no word of complaint, just massaged my forearms whenever we halted, although his, too, had become as hard as the rock we clung to. My legs trembled from fatigue, and my buttocks ached from all the pushing up and down and sideways.

He whispered. "Look, love. Look. We've made it to the edge."

Below us a path paved with gems meandered alongside the moat. On its far side rose the outer wall, looking to my eyes like the forbidding face of an ice cliff. On the path roamed the personages of the courts, resplendent in their vivid robes and changeable aspects. Groups flashed along more distant bridges and ramps toward us, as if gathering to hear a poet sing.

Vai unwound the kerchief he'd knotted around his neck. Easing his sword partway out of the sheath, he cut his skin for the first time.

Red blood welled up.

A cry shivered through the air. Dust spattered from the walls.

Vai pressed the kerchief to his wound to sop up the blood. The greedy whispering of the courts scraped the air like fingernails down a chalkboard. Hadn't they had enough blood? Could they ever be satisfied?

"Catherine." He handed me the kerchief, then clambered to where the moat ran narrowest. The liquid in the moat was churned into a froth of pinkish foam like spume bubbling from the mouth of a dying man. I probed with a foot down a wall I could feel but not see, and found a toehold. Easing myself down, I settled my weight on one aching foot; my calf cramped but I had to grit my teeth and endure it. I let go with my upper hand and groped for a lower place to grab. A hand, or claw, slammed up, dislodging my boot.

So I leaped down among them. Cats always land on their feet. I plunged forward, smearing the blood that stained the kerchief onto any surface I could find: their robes, their outstretched hands. I rubbed a speck of blood on the path, feeling dirt beneath my fingers instead of the smooth silver walkway I saw with my eyes.

The fine, elegant people turned on each other in a frenzy. I jammed the kerchief into the gaping jaw of a being wearing the face of a distinguished elderly man and dressed in the formal court clothes a man would have worn a hundred years earlier, all silk and gold-threaded embroidery.

I shoved my way out of the clawing, jibbering crowd as they converged to tear at the one who was suckling on the cloth. A few had enough sense to smell Vai's escape. I raced out in front of them.

The interior maze ended without touching the outer wall. It was this gap we had to cross. He dashed across the moat as if there were no liquid in it and started climbing the outer wall, but he was still within reach of their teeth as he tested a grip. I followed him into the steaming waters, but the molten fire in the moat was an illusion. It was all grainy dirt.

A creature glided toward me. She had the seeming of a woman whose coiled hair was laden with gold coins. I thrust. My sword pierced her. Pain shivered up my arm, but I pushed, leaning my full weight into her.

She shattered, coming apart like a pouch of sand when it is ripped open.

Where the grains soaked into the ground, the veil of illusion cleared. As if through glass, I saw the dusty surface of salt. I smelled the sun of the mortal world, and heard the shrill whistle of wind blowing beneath an empty sky.

"Catherine!"

The exhalation of their breath iced my neck. To climb I had to sheathe my sword. Fear propelled me. I swarmed up the face of the cliff as he hoarsely called directions so I need not pause and look, for if I had hesitated, they would have grabbed me.

"Up three hands, now right, another hand farther, so you see it? There! Your foot to where your knee is. In a half step. There, that's right. Push up, it's wide enough to hold you. See my left foot? Let go with your left hand. You grab where my foot was..."

So we climbed, me sweating from the pain that flamed in my arms and hands. I was so exhausted I was shaking, but I was not going to lose him.

He disappeared over the rim, then reappeared to haul me up beside him. I shrugged out of the pack. We lay panting side by side. The length of my blade was pressed into me by the weight of his leg alongside mine. I rested on my back, staring at the pewter bowl of the sky and what appeared to me now as the high white wall of the palace rising behind my head exactly as I had seen it before I had entered. Vai lay on his stomach, and he appeared to be looking over the edge of an escarpment as he stared into the pit we had escaped. I had to shut my eyes because I could not tell which direction was up. I felt dizzy. His ragged breathing was all the sign I needed to know that he, too, was fighting the toll taken by our exertions.

"We've got to keep moving," I said. "We've got to reach the jade doors and retrieve Queen Anacaona's head. Someone is sure to come after us."

"We need to retrieve *what*?" Vai sat up as if he had finally woken out of a bad dream.

I opened my eyes. "I'll explain later. There's a jade door with warded ground somewhere along this exterior. We can cross there."

We stumbled to our feet as I hoisted the pack. Vai stowed the tools and slung on the carpenter's apron. His face was gray with exhaustion, but he trudged forward stubbornly. My entire body hurt as we staggered along the rim of the palace.

I wanted to ask Vai if he saw the white stone walls rising beside us, if he saw a plaza stretching to all sides like a sheep-mown pasture, but the effort of forming words was too great. All I could do was look ahead, hoping we would soon reach the jade door and its warded ground.

A cloud of crows swept past, flying as before a blow. Wind sheared across my back. I faltered, looking over my shoulder. A wrath of clouds boiled toward us. Lightning flashed, although no thunder sounded. Rain lashed the ground in sheets.

I had seen that storm before. I knew what it portended.

I grabbed Vai's hand. "It's my sire coming. We've got to run."

Light flashed on the horizon ahead of us. It splintered into a smoky tide like the crests of multiple waves tumbling toward us: a dragon's dream.

Vai's hand tightened on mine as he sucked in a harsh breath.

We were caught between Hunt and dream, between death and obliteration.

A plain black coach rolled up, pulled by four white horses whose hooves did not quite touch the ground. A coachman sat on the front of the box. He had the white skin and short, spiky, lime-whitened hair of a man of Celtic birth. He wore a plain black coat, thin leather gloves, and a hat that he tipped up with the handle of his whip, greeting us. The footman hanging on at the back of the coach was no man but an eru; she appeared as a woman with black skin, short black hair, a third eye in the center of her forehead, and her wings neatly furled. She did not let go of the coach. Instead the door swung open. My sire beckoned from the interior.

"Best hurry," he said with a calm smile. "This coach is a refuge, a sort of warded ground all on its own. The tide is coming in fast. You'll be safe inside here."

His sober dash jacket and neat black trousers made him look like a humble clerk on the way to his day's work at his master's offices. You would never have guessed he had recently hunted down and killed some poor soul in the mortal world, and then been forced to bow before the spirit courts and have all that power ripped from him to feed them instead. Not until you looked into his eyes. His gaze had as much mercy as a knife in the dark.

"Do you imagine we believe you?" asked Vai in the tone of a man at his supper who has just been told that the crust of bread set before him is the haunch of beef he requested.

"I imagine you have no choice but to join me. I have something of yours, Cat." He indicated the Taino basket in which I kept the cacica's head.

"How could you get that?" I demanded.

"I saw you hang it on the tree. Best hurry, Daughter."

I looked at Vai, and Vai looked at me.

A smile brightened his weary face too briefly, but it was enough to strengthen me. There is more than one way to skin a cat. There were two doors in the coach, one that opened onto the spirit world and one that opened into the mortal world.

Vai nodded.

I swung up into the interior of the coach and gripped my sire's arms so he could not slam the door in Vai's face and thus leave him outside at the mercy of the tide.

"Father! I missed you so much!" I leaned in to kiss him on the cheek, my lips warm against his cold, cold skin.

I had the intense pleasure of watching my sire blink in bewildered astonishment.

Before he could react, I snatched the basket off the seat and slung it over my body. Then I clambered past him. Grabbing the latch, I pushed down with all my strength.

It did not budge. It did not shift at all.

I hissed, "Open up, I beg you."

The latch's eyes glimmered into life as two stripes of light on brass. Its mouth was a flat line. It said nothing. And it stayed stubbornly locked.

The other door slammed shut. The coach lurched forward, swinging in a wide turn. I tumbled onto the upholstered bench opposite my sire as Vai pushed past me and, in his turn, grabbed the latch. Sparks spat with a cracking cascade of pops. With a grunt of pain Vai hit the bench and sat down hard next to me. He swore as he shook his hand.

My sire touched fingers to the spot I had kissed. "A transparent ploy. Truly, I thought better of you, Cat. You might have known I would have anticipated such a move."

He rapped on the ceiling of the coach with his cane.

"Back to the pit," he said in a conversational tone I knew the coachman could hear. His gaze settled on me. "You've done well, Daughter. You've proven you are strong and stubborn, but still not quite smart enough. You're still not quite thinking things through. Affection weakens you. I gave him a chance to survive so he would still be living when you found him. This time I will dump him straight into the pit. I don't need him any longer. Let me assure your tender heart that he will feel no pain once they've drained his blood, for the blood of mortals is the force that gives the courts power over the rest of us. He'll become something like them, only without a mind."

201

I hadn't known I could move so fast. My sword slid like lightning out of its sheath. I knew exactly where to aim: up under his ribs at his heart.

Vai slammed into me, jostling my point so it skipped off the upholstery and lodged in a corner. I cursed and tugged it free.

"A killing blow will kill you, not him!" He kicked past my legs and shoved open the door that led back into the spirit world. "Stay where you are, Catherine."

"Vai!"

"Better this than the salt plague, love."

He jumped out of the rushing coach into the path of the incoming tide of light.

I did not think. I leaped after him.

The dragon's dream roared down over us in a rainbow of violent colors. The call of a bell split the world, air from water, fire from stone, flesh from spirit. The vibration rang up through the ground and down from the sky until there was no existence except the tremor of sound shivering the entire world as if the world were the drum being beaten.

I threw my arms around him, and I kissed him. Let his embrace be the last thing I knew. He held me tightly. A cloak of magic rippled from around his body to envelop me as within wings.

The tide ripped over us like sea spray followed by the pounding of a huge crashing wave. We were driven down as an abyss opened. Every part of existence yawed sideways, then tipped upside down. We fell into smoke as the world around us vanished.

20

Death wasn't all bad, because it felt a lot like kissing Vai. Our embrace distracted me for longer than it should have. Then I remembered what had happened. Still clutching him, I broke off the kiss.

Inhaled.

I could not breathe.

I could not breathe.

I could not breathe.

An undertow sucked me down.

The abyss of the past is a black chasm. It is too dark to see clearly, yet its waters run all through us.

I am six years old. In the drowning depths of the Rhenus River, my papa and mama are dying. As the water closes over my head, my mother's strong hand slips out from mine. She has lost me, and I've lost her. I open my mouth to cry for her, but all that rushes in is smoke.

We were going to die in the smoke unless I could find a gate and cut our way out.

"Mama," I whispered, clawing my way through dense fog toward a half-glimpsed beacon.

For there she was, she and Daniel, in the shadow of the ice cliff. They were striding across a stony shore to meet the men who were pushing a boat down to the ice-gray waters for their escape.

"Mama," I said, louder, finding strength in desperation.

She halted, dragging Daniel to a stop. "Did you hear something?"

He looked up at the face of the ice. "Just the wolves and the wind."

"No, something else." She rested a hand on her belly and extended the other arm as if hoping to touch something she could not quite see. "A child. I heard a child calling to me."

Blessed Tanit, keep me in your heart. Do not let me die.

I will not die.

I bit my lip hard enough to raise blood as I reached for and grasped the memory of her hand.

21

"*Catherine!* Stop fighting me! You're impossible to keep hold of when you wriggle like this."

I slithered out of a grip that was dragging me through icy water, but my numb limbs had no strength. The tide dragged me under as it hauled at my skirts.

A man lifted me above the water. I spewed all the cursed salt water I had swallowed. My bitten lip stung. I sluggishly realized that Vai was carrying me out of the sea. He dumped me onto a stony shore, then slapped me repeatedly on the back as I retched.

I found my voice, although it was sadly thin and mewling. "Why must I always swallow seawater? It tastes so foul."

Vai collapsed beside me onto the pebbled strand. He fumbled to unbuckle himself from his carpenter's apron, wheezing as he gulped in air.

I thought the weight of the pack was going to crush me. Rolling onto my side took all my strength. The hard stones felt heavenly because they were solid. The sea sloshed up to tickle my boots, then receded. Fiery Shemesh, but I was freezing!

The wind was coarse and unforgivingly cold.

Vai was still wheezing. I tugged my arms out of the straps to shed the pack. With the sodden basket bumping on my rear, I crawled over to him, only to realize he was not wheezing but laughing in a hoarse sort of way.

He smiled at me. *Smiled!*

His smile acted as an infusion of hope. My lips twitched, fighting upward.

"Look!" He gestured.

A blustery gray sea stretched away from the shore. Across the channel, barely visible under a haze of cloud, rose the blue-dark shore of another land. But that was not the strange thing. A ship glided atop the waves, three-masted, sails unfurled but unmoving despite the stinging breeze. As I gaped, wondering why I could not see any sailors racing about on the deck or climbing the masts, one of the sails began to ripple, then the second, and then the third. Where there hadn't been one before, a man appeared halfway up the mainmast.

It was illusion, taking form in front of my eyes as he wove cold magic with a speed and dexterity that astounded me.

"We've been washed back into the mortal world, love." The ship vanished as he sat up and spat. "Gah. What I wouldn't do for a glass of my mother's hoarhound tea sweetened with honey. Catherine! You're shuddering."

He pulled me against him. I could have sworn warmth radiated from his body, although it was hard to feel anything. My wool skirt clung to my legs, the fabric crackling as if it were actually beginning to freeze.

"There's shelter," he said. "Walk with me."

The shoreline was stony beach. A little peninsula of land sloped up to a cliff of ice that loomed over us like fate. There was no vegetation, nothing but rock and ice and sand. Crevices and canyons had dug staircases into the ice cliff, pocked with boulders. On the tiny peninsula, lying between ice cliff and icy sea, a deposit of huge rocks formed a low cave.

"See if there's any driftwood to build a fire," he said. "The cave is the sort of place it might get swept into and caught."

"I c-c-can't build a fire."

"Did you pack no flint?"

"You'll k-k-kill the fire."

"As long as I can work cold magic, I will not freeze to death, but you will. Do you hear me, Catherine? Tell me you understand what I'm saying."

The wind gusted out of the north, sweeping over the lip of the ice. A voice flew on that wind, dangerous and wild. A howl rose.

206   I staggered to a halt. "Do you hear that?"

"Come on, love. Just a little farther. We'll see if there's fuel for a fire and then I'll go back and fetch our gear..."

Wolves.

We hadn't escaped. The Hunt was after us. My sire had already found us. What did he want from me? Or was he just angry that I had rescued first my cousin and then my husband from him?

The presence of beasts stalking a person concentrates the mind wonderfully. The landscape before me settled and I knew where I was. I had reached for my mother, and somehow the connection between us had brought me to a place she had once walked. "They left the other boat in the cave. We've got to drag it down to the water and get out of here before the wolves come."

His grip tightened on my arm. "Love, you're raving. There's no wolves, and no boat..." I curled my lips in a silent snarl that made his eyes widen. "But let's just go see about the boat."

We picked our way up the slope and in under the dank shadow. A huge slab of a boulder made a weighty roof, giving the cave the look of a crude shelter of stone built by a giant. I cleared debris off a hump to reveal canvas stretched taut over a rowboat. The boat had been turned over and raised off the ground on stones. Two oilcloth bundles with oars and oarlocks had been tucked along the underside of the benches, together with an unexpected bounty of a spare flint, an iron pot, and a hunter's knife.

"Lord of All. How did you know this would be here?"

"My mother reached out to me from the past and pulled me here." I dragged the canvas off the boat. It was big enough to seat six men, but I thought we could handle it. Howls drifted off the height. "We have to get out of here before the wolves come. Can't you hear them?"

"It's just the wind." He rubbed my hands between his. "You need to warm yourself at a fire before we try to cross the water. Your lips are blue. People can die just from exposure to cold."

Through chattering teeth, I spoke. "You have to believe me about my mother."

He paused, then resumed chafing my hands. "I don't see why not. The chain that binds our marriage pulled you to me in Expedition."

"That was the machinations of General Camjiata and James Drake."

"Yes, that as well, but didn't you ever wonder why you found me so easily the moment you stepped onto the jetty? The chain that binds us drew you to me. You'll always be bound to your parents as well. We'll rig these ropes so we can pull the boat over, then haul it down on the canvas. But once we get it down there with everything in it, then you must promise me if there are no wolves you'll build a fire for long enough to warm up and dry out that wool a little bit, and my coat and gloves, which you so wisely brought. By the way the light falls I'm pretty sure it's late winter or early spring. It's still morning, so we'll have time to cross before dusk. Catherine? Are you listening?"

"Yes," I said, for the sound of his voice was so comforting.

We rigged the rope, flipped the boat, and dragged it over the stone beach to the water. The work warmed me but at the same time sucked all energy from me. Afterward, it was all I could do to stay upright, leaning on the stern, as he fetched our gear and arranged it as ballast. The cold gnawed through my flesh to the bone. He set the oarlocks and oars. Out of the dripping pack he unfolded the winter coat I had carried just for him and put it on me. He looked me up and down. He had the worst frown on his face, startling in its intensity. I had never seen that expression on him before. I had no idea what to make of it.

"Catherine." He spoke my name with what sounded like anger. "You are now returning to the cave. I'll build a fire and leave so you can light it and get warm..."

A howl skirled down on the wind. I watched him register the sound. His brow wrinkled. Anger flickered in the twitch of his cheeks. His gaze lifted to the rim of the ice shelf.

High up on the path, three shaggy wolves nosed into view. Four more wolves were already most of the way down a canyon path that led from the rim to the beach. In our effort to shove the boat to the shore, we hadn't noticed them. They were huge. I smelled their hunger.

Desperation sheared through me. I braced and shoved, but the boat shifted barely a finger's breadth. "We've got to go..."

"Wait."

My cane stung my leg, woken by Vai's cold magic. A change in pressure made my ears pop. I dropped to my knees, sure I was about to be slammed into the ground.

A *crack* ripped through the air. A weird moaning noise followed, succeeded by a rushing whoosh, and then by a rumble. His mouth curved into the sort of smile a man gives to his hated opponent when he knows he has won and can rub it in the other man's face. It was the smile that had driven Drake to hate him so much that the fire mage had tried to get revenge on Vai through me.

"Move!" he said with a laugh, throwing his shoulder to the boat.

The rumble grew to a roar. Vai slung me into the boat and hopped in, scrambling to the oars. He rowed hard. I turned to look behind.

Ice calved off the high cliff. Caught in the collapse, the wolves tumbled and vanished into the crash of ice. The boom of the avalanche filled the world as it buried the canyon. White mist boiled up in sheets.

"Brace yourself, Catherine."

A rolling tongue of ice and frozen snow spilled across the tiny peninsula, hissed over the beach, and slumped into the water with a crackling roar like a hundred muskets going off at once. A wave pitched us backward, but Vai kept the boat steady as we were driven partway across the channel. Out in the middle of the water, the choppy waves and wind caught us in a buffeting pitch and yaw. He set to, rowing hard, as I shivered inside his wet wool coat.

"Can you row, Catherine? It would warm you up."

Looking at his bare hands on the oars made me want to weep. Cold had dug its claws all the way to my heart. Strangely, the bitter air and cold spray off the sea had no effect on him. If anything, he seemed invigorated. "I c-c-can try, but I haven't before."

"Then not in these conditions, love."

The rocking and tipping of the rowboat was beginning to make me feel queasy. "Can't you make a wind to blow us?"

"You don't want wind out on the open water in a rowboat. Anyway, it's not like that. Wind can't be confined or channeled. I can shift masses of air and freeze rain in the clouds so it falls as sleet or hail…" He glanced past me, eyes widening.

More wedges of ice shook free from the ice shelf. Mist sprayed. The sound of their crashing fall rolled over the channel. A swell rose under us, then a second and a third. He swore in a low voice. I huddled in the wet coat. It would be easier just to go to sleep.

"I didn't mean that to happen, and I'm not sure what just did." He frowned at me as if I had said something to offend him. "Talk to me, Catherine. Tell me about your father."

Fury shook me awake. "I never want to speak of him again!"

"I don't mean the one who sired you. I meant your father. Daniel Hassi Barahal. The one whose portrait is in your locket. Did you see your father on the beach?"

My father.

Words emerged, although I scarcely knew what I meant to say. "They had just come down from the ice shelf. They were fighting wolves. There was a dead man all bloody. I think his name was Gaius. The Baltic Ice Expedition ended in disaster. Most of the explorers died on the ice, but some survived. Most of the other attempts to explore the ice have ended with the expeditions vanishing forever. I wonder if they accidentally cross into the spirit world and get eaten there. Probably it was just wolves who caught them."

"Are you suggesting this boat is left over from the Baltic Ice Expedition?" he asked in the calmest voice imaginable, although he looked annoyed and stern in that way he had when he was overcome by a strong emotion. "Tell me about that, Catherine. Keep talking."

If there was one thing I was good at, it was talking. So I kept talking, even if I stumbled and lost my train of thought. He persisted in asking questions, prodded and poked in a verbal sort of way since obviously because he was rowing the entire time he could not actually poke and prod me, although I had a vague memory that I ought to wish he ought to be able to, but that was a long time ago and anyway it was so very cold and my body ached so much and I was so very tired that eventually I lapsed into silence.

We bumped up on a shore in the lee of a tiny inlet. Ice rimed the shallow water where a stream burbled through a tumble of rocks. A blanket of snow carpeted the hollows, but the wind had swept most of the land clean. There were no trees and little vegetation, only lichen and moss. In the sheltered lee of forgotten boulders and clefts in the earth, waxy-leafed plants spread, laced with frost. Nothing stirred, not even birds a-wing.

Pull up the boat. Turn it over and stow the oars. Fill the bottles with stream water. Walk. Walk. Walk.

I did what he told me to do, as a goblin's automaton obeys. Was that how the coachman functioned? Was the coachman truly of a goblin's making, or was that just a story he had told me? Would I ever find out?

There was no wood or we would have stopped to make a fire, even though Vai would have had to leave me. By following the stream, he found an animal trail that he tracked like a hunter.

We rounded a boulder to find ourselves face-to-face with a huge woolly rhinoceros. Its twinned horns dipped as it gave a growling snort. A muzzy instinct woke in the pit of my stomach that the creature could trample and gore us. Vai placed himself between me and the animal. He spoke words I did not know in a cadence whose rhythms sailed past, as if he was politely greeting the beast. It snorted as in answer. As Vai eased us past, it silently watched us go.

For an eternity we walked. Once we ran across a fire pit ringed with stone, sheltered on the lee side of a slope, but there was nothing to burn except straggling patches of gorse, so he decided we should go on.

It was just so hard to put one foot in front of the other because I kept staggering off the path and catching myself at the last moment on the point of my cane. An idea grew in my head, a very compelling idea that I ought to have thought of long before.

"I would be warmer if I took off these wet clothes," I said.

He was striding up a slope amid winter-whitened grasses and hardy sedge. The thought of trudging after him up such a brutal incline made my legs congeal, so I stopped moving and fumbled at the coat.

He ran back to me. "No! Absolutely not, Catherine." He kept talking as he dragged me along. "Do you see the prints? There have been hunters or trappers here. The track leads to a place people go. There's likely a sheltered spot where they camp."

He broke off as we reached the top of the slope. I really wanted to find a small hole to crawl into. Instead I looked up.

The land ended at a flat shoreline. Beyond it silver waters spread like a mirror. The distant haze of the far shore melted into the encroaching dusk. Maybe there were trees on the other side, but I couldn't be sure. The near shore was dusted with snow, so the whole land radiated a white sheen. A wide stream was crackled over with a skin of ice. Someone had built a crude wooden pier where the stream flowed into the wide water. Just inland from the pier stood a shed, and next to it huddled a small log house with a sod roof. A rowboat had been tipped onto its side under the low eaves of the hut.

He thought it was a good idea to go down. I slogged along, steered by his grip. My sword flared as he shaped bulbs of cold fire. A door gave way to a narrow entry hall with a stall for animals, where he dumped our gear. Inside a second door lay a bench and table and a bed tucked into an alcove with cupboards built in beneath. The hearth was empty but for a large kettle and roasting spit. The room was cold, windowless, and dark, with barely enough room to turn around in.

While he explored, I drifted, reflexively setting my cane and the basket on the table. Hadn't I been carrying a pack before? I couldn't remember how he had come to have it. Fortunately I was no longer cold. His exclamation roused me. He was pulling skins and furs from the cupboards beneath the bed.

"This is a hunters' refuge. A place men can take shelter if they're caught out in bad weather. There's bound to be a village within a few days' travel. My village keeps the same sort of shelters." He glanced at me. "Catherine, now you must take off your wet clothes."

My fingers were too numb to unfasten buttons.

He undressed me, dried me roughly, and wrapped me up on the bed in the furs. Then he went outside with the kettle, brought it back full, and laid wood onto the hearth although obviously he could not light it. Our wet clothes and gear he spread over the table and bench.

He stripped and got in with me. His skin was so warm that after a while I began to hurt all over. Chafing my hands, my cheeks, my legs, he talked a stream of words that I did not fully understand except that I loved to hear him speak. I began to shiver, and at length the shivering subsided as a frail glow of warmth took root in my frozen heart.

Blessed Tanit! We had escaped the spirit world! We were going to live!

As I relaxed, so did he, and I slid into a sleep without dreams.

22

I opened my eyes to darkness. A night breeze whistled in the chimney, but nothing else stirred. The air was wintry cold except where we were bundled warmly together, skin to skin. I lay for a while, wondering about him. He had rowed and tramped for miles in wet clothes after being half drowned in the icy sea, just as I had. In all the time I'd known him he had never seemed particularly affected by cold. Hadn't he once told me that magic fed him? I had thought it a figure of speech but now I wondered if it was true in a strange and secret way.

He shifted but did not wake as his hand settled on my hip. *I had him back.*

My spirit exulted, and I was surprised at how amorous I felt. However, my throat was raw, my mouth tasted like a stew of brine and bile, and I wanted a bath. I was ravenously hungry and still tired, and well aware of how desperately we needed drink, food, and dry clothes. And then?

Then I must have fallen asleep, because I woke up as he moved, rubbing his head.

"I feel I've been hit by a hammer," he muttered hoarsely. "My muscles ache, and I'm a little dizzy."

He swung out of the bed. The shutters were closed, but I knew it must be day because my sword was a cane. As he shaped a globe of cold fire, the sword flared to life. I admired his backside as he stretched and then walked to the table to touch the clothes.

He winced. "Ah! Cold and clammy!"

"You're a lot of trouble, Vai. I could have had a fire roaring all night."

"I'll keep you as warm as you could ever hope to be," he said with a provocative look. "But not right now, love. I'm sure this headache comes from thirst and hunger. You must be starving."

I tested the puffy, tender bruise where I'd bitten myself. "I'm so worried about Bee and Rory. We've got to get to Havery. The family won't protect her from mages, princes, or generals, not if they're offered an advantageous agreement in exchange for her person. Bee thinks she can scold powerful men into obeying her but that only makes them want her more...Noble Ba'al, Vai!"

I told him about Amadou Barry.

He whistled, shivering as he dressed in the damp clothes. "Washed away in the tide! What a fool! Anyway, we can't go on until we've dried our clothes. You must light a fire. I'm going to see what's in the shed. Maybe there's something I can use to snare a rabbit or catch a fish."

"You could stun some poor unsuspecting beast with your magic, couldn't you?"

He kissed me on the forehead. "I already have."

Clearly I hadn't yet recovered from yesterday's travail, because my mind had barely managed to trudge past several bland retorts before he returned to inform me that he was headed out to hunt and there was meanwhile a treasure-house of provisions in the shed. Then he was gone.

I gasped as I set my feet on the packed earth floor. The cold seared right through my skin. I ached all over, but I knew that would fade. With a blanket sewn of lusciously soft beaver pelts wrapped around me, I got the fire going and the kettle heating. The bench shoved right up against the brick of the hearth helped the clothes dry more quickly. Wool steamed, its scent rising. The worn cotton cloth I had stolen on Salt Island fluttered as the fire roared.

Shivering in wet wool, I ventured out of the hut and ransacked the shed. Right inside the door I found a large tin tub and a pair of wooden buckets. From the evidence of the frames and troughs, I supposed the hut and shed to be a haven where winter trappers and hunters could deal with their kills. Since the winter pelts of animals were thickest, it made sense that winter was the best time to hunt and trap for furs, and if villagers came there every winter, they likely stocked it late in the autumn. Crocks and baskets sat on frames out of the reach of rats. Parsnips! Barley! Lentils and broad beans! Nuts in the shell, already dried! Withered bunches of dried nettle and hoarhound hung from the central beams. Dried vetch for animal fodder was bundled in sheaves. When I discovered a stoppered jar of linseed oil, I almost wept.

Would the villagers who used this hut consider us thieves? It didn't matter. Our canoe had hit the sand. We simply could go no farther right now.

Quite some time later I had barleynut-cakes baking on the bricks, a pottage of parsnips, lentils, and barley simmering, and a pleasing tisane of nettle and hoarhound at brew. I made a place for the cacica's skull at the back of the table, against the wall, and set before her a slice of parsnip garnished with a drop of the tisane. After this offering, I drank the first infusion of the tisane to soothe my raw throat and gobbled down two bowls of soup.

Eating and drinking improved my mood and constitution immeasurably. I sorted out all our gear to repair later. It seemed prudent to carefully test the sheaths to make sure they hadn't cracked from the cold, and to rub them with a little oil; if one was careful, perhaps they could be reused. I pinned up my braid and bathed using the lavender soap we had taken from our old home. Afterward, I washed out my filthy clothes, dumped the dirty water, and combed out my hair. The cotton from Expedition dried quickly, so I dressed in my bodice and a wrapped skirt. The tub was half filled with steaming water for Vai, and more was heating.

I was contemplating a rock-hard slab of dried whitefish when the fire flickered. With a disgruntled sigh the flames went out on a puff of ash.

I pulled on my boots and dashed outside. It took me a moment to spot him trudging along the shoreline with three dead grouse slung on a line. He was farther away than I would have expected, until I saw what trailed behind him.

A mage House troop of turbaned riders pursued him. They wore gray wool winter coats cut for riding, and their heads were wrapped in bright green turbans. The horses picked their way over the uneven ground. My heart pounded as I cursed under my breath, rage and frustration exploding. How had the mansa found us so quickly?

I counted forty men before I noticed Vai glance over his shoulder to measure the distance between them and him. A lance that had been nothing more than a long spear with a wicked steel point unfurled a banner marked with the four phases of the moon, the sigil of Four Moons House.

The moment he saw me waiting, the soldiers vanished in a patter of sleet that doused my rage. My heart fluttered as his step quickened. He was disheveled, dirt smeared like paint down one side of his face. His once-elegant clothes looked like a beggar's chance-met rags. He dazzled me.

"I thought the soldiers were real!"

His face shone, dark and beautiful. "My magic is unbelievably strong here."

"Didn't Professora Alhamrai say cold magic is stronger when the mage is close to the ice?"

"Cold mages have always known our power lies in the ice. There's so much nyama. I could do anything, love." He laughed again as he hung the grouse from the eaves.

"Not that thinking poorly of yourself has ever been a problem for you," I remarked.

His eyes flared as he looked me up and down. He had the dizzy good humor of a man who is half drunk. "Not only do you look clean and fed, but you obviously have no idea how beautiful you are, especially with your hair down and that mouth of yours talking. Are we going in?"

The interior seemed dim after the bright sky and the snowy landscape. The lingering heat warmed me right up, or maybe it was hearing him stamp about in the entry hall behind me. I tested the water in the tub. He came in, shedding his coat.

I was not minded to be subtle. I helped him out of his clammy garments and wrapped him in a fur for long enough to make him drink the hot tisane and eat soup and barleycake, although he wasn't much interested in the food. The tub interested him more, where I washed every bit of him with the sweet-smelling lavender soap. I managed to dry most of him with one of the pagnes before he picked me up.

"The problem, Catherine, is that if you want a fire, I have to be
216 outdoors away from the hearth. And if you want us to be together

indoors, then"—he dumped me on the mattress—"we are going to have to spend most of our time in this bed."

He braced his body over mine, his arms on either side of me. He lowered himself to brush a kiss over my lips, then pushed back up. The feel of him a hand's span above me made me wriggle. I had to put my hands all over him before finally pulling him down on top of me so we could kiss. When I was breathless, my heart racing and my body aflame, I broke off.

"What I don't understand is why you still have clothes on," he murmured in a voice like honey.

I nipped at the lobe of his ear. Did I have to inform the man of everything I wanted?

He sat up, although he left a hand cupped over my right breast, fingers teasing absentmindedly through the cloth of my bodice in a way that made me squirm. "You can't be waiting for me to undress you, can you? Perhaps there was something else you wanted to discuss? I had many long conversations in Expedition on the fascinating subject of the properties of heat, whether heat is dynamic or perhaps undulating a little bit like you are now."

"If you are going to do nothing but taunt me, then I am done speaking to you, Andevai."

His eyebrows arched. He leaned closer. "Not one more word?"

I lifted my chin defiantly as I pinched my lips together.

His lazy smile was more challenge than sweetness. "We'll see about that."

23

Much later, we lay quietly together. For the longest time I luxuriated in the feel of his arms around me. A light fall of snow drifted down outside, flakes dusting along the roof with a hiss.

"Vai?"

"Mmm?" He kissed my neck.

"Our efforts have left me hungry." I stuck a foot out from under the blankets, and sucked in a breath. "It's cold out there. You're such a nuisance, you fire banes."

Arms tensing, he stopped nuzzling. "I never got used to that name. It always seemed like mockery to me, even when none was meant."

I really was hungry, but his confession fell so unexpectedly that I thought of how Kofi had seemed to understand Vai in ways I had never glimpsed. "People in Expedition respected you."

"Because I worked hard and was a good carpenter. Not because I am a cold mage."

"How did you become such a good carpenter?"

I felt his smile in the tilt of his head against my hair. "My father and uncle were carpenters. They were teaching me the trade. Remember, my magic didn't bloom until I was sixteen."

"I thought your father and uncle were hunters."

"They were also hunters. But a person must have a trade. Before she became ill, my mother was renowned for her basketry. Did I ever tell you that?" He did not wait for my answer. "When things got bad for me in the youth hall at Four Moons House, I started sneaking out to the carpentry barn. The mansa's uncle let me work there." He began stroking my belly with a motion similar, I supposed, to that he might delicately use to plane a surface.

"The mansa's uncle was a carpenter?"

"An architect. He was educated in Camlun and had studied with learned masters across Europa. He said knowing the carpenter's craft helped him understand how to build. In a mage House, many sons and daughters have no magic, so they serve the House in some other way. Because he was the uncle of the mansa he was willing to defy the mansa by teaching me, since it was seen as lowborn of me to wish to work with my hands. But the work helped me concentrate on my studies. I couldn't be angry or fighting if I was working with my hands." His stroking hand clenched.

"How did things get bad for you in the youth hall?"

He pushed to sit. "Can you heat enough water to scald and pluck the grouse? The sooner we can leave here and get away from the ice, the better. Next Hallows' Night your sire will come after us. I can hide from the Hunt in a troll maze, but you can't. We must find a way to protect you from him."

His sudden change of subject forced me to ask a question whose answer I feared. "Did my sire harm you?"

He gave a curt laugh leavened by a self-mocking smile that reassured me that he had not been hurt. "He did an injury to my pride, that is certain. My magic counts for nothing in comparison to the magic he wields as easily as breathing."

"Yet you had the courage to stab him. Even knowing how strong he is."

He pulled down the blankets to expose my right shoulder. I had once thought him the pampered, privileged son of a mage House, as highborn as he was arrogant. The callused touch of his fingers, however coaxing and sensual, reminded me that he had been born to a very different life. With kisses, he traced the two seamed scars on my shoulder. "I hurt you instead. How could you know that horrible thing your sire threatened you with?"

"The latch of the coach conceals two gremlin spirits, one inside and one outside. They can see and talk. When I was climbing up the tree in the spirit world, I saw through its eyes."

"Ah, yes, I remember you talking about the latch."

"Are you saying you don't believe me about the latch?"

He kissed my forehead. "Love, why did you try to kill your sire? You would only have killed yourself."

I brushed my fingers across his lips. "I was so angry and afraid that I forgot." I swung out of bed and padded over to the table to dress. "Although now that I think of it, if you hadn't stabbed him the first time and he hadn't boasted that the injury would fall on his children, then you wouldn't have known to stop me from trying to kill him."

"That is convoluted logic even for you." Sitting up, he shaped four globes of cold fire as easily as I might inhale. "Love, how did your mother get pregnant by the Master of the Wild Hunt?"

I got into my undergarments. "He threatened to kill Daniel, and the other survivors, unless she allowed him to impregnate her."

He nodded gravely. "The women in my village suffered much the same. My grandmother was sent up to the mage House to work in the hall. One of the men fancied her. Village girls like her weren't allowed to say no. He kept her as his mistress until he got her pregnant and discarded her."

"Is that why you bloomed with cold magic? Because your grandsire was a magister?"

He smiled as at an old joke. "The man who sired my father on my grandmother was a clerk, not a mage. He was sent to Four Moons House as part of the retinue of a woman from another mage House when she married the mansa's father. Who's to say the magic came from his breeding? It might have bloomed from an unknown seed. It might have come from my grandmother."

"The same place you got your looks? From your grandmother?"

"My mother did once say my father was the handsomest man she had ever seen. Of all his children, I resembled him the most." He looked very appealing, sitting naked on the bedding. The light cast a sheen on his skin that made me want to rub my hands all over him all over again. The curve of his knee drew my eye to the line of his thigh. He had a way of looking at me that meant he knew I knew he knew I was admiring him, and that he was perfectly happy to be admired. He was like Bee in that way: That people enjoyed looking at him gave him satisfaction.

"You're sitting there hoping to tempt me back into bed, aren't you? But if we want to dry out your clothes, I have to light a fire." I glanced at the skin nailed over the window. "It will be dark soon, so I won't make you stay out for long."

"How can you dry out my clothes? To go outside, I must have something to wear."

"You can wear the clothes I brought for Rory. They've dried out—"

"Rory?" The courting Vai who had sat patiently through many evenings at the boardinghouse while I flirted with customers had never spoken quite this sharply to me.

"One of my sire's other children. The saber-toothed cat. You met him in the spirit world, at the hearth of the djelimuso Lucia Kante."

He lifted his chin, gone a little prickly as if embarrassed he had revealed a spark of jealousy. "I remember the cats. The male is your half brother?"

"Yes. My sire can change form as he wishes."

"I can guess the details."

"I can understand why my sire would breed children in the spirit world. Not all of the predators in the Wild Hunt are his children, but at least some are, and he can bind all of us whenever he wishes, as he did Rory. But why did he want Tara Bell?"

"Perhaps he is one of those men who delight in knowing they can take a person who does not want them."

"I'm not sure we can call him a man. I don't think he feels what we feel. He must have had some other reason. Think how useful I proved because I was able to cut a fence for him into Taino country." I told him about the way my sire had enfolded me in his wings, the words he had whispered, and how I had thought at first that he had been speaking of Vai. "But now I think he was talking about himself. Mortal blood feeds the spirit courts and gives them the power to bind their servants to them. He's bound to the courts, just as I'm bound to him. Just as you and your village are bound to Four Moons House. Why tell me that a prince among slaves is still a slave if he does not chafe at his chains?"

As he considered my words, I could not help but note what a decorative thinker he was, with his chiseled shoulders and those inventive fingers splayed along his chin. "So 'the palace where those without

221

blood cannot walk' was the pit. Our ancestors whose spirits walk in the spirit world can't cross into the palace—the pit—because they have no blood."

"Yes. That's why the cacica couldn't cross and I had to leave her hanging…" I trailed off as I realized I had positioned the skull with a full view of the bed.

Vai followed the line of my gaze. "Catherine, why is there a skull on the table?"

My cheeks burned.

"I don't remember seeing a skull when we arrived here yesterday," he added.

"Blessed Tanit," I murmured, blushing even more scaldingly as I turned the skull to face away from the bed and toward the hearth.

"I thought you were telling one of your jesting tales to entertain me, like you do. I didn't think the basket really had a head in it."

Was her vision confined to the spirit world? Could skulls see? Could a skull close its eyes if it had no eyelids? Or would it be forced to watch *everything*?

"Why would you even have the head of the cacica if the Wild Hunt killed her?" he asked.

"The Taino ancestors put me on trial for her murder but I talked my way out of it."

"Naturally."

"The council of elders recognized the merit in my arguments!"

His shoulders tensed. "You mean it. It's really the head of Queen Anacaona."

"Of course it is! Why would I say so otherwise? I have spoken more to her after she was dead than I ever did while she was living. She admires your good manners and your…attractive disposition. She told me that an unusually powerful fire bane like yourself would have been a challenge she would have savored."

His jaw tightened. He pulled the fur blanket around his torso and stood, primly covered from armpits to calves.

"Gracious Melqart, Vai. Are you *embarrassed* that the skull has seen you naked?"

"You're the one who turned her to look away from the bed." His look of offended hauteur only emphasized his grip on the blanket.

I laughed so hard that I cried. With a mumbled apology to the cacica, I draped cloth over the skull to cover the eye sockets.

"Oh, Vai," I said, wiping tears off my cheeks. "I adore you when you're indignant."

He was looking very smoky and irritated in a way that made me bite my lower lip lest I laugh again. The man looked delectable when he had been driven up the pinnacle of disdain by feeling his pride and dignity had been slighted. Without a word of warning, he hauled me to the bed and strenuously, if very quietly, worked through his wounded feelings with my full cooperation.

Afterward he left me a sphere of cold fire and went outside. I uncovered the skull. I had grown so accustomed to the skull that it was easy to chat to her, although I was grateful there was no actual conversation or the chance that she would reveal by expression or unguarded comment what she might have seen. As I lit a fresh fire in the ashy hearth, I remarked that as difficult as it was to cope with the lack of fire, it certainly was pleasant to have cold fire as light. I explained that I had grown up in an impoverished household where beeswax candles were too expensive and tallow candles so smoky and foul-smelling it became a chore to sew or read by their light. I set a slab of fish to soak, and softened the dry barleycake in a hot parsnip-and-bean soup.

The water in the tub held a ghost of warmth in which I scrubbed his clothes. I went through them first, but I did not say anything to the cacica when I discovered three of the prophylactic sheaths tucked up one of his cuffs. The rascal! On Hallows' Night he had been prepared to reunite with me. Of course, he hadn't known I'd been imprisoned on Salt Island.

Washing done, I tidied up part of my sewing kit, and mended one of the tears in his much-abused dash jacket. The fire roared, drenching me with blissful heat. But I missed him.

How Bee would mock me!

Let her. I had faced worse than her mockery.

I dressed as warmly as I could and went out. Snowflakes spun on a trickle of wind. With clouds overhead, the air wasn't nearly as frigid. In summer this shoreline would be marshy and plagued by bugs, but it was breathtaking in the winter evening with the snow shining and the water sparkling with the reflection of the magic he casually unleashed   223 in cascades of bursting rainbows. He was throwing the illusion of light around in gouts of color that fell in waterfalls, spilling from image to image. A magnificent stag lost its antlers to become a horse pulling an elaborate chaise that became a Kena'ani ship with its prow cutting through the waves in the shape of a leaping horse. There was no reason or purpose for it. He was just doing it because he could.

He walked to meet me.

"It's so beautiful, Vai."

"Mmm," he agreed as he kissed me with unexpectedly warm lips.

"I missed you."

"Of course you did, love." He put an arm around me as we stared south toward an unknown shore. Snow winked where it dissolved into the water. "We need to find a mage House or inn, or we won't last long in this cold. Even with a fur blanket."

"I feel like a thief taking the blanket with us. A fine beaver pelt blanket like that costs a year's wages in Adurnam."

"I'm taking no chances with you and the cold, love. Now go in. You're shivering."

We set out at dawn, glad to be moving. It took all morning to row across the sound. The water was so formidably calm that I was able to take several turns at the oars. By sighting on an unusually tall tree, we came in fairly close to straight across from where we had started, working back against a placid current. There we found a pier and cabin very like the one we had just left, except it had a shed for drying fish.

A path led south through woodland of stunted pine and scrub birch. We stowed the boat and started walking. When a freezing mixture of snow and sleet began to fall on the wings of a stiff east wind, we were forced to turn back and shelter indoors for the rest of the day and night. To be snuggled together with the fur blanket wrapped around us was no hardship, but in winter we could not survive long on love alone.

Thank Tanit, the next morning dawned clear. We walked all morning. I was hungry, and he actually looked tired, although I was not about to tell him so.

Instead I talked. "Kofi said you would be the net that Expedition's radicals threw across the ocean to Europa."

"If the charter the Assembly is writing in Expedition can be displayed in towns here, that may encourage people to demand that communities should have a say in ruling themselves."

"That's why Kehinde wanted the portable press from Expedition so badly, isn't it? To escape princely censorship of her pamphlets."

"Kehinde?"

"Professora Nayo Kuti, the scholar and radical pamphleteer. The prince of Adurnam imposed martial law when the people demanded the right to elect a single tribune to the Adurnam council. If electing a single tribune to represent all the people is too radical for such a prince, imagine what he would say to the idea of an Assembly!"

The trees and ground with their coat of snow sparkled in the sunlight. The sky was so blue it seemed to have no limit, only to fall away forever as into a spirit world where every layer fit inside another layer without ever reaching an end.

"That's not the only thing I carried away from Expedition," he said. "In Europa, cold mages have always stood at odds with the blacksmiths who wield dangerous fire. What if cold mages and fire mages could work together, as they do in the Taino kingdom?"

"I thought fire banes were slaves in Taino country."

He smiled as at a jest I ought to understand. "The situation is more complex than that. In the Antilles those with cold magic are generally so weak and untrained that it's no wonder they are considered an inferior breed of magister." He indicated the basket. "Even the cacica was startled and impressed by my magic."

I opened my mouth to joke about how she had been ogling him on Hallows' Night, but when I considered the contours of his pride and the respect due to her dignity, I decided against it.

Fortunately he had gone on. "She explained to me how catch-fires work. It is exceptionally dangerous both to the fire mage and to the catch-fire. That is why when a Taino man or woman first blooms with fire magic, a kinsman volunteers to become their catch-fire. To the outside eye it may look like slavery. But it is just the family taking responsibility until the new fire mage learns to properly control the weaving."

"But I heard of fire banes being sold against their will into the Taino kingdom."

"I don't know, love. It may be. People also act wrongly at times. But

225

I can't help but think about how much more we could do in Europa if cold mages worked in harness with fire mages. Not that the mansa would ever listen to me."

"Honestly, Vai, the prospect of fire mages and fire banes working together alarms me. We've seen what James Drake is capable of."

"Not every person is like James Drake." His breath misted the air before its heat faded.

"If cold mages and fire mages worked together, then people would fear them more and hate them worse. What would stop magisters from taking over everything? I mean, besides the Wild Hunt? Any magister who learned how to hide from the Hunt in a troll maze would tell every other magister. If mage House magisters hide, then someone else will die. Someone has to die to feed the courts. As some unknown person did when we were in the spirit world. As Queen Anacaona did." I tapped the basket.

"People will die regardless."

"Yes, but we don't have to accept the things we might change. 'Risks must be taken if we mean to get what we want,' as Brennan Du once said to me."

"No doubt hoping to impress you so you'd give him a kiss," muttered Vai ungraciously.

"Not every man admires me just because you do."

"That is exactly my point, Catherine. As long as clientage remains part of any legal code in Europa, as long as princes and mage Houses can bind entire villages into generations-long servitude, then how can things truly change? Camjiata is the only one with a legal code that will abolish clientage. There is no benefit to the princes and mage Houses to abolish clientage, because they prosper by it."

The skin of frozen snow crunched satisfyingly beneath my boots as I smashed each step into the ground just as I planned to smash my foes. "Did Camjiata charm you like he charmed Bee? He's not our friend."

"Perhaps not, but he is our ally in the fight to abolish clientage. "

"How can you say so? He shelters Drake. Who, may I remind you, wants to kill you, after you've witnessed me being humiliated!"

"I can crush James Drake."

"Never let it be said that you lack confidence."

His tone sharpened. "Do you doubt me, Catherine?"

I halted in the middle of the path. "Of course I don't doubt you! But James Drake nearly burned me alive. The backlash of his magic didn't pour harmlessly through me as it did through you. Even so, the worst thing was that he meant to kill you, if he could have. When I saw him again, I was so angry and scared that I kept insulting him until he lashed out at me. He would have done something dreadful if the general hadn't stopped him. I don't know how to stop myself from provoking him if we see him again."

He grasped my arms. "That man will never hurt you, Catherine. Never."

"That's right, because I will kill him."

He was silent for so long I thought he might be displeased by my bloodthirsty rejoinder. At length, with a frown, he spoke.

"I know you hate your sire, love, and I understand why you do. But don't forget there is a part of him that gives you strength."

"He'll never truly let go of me," I murmured, shuddering, for an unreasoning fear seized me. What if he could hear and see all I said even here in the mortal world? How could I ever escape, with his claws already in me?

"James Drake?"

"You're the one James Drake can't let go of. He doesn't really care about me. I meant my sire will never let go of me, never stop hunting me..."

Perhaps the wind whispered. Alarm, like a dagger, pricked my neck. I pulled away from Vai to examine the woodland. Flakes of half-forgotten snow drifted among the slender trunks.

Vai drew cold steel and spun a breath of magic to waken my sword.

Sometimes the danger that stalks you stays hidden because it comes in plain sight.

A black wolf trotted down the path toward us, out of the south. When its uncannily golden eyes met mine, I knew it was some manner of kin. The wolf flicked a look over its shoulder and loped into the trees. A chittering bird fell silent. Tremors brushed the soles of my booted feet. A metallic jingle chimed.

"There's someone coming," I said. "Horses and men."

Where the path dipped, curving to the right, nine men came into view. Four riders had spears braced in their stirrups, with bowcases slung from their saddles and primed with arrows. One carried a musket. Five men walked alongside lugging packs and traps. They wore sturdy winter clothing and fur hats. Some had the white skin of northern Celts, while others had mixed coloring. Seeing us, they halted in surprise.

Vai touched my arm. "Be ready to hit the ground. I will stun them all."

The man with the musket gave a curt command. The horsemen dismounted, and all knelt submissively. The leader handed his musket to a comrade. With hands open and extended in supplication, he walked forward. He was an older man with a dusky, weathered face and a beard streaked with gray. Something in the shape of his blue eyes and the cut of his cheekbones struck me as familiar, although I had never seen him before.

Where I had grown up, young people showed respect to their elders by never looking them directly in the eye. Although we were younger than he was, the man kept his gaze lowered subserviently. Twenty paces from us he pulled off his hat to reveal a thick head of dark red hair, veined with white and pulled back into a braid. Ten paces from us he dropped to both knees.

"Salve, my lord." He enunciated each word carefully. "Of your presence, we know nothing before we are coming upon you. We would not be displaying our spears in your face if we knew. To us, grant forgiveness, at your pleasure. To our households, your coming brings honor. What do you desire?"

"Who are you?" Vai demanded.

The man glanced up as if to gauge how angry Vai was. In that moment, his gaze skipped to take me in. He ducked his head, hands clenching into fists.

"My lord, I am of the people called the Belgae. I am Devyn, son of the priest Mad Kirwyn, he who is beloved of Carnonos the god." He studied me. "Your pardon I ask, my lord. How is this beast come to be walking beside you? Have you caught a spirit woman on the ice? She wears the black hair and golden eyes of the hunter. But the face she wears is the face of my dead sister."

Vai looked from the man to me and back to the man. The shape of Devyn's face was familiar because it was the same as my own.

24

Vai knew he could hammer them into the dirt, and because he knew it, they believed it.

"I am a magister of rare potency and considerable influence. My wife and I washed ashore north of here under unexpected circumstances. We seek shelter and assistance in continuing our journey south."

"Your *wife?*" Devyn glanced at me with a puzzled frown. The other men cast surreptitious looks at me. "My lord, if you say so, but no shame is there to a man who is capturing a wild beast to burnish his standing in his House."

Vai stared down the man until Devyn opened both hands and bent his head. "I expect my wife to be shown the same courtesy as you show to me."

"Your pardon, my lord. My duty it is, to be escorting you." He spoke to the others in a lilting run of words I could not really understand. To judge from Vai's look of concentration, he was having a better time picking out meaning from the heavy dialect, and it didn't appear he liked what they were saying.

Nevertheless, he handed over the food supplies we had taken from the cabin. In exchange they gave us all four horses, one for our gear. The two groups separated: We and Devyn rode south, while the village men continued north.

"How can they know you're a cold mage just by looking at you?" I said in a low voice. "It can't just be your good looks. Not every handsome man is a cold mage."

"You can be sure I am wondering that myself."

"Why every handsome man is not a cold mage?"

He smiled but did not take the bait. "We're fortunate they were headed out to trap."

"I thought with the horses and bows they might be hunting the wolf."

"They consider the wolf to be the servant of their god, Carnonos. The god's servant cannot be hunted. They're troubled by you."

"That wolf could be my half-sibling," I muttered. "Blessed Tanit, Vai. Are these my mother's people?" I glanced toward Devyn to find him watching us.

"The resemblance is remarkable."

"If this is her village, and the channels we crossed are part of the Baltic Ice Sea, then it makes sense that the expedition she and Daniel were part of used her home as a staging point."

"An interesting consideration. I will ask."

But Devyn put off Vai's questions by insisting only the priest could answer. We rode with little conversation for the rest of the day and well into the evening.

Night wrapped the world in silence. A full moon bathed the trees and the snow-clad earth in a glamour, painting the world in contrasts: the white shine of birch bark and the heavy branches of dark spruce. I felt like a forgotten ghost drawn back to an unremembered grave. It was so cold. Vai wrapped the fur blanket around me.

The road brought us to a clearing.

The moon overhead poured light on a princely hall that sat amid untended shrubbery gone wild. Its arched doorway was staved in as if kicked by a giant. Every window had shattered, and the roof had collapsed. On the lintel above the entrance was carved a crescent moon. Though the manor house rose two stories and had wings flying back on each side, a coat of ice as clear as glass encased the entire building.

Vai sucked in a breath. The mare, taking his mood, sidestepped skittishly before he brought her back under control.

Not a single plant had woven its way inside, despite the age of the ruin. The smashed floor revealed the rubble of a hypocaust beneath. Intact corpses were caught and preserved within the ice as if they had been frozen as they tried to escape.

"Blessed Tanit!" I murmured. "Gracious Melqart, protect us. Noble Ba'al, watch over your faithful daughter."

"The spirit knows this place because she visited here before in her other form." Devyn signed a ward against evil tidings.

"I am not a ghost or a wolf," I said in a choked voice, but he would not look at me. To look at his face slammed me with the axe blow of memory. As a child, I had looked into a similar face, my mother's face, as she bent to kiss me. A scar had ripped a lightning-like seam across the right side of her face, and she was missing one eye. The hole gaped like a skull's socket, a gate onto the pain she had suffered. Yet her expression was serene and loving.

"Tell no one. Keep silence," she had murmured. "Just until we tell you we've reached the safe place we're traveling to. Sleep, little cat. Your father and I are right here beside you."

The memory opened a pit inside my heart. There was no safe place.

"Bad fortune to be here at midnight, haunted by spirits," said Devyn. "Best we ride on."

Vai did not budge. "This is the mage House that was destroyed by the Wild Hunt. Crescent House, it was called."

"To this place the Hunt came, it is true, my lord. On Hallows' Night, they were riding with claws and teeth. Bad fortune it is, my lord, to be lingering. Please let us be moving on." He glanced toward me as if expecting me to turn into claws and teeth, and rend him.

I hated him for fearing me. The frozen shell of the House was a grave for those trapped within, woman, man, and child. The ice had spared no one.

"I am Tara Bell's child!" In the muffled night my voice rang like a shout. "That's why I look like her! I'm your niece!"

He looked at Vai. "I have no niece."

"Don't you understand?" I cried. "Don't you see who—?"

"Silence!" Vai's voice snapped.

I dragged in a bitter breath, fighting a flood of anger and an ebb of despair. Of course he was right: The last thing I needed to do now was make them more suspicious by informing them that their worst fears about me were true.

Devyn clipped his horse forward.

In a softer voice Vai said, "Catherine, I'm tired of the cold, love.   231

I'm exhausted, and I hurt. I need to know you won't freeze to death. Please, let's get out of here."

The sight of the ice-caged ruins and trapped corpses had truly shaken me, but it was his effort to disguise the tremor in his voice that made me realize that will alone was carrying him. I rode out of the ghost-ridden clearing, for I knew he would not leave if I did not go.

As if our movement unleashed it, the moon began its slide westward.

Soon the road passed pasture walls built of peat. If there were fields awaiting spring planting, I did not recognize them. Everything was strange to me. My moorings had slipped the dock and I had drifted free. I was riding the road my mother and father had traveled. We had just ridden past the estate where Camjiata's wife, the dragon dreamer Helene Condé Vahalis, had been born and raised and had died. The general had been here, too, back in the days when he was merely Captain Leonnorios Aemilius Keita.

Why had it all happened? How had the four of them met: the ambitious captain, the loyal soldier, the half-blind oracle, and the restless traveler? Was there ever a reason, a destiny, as Camjiata claimed? Or were the Romans right that the goddess Fortuna was veiled and blind and therefore capricious?

We passed stone walls and winter-seared pasture. Barking dogs gave notice of habitation. Under the brilliant light of the moon rose long houses with peaked thatching, flanked by sheds with sloped roofs. Torchlight flared ahead. As we reached the village, Vai's magic guttered the torches one by one. The doors leading into the houses opened, and dimly seen faces peered out. Although we didn't need light on the night of the full moon, Vai extended his right hand in a gesture meant to be dramatic, and pinched four globes of light out of the air. Devyn mumbled a prayer.

We rode down a dirt street through the center of the village. In spring the main street would be nothing but a strip of sloppy mud. There were no modern chimneys, only smoke holes, and no glass windows set in the wattled walls. To judge by the bleating of sheep, the flocks were being wintered over in the same houses the people lived in. Two thousand years ago a Roman legion pressing forward to find tin, fur, and slaves for trade had probably seen the same sights we did now.

Had my mother truly come from this barbaric place? How different Daniel must have seemed to her, with his sophisticated education and his years of travel!

Watchmen paced us through the streets, holding their blackened torches. People slipped out of their homes to follow Vai's mage light. We halted in front of a substantial house with a high roof. An elderly man dressed in an embroidered wool gown and a calf-length sleeveless leather tunic appeared on the porch. He greeted Vai with incomprehensible words.

Devyn translated into his weirdly archaic and broken Latin. "To you, Magister, we are honored to be giving guest rights. Your magic is strong. You have captured the god's beast and trapped her in the form of a woman. But in this village the beast cannot be staying. She bears malice toward us by wearing the face of one of our dead."

"She is my wife," Vai repeated. "Not a beast. We need shelter for the night. We will go on in the morning."

"No shelter can we be giving you unless the priest pours the offerings and the god grants his blessing."

Vai's lips thinned. I had a feeling that he was trying to decide whether to terrify them with a frightening display of cold magic.

"It can't hurt to go to the temple." My teeth were beginning to chatter even with the fur blanket wrapped around me.

"Very well, love. But only because you say so." He turned to the headman. The arrogant tilt of his chin lent curtness to his words, reminding me of when I had first met his withering disdain. "Because the hour is late and I do not engage in debate on the street, I will allow you to escort us to the temple. You personally will attend me, as befits my consequence and your hospitality. I expect a decent meal, hot drink, and fur cloaks and gloves to make up for this unwarranted insult."

The old man was obviously unaccustomed to being spoken to in this manner, but he touched hands to his bowed head and, to my surprise, himself took the reins of Vai's horse as would a servant. Villagers followed us in procession: women draped in long shawls, men wrapped in wool capes, children swaddled in pelts. At the outskirts of the village we passed between a row of granaries set up on stilts. Beyond the granaries a lane entered a rocky pasture. The moon's light was so bright I could see the shape of every rock tumbled in the field, every face breathing into the frigid night.

The temple grounds were surrounded by a ditch and stockade. The procession halted in front of a plank bridge that spanned the ditch. Vai dismounted, so I did as well.

He turned to the headman. "You will accompany us."

The man answered, and Devyn translated. "We are forbidden."

"Then we will go alone." Vai took the reins of the horse that carried our gear and led it over the bridge. Moonlight gleamed on the skulls of cattle set in rows at the bottom of the ditch. I touched the hilt of my sword.

"Do not draw your blade in this holy place unless you are threatened," he said softly.

"I feel threatened."

The stockade had no gate, rather an opening framed by two stone pillars. The pillars each had three niches, and in each niche rested a human skull. Their staring silence made my skin crawl.

"Let me sneak in ahead to make sure there's no ambush," I whispered.

His cold fire vanished, leaving him and the horse like ashen ghosts under the moon. I wrapped myself in shadows. Beyond the gate a path sprinkled with white stones led down by stair-steps into a hollow. I crept not into a stone building as Romans would have built nor the kind of open-air sanctuary lined with pillars in which Kena'ani worshiped.

I walked into a grove of oak trees. Oaks certainly could not flourish this far north, yet here they were, fully leafed as if with summer, their canopies meeting over my head. Between the trees rose poles from which hung lamps, each one burning a sweet-smelling oil. The smoky heat breathed like summer. Had I passed back into the spirit world?

No. For they were not living trees. They were dead trunks decorated with tin and copper foliage. Wind brushed a tinkling whisper through the metal leaves.

Beside a bricked-in hearth, a man sat on a stool. A huge bronze cauldron hung over the fire. Its polished surface glimmered in the twisting light of the flames. The face of a horned man shone in the curve of the cauldron, and it watched me as with living eyes.

The man at the fire turned. He heard me, although I could sneak as quietly as any mouse. He saw me, although I concealed myself within the shadows. I knew at once who he was. I resembled him in some ways more than I did my mother, for he was darker than his children. There was mage House blood in him.

I did not know what language he spoke, yet I understood him perfectly.

"Beast, we have not invited you to enter. Trouble us no longer, you who come to haunt us wearing my dead daughter's face. Begone. I banish you."

"I'm not a spirit! I'm Tara Bell's child. You are my grandfather."

"Tara is no longer my daughter. Her home and her family she gave up to follow the Roman goddess Bellona, the lady of war. All men she foreswore except the captain who took her oath to serve him, Captain Leon. She marched south into his service. Her child you cannot be, because the Amazon soldiers bear no children."

"She did bear a child, because I am hers and in your heart you know I am hers!"

He raised his hands as if warding off an attack. "If you speak, the god will be hearing you!"

"Who will hear who does not already know?" I cried. Would my own grandfather reject me?

"The anger of Bold Carnonos fell upon this village. The magisters of Crescent House made offering of their magic to build an empire. So the god destroyed them."

"He's not a god! You just call him that because you fear his power."

He raised the knife of sacrifice. "We do not want your poison here to call his anger back on us. Begone. Begone. Begone."

Down the avenue of oak trees, lamps flickered and began to go out one by one. Vai appeared in a nimbus of cold fire, leading the pack horse.

"I heard you shout, love." He tossed the reins to the ground and, drawing his sword, stepped between me and the man who refused to be my grandfather. "Holy one, you cannot possibly wish to anger a magister, and you especially do not wish to anger me. Because I promise you, no magister you have ever seen or heard tell of has done what I have done. For I have defied the hunter, and stolen his own daughter out of his very nest. Of course she has fallen in love with me and chosen to become my wife. She is no threat to you or to this village. You ought to rejoice and lay a feast to celebrate her arrival, for I assure you that everything about this woman ought to make you proud to call her your kin."

The priest lowered the knife, his gaze fixed on Vai's cold steel, which needed only to draw blood to cut his spirit out of his flesh and send him screaming into the spirit world. "The girl has bewitched you, Magister. The god toys with you. It will end in grief and blood. I see it in the cauldron."

"You see your own fears," I said hoarsely. "You know what happened to your daughter on the ice, don't you?"

His pitiless gaze seared me. "I told her to smother the child the moment she gave birth. Do you know what she said to me?"

My heart dropped as if into the pit of my belly. I feared to know. Yet I had to know.

The old man's malice gleamed in a face so much like mine. "She said, 'Do you not think I did not try to rid myself of his hateful seed? Yet nothing I did would dislodge it.'"

"You don't need to listen to any more of this, Catherine. We can walk out of here now."

My feet would not shift. My grandfather's hate pinned me to the earth. The memory of Tara's defiance still enraged him.

"Yet after that, the shameless whore spoke of *pride*! She said, 'But then I realized that it was loyalty that made the child, because I went willingly to the hunter to save the lives of the others. Loyalty will be her birthright. Do not think I will be ashamed! I will be proud! Because loyalty will be the bright light this child will bring to the world.'"

The glimpse into my mother's heart stunned me.

"I told her she would come to a bad end," he went on in a rheumy whisper. "The hunter never stops hunting. His children belong to him only. Blood binds them forever and always."

He shut his seamed old eyes, pressing fingers onto the closed eyelids.

"I see the Hunt in the cauldron every Hallows' Night. I saw Tara and the Phoenician, dragged down into the river. I saw a child torn from their grasp as Tara reached for her with the only hand left to her. I saw the water choke them and kill them. "

236

"Enough!" snapped Vai. "I do not fear you, holy one, although I respect your age, as it is proper for the young to respect the old. You have poisoned your own well with fear and hate."

The priest opened his eyes. Unlike Tara and Devyn he had dark eyes, and in the firelight they seemed to gleam with a golden brown almost like mine.

"They tell me you walked out of the north, Magister. Surely on the road here you passed Crescent House frozen by the breath of the Wild Hunt. That is not fear. That is truth. Take her, if you must, for you are young and arrogant and you believe all will bow before you and your magic. But you are nothing but dust and salt, and less precious than salt. Go, as did my daughter Tara. Go, as did the Phoenician, Daniel, who believed he could stand beside her. Go, as did the captain who thought he had found a woman whose dreams would deliver up Europa to his ambition. The hunter will crush your defiance and destroy all that you love. The hunter cannot be defeated, because he is death."

"Come, Catherine. We are leaving this cursed place."

I followed Vai past the dead lamps and out of the sanctuary to where the village waited in silence. Snow drifted like frozen tears. I feared that the villagers meant to abandon us on the road to die of exposure, but even in this isolated place, respect for cold mages was akin to awe. Hot wine and a platter of warm porridge awaited him, which Vai forced me to share although I was neither hungry nor thirsty. Vai was presented with two pairs of fur-lined gloves and two voluminous fur-lined cloaks. He helped me into mine before wrapping himself in the other. Fresh horses were brought as well as a donkey to haul our gear. Devyn was assigned to accompany us with three older men, grim fellows bearing spears in a way that made me think they had once been soldiers in whatever war had brought Captain Leon to the north, before he became General Camjiata.

People stood with breath misting to watch us depart. I couldn't tell if they expected a calamity to befall us before we left their sight, or if they wished to store away the memory to tell as a tale over and over again at the winter hearth: how they had seen the lord magister and the beast ride away into the night. It was as quiet as if death had blown a kiss over the world. The only sounds were the crunch of hooves on crusted snow and the moan of the wind. I could not stop shaking.

Our road was a broad cart track glistening with a lacework of frost under the moon's light. We halted at daybreak in a hamlet of two farmsteads to feed and water the horses. Vai suggested I go indoors to warm myself at a hearth. The women hustled their children out when I came in, so I went back out again, not wanting the children to get cold. My hands hurt, and my lips were numb, and worst of all, a pair of crows now followed us. I was sure they were my sire's spies.

It was a long, silent, cold day as we rode south. At midday, when we halted in an abandoned shelter for a short rest, Vai sat next to me on a crude wooden bench. I huddled in a shawl of misery, as mute as if the priest in the temple had cut out my tongue.

Vai addressed Devyn. "Is there no mage inn in your village? Surely magisters ride through your village every year or two to claim their tithe in servants and in furs. Now and again a child must bloom with cold magic. Why would Crescent House have built in such a forsaken northern place if there was not something they deemed valuable there?"

Devyn stared at his hands as he answered. "To our village, no magister is now coming. The death of Crescent House has to us brought the curse of the god. Each year after the night of bonfires when the sun turns south, we bring our trade goods and our children to the trade fair at Kimbri. There will you be finding House lodging, Magister."

"It was the ice, wasn't it?" said Vai suddenly. "The mages of Crescent House wanted to be close to the ice. Because our power is strongest here."

Devyn gestured a sign to wipe away the secret knowledge he had unwillingly overheard. "If we wish to be reaching Kimbri before nightfall, then we must be riding, Magister."

Afternoon shadows lengthened. We passed fields covered with rotting straw against the cold. As twilight sank down over us and the moon rose, a substantial village rose like illusion in the evening mist. Past clusters of thatched huts rose wood buildings with glass windows through which lamplight shone. We turned aside and rode to an ice-rimed meadow. Two cottages posed picturesquely on the bank of a stream, linked by a long enclosed walkway. Smoke rose from the chimney of one cottage. Devyn led us to the cottage with no chimney and thus no fire.

Lamps, seen through glass windows, guttered out as we approached. The door opened and men hurried out who had clearly been making everything ready for us. Their faces looked ghostly in moonlight. They made a deep courtesy.

My body ached, stiff with cold and with emotion I dared not claim.

Vai touched my arm, his forehead wrinkled with concern. "Catherine, let's go in."

Yet then my mother's brother spoke. "Was there ever peace for her, before the hunter came to kill her?"

My gaze flashed to him. "They knew peace for a few short years."

"The magister calls you Catherine. Is that the name Tara gave you?"

"Yes. She named me Catherine."

His mouth was creased with sorrow; his weathered face held many lines, and none made me think he had ever laughed much. "Catherine," he repeated. "Named after Hecate, the goddess of gates, who guards the threshold between the living and the dead. True it is, that the hunter sired you. But it is sure you are my sister's, for I see Tara in every line of you. I loved her once. But she left us and she never looked back."

"They loved me," I said hoarsely, for I needed him to know that. I clasped the hilt of my sword in one hand and pressed the other to the locket hanging at my breast. "She was pregnant again with another child, with Daniel's child, who would have been my brother or sister. They didn't mean to leave me behind. They meant us to all be together."

His words slipped into an older rhythm, as if only he and I were awake in the whole wide gloaming. "From what cloth is longing woven? Is it silver? Is it gold? Yet even fine garments wear out, while longing still clads me."

His words caught in my heart and, on an impulse I could not control, I extended a hand toward him. He reined his pony away as if even the thought of my touch might contaminate him.

"Catherine, let them go," said Vai, grabbing my mount's bridle.

I was too stunned to protest as Devyn and his soldiers rode into the village for the night. Vai sent the local men away, then drew me inside the cottage and shut and latched the door.

The cottage had two chambers, one on each side of a central passage. A back door opened onto the enclosed walkway that led along the hypocaust to the attached cottage, where the stove burned. Heat poured up from beneath the floorboards.

In the parlor a knotted carpet had been rolled back to leave space for a tub of steaming water, buckets for rinsing, and a bench heaped with linen towels. Our gear had been set on a table next to a folded stack of clean clothes. By the light of cold fire Vai closed the curtains while I stared at the unexpectedly luxurious surroundings, feeling as if I'd found silk in a ragged shepherd's hovel.

"Love, come here."

He undressed himself and then me, pinned up my braid, and coaxed me into the tub with him. As the water warmed my numb limbs, he just held me. My thoughts had hit a wall. I could only comprehend the lap of water sloshing against the side of the tub, the steady rhythm of his breathing against my back, and the pressure of my head resting along his cheek.

In the other chamber waited a spacious curtained bed with an astounding feather quilt of exquisite construction. Dressing in the linen bed robes they had laid out for us, we snuggled together under a wool blanket on a settee. We shared a tray of honeycakes, a bowl of porridge garnished with butter, and a bottle of bold red wine. A part of me was hungry, but it all tasted like sand.

He spoke at random. "I can only figure one reason they thought me a magister the moment they saw me. Most people here have the pale skin and hair of Celtic ancestry, although some like your grandfather are more obviously mixed, likely the bastard descendants of Crescent House. To their eyes I must be a magister and thus a nobleman."

"Why would cold mages want anything in this terrible place?" I said angrily.

His lips crimped down. He pressed a hand over mine. "Love, you're very tired. We both need to sleep. Some things are better examined in the morning."

"I don't even know what day it is. We don't even know what year it is…" Days and years were not the pain clawing up out of my bruised

240

heart. "First Aunt Tilly and Uncle Jonatan gave me away. Now the man who is my uncle fears me and my grandfather wishes I had been smothered at birth. My mother and father are dead. My sire is a monster. And I miss Bee. I don't even know where she and Rory are or if they're all right."

Tears welled out of the pit exposed by the half-remembered whisper of my mother's voice in my heart. She had reached for me. She had cherished me despite everything.

Vai tucked us under the bedcovers and let me cry in his arms. He said nothing, and when my tears at long last dried up, I knew there was nothing he needed to say. Any man or woman can speak words and not mean them, or mean them and not have the strength to carry them through. Instead he kissed the tears from my cheeks and sighed with weary satisfaction as he settled me comfortably against him. Strange it was how his silence brought a measure of peace to my heart. We had traveled such a long way, and even farther if one measured from the first day we had met.

"Vai?" Seeking another form of comfort, I dropped kisses along the curve of his neck.

More worn out than I had guessed, he had already fallen asleep.

25

Vai's twitching and muttering woke me. He was slipping in and out of his village patois, obviously dreaming. He was very warm, possibly feverish, trying to throw off the blankets and quilt as if they were weights he had to free himself from.

In a rough, desperate voice he said, "Ah kill 'ee." Then, more clearly, flat with rage, "I will kill you."

"Vai. It's me. It's Catherine. I'm here with you. You're safe. We're safe." I stroked his hair and face until he relaxed.

He sighed, barely awake. "My sweet Catherine. You're safe. I'll keep you safe."

Between one breath and the next he dropped back into sleep.

The air was pleasantly warm, heat rising from below. I slipped on the linen dressing robe and peeked out the closed curtains to see the sun almost at zenith. Gracious Melqart! We had slept a long time. Voices murmured in the passage. I opened the door. Men were in the parlor, tidying up. When they saw me they averted their gazes.

"Salvete," I said, speaking slowly. "May we have food? Broth and porridge to start with, and a heavier meal later. Wash water, please. Also, if you can clean our clothes and gear . . ."

Our things were taken away and food delivered. I ate, but Vai did not wake. He tossed and turned, shivering and then sweating. I washed him down repeatedly with cool water. Once I was able to wake him for long enough to get some broth down his throat, but he fell back asleep as in a stupor. It frightened me that he had driven himself to collapse and I hadn't noticed. To pass the day I mended his dash jacket, ate, washed my hair, and enjoyed the comfort of a furnished and heated domicile, although I kept a chair shoved under the door latch as a precaution.

Without his cold fire to light the evening, I crawled back into bed at dusk.

What woke me I did not at first know, only that I came awake groping for my sword. The hilt shivered in my hand as I drew it out of the spirit world. Vai was sprawled across half the bed, dead asleep but breathing comfortably. The door's latch jigged down, and the door bumped against the chair. Veiled in shadow, I padded to the door.

A male voice muttered to his companions in words I understood well enough to get the gist: The mage was ill, the black-haired beast was alone and trapped in the body of a woman, so the cursed magister could be slaughtered like the pig all mages were and his possessions shared among men bold enough to take action.

A hand groped through the crack where the door gapped open, seeking to shove away the chair. I stabbed, pinning the hand to the wood.

"I never sleep. After I kill you, I'll paint my face with your blood and come after the rest."

I pulled the blade out.

Whimpering in fear, the men stumbled out the front door. I grabbed the linen dressing robe, tied it around myself, and went after them. By the time I reached the open door, my attackers had vanished into the night. A lamp carried by a single person approached across the snow. With sword raised, I waited. A middle-aged man halted at the bottom of the stairs. His lime-whitened, spiky hair glittered with snowflakes. In his ears shone the gold earrings of a djeli. He spoke with an educated accent as he measured me with a tale-teller's curiosity and an icing of fear.

"My apologies if the magister was disturbed. I heard too late that ruffians were up to mischief. They will be punished." There drifted from the village a shout, followed by a scream. "Do you wish to kill them yourself?"

Anger made it easy for me to strike. "No. Give them a year's punishment at hard labor so they live to tell the tale of how no man can attack a magister. How are we to sleep, knowing the hospitality we were offered has been violated?"

243

"It is our shame that the magister was insulted. No doubt he keeps one such as you as protection."

"One such as me? What do you mean?"

He hesitated, looking as if he were trying to decide whether it would be better to answer or to plunge his head into a cauldron of boiling oil. "I mean no offense. Your hair and eyes stamp you as being born with the mark of the Hunt. Such children are known to be unseemly wild and ungovernable, lustful and violent."

"Are there many like me here in the north?" I demanded, much struck by this revelation. Was my sire tomcatting about every Hallows' Night? Or was the wolf we had seen capable, like Rory, of walking in human skin?

"Not so many. Most such ill-omened children are set out in winter for the wolves to eat. I will watch here by the door through the rest of the night myself, if you will allow it."

I let him into the passage to sit on a bench. Once back in the bedchamber I shoved the chair back up against the door and then sat under the quilt in the bed, unable to sleep for the way my blood was pounding. Set out in winter for the wolves to eat! I would just eat those cursed wolves first! Not to mention skewer every night-stalking criminal who hated cold mages.

Vai hadn't stirred. Asleep, he was so vulnerable. I had once heard him describe to his grandmother the impossibility of a cold mage making his way in the world alone, without a mage House to protect him. Was there no safe place for us?

I meant to keep watch until he woke, but as dawn lightened night to gray, I dozed off.

A spill of water woke me. He stood naked at the side table washing his face at a basin. Seeing me awake, he slipped back into bed.

"Vai!" I cradled his face in my hands as I studied him for lines of illness. "I was so worried about you. How do you feel?"

"Rested and warm, although I'm hungry. Why would you be worried about me?" I loved the way his hands roamed, knowing just how to touch me. "Ah! You're worried because I fell asleep last night instead of—"

"Last night? You slept two nights and a day!"

"Did I? I collapse sometimes when I weave too much cold magic for too long without rest." His casual tone reassured me, as did the kisses he flew along my cheek. "It's no wonder you're disappointed and fretful."

"To be sure! Now that you mention it, I suppose I am a trifle sulky and out of sorts, and not just because I spent all day yesterday as an adoring wife ought, lovingly mending your dash jacket while watching over you in your sickbed, and afterward stabbing a man in the hand."

He drew back. "What?"

"Last night I stopped three men from breaking into this chamber and killing you."

He got back out of bed and pulled on trousers and shirt before opening the curtains. The view revealed a snowy meadow and ice-spackled stream but no people, although I heard the hum of troubled voices. "I had hoped to stay here a few days to rest, but we'll have to move on at once. If you feel strong enough after staying awake all night and stabbing miscreants."

"Of course I feel strong enough! Do you think I am some delicate flower?"

He buttoned up the dash jacket. "Of course not, love. *Delicate* and *flower* are two of the last words I would ever consider using to describe you, along with *quiet, placid, cautious,* and *frail.*"

"That's six words."

"So it is. You did a fine job mending the jacket, love."

"My thanks," I replied primly, although I was secretly relieved the work satisfied his fastidious eye. "By the way, the town's djeli spent the night in the passage."

Vai drew his cold steel and spun a shiver of cold magic so I could draw mine. Then he pulled the chair away from the door and threw it open.

Seen through the open door, the djeli rose from the bench. "My lord!"

"Is this the hospitality your village offers?"

"My lord! We feel nothing but shame. The malcontents who attacked you are dealt with."

"As they should be. By what means will you see us safely conveyed to our destination?"

245

"The headman has already told me to offer his carriage and outriders to convey you to White Bow House in Sala, my lord. Will that be acceptable?"

"At once! We require provisions for the journey. I assume there are staging points and mage inns along the route?"

"Yes, my lord."

Vai shut the door and turned to me. "The sooner we're out of here, the easier I'll feel."

"Probably he means the outriders to slaughter us on the road."

"I doubt it. This is a well-maintained cottage. The arrangement with the cold mages must benefit the headman enough for it to be worth his while to take so much care. Our gear?"

"Everything has been capably cleaned and repaired."

The coach arrived so quickly that I suspected they had been waiting for us to wake up, meaning to get us out of town before there was more trouble. People gathered under the cold lens of the sky to watch as we left the cottage. Women covered the eyes of their children, as if my gaze might wither the innocent. At the back of the crowd, thin young men stared at the coach with sullen contempt. The djeli handed in heated bricks, a basket of provender, and a bottle of wine while offering a fulsome apology for the disrespect we had endured. Vai thanked him, shut the door, then leaned across me to close the shutters as a whip snapped and the coach began rolling.

"I see no point in allowing them to stare. We can't change the minds of the ones who hate and fear us, not like this. Are you feeling better, love? I mean, after everything we saw."

"If you mean the ugly words that hateful old man said to me, I see he meant to poison me against my mother. All he did was make me love and admire her more. Do mages simply kill anyone who tries to assault one of the Houseborn?"

"At Four Moons House, criminals were sent to the mines."

"I wonder under what conditions they labor there."

"I don't know," admitted Vai, "but everyone in my village knew that people sent to the mines never returned."

On the first day the carriage rolled uneventfully through the winter countryside. An outrider went ahead to alert each next stage that we were coming. By the second day I was surprised at how good the roads were, until the coachman informed me that they had been built in the last ten years with indentured local labor under the supervision of soldiers. Before that, he said, the journey would have taken a month on a cart track.

At dusk on the third day we rolled into the courtyard of an isolated inn out in the middle of nowhere. No one bustled to assist us. The watering trough had been smashed to pieces.

An outrider came running from the stables. "My lord, the place has been ransacked and defaced."

Vai and I drew our swords. Under Vai's mage light we investigated the two-room inn and the stove house and kitchen behind. Every piece of furniture had been stripped out except a wooden slops bucket with a leaking bottom, filled with frozen excrement. Shattered floorboards exposed the pillars of the hypocaust system, on which were painted curses. Amulets plaited with animal bones, withered leaves, and chicken feathers caked with dried blood hung from the lintels.

Outside, Vai called over the most senior outrider, a quiet man who performed his duties and kept the younger men in line. "Speak honestly and I give my word I will hear your speech without reprisal. Why do the people here hate cold mages so much they would do this?"

The man considered his gloved hands. "My people have been living in these lands since the dawn of time, my lord. Then in my father's youth, the outsiders came. You mages brought down the anger of the god over all the countryside." He glanced at me. "The mage houses and their princely allies rule us now. They take our young men to build roads and to fight, and our young women to be servants and to be shamed. For this privilege, my lord, we must be paying a tithe of our furs and meat to the mages likewise."

Snow dusted down over us. The men watched with the caution of servants. They were five and we were two, and yet they showed no sign of being eager to attack us.

Vai spoke. "Did you know there is a man, General Camjiata, who has written a legal code that outlaws clientage? A law that says no person may own another person as property or claim another community as its possession?"

"Do you mean the Iberian Monster, my lord?" asked the senior man. Unaware of how he was twisting his hands, he had almost pulled off one of his gloves.

"You have the look of a soldier about you," I said. "Perhaps you fought in the war twenty years ago."

His gaze flashed to me before settling back to Vai. "We should go on, my lord. We'll nurse the horses along and get to the next hostel. There is moonlight, and your magic, to light our way."

"I'll scout ahead." In full sight of the riders I wrapped the shadows around me. They exclaimed as I vanished, and I was glad of it, because if they refused to like or trust me, then I wanted them to be scared of me.

Vai walked in front of the horses with a lamp fashioned of cold fire. The clop of horses' hooves and the stamp of the men's footfalls faded into winter's silence as I ran ahead. It was so quiet that the ambush revealed itself by the heavy breathing and restless shifting of men hiding alongside the road in a ditch. There were only ten, armed with iron weapons. I trotted back to the coach.

"Wait here," Vai said to the attendants. "By no means come forward until you hear sounds of fighting. Catherine, no killing unless we have no choice."

"They mean to kill us!"

"Maybe so, but they are not without fair grievances and no means to gain a hearing. If we have no choice, we won't spare them."

I acquiesced rather than argue; I would do what I must when the time came. Sparks of cold fire bobbing along the ground gave us just enough light to creep off the road and thus up behind them. At the ditch I stalked in among them where they shivered, waiting patiently.

"Did ye hear a footstep?" one whispered.

"Hsss! Look!"

A carriage and horses glided down the road, fitted with a coachman and footman. It was an astonishing illusion, except for a lag in the turning of the wheels. Still, the ambushers should have been instantly suspicious of it for the lack of sound. Instead, wound up and eager, they leaped.

The carriage and horses dissolved into a hiss of falling ice.

Cold magic hits like a hammer, so sing the bards and the djeliw. Air becomes ice. Iron groans. I dropped to my knees just as all the iron in their weapons shattered in a burst of shards and screams. Only cold steel was safe.

Wreathed in my threads of magic, I ran among them. The smell of their hot blood and the scent of their panic lanced through my veins like lust. My sire was a killer and my mother a soldier, but I remembered what Vai had said, so I only pricked them in shoulder and thigh. Many were already bloodied. Two had to be carried by their fellows. Routed, they fled into the night.

When I gave the all clear, Vai joined me on the road. I laughed, exultant at our easy victory.

He looked grim and said only, "You are unharmed?"

"Yes. That was spectacular!"

He sighed. "I cannot help but think there would not be this kind of trouble if not for the inequity of the law and the burdens placed on people bound into clientage."

"You're kinder than I can be toward people who meant to do us harm! Bandits and troublemakers! You need to work on the wheels of the carriage. They didn't quite look right."

In the light of a perfectly shaped illusion of a candle lantern, we walked back the way we had come as Vai rolled illusory wheels ahead of us, trying to fix the lag. Soon we met the outriders approaching at a brisk trot, for they had heard the screams. When the servants saw the stains of blood upon the ground and the fragmented remains of the weapons, they turned as grim as Vai.

The night hung suspended as we traveled on as through a dream.

After some time one of the young men abruptly asked Vai what he had meant by "a legal code." The senior man harshly told the lad never again to speak of such matters.

26

Sala's wide avenues, packed districts, and tall houses spoke of prosperity. Coffeehouses with big glass windows were crowded with chattering men. A market bustled with women in head wraps and winter cloaks.

I tugged on Vai's sleeve as I looked out the carriage window. "Look! An airship!"

Vai leaned over to follow my gaze. Ahead rose three scaffoldings. Taut lines tethered a gleaming airship to one of the towers. Figures moved on the tower with a grace that was not human.

"Fiery Shemesh!" I pointed. "Those are trolls! Did I tell you the prince of Tarrant expelled all trolls from Adurnam? It's strange to see trolls—and airships!—here in the eastern wilderness. I wonder where they came from."

We rolled along a street lined with offices whose signs advertised solicitors, architects, and civil engineers. A door to one of the offices opened and a pair of trolls dressed in drab dash jackets stepped onto the sidewalk. One looked as we passed. Quite unthinkingly I met its gaze directly. Its crest flared as threateningly as if I had challenged it, and it lunged. I slammed the shutter closed.

"Catherine?"

"Nothing." I eased open the shutter.

All the main streets converged on the prince's palace, a building ornamented by two towers surmounted by huge gilded eggs. *Eggs?* I stared at the towers until the gates of White Bow House cut off my view.

Our arrival in the carriage yard of the mage House brought first a startled groom and then a steward who took one look at us and hurried back inside. A bevy of young women emerged from the depths of the House, giggling behind painted fans in a fashion fifty years out of date. A coterie of young men strutted into view as they sized up Vai and then me. Last, children were marched out as if we were glorious visitors come for a festival who had to be greeted by the entire community. They had the mixed look typical of mage Houses, with complexions ranging from pale to dark, and hair all shades but none as straight as mine. By their expressions of delighted interest, it was obvious White Bow House did not get many visitors.

An old woman appeared carrying a bowl of water, which she offered to us in the traditional greeting. A pair of modest youths held basins so we could wash our hands and faces.

"Be welcome to White Bow House, home to the Cissé clan," the old woman said. "Be sheltered and fed here, as our guests."

"I am Andevai Diarisso, of Four Moons House," he said. I was surprised he erased his village origins. "This is my wife, Catherine Bell Barahal. Your hospitality honors us."

A man not much older than Vai stepped forward with an assertive smile. "Let me greet you, Magister Andevai." His accent softened *Ahn-de-vai* to *Ah-theh-nay*. "I am Viridor Cissé, grandson of Magister Dyabe Cissé, who founded White Bow House. I am mansa. I welcome you, my slave."

As surprised as I was to find so young a man as mansa, I was more shocked when Andevai laughed at this blatant slur with the greatest good humor.

"Ah, you thieves! What do you mean to steal from me?"

"We will steal you away to the men's courtyard, for you are come just in time for the Feast of Matronalia. A good feast for young married men to celebrate, with its hope of fertility and fruitful childbirth," Viridor added with a sidelong look at me.

Vai grasped my hand, leaning close to whisper, "We're safe, love. We're safe here."

With a parting smile he abandoned me, tramping off with the menfolk to the tune of a great deal of manly joking and laughter.

Whether out of politeness or because she sensed my consternation, the old woman took my right hand in hers, not to shake but to hold. 251

"I am Magister Vinda. We have a modest suite of rooms for visitors, nothing like what you must be accustomed to at Four Moons House, but I will see you made comfortable." Her speech was cultured, burred by old-fashioned pronunciations.

The "modest" rooms luxuriated in richer furnishings than anything I had grown up with. Blue fabric embroidered with sprays of silver stars upholstered the couches. The bedchamber was decorated in lovely shades of yellow.

"Everything is very lovely and of the finest materials," I said, quite honestly. She looked so pleased I wondered if they had ever received any guests at all in this frontier town.

"These are all your belongings?" she asked with obvious surprise.

"We met with unexpected difficulties on our road and were separated from our companions and the rest of our things," I temporized.

"It is clear by the state of your clothing that you have traveled an arduous path," agreed Vinda. "By which I mean no disrespect, Maestra."

"None taken!" I smiled. In my experience, smiles had a great deal of utility when it came to smoothing over an awkward question. "I was surprised when the men called each other slaves and thieves."

"The Cissé and the Diarisso are cousins who may joke with each other. Are you only recently come to the mage House, to not know this? I find it curious that a young mage of such rare potency has been chained to a woman not Houseborn and with no magic."

She was no djeli, to see the threads I wove so easily. "No one could have been more shocked than I was," I agreed politely. "How do you know he is so...potent?"

"I can divine cold magic in others." My blank expression prodded her into an enigmatic smile. "Diviners like me seek out blooms of magic among people not born into the mage Houses. When we find them, we bring them into the House to strengthen our lineage. Have you any children yet?"

I blinked, not sure how to answer this without seeming acerbic. "Why do you ask?"

"It is not usual for a young man to be sent on his Grand Tour with a young wife accompanying him. I thought you perhaps had borne him children already and sought a child by another magister. But if you've as yet had no children with him, then there can be no reason for you to seek to be impregnated by any of our men. Perhaps you are of the Sapphic persuasion, in which case I can let you know which women of the House may be interested in your attentions."

I stared at her in confusion, as bewildered as if she had started to speak in a foreign language.

Her brow wrinkled. "I beg your pardon. Some people have no interest in sexual liaisons, nor is there any reason they should. Perhaps you prefer to choose for him from among the women who seek a child? I assure you that we keep careful records so no near relatives inadvertently mate."

"Choose for him? I don't understand..." Then, of course, I did. My eyes must have gotten very round, and then very narrow. She took a step back. I reined in my temper, trying not to snap, for I sensed no hostility. If anything, she seemed puzzled. "Is this the way you greet every male visitor? By offering to let him impregnate the women of your House?"

"Yes. It is the custom among the mage Houses when the visitor is a powerful cold mage." She studied me as if I had sprouted antlers: a surprising turn of events but not yet a threatening one.

"What do you mean by the Grand Tour?"

"You truly have no idea." She folded her hands at her waist in the manner of a governess about to launch into the day's lesson. "Exceptionally potent cold magic is vanishingly rare, despite how it seems to people outside the mage Houses. Promising young men are commonly sent all around Europa, visiting other mage Houses and offering their services to young widows and to married women who have already had several children out of their husbands. Many years ago some wit called it the Grand Tour, and the name stuck."

"You send them around like you would breed livestock."

"Not at all. No one is forced to the task. It is a sensible way to attempt to increase the number of cold mages born within the Houses."

I remembered a thing Vai had told me on the night we had consummated our marriage. "Might women travel to a mage House where it is said a promising young cold mage resides? To see if they can get pregnant by him?"

She smiled with relief, at last assured my intelligence was not wanting. "Yes, that also happens, but only among those Houses who have both wealth and prestige enough to make such visits. Please excuse my plain speaking, since I comprehend I have surprised you. We are a small House, very isolated and not rich, a trifling country cousin compared to Four Moons House. We have struggled for over fifty years to survive here in the frozen north among savages. Our mansa is unseasonably young because we lost all of our experienced magisters in a cholera epidemic ten years ago. Our djeliw died as well. For us the arrival of a powerful cold mage is a precious opportunity to strengthen our lineage."

I did not want to get us tossed out into the cold, and furthermore, she had a point. "My apologies if it seemed otherwise to you, but we are not here on a Grand Tour."

She seemed more curious than annoyed. "Your ignorance of mage House customs and that blush in your cheeks suggest you are newly come to the marriage bed and that your husband pleases you, as well he might, for he is certainly handsome. I shall not press you further on this account. It would be an inauspicious time."

Apparently without having taken offense, she changed the subject to practical matters. Not that cultivating a new generation of mages wasn't, at root, a practical matter among people whose wealth and station depended on the presence of intimidating magic.

"Let me take you to the baths. We'll launder your clothing and fit you with clean things. I can see the magister's clothes need replacing. There are a number of good tailors' shops here."

A tailor's shop called Queedle & Clutch. Towers surmounted by gilded eggs. A cat waiting in the shadows. Bee had drawn these things! As the memory struck, I gasped out loud.

"Maestra, are you well?"

Palm pressed to my chest, I smiled, made tremulous by hope. "I hope and pray we might stay here a few days to rest," I said, a little hoarsely. "It has been a long and difficult journey."

"Of course. Come along. The women are eager to welcome you. We have turnip stew."

Having become accustomed to the free and easy manners in Expedition, I had to remind myself that I once would have found it unexceptional for men and women to dine in separate chambers. Anyway, I was grateful for the friendly greeting I received in the women's hall. The young women plied me with so many questions about Vai that I prudently entertained them instead with tales of Expedition and the Taino kingdom. They demanded to know if it was true that a woman had ruled the Taino kingdom, and that the new Expedition Assembly would include women as assemblymen, with the right to speak and vote just like the men.

"Of course it's true. No troll clutch in the city of Expedition would support the Assembly if females did not have the same rights as males. Do you not speak to the trolls who live here? As we came into town I saw trolls and airships. Where did they come from? Does your mage House support their presence here?"

"Of course," said Vinda. "Our House and the *ghana* work hand to glove to cultivate all the riches of this territory and in that way encourage more people to settle and work here."

"Truly? I had always understood that the technology of combustion is anathema to cold magic. Why, you are quite at the forefront of the tide of change!"

They were shocked their tedious backwater could be seen as a place where interesting things were happening. Twelve years ago the first trolls had arrived from North Amerike. They had petitioned at the ghana's court—*ghana* being the local word for the prince—for permission to mine and log in the mountainous regions near the sister cities of Sala and Koumbi.

"What do they mine?" I asked.

Vinda said, "Iron and silver. The early settlers fifty years ago got rich on silver, but the trolls brought in more efficient methods. They're building manufactories. They pay wages by the day."

"Yes, but you have to live in one of their settlements," objected a girl. "Who wants to live out there in the wild where they might eat you if they felt like it?"

"Have you heard rumors of trolls eating their employees?" I asked.

"No," said the girl, her cheeks flushed with excitement, "but we hear bloody tales of trolls gone out to survey the land who get into violent altercations with local tribesmen. The tribespeople are angry that foreigners are disrupting their hunting and trapping. Are you well acquainted with trolls?"

"I have been adopted into one of their clutches." It was remarkably gratifying to see how they quieted, quivering with anticipation.

Really, I could have talked all night, but I wanted to tell Vai about Bee's dream. At last I retreated to the guest suite to discover Vai not there. Gracious Melqart! How late did the men intend to celebrate? Had he let down his guard too easily? Had we fallen into a trap?

Knowing White Bow House had lost all its djeliw made me bold. I drew the shadows around me and went in search of the men's courtyard, even though I knew I ought not to venture there. The corridors lay empty. Elsewhere in the compound, children were being sung into their sleep, the youths were reciting their lessons before bed, and an old man was snoring. Drums tapped a festive rhythm. The scent of liquor spilled through the air as the seal of friendship. Like a hunter I followed its trail.

An open door admitted me into the mansa's formal audience chamber with a carved stool and several cushions. Past another door I entered a formal dining chamber with a table and about thirty chairs, all undisturbed. Past that lay an informal receiving chamber. Here the remains of a generous supper littered the low tables, cushions all awry. Beyond glass-paned doors lay an inner courtyard lit by cold fire. Snow glittered on the shrubs and trimmed hedges.

Four drummers laid down a rhythm. Every dance has a story, every rhythm a meaning, through which it converses with the pulsing heart of the world. Like the other men, Vai had stripped off his winter coat and his dash jacket. They were all very fine, for they were men who had grown up with dancing, but he had a supple and energetic way of moving that naturally drew my eye as I admired him. Although normally he would have known I had crept close, he showed not the least sign his thoughts lay anywhere except within the rhythm and the camaraderie of the men laughing and egging each other on to show off.

This courtyard was not meant for my eyes. I was trespassing.

I padded back to the lonely refuge of our rooms. In lamplight I set out the cacica's skull and poured her a little wine. As I cleaned and sorted my sewing kit, I told the cacica about my evening with the women of White Bow House. I had stayed away from discussing Camjiata or radical philosophy and stuck to a theme of women speaking out and taking a place in governance. Everyone had paid attention, even if most had been skeptical that such a thing could ever happen. Maybe there really were times when words were more effective than a sword.

Men's laughter gusted up the hall. I grabbed my sword as the lamps guttered out and the door swung open. Vai slammed it behind him as he stamped snow off his boots. Baubles of cold fire bobbed erratically over his head. He shed his coat and tossed it over a chair to reveal his dash jacket unbuttoned and disheveled as if he had carelessly dragged it on.

"I could just eat you up," he murmured, pressing me back against the wall to kiss me.

I wrestled free. "Blessed Tanit. You are drunk!"

"Given my previous experience with you when you were drunk, I can't help but wonder what you will be like in bed when..." He noticed the skull sitting on a side table. With a visible start he recoiled a step. Then he grabbed his coat and draped it over the skull. That he looked inordinately pleased with his cleverness confirmed my belief that he had imbibed too much liquor.

"I felt it prudent to maintain my wits in a strange household. Why were you outdoors?"

"We drummed the festival dance in the courtyard. It started to snow." He tugged me into the bedchamber, steered me to the bed, and grappled me down on it. "Since it is the Feast of Matronalia to honor the Roman goddess of childbirth, they all wanted to know if I have gotten you pregnant yet. I had to tell them it was not yet the auspicious season for us."

"They do seem inordinately interested in your fertility. Magister Vinda asked if you were here on your Grand Tour."

He stiffened, and not in an amorous way. His mood lurched from lasciviousness to fury as he sat bolt upright. "Our offspring is not the mansa's to sell or trade as he wishes."

"I set her straight, I assure you," I said soothingly, stroking his arm.

He leaned against the headboard, looking away from me and thus forcing me to contemplate the beauty of his eyes and strong cheekbones. The sulky set of his lips made me want to kiss them. "Do you have any idea how insulting it is to be treated as if you are nothing more than a highly regarded stallion with desirable conformation?"

Several jesting comments raced against each other in an effort to reach my tongue first, but I yanked on the reins and tried another tactic to calm him. "When I was waiting tables at the boardinghouse, some men treated me as if I were nothing more than a womanly form they'd like to fondle and take to bed."

He glanced sidelong at me with a swift measure to take in exactly those conforming attributes. His thunderous frown eased slightly. "They surely did."

I bit down a smile. Levity would be fatal at just this moment. I chose a feinting attack. "Magister Vinda wondered if I was looking to dally with one of their women. Or get pregnant by one of their men."

He put an arm around me. "Why would they think you would be interested in anyone else when you're married to me?"

That he could speak such conceited words with such humble sincerity never failed to delight me. "I suppose it would depend on whether I can get satisfaction. If I must dash the hopes of the many, then you must accommodate the desires of the one."

"Must I, Catherine?" He had a way of saying my name that made it seem like the most burning caress whose touch inflamed my entire body.

"Yes. You certainly must."

27

My growling stomach woke me. Both bed and window curtains had been pulled back to admit the light of a sunny winter morning. Vai sat at a dressing table in front of a large mirror, shaving. He wore trousers but nothing else, so I ogled his back, with his workman's muscles. There was an old scar across his mid-back, as well as a fading bruise on his left shoulder that he had acquired during our escape. I admired the way he turned his head by degrees to get a new angle, and the methodical way he trimmed using a comb, razor, and tiny pair of scissors.

Then I got bored.

Was the man trimming hair by hair to get the exact look he wanted?

"Gracious Melqart, Vai. How much time do you spend on your grooming? Wouldn't you rather come back in bed with me?"

He met my gaze in the mirror. "Of course I would, love. But I'm meeting Viridor and the lads for breakfast. They're going to show me the schoolroom—"

"The schoolroom?" Dumbstruck, I contemplated a new side to his character.

"They lost most of their older mages in an epidemic of cholera ten years ago. They've had to rebuild their schoolroom without the teachers. I told them I would outline the lesson plans used at Four Moons House so they can institute a rigorous curriculum."

"I thought the secret belongs to those who remain silent."

"The mansa always says that every mage, no matter how young or old or how he came to Four Moons House, must be educated in mage craft. To instruct every mage helps all mages regardless of what House they belong to. Anyway, if we mean to speak of freedom as if we believe it is a right for our communities to claim, then we must mean it for all communities, not just our own. The children here deserve the same education I received, don't you think?"

With a startled frown he paused to examine his face in the mirror, as if he had just discovered an impertinent flaw. He slid the comb into his beard and trimmed hairs by shaving the razor along the comb.

A plain linen dressing robe lay folded by the bed. After slipping it on I padded over to stand behind him. The floorboards breathed a comforting heat. I felt truly relaxed for the first time since the morning he and I had woken up on the bed he had built for us, after the night we had consummated our marriage. How I missed that bed!

I traced the angled scar on his back. "How did you get this?"

His hands tightened as he caught in a breath. After a moment he blew away the hairs on the razor with an exhalation. "In the youth hall at Four Moons House."

"Bad enough they were allowed to taunt and bully you with words. They were allowed to actually beat you and harm you? This looks like a knife cut! No one put a stop to it?"

His frown sharpened to an arrogant sneer as he fastidiously wiped off the shaving kit and packed it away into a tiny wooden box in which each tool fit exactly. "I was the village boy, remember? Did Magister Vinda really think I was here on a Grand Tour? Viridor said nothing about it."

In the face of this uncomfortable shift of mood, it seemed wise to calm him. "Vinda is a diviner and can tell perfectly well how powerful a cold mage you are. She can't have known you would see it as an insult. To her it would seem a compliment. There was a time you didn't refuse."

"Because I was young and ignorant. I boasted about how women offered themselves to me. For the longest time I thought I was so irresistible that women would travel to Four Moons House for a chance at my bed. What a fool I looked to everyone! How they laughed and mocked me."

"Yes, and that's all in the past now, love. White Bow House has been very hospitable. It's not fair to be angry at them." I fetched his shirt and jacket, thinking that clothes would distract him.

260   His frown faded as he pulled on his shirt. "I'm not angry at them.

Viridor has been more than generous. He'd like to have us stay as guests for as long as we wish. I know you want to get to Havery as soon as possible, love, but I do think it wise for us to recover from our arduous journey before we go on. Just a week or two."

"Yes, of course we must stay. We need to find a tailor's shop."

"That's already arranged." He buttoned up his much-abused jacket. "After breakfast and the schoolroom, Viridor and the lads and I will be going down to Cutters Row. That's what they call the tailors' district here. Viridor offered to see that I have decent clothes to wear."

I managed not to burst out laughing. "That's exceedingly generous, especially since he can have no conception of what you mean by 'decent.' But I meant that we need to find a particular tailor's shop, one that's opposite a troll-owned shop called Queedle and Clutch." I explained about Bee's dream. "I'm hoping it might be her I'm meant to meet. Just as she dreamed she and I would meet at Nance's that night in Expedition after the areito."

He smiled as if our fierce misunderstanding at Nance's had attained the glamour of a fond memory, for he was the sort of person for whom an unconditional triumph quite eradicates any troubling defeats. "Well then, my sweet Catherine, I shall insist we patronize whichever tailor shop sits opposite Queedle and Clutch. Come here. I don't have to leave quite yet."

White Bow House's hospitality could not be faulted. With plenty of food and a comfortable bed we regained our strength quickly. The hypocaust system built under the well-appointed house made it easy to weather a short but ferocious cold snap that would have killed us had we been caught out on the road.

Yet fourteen days passed, the weather warmed up, and still there was no sign of Bee. I busied myself earning a little money by writing pamphlets for a troll-owned printer. Vai took for granted that the mage House would provide for all our needs, but I wanted funds of my own in my purse.

On a cloudy afternoon I trudged through sleet along Printers Lane with a sheaf of papers tucked in a satchel. Magister Vinda accompanied me together with two male attendants as guards and two young women to hold umbrellas over our heads. I was sure the four servants were slaves in all but name, clientage-born as Vai had been. But since

261

they were country-born youth who could not speak anything but the garbled rural dialect, I had been unable to hold extended conversations with them.

"I must admit, Magister," I said to Vinda, "you are the last person I thought would embrace so enthusiastically such radical principles as an elected Assembly and the right of women within a community to stand for Assembly just like men."

"Why should that surprise you?" she asked. "I see no reason women should not act in the same capacity as men. Is the mage craft within a woman's body worth less than that in a man's? Has the Lord of All not given both women and men voices with which to speak and to sing?" She paused. "You look surprised."

"I thought the mage Houses objected to anything new, like the combustion engine or airships or any sort of radical philosophy. In Adurnam, it's only been in the last fifteen years that girls were even allowed to attend the academy college. Of course we sat upstairs in the women's balcony, or at separate tables on the other side of the room from the boys. I thought mages must therefore also object to educating women."

"Where do you think the fashion of educating girls alongside boys comes from, if not from mage Houses? We have always trained our girls as well as our boys."

As we arrived at that moment at the establishment Pinfeather & Quill, I had no opportunity to reply that my own people had done the same. A bell tinkled as we entered the front room. Its counter was covered with printed pamphlets, and a press thumped in the back. The smell of ink and dust pervaded the air. A drably feathered troll pushed through the curtain separating the two rooms.

"Magister Vinda. Maestra Bell Barahal." Tewi had the facility of all trolls to mimic human accents exactly and had quickly adapted her speech to mine, so she was much easier for me to understand than were most of the residents of Sala. "How is it with you this day?"

We shook hands. She had a bitter scent, like aniseed, not unpleasant but not attractive. Her head swiveled almost back-to-front to mark the entrance of a second troll, a shorter, brightly plumaged male. He gave a bobbing courtesy, but his gaze tracked us in a most alarming way. With ink-stained talons he poured out tea and uncovered bowls to reveal nuts and dried fruit, then stood by the door measuring the four nervous servants as for dinner. Tewi paced through the formalities in a rote way different from Chartji's or Keer's, as if she had taught herself rules for how to deal with humans rather than having grown up among them.

After the preliminaries Tewi indicated the papers. "You are finished with the third article? The pamphlets describing the Taino kingdom have sold well so far."

"This is my description of how Expedition's radicals overthrew the Council and instituted an Assembly and charter. General Camjiata figures prominently in the tale."

"Timely!" Tewi paged through the text. I liked watching her taloned fingers shift each sheet with a flick that stubby human fingers could not match. "We have just received news from Iberia."

"You have news of General Camjiata?" This was the first I had heard of the general since the mansa's declaration—almost a year ago, in Adurnam—that Camjiata had made landfall at Gadir.

Tewi went on. "A coalition of southern Gallic princes marched into northern Iberia. They hoped to take the general by surprise before he could consolidate his allies and raise an army. However, the general defeated the coalition in a battle near the city of Tarraco. We're printing a broadsheet with the sensational news now."

Vinda leaned to look at the broadsheet with its screaming headline "Iberian Monster Devours His Enemy!" Her sudden motion caused the male troll to take an assertive step forward with feathers fluffed out. I grasped at my cane just as Tewi whistled. The male checked himself and flattened his crest.

Vinda was so intent on the broadsheet that she did not notice. "I thought Camjiata was killed fifteen years ago when the Second Coalition defeated him at the Battle of Havery."

"No, they took him prisoner and held him on an island," Tewi answered. "He escaped over two years ago and found refuge in the Antilles before returning to Europa."

Hard to believe it had been over two years ago that Vai had walked into my life! The spirit world had stolen so many months from me.

"Maestra Tewi, where do you get the news?" I asked. "The princes and mages who oppose Camjiata will wish to suppress such tidings, lest discontented folk think to quarrel on his behalf."

Tewi did not bare her teeth in an imitation of a smile as Chartji did. She bobbed her shoulders in a movement perhaps meant as a show of agreement but which I found threatening. "What the ghana of Sala knows, he keeps to himself. But other rats travel the roads, and other rats talk."

"Beware lest you find yourself in trouble for disseminating radical literature and censored news," said Vinda. "The ghana arrests radicals and throws them in prison."

"The ghana will not be so eager to arrest ones who make the swords and rifles with which he arms his troops."

"No, indeed, it seems unlikely," I replied, amused by her blunt assessment.

"Regardless, the ghana has not decreed a minister to approve or censor all printed materials, such as the emperor has in Rome. Our consortium tried to set up a printing establishment in Rome. Our petition was refused."

"Fiery Shemesh! I never heard there were trolls migrating to Rome!"

Tewi bobbed again, making me wonder if it wasn't after all her way of showing amusement. "We people like to stay busy and see new things."

After Tewi paid me my share of the profits from the week's sale of the first two pamphlets, we took our leave.

Vinda shook her head as we walked along. "There will be trouble when this news becomes known on the street by every rough laborer and laundress, but the troll is right. The ghana will not wish to offend those who make the weapons he needs."

The rain had stopped. Wheels slicked through puddles as carts and wagons passed. Through a window I glimpsed a man seated in a coffee-house reading my first pamphlet aloud to his companions while they laughed and commented. Well! That was gratifying!

"I shall leave you here," I said as we reached an intersection. "The tailor sent me a note asking me to come by at the same time Andevai has an appointment. The tailor has never specifically asked before, so I really must see what he wants."

"You are brave to venture into such a lion's den. I should not like to come between the magister and his clothes. He is strict about how he likes things done."

"Have there been complaints of his teaching?"

"Only by the weak-willed and lazy. He can be exacting, it is true, but he always shows deference to his elders and asks us, we few elders who are left in White Bow House, to share our knowledge. His manners are so very good that I should like to meet his mother!"

Since Vai had never mentioned his village-born origins, I wondered what Magister Vinda would say if she knew the well-mannered young man had been born to the same rank of people as her own lowly servants.

"I will send two attendants with you," she added.

"My thanks, but I would prefer to go on my own way, if you don't mind, Magister." In truth, the tailor's unexpected summons had raised an unreasonable hope in my breast.

Vinda's smile was both gracious and skeptical. "You're a bold girl. The young women in the House think you quite the most exciting person they have ever met and wish only to have adventures like you, but I have told them a hundred times in the last two weeks that the tale gives more delight than the living of it."

Her words made me think of Luce. Was Luce resigned to helping her mother at the boardinghouse? Had she decided to take a factory job, maybe in the hope of saving up enough money to buy an apprenticeship into a troll consortium that might offer her a chance to travel?

"True enough, Magister. I hope you do not consider me a bad influence."

"I like the way you speak up, even if I do not always agree." To my surprise she kissed me on the cheek as she might a niece. "Go on. It is certain you can take care of yourself."

Sala's central district was not large, so it did not take me long to reach Cutters Row and the tailor shop opposite Queedle & Clutch. The bell jangled as I entered. Two men sat cross-legged on a raised platform in front of the shop window. The straw-haired man was sewing buttonholes and the black-haired man was finishing a collar. They greeted me with friendly smiles before glancing toward a screen that concealed the other occupants of the room.

"No, the cuffs should not come to the crease of the wrist," Vai was saying in a tone whose self-indulgent fastidiousness might provoke a less patient man into taking scissors to every garment within reach. "They should be a finger's width longer—no more!—so the wrist is not exposed when I extend my arm to its full length. You see how that ruins the look."

I shook out my cape and hung it from a hook at the door.

"I can't possibly wear this! Please tell me you have not cut the other two to this same length."

"I have not cut the third one yet, Magister, for I am not sure of the fabric."

"I have already told you which fabric I want. Did I not make my wishes clear?"

I smiled at the two men, who smiled knowingly back at me. They had obviously endured many of these harangues; I quite wisely never stayed long in the shop when I did come with Vai.

"Of course, Magister, I have already taken care of the problem with the other dash jacket, if you would like to try it on. Let me help you. Just a moment, if you will."

The tailor emerged from behind the screen to see who had come in. He was a bent old man with the wry demeanor of a person who has for his entire life successfully done business with overly particular customers. "Salve, Maestra," he said. "Thank you for coming."

"You are a patient man, Maester," I said in a low voice, with a glance toward the screen.

He inclined his head, thankfully not denying the sentiment. Like me he kept his voice low. "He holds others to the exacting standard to which he holds himself. The first dash jacket I made to his specifications he wore when Magister Viridor introduced him at the ghana's court. In the ten days since, my custom has tripled and I have had to advertise for more sewers and cutters."

Through an open door I could see into a sunny room in back, where men bent over garments in various stages of assembly, conversing in a merry rumble of masculine voices.

"The work out of your shop is very skilled."

"So it is, Maestra, and my thanks for mentioning it. But men will believe the illusion that if a well-formed man looks good in a garment, then they necessarily will also. It takes all my power of persuasion to convince some of these new customers that a different style of clothing would suit them better. Which brings me to my purpose." He indicated bolts of cloth unfurled across the cutting table. A length of dove-gray woolen broadcloth covered the other bolts; it was exactly the sort of sober fabric Vai despised. "He was insistent about the green floral print but I cannot think the color suits his complexion. Now he has brought in a fabric that is too, ah, decorative for the style he prefers. I intend no offense, but perhaps you could persuade him to a less flamboyant…"

Vai stepped out from behind the screen. The top five buttons of a tepidly green dash jacket were undone. It was indeed not his best color. "Catherine? What are you doing here?"

"Just passing by," I lied, to protect the tailor. "Goodness, Andevai, you look like a fern." To give myself something to do before he exploded, I twitched aside the gray cloth to see the fabric hidden beneath. "Gracious Melqart!"

Distracted, Vai looked down, then smiled. "It's perfect," he breathed so ardently that the sewers had to conceal snickers.

The cloth beneath was finest wool challis, dyed a deep blue in which whispered all the soft promise of a twilight sky, which subtlety was entirely overwhelmed by its being embroidered with flagrant sprays of bright color depicted as flowers bursting open like fireworks. A person might call it *decorative* as a euphemism for *gaudy*.

But what shocked me was that it matched the fabric of the dash jacket worn by the man meant to be Vai in the false dream sketched by Bee to convince Caonabo not to arrest me.

The bell jangled as the door opened. A swirl of chilly, damp air shivered into the shop like a big cat with a cold nose nudging your cheek. A remarkably attractive man with blond hair, a thick mustache, and scarred knuckles stopped short.

"Bold Diana! It is peculiar to find you exactly where I was told you would be."

"Brennan!" Elation throbbed through my chest. Brennan Touré Du was the first man who had ever truly flirted with me, however mild a flirtation it might have been that night at the Griffin Inn when I had met him, the trolls Godwik and Chartji, and Professora Kehinde Nayo Kuti. I had understood at the time that he was being kind, for a man of Brennan Du's experience and reputation was quite out of the reach of a girl like me.

Vai's hand settled possessively on the small of my back as he stepped   267 up beside me. "I believe we have not been formally introduced," he said in his most coolly belligerent tone. "I am Magister Andevai Diarisso of Four Moons House. Perhaps you will be so kind as to inform my wife and me why you are here."

The infamous radical called black-haired Brennan had a history of fighting, whether in taverns or in the service of his radical philosophy. He also had a brilliantly charming grin, which he deployed with blinding good humor as he approached Vai with an outstretched hand in the radical manner, man to man as an equal.

"Magister! It is an honor to make your acquaintance formally. You must have quite a rousing tale to tell, if everything Beatrice has told me is true."

Good manners won out, as they always did with Vai when it came to the point. He shook hands, but watched like a wire strung taut as Brennan shook my hand.

"She told me to look for the tailor shop opposite Queedle and Clutch."

I just could not stop grinning. "Where are Bee and Rory? Can I go to them right away?"

"Immediately!" When Brennan turned that smile on me, I realized he was striking in large part because he was at ease in himself. He was not burdened by the insecurities and vanities that plagued Andevai.

"Let me finish here before we go," said Vai, again settling a hand against my back.

"No need to accompany us if it's any trouble for you, Magister." Brennan examined Vai with a distinct crinkle of laughter about his eyes. "I will return your wife to you by nightfall."

"It is no trouble for me to accompany you," said Vai in a fruitless attempt to sound unconcerned: His tone came off as threatening. "Indeed, I insist on it."

"You can't wish to wear that dash jacket in public," I said.

Unfortunately the tailor sailed into the breach. "I have the other dash jacket ready, Magister, if you will just come back with me to try it on. I assure you, it will fit exactly as you wish."

I followed Vai back behind the screen, where we chanced to have a few moments alone as the tailor went to the wardrobe to fetch the

other garment.

"I don't know that I would call him the handsomest man I ever met," he muttered with such ill temper that I was tempted to smack him. "But the enchanting smile has a certain stark effect."

"Jealousy ill becomes you," I whispered as I unbuttoned his jacket. He glared.

"Also, I don't like it." I slipped the fourteenth button free and pressed my hands to his shirt, beneath the jacket. "It makes it look as if you don't trust me."

His chest heaved. "Of course I trust you."

"Do you?"

The tailor returned with the finished dash jacket, this one sewn out of a fine damask dyed the color of a ripe peach. I stepped back hastily.

"Had you some remark upon the floral fabric, Maestra?" the tailor asked with a hopeful bow.

"I think by all means it is entirely appropriate for a dash jacket," I said as the old man strove to contain his unprofessional wince at my unprofessional judgment.

Vai was too preoccupied by his own struggle to notice our aside. His tone could have been chiseled from granite, it was so hard. "Go on, Catherine. I don't need to accompany you. Will Beatrice and your brother be returning to stay with us at the mage House?"

I took his hand. "It might be best to join them for supper at their domicile."

The bell tinkled again as the door opened. A familiar voice said, "You've been in here a long time, Brennan. You said to come in after you if there was trouble. Is there trouble? Cat! I can smell you're in here! Begging your pardon, Maesters. I didn't see you there. I'm Roderic Barr. It's a pleasure to meet you. You're sewing! I do admire people who can sew. They have such nimble fingers!"

"Rory!" I shrieked, dashing out from behind the screen and into Rory's arms. I looked up into his smiling face. "You're all right, both you and Bee?"

He kissed me soundly on each cheek in the traditional Kena'ani way. Still close, he sniffed. "Goodness, Cat, that man has put his scent all over you!"

My cheeks must have flamed red, for the sewers turned their heads to hide their chuckles. Brennan looked past me with a warning lift of his chin. I released Rory as Vai stepped out from behind the screen in his unbuttoned jacket.

"So she did rescue you!" Rory walked up to Vai and stared him down eye-to-eye. Rory was a touch taller and he had puffed himself up in that odd way he had of making himself seem bigger. "I am her brother. I look out for her."

Vai did not budge. "Catherine is capable of looking out for herself."

"You have sisters. You know what I mean."

"How do you know I have sisters?"

"Cat tells me everything." Rory made the words a challenge.

Brennan put a hand on my arm to keep me out of it. The tailor put a hand on the screen to steady it in case there was an altercation.

Vai took in Rory's black hair and golden eyes, and the badly mended and faded dash jacket he was wearing. "Lord of All! That's the jacket I wore the night of... it's ruined!"

Rory's smile was almost a wink. "It was this, or go naked. Not that I mind going naked, but it does get cold. Be assured Cat already scolded me for ruining it and scolded Bee for letting me wear it in the first place. I do like it when Cat scolds Bee, because no one else does and I can assure you that nothing is more tiresome than Bee let loose in the world with no one to scold her." Without asking permission, he smoothed the sleeve of the jacket Vai was wearing as Vai's eyes widened in disbelief at the familiarity. Rory practically purred. "I really like this color. You have the most beautiful clothes."

"Roderic, why don't you accompany the magister so you can bring him along this evening," said Brennan in a hearty voice as he grabbed my cloak and tugged me out the door.

I resisted. "But I... what if...?"

He cut me off as the door shut. "Nothing Rory can't handle. Better to leave the two of them to get acquainted without you there, for I perceive they are each in their own way a bit... shall we say... protective of you, Maestra Barahal."

"Call me Cat, please," I said, for I perceived it was time to turn the subject entirely.

"So I shall, Cat, for that is what Bee calls you, and since she talks about you a great deal, I rather feel I know you better than I ought."

"Oh dear," I muttered.

He indicated a ramshackle carriage waiting at the intersection, driven by a young man burly enough to be a boxer, who was accompanied by a scarred fellow armed with a stout cudgel. The driver acknowledged us with a nod. The carriage started forward the moment we settled in the seat. Grimy glass windows rattled as if likely to shake right out of the frames.

"Are you the rats who brought news of Camjiata's victory to Pinfeather & Quill?" I asked.

"I mean no offense, but before I take you into my confidence, I must know if the magister means to support the radical cause. Bee has repeatedly assured me that in Expedition the magister declared his intention to break from Four Moons House. Yet you are guests at the local mage House."

"If you were a cold mage traveling in winter, you would stay at a mage House, too, or else you would freeze to death!"

He chuckled. "I am not accusing the magister of anything, Cat, although I appreciate your spirited defense. I am sure he would appreciate that defense, too, if he were here, for I have a suspicion he was a little reluctant to allow you to leave with me."

We pulled into the heavier traffic along a main thoroughfare. Enchanting as Brennan Du might be, I was not about to discuss Andevai's character with him!

I changed the subject. Ahead rose dark clouds, the surly smoke of iron furnaces and bustling manufactories. "I am surprised to see so many trolls in Sala."

"The trolls see forests that need to be managed and mines that have been left untapped. Laborers who owe their service as a tithe to their prince or House masters travel here for the chance to be paid a wage for their labor."

"And you've come to agitate for revolution among the laborers. Never in all my childhood dreams did I imagine I would one day conspire with radicals!"

His answering grin kicked me right in the gut, for he really was quite attractive.

"Yet you've grown up, Maestra. You were a girl when I met you at the Griffin Inn. I would say you are a woman now." He reached inside his coat and withdrew a printed pamphlet. "Did you write this account of the Taino kingdom? As Beatrice would say, it's splendidly engrossing. Especially the bit about the shark."

I accepted his compliment with a calm, sensible smile. "It is true I have had some unexpected adventures."

I had not set foot in the easternmost district of Sala because it was known as a rough-hewn laborers' camp where restless men congregated. As Brennan had explained, many came from principalities to the west, escaping indentured servitude in the hope of finding employment in the manufactories. A Venerday market had been set up under shelters. Braziers heaped with wood burned merrily to cast a bit of warmth on passersby. I was grateful for my cloak.

The carriage rolled along lanes where butchers and bone-boilers hung their signs. We pulled up by empty livestock pens. On one side stood trolls like berries on a bush; no troll stood alone, and most stood in clusters of three or four, while each group kept at least three arms' length from any other. They wore garments that mimicked human fashions, but their clothing was so adorned with bits and baubles of polished metal, glass, and beads that I had to look away or get a headache.

On the other side, the fences were crowded with men shoulder to shoulder on the rails and in the pens. They had the unwashed look of men who haven't the coin to pay for a tub of water in which to bathe. A few shawled and cloaked women moved through the outskirts of the crowd, selling food or, judging by the furtive movement in the shadow of a half-hidden alley, their own bodies.

The heat of so many people had churned the frozen dirt into a mire. Yet despite the crush, and the occasional bark of a dog, the crowd seethed in a remarkable silence. All stared at a barrel on which a petite young woman stood giving an impassioned speech.

Bee had raised her voice in the cry for revolution.

28

As I reached for the latch, Brennan caught my arm.

"Don't get out. The ghana has spies in the crowd."

He pulled down the glass in the window so I could hear. Bee's voice carried easily, for she certainly never had any trouble making herself heard. She spoke in clear schoolroom Latin meant to be widely understood.

"Our demands for new laws will not cede to the demands of blood and birth. We dispute the arbitrary distribution of power and wealth which is claimed as the natural order. We know it is not natural. It is artificially created and sustained by ancient privileges. Why should those privileges be reserved to only a few communities? By what judgment do the patricians claim they stand above the rest? It is on our backs and our labor and our blood and our children that they rise. We need not stand bent beneath. We can stand straight and say—"

"Kiss me, sweetheart!" shouted some wag in the crowd. "That's what we say. You're the prettiest girl I've seen in an age."

Raucous laughter followed this sally. I glanced anxiously across the crowd. Brennan pointed to two trolls stationed intimidatingly behind Bee: Chartji and Caith.

"Kiss you!" Bee exclaimed without losing a beat. "Why would I kiss *you* when a Roman legate begged me to become his favored one and yet I turned him down? Do you think you are as much of a man as a Roman legate?"

"More a man than any legate, as I can show you!" the fellow called to shouts of laughter.

"Thus you prove my point. If you wish me to look upon you as the amatory equal of a Roman legate, then you must surely believe that justice is no different from love. You cannot chain one community into clientage and call that justice while you let another community enrich its coffers and feed its children off the blood and toil of the first. The blood of a poor laborer flows as red as the blood of a prince. Death hunts them both equally, for a corpse knows no rank. It is only those who survive the dead man who dedicate themselves to making such distinctions. There should be one law that treats all communities in equal part, so every person has honor and dignity."

"She's quite remarkable," said Brennan, keeping his face in shadow as he gazed out the window. "A natural orator. I've never seen a heckler get the better of her, and they do try."

"I had no idea she would ever be giving speeches!" I stared in rapt admiration at the way she exhorted the crowd to consider how unjust laws and antiquated customs were the means by which the many were sacrificed to exalt the few. Yet it was not Bee's bold voice I had doubted but the idea that people like us would ever get a chance to speak at all.

"We do not need nor do we desire their false generosity or their dishonest counsel! We seek only the honor and dignity that by right fall upon every person. The law must unchain all communities from clientage, from indenture, from slavery. That is what we ask you to consider."

A rumble stirred the air. A troop of soldiers swung into view at the far end of the livestock yards. Their flowing tunics and feathered caps gave them an imposing presence.

"Consider wisely!" cried Bee with a glance at the approaching cavalry. "Your ghana wishes to enforce my silence and compel your obedience." She jumped down from the barrel.

A voice rang out. "There's a reward for the man who hands seditionists over to the ghana!"

Brennan rapped on the ceiling, and the carriage began rolling.

"I'm not leaving her out there in that!" I grabbed the latch.

He slammed me back against the seat. "Stop! You'll never find her in this crowd and will only make things more difficult by going in search of her."

I twisted, trying to get free, but he knew the same dirty fighting tricks I did. "Ow! You're reckless to let her go into a crowd like that!"

"I am reckless with my own life, but never with the cause. Stop fighting me, and look!"

As the men began to run, dissolving into a din of fright and panic, the trolls blocked the lanes down which the soldiers rode. Their heads swayed as they scanned the formation. There was something uncanny in the way the trolls bent forward from their usual upright stance, bodies lowering. The riders slowed. I sucked in a breath, gripping the edge of the window.

A gun went off. Spears lowered and swords flashed as the soldiers rode down the unarmed trolls. If trolls could ever be said to be unarmed.

They scattered. Whistles shrilled. A cascading melody lilted like a pretty aria, yet its spill of notes made me shudder down to the bone. Some charged, while others easily overleaped the fences and bounded to circle in from the side. I had never seen anything like it. They were so quick that the frontmost simply dodged the thrust of spears. The movement and scent of the trolls panicked the horses, and the lead mounts bolted, throwing their riders or slamming into the pens on either side in an effort to get away. A sword flashed, cutting into a feathered hide.

Was that blood I smelled, hot and dark?

A shriek tore the air. The clamor of men was drowned under a cacophony of whistles so loud I clapped my hands over my ears. A troll ducked under the belly of a horse and slashed upward. As the horse screamed, its guts spilled.

Brennan shut the window as the carriage lurched around a corner. "That's torn it!"

"I can't leave Bee out in that—!"

"Trust that I know what I'm doing. We have a meeting place already planned."

Knuckles white, I held my cane, wanting to batter him over the head with it, but instead I took in one slow breath after another, trying to calm myself.

He shook his head. "It's a good thing Bee warned me that you leap before you look or you'd have gotten out there and caused ten kinds of trouble. For one thing, what if the ghana's spies recognized you as the magister's wife living on the hospitality of White Bow House? What 275 kind of questions do you think they would start asking? You can't just jump. You have to consider the consequences of each action."

"I thought the more you skate onto thin ice, the better you like it. That's what Kehinde says."

A flash of real irritation tightened his lips and eyes. The force of his anger silenced me. I had no idea what Brennan Touré Du thought of me, and I feared he wasn't thinking very highly of me at all.

We trundled along as an appalling noise chased us with the pitch of an ugly fight. The carriage jolted to a halt. The door opened, and Bee flung herself into my arms. My eyes grew damp, but after a struggling pause she sat back with one arm gripping my waist and the other holding my hand. The carriage dipped as several people swung up onto the foot-rail in the back.

"I couldn't see anything, but I heard the screams," she said to Brennan.

"Does that happen every time you speak?" I demanded, still trembling.

"The ghana's troops should know better than to draw blood," said Brennan. "It's why we like to have a crowd of trolls at our gatherings. They're curious about the way the rats behave, and by being there they are the best protection radicals can have."

"Bloody Melqart!" I whispered. "It disemboweled a horse!"

I pressed a hand to my mouth, then lowered it. While the thought shocked me, my body did not respond with revulsion. Instead I thought of how much moist, raw flesh was thereby exposed.

Bee crushed me against her. "Oh, Cat, I'm so sorry you saw such an awful sight. I didn't know we would be separated for so long. It's been almost a year since you and I were in Adurnam! I became so afraid I had lost you. Let's never be parted again." To my surprise, she burst into tears.

I fussed over her. Despite my tears and the fading chaos of the battle, I was swept with an intoxicating happiness. I had rescued Vai and now I was reunited with Bee and Rory. For this hour, at least, I could luxuriate in knowing I had reclaimed the ones I loved.

"As long as you're safe that's all that matters. Have you been well, Bee? Have you had quite a bit of trouble?"

"Yes. It's not the first time a public meeting has been attacked in that aggressive way. I can't get used to it."

"You're not meant to get used to it! What happened after you and Rory left me in the spirit world?"

She wiped her eyes with the back of a hand. "Rory and I swam ashore in the city of Camlun at the festival of Beltane. We traveled to Havery, where we were courteously received at the law offices. We've been with the radicals ever since. It's been more dangerous than I imagined. Professora Nayo Kuti was arrested in Lutetia for the crime of spreading sedition!"

"What happened?" I demanded.

"We believe the mage House in Lutetia pushed the Parisi prince to take the step," said Brennan with a crooked smile meant to remind me of why he had to be careful with mages. "However, her husband is a man of considerable status in Massilia. Through his efforts she was released and sent back to Massilia."

"Professora Nayo Kuti is married?" I said. "I thought Kehinde was an independent woman."

Bee's gloved hand slipped from mine and she leaned over to rest a hand on Brennan's knee in a gesture so intimate and familiar that I looked sharply away lest I blurt out an inappropriate question that would embarrass us all. My thoughts whirled dizzily.

"I am sorry regardless to hear she was arrested," I lumbered on, "but I am glad to hear she was released in a timely manner to a safe place. I hope she is still writing."

"She is still writing and her pamphlets travel across Europa." Brennan nodded at Bee.

She withdrew her hand and tucked it into the bend of my elbow. "I pray your escape was not too much of an ordeal, dearest. Is Andevai unharmed? I hope we will have time to prepare him before he sees Rory wearing his ruined dash jacket."

Brennan chuckled.

I sighed. "He is much the same as ever, as you will see. Bee, where is your sketchbook?"

She had it with her, for her sketchbook was like my cane: We never went anywhere without them. I paged through to the sketch of the tailor's shop.

"When Maester Godwik recognized the eggs atop the towers as the architecture of Sala's palace, I knew I had to come to Sala," she said. "I hoped you would remember. And you did!"

I flipped to the sketch of the false dream.

"Cat!" she whispered, with a glance toward Brennan, who had closed his eyes in a kindly attempt to give us a little privacy. "Why do I need to look at this? I try to forget I ever drew it."

For the longest time I examined the fabric of the dash jacket worn by a man seen only from the back. Shading and hatching became petaled flowers, while dots and lines evoked the spray of fireworks exploding joyfully out of the flowers' blooming splendor.

I said in a low voice, "Quite by chance and not by my doing, he is getting a dash jacket made in this fabric. Can you bring about the future by drawing it?"

She snatched the sketchbook out of my hands and snapped it shut as if to close off the drift of my thoughts. Brennan opened his eyes, looking startled.

"I have no power to bring about the future. I only have the curse of sometimes glimpsing the future in visions that usually make no sense."

She looked at Brennan in a way that made me realize she and he had discussed the subject at length. I caught my breath, waiting for some confession, but she only turned back to me with hands pressed together, palm to palm, as she spoke.

"I have done a lot of thinking about what you and I have seen, and what Queen Anacaona told me. The women who walk the dreams of dragons walk unscathed through the Great Smoke, which we might also call the ocean of dreams. People have long gone to augurs and priestesses to have their dreams interpreted, because they believe dreams are windows into the gods' intentions. Yet surely most dreams are merely a jumble of thoughts and images and fears and hopes. Or nothing more than indigestion."

"Or brought on by too much whiskey," murmured Brennan with a smile that brought a rose's bloom to Bee's cheeks.

She went on as if he had not spoken. "I think the Great Smoke is very like the ocean. It has shallows, and depths, and a shoreline. I believe it also has currents just as mariners tell us our own oceans do. I now believe all strands of past, present, and future commingle in the Great Smoke. Dragon dreamers walk the currents of the future, even if we do not know what we are seeing." She paused to brush her cheeks. "Why are you staring, Cat? Is there something on my face?"

"No." I struggled for a jest but could not find one. She looked so grave and scholarly, quite unlike my bombastic and passionate Bee but exactly like a woman I could love and admire just as much. "Was the leviathan that conveyed us across the Great Smoke truly a dragon?"

"*Dragon* is a word we use to describe something we don't understand. But to truly answer your question, we must speak to the headmaster. To speak to the headmaster, we must travel to Treverni Noviomagus."

"Are you sure that's where he is?"

Brennan nodded. "We have learned through our network of intelligencers that a man answering to the description of the headmaster and bearing the name Napata is headmaster of the New Academy in Noviomagus. The New Academy was founded two years ago."

"Which would be the right time if he left Adurnam after we fell into the well," added Bee. "Furthermore, Cat, I think we will find him in Noviomagus on the Feast of Mars. In nine days. That's what I dreamed. Remember?"

I clasped her hands excitedly. "The secrets of the Great Smoke aren't the only thing he can tell us. He saved his assistant from the Wild Hunt. We need to find out how he did it. He might be my only chance to save myself from my sire."

Bee squeezed my hands in reply, for I could tell by her expression that she had not told Brennan any of my secrets.

Brennan was tapping his thigh rather as Vai did when he was wound up, counting a drum rhythm as if it helped him focus. "We will have to leave Sala tonight regardless, before the ghana can close the roads." He opened the window.

Dusk bled darkness over a street of tightly packed row houses. The carriage slowed, and Brennan cracked open the door. As we passed the awning of a hat shop, he jumped out and caught Bee as she sprang after him; I leaped likewise, and dashed through the open door. The elderly shop attendant nodded as I followed Brennan and Bee through the front room and out the back into an alley.

Several streets over, we entered a humble, whitewashed inn whose front room was swept clean of customers. A young woman wearing a head wrap, wool gown, and calf-length leather vest was bent over the stove, lighting a fire. She carried a baby in a sling against her back.

As the door creaked open she said words in the local dialect that I understood as "We're closed." When she glanced up she switched to the bastard Latin common among laborers who had to speak to people from different regions of Europa. "In the back upstairs. Ye was never telling us ye mean to be bringing a cold mage who would be killing all the fires in the house, did ye?"

"My apologies, Maestra." Brennan gestured for us to go ahead. "We intended no inconvenience. I must warn you, there's been fighting at the livestock market."

"Angry Carnonos!" She stood with a gasp of outrage. "My brother is gone there! If the ghana's men come searching, ye cannot be staying...!"

Bee drew me down a passage and past a kitchen where a woman was cursing most alarmingly about plague-ridden cold mages, and thence into a back wing of the building.

In a chilly passageway she took my face in her hands, forehead wrinkling as she peered at me in the dim light. "Is all well? You escaped the spirit world unscathed and unbound?"

"Not unbound, but unscathed except for the ruin of one of his favorite dash jackets."

With a hiccupping laugh she crushed me against her in an affectionate embrace. "Oh, Cat! I've had all sorts of adventures but I felt so lonely without you."

I pulled her hands down and squeezed them. "Not as lonely as all that, it seems. Answer me truly! Is there something between you and Brennan?"

Her hesitation told me everything I needed to know.

"Blessed Tanit! Are you sleeping with him?"

Her fingers tightened on my hand. "We have been traveling together for months. I must say there are benefits to being a young woman who knows she is barren, when it comes to activities of the amatory sort. But I'm not in love with him, not in that way. We're more like attentive companions."

"Attentive companions! Are you telling me you're engaged in a companionably attentive affair with one of the most notorious and dashing radicals in Europa?"

"Shh! Lower your voice. This isn't the place to have this conver-

sation!"

"Does he want to marry you?"

"Strangely, Cat, not every man wishes to marry me, starting with your husband and ending with Brennan Du. I find it's a relief to negotiate a relationship that is based on respect and friendship rather than all this overheated romance." Her voice dropped so low I had to lean my head against hers to hear. "The truth is, he's been in love with the professora for years, but she is married. I heard Brennan and Kehinde arguing once. She admitted that she dislikes her husband. It was a marriage arranged for her at a tender age. You would think an intellectual of such radical sensibilities would take it upon herself to shed such imprisoning traditional customs, but she refuses to do anything that would bring dishonor upon her family."

"There's a great deal I do not understand about this situation!"

Brennan's laugh floated from the kitchen, where he was evidently soothing the cook.

"I do not want to be discovered gossiping with you!" Bee finished, dragging me on.

Upstairs, at the very back, we entered a modestly furnished dining chamber lit by cold magic and cooling rapidly. Rory lounged under a blanket on a threadbare couch situated beside the brick chimney and its dead fire.

Vai rose from a chair. "Catherine! You look...confounded. Was there trouble? Beatrice! Is all well with you? Have you peace and good health?"

Bee kissed him on either cheek in the effusive Kena'ani manner. "Andevai! Here you are! What a startling color that dash jacket is! Please allow me to tell you how very glad I am that you are back with us."

"My thanks, Beatrice," he said stiffly, taken aback by her enthusiastic welcome and perhaps wondering if she disliked his new garment. The distinctively rich orange-red damask did look well on him. Because the sleeve length was just right, I wondered if the tailor had shortened the sleeves on the green jacket on purpose so he wouldn't wear it. "Catherine has been worrying about you."

"Of course she has! I'm sorry to say we had trouble today. A violent altercation broke out between the ghana's troops and some loitering trolls."

Rory whistled under his breath. "Glad I missed that."

"I am sadly sure the town is in for a very bad night. Can you and Cat be ready to depart within the hour, Andevai?"

He took my hand and looked me up and down to make sure I was all right before releasing me. Footsteps in the hall brought me around with my sword half drawn.

Brennan entered the room. "Magister, next time we'll bring you in through the stables so you don't put out all the fires. Can you be ready to leave within the hour?"

"No. Nor do I see the need to do so."

I cringed at Vai's brusque tone. Rory smirked, as if he found the situation amusing. Brennan sighed wearily, and Bee opened her mouth to make a scalding retort.

Vai sailed right over her. "However the ghana reacts to this disturbance, I will have no trouble leaving Sala. I see no need to go sneaking off and freezing and besides that leaving disgruntled innkeepers at every stop because I kill their fires. Nor will I agree to camping out in the woods in this damp and cold. Not when I can have every expectation of peace traveling as a magister in a coach generously provided by White Bow House. No prince or ghana or lord—or radical—will prevent me from making sure my wife travels in comfort to Noviomagus."

"Goodness, Cat!" said Bee. "He still talks in exactly that same pompous way."

His gaze flicked to her. "If you are trying to irritate me, it won't work."

"How could it, when you are already so very irritating?" she muttered.

"Because as I was just about to say and now will say, there is no reason the three of you cannot travel with us. We told our hosts we were separated from our servants, so you will pose as our retinue. All of us can leave Sala in a way uncomplicated by searches, seizures, and concerns about where we will sleep every night."

"Pleasant to have all such mundane details settled," said Brennan with a wry grin.

"How do I get to serve?" Rory fluttered his eyelashes in a way that made Brennan chuckle as at an old joke that hasn't lost its charm. "By the way, Cat, you were so very wrong when you told me that first day in Lemanis that I can't wear women's clothing. I have made several friends in the last months who enjoy it when I dress in women's drawers and other garments."

"Rory!" Bee cried in a long-suffering tone redolent of many shared experiences I would likely never know anything about. "You need not say just whatever comes into your mind, as I have had reason to tell you before."

"I just wanted Cat to know! I don't mind being scolded for something I did wrong, but I don't think it fair to be scolded when I did nothing wrong!" Oblivious to the stupidity of poking an already annoyed wasp, he addressed Vai. "Do *you* wear women's drawers?"

I braced myself. Bee pressed fingers to her forehead, wincing. Brennan rocked forward on his toes, clearly expecting the same outcome I was.

Vai smiled indulgently at Rory, as if they were the best of joking friends. "No, I do not. But I can't see why you shouldn't wear them if you wish to. It's just that they're cut for a different shape."

I exchanged startled glances with Bee at this unexpected display of relaxed camaraderie, for if there was one word I would not have used to describe Vai, it was *relaxed*. Footsteps scraped down the hall. Rory stood, the blanket sliding off to reveal him wearing the green floral dash jacket. Blessed Tanit! Had I gotten hit on the head and was I now dreaming that Vai had given one of his precious jackets to someone else?

"Chartji and Caith cannot believably pose as your servants, Magister," Brennan went on as the door opened to admit the lawyer Chartji and her clutch-nephew, the young troll Caith.

I took a step back, a shade too abruptly, because Caith's head slewed around like that of a predator spotting the furtive skittering of its hapless prey. A vivid memory of the troll ripping out the belly of the horse, guts spilling, steam rising from the hot innards, blinded me for a blink of an eye.

A blink was all it took for them to take the leap and make the kill.

"The feathered people need not pose as my servants," said Vai, startling me back to myself. He crossed to shake Chartji's hand. "Chartji is my solicitor, after all. A pleasant coincidence that we stumbled across each other here in Sala. We have a great deal to discuss." 283

"I have not neglected your case, Magister. However, my case file is in Havery."

"All the more reason I would be pleased to offer you and Caith conveyance in a comfortably sprung carriage and lodging in respectable inns for as long as you choose to accompany me."

Chartji bared her teeth to mimic a human smile as she approached me to shake hands. "Catherine Bell Barahal. I am pleased to flock with you again. Our clutch-cousin, Keer, has written of your doings in Expedition."

I hesitated, bruised by the memory of the dead horse. "Truly, I am glad to be reunited with you all. I was just so . . . stunned by the fight at the livestock market."

"It is not to be wondered at," agreed Chartji. "Trolls from the north country in Amerike have little understanding of human behavior and custom. They are brutish and abrupt. They don't properly know how to behave around you rats. Why, they don't even take rats as clutch-cousins or allow them to buy stakes in their consortiums, as we Expeditioners do."

As I grasped her hand I was overtaken by a distinctive scent of summer sun, hot stone, and dry grass touched by the gentle spray of falling water. Keer had felt the same to me. I liked it. The other trolls hadn't smelled this way.

She bared her teeth again, sharing a smile as if she could smell my settling nerves and wanted me to feel reassured. "Regardless, Cat, you have certain rights and privileges now, for you have given up your weaknesses to the clutch and not been consumed."

"Does that mean you and I are clutch-cousins also, Chartji? And me and Caith, too?"

"Ooo!" said Caith, who had been circling in with his bright gaze on my cold steel. "If we are clutch-cousins, then can I hold that shiny blade?"

Chartji whistled, and Caith bobbed apologetically and retreated to the table, where he tapped his talons so fretfully on the wood that he cut shallow gouges.

"That might just work," said Brennan to Vai with a nod of appreciation that melted Vai's frosty manner a trifle. "How are you going to explain how you suddenly picked up your three servants after being here two weeks with none?"

"What makes you think I have to explain anything to anyone?" Vai tugged on his sleeves.

Rory tugged on his with exactly the same movement. "The sleeves were too short," he said, "but the clever tailor put lace on to lengthen them. Don't they look nice?"

Vai gave me a stern look to remind me not to criticize.

I said, quite truthfully, "The color looks well on you, Rory. The fit is good, too, although you might need to have it let out a little at the shoulders. I'm delighted"—if astounded!—"that Vai has seen fit to make sure you are properly clothed."

"By the way, Magister," said Chartji, "several letters came to you from Expedition."

"Have they?" Vai grinned with such unfeigned delight that Bee looked as startled as if he had turned into a different man. "Kofi said he would write! I don't suppose there is any chance you have the letters with you?"

"No—" Chartji broke off as I raised a hand for silence.

Footfalls sounded from the passage. The woman with the baby entered, carrying a tray.

"Cook will be having the soup hot soon now, Maester," she said to Brennan, "meaning no disrespect to the magister." She glanced at Vai and then took a second look up and down in an admiring way before she began unloading the dishes.

Bee cast me a look, rolling her eyes. Fortunately Vai was speaking to Chartji in a low voice about sending letters back to Expedition, and did not notice. Youths brought the food, a hearty fare of mutton stew and cabbage mashed up with turnips, and we sat. I half expected Bee to be casting sly glances and arch looks at the man she had confessed was her lover, but she treated him no differently from the rest of us.

"We radicals are not working *for* General Camjiata," Brennan explained to Vai. "We are working *with* him to achieve those goals we share in common. He will soon march his army north over the Pyrene Mountains into the Gallic Territories. We need to discover the plans of the Alliance of princes and mages, where and when and with what numbers they mean to fight him, because they will fight him. The general simply cannot have raised as large an army as his enemies will. He will need our help to defeat them."

"Have the radicals no spies?" I asked.

"We have successfully insinuated a few spies into the princely courts. What we lack is any knowledge of the plans of the mage Houses, for they are closed to us."

Vai considered his bowl of stew, then met Brennan's gaze. "I can move easily into any mage House in Europa. But I do not stand so high in mage ranks that I would ever be admitted to councils of war." He glanced sidelong at me in a way meant to make me smile, and it did. "However, once I introduce my wife into those halls, she can eavesdrop."

"Are you truly willing to do this for the radicals, Magister?" Brennan asked.

"I don't do this for you. I do this for my friends in Expedition, and for my village."

"If the mage Houses discover you are acting as our agent, they will kill you."

He shrugged. "If I am willing to risk nothing for freedom, then I am not a man."

"Spoken like a radical, Magister." Brennan set down his cup. "We had best get out of Sala sooner rather than later. I won't travel with you all the way to Noviomagus. I need to deliver news of the general's victory to printers and allies in Koumbi. We'll meet in Havery after we have both completed our other business."

"Caith and I are not going to Noviomagus," added Chartji. "Not if one of our older brethren is nesting there."

"Keer also used the phrase *older brethren*," I said. "By which I collect you mean the creatures we call dragons. Why can you not go to Noviomagus if the headmaster is one of them?"

She showed her teeth again, all white and sharp, and chuffed in a way meant to show amusement or, perhaps, a shiver of what a human would have called nervous laughter.

"Because he would eat us."

29

On a cold late Martius day, slushy and stinging, we reached the mighty Rhenus River. The town of Noviomagus had been founded as a far-flung outpost of the expanding Roman empire and was now a thriving center of trade and textiles. The central district was crowded with opulent four-story edifices, the homes of rich lords and merchant families. In contrast, the mage House was ostentatiously single-storied, its sprawling wings and courtyards eating up several city blocks.

The palatial forecourt of Five Mirrors House looked every bit as grand as the estate of Four Moons House. Even decently dressed in well-tailored clothing I felt utterly out of place. Vai slapped his gloves repeatedly onto his palms as he examined the sweep of the steps, the pillared portico, and the double doors.

"Keep silence and follow my lead." The press of his mouth gave him a sneer.

A steward starched to perfection in a magnificent orange boubou appeared at the door. He was tall, broad-shouldered, and as dark as Vai, the patrician height of all that is cultured and impeccable.

"We interview for servants in the kitchen wing. You may go around to the left."

Vai crushed his gloves in his hands. "I am Andevai Diarisso, a magister of the Diarisso lineage, out of Four Moons House. I suggest you escort me to see your mansa as soon as we are properly purified and have made the rightful courtesies."

The steward's eyebrows flew up in an expression of astonishment. "Is this all an honored magister of Four Moons House travels with? A satchel and a woman?"

A chilly blast of air huffed over us as a few stray hailstones clattered down.

"I am on a Grand Tour. My coach overturned this morning. It will take days before it can be repaired. Likewise, my servants were injured. I left them behind with the coach and driver and came ahead myself with my wife to have a hope of acceptable accommodation and some manner of edible food. Really, the fare at the mage House hostels in this part of the world is unpalatable. I had heard that the magnificence of the architecture and the lavishness of the table fare at the mage Houses in old Roman territory were beyond description, but I admit myself sorely disappointed in what I have so far experienced."

Here stood the Andevai I had first known and loathed!

The steward's stare made my neck prickle. "Ah, of course. This way, Magister."

He ushered us into an antechamber furnished with plain wooden benches and a set of tapestries depicting the diaspora from the Mali Empire. A heavyset woman in an indigo robe offered us water in the traditional way.

"Magister, you must be purified through water." She indicated that Vai should go with the steward. "I will myself attend you, Maestra."

The House had splendid baths in the Roman style, split into a men's and a women's half just as they had been at the gatehouse of Four Moons House.

"Tell me what happened," she said after I immersed myself.

We had deposited Bee and Rory and our luggage at a modest hostel at the edge of town and sent the carriage back to Sala, but naturally I was not going to tell her any of that.

"It was so frightfully rough to be tumbled in such a vile manner. And I had to leave all my gowns behind." I simpered into a digression on why I preferred wool challis to damask that soon caused her expression to glaze over in a satisfactory manner.

Servants brought clean underthings and a shapely gown with a shawl. In this pleasing garb I was escorted to a parlor fitted with low couches. Attendants brought a tea tray with tiny almond cakes and jellied berries. Vai was shown in, and we were left alone. He wore the same dash jacket he had arrived in, although it needed to be cleaned

and pressed.

"Did they not offer you a change of clothes?" I asked.

"Nothing I could lower myself to wear," he said in a combative tone.

Refusing the bait, I reclined on the cushions and drank three cups of tea and ate four almond cakes and all of the jellied berries while Vai glared over the bare branches of a winter courtyard as if his gaze had ripped the leaves from the shrubs. The way he tapped a drumbeat on his thigh was a sure sign he was churning with restlessly unpleasant thoughts.

"Vai, you need not use that expression when there is only me here to see for I can assure you it no longer intimidates me although it does make me want to bite you. And not in an amorous way."

My wit did not raise even the ghost of a smile.

The door opened. I rose. A wiry man in an indigo boubou walked in; his gold earrings marked him as a djeli. He was followed by the woman and the steward. An elderly man wearing a modern dash jacket and trousers entered and took a seat.

"To our House we give you welcome, son of the Diarisso lineage." The djeli slipped into a melodic chant heavily infused with Bambara. By the way Vai's hands stilled, I could tell this elaborate greeting mollified him.

At length the djeli finished. The elderly man raised a hand to indicate he meant to speak with his own voice. "The Diarisso lineage has a reputation for strong cold mages who are proud to the same measure that they are powerful." The mansa's gaze slid from Andevai to me. "You are not mage House born, Maestra."

"I am Kena'ani, Your Excellency," I said, dropping my gaze respectfully.

"What is your name?" asked the djeli.

I heard Vai's intake of breath but to lie to the face of a djeli was to invite disaster. "I am Catherine Bell Barahal, Your Honor."

"You're chained," the djeli said. "Such a marriage is unusual these days."

The mansa pressed his fingers together. "I had no idea any Kena'ani clan had the means or opportunity to interest a mage House in a marriage contract."

I had not worked at Aunty's boardinghouse for two months without learning how to handle old men. "It is certainly not anything I can speak of, Your Honor, for having been but a child of six at the time the marriage was contracted, naturally I knew nothing about it. Indeed, you may imagine my consternation when I was suddenly informed but a week before my twentieth birthday that I was required to marry a man I had never met and indeed never before heard of. In fact, I only discovered my fate when the magister himself arrived at my aunt and uncle's house to claim me. I was speechless."

Vai's lips twitched but he did not quite smile.

"Most would marvel at your good fortune," said the woman. "I hope you appreciate the unexpected bounty you have received."

"I make sure she appreciates it every day," Vai said in a stern tone belied by the flicker of his eyes.

The woman chuckled.

The mansa was less amused. "I should like to see how powerful your magic really is."

Vai's frown returned. "I can prove myself in any manner you request."

My cane trembled to life as he spun a rainbow into a carriage drawn by horses and then into the horse-headed prow of a ship and then into an antlered stag.

"If nothing else, you can earn a living entertaining in the taverns," remarked the steward. "I hear that is how village-born cold mages make their living in the circuses of Rome."

A crashing cold made me hasten to Vai's side. His hands were in fists, and I was afraid he might draw his sword.

The mansa raised a hand in a gesture of peace. "You are no impostor. Be welcome here as our guests. It will take us a few days to properly consult our records to determine which women might be best cultivated by your seed. I'll need to know the names of your forebears, likewise."

The steward opened the door. "Do you prefer to take supper in the hall or a tray of food in the guest suite so you may recover from your travails in comfort and quiet?"

"A quiet evening tonight, if you will be so kind," said Vai.

We took a polite leave and followed the steward past the school-room wing with its echo of children reciting in loud voices. People paused to watch us pass. Their reserved expressions were as intimidating as their highly decorative and rather old-fashioned clothing.

As the door of the guest suite closed behind us, Vai sank onto the silk-covered couch.

"Cultivated by your seed! You are reduced from animal to plant!" I pressed a hand to his forehead. Ashen shadows dulled his eyes, and lines of weariness soured his mouth. "You're warm."

"She piled her cold magic on top of mine to try to cut the threads of my power."

"She did? The woman?"

"The mansa could not be bothered to test me himself...yet what if he didn't challenge me because he already knew his cold magic isn't powerful enough to challenge mine? Perhaps the woman is the more powerful cold mage."

"Then wouldn't she be mansa?"

"A woman can't be mansa. The mansa is a man who rules the House as a prince rules a territory or the emperor rules Rome."

I placed the cacica's skull on the side table, positioned to stare directly at Vai. "What do you think of this argument, Queen Anacaona?"

"Catherine!"

"Why should I not appeal to a woman who ruled a powerful empire? Either the most powerful cold mage in any House rules as mansa, or the mansa is chosen by some other criterion. But you cannot say that the mansa is the most powerful, if he is not. I would like to hear what Chartji would make of your argument."

"Lawyers are paid to make arguments. Furthermore, the feathered people love nothing more than picking through the most arcane details to find things to quibble over."

"You have no answer to my perfectly reasonable point, have you? For that is exactly why you hired Chartji in the first place."

He beckoned. I returned the skull to the basket. When I sat next to him, he pulled me close and whispered, "So much for our attempt to spy. The steward said 'village-born.' The mansa knew you aren't Houseborn. I think they know who we are."

His words fell like stones, unpleasant because they were so hard. "How could they know? I'd better go see what I can learn."

"You need not look quite so eager, love. Although I suppose it is natural that you do."

He released me as a parade of solemn servants entered bearing 291 platters. As they readied the table I retreated to the bedchamber, drew the shadows around me, and walked unobserved back through the bustle in the sitting room and out the open door.

Near the entry hall I recognized the djeli's distinctive tenor. I peeked around a corner. The djeli and the steward were speaking to a soldier who had saddlebags slung over a shoulder. Although their speech had a rhythm different from that of Adurnam, I could string together sense.

"Ride to Four Moons House. Tell the mansa we have the young magister he seeks. Go in haste. Do not rest."

Four men armed with crossbows stamped in from outside and bowed to the steward. He directed them down my corridor. They walked past without seeing me.

The djeli was holding a sheet of foolscap, which he read. "There are four fugitives, my lord," he said to the steward. "We are advised to keep the wife as hostage for his good behavior, but that she has peculiar abilities and must be watched by a djeli at all times. Also, remove all mirrors. Kill her rather than allow her to escape. There may also be another man and woman. Shoot the man and capture the woman."

The steward made a sign to avert evil spirits. "Ill-omened! Strange to have them turn up a year after we got the letter."

The djeli perused the letter again. "The four have become partisans for General Camjiata."

"If they are partisans for the general, why are they not with his army?" asked the steward. "Why would the young Diarisso come here in such disorder? He is not on a Grand Tour, although no doubt the women will wish to pursue the matter."

The djeli nodded. "Above all, we must not make them suspicious. We will coax them to stay."

Pursue the matter! Coax them to stay! I retreated to the sitting room, still in my shadows. The table had been tastefully laid and a side table arranged with platters: spiced beef with apples, fish in a pepper sauce, and winter parsnips stewed with leeks and garnished with freshly bloomed violets for decoration. Three servants awaited orders.

"We will serve ourselves, as we prefer to dine alone." Vai spun cold fire into lamps of fluid silver shaped like a lion, a crocodile, a stag, and a horse. This casual feat made the servants murmur as appreciatively as if he had done it to entertain them, and maybe he had. "Do not disturb us unless we call for you."

Dusk was settling over the garden. People paced its confines, lighting stone cressets with cold fire. I shut the curtains. Yet I could not despair, for the food smelled delicious. I again set out the skull and placed a spoon with a bit of meat, fish, and parsnip by the white jaw, then steered Vai to the table.

"I'm not hungry," he said, with the burning look of a proud man who is preoccupied by feeling he has allowed himself to be outmaneuvered by his enemies.

"Yes, yes, magic feeds you. So you told me before, although I'm sure I don't understand what you mean by it. You will eat to keep up your strength." I shoved him into a chair and whispered. "They've sent a messenger to Four Moons House."

With my own plate piled rather higher than his, I savored a fine meal, and he did at length start eating. I demolished the remaining dishes and afterward, before I quite realized I was doing it, cleared the table and set everything in stacks on the side table as I had become accustomed to doing at Aunty Djeneba's. Closing my eyes, I allowed my senses to range afield. The vast compound was deeply woven with threads of pulsing magic. By the sounds of boot-heels, I could track the guards patrolling the garden and passage.

I led him to bed and undressed him. Beneath the covers we snuggled close.

"We're under guard," I whispered in his ear.

"It will take at least a week for a courier at speed to reach Four Moons House and return," he said, in a better mood now that he had eaten and had his arms around me. "Our difficulties are threefold. They know who we are, so our attempt to spy has already been thwarted. You must warn Bee and Rory they're in danger. You and Bee must have time to speak to the headmaster before we leave Noviomagus, so it may be best to play along for a day or two before we break out. Also, this is a very comfortable bed, do you not agree?"

"A woman does not have to walk the dreams of dragons to foresee you plan to enjoy its comforts tonight."

"So I do!" he remarked, as if surprised at my perspicacity. "I'm not sure you're appreciative enough of your good fortune. As for tomorrow, I have a plan that plays to both our strengths."

"I can't wait to hear what you imagine those to be."

"Nor will you wait. I am methodical and persistent. You are impulsive and unpredictable. Ouch! Not to mention wild and ungovernable."

That was true enough, as he soon discovered.

It was a simple plan with room for precipitous change. In such a sprawling compound there were layers of propriety meant to separate the high from the low. The mage House had a lovely breakfast room where a select group of adults broke their fast. There Vai insisted we would go, although the steward asked us four times if we would not prefer a comfortable tray of food in our suite. As we walked through the corridors I could not help but notice they had taken down all the mirrors.

Vai wore the dash jacket of midnight blue with exploding flowers, which he had brought along in the satchel precisely to overawe the House residents. To my surprise it looked splendid, not at all ridiculous. As good as the man looked out of his clothing, he looked particularly fine when he was well dressed and with his beard and hair trimmed the way he liked. He had a way of moving meant to draw the eye. As we entered the dining parlor, shadowed by the steward, everyone looked up. Men and women sat at separate tables, and the women in particular watched as Vai paced the length of the side table with its platters of apple and yam pudding, various porridges of rice, corn, millet, or wheat, warm bread with butter, fried beancake, a haunch of moist beef, and a dozen other mouthwatering trifles. The coffee looked sweet and milky.

"Is this all?" he demanded. "I expected a repast fitting to a House of stature, but..."

I picked up a plate, because the beef was whispering seductively to me.

"Catherine! I cannot allow you to partake of inferior comestibles." His breathtaking obnoxiousness commanded the entire room. Even I disliked him a little, and that was saying something considering what we had shared in the night. "Is it possible your cook can bestir herself to deliver something edible?"

I hadn't meant to, but I whispered, "Please, I'm so hungry."

294

The next thing I knew a tear was trickling down my cheek. The effect of the tear on the patrician mages was remarkable. They reacted as if a large saber-toothed cat had leaped into their midst: Some froze, while others made ready to flee.

"What is your desire, Magister?" asked the steward in the tone of a man who is never awed by the fits and starts of the powerful, because he is their equal.

"I desire a tour of Noviomagus," Andevai said not as a request but as a demand. "What sights there are to see, if indeed there are any in such a town, for I recollect my lessons that once this was nothing more than a frontier outpost of the Roman Empire, now sadly fallen. Catherine! Put that down!"

I had taken advantage of his speech to creep over to the side table and fork a slice of beef onto my plate.

"Lord of All, Magister," said one of the men, goaded into speech, "let the girl eat."

My husband smiled in the most condescending way imaginable as he turned his dark gaze on the other man, who was not much older and had the look of a person gone a little soft from having lived in luxury all his days. "That is how revolution starts. You give them one scrap of beef out of pity and suddenly they wish to eat rich food that isn't good for them and is likely spoiled besides."

I could not help myself. Right in front of their astonished gazes, I wolfed down the slice of beef before he could take the plate away from me. His eyes flared. The chamber grew so cold so fast that my next exhalation made mist.

"I am sure a tour can be arranged," said the steward hastily.

Vai's eyebrows rose as the cold eased fractionally. "I am sure you can arrange such a tour, but have you any decently sprung carriages in which we may be conveyed in comfort? I was shocked at the condition of the bed. It was not adequate to my wife's needs."

I choked down a laugh, and tried to turn it into a coughed sob.

At the far table one woman whispered to another, "See how he dresses himself like a peacock and fits her in dull, ordinary feathers!"

Ordinary! Blessed Tanit! In Sala I had myself overseen the making of this sensible ensemble of mock-cuirassier jacket and perfectly tailored traveling skirt with a double row of buttons in the front for ease of dressing and sewn of the finest challis dyed a sophisticated rich spruce green that exactly complemented my coloring.

The steward was by now looking angry. "You may be assured that our carriages are of the first quality, Magister."

He tried the bread. "Sadly, the same cannot be said for your cook. I will endeavor to accept what you set before me. My wife has begged me to break our journey here for some days of needed respite, for she has a frail constitution and the coach accident quite overset her delicate nerves, but I am not sure I can endure these conditions for even one more night, much less perform other duties."

As the steward assured him that all would be arranged to his satisfaction, I stealthily ate two slices of bread magnificently flavored with a tincture of garlic and dill. Then I managed to eat my way down the side table as Andevai complained at length about the unlikelihood of anything being arranged to his satisfaction.

Not long after, we were seated in a spacious and exceptionally well-sprung carriage taking a tour of the city under the guidance of the steward. He was, he informed us imperiously, the son of Five Mirrors's mansa. He did not like Andevai, that was obvious, but best of all, he had begun addressing gentle comments to me as if he felt sorry for me. The djeli had come along, ostensibly to narrate our tour. Although he glanced at the laced-up basket and my cane, he did not remark on them.

Noviomagus had the look of a prosperous town. Folk were out shopping. Servants pushed carts along the cobblestone streets. Like most urban centers that had survived the collapse of the Roman land empire eight hundred years ago, the old forum of the Roman city had developed into a civic center of a new town. A clock tower and a council house identified the public square where festival dances could be held, soldiers could parade, and princely bards and djeliw could declaim to large crowds. My husband compared these agreeable surroundings unfavorably to the superior architecture of cities I was pretty sure he had never visited except in prints collected into books. He then demanded to see New Bridge, whose splendors the djeli described in lengthy detail as we rolled through the streets toward the

river. I enjoyed the djeli's resonant speaking voice and fluid delivery not least because it meant I didn't have to listen to Andevai go on in that appalling tone.

It was a mercy to get out of the carriage at New Bridge. The air was cool, and the cloudy sky was rent by wind. Andevai asked question after question about the design and engineering of the bridge. He sounded as if he actually knew what he was talking about, as perhaps a man trained in carpentry by an architect would. I lagged behind. The moment the djeli turned his back on me, I slipped away behind a passing wagon. The men attending us shouted in alarm, but I had already hidden in the shadows and raced away. Because the Feast of Mars Triumphant began this evening, shopkeepers had hung the red festival wreath pierced with a short sword from their doors or over their windows. I saw no ram's masks in honor of the old Celtic war god Camulos, as were customary in Adurnam. Here, Mars Intarabus was known as the wolf-killer because he wore a wolf's pelt for clothing.

It was a comforting thought, soon succeeded by annoyance as I dodged out of the way of wheeled vehicles and hurried onto quieter lanes behind a man pushing a wheelbarrow full of bricks.

Gracious Melqart! Andevai's high-handed style really did display him in a most unflattering light. Four Moons House had a lot to answer for in its treatment of him, but he was not innocent of fault. His vanity dovetailed with his pride to make arrogance easy for him. Yet his plan had worked. Now he could keep them off guard with raging and sulking until Bee and I completed our business.

Rory was lounging in the hostel's parlor with a mug of beer in one hand and a dozing toddler on his lap as he charmed the woman who ran the place. With her ash-blonde hair and skin the color of milk, she looked as if her ancestors had lived in this region since before the Romans came.

"Where is Bee?" I asked.

He waggled his eyebrows. "She went for a walk, though I begged her to wait until you returned. Maestra Artia says there's been a dreadful epidemic at the New Academy."

"All the pupils were sent home!" The woman was eager to tell the tale again. "When my husband's cousin's wife's nephew went to deliver a wagonload of turnips and onions in his usual way, he was turned back from the gate by that strange young man who looks like 297 a ghostly spirit. Several of the servants have died. On no account is anyone to enter the grounds."

"What of the headmaster?"

"A high and mighty nobleman, they say, though I never saw him. He lingers on his deathbed!"

"How frightful!" I exclaimed, and seeing that she was not likely to leave the room without provocation, I surreptitiously pinched the toddler so hard the poor child woke up wailing.

After she apologetically carried off the screaming baby, Rory turned on me. "Cat! How could you? He peed on my arm!"

"Bee won't be able to stop herself from poking her nose in a little farther. I'm going after her. You must lie low until we return." I explained the situation.

"How can they wish to shoot me? They don't even know me!"

"Go wash your jacket. Stay alert and stay inside."

I walked out of town on the old Roman road that led south along the river to the city of Colonia. For once it was pleasant to have only my own thoughts for company. As much as I loved Vai and trusted his strength and loyalty, Bee had been right: He was not always a restful person to be with. Bee was not a restful person either, but my heart could never truly be at peace unless I knew she was safe, and I wasn't ever wholly happy except when she was near. I hurried, eager to reach her.

At the third mile marker I reached a large estate. A towering hedge blocked my view of the land. I passed a massive iron gate closed across a pretty lane lined by evergreen cypress trees. The drive cut through landscaped grounds to a distant compound house set back by the river. On the opposite side of the gate, the impenetrable hedge gave way to a row of larger cypress grown close enough to block the view toward the river.

"Cat! Here!" Bee peeked through cypress branches.

I hopped over the roadside ditch and shoved through the branches. Before I could inform her of what an idiot she was to go tramping off without me, she dragged me out of sight behind the cypress. Inside the estate grounds, we hid in a copse of trees of white-barked alder, ringed by yet more cypress. The trees concealed a set of marble benches whose bases were carved with what I first took for serpents and then realized depicted swimming dragons with tapered wings, elongated muzzles, and smoky breath.

"Why didn't you wait for me?" I demanded. "Any terrible calamity could have befallen you! Anyway, I'm so aggravated, Bee, because nothing is going as planned!"

She listened as I explained what had happened. "I trust you did not suffer any mistreatment while staying overnight there!"

Sadly, I blushed, thinking of how we had started on the bed and ended on the table.

"Not that I need hear any details!" she said, laughing. "I have come to agree with the Romans in this. An excess of passion is clearly the sign of a undisciplined mind."

"Vai is not undisciplined!"

She smiled in the manner of a general contemplating sweet victory. "I wasn't talking about him."

In the distance dogs began barking, a clamor that built to a frantic yipping. We leaped to our feet.

"Fiery Shemesh!" Bee exclaimed. "I thought we would be safely hidden here!"

A huge dog with teeth bared charged through the trees, followed by a slavering pack of equally gigantic hounds. They erupted into a deafening frenzy of yips and barks as they surrounded us. I brandished my cane, wishing desperately that it were a sword.

"Behave!" she proclaimed in her orator's voice. They ceased barking and flattened themselves, ears back. Waggling forward, they acted like courtiers who have fallen out of favor and wish to regain the approval of a mercurial queen. She deigned to allow them to lick her hand and grovel at her feet.

"Gracious Melqart, Bee! You have always had a way with dogs, although I cannot imagine why except that dogs have no discrimination whatsoever, for they will adore anyone who feeds them!"

At the sound of my voice, several growled.

"Down!" she cried. Their growls ceased. She glanced at me with a triumphant smile. "Didn't Andevai win your heart by feeding you? Care to try your fortune with these? I swear on Melqart's Axe I will only let them bite off one of your hands."

"Bee, someone is coming."

299

My warning came too late. The cypress branches parted to reveal a ghost-pale figure wearing a midnight-blue dash jacket under a plain wool coat. The headmaster's assistant stared, mouth agape. Kemal Napata was an albino of Avarian ancestry, which meant he had extremely pale skin and straw-colored hair but also broad cheekbones and eyes with an epicanthic fold to mark him as a man whose ancestry resides in the distant East. His surprise was certainly greater than our own. After all I had done and said in the last year, I could easily recognize the look of frustrated longing and struggling restraint that tightened his expression.

"Beatrice Hassi Barahal!"

"Maester Kemal Napata," she echoed with a graceful courtesy. "Please, if you will, call off your hounds. I do not fear them, for they are quite loving, but I confess to some anxiety that they have taken a dislike to my dear cousin Cat, mistaking her name for her character."

At the academy we had jokingly called him the headmaster's dog for his doglike loyalty, but I examined him with a fresh perspective now. He had a stocky frame and an appealing face once you became accustomed to his unusual coloring. More importantly, as the headmaster's assistant, he must know things most people did not.

I said, "Begging your pardon, Maester Napata, but is the headmaster a dragon?"

His gaze skipped off Bee and landed on me. "Amun's Horns! You both must leave at once."

A gust of wind thundered through the cypresses. The white branches of alder lashed. A heavy weight thumped. Whimpering, the hounds huddled behind Bee.

A claw with talons as long as my arm raked between two cypress trees. Smoky mist spun through branches, which crisped to brown as if scorched by heat. The thin carpet of snow in the circle melted so fast that one moment we were standing on white and the next in seeps of water. A very large creature gave a very large *huff* that so scared me I dropped my cane.

Trees parted as a head thrust through. Its skin was scaled with obsidian flakes that both devoured and reflected light. Its eyes were as big as my head, so fulgent a green that they shone.

My enemy.

What instinctive force clawed up from my gut I did not know; I only knew that this was my enemy and I had to kill it or be killed.

Yet its gaze paralyzed me. In its eyes lay memories like shadows.

I saw a curly-haired man lift a little girl up to stand on the lower railing of a large, flat ferryboat. He braced himself to steady her. A crippled woman limped up next to them as they stared across a wide river. The little girl was babbling nonstop about her lovely new boots and whether there were any biscuits left to eat and if they would have to sleep in the coach once they got across the river and could she possibly hold on at the back of the next coach with the guard if she was very very good. Her parents smiled fondly at her and apologetically at the other passengers crowding on, some of whom winced away from the woman's scarred face and empty sleeve. The ferry juddered as it cast off from the shore and began tacking across the powerful current. The woman pressed a hand protectively on her rounded belly. Wind whipped up the girl's long black braid. The ferry bucked as if wrenched by an invisible hand, and some passengers cried out in fear. But with each tilt and dip of the boat, the girl shrieked with excited glee as she leaned trustingly into her father's arms. She galloped her little carved horse through empty air, and with a bright smile at her mother, she said—

"Cat! Step back!"

Too late. The vast jaws of the predator opened as the ferry tipped, took on water, and sank as quickly as a stone, so fast that no one had a chance to scream. The railing scraped the girl's hand as she clung to it, then lost hold. A rumble was all the voice the river had as it tore her father away from her. Her mother's hand gripped hers with such desperate strength, but as her blood welled up from the scrape and dissolved into the water, she faded out of her mother's grasp.

Delicately the beast closed its mouth over my body. Then I was drowning in a sea of smoke.

30

In the depths of the ice, wreathed in ice, sleeps the Wild Hunt. When it is woken, all tremble in fear.

In the depths of the black abyss, there drift in a watery stupor the Taninim, called also leviathans, and when they wake, their lashing tails smash ships into splinters and drive the sundered hulks under the waves.

In the depths of earth, wreathed in fire, lies coiled in slumber the Mother of All Dragons. Her smoky breath fills the ocean of dreams. She stirs, waking, and the world changes.

So we are told.

But of all the great powers in this world, one thing was certain.

No one could screech as loudly as Bee when she was truly outraged.

"LET. HER. GO!"

Thumps hammered its body, small fists pounding the leviathan's massive flanks.

"How dare you? After I almost died unearthing a nest, is this how you repay me?"

Then she kicked him.

I wasn't sure how I knew she had done that, only that I was spat out amid a rain of pebbles. After a moment the hail ceased. A dog crept up to me, ears down, and apologetically licked my face.

"Pah!" I shoved the animal away when it looked as if it meant to lick me again. Grabbing my cane, I staggered to my feet and spun to face the monster.

Bee sat on a bench beside the headmaster as Kemal Napata hovered anxiously behind. The headmaster had his hands on his knees, looking winded. His seamed black face and tall, slender frame looked exactly as I remembered them from Adurnam: those of an elderly man of Kushite ancestry with a scholarly demeanor and a calm heart. Sparks of green lit his eyes before fading into brown. The hounds swarmed over to press close to his feet.

Bee was in full spate, like the spring flood.

"I don't care if her sire is the Master of the Wild Hunt and if the spirit courts are the most ancient enemies of your kind. I never asked to walk the dreams of dragons! Someone else decided on my behalf! Furthermore, when you tricked me into crossing into the spirit world, I almost died to save those hatchlings! And after all that, I am meant to watch while my dearest cousin is *eaten*?"

"Maestressa, you cannot speak to the noble prince in such a tone," said Kemal, aghast, for Bee was leaning toward the headmaster as if her next move would be to punch him.

"What do you mean, I can't speak to him in that tone? I *am* speaking to him in that tone, now that I know he is not a prince of Kemet at all but rather an impostor slithering about the world with some manner of secretive plot in hand that involves the death of perfectly gentle, mild, and blameless young women!"

By the angry flush mottling his cheeks, Kemal appeared as if he might be reconsidering his infatuation. Trying to gather up enough breath to speak, I wheezed my way into a coughing fit.

Bee ran to me. She patted my face. "Dearest! Are you going to live?"

"Really, Bee," I said in a hoarse voice, "I was quite impressed by that diatribe until you described yourself as gentle and mild." I eyed the evidence of the broken branches.

The headmaster got to his feet. Bee and I jumped back. I raised my cane defensively.

"Maestressas, might we retire into the house for a cup of tea? The warm fire would be welcome to my old bones."

Bee squeezed my hand. "Surely you can understand that we may be reluctant to enter a den within whose walls we may be devoured at your leisure."

"I fear you have read too many lurid tales, Maestressa," he said in so kindly a manner that I began to think he must have reached the little grove of trees just in time to banish the monster, for this harmless old 303 man could surely not have been the monster himself. "You will be safe within the house. I do not eat human flesh."

"I heard half of your manservants have died," Bee said rudely. "Did you eat them?"

He sighed. "Yes."

Bee opened her mouth and then, after all, could grapple no words onto her tongue.

I pushed her behind me and swashed with my cane. "Back away slowly and we'll make a break for it," I muttered.

"Yes, I ate them," he repeated, "but they were not men."

"What were they, then?" she asked. "Trolls? And why did you try to eat Cat?"

"I did not try to eat her. I hoped she might see a memory in the tides of the Great Smoke."

I had always respected the headmaster because his easy demeanor and impressive erudition stood in such contrast to my Uncle Jonatan's short temper and small-mindedness. I didn't truly know what sort of older man my father Daniel would have become, had he lived, but I had liked to believe he would have been something like the man who had patiently satisfied all factions whose children attended Adurnam's academy college, without giving way to any one.

Only evidently he was no man.

"How can we trust you?" I asked.

"A reasonable question, Maestressa. I apologize for our unfortunate way of meeting just now. You surprised me at a vulnerable moment."

"Are you a dragon?" I asked.

"I find I am rather weary. Will you take tea on this cold day?"

Bee said, "You choose, Cat. I'll do as you say."

I had seen what I had been too young to understand at the time, that I had survived because I had accidentally fallen into and out of the spirit world.

"I think it is safe to go," I said.

"Are you sure?"

"Strangely, I am sure." I could forgive a lot for having been given the chance to see the loving way my parents had smiled at me and at each other, the way I had looked at them with such wholehearted trust. The way my mother had tried to hold on to me.

The house was a stately lord's home with two wings and three stories plus tiny attic windows. It was set near the river's edge flanked by a second band of trees. The gravel drive led to the imposing front entry but we walked around to the side, where a man took charge of the dogs and chivvied them away to a kennel.

We made our way through the house to a pleasant library. Bay windows overlooked a field of sheep-mown grass that sloped to the bank of the Rhenus River. A door opened onto a garden alcove. In the little garden, rosemary surrounded a flat granite rock where a sun-loving creature might bask in summer.

The walls were lined with bookshelves and enough mirrors that every part of the room could be seen within a reflection. There were two hearths instead of one, both fitted with the most modern circulating stoves; the room was too warm for my liking. Worktables were heaped with scrolls, books, and ridges of stacked letters, the usual detritus of a scholar. The chamber looked nothing like the study in Adurnam.

The headmaster sat in a chair situated by the windows and gestured toward a couch placed opposite. He shifted restlessly, as if he wanted to leap up again. Cautiously we sat. I saw no point in pleasantries, given everything that had happened. I asked what I needed to know.

"How did you drive off the Wild Hunt and save Kemal?" I asked.

He lifted a hand to indicate the nearest mirror. "In mirrors we can see the threads of magic woven through the worlds. Because of this, mirrors can be used to confuse and conceal."

My hope crashed. He could not save me any more than a troll maze could.

"Ever since the day you and your cousin arrived at the academy, I saw that the threads of both worlds run through you," he added. "I have always known what your cousin is, but I long wondered why your blood and bone are mixed of both mortal and spirit kind. The day the head of the poet Bran Cof spoke, I realized your sire must be a powerful spirit lord."

"You had no idea before?" I asked.

His mouth parted as if he were about to hiss, but he coughed instead. "I know less than you might think about the spirit world. I cannot walk there."

"But you hatched there," said Bee.

"I hatched there, although I have no memory of the event. We have no thinking mind until we swim through the Great Smoke and come to land in this world. The creatures of the spirit world live in their place, and we live in ours. The two are not meant to mix." He examined me as he might a curiosity. "Before I met you, Maestressa, I would have said someone like you could not exist. Everything you are and can do rises out of the mingling of two worlds in your flesh."

"Not everything, Your Excellency," I said. "I was given love and strength by the actions and example of the mother and father who meant to raise me and were killed because of me. I know affection and constancy because of the loyalty of my dear cousin Bee. My aunt and uncle fed and clothed me in the same manner they fed and clothed their own girls, so I learned fairness from them. We girls were taught deportment, fencing, dancing, and sewing, as well as how to read and write and do accounts and to use herbs to make the last of winter's store of turnips and parsnips taste palatable. So I learned both a trade, and how to make do. I refuse to agree that everything I am is due to my sire breeding me on my mother. I am not a horse or a dog, to be described in such a way. Even horses and dogs can be raised poorly, or well."

Perhaps, becoming heated, I had raised my voice.

"Passionately argued." A faint smile calmed his face. "Very well. Your actions and your loyalty to your cousin have convinced me you are not a servant of the spirit courts, they who are our implacable enemies. I believe you have earned the right to have a few of your questions answered."

Bee touched clasped hands to her lips, then lowered them. "From everything I have learned, it seems your people somehow bred or created the women who walk the paths of dreams. Your people infested us, if you will, with the curse of walking the Great Smoke in our dreams. You did so because you want us to walk into the spirit world and unearth a nest and guide its hatchlings into the mortal world."

"That is correct."

"But we can also glimpse meeting places in the future."

"Your visions allow you to find a nest. All the rest is coincidental, not of importance to us."

Bee's expression sharpened to her axe-blow glare, and I was sure she was about to say something cutting, but instead she sat back. "Surely nests hatch without our help."

"They do. And they have across the passing of many generations. Understand that we are far older than your kind. It is the way of my people that our mothers live in the Great Smoke. They lay their eggs on the shore of the spirit world. The eggs hatch in the spirit world, and hatchlings seek water, through which they fall into the Great Smoke. After a time swimming there, those who survive surface into this world, for it is here we must grow to maturity. Thus the cycle starts over. But in recent ages, our ancestors began to notice that fewer and fewer were reaching this world. We came to believe that the creatures of the spirit world were deliberately devouring the hatchlings in the hope of eating them all and thus causing us to die out completely."

"Why would they want your kind to die out?" Bee asked.

I said, "Probably so there will be no more tides. That's why the eru and other spirit creatures build warded ground, so they won't be changed when a tide sweeps over the land."

He smiled as he once would have at the academy, approving a pupil's correct answer. "That is what we believe. We can only know what we have learned from humans who have walked there."

"How did you make the dream walkers?" Bee asked.

"Only the mothers know. I do not."

Kemal held open the door to allow a woman to carry in a tea tray. As she set down the tray on a worktable and poured, I recognized her. She had been the housekeeper for the dying man we had stumbled on while escaping from the Barry household, an old man who had exuded heat, sheltered loyal hounds, and asked Bee for a kiss. Now she was working for the headmaster.

"You may go, Maestra Lian. Kemal, you may also leave us. I will ring if I need you." When the door had closed, the headmaster took a sip of tea. "For a very long time now our numbers have suffered, and we have become few. We have come to expect at best three hatchlings to survive from a mating swim. Two days ago, on the equinox, eleven hatchlings swam ashore from the nest you unearthed, Beatrice. They were all brought safely to the house. Quite astonishing, and a reason for us to hope our numbers may increase."

I thought of how many had been eaten and crushed in their race through the spirit world. Truly, few if any would have survived if Bee had not been there to shepherd them into the river.

"Why would they only be coming ashore now when it was so long ago that Cat and I dug them up?" Bee asked.

"While they are swimming in the Great Smoke, hatchlings cannot sense the mortal world. However, here in the mortal world, a male announces his readiness to crown by marking a river's shore with a scent. That mark attracts any rivals who wish to challenge him. The scent is so strong that it penetrates the Great Smoke as well. Hatchlings follow it into the mortal world."

"What does it mean to crown?" I asked, for I could not help but wonder if the word was a euphemism for mating.

With a frown, he glanced out the window as if to suggest I had been rude for asking.

We sat in an uncomfortable silence. I did not know what to say, and Bee did not speak.

"Can it be?" He sat forward abruptly. An unexpected grin brightened his expression, and he rose. "What rich bounty showers on us! Yet more arrive!"

He limped into the garden and down the lawn. Bee and I ran to the window.

A spout of water swirled up from the river like an unraveling thread pulled off the fraying hem of a piece of cloth. The water poured into the headmaster. His human shape changed. I suddenly understood that his human form was nothing more than an elaborate illusion. The body absorbed the water and grew into a glistening dragon, one with a mouth large enough that it could eat me in one gulp. The slippery texture of its black scales swallowed light. Its head had a whiskered muzzle, and a shimmering crest ran down the length of its spine, waving like grass in the wind. Its body tapered into a flat tail more like a fish's than a bird's. Yet despite the creature's perilous aspect and daunting size, it waddled in a remarkably ungainly way down the sloping ground.

A roil of movement stirred the river. Creatures surfaced.

"They're mine!" Bee's face had the shine of a mother's smile. "Don't
308   you recognize them?"

She ran outside.

I halted in revulsion by the garden door. Eleven silvery-white eels the size of children humped up onto the shore, blowing and wiggling as they snuffled along the grassy bank. They were the ugliest things I had ever seen, except for their startling gem-like eyes. The dragon huffed a smoky breath that stopped them in their tracks and compelled their attention. Every pair of glowing eyes fixed on him.

A twelfth grub squirmed unremarked onto the shore farther down the bank, beyond a small wooden pier to which a rowboat was lashed. A hawk dove down to investigate its movement. The stray hatchling's sapphire eyes tracked the hawk's flight as the bird settled on the bare branch of a tree. The raptor and the grub studied each other. Then the hatchling lunged forward. In the time it took me to suck in a shocked breath, not sure who was going to devour whom, it changed.

As if the tide of a dragon's dream swept its unformed body, it molted its ungainly larval form and rose as a large hawk, beating for the sky. The true hawk followed.

I dragged my gaze away from the birds to see the eleven hatchlings molting their ugly grub forms. They transformed into smaller versions of the scaled beast. The air around the headmaster shivered as if rippled by a blast of heat. The shining black body of the beast turned in on itself and became that of the man we knew, thankfully in his clothes. A brief circle of dense rain splashed around him, as if he were raining away the water he had earlier absorbed.

In a frenzy of imitation, the grubs also changed, although they did not change size.

Eleven youthful persons stood dripping wet and naked on the shoreline, with no thought for modesty. They had the size and features of innocent boys who are no longer children but not yet grown. They surged forward to crowd around Bee, touching her, patting her, sniffing her.

Maestra Lian came striding down the lawn. With brisk gestures and snapped words she herded them away from Bee and toward the house.

Bee ran to me, her face so opened by joy that she seemed ready to fly. "Did you see, Cat? They know I'm the one who hatched them!"

She glanced past me, and the brilliance of her gaze softened. I turned. Kemal stood in the garden door, watching the youths flock into the house. An expression of unimaginable grief seared his pale features.

"Maester Napata, I hope we have done nothing to disturb you," said Bee in the same tone she might use to coax a wounded dog out of its hiding place.

He muttered, "What have you not done to disturb me?"

"Are you a dragon, too?" she asked, more lightly.

He flushed, glancing away, then took in a sharp breath and faced her. "This is the only body I have ever been able to wear. Since it is a man's body, can I then call myself a dragon?"

Her frown usually presaged a scold, but she spoke in a mild voice. "If you hatched as these others did, out of a nest in the spirit world, then aren't you a dragon regardless of what body you wear?"

"The others say I am too much of a weakling to change," he muttered in a low, shamed voice.

"I hope they shall say no such thing where I can hear it!" she retorted. "I am sure there is some other explanation."

The headmaster walked into the garden alcove. "There is an explanation."

He ushered us back into the study. There he sat at the desk and sipped at his cooling tea as if our conversation had not been interrupted by the arrival of eleven—twelve—inhuman creatures out of the unseen smoke of the spirit world's fathomless ocean.

"As with all that is born into the spirit world, our essential nature is one of change. When a hatchling first emerges into the mortal world from the Great Smoke, it does not comprehend that it has a true nature, the kernel of its being. That is why we must meet our young ones at the shore, so we can shepherd them into their true shape. Kemal came to shore among humans. It is remarkable he was not killed the moment he breached the water, for that is usually what happens if a young one wades onto land where no kinsman is there to aid it. But he was not killed. For all his childhood he thought he was human. I am not sure if the family that took in the small orphan child did so because they felt pity for him or because they knew in time they would be able to receive a substantial pension from the emperor. In the Empire of the Avar, any child with the white skin and hair we call albino must be handed over to the emperor. Those who bring such a child forward are rewarded, while those who try to hide such a one are punished. I found Kemal in a sacrificial lot being made ready for the Wild Hunt. It is known among the Avar that in rare cases these albino children are dragons, although most such albino children are perfectly human. However, that is why the empire exposes them on Hallows' Night, because the Hunt will always kill one of us if it can."

"How awful," said Bee, glancing at Kemal.

"A maze of mirrors will always confound the Hunt," the head-master went on. "I rescued Kemal by this means, but I had found him too late. He had spent so many years in a human body believing him-self human that he was too old to learn how to change."

Kemal stared at his hands as if trying to pretend we were not talk-ing about him.

"Your Excellency, just now on the shore, I saw one turn into a hawk and fly away," I said. "What will happen to it?"

"It will live a hawk's life and die a hawk's death. It is impossible to find those of our children who are lost in this way. These examples illustrate how important it is that we be the ones who greet our own children and welcome them to this world. If they do not know we are what they can be, then they will never know and are lost to us regardless."

"Can the rest of you change shape at will?"

"Yes. All except Kemal."

"Then why do you live in human form, Your Excellency?" Bee asked.

"As your kind spread across the lands and began to discover our young ones and kill them out of fear, we discovered our best camou-flage was to walk in the world in human form, and to live among you."

"How do they know whether to be male or female?" I asked.

His smile reproved me. "It is not the same for us as with human-kind. When we hatch in the spirit world and swim in the Great Smoke, we are grubs, neither male nor female. When we come ashore in the mortal world, we become male."

"How do you breed and produce nests, then, if you are all male?" Bee demanded.

"Would I ask you such a intimate question? Do not presume to ask it of me." The brown of his eyes flashed with the spark of emeralds, as if his control of his human shape was slipping. He spoke in an edged tone I had never before heard from the man who had famously not once lost his temper at the academy. "I am weary, and growing restless. Is there some favor you came to ask that you believe I can help you with?"

Bee twisted her hands together. Her hesitation surprised me, as did the way she chewed on her lower lip as if nerving herself to speak.

"Your Excellency." Maestra Lian appeared at the door. "They are clothed and settled in the upstairs room for safety. A fifth claimant has arrived."

He leaped to his feet with such a hiss that Bee and I both jolted back. I grasped the basket, wondering if I would need to throw the skull at him.

"We are done here," he said in a hostile tone that killed the interview. "You must go."

Bee sucked in a huge breath and let it out all in a rush.

"Your Excellency, how do I stop dreaming?"

"Bee!" I whispered, shocked by her words.

He shrugged his shoulders uncaringly. "How do you stop dreaming? In the same way you stop breathing. You die."

"We must leave now," said Kemal firmly, waving us out. "I will escort you to the gates."

We walked out of the grand house in silence.

Once on the drive, Bee spoke. "Maester Napata, how many people know that dragons roam the earth in the guise of human beings?"

"In this part of the world, I should be surprised if anyone knows, for we keep ourselves hidden."

A coach passed us, driving toward the house. A distinguished man of middle years stared at us from the coach. Was this the fifth claimant? Certainly he was an adult, not a hatchling. What crown was he challenging the headmaster for?

At the massive wrought-iron gates, the two guards cast sneering glances toward Kemal but allowed in an insulting manner that Bee and I might pass through the gatehouse. After a formal courtesy she and I departed.

"The guards must be dragons, too," said Bee. "They were very rude to Maester Kemal."

"You are his champion now! I wonder if any of the attractive men at the academy college in Adurnam were secretly dragons. How does it feel to know a dragon is infatuated with you?"

"It's nothing to joke about," she snapped. "Imagine being orphaned in such a way, and never even having a single memory of your parentage or what you truly are! You of all people should feel sympathy for the young man's plight."

"Blessed Tanit! This is a change of heart! I am sure it was you who first conceived of calling him the headmaster's dog back in Adurnam."

"I am sorry I was too selfish to remark on the sorrows and griefs of others. People must do better in being kind to others, for I am come to see that the temperament that looks suspiciously on any person who does not wear the garb they believe is proper, is the temperament most apt to punish the unfamiliar and least apt to see justice done. Do you not think so?"

I caught her hand. "Bee, do you really wish you could stop dreaming?"

"Of course I do! What has it brought me except trouble?"

"Is that why you wanted to see the headmaster?"

"The most pressing reason, yes. But it was a foolish question, wasn't it? Even if there were a way for me to stop dreaming, no one would ever believe me if I said I had stopped. So I may as well keep my gift and learn to use it for our purposes, not theirs. Why should we be theirs to command? We belong to ourselves!"

At the hostel we shared a supper of thin gruel with a turnip for garnish. I offered a bit of turnip to the skull, then dug in. The appearance of the skull merely made our hosts think us visitors with arcane powers, for severed heads had a peculiar mystery and importance among those of Celtic lineage.

We hadn't the extra coin to pay for a tallow candle, and without Vai we had no cold fire, so we retired to our tiny room at twilight. Bee and I sat cross-legged on the bed, facing each other with knees touching and heads bent together. Rory stretched out beside us clad in trousers and shirt. Bee wore a practical night shift, and fortunately the women of White Bow House had gifted me with a pretty night shift decorated with lace, although this was the first night I had worn it. I was fretful, worrying about Vai. Did mage Houses have some secret means by which to imprison rebellious sons? Iron shackles and iron bars could not contain the most powerful of their kind. What could?

Bee twined her fingers through mine. "I miss Mama and Hanan and even Papa and wretched little Astraea. I miss the quiet life we had in Falle Square. Can you even believe I'm saying that? When I was there, all I could dream about was having a wealthy and handsome prince rescue me from the dreary poverty of our lives. Now a quiet life doesn't seem so ill-favored."

"It wasn't as quiet as you remember. Aunt and Uncle were always scrambling to make ends meet. Not to mention the constant trouble they were in for buying and selling information. I expect they found the life more wearying and anxious than quiet, whatever it may have seemed to us. They kept us very sheltered, Bee. As I am discovering!"

"I wish I could have spoken to the hatchlings. I feel I am their midwife. All this time dragons have lived among us and yet we have never known."

"I could have told you," muttered Rory. "I expect the only reason the dragon didn't eat you is that you taste sour, not at all to his liking. But who ever listens to me? Besides Vai, I mean."

"Andevai listens to you?" Bee said with a snorting chuckle.

A board creaked in the passage. Fingers tapped lightly on the door. Rory rolled off the bed with unseemly haste, and slipped out. I heard the husband's murmur, and they padded away.

"Does he do this everywhere he goes and every place he stays?" I asked.

"Yes, he's incorrigible. But you know, Cat, he's right. Andevai does listen to him in a way you and I don't. Simpering Astarte, they're actually rather sweet together, just as a man and his wife's brother should be. Rory makes Andevai likable."

"Vai's not likable with me?"

She laughed. "Watching you soothe his ruffled feathers amuses me, considering if it were anyone else you would cut him to pieces with your tongue."

"I tell him what I think!"

She squeezed my hand. "Yes, dearest, and he adores you for it. Still, I expect Andevai particularly likes Rory because he has discovered Rory can tell when you are fertile and when you are not. A useful sort of person to have around, don't you think? Given that you don't want to get pregnant yet but wish to enjoy sexual congress."

"Blessed Tanit! Now that you mention it, Vai has conversed upon that subject more than once since he and Rory met. I ought to have suspected. Anyway, Rory has the knack of flattering people in exactly the right way, so that it's true but not condescending."

"Yes. It's like he's hunting for the kill, only the kill in this case is winning people over to like him. He always seems to leave them in better spirits than when he arrived. Don't you think that is a rare gift, the ability to make people happy?" She sighed.

"Haven't you been happy as a radical? Sleeping with the infamously handsome Brennan Du?"

She released my hands. "Yes, as for adventure and the admiration of men swept off their feet by my brilliant rhetorical abilities, I would say that the last nine months have been eminently satisfactory."

"Goodness, Bee! Were there other men?"

A smack of sound against the windowpane startled me; someone was throwing pebbles at our room. I got off the bed and peered down to the street. With clouds overhead, no moon or starlight limned the street, and although the houses on this lane had night lamps burning on their porches, not a single flame now illuminated the dark. I recognized the shadowy form from the drape of his winter coat over his shoulders. Alarm leaped like a deer bolting from the scent of wolves.

"It's Vai!"

I crept downstairs, unbarred the door, and let him in. In the back of the house the fire in the kitchen stove, sealed for the night, groaned with a resigned huff as the presence of a powerful cold mage sucked all combustion from the flames. We tiptoed upstairs.

"Andevai!" Bee whispered as he shaped a spark of cold fire into the shape of a candle. "Why are you here? What went wrong?"

He shook off the coat. He was wearing a rough workingman's jacket and trousers we had smuggled into Five Mirrors House as cushioning for the cacica's head, which he had pulled on over his other garments.

"I told them it wasn't the first time you had run away from me, which statement has the added benefit of being the truth. I spent all day nagging at them to find you, thinking that would relieve their concerns about me. Then they paraded four women in front of me and asked which one I wanted in my bed." He sank down on the bed and rubbed his head as if it hurt. "They were so insistent, reminding me of how every magister owed it to the vigor of the Houses to do his part. The only way I could get rid of them was to reduce them all to tears by enumerating their flaws and shortcomings at length."

"That can't have been difficult for you, Magister," said Bee with a sting in her smile.

He looked up so quickly I thought he meant to cut her with an edged retort. She braced herself, ready to give back what she got.

"For over seven years I worked to become the magister they would accept in Four Moons House, so I could prove I was more powerful than them, smarter than them, better than them. It was so easy to become him again. But I don't want to be that man."

Bee's mouth parted in astonishment. Mercifully she said nothing, for above all things I could not imagine Vai accepting sympathetic platitudes.

"Then you won't go back, love," I said.

He looked away. "None of that matters," he went on in a curt tone that another might have heard as a rejection but that I knew came from pride. "As I was leaving the parlor after getting rid of the women, I saw a messenger wearing the colors and badge of Four Moons House."

"The courier I saw leave last night can't have gotten there and back so quickly."

He nodded. "Yes, it seemed odd to me. I followed, but I'm not a skilled spy. I never discovered what the messenger was there for because I was caught just as the steward was ordering the captain of the House guards to start a house-by-house search of Noviomagus to look for you, Catherine. I pretended I had come to insist on that very thing, and demanded to go with them. I slipped the laborer's clothes inside my coat and changed in a tavern." He laughed mockingly. "I pulled an old cap over my head and slouched out past them. They look only at posture and clothes. They didn't even see me go past."

Sleet hissed along the roof. He glanced at the window.

"I expect their magisters are bringing down a storm to keep travelers off the roads. It will take some time to search, but they're bound to check hostels and inns first. We've got to go."

316   "Very well," said Bee decisively. "We'll return to New Academy and

demand refuge. The headmaster was singularly unhelpful, but we are owed that much, surely!"

"What about Rory?" I asked as I began collecting our belongings. "He went to the innkeepers' chamber."

Vai's amused grin was so rare a sight that Bee actually stared. "Ah. I take it he is out prowling. I shall fetch him while you dress."

As we dressed, he descended the creaking stairs. I heard the hard rap he gave on a closed door and his voice raised without the least embarrassment. "I beg your pardon, but I need Rory immediately, for we've had urgent news."

The baby woke and began sobbing disconsolately. Rory made apologetic fare-thee-wells as Bee and I got everything ready. We had a lot to carry, a bag each plus Vai's carpentry apron, which he wore under his coat. Foul weather dogged us as we strode miserably along the road beneath a biting sleet that made my nose go numb. Not a single soul braved the road except for us. The night lay as dark as if pitch had been poured over the world, but Vai's mage light lit our path.

Wind tangled in the trees with a rush like wings. Between gusts I heard hoofbeats. Bobbing lights approached from the direction of town, not lantern light but cold fire. Mages pursued us, riding with soldiers. Ahead the impenetrable hedge gave way to the academy gates, where a real lamp burned. We reached the gates before the troop got sight of us. A burly guard with a bored expression slouched out from the gatehouse. The gate lamp burned steadily despite Vai's standing next to it.

"You must let us in!" Bee cried.

"You can't enter." The guard eyed Rory with a look that made Rory curl his lips back. "The master is dueling the last challenger. After that, the winner will banquet on the remains. Go away, and be grateful I do not eat you, which I do not do solely because of the nasty stink of your flesh."

"Who do you think I am, that you speak to me in such a dismissive way!" Bee exclaimed. "What of all those youthful hatchlings for which I am sure your kind ought to be grateful, lest you otherwise die out like ash on a dead fire? Do not condescend to me. Take us to Kemal at once."

"That hapless worm!" He grinned to show his teeth. I could not help but think of Chartji, whom I liked so much better! "He is no man. Or I should say, he *is* a man. A sad creature that makes him, so shrunken and weak he cannot become his own self."

Bee lifted a fist, ready to slug him. He hissed at her in a way that made Rory snarl and me grab for my sword.

Vai stepped between them. "If you do not wish your master to be disturbed, you do better to hide us than to let the soldiers find us. If they do catch us here, we will tell them everything. Then the entire mage House will descend upon you."

This argument, delivered with Vai's magisterial self-confidence, so struck the man that he hustled us into the gatehouse and out the back way onto the grounds just as the troop rode up. We hid in the dripping shadow of the hedge as soldiers tramped through the gatehouse and back out again while the guard complained vociferously at being rousted from his warm hearth.

Soldiers and mage continued south, still on the hunt. Without waiting for permission Bee ran down the drive toward the house. That the guard did not chase her made me hasten after.

"We must be cautious, Bee," I called, trying to grab her sleeve. She could really run when she wanted to. She slipped out of my grasp as she put on a burst of speed despite the pack bumping on her back. Rory was lagging behind, reluctant to press on, and weighted down with a bag in each hand. Vai had dropped back to prod him forward. They faded into night's gloom. Ahead twin lamps burned.

A large shape passed so close over my head that I ducked instinctively. An exhalation of smoky mist spilled fiery sparks above my head. A second shape, bigger than the first, swooped down. I tackled Bee. Rising to my knees, I twisted the hilt of my sword to draw it, but the weapon hung inert in my hand, as heavy as lead.

"Down!" I cried.

With a dreadful smacking thunk, the second beast slammed into the first one and smashed it to the earth a stone's throw away. The impact shuddered through the ground.

Bee staggered to her feet. "We've got to get to the house!"

Thrashing and roaring, the beasts rolled toward the drive. Claws and teeth flashed as deadly daggers, moist with fluids. A scaly tail thwacked down on the gravel drive no more than three body-lengths from where I was gaping like a lack-wit. Coming from out of nowhere, hands dragged me backward.

"Run!" Vai shouted.

"Where's Rory?"

"I sent him back to the gate. We're cut off. Bee! Move!"

We abandoned our gear as we bolted for the safety of the building. A harsh shriek scraped the air, curdling my blood. So frightful was the sound of teeth crunching bone that I staggered, for the vibration of the noise ground through my own bones in sympathy.

Dying.

I am dying.

My blood is hot and harsh, pouring into the throat of my remorseless rival. The strongest has won the right to the crown.

Vai did not let go of my hand as he kept us running. A gusting trumpet cry chased us. A dark shape launched into the air and, twisting, landed with a ground-shaking thud right in front of us. Together we stumbled to a halt and stared down Leviathan.

Rory stalked up beside us, trembling but determined to stand with us.

The dragon was now far larger than it had been on the lawn earlier in the day. Although clouds shrouded the sky, stars glimmered in its scales like a vision of unknown shores. The head lowered to peruse us. Eyes like emeralds spun in dizzying circles. Through those spinning eyes I watched as through a window into a hazy mist where shadows of figures shuddered into view and melted away. Was that my mother, staggering through a chaos of battle, one eye bleeding and her lower arm horribly shattered so bone stuck through the torn flesh? I swayed at the sight of her blood and pain.

"Lord of All!" Vai shut his eyes so as not to be caught in the whirlpool. "The creature has cut the thread of my magic. I can't touch the ice."

He tried to push me behind him so it would eat him first, but I twisted out of his grasp and stepped forward. Bee yanked me back.

"Both of you, move away!" Stepping in front of the beast, she had the look of a scrumptious honeycake set before a ravenous dame.

"Salve, Your Excellency! Our apologies for interrupting your dinner. I am sure you recognize us as harmless bystanders. Please let us

319

pass to the safety of the house. We will be perfectly happy to stay out of your way until the soldiers who are trying to arrest us have gone."

The leviathan exhaled with a snort of smoke. Sparks glimmered before dissipating like cooling steam. It heaved itself one big flop toward us.

Never run when they have you in their sight. If you ran, they couldn't help but chase you.

Its maw opened to reveal a predator's teeth slimy with fluids and moist substances I did not care to name. Fetid carrion breath mingled with smoke to bring tears to my eyes. Vai's hand tightened on mine, and I knew he was going to throw himself forward to give me time to escape, so I snaked my foot out, meaning to trip him as soon as he lunged.

"Don't move, you idiots!" said Bee without looking at us.

A pale man crunched into view on the gravel drive, skirting the flank of the beast. "Move slowly off to the side so you do not stand between him and the challenger," said Kemal.

We edged sideways onto the grass as Kemal calmly collected our abandoned gear. Vai had sheathed his sword and now had one arm around me and the other around Bee. My panic had ebbed enough that I guessed it soothed him to feel he was protecting us. I even leaned against him, and his hand tightened on my waist to comfort me. I was shaking, it was true. I did not mind a bit of manly comfort. Rory nudged up against me, and I caught his hand in mine.

Gravel ground under its belly as the beast squirmed forward. It nosed up to the steaming carcass of the beast it had just killed and began to feed, ripping and swallowing the tender flesh and sucking at streams of blood and internal fluids. Bee hid her eyes. Vai grunted, looking down.

"It can't possibly still want to eat us after it eats all that," Rory muttered, watching with a predator's measuring interest.

Kemal set the bags and packs beside us. "My apologies, but you cannot stay here."

Bee pleaded with a fervent gaze. "The mage House troops are going to arrest us. Please."

Her pleading surely seemed like torment to him. "You cannot stay
320 here."

"The headmaster owes me a favor," said Bee.

"The headmaster is gone. That he spoke to you earlier today is astonishing enough. It was the last time he appeared in human form. Any adult male who challenges for the crown does so in our ancestral form, what you would call a dragon. Those males who refuse to compete remain in the form of a man so they pose no threat. The flesh of each rival who is consumed strengthens and grows the winner. The last survivor earns the right to crown."

Vai's gaze flashed up. "Is that a polite euphemism for mating?"

I was pretty sure Kemal's skin darkened with a flush. "We are not like you. The strongest male proves he has the strength and therefore the right to crown. To crown means to become female. Thus will he enter the river and become she, and thus she will cross by water into the ocean of dreams, what you call the Great Smoke. The mothers live there. Now I have told you more than I ought," he finished, with a glance at Bee. "You must leave at once."

Bee had not given up. "Is there some other refuge? A boat? Horses? A hidden path?"

"No." He hustled us back up the drive. The noise of feeding mercifully faded behind us.

Lamplight winked as the gatekeeper peeped out. "I can't open up. Trapped inside and like to be crushed and spat out is what you get for demanding the right to go where you ought not. Fools!"

"Let them out," said Kemal.

"You're not even worm enough to make me," said the gatekeeper, with a laugh.

Perhaps the night's fraught events had worn Kemal's mild temperament threadbare, but I thought it more likely that he responded as a young man might who feels he has been insulted in front of a woman he wants to impress. Kemal punched him up under the ribs with a strong undercut from his right, followed by a swift uppercut to the jaw from his left. The man went down.

"That was bruising!" said Rory, shaking out of his anxious slouch. "Have you studied the science of boxing?"

A horn shrilled from the road. Behind, the leviathan trumpeted in answer to its challenge. Heat grew at our back. The dragon was dragging itself closer.

"Hurry!" Kemal pushed us through the open door of the gate-house. Even in such dire straits, I could not help but notice that the hearth fire burned unstintingly as Vai passed. We tumbled out on the other side of the gate as the gatekeeper skittered back into the safety of the gatehouse and slammed and locked the doors. The bellows breath of the dragon sucked in and out like the rhythm of the forge. It was definitely larger than it had been before it had eaten the last claimant.

Worst, the soldiers were closer than we had realized.

"There is the Diarisso mage!" In the aura of the gate lamp, soldiers clattered out of the night even as the cold fire guiding them vanished as though blown out.

The mage House troops spread into a semicircle that pinned us in front of the gate. We were caught between the claw and the teeth, as in the old tale of the slaves fleeing ancient Kemet who were trapped between the pharaoh's army and an uncrossable sea.

"How could you abandon us like this!" Bee cried accusingly at Kemal.

Rory muttered, "Eaten or shot, which ought I prefer?"

Vai swore out of bitter frustration as his magic failed him.

I could barely lift my cane.

"I can't reach my magic!" cried the mage riding with the troop. "What power traps it?"

"Kill all but the Diarisso," shouted the captain.

Soldiers dismounted and swarmed forward with swords raised. Anger kindled in Kemal's face, like buried light cutting through a concealing veil. He feared for Bee, certainly, but the knowledge that he had unwittingly walked her to her death surely scoured his pride as well. Or maybe it was only years of frustration at being told he must not desire what was so completely out of his reach and which was now to be torn from him forever.

He forgot himself.

And became what he really was.

First a pale man flashed as if he had become mirrors all catching tomorrow's sunlight. The iron of the gates crumbled and, in a rush as of wind, poured into an eddy that he began absorbing. The substance filled and changed him. A creature formed as of polished iron swelled out of the vanishing figure of the man. It grew so monstrously fast that as I took in a breath I still saw the man, and as I exhaled a dragon filled the open gateway. Its mouth could have swallowed a pony. Whiskers like ropes lashed in a wind I could not feel. A crest rippled along its ridged spine in a delicate lacework of steel. Its tail whipped around and toppled several of the cypress trees. Its roar crackled like the fury of a blazing fire sweeping over us.

The soldiers fell over each other in their haste to retreat. The horses scattered as one rider sounded the alarm on a horn: *Ta-ran-ta-ta!* A distant horn answered, echoed by a third.

Close at hand a trumpet cry shook the air. Huddled against the door of the locked gatehouse, we turned to see the black dragon rise to confront this new challenger.

31

Once I had feared the fury of a magister powerful enough to rule as the head of a mage House more than I had feared the frightful tales of the great powers that lie invisible to us.

What a naïve girl I had been.

Two monstrous dragons reared up to attack each other, heedless of the tiny mortals scrambling away beneath them. Heat poured off them in battering waves. The tops of the cypress trees caught fire.

I grabbed Vai's arm, for Bee's comment had jogged my memory at last. "There's a rowboat at the river's edge. Bring everything. Rory, hurry!"

We dashed past the ruined gate and the closed doors of the gate-house, heading toward the house. With a shrill scream the black launched itself against the smaller iron dragon. When their bodies collided, the ground actually shook.

Ash and burning needles spun down over us as we ran down the drive. Vai was cursing; he was a man unaccustomed to being rendered impotent in such a devastatingly comprehensive way. When I looked around, Bee wasn't with us.

"I have to go back and look for her!" I shouted.

"Rory, find the boat, make sure there are oars." Vai shoved the bag he was carrying to Rory. His apron of carpentry tools wrapped him like armor. "Catherine, I won't leave you, so don't ask it of me."

Heavily laden, Rory staggered toward the river. Vai and I hunkered in the cover of the trees as the two dragons came rolling past in a frenzy of talons, teeth, and lashing tails. They broke apart. The dragon who had been Kemal beat its wings, the draft driving us to the ground. A thread of blood trailed past my hand with a stench like the forge. The black dragon rose onto its hind legs; its body blocked out half the sky.

A small person ran into the gap between them.

"Bee!" I screamed.

Vai threw me onto the ground, and himself on top. I squirmed and poked but his weight and that of the laden apron trapped me. "Hate me if you wish, but you can't save her this time. She can only save herself."

She was refulgent with anger. "Enough, Your Excellency! You have triumphed over all your challengers! Now go and do what things your kind do when all this rending and roaring is over!"

As she spoke she retreated until she stood beneath the iron-gray dragon. It could have crushed her with its talons or snapped her up in one gulp, but fearlessly she pressed a hand on its belly.

"Please, Kemal. You don't need to challenge him. Turn back into a man, and I'll give you a kiss."

"That will work," said Vai, his mouth against my ear.

It took me a moment to realize he wasn't being sarcastic.

The black dragon inhaled so deeply that the sparks and smoke swirling around us were sucked into its nostrils in a prelude to a fresh attack. Hail peppered down. Vai took the brunt of the impact but uttered not a sound.

The hail ceased, leaving the ground covered with iron pebbles. Vai rolled off me, rubbing his head and cursing under his breath.

The gleam of the black dragon's scales cast a hazy light over the two figures on the gravel drive. Kemal had become a man again. He knelt, head bowed, his left arm and leg streaked with blood.

"Come with me," Bee said coaxingly. She helped him to his feet and toward us along the drive. Their shuffling progress spun in the mirrors of the dragon's eyes as it watched them go.

I would have run forward but Vai held me back. "Catherine, there are times when you must stop and think and not just leap. If you rush out there, your movement or whatever scent you have of the spirit world may startle it into attacking."

"Thank Tanit!" Bee staggered up. She listed heavily to one side with Kemal leaning on her. "Help me. He's injured, and stunned."

Vai got an arm around him, and Bee let go.

"I was so frightened!" I hugged Bee so hard she grunted.

"Ouch! Cat! Let me go. Where's Rory?"

"We sent him ahead to secure the rowboat."

The dragon bellowed so loudly we all cringed. A horn cry answered, followed by a second and a third. Drums pulsed from the heart of the city. Was the Treverni prince raising his militia?

"Will the mages be foolish enough to attack?" I asked. "Can weapons hurt a dragon?"

"Best not to find out," said Kemal. "My people are few in number. He has now ingested the seed of five males. We must coax him to the river. Once in the water, he will crown. Once he becomes a female, he will dive for the Great Smoke."

"Very well." Bee boldly walked onto the drive. "Your Excellency, a part of you must surely still be the headmaster. I need that part of you to listen attentively. Soldiers are coming. You must depart. Otherwise the soldiers will attack the academy with the hatchlings in it. You are a rational and educated man. You can't want all those young ones killed. So let us move."

"She's magnificent!" Kemal breathed.

"Or insane," muttered Vai under his breath. "Are you sure she's safe from him?"

Kemal grimaced. "We do not eat people. They smell bad and are not at all nourishing. Among the lore of my kind, it is said humans are poisonous. Cold mages most of all."

"How have you cut the threads of my magic?" Vai asked.

"I know nothing of such secrets. Why would I?" Bitterness shaded his expression but then, remembering what he had just done, he smiled.

After a hesitation, Vai spoke. "My apologies for any discourtesy I showed you the first time we met, Maester Napata. I'm not just saying that because you saved our lives."

Kemal staggered along between us, looking unaccountably cheerful for a man who had taken several gashes to the flesh. "My thanks, Magister. Be assured I am accustomed to such treatment from cold mages. Although to be honest, your arrogance had a particularly memorable flair that made it all the more striking."

I glanced past Kemal to Vai, not sure how he would react to this gentle sarcasm.

"My thanks," he said with a slight flutter of his eyelashes. I wasn't sure if he was suppressing a sneer or a laugh. Then he smiled. "I often practiced for many hours in front of a mirror to be sure of bringing it off to its full effect."

Both Kemal and I laughed.

We hobbled around the kitchen wing. In front of the pier, guarding the rowboat, we discovered Maestra Lian holding a burning lamp in one hand and in the other a poker with which she was threatening Rory. He had an oar in each hand as he tried to dodge past her.

"Maester Kemal!" she cried. "This person steals the boat!"

He let go of us and limped to her. "Maestra Lian, let him pass. His Excellency is about to depart." He took the poker from her to use as a cane. "Some ruse must be devised to confuse the soldiers and send them away. I fear for the hatchlings."

"Tell them I wove the illusion of a dragon with cold magic as we were escaping," said Vai. "Their belief in my exceptional abilities will trouble them for months."

"If not years," Rory said, lowering the oars. "Can I get in the boat now, or is that dragon-stinking man going to poke me with the iron stick?"

I poked him. "Rory, don't be impolite! Maester Napata, my apologies. What will you do now?"

Kemal gestured toward the building. "I inherit the position as headmaster. That was always His Excellency's intention."

A shape like the void of night thumped down to the shore. I felt as with the skin of the grass that crushing weight, the ancient fire of its soul, and the spark of a new being about to shed the husk of its old form.

Bee's flow of words was the leash on which she led the beast to water. "I do not mean to sound inconsiderate or ungrateful, but I do think it most unfair that I should risk so much and yet be told so little. I realize human people are of little interest to your kind except insofar as we hinder your lives or aid you. But, for example, I would wish to know who that very old man was who kissed me and then died! Was he one of your kind, for I am sure he must have been. Why did he say he was waiting for me? He called me his death!"

327

Because of the cloudy light chasing along its black scales, she was able to see us standing by the pier. She waved cheerfully, looking not one bit frightened.

The dragon slid into the river. The touch of the water peeled away the skin of the beast. As his old skin sloughed off, a slender creature with pearlescent scales unfolded sleek wings. Its crest fluttered in a rainbow of shining color. It looked very like the leviathan that had carried us across the Great Smoke, only much smaller. The water boiled white as she swam in a wide arc out into the current and back to the shore.

Stars peeked through rents in the cloud cover. The head breached. Water poured off the long neck as she towered above us. Her scales reflected us as in a mirror:

The shadow of Rory's cat spirit limned his body like a cloak.

The glittering threads of Vai's cold magic flowed like sparkling ribbons that were being sucked into the void of the dragon's massive weight.

Maestra Lian and Bee each bore the ghost of a third eye shutting and opening on her forehead.

As for me...two Cats melted together, one wreathed in the shadowy threads of magic that bind the worlds while the other was plain, solid flesh.

Bee turned to Kemal. Unfolding around him in the manner of a male peacock's bright tail, he wore a fan of brilliant colors shaped into the translucent illusion of the dragon that was his true nature. I thought it unlikely he could have looked away from Bee's smitten regard even if the world had ended and we had all been swallowed by fire and ice.

Her voice's hoarse tremor was no doubt enrapturing to a man who had been hopelessly infatuated for so long. "I have never seen anything as magnificent in my life as you becoming a dragon."

She tipped up her face.

I thought he would crush her to him and kiss her searchingly and deeply and with the release of all that frustrated longing, as Vai had kissed me so angrily and passionately on the stairs at Nance's boarding-house in Expedition.

Kemal was not that man. As if he feared she was too fragile for his pent-up emotions, he brushed his mouth over hers in a shy, tentative kiss.

"Gracious! Is that the whole of what you mean to do?" Bee hauled him bodily into her, pulling him down for a very different sort of kiss.

I looked away. As my arm brushed the basket, I remembered how General Camjiata had pieced together disparate images from Bee's purloined sketchbook to guess how to capture me on the jetty in Expedition. Hastily, I unlaced the basket. I held out the skull so it faced the shining column of the dragon.

The cacica looked back at me. In my hands she was still a skull, but in the reflection I saw in the pearl mirror of the dragon's scales, she was a living head.

"Your Highness!" I cried, startled by the apparition. "We are still traveling. I assure you, I mean to find your son Haübey and return you to him as soon as I am able."

Her gaze fell on Bee locked in a fervent embrace with Kemal. "Distracted by kissing, as the young are wont to be. My thanks for the proper respect you have shown me, Niece. I give you warning. Trust not in fire banes. The ones you thought were your friends have betrayed you. People will speak and act in all kinds of ways because they do not believe there are ears or eyes to witness."

"What do you mean?" I cried, but the creature that had once been the headmaster plunged beneath the surface and I was left with a skull in my hands.

The churning deeps turned as into glass. I saw through it into an unfathomable sea. Humble fish swam through currents made by memories of that which has happened, which we recall imperfectly, and that which is yet to come, which we cannot foresee.

James Drake laughs as he stands with a foot on the limp body of a man. Blessed Tanit! The fallen man is Vai. Drake shoves the body with his foot and beckons for a soldier to bring a horse.

"Catherine!" called Vai from the boat.

I shoved the cacica's skull into the basket and ran onto the pier. The dragon flashed away into the chasm, out of the mortal world and into the Great Smoke. As the waves of its departure slapped the shore, Vai raked six fat spheres of cold fire into the air. Light coalesced into gleaming columns so bright I could discern the green of the grass.

I kissed and then released him. "If soldiers are coming, they'll know right where we are."

"That is my intention. I want to draw them off from the academy."

From the road, a horn blatted and was answered thrice.

Kemal set Bee back from him. "When I have made all safe here, I will find you," he promised her. He turned to us. "I'll tell them you stole our horses and fled by road. Go!"

I dragged a speechless Bee into the boat. Vai pushed off and set to the oars as Rory coiled the line. The current caught the bow, spinning us halfway around until Vai pulled us back. Bee stared toward the bank. A lamp caught flame. Kemal stared after us until Maestra Lian took his arm to help him back up to the academy of which he was now headmaster.

32

For the longest time no one spoke. Rory sat cross-legged among the gear, his head buried in his hands. Bee stared back the way we had come. A candle of light floated by Vai's knee, casting a gleam onto his beautiful face and intent expression. I watched the way his fingers tightened and relaxed on the oars, the way he glanced up between strokes at me, as if he was never quite sure he would still see me there, as if I might vanish between one breath and the next.

All my breath spilled out of me as I forced the awful vision of James Drake out of my head. I could kill Drake. If he tried to touch Vai, I would.

"Well!" said Bee. "Not every young woman has a dragon fall in love with her!"

I laughed, for her gloating tone scoured fear from me. I counted off on my fingers. "Goodness, Bee! A legate. A prince. An infamous radical. Even the mansa seemed inclined to fall for your prodigious charms. It seems unthinkable a dragon in the shape of a man would not do so likewise."

"How can you speak to me of any of those others!" she cried. "They are but...trifles compared to..." Words failed her.

Vai's gaze flashed up to meet mine. He smiled the intimate smile meant for me only, the one that made my cheeks grow warm. "I would have demanded more than a kiss."

"I must say that in your case, Andevai, I do believe that horse has already left the stable," retorted Bee in the most dignified manner imaginable, after which she spoiled the effect with a toss of her curls and an audible sniff.

Rory lifted his head. "Wouldn't it be more precise to say in that case that the horse has already entered the—"

"Rory." Vai's tone was genial, but he cut him off.

I cut in. "Maestra Lian is a dragon dreamer. Both of you have a ghostly third eye."

Bee touched her forehead, then giggled giddily. "Don't joke, you beast! Think of how unsightly that would look! I wonder why the headmaster never revealed the truth to me while we attended the academy."

"If he had told you what he was and what you were, back before all this happened, would you have believed him?"

"I suppose not," she said with a grudging sigh. "Anyway, my dream was wrong, about meeting the headmaster in his study."

"We found the headmaster in Noviomagus on the Feast of Mars Triumphant. He ate fire challengers. I spoke to the cacica as in a mirror. If you didn't truly understand the dream you were having, you might have interpreted it in a more familiar way."

"Why, Cat," she said in surprise, "I do believe you are right for once."

A horn's call rose and faded. Rain spattered over us. I clutched Bee's hand more tightly.

"Catherine, are you cold?" Vai pulled the left oar to steady us in the current. A bauble of cold fire chased out in front of us to light our way.

"I'm scared of being out on the water, to be honest."

Bee put an arm around me, but her attention was fixed on the globe of cold fire. "Andevai, how far can you push the cold fire away from you before you lose control of it? For that matter, how close must you be to a fire to kill it?"

"In Expedition we did a number of experiments to study exactly these issues."

"Did you?" said Bee, shifting excitedly beside me on the facing bench. "What did you do?"

"Everything will be different here because of the proximity and mass of the ice, but..." He described how the troll scientists he had worked with had set different combinations of things on fire and adjusted him for distance, angle, and substances placed between him and the fire. They had tested his ability to manipulate cold fire at distance, and how long the brightness would last after he had let go of it. "And both the feathered people and the dragons have an effect on my cold magic."

As they talked, I shut my eyes and pretended we were in a carriage.

After another hour we put in at an isolated sandbank. The boat became our roof as we huddled beneath like kittens under the beaver-pelt blanket and our winter coats, with Vai and Rory on the outside and Bee and me snug between them. Rory fell asleep at once.

"No kissing," said Bee.

Vai kissed me anyway. The touch of his lips was as soft as the caress of flowers.

"The cacica warned we must beware cold mages pretending to be our friends," I said. "But we already know the mansa of Five Mirrors House sent word to Four Moons House."

He sighed. "Yes. I should have known better than to believe I could return to the Houses."

"To think dragons walk among us and we never knew!" whispered Bee. By the lilt in her voice I could tell she was wide awake. "It seems to me the spirit world and the Great Smoke are locked in a struggle that neither can win. One grows powerful while the other grows weak, and then they reverse, back and forth endlessly."

"Perhaps the interlocked worlds are like steam engines, ever heating and cooling," said Vai.

"Gas expands as its temperature goes up, and a balloon deflates as its temperature goes down," she murmured. "What if cold mages are moving the vital energy from one place to another?"

"I'm trying to sleep," said Rory, and they lapsed into silence.

Tucked against Vai, I listened to him think by listening to the way he breathed steadily, sucked in a breath as a thought struck him, then slowed again as his mind waded through the possibilities. The river flowed with a soothing voice that pulled me into its drowning waters. Held in his arms and with Bee's back pressed against mine and Rory's soft snuffling just beyond her, I did not fear. My mother's hand and my father's voice had guided me home. I slept.

I woke alone in the frosty chill. A pallor of gray brushed the edges of the night, promising dawn to come. Wisp-lights trailed along the far bank.

Vai knelt beside me, a gloved hand shaking my shoulder. "Catherine, wake up."

"I'm awake. What are those lights?"

"Troops searching the shore. We've got to get back out on the water."

The Rhenus River flowed north before its final curving southwest plunge toward the vast marshy delta we in Adurnam called the Sieve, which poured through a hundred channels into the Atlantic Ocean. On this stretch of the river the current was steady but not treacherous. Vai gave us each turns at the oars. The banks were overgrown with bushes and woodland. All morning we saw no villages or fields, and only once a rider on horseback.

Just past midday and by now exceedingly thirsty and hungry, we spotted a village on the western bank marked by the round houses typical of northwestern Celts. It appeared to be a peaceful place, folk about the spring business of sharpening plowshares and milking ewes. We pulled into a backwater and tied up.

The village was larger than it seemed from the river, with a pair of temples and a blacksmith's forge at the intersection of two cart tracks. The crossroads was marked by a stone carved with the image of a seated man with antlers on his head, who held a snake in one hand and an armband in the other. Called Carnonos in my mother's village, he had other names elsewhere and was often called a god, but I knew the figure was a depiction of the Master of the Wild Hunt, who in the old tales guided the souls of the dead across the veil that separates this world from the spirit world. My father had recorded one such tale in a journal: *Everyone knew the worst thing in the world was to walk abroad after sunset on Hallows' Night, when the souls of those doomed to die in the coming year would be gathered in for the harvest.*

The Hallows' Hunt was, my father had opined, a way for people to comprehend the unexpected nature of death. The old tale had not spoken of blood and chains. Had the Wild Hunt always hunted blood to feed the courts? Not according to the old tales. Likewise, had young women always walked the dreams of dragons? For it certainly seemed that dragons had somehow planted a seed whose fruit had become dragon dreamers.

Had the worlds always been one way, or did the worlds also change, shifting and transforming?

A hammer's pounding started up at the forge.

"Maybe we'd better go back," I said.

"Blacksmiths have no love for cold mages, it's true," said Vai, "but we can use this to our advantage."

"How is it to our advantage to have a blacksmith have no love for you, Andevai?" Bee asked.

"Why would you give speeches to gatherings of people, Beatrice," he responded in exactly the same tone, "when so many are hostile to what you have to say?"

"Because I may change their minds if only they hear and understand the important things I have to tell them!"

"Just so," he agreed.

Folk gathered to watch us approach the forge. Inside, the bellows kept pace, and the fire kept burning despite Vai's halting twenty paces away. That was part of the blacksmith's magic. A white-skinned man with a burn-scarred face and work-marred hands emerged, wiping his palms on a cloth. He spoke with a rough dialect, but I was beginning to get an ear for it.

"Ye is a magister," the man said. "We like not having truck with yer kind, mage. Some of them mage House soldiers was a-coming through here yesterday. They carried the banner of Five Mirrors, but they had riding with them some men wearing tabards marked with the four phases of the moon."

Vai showed no emotion, but it was all I could do not to react to the mention of soldiers from Four Moons House. The courier simply could not have gotten there and back so quickly.

"We thanked them kindly and showed them the road out of here. Yet they still went a-taking a lass and a lad and four stout sacks of turnips with them, as they are having the right to do. So if ye must take anything from our peaceful village, take it, and then with our favor, ye may walk out that road likewise, and be quick about it."

"Perhaps I am the one the soldiers are looking for," said Vai.

The blacksmith looked him up and down, for he was wearing his laborer's clothes, having packed away the precious dash jackets. "Ye is a workman's son, not a fancy magister."

"I am a village-born lad, but I am a cold mage likewise. You know how it is with the mage Houses. They take what they want and bind it to them."

"That, indeed!" said the blacksmith. The village folk murmured in agreement, as they would make interjections when a djeli told a tale. I could not help but notice that men stood in the front ranks with the women and children in a separate group at the back.

Vai went on. "Besides that, I have something to tell you. For many generations have blacksmiths and cold mages stood at odds. You know this to be true."

"I know it," said the blacksmith, and from within the crowd people echoed, "I know it!"

"Blacksmiths keep the secret of fire, and a dangerous secret it is," said Vai.

"That's true," said the blacksmith, "but ye must be knowing it is no fit subject for standing out in the public square, to be speaking of such mysteries. Especially not in front of women."

"There is a way for fire mages and cold mages to work together," said Vai, "as I have had reason to learn in the western lands across the ocean, which are ruled by a people called the Taino."

The blacksmith's blond hair was shaved to stubble, although he had a long beard. He scratched his bristly hair now. "Ye speak like a madman. Why have ye come here?"

"I speak truth. We seek to escape the mage House. I admit we need food and drink, but that is not all we are about." He glanced at Bee with a lift of his chin.

As in the game of batey, she took the pass. "Are you a free village? Do you rule your own selves? Or are you bound to a prince or a mage House, all that you have and your own labor and children besides chained by law and custom as their property? I know the answer from the words you have already spoken." Some nodded, while others stared with frowns, wondering what path her speech would take. Perhaps they weren't sure they wanted to hear such words from a woman. "You are not the only ones who dislike the tithes and chains by which people are bound. We are bound likewise, yet we fight."

"How can ye fight?" said the blacksmith with a curt laugh. "Best to give them what they want and see their backs as they are leaving."

"Words can fight when enough people know there can be another way," I said.

Vai said, "Let fire mages and cold mages work together, and we can break down the power of mage Houses and princes."

The blacksmith's sneer stung like the ashy smoke of the forge. "And raise up ourselves in their place? A friendly offer, lad, but this thing cannot be done. We of the brotherhood hold our secrets close to keep ourselves alive. We who live with the fire burning within us live one breath away from our death. This ye are knowing, and likewise I have said more than enough. We are wanting no trouble here. Begone, and we will pretend we never saw ye if any are come to ask."

"I do not know by what secrets and rituals blacksmiths protect themselves from the backlash of fire, but I do know there is a way for cold mages to protect fire mages. If they trust each other."

Several of the old men laughed, as if this were the greatest joke they had heard in an age.

The blacksmith's frown made me think he might melt into white-hot slag just from anger. "Ye's a tale-teller, lad, is that it? A wanderer trying to taste a piece of bread with what words ye have to spend. The two lasses' pretty looks are a better lure than yer blasphemous promises."

The old men gestured for the villagers to move away as from a fight.

Vai did not budge. "You know better than to speak insultingly of another man's wife to his face, much less to hers, so I will let that pass for this once. This is what I know: Cold magic feeds me, but the backlash of fire magic devours itself. Yet I can teach you how to pour the backlash of fire through the threads of my magic and thus harmlessly into the bush—the spirit world—where it cannot harm you. This is the truth. I swear it on my mother's honor."

By no other vow could he have so forcibly impressed them. The blacksmith looked startled, but the outright hostility drained from his face.

"I will talk to ye in the forecourt of the temple of Three-Headed Lugus," he said at length, "if ye are willing to enter the god's sanctuary."

"I am a carpenter's son. My father and uncle made offerings to thrice-skilled Lugus, whom they called Shining Komo with three hands and three birds."

The man indicated me. "This one? She is truly yer wife?"

"She is. And the other is her cousin."

"My apologies," he said as politely as anyone could please. He beckoned Vai over and spoke in a whisper, but of course I could hear them perfectly well. "To enter the forecourt of the god, ye must abjure the touch of woman."

"For how long?" Vai asked with perfect seriousness, as if the request were not at all unreasonable.

I knew that hunters held various proscriptions, as well as hanging amulets about their bodies before they entered the bush to hunt, so I felt it prudent not to listen to their secret business. Instead, Bee and I introduced ourselves to the women.

In a village like this, still fixed in the traditional ways, women and men kept most aspects of their lives separate. The women took Bee and me to a little temple dedicated to Mother Faro, the name they gave the deity of the river, where we poured libations over the stone altar. Afterward we settled into a common room lined with pots made by the most prestigious woman in the village, a potter who had married the blacksmith. The potter was black in complexion, a woman of renown married in from another prosperous village. Food and drink she offered in plenty, although no beef, as that was reserved for the men at this time of year. Women and children wandered in and out to observe us. I brought out my sewing kit, and they exclaimed over my steel needles, commonplace in Expedition but precious here. I sewed while Bee talked.

It was just so interesting to watch how Bee coaxed people into thinking about things in a new way. The women had never heard of Expedition or the Antilles, nor even of General Camjiata, although they had all heard of the Iberian Monster, known as a marauding general whose troops ate babies and who magicked women into men to make more soldiers for his army.

338   "All this talk of an assembly in a far country makes little difference

to us," said the potter. "What I want to know is how a man can write a law code and suppose any mage or prince will care what it says? They can ignore it easily enough."

"Not if you do not ignore it!" said Bee.

"Words scratched on paper do not a binding make. Only blood makes a binding."

"We are bound if we believe there is only one way things can be," said Bee.

"Do you think we can stand against their soldiers?" asked the potter as others nodded. "You are young and innocent to not know the way of things."

Regardless of how little agreement Bee fostered among the women who stayed up late to listen, she kept them listening, even if only for the novelty. She and I slept together in an alcove bed tucked into the wall, with a pair of dogs curled at our feet. In the morning I gave the potter a steel needle, and the women provisioned us with enough barley-cake, turnips, and beans to last three days.

"What did you discuss?" I asked Vai once we were back out on the river.

"I can't speak of it." To a man raised as he had been, such secrets were sacred. He was careful not to touch me. Even Rory was unusually solemn, in a mood I might have called brooding.

Bee said, "I did not see you, Rory. Were you with the men?"

"I don't like temples. They make my skin itch." He perused our faces as if he expected to uncover a rebuke. "I saw a terrible thing while you three were about your feasts and friendly talk! These people wish they were not bound to the mage House, but they bind people in their turn, don't they? While they feast and sing and sleep, aren't there people who serve?"

"Everyone must work," said Vai, with a shake of his head.

The river's voice almost drowned out Rory's words, for he could barely choke them out. "I heard a noise in one of the byres as I was sniffing about as I like to do at dusk. There was a man handling a woman who did not want him. He pushed her down into the dirty straw and pulled up her skirt and shoved his part into her. She did not cry out for help or fight but I could smell her humiliation and shame. So I pulled him off. I told him I was the spirit of vengeance visited upon men who abuse helpless women. He laughed at me. He said the woman is a slave and thus a whore because slaves have no honor. So I showed him my true face. And he pissed himself and ran off. Then the woman reviled me. She said she was taken from her village by soldiers when she was young and sold months later to the blacksmith's father. Any man in the village can use her as he wishes, just as he said. She will be punished now for what I have done. So I was ashamed for having done a thing to bring trouble on her. I told her she could escape with us."

"Lord of All," muttered Vai.

"But she refused! She said she has a healthy boy child who has been adopted as a son by a village man who has only daughters. He means the boy to marry one of the girls and inherit his cottage. If she runs, the boy will be turned out. She cannot let the chance go that he will have a good life. How can this be true? How can people live, with their spirits crushed day after day?"

"Blessed Tanit protect her!" murmured Bee.

Rory trembled with hissing fury. "I thought the radicals mean to free people who are bound to serve others. But what of people like her? I should have stolen the boy and made them both come with us, but I was a coward."

For a long while we floated downstream in silence.

At last I said, "You're not a coward, Rory."

"Such a woman would fare worse as a stranger in a town with a child in tow and no family to protect her," added Vai. "That the child may flourish gives her hope each day."

Bee said, "You can't save every mistreated person, not alone and with the law against you."

Rory shifted onto the bench beside Vai. "I want to row now. I'm too angry to talk."

Though our hearts felt wintry, signs of spring had crept into the landscape: buds greening on trees, violets in patches of color beneath the stark woodland, birds flocking north as they honked or trilled. In this flat country the river split into channels separated by long, flat islands. We passed several villages. At midday we saw riders on the eastern shore. Later in the afternoon a man with a spear watched us pass. Sheep worked their way over a greening pasture still damp with yesterday's rain. As we swept around a wide bend, the sun peeped out from behind a patchwork of clouds.

Open land breached by a canal spread away from the eastern bank. Through this grassy expanse a troop of mage House soldiers picked their way toward the water's edge.

"Curse it," said Vai. "Bee, you've the steadiest hand. Keep the prow in line with the current. Rory. Catherine. You two sit close in the middle."

He shifted up to kneel at the prow as Bee settled to the oars. Rory and I weighted the bench at the stern. My cane flowered into a sword as two boats exactly like ours appeared alongside us. It was an impossible illusion to hold through every shift and nuance, and Vai meanwhile kept glancing up at the sky. Thunder rolled although the sky hadn't the weight of storm clouds.

The soldiers parted to let through a man on a horse. In his flowing robes and with his height and hair, I knew him at once as the mansa of Four Moons House. Soldiers with crossbows knelt to take aim.

"How could the mansa have come after us so quickly?" muttered Vai.

"The dragon betrayed us," muttered Rory.

"Kemal never would!" Bee glared, but her steady rowing and skillful piloting did not slacken.

A force both terrible and strong was grinding within the clouds drifting innocently above. On the shore the mansa raised his gaze heavenward as snow began to fall. Vai was going to hide us in a blizzard. All we needed to do was get beyond the range of their bows.

More soldiers rode into view. They were wearing three different uniforms: the black-on-white squares of Five Mirrors House, the four phases of the moon of Four Moons House, and the strung bow of White Bow House. Mansa Viridor trotted up to greet the mansa and look across the water toward us. I was too shocked to utter a word.

"I should have known better than to trust friendship offered by cold mages," Vai muttered.

Snow began to fall in earnest.

Soldiers bundled two slight figures to the shoreline, making sure we could see the swords held to their throats. Vai's hands gripped the gunnel. The illusions of the other rowboats dissolved.

"Who are those terrified girls?" said Rory. "Do the soldiers mean to kill them?"

"Those are my little sisters," said Vai in a voice I scarcely recognized because it was flat with fear and rage. "Lord of All, he will kill them. They are nothing to him. Love, go on to Havery. I will find a way back to you, but I cannot abandon them."

He cast me a desperate look, shed his coat, and plunged into the river with his sword.

A crossbow bolt plopped into the river near him. A captain shouted at the troops to stop shooting because the man they wanted was in the water. The girls could not have been more than thirteen or fourteen. They clung to each other as swords caged them. I looked at Bee, and she looked at me. I knew what she would say before she said it.

"Cat, you have to go after him while he's still in the water so they can't shoot you."

"I have to stay with you to protect you, Bee."

Her gaze held me. "Rory and I can protect ourselves. Look how frightened the girls are. Together, you and he can manage an escape with them. You know where to meet us. Go!"

I shed my cloak. This river had drowned my parents, but I plunged in anyway. Fear drove all thought from my mind as I came up floundering and gasping to the surface.

Rory called, "Swim! Don't paddle like a dog!"

I churned my arms through the current and did not gulp down more than four or five mouthfuls of water before my feet scraped on river bottom. I crawled onto the bank, trying to hack out the water I'd swallowed. A crow flapped down from the sky and landed so close to me, watching me with its black eyes, that I shrank back. Then it fluttered off, cawing. Soldiers surrounded me as though I were a cornered boar, their spears ready to pierce me through.

I leaped up, fumbling for my sword. A whistling hiss spat past my ear. Something pushed hard on my shoulder, spinning me backward.

A crossbow bolt stuck out of my flesh, right below the collarbone. Where had that come from?

I toppled to my knees. The world filled with a whirl of snow. An imposing man loomed before me out of the blizzard. His voluminous robes rippled across my sight like the wings of death.

"Don't kill her," the mansa said.

342   I fainted.

33

I woke to a warm cloth wiping my face. Opening my eyes, I looked up at a woman with gaunt cheeks and short wiry hair more gray than black.

"Do not speak," she said in a raspy voice, careful not to jostle the crossbow bolt sticking out of my body. Stabs of pain pulsed through my right shoulder. "Here comes the surgeon."

Over her shoulder I caught a glimpse of a man in a traditional bou-bou, carrying a leather bag and a small drum. I lay on a cot in a hospital tent spacious enough to house a dozen soldiers, although I was the only patient. Before the doctor could reach me, a soldier cut him off.

"Catherine Barahal. I have been looking for you." Lord Marius stared down at me with such loathing that I whimpered. "Where is Legate Amadou Barry?"

My nurse looked up with no sign of servility. "My lord, she will do better once the arrow is out and the wound cleaned."

"Ah." He cut away my clothes and probed the wound in a way that made me almost stop breathing as I struggled not to cry out. "It's hit the bone, but the bolt must have been at the end of its range. Nothing I haven't dealt with on the battlefield."

He fixed a hand around the shaft and pulled it out. The pain made me go blind and deaf for the longest time, oblivious to everything except the pulse of my heart, or the earth, or a drum: I was not sure what I felt. Nor did the pain ease as my body was washed and handled, wet clothes stripped from me, and a stinging poultice laid atop the red-hot center of the wound.

After an agony of time I sought with my mind along the length of my body and found my right foot. Focusing on the foot, which did not hurt, I opened my eyes. The roof of the tent billowed with odd patterns of light that made my eyes water. I was naked, a blanket tucked modestly around my body and folded under my armpits. My right shoulder had been bandaged. When I shifted, a wave of pain spilled outward from the shoulder, and I whimpered.

"Here you are," said the gaunt woman, still seated beside me.

Two girls stood behind her with huge dark eyes a-goggle. Their striking resemblance to Vai snapped me into full wakefulness. One girl was a head shorter than her sister and as thin as a reed; she leaned on a crutch. The taller girl was robust.

The woman leaned forward. "Drink this. It will ease the pain."

Again Lord Marius appeared, a god out of a Greek tale, ready to smite. He snatched away the cup before it could touch my lips. "I want an answer to my question."

She nodded calmly. "Of course, my lord. But it is hard for the young woman to speak with dry lips."

I could speak!

"The Legate Amadou Barry is responsible for his own death." My voice emerged as more of a hoarse croak. "It was his choice to follow us into a dangerous place. He thought he had the right to possess Bee simply because he wanted her. Yet he didn't respect her enough to trust her when she tried to save him. He was swept out of the spirit world by the tide of a dragon's dream. I don't know what happened to him after that."

"My lord, if you will allow her to take willowbark tea to ease the pain, she will come to her senses."

"She is not delirious." White-lipped, Lord Marius glared at me. "The punishment for murdering a Roman legate is death. The punishment for murdering my beloved brother is that I will hound you until you show me his grave and then I will water it with your blood."

From outside I heard men shouting angrily. Lord Marius turned to look at the tent's entrance, where two soldiers in the colors of the Tarrant militia stood guard.

"No! They're saying one of them was shot! I will see my sisters!" The voice was Vai's.

A second male voice replied in the loud and mocking tone of a highborn man who means to be heard by as many people as possible. "Your sisters, or your daughters? I know how your kind are. Everyone sleeps in the same bed."

"I'll kill you," said Vai in a raw, ugly tone I had heard only in his nightmares. The smack of a fist hitting flesh was followed by the thud of a body hitting dirt.

The other man shrieked, "Get the stinking goat off me!"

A commanding voice I recognized as the mansa's spoke. "Enough! Tie his arms back if he can't control his fists." The grunts and curses of a scuffle faded to silence.

Vai burst into the tent. His arms were trussed up behind his back with rope bound around a stout stick that could be twisted to control him. The brawny soldier who had hold of the stick brought him up short as he saw the girls.

"Bintou! Wasa!"

The bigger girl bolted to him and pressed her face against his shoulder. He kissed her hair, then looked with a frown toward the other girl who, with her too-short crutch, hadn't tried to move. His glance skipped from the invalid girl to the woman. His lips parted. A jolt of stunned shock rolled through his body. But he recovered quickly. In a cunning move worthy of a sly Barahal, he slammed back into the soldier, jostling the stick. With a wrench, he freed himself and staggered forward to drop to his knees before the woman.

"Mother." He rested his forehead on her knees. "Forgive me for bringing this trouble on you and the girls."

"Son." She laid a hand on his head in a blessing. Tears rolled down her cheeks, but her tone was implacable, even a little aloof. "You will be strong, as I taught you. I am told this woman is your wife and thus my daughter."

His head and shoulders came up as if yanked. With an intake of breath, he stared into her face to read the truth of the words. Then he turned and saw me.

"Catherine!" He leaped to his feet. "What can you have been *thinking*? You weren't to follow me...did they capture...?" I recognized the moment he saw the bandage because of how his entire body shuddered. He was not speechless. He spoke through his magic. A grinding roar of noise rumbled far above as masses of air crashed and cooled. A waterfall of illusions spilled around us like deformed creatures writhing as they were twisted inside out.

"Andevai, this is not the behavior I expect from you." His mother did not raise her voice, yet her tone cut right through the fury of his emotions.

He fought down from the storm, but it was a hard descent. He was so passionate about things. My shoulder hurt horribly, but I had my wits tucked about me like the blankets. He needed a task to take the edge off the surge of frustrated feelings of impotence and wounded pride.

My voice scraped out a whisper. "I thought you would need someone to help take care of the girls. They looked so frightened. But honestly, Vai, I wish you would get Lord Marius to stop threatening me. Bee and I truly did try to save Amadou Barry in the spirit world, but he wouldn't listen to us. She wept buckets of tears when he was swept away in the tide. Now Lord Marius says he means to kill me to get satisfaction. But it was the legate's foolish choice and not any scheme of ours. And he won't let me drink my willowbark tea."

Illusions vanished. Even with his arms tied behind him, Andevai could draw himself up with the arrogance of an exceedingly powerful cold mage who does not expect to be crossed.

"Lord Marius, my wife is not to be bullied or threatened. The legate should never have believed he could walk into the bush as if it were a country garden. Even those who have studied its secrets and passed down this lore know how dangerous it is to walk there. He was a fool twice over. Once to rush after them. Twice to not heed them."

"Were you there, Magister, to see how it all transpired?" Lord Marius asked. "How can I even believe such a wild tale?"

"I have told you the truth. Give me the tea so I can give my wife relief from the pain of her injury."

As angry as Lord Marius was, he also had a sense of the absurd. "How will you manage that, I wonder, with your hands bound behind you?"

Vai's mother rose. That she scarcely had the strength to stand was evident by the tension in her frail frame, but to look at the stately lift of her head and the pressure of her gaze, one might never guess she was anything but a woman of power.

"I will take the cup, my lord, and minister to the young woman, as was my intention." She held out her hand.

Something in that voice struck him. His forehead wrinkled as he obediently handed over the cup. "Are you mage House born, Maestra? For you have something of the manner about you, although I can't quite figure your accent."

"I am a peddler's daughter, my lord. Not even a garden or hut to our name. We were the least among people you could ever meet. Lift her head. Gently, if you will, my lord."

To my astonishment Lord Marius tucked a strong hand under my neck and carefully raised me. Obviously he had practice assisting wounded people to drink. The cup she set to my dry lips did not interest him. He examined her. "Ah. Then some Houseborn man took a fancy to you, did he? I know that happens."

She did not look at him, not from shame, I thought, but because she considered the tea more important than the answer. "No, my lord. I am no man's jade. I was the third and last wife of a village man who was born into clientage to Four Moons House. Lest you wonder, he was the only man who ever touched me. The boy is his, and mine. You may lower her head now, my lord."

"Proud Jupiter," muttered Lord Marius, setting me back. He looked Vai up and down. They had given Vai dry clothes, now scuffed from whatever fights he had been in, but for all that he wore someone else's clothes and a smear of mud on his cheek, he still looked magnificent. "I had no idea the magister was not born to the House."

She handed the cup to the tall girl, and then sank onto the chair. I could hear the hoarse crackle of her labored breathing. Yet when she found breath to speak, her words were firm. "He is not of their making. So powerful he is that they must bind him lest they lose him."

"Mama," muttered Vai.

"I did not raise you to be ashamed, Andevai. Now go, you and the lord both. You can return at a more proper time, and when you have wiped the mud off your face, for I am sure I did not teach you to appear so slovenly in public."

Lord Marius whistled under his breath, but his amusement was a blade, flashing and then sheathed. "I will return to hear a full accounting."

347

Vai stepped forward to kiss me, but before his lips met mine his mother's voice cracked over us.

"Son! Are these the manners I taught you? To insult your wife by touching her in public before the eyes of others?"

He jerked away from me. The girl with the crutch clapped her free hand over her mouth to hide a smile. She had a rascal glint in her eye, that one. I had seen its like before.

"Go on, Son."

He kissed the girls and left obediently. All the men fled, leaving the four of us and a pair of womanservants. His mother coughed with a dry wheeze. At length she could speak again, if barely in a whisper. Her proud aspect did not waver. Had she worn cloth of gold and sat on a throne, I would have called her a queen.

To the tall girl she said, "Bintou, fetch some of that broth we were brought this morning."

To the short girl she said, "Sit down, Wasa. You will need your strength later."

To me she said, "Bad enough you use his name, but I suppose your ways may be different."

"What am I supposed to call him if not by his name?"

"A woman does not call her husband by his name. After her first child is born, she may address him by the eldest child's name, as I did my husband, as 'Andevai's father.' Despite your ignorance in such matters, I can see you have an idea how to handle him. I must warn you that his father and grandmother spoiled him."

"Did they?" I ventured.

Her frown was daunting! "It is so easy for good-looking boys to be ruined by praise. It has taken all my effort to make sure he has learned proper manners. You must resist any inclination to let him have his way in things beyond what a man has a right to ask for, cooking and children."

This hard speech did not upset me. Indeed, I found it enlightening. I stirred, wishing I dared sit up. "Maestra, I beg you, please lie down, for you are looking exhausted. Bintou, please bring your mother some of that hot broth, for I hope it will soothe her lungs."

The grim line of her lips softened. The ghost of a younger, healthier woman danced briefly in her face, then vanished, but it was the way she carried herself that caught the eye. All this time I had been thinking that Vai's pride came from his close study of the mansa.

Bintou brought her mother broth, then settled her on a cot. Meanwhile Wasa took my hand in the familiar manner of a little sister, tracing my fingers with her own. As her mother's harsh breathing gentled to sleep, the girl spoke.

"Was he really going to kiss you right in front of Maa?"

I met her gaze gravely. "I think he was."

She leaned closer with a smirk on that seemingly innocent little face. Her fingers crept up my arm. "He likes you."

I grabbed her ear with my uninjured hand. "He does like me. What do you really want?"

"The locket."

"You can't have it. My father gave it to me."

"I never met my papa. He died while my mama was big with us."

"I'm sorry about that. I lost my father when I was six. I might let you look at it later if you're very good." I released her ear. "Where is my cane? And the basket?"

"No one can touch the cane. It bites. Also, there is a skull in that basket. I looked, even though Bintou told me not to. Then it talked to me." She eyed me. "Do you believe me?"

"It would depend on what the skull said to you. Then I would know for sure."

"She spoke like a foreign person. She was hard to understand. I think she asked me to tell her who I was and why I was staring at her so rudely."

Hard to say if Wasa had a gift or was just exceedingly quick-witted. "If you are very well behaved, I will introduce you to her."

She glanced at her sleeping mother. "I am always well behaved. Or at least, I am when Maa is awake."

I smiled as she sat back to allow Bintou to bring a cup of broth. I sat up with a bolster propped behind me and handled the cup with my uninjured arm. Afterward, with my right side held motionless along a rolled-up blanket, I was able to doze.

Later I heard the girls whispering in the village dialect, and their mother scolding them.

"They will despise us no matter what we do. But we will give no cause for scorn by speaking like uneducated people. Recite to me from the primer."

Pronounced with careful enunciation in the sweet, high voices of the girls, the simple, rhyming phrases spun me down into sleep.

Candle flame is candle bright.
Can you quench the candlelight?

At dawn the entire camp was taken down. My skirt and petticoat were dirty but wearable. The lovely cuirassier's jacket was a loss. An ill-fitting and homespun wool tunic replaced it, although I had Bintou salvage the jacket in case I could repair it.

We traveled in the bed of a wagon. The jostling caused me so much pain that it was all I could do not to sob the entire weary day and the next and the next. I became feverish as the wound throbbed. Not a word of complaint passed the lips of Vai's mother, although her cough got worse, shaking her entire frame, and sometimes she went gray as she struggled to suck in a breath of air. At night Bintou dosed her with a syrup that drugged her into a stuporous slumber.

Days passed. We slept in the hospital tent, in servants' quarters, in stables, always under guard. Of Vai I saw no sign, but the locket's warmth told me he lived. With what tendrils of thought still remained to me, I imagined we were returning to Four Moons House. Instead we came to rest at last in a locked room with a hypocaust floor. Wood-barred windows overlooked a walled courtyard past which I heard the sounds of city life. The room had four rope beds and a table and bench. Wasa set the cacica's skull on the table, as she had started doing at every stop on the way, careful to ornament her with a flower or bit of greenery.

Once the incessant jostling had ceased, I slowly recovered. A digni-fied older woman in a head wrap and burgundy boubou applied poul-tices to my shoulder and prescribed a diet of broth, beets, and barley. After some days I was strong enough to ask where we were.

"In the city of Lutetia."

"Lutetia!" Twenty years ago, in this very city, General Camjiata had overseen a committee of legal scholars and bureaucrats who had written up his famous law code. My father had written extensively on the meetings in his journal. "Why are we here?"

"No more can I say, Maestra, except that you bide in Two Gourds House by the courtesy of the mansa of Four Moons House." The healer spoke slowly so we could understand her. "The woman's lungs are stubbornly inflamed. The syrup of poppy has weakened her badly. The girls tell me she has taken it for four years. No person ought to drink the syrup for so long. I am surprised she has survived this long. As the gods will, so will it be."

I did not like to hear talk of dying. "Might we wean her off the syrup?"

"It would be difficult with her so weak."

"But we can try!" The cacica would not give up so easily! With her training as a healer, she might know how to help. "Might we get a mirror so we can tidy our faces?"

"I have been told I may never bring a mirror into the room."

I refused to give up. Obviously Vai's mother needed a degree of nursing the mage House had never been willing to provide and that her daughters were too young and inexperienced to manage. First I begged for richer food and more of it. I asked for pen and paper so I could record dosages of the syrup. I held a pot of water steeped with the needles of Scots pine so she could inhale its steam. We rubbed oil of mint into her chest. Day by day, one drop at a time, I cut down on the amount of syrup she ingested.

She was not an affectionate or genial woman, nor was she easy to talk to, so I talked. She could never hear enough about what Kayleigh had done and said in Expedition, and what manner of fine, honest, loyal, and hardworking man Kayleigh's husband Kofi was and what sort of people his household had in it. I would have sewed, but our captors refused me needles and pins. They had no idea that my cane was a sword at night.

I acquired a schoolbook primer and slate tablets for the girls. When I noticed how avidly their mother watched them recite, I informed her that the girls would become better readers if she would allow them to teach her the letters, for I was sure she would never ask for her own sake.

She was very proud. I liked her for it.

As it grew warm, we took her outside to sit in the sun.

"How did you come to marry Andevai's father?" I asked her one day in the courtyard as I bounced a rubber ball from knee to knee. I 351 had coaxed the attendants with stories of Expedition until they had managed to find me a suitable ball. With but a single flower trough of withered stalks for decoration, the walled and paved courtyard offered just enough space to play.

Vai's mother was strong enough now to weave stems of grass, and could plait anything into marvelously decorative baskets. "My father sired ten daughters. My mother was dead with the last. A peddler's daughter may not hope for much. My eldest sister married our cousin. That was accounted good luck. The others had no such offer. My father was a good man but he had not the means to feed us all..." Her eyelids dropped, shuttering a memory. "I would not become what they were forced to. I was not wax for candles to be dipped in."

Seated on a stone bench bent over the schoolbook, Bintou and Wasa looked up with wide eyes. I caught the ball and held it against my hip.

"Then you came to Haranwy," I prompted.

"Not then. We came to the Midsummer market outside the city of Cantiacorum. Andevai's father had come there on behalf of his village, with cattle to sell. Men who walk in the world will take their fancy where they can. I was then about the age Kayleigh was when she left for Expedition. Men do fancy the young ones they guess are untouched. More than one man offered money to my father, but I refused. Then Andevai's father came and made the same offer. He was a rich man to our eyes. By this time my younger sisters were crying from hunger. My father beat me when I refused again. The man said, 'I can feed a third wife if she will cook for me and give me strong children.'"

"So you agreed?"

"I never thought I would find such fortune. He gave my father a cow as my bride price. I saved my sisters with that cow."

I managed to keep my eyes from popping open. For the daughter of a man forced to sell his own daughters rather than starve, this was astoundingly good fortune indeed. "Your son says you once told him that his father was the handsomest man you ever saw."

There crept a reminiscent smile to lighten her expression, but her tone remained cool. "My husband was a good man. He treated me well. I was a good wife to him. I did not listen to what people in the village spoke about me. Their spite could not bow my shoulders."

352   I thought of how Andevai's brother Duvai had told me his own

mother, the second wife, had left Haranwy and returned to her own village after the arrival of Vai's mother. I dared not venture into such turbulent waters. However, there was a thing I was curious about.

"Maa, you love to hear me speak of Kayleigh, but you do not like it when I speak of your son. May I ask why that is?"

She lifted her chin in a proud gesture so like Vai that I knew he had picked it up from her. "He can no longer be part of my thoughts. His life is lifted beyond ours now."

I knelt on the gravel, looking up into brown eyes. "Maa, he will not leave you behind."

"He must. So I have told him."

I pressed a hand to hers. "He cannot. Don't demand that he turn his back on you and the girls and the village. The mage House almost ruined him."

"He will stand high in the world!"

"Don't destroy the good man that he struggles to be. Don't dishonor that man by asking him to become the mage the mansa wants him to be and that you think is best for him. Let him fight in the way he must."

Her fingers crushed the basket she was weaving. I had not known she had such strength in those frail hands. "I am weary. I must lie down."

Bintou and I helped her in, and I washed her face and sang a lullaby until she went to sleep.

In the first days of our captivity, several attendants had remained in the room at all times, but as the weeks passed they had grown complacent. Seeing no one around I steered Bintou to the garden wall. She made a basket with her hands and hoisted me up. My shoulder still twinged, and my illness had weakened me, but I got my stomach atop the wall they thought was high enough to pen me in. Of course it was not high enough.

From the height, hidden in my shadows, I surveyed a sprawling compound of courtyards, wings, and separate buildings. I balanced along the wall, looking into an herb garden, an open ground where children were playing in the sun, a well-tended rose garden where two richly garbed and very pregnant women were holding hands on a bench. Their affection for each other was so tender. How I missed the ones I loved!

What ought I to do? Summer had come, and autumn would follow. If I was stuck here on Hallows' Night I had no hope of escaping my sire's anger. Yet should I run, Vai's mother and sisters would receive the brunt of the mansa's punishment. Like Vai I could not consider myself free as long as others were in chains. The mansa had known exactly how to trap him.

"Are you sorry you swam to shore, now you're stuck with us?" Bintou asked when I returned.

"No," I said truthfully. "I met you, Bintou. That made it all worthwhile. Wasa, of course, I might easily have lived many years longer in peace for not meeting."

The girls giggled and hugged me, then reached around me to try to pinch each other, as Bee and I used to do. The press of their bodies against mine brought tears to my eyes, not of sorrow but of sweetness.

"Vai and I will find a way. I don't know how yet. But we will."

The scrape of a foot at the open door brought my head around. Vai's mother leaned against the door frame, watching us with the haughty look that was a cloak for her vulnerability. Just like her son. I no longer wondered that he had found the strength to survive the misery heaped on him in his first years at the mage House, or how he had endured without getting melted down into slag.

In the last week the trough of flowers had finally bloomed, stalks and branches blasted with color like fireworks exploding. Was this what it was like for a person, who had drifted all the years of his life without magic, to bloom with power? One day you are closed, and the next you are open.

Vai's mother smiled at me.

I shook off the girls and hurried over to take her hand. "Awake so soon?"

"I heard you laughing," she said in the tone of a woman who has only just remembered that she once knew how to laugh. "My son is fortunate to have found one such as you, Catherine."

I laughed, because otherwise I would have cried. "Have you not heard the story of how we were forced to marry, and then he wouldn't let me eat my supper? Look! Here they are come with our supper! Mmm! Is that yam pudding? I'll tell you while we eat."

34

Some days later, on a sunny afternoon, I read sentences aloud as the girls wrote them out on slate tablets. Vai's mother rested on her bed. In this isolated wing of the huge complex, the sounds and smells of each day had a familiar rhythm as the servants went about their tasks. An unexpected drum of footfalls surprised me into setting down the schoolbook. The door opened and four guards entered. I grabbed my cane.

The mansa strode in. The damask of his flowing indigo robes gleamed. His hair was braided into canerows, the ends ornamented with white beads that clacked softly. I looked in vain for the old djeli, Bakary, who I was sure liked me. In the passage waited a younger man with a djeli's gold earrings; he wore a dash jacket instead of Bakary's traditional robes.

Vai's mother got to her feet as Bintou and Wasa rose, Wasa fumbling with her crutch.

The mansa barely glanced at them. He studied the cacica's skull briefly, but in truth his interest was all for me. "Catherine Bell Barahal, I have been blind to how valuable a person you are."

He glanced toward the door as Lord Marius walked in. The soldier had an arm in a sling and a lurid but healing cut across his forehead and the bridge of his nose.

I made a pretty courtesy. "Your Excellency. My lord! You arrive with no warning, quite to my astonishment. I find surprise has made my mouth too dry to speak. Surely a soothing pot of tea and some news of my husband might help me find my voice."

Lord Marius slapped me.

The force rocked me back. My skin stung so fiercely that tears welled in my eyes.

Wasa lost hold of her crutch and fell. Lord Marius grabbed my arm to stop me from going to her, so Bintou had to help her sister to her feet, both girls crying with fear.

"For shame," said Vai's mother. "The girl is defenseless and a prisoner."

"Enough!" The mansa signaled toward the door. "Bring tea." He regarded Vai's mother with a considering frown. "I was told you were likely to die on the journey here to Lutetia, and sure to die within a week. Yet here you stand, still living. How does this come about?"

"Mansa," she said, not answering, although she kept her gaze lowered.

"Stubborn, like your son. He lives," he added, looking at me. "Satisfy me, and you will be allowed to see him. Defy me, and he will bide here never knowing you are held so close."

I kept my chin high, for of course if Vai were here, he knew I was here.

The mansa chuckled, reading more into my expression than I intended. "Do not think to be prowling about to find him with the curious magic you possess. We have djeliu set to watch you. Right now, I have promised Lord Marius a full accounting of the fate of Legate Amadou Barry."

"Will you be seated, Your Excellency, so Andevai's mother may be seated?"

"They may sit, for whom standing is a burden," he agreed magnanimously. A chair was brought for him. The moment he sat, Vai's mother sank onto the bed, the girls pressed to either side.

With the chair came a pot of tea with two cups only. I took the pot from the servant and poured for the men. Lord Marius paced as I described Amadou Barry's brief sojourn in the spirit world. He asked questions, and I answered each one in such excruciating detail that eventually he admitted defeat. Never let it be said I could not talk longer than they could listen!

"We shall never know the truth," Marius said with the narrowed eyes of a man who has decided you are a liar.

"Perhaps not," said the mansa, "but her account tallies with what Andevai told us."

"They have colluded on their story. The magister never saw Amadou Barry at all."

"If we colluded," I pointed out reasonably, "then we might as easily have woven up a tale in which the magister was present for every part of the business. Or I might have claimed we never saw the legate at all in the spirit world, thus leaving you to wonder if he became lost in some benighted realm. But I did not. I am telling the truth."

"Yes, I think you are telling the truth, if not all of the truth." The mansa studied me across the rim of his cup before he drained the last.

"More tea, Your Excellency?" I asked.

"I have quite underestimated you. I daresay the Hassi Barahals sent you to spy on us. But I wonder if even the Hassi Barahals know the whole. I am certain we do not. Perhaps Andevai does."

I smiled politely.

The mansa rose, gesturing for Vai's mother to remain seated. "Do you dine with us this evening, Marius?"

"I do not. I am summoned to the Parisi court to give a report on the campaign. The prince was angered I did not come to his palace the moment I set foot in Lutetia, but this business of Amadou took precedence. I will call on you tomorrow." He did not take his leave of me, and Vai's mother and the girls were too far beneath a man of his rank for him to notice them, any more than he would have deigned to say goodbye to the servants.

"You will accompany me, Catherine," the mansa said as he went to the door.

"Will supper be brought for Andevai's honored mother and his innocent young sisters? Who will watch over them if I am not here to make sure they are safe?"

He paused under the threshold. "Do you think it is your presence that has made them safe? Please disabuse yourself of that notion. It is my word that makes them safe. As long as Andevai obeys me, they remain safe. Come."

I kissed the girls and knelt before Vai's mother to get her blessing.

Then, with my cane, I followed the mansa through long corridors into a grand part of the House.

"It is the opinion of the healer of this House that you saved the woman's life," he said. "Your stubborn persistence brought her through the crisis."

"My thanks, Your Excellency," I said. He stood a head taller than me, big-boned and meaty without being ungainly. He went beardless in the Celtic fashion, which made him look younger than he probably was. His praise made me nervous. "That is a very fine damask. The color suits you."

He chuckled. "Flattery may work on your husband, but it does not work with me."

We halted before a set of doors carved with scenes of wolves leaping upon hapless deer. Attendants ushered us into a private parlor and shut the doors, leaving us alone. Dusk had settled over a garden outside. The mansa casually pulled a spark of cold fire from the air and let it grow to the size of his head. The chamber had gilt wallpaper and a ceiling painted with running gazelles and turbaned horsemen in pursuit. A second set of double doors, also closed, led to an unknown chamber on the right, while a single door on the left marked another unseen room beyond.

"You are an interesting creature, Catherine Bell Barahal. What do you want?"

"Your Excellency, do not think I am being disrespectful when I admit I am startled to be asked such a question by a man who previously sought to have me killed."

"I am not often wrong, but now and again I make a mistake. You have many strange talents, and a command of magic outside my knowledge. As well, quite unexpectedly, I have seen changes in Andevai. It is true you brought him to defy me, when he never had before. But in showing complete loyalty to you, he has comported himself with remarkable discipline. A mansa would be well served with a wife like you." My wince made him chuckle. "Do not misunderstand me. I have no interest in you on my own behalf."

He clapped his hands thrice. The single door opened. A dignified and beautiful young woman entered. She wore a truly magnificent purple boubou with patterns of white roundels and a matching head wrap elaborately towered and knotted. Beside her, in my worn skirt and village tunic, I looked like the drab girl I was.

"What is your wish, Husband?" Her voice was elegant and cultured, her black complexion flawless, her wrists weighted with gold bracelets. "Ah, yes, as we discussed. I will take charge of you now, Maestra. I am Serena. You are Catherine. Please come with me."

She offered a hand not to shake but to clasp in a sisterly greeting as she drew me into a woman's sitting room decorated with low couches heaped with embroidered cushions on which people might comfortably relax and converse. Under one window stood a table with a chess set. Attendants hustled me behind a screen. They stripped me, washed me in scented water, dressed me in new underthings, and combed and braided my hair. Last they dressed me in a burgundy challis skirt, cut for striding, with a short jacket in thin stripes of rose and burgundy. I was no peacock, but then, I had never wanted to be. These well-tailored and sober clothes suited me perfectly.

Serena led me back through the parlor and through the double doors into a splendid dining room decorated in the old style, a long table surrounded by twenty-four cushions. Past another door I saw a staging area where male servants were arranging a veritable army of platters. At a side table an elderly steward supervised the decanting of multiple bottles of wine. After washing and drying our hands in a brass basin, we waited by the wine.

"I am told you are not House-raised, Catherine. In the mage Houses, when the mansa presides over a meal with important guests, it is customary for his wife to pour the wine and keep the glasses of the guests filled." She sighed with a hint of exasperation. "I told the mansa it would be best to give me time with you to instruct you in the proper handling of the carafe and how to pour. Under the circumstances he cannot wish you to stumble, but..."

The far doors opened and the mansa entered. In his wake men streamed in, chatting as stewards showed them to their seats and brought bowls and towels for them to wash their fingers. No doubt the mansa had his own reasons for throwing me straight into the fire. Well! There was a lot about me he did not know!

As host of the gathering, the mansa naturally sat at one end of the table. The older guests were placed next to and then down from him in, I had to suppose, declining degrees of importance. The younger men were seated at the other half of the table. I recognized the mansa's nephew, who had tried to kill me at Cold Fort and whom I had met again in Adurnam. When a steward directed him to a place midway down the table, close to neither end, the nephew cast me such a hostile look that I flinched.

Serena patted my hand. Under cover of the men's talk she whispered, "Be gracious and silent. You must expect hostility from those who expected they were to be raised highest."

To my surprise Mansa Viridor entered. He was seated in a place of honor among the younger men, to the left of the empty end cushion. Viridor saw me, then glanced toward the door.

Just when I realized Vai had not the status to be invited to such an exalted gathering of august magisters and princely allies, he walked in, last of all. His beard was freshly trimmed. He had let his hair grow out a little. He wore a long black-and-gold riding jacket trimmed with soldierly red braid, slim trousers, and gleaming boots. Possibly, I might have sighed longingly.

Serena's fingers caught mine as she whispered, "You are staring at him. Do not. It makes you look like the cheapest sort of serving girl in a tavern where laborers congregate after work."

Vai glanced at the mansa, already seated, and dipped his chin respectfully as he looked down at the only cushion left, the place at the opposite end that faced the mansa down the length of the table. He paused there for long enough that every man had to acknowledge that Andevai Diarisso Haranwy would take the seat that mirrored the mansa's. His gaze flashed up to mark me, the message in his beautiful eyes so searing in its intensity that Serena sucked in a sharp breath. Maybe he meant it to be a private intimacy shared between us, but he hadn't my years of experience in effacing myself in order to let Bee absorb all the notice. Every man at the table turned to look at us two women.

"I serve the elder men, you the younger," Serena murmured, careful not to look any of them in the eye. "Be graceful and serene."

With an aplomb I admired, she picked up a carafe and swept over to the mansa. The steward indicated another carafe, which I carried to the other end where Vai was seated. This was no different from serving drinks at Aunty Djeneba's boardinghouse, except any mistake here would reveal me as a waddling duck pretending to be a swan and allow every mage who hated Vai the chance to laugh at him.

I watched Serena kneel behind the mansa to pour into the offering cup and then his cup. She poured for the older men in a zigzag order according to their proximity to the mansa. A steward hovered at her right hand to replace the emptying carafe with a new one. Only when she had finished did I kneel just behind and to the right of Vai and reach past him for his wineglass. My arm brushed his, and his eyes closed briefly. After filling his cup, I poured for the young men in the proper order, copying her movements in reverse, and retreated to the side table. Serena's approving nod saturated me with an unreasonable amount of satisfaction.

I could be serene!

Male servants carried in platters of delicacies never seen in our weeks in custody: chicken simmered in onion and mustard, fish cooked with tomatoes, a haunch of peppered beef, and skewers of grilled goat on beds of spinach, a constant stream of dishes. The men set to their meal.

Young men drink faster than their elders, and my job was to anticipate before any glass was emptied. Conversation flowed as steadily as the wine, the older men in serious discussion and the younger men jesting in quiet voices among themselves, for they had not the right to interrupt the older men's conversation. Vai spoke rarely and only in answer to questions put directly to him. Not that I was looking at him all the time. I was too busy pouring wine.

How the men did stare at me as I moved around the table! Not in the flirtatious way I had enjoyed at the boardinghouse but as a man may measure an ill-fitting suit of clothes he is surprised to see offered to him as one of good quality. The mansa's nephew and several cronies seated beside him were the worst, calling me over before their cups were empty as if to suggest I had not noticed. I did my duty in as patient a manner as possible, for I was determined not to shame Vai. Furthermore, at last I had the opportunity to spy in the mage House.

Confined in the chamber and garden, I had heard no news at all for over four months. Now I heard every word they said.

War had come to Europa.

General Camjiata had united the Iberians and marched an army over the Pyrene Mountains. In a series of running battles he had pushed north and, with a mastery of strategy and tactics that utilized his modern rifles and cannons to best effect, he had defeated every force sent against him. Worst, several Gallic princes had declared neutrality or even shifted allegiance to support the Iberian Monster. Inflamed by radical agitators, towns and villages had risen up against their masters and welcomed the general's troops.

A month ago, on the Midsummer solstice, an alliance of princely and mage House troops under the command of Lord Marius had fought Camjiata's army to a standstill at the city of Lemovis. Both sides had been forced to withdraw without a clear victor. Lord Marius had pulled his troops back to Lutetia to resupply and to wait for help from Rome.

"The Romans have fielded their legions at last," said the mansa. "They have taken their time, considering we princes and mages have borne the brunt of the monster's aggression for four months." He looked down the length of the table. "Andevai, by the quiver of your eyebrow I discern you have a comment you wish to make. You may speak."

Vai's gaze skipped to me, where I stood holding a carafe, and back to his master. "Mansa, no useful campaign can be planned without taking into account that the general is using fire mages."

The mansa's nephew leaned forward with a sneer. "What proof have you for this insane assertion? To call fire is to die in fire." He turned to the mansa. "Uncle, the village boy is either trying to impress you with lies or is simply too ignorant to know he is wrong."

No wonder he hated Vai, for no man at the table could mistake the privileged place at which the mansa had seated the village boy.

"What do you think?" the mansa asked the table at large.

Vai sat in perfect rigid silence as they debated the question, some mocking, some serious.

To my surprise Viridor spoke in Vai's defense, exactly as if he had not betrayed him. "I have seen these troubling incidents also. We cannot ignore them."

"Blacksmiths forge weapons, and weapons are used by troops," said the mansa's nephew, pressing his point with the snicker of a belligerent man who believes he is being challenged by a weaker opponent. "That is not the same as mages who wield fire magic, which is an impossibility. The people in the Amerikes gulled him with tricks and illusions. One such as he cannot help believing anything he is told."

Vai fixed his gaze on his hands, which he had laid flat on the table as if to remind himself not to clench them into fists. "I do not *believe* this is going on. I know it. Mansa, I have given you numerous examples, the most obvious of which are the burned estates and palaces of enemy princes, and the burn-scarred bodies of dead soldiers."

The mansa said, "Burning down buildings is the work of the angry mob. It needs no magic. Likewise, men will deface the bodies of those they hate and fear."

Vai nodded. "It is true that to tell the difference between what is begun by a fire mage and finished by angry men is difficult."

The mansa's nephew snorted. "How convenient! If it is difficult, then one can keep claiming it is true! Why would a fire mage not just burn all enemy soldiers alive, if they could do it?"

"I do not know if blood protects the living body, or if no fire mage dares unleash such a monstrous power. But regardless, all who with their own eyes witnessed the death of the mansa of Gold Cup House at Lemovis know of what I speak." Vai looked directly at the mansa, his gaze not quite a challenge. "If the Coalition Army and the Romans do not recognize the threat of fire magic and change their tactics, they will lose."

The mansa's nephew drained the last of his wine, then laughed as I hastened to refill his cup before he could complain of my incompetence. "The wrath of fire mages is a story told by credulous villagers who know no better than to believe the pap they nurse from their mother's breast. If, indeed, they even know who their mother really is."

Vai looked up. "A man can bray like a jackass, but that doesn't mean his noise means anything."

Every man tensed. In a chamber full of cold mages, the temperature's drop came as no surprise. Vai's expression remained impassive, except for the stab of fury that twitched in his cheek.

The mansa's nephew raised his newly filled wineglass in mocking salute. "Rumor has it you're the only magister on campaign who sleeps alone every night. If you need some help to make a woman of the Phoenician girl, I would be happy to oblige. Most of the time they like it best when they claim they don't want it. Just like you. I haven't forgotten how I had to make a woman of you when you first came to Four Moons House because you stubbornly refused to acknowledge your betters. Someone had to put you in your place."

I had a moment of stunning clarity as Vai rocked back as if he had been punched.

The gods do watch over us, even if we cannot always recognize the shape their hand takes. A serving man bearing a tureen of beet soup had halted in embarrassment an arm's length from me. I snatched the tureen out of his hands and dumped its contents over the head of the mansa's nephew.

He shouted, staggering up so off balance that I needed only to nudge his knee to send him tumbling ignominiously onto his backside.

"Noble Ba'al, forgive me, Magister!" I cried, slapping a hand to my chest in an exaggerated gesture worthy of Bee. "From the garbage that came out of your mouth, I mistook you for the slops bucket."

The older men laughed appreciatively and the younger nervously, while the servants looked as if they wished they were anywhere except in the dining room.

I knelt under cover of laughter. "One word more, Magister," I whispered, "and I will tell the tale of what a fool the Phoenician girl made of you, the day you and your soldiers and your highborn magic could not catch me when you found me unarmed on the road. I'm sure every man here wants to hear the part about how I mocked you and then stole your horse."

Picking up the fallen wineglass, I rose, handed the empty tureen back to the stunned serving man, and to my surprise was greeted by the head wine steward handing me a full carafe.

"Well done, Maestra," he murmured.

"Do go clean up, Jata," said the mansa to his fuming nephew, who was picking bay leaves out of his hair. "Now, Andevai, describe in greater detail for our guests why and how you believe General Camjiata is using fire mages to fight his battles. More wine."

As if more wine were what a pack of half-drunken men needed! But Serena nodded at me, so I poured, one eye always on Vai. He did not drink or eat a single morsel more. He explained crisply and in detail what he had seen and what conclusions he had drawn. Someone who did not know him might have mistaken the edge to his voice as arrogance when by the set of his shoulders and the angle of his chin it was clear he was covering humiliation.

The meal dragged on long past my patience for it, but I smiled and served to the end. The men departed in a mood half martial and half jocular, soaked in wine. Vai was sent out with the visitors to see them safely on their way home.

The mansa remained, lost in thought as the servants cleared the table around him and themselves departed. When only the mansa and Serena and I were left in the room, she poured three glasses of wine. The first she gave to me. She set the other two on the table and seated herself on a cushion next to her husband with an enigmatic smile.

I was so thirsty and angry that I drained the wine in one swallow, a rush like wet earth and giddy flowers. "Why do you let the powerful abuse the powerless? Why would you allow the one who had the least to fear to abuse the one who had no one to help him?"

"The magic should never have bloomed so strongly in a common-born slave like him, a boy whose own mother has not even a village lineage to claim," said the mansa harshly. "When it did so, he ought to have been grateful we brought him into the House."

"Where he was mocked and reviled every single day?"

"Boys will fight and compete to prove who is strongest. He should have bowed his head to those who stand above him, as a courtesy if nothing else. He would have done better with the youths he took his lessons with if he had not insisted on besting them in every trial."

"That excuses it? Did all of you just look the other way while this kind of thing went on?"

A chill shuddered the air as his gaze tightened, but I did not retreat. "Do not be insolent, Catherine. One time it happened, in his first year at the House. Never after. The youths were warned they had gone too far in this instance."

"Because you saw how powerful his cold magic could be? How useful he could be to you? Had he been a village child with no such promise, would anyone have cared?" Serena gave a shake of her head to remind me to be serene and placid. But I could not. "His own grandmother was impregnated against her will! She was not the only woman so used!"

He shrugged. "You will understand better when you must supervise the whole."

"When I must supervise the whole…" I stared at the brilliant stain of beet soup mottling the rug. A dreadful fear gripped my heart. "What do you mean?"

He rose, leaving his full cup untouched. Serena rose gracefully alongside, a superb ornament, the sort of polished and splendid young woman of high rank a man may marry as his third or fourth wife, when he can choose for his own desire rather than the House's needs and convenience. But he did not look at her. He was sure of her. He looked at me.

"You would do well to remember that he belongs to me, Catherine. Not to you. Not to himself. I will keep him in Four Moons House by whatever means I must."

He clapped his hands. A steward appeared to escort me back to my prison.

I found Vai kneeling before his stern-faced mother, his head bowed. He had an arm around each sister. Servants collected our things.

Seeing me enter, Bintou leaped up. "Cat, we're leaving."

"Leaving Lutetia?" I asked, watching Vai. He did not look at me.

"No, we're leaving this room. Vai says we are to have a grand set of rooms with a large garden! What do you think of that?"

Grand they were, as we soon discovered. An invalid chair was wheeled in, big enough for Wasa to sit on her mother's lap. Although servants now swarmed everywhere, Vai himself pushed the chair through the corridors to the guest wing and a suite of rooms just down the hall from the parlor and dining hall where the mansa and I had had our conversations. A lovely entry and a charming little audience room gave onto a sitting room, off of which lay two bedrooms.

One of the sleeping chambers had been arranged with two beds, one for the girls and another for Vai's mother. Its glass doors opened onto a courtyard lit by cressets of cold fire to display a fountain, benches surrounded by troughs of blooming flowers, and an arbor that screened a garden beyond. The girls hung on him, whispering secrets to him and giggling at their own jokes, as I settled his mother comfortably for the night and placed the cacica's skull to watch over them.

After we kissed the girls he took my hand. He led me past the arbor and into the garden to a tiny summer cottage, a gazebo hung with cloth walls. Inside stood a bed draped with gauze curtains and flanked by two privacy screens. Bowls of food crowded a small table set for two people. Servants waited. He thanked and dismissed them, and they left.

"You must not have eaten," he said. "There is fish, and fruit. And yam pudding that I had the kitchen make specially for you."

Looking at the proud lift of his chin and the mulish set of his lips, I knew he would not speak of it, not now and maybe not ever.

"Vai, do you remember the Griffin Inn, in Southbridge Londun? When I came out from the supper room and you took one look at me and got up and came over to me? Why did you just get up like that and take my word there was trouble?"

He blinked. "But there *was* trouble, Catherine. It seemed obvious by your haste and tone. I could as well ask why you warned me. You could have said nothing and hoped they killed me, since they vastly outnumbered me. The people at the inn were not inclined to take my part."

"Think of how many people would have been hurt or killed if you had unleashed your magic! It was better to go on with you than to risk injury to people who had no part in the fight."

He slipped his fingers between mine until our palms touched. "You chose their safety over what you must have believed to be your own happiness. That is how it is with you, Catherine. You never questioned what your aunt and uncle thrust on you. You stayed loyal to their wishes up to the moment the mansa commanded me to kill you. Even then, love, you stayed loyal to your cousin. You didn't run away to save yourself. You ran back to save her. Just as you jumped into the river because you thought my sisters looked frightened, and probably because you thought that together you and I could rescue them. Just as you tirelessly nursed my mother." I thought he was going to kiss me, but that was not what he was about. "Your mother was right about you. 'Loyalty will be the bright light this child will bring to the world.' Never think otherwise, my sweet Catherine."

A balmy night breeze chased through the cloth hangings that shielded us from view. Every cresset of cold fire in the garden went out.

I leaned into him.

He kissed my hair.

I raised my head and brushed his mouth with mine.

For a very long while neither of us spoke a single word, except what was in our hearts.

Much later we lay in the bed, drowsy and contented, yet I could not stop caressing him. I traced his lips, his chin, his throat, and then his shoulders and up the back of his neck.

"You've kept your beard trimmed but decided to let your hair grow out."

"I promised myself I would not cut it until we were reunited."

I would have made a joke about it, but my heart was too full. He held me as I lightly stroked his chest, and after a while I thought he had fallen asleep.

"Catherine." His whisper made me shiver as from a touch of winter. "Everything has changed, love. Everything."

My wandering hand stilled. "What has changed, Vai?"

I wished I could see his face, and then, after all, I was glad he could not see me.

"You must have suspected when you were brought in to pour wine. That honor is granted only to the mansa's wife or daughters. When you saw where I was seated. The mansa has adopted me as his son and named me as his heir."

"But...what about...your village, and clientage, and Chartji's court case, and Camjiata's legal code, and Kofi and the radicals?"

"It's not even that I've bested them, every cursed one of them. For all those years the mansa scorned me as the village boy. He never thought I would amount to more than a lamplighter who renews cold fire each night at mage inns. No matter what I did, it was never good enough. But now he knows. Think of the honor to my mother! I will become mansa of Four Moons House."

Exhausted by his climb up Triumph Spire, he fell asleep in my arms. But every time I closed my eyes, I remembered the troll lunging to rip out the belly of the horse.

The mansa had trapped him in the most gilded cage of all.

35

In the gray light of dawn, the singing of birds woke me. I eased out of his embrace, pulled on his shirt for modesty's sake, and crept to the table to pick my way through the untouched food, for I was ravenously hungry. He stirred soon after and propped himself up on an elbow.

"You look very fetching in my shirt, Catherine," he said in a tone that fetched me right back to bed.

Afterward I fell asleep. He woke me some time later by pulling a cover up over us, and I pretended to be asleep while servants bustled about the space.

When they left we washed each other behind a screen where pitchers and a basin were set out for our use. He presented me with a linen dressing robe dyed a sumptuous midnight blue, while he slipped on a dark-gold silk dressing robe embroidered in bold geometric designs. The table had been laid with sliced meats and cheeses, fresh bread, and berries smothered in cream. A cup of coffee woke me right up.

"Why is my dressing robe so plain and yours so excessively decorative?" I asked.

He fed me a spoon full of nothing but the sweetened and whipped cream, and smiled as my eyes rolled back in ecstatic delight at its melting goodness. "You may have whatever you wish, love."

"Did you arrange for the clothes?"

"As it happens, I did. In the field, I received a report every week, so I knew you had recovered and that my mother's health was improving. When I heard we were coming to Lutetia, I insisted you be fitted with clothing suitable to my station. I remembered the dressmaker's measurements from Sala. Do you like the style and cloth I chose?"

"They're exactly what I like. Andevai…" I hesitated, not sure how to start.

"Why is it you only say 'Andevai' when you're annoyed with me?"

Daylight revealed the cloth walls as canvas embroidered with elaborate garden scenes. I peered out through the slits to make sure no attendants waited within earshot, then sat back down.

"Vai, my love, I'm not annoyed with you. Far from it. Can I have shown you my feelings any more clearly than I already have?"

Because it pleased him to do so and it pleased me to accept, he fed me another fat spoonful of the glorious cream. A bit smeared on my lip. He leaned over the table to lick it off.

I had to forge forward before he mistook the nature of my hesitation. "I know the mansa has shown you an unbelievable honor by naming you as his heir. But it troubles me. He told me last night that you belong to the House. To me, this looks not as if he is freeing you but as if he is binding you more tightly to him."

He tapped the spoon against the rim of the bowl half full of cream and berries. A pure faint tone rang. "I know, love. But…you should have seen my mother's face when I told her."

He bowed his head and covered his eyes with a hand. He said nothing, did not move at all except to breathe. I dared not move for I felt to do anything would profane the tears I doubted he had ever let anyone see except perhaps his beloved grandmother.

At length he took in a deep breath and wiped his cheeks. I buttered a piece of bread and handed it to him wordlessly. He ate it.

"I think I comprehend a little of what it must mean to her. And to you. But I cannot be easy with it. In fact, I think it is a mistake."

A frown flickered. "How much choice do you think I have in this, Catherine? What was I to say to the mansa?"

"Doesn't the mansa have sons?"

"He has four living sons. None have more than a candle's worth of cold magic. That's the first test, you know. Quenching a candle's flame without touching it. But consider the advantages. As heir to Four Moons House I can change the customs of the House. I've already written to Chartji to ask her to meet with me here in Lutetia to discuss how we might go about it. I can walk among the magisters and elders and speak to them of why clientage is wrong and how it harms the mage Houses more than it helps them."

"Have you done so? What did they say?"

"It has only been one month! People are naturally fixed on the crisis created by Camjiata."

"Whose legal code you were once so determined to champion!"

"Camjiata is using *James Drake* to fight his war."

I grasped his hand. "Bold Melqart! You've seen battle, haven't you?"

His eyes shuttered. Then he spooned up another mound of cream. The way he fed me, with his lips slightly parted and his body leaning toward mine so his dressing robe gapped to give me a splendid view of his chest, was as delicious as the cream.

"I was never in danger. As for the war, you heard a great deal last night. You may be surprised to hear I have seen Professora Nayo Kuti's pamphlets being passed among the soldiers of the Coalition Army. The radical philosophies are being talked about in our army, not just theirs."

"*Our army?* The last time we were together, we were *running* from 'our army.' When exactly did the mansa make you his heir?"

"After the battle of Lemovis, a month ago. He saw that no one else had enough imagination to realize what was going on, much less the discipline and intelligence to discover ways to counter it. Furthermore, I am the only cold mage in Four Moons House besides the mansa who can truly build and hold a thorough illusion. There are other forms of cold magic that take more reach, but for illusion you must marry intense skill and discipline with the ability to reach deep into the ice."

"You are the only one besides the mansa? Even including the women?"

To his credit he paused, forehead wrinkling. "I suppose I don't know about the women. Although honestly, Catherine, to hear that anyone besides the mansa could best me in this would surprise me."

I leaned across the table to give him a kiss. "Of course it would surprise you. My point is that the mansa may yet sire more sons and choose to replace you with one of them. Furthermore, you said Five Mirrors House in Noviomagus is ruled by a mansa who is not as powerful as the magister who tested you. She happened to be a woman, and thus according to House custom ineligible. So let us say the mansa truly wishes for you to become mansa after him. If you do not have the support of the elders of Four Moons House, what is to stop them from demanding a more eligible if less powerful man once the mansa has passed on? Then you would have waited for all that time, perhaps for decades, only to find yourself just as powerless as you were the day you came to Four Moons House. All that time when you might have been working for a greater cause. It is the perfect means to keep you in harness."

An eddy of cold air pooled around us. "Do you suppose I am too uneducated and common-born to have thought of exactly these sorts of complications?"

"Of course I don't! I will thank you not to pretend that I do so you can wallow in your wounded feelings! You have just bested the rivals who tormented you for so long. You have raised your mother to a position of honor beyond anything she can ever have thought to expect. And you have been proven in the starkest way possible as exactly the rare and uncommonly potent cold mage you have always known you are. All laudable things. I want to know if you have forgotten your promise to Kofi."

Ice crackled as frost across the surface of the cream as he pushed back his chair and rose with a curl of his lip. "I think that is enough! Do not believe you understand my promise to Kofi."

"I've just gotten started!" I shoved back my own chair and stood. "Either you want a wife who respects you enough to challenge you when she thinks you may be wrong, or you want a wife like the gracious Serena, whose manners are beyond impeccable, and whose desire and purpose is solely to serve the wishes and needs of a husband who chose her for her beauty."

"How do you know she doesn't challenge him in private? How do you know she didn't desire and even seek the marriage? It may not seem so to you, but marriage to the mansa of Four Moons House gives a woman's lineage significant prestige and valuable connections. For that matter, how do you know she isn't a magister herself, married for her magical potency and not just her signal beauty?"

"How would you know what she is like in private?" I demanded.

He blinked. With a shake of his head the contemptuous mage

vanished, and the Vai I loved returned. "Why, Catherine. Here is an unexpected sting of jealousy!"

How I hated that particular smirk of his. I fumed, not wanting to admit he was right or that I had simply assumed a dazzling beauty could not also be an accomplished magister.

"In fact, as the mansa's heir, I am allowed to sit in his private parlor in the most casual manner imaginable. I may even converse easily, like a son, with his charming wife." He slid into a light Expedition cant. "I reckon that gal's a little lonely and like me company."

"Peradventure some maku is going to find he own self a little lonely sleeping on the floor!"

He glided so quickly around the little table that I did not have time to step away before he pulled me to him. "Is he, now?" he murmured caressingly.

"Do you want to provoke me, Andevai?"

"Now that you mention it, I rather find that I do. You have no idea how attractive I find you when you get like this." Given that he held me against him and his dressing robe had fallen half open, I had some idea. "I have been promised this whole day is mine to do as I wish."

"To argue with me?"

"We can argue as much as we need to, love, as long as it is understood that we trust each other. I know this is unexpected and that it may seem like the wrong path that goes against everything we have discussed at such length. I admit I have some reasons that are not the right ones and that I just...to do this, to receive this...heir to the mansa..."

He kissed me in a tumult of emotion that he had no other way to express. I struggled not to give way to the intense desire I felt for him, to think with my mind instead of my body, but the two were woven too intimately together.

I eased the dressing robe off his shoulders. "I shall need more of that ambrosial sweetened and whipped cream when I am done with you."

"Not yet, not yet," he whispered in a hoarse murmur that made me wild.

All entangled and kissing him, I nudged him toward the bed.

"Announce me."

The mansa's voice fell like the stroke of a sword. Vai would have leaped back as if cut from me, but modesty made me cling to him. The mansa had in fact already announced himself, standing on the upper step with the entry curtain held away in his left hand and his thick eyebrows raised interrogatively. I thought he looked amused or, perhaps, relieved that the young man he had chosen as his heir was capable of the deed. He stepped back and dropped the curtain to give us privacy in which to straighten and retie our dressing robes.

"Thank Tanit we hadn't made it to the bed," I muttered, my face aflame.

But after recovering from his surprise, Vai did not look displeased. He lifted the curtain. "Mansa, please. Come in." To a servant beyond, he said, "Bring more coffee and a fresh cup. Another bowl of berries and cream."

The mansa sat in my chair and Vai opposite him, leaving me to accept the new pot and cup when it was expeditiously brought. I squelched an urge to pour coffee over both their heads and instead poured for them and afterward for myself. I heaped my cup with two spoonfuls of the cream, after which I retreated to stand off to the side.

"There is news," said the mansa, careful not to look at me, for although I was covered from neck to ankles in the dressing robe, his presence in the gazebo felt strangely intimate. "Camjiata's skirmishers have been sighted in Cena. He may intend an assault on Lutetia."

"He proclaimed his legal code here in Lutetia in the year 1818," I said. "Twenty-two years ago. That must mean something to him."

The mansa sipped thoughtfully at his coffee. "Indeed. Handbills and broadsheets and seditious pamphlets circulate in the streets. They claim to be the text of a declaration of rights. By this means he has deluded gullible villagers and illiterate laborers with an idea they will be better off with his imperial rule than with the rule of local lords and mages who know their people and are concerned for the health of their lands. Can you imagine?" He paused to give Vai a long look.

Vai would never stare down an elder, but his respectful manner was not meek. "I would not call them gullible, Mansa."

"I suppose you would not. Yet should the general succeed, he will need governors to oversee provinces. Such people will skim off bribes for themselves and hand the right to collect taxes and tithes to their cronies and favored underlings. A great deal of petty and grand corruption will ensue. Meanwhile, there is the problem of fire mages. You are sure he is using fire mages, Andevai? The mansa of Gold Cup House was an old man. His heart might simply have given out."

"You saw what happened. You know I am right. Furthermore, I know exactly what manner of unscrupulous and callous man is being allowed to have his way by the general."

With a faintly mocking half smile, the mansa examined Vai. "One thing you have never lacked is certainty that you are right. I will be sending Serena back to Four Moons House immediately with an escort. See that your mother and sisters are ready to depart with her at midday."

"Will my wife accompany them?"

"No," said the mansa, at the same time as I said, "No!"

Vai's rigid posture did not ease. "Mansa, I have some concern over how my mother and sisters will be received at Four Moons House if there is no one there to see to their comfort, nurse my mother properly, and protect them from disrespect."

"Be sure I recognize your concern, Andevai. At my request and command, Serena will take charge of ensuring they be received in all ways appropriate to my heir. Understand that disrespect shown to them is now the same as disrespect shown to me."

"The girls should be allowed to take lessons," I said. "Even if they have no cold magic—and of course that is not yet determined—they should be educated as any girl in the House would be. Wasa should be treated no differently just because she's undersized and her legs don't work well. She's a very intelligent girl, and it would be a mistake to allow her to languish. Forcing her to study will also keep her out of mischief. Also, the crutch she has been using is too short and heavy. I asked several times if it might be replaced with something better, but the attendants said they had no authority to replace it. If she had one made to fit her frame she would be able to get around more easily and that would allow her to gain strength."

The mansa lifted his cup to indicate that I had not anticipated that he needed more coffee. "It has come to my notice, Andevai," he said, ignoring me as I poured, "that your wife has a mouth on her, as I would have crudely said when I was a lad."

"Yes, Mansa."

"Are you going to teach her to curb her tongue?"

"Mansa, it is her place to determine whether and when she speaks, not mine."

"Are you going to continue talking about me as if I am not here?" I demanded.

"Curbing her tongue would surely be a difficult task for anyone," said the mansa. "Some of that cream, if you will, Catherine. As you put on yours. I want to try it. Andevai, you have not touched your cup."

"No, Mansa." He picked up the cup, looked at it, and set it down without drinking.

"You don't eat enough," added the mansa, "as I have had cause to observe."

"I tell him the same thing," I said promptly. "Would you prefer tea, Husband?"

He shot me an accusing look, and the mansa actually chuckled.

Blessed Tanit protect me! A few more steps down this road and I might start believing it was possible to like him, the cunning architect of our prison! Perhaps it was only coincidence or perhaps Noble Ba'al saw fit to remind me that I stood garbed in false clothes in the palace of my enemy, for a rumble like thunder drifted in the distance.

Vai leaped to his feet.

The mansa rose. "See to your family, Andevai. I want them on the road within the hour."

As I held away the curtain for him to leave, I puzzled at the blue sky, where I saw not a trace of storm cloud.

"How can it be thundering?" I said to Vai.

"It's not thunder. It's cannon."

Servants hurried in. They stripped the table bare with the speed of locusts. A manservant appeared with a fresh set of clothing, including a brown-and-gold dash jacket I hadn't seen since we'd had to abandon most of Vai's garments in Adurnam.

"Gracious Melqart, Vai! How did you get your clothes back?"

Vai stepped behind a screen to dress. "The mansa had them delivered to me one day. I admit, I was surprised. I had riding clothes made for you, love, so we can go out today."

A woman helped me into a split skirt cut in an exceedingly practical and flattering style with buttons down the front, and a long jacket in an amber-brown challis. Expensive calfskin gloves and a saucy hussar's shako crowned by a jaunty feather completed the ensemble, although it was Vai's smiling admiration that made me preen.

We traversed the garden on a path of white gravel through a stand of ornamental fruit trees. Bintou and Wasa sat on a bench by a fountain, playing with an adorable puppy that licked their faces as they giggled. They were wearing new clothes, neatly made and brightly colored.

"Vai! Cat!" they shrieked, seeing us. Bintou leaped up and ran to him while Wasa bounced on the bench in excitement. Vai released Bintou to pick up Wasa's crutch and give it a frowning examination. Then he carried Wasa into the breakfast room, where his mother sat on a couch, watching our arrival through the glass. She, too, wore new clothing. When he knelt before her in greeting, she did not effuse over him but merely laid a hand on his head. Excluded, the girls swarmed me. I held one in the curve of each arm and watched as he raised his head to address her.

"Mama, I have news." The rumble of a distant cannonade stirred the air, then faded. "You will return to Four Moons House with the girls."

"To Four Moons House? You cannot think of taking us to live in the House."

"It is appropriate for you to live on the estate in a suite of rooms like this one, suitable to your consequence."

Her slender frame tensed. "How will the girls be comfortable in that place?"

"You must be shown the honor and respect that is due to you," he said, a little exasperated. "If you don't live in Four Moons House, it looks as if I am ashamed of you. You never liked the village anyway."

"To live in a prosperous village was my greatest dream! I was satisfied."

"After Father died, I don't think you were happy." He glanced at the carpet and muttered, "I certainly couldn't make you happy."

Her thin shoulders trembled.

He drew in a breath as if he had been struck. "If it does not please you, Mama, if you prefer to return to Haranwy, then you shall do so."

Her chin lifted. "With your father's passing, there is nothing in Haranwy I shall miss. We will do what suits you, now you have been raised so high."

If I hadn't been looking at her I would have missed the shine of pride that brightened her face, quickly limned and quickly gone.

Vai saw it, too. His smile blended relief and satisfaction. "That's settled, then. The girls will receive schooling, and they will not be bullied as I was." He glanced toward us, without a trace of teasing smile. "They will work hard and comport themselves with good manners."

"No child of mine will embarrass our family with poor manners." Vai's mother spoke the words in such a stern tone that I would have feared to disgrace her.

Bintou nudged me. "The girls in the House won't want to be our friends."

Vai rose. "Your trouble will be that the girls in the House will want to be your friends, and some of them will want it for the wrong reasons. You two shall have to discover which are honest and which false. As for your friends in Haranwy, it can be arranged that they visit you. In fact..." He looked at me, radiant with triumph. "I see no reason I cannot ask the mansa to consider expanding the school to include the village children. It is not too far for them to walk. It would not tax the resources of the House to admit thirty more children to the school during the day."

"That is a fine idea in principle, Husband," I said, "but what about the House's other client villages? Will they languish, while you favor Haranwy?"

His mother said, "The children in the village are needed to work at chores."

"I will find a way to do this," said Vai with a stubborn pinch of his lips.

Fortunately an attendant announced Serena, who came accompanied by two other women. I greeted her with clasped hands. She greeted Vai casually, like an equal, then introduced me to her companions: One had married into Four Moons House and one been born into it. I escorted them to Vai's mother, who remained seated, which was the privilege of an elder, although I was pretty sure Vai's

mother was younger than the mansa for all that she looked much older from years of illness. She accepted their polite greetings with a rigid aspect of seeming calm. The girls were so stricken by shyness that they barely whispered.

"They will ride in my personal coach," said Serena. "If there is trouble, I can protect them."

"That's very generous," I said, in genuine surprise.

"Is it?" she asked with lifted eyebrows. She turned back to Vai's mother, bending over her to clasp her hands. "Maa, be sure I will take proper care of you and your girls, both on the journey and once we return to Four Moons House. Now I must go and make ready."

She kissed me on the cheek and departed with her companions. Going to collect the cacica's skull from a table by the door, I heard them murmur as they walked away down the passage.

"Really, Serena! He is certainly the epitome of a man in looks and dress, and we have all heard more times than we could possibly wish about his cold magic, but the family! How could you not laugh at seeing his mother's rustic simplicity? They say she was born in a cart."

"My grandmother would slap me for any such display of poor manners. Nor do I forget that my children will one day need the favor of the new mansa to make their way. Besides that, now my husband has chosen his heir, disrespect shown to them is like disrespect shown to him."

"Catherine, what is it?" Vai murmured, coming up beside me as I laced the basket shut. Seeing his mother distracted by a steward's quiet instructions, he caught my hand in his. "That's a brilliant idea you have about opening up the school to all the children of the local villages."

"Yes," I said dreamily, imagining the consternation at the introduction of so much rustic simplicity when Vai and I announced our new plan.

Noble Ba'al! Had I already acquiesced? Had the mansa defeated me so easily? Or was it the look on Vai's mother's face that had weakened my resolve? How could Vai and I possibly manage a household if we started from nothing among people hostile to cold mages? How would we even keep warm in winter? To build a house with a hypocaust system was ruinously expensive even if Vai did much of the carpentry himself. We hadn't a sestertius to our names.

He allowed a servant to push his mother and Wasa in the invalid chair so he could walk behind them arm in arm with me. As we paced through the compound along corridors I had never before seen, he smiled, for the people who lived in Two Gourds House did pause to look. Blessed Tanit! The man meant to make sure everyone saw him. I was both amused and embarrassed. I did not like so many people staring at me. I did not like the feeling that I was being seduced into the clutches of the mage House with lovely clothing and flattering admiration, even though I knew that was not Vai's intention. No doubt he simply wanted to give things to me to show he could, like the sandals he had bought for me at Aunty Djeneba's and the bed he had built for us.

The troubling confusion of my thoughts made it therefore a relief when we settled the family in the coach. When a big basket appeared with the puppy in it, to be conveyed with the girls in the coach, I thanked Serena so profusely that she smiled in a way that made me feel gauche, an emotion I would never have believed I could experience.

"The creature will give them something to keep their minds off the journey and whatever trouble lies behind us."

The girls wept and clung first to me and then to Vai before he gently reminded them that he relied on them to take care of their mother.

Vai's mother took my hand in hers, speaking in a low voice. "You were right. He did not leave us behind." To my surprise she kissed me on the cheek.

From the steps we watched the cavalcade depart. The spears of the escort flashed under the bright eye of the sun. The Four Moons banner rippled in a brisk wind. Distant thunder rolled, and everyone waiting in the courtyard looked up at the cloudless sky.

Vai spoke. "The cannonade is not battle. It's Lord Marius's army at field maneuvers. We shall take a tour of the city today. The river walk is lovely in the sun."

"Vai, yesterday Viridor acted as your ally, yet he is the one who betrayed you."

He shrugged. "He did what he thought was best for his House, not out of malice. I can't fault him for that. In a way he helped me, for none of this would have happened had I not fallen into the mansa's hands. He and I talked it all out."

"You are friends again? You trust him?"

"Yes."

A steward dressed in the brown livery of Two Gourds House approached Vai. "Magister, you are required in the men's hall. Maestra, if you will, the steward of the women's hall attends you."

Vai went his way and I went mine, accompanied by a young djeli-muso with jangling gold bracelets on both wrists and gold earrings. In our guest suite a formidable woman stood examining the cacica's skull. Her resplendent starched boubou and head wrap marked her as Houseborn. After a suitable exchange of greetings, she cut to the point.

"As long as you remain here in Two Gourds House, you will need persons to attend to your needs and those of your husband. Have you any particular requests, Maestra?"

I thought I might as well take the bull by the horns. "I am newly married, Maestra, and I was not raised in a mage House. As you must surely know, I am only recently released from confinement in another wing of this magnificent establishment. If you could assign me an experienced and patient woman to help me make my way, I would be grateful."

She nodded. "Yes, you must learn to do things in the proper way. There was some talk in the servants' quarters about the unseemly way you laced up your skirt and bounced a ball around the back courtyard. Yet Magister Serena said you acquitted yourself well when you poured wine for the men's supper last night. So you cannot be unversed in all aspects of a woman's duties."

I just could not resist. "The game with the ball is called batey. I would be happy to teach it to anyone who wishes to learn, boys and girls alike, for everyone plays in the Antilles."

She sighed. "I will be blunt, Maestra. It is my understanding that his origins are very low. The honored mansa of Four Moons House and my own cousin, who is mansa here, believe your husband to be crucial to the effort to defeat the Iberian Monster's greedy ambitions. For him to be raised to such a position of honor is an unexpected act that speaks to his exceptional promise. If you will allow yourself to be guided by me, then you will avoid doing things that could shame your husband. As it is said, a well-behaved wife will bear well-behaved children."

My lips closed over several imprudent retorts. I plied a different stitch. "Goodness, Maestra, I am only thinking of my husband and future children when I play batey. In the Antilles, they encourage girls and young women to play so as to strengthen themselves for childbirth."

She frowned. "In that case, I suppose it must be seen as unexceptionable."

Servants were assigned to guard, serve, and clean our suite, and a steward was on duty at all times to advise me in matters of propriety. No mirror graced the suite. Except when Vai and I were in the bedchamber, a djelimuso would sit in formal attendance, so it was clear the mansa did not trust me.

Playing batey along the garden wall distracted me from the intense boredom of the next many days. When I asked for books and newspapers to read, I was brought accounts of household management and plates of the current fashions, which I would have enjoyed had I had companions to share them with. The attendants kept a formal distance from me at all times despite my efforts to draw them out. In the end I sat next to the skull and browsed the books while keeping up a one-sided conversation with the cacica about my reading.

I saw Vai only at night in the intimacy of the summer cottage and our gauze-curtained bed, where he was diligent in his attentions. Afterward he fed me scraps of news before falling asleep, and kept promising we would talk more the next day. But the next day never came because after we had eaten our breakfast of rice porridge garnished with berries and cream, he would be called away. Everyone in the women's hall treated me politely, but they weren't friendly and confiding, and no one was interested in my stories of Expedition and the Taino or even my store of tales from my father's journals. Two Gourds House had an ancient lineage and a vast treasure-house of wealth and power to give it consequence in the world. One thing I did not have, in that world, was anything but borrowed consequence. It was pretty clear they thought I talked too much. When I thought of how the gals in Expedition had taken me in, it made me want to cry.

Fortunately I was allowed to sew in the women's courtyard, under the eye of the steward, who counted out needles and pins and collected them at the end of each day. I amused myself by piecing together the cut-up parts of my ruined cuirassier jacket into a serviceable garment.

One day one of the younger women ventured a personal question. "Is it true you are Phoenician, Maestra? That your marriage contract restricts him to only one wife?"

"I was born and raised in a Kena'ani household," I replied, aware that this point was of particular interest to the unmarried woman, for a mansa's heir might normally expect eventually to take three or four wives. "But naturally I knew nothing of the contract or the marriage until the day it happened. It was all properly arranged for us by our elders."

In a whisper I could hear perfectly well, a sour-faced young woman murmured, "A shame the man is wasted on a trifling girl like her. You know what they say about Phoenicians. They sacrifice their children to their bloodthirsty gods, and whore out their daughters."

"No matter, I suppose," her friend replied with a scornful smile, "for as soon as the Iberian Monster is dispatched, they'll send him on a Grand Tour."

I stabbed the needle into the wool, pretending I was sewing tongues together. If only Bee had been with me, we could have demolished them.

With the first flight of barbs unleashed, they were not done with me.

"Yet I have heard a strange tale from the servants, Maestra, which I cannot believe could possibly be true. They say you strip down to almost nothing and bounce a ball on your knee. Like a savage. Or a man."

My gaze flashed up. I was glad to see their hesitation as I took notice of them. They were right to be scared of me! Their trembling made me pounce. "Did no one tell you? My father is a spirit beast who stalks the bush but walks in this world in the shape of a man. No man can tame me, and only one man has enough strength and charm to coax me into loving him."

The benefit of telling the truth, as Rory had once said, is that no one believes you.

The young women tittered and smirked. The steward frowned, her gusty sigh a whip of disapproval. But the older women looked thoughtful, and an elder abruptly declared she had it in mind to have a story. A djelimuso sang the tale of Keleya Konkon's prodigious cooking pot, which was, in truth, an exceedingly grand story. I did not get to hear the end of it, for a male steward arrived.

383

I had been summoned by the mansa of Four Moons House.

I thought I would be asked to pour wine for the mansa's noonday dinner, where at least I would get to see Vai even if I was not allowed to speak. But the steward escorted me instead to the most splendidly decorated suite of rooms I had ever seen, all gilt trim and ceilings painted in a distinctive style that intermarried Celtic knotwork with the arcane symbols of the Mande hunters. An armed attendant locked me into a small antechamber, where I paced rather than sitting on the cushioned bench. A latticework window overlooked a parlor, from which double doors opened onto a larger audience room beyond, where men circulated, talking. I looked for Vai but did not see him.

The mansa entered the parlor together with the Two Gourds mansa, an elderly man with a seamed face and black hair shot through with white. They stood by a window overlooking a garden, too far away for any ordinary mortal to overhear, but I cast my threads through the tangling magics of the House and listened.

The mansa of Two Gourds House spoke in a low voice. "His birth is low but his power is clear, so I have not questioned your plans. But now Lord Marius returns and tells me the girl has been working with Camjiata. That she was the general's agent all along, and seduced your young magister into doing the general's work. Are you certain this course is the wise one?"

"Leave him to me. I have him coming along just as I wish. He will guard his mother's honor with his own."

"And the girl?"

"She is part of my plan. He is badly infatuated with her."

The Two Gourds mansa clucked his tongue disapprovingly. "A woman is wet clay. If he does not shape her to obedience now, he will have trouble later."

"Lord of All, my brother, you must have felt ardent about one woman or another in your youth! Never mind. What matters to us is that for all he is the most cocksure of young men, he desires above all things to seem a man in her eyes."

"Yes, yes, I vaguely recall how it was to be young and led by my passions. I suppose he will get her pregnant soon enough. But a Phoenician mercenary house is not a worthwhile ally. I understand it was your council's only way to bind the Hassi Barahal clan back when they had information about the general at the end of his first campaign. I can see why you married her to him when you thought he was of little utility to your House. But now he is your named heir! If you mean to follow through with it."

"Despite every hesitation, there is no better candidate. You know what he did at Lemovis. It would be better to kill him than to see him defect to the general. But to kill one as powerful as he is would be a terrible deed we would all regret. He belongs to Four Moons House, and now I have made sure of it."

A chill of horror spun through my bones.

The Two Gourds mansa went on, "Is it true the marriage contract constrains you? I would give you my youngest daughter for him, even as a second wife. She has seen the boy and approves."

"It was a chained marriage. Magic binds our hands in this regard."

"Is the Phoenician girl truly worth that much to you?"

"You will soon see."

A steward appeared at the far doors. "Your Excellencies, if you will."

The men flowed away into a room I could not see from my unlit prison. I heard men's laughter and the clink of utensils as they sat down to their meal.

"You will soon see."

That sounded ominous.

Footsteps scraped the corridor. The lock clicked, the door opened, and a steward led me into the dining room. Two Gourds was a traditional household. The old mansa's young kinsmen served their elders while his wives and daughters poured wine for the more than thirty men in attendance. Vai was describing how a cold mage might defuse a square of riflemen without getting killed.

"The risk to the cavalry will be great, but that risk arises regardless. If the cold mage is placed at the center of the horsemen, the riders can sweep in and out at speed. The proximity of the cold mage to the combustion will kill their shot. If it is coordinated properly, then a second cavalry charge can break the enemy square during that interval when the riflemen and cannon cannot fire."

"An excellent idea," said Lord Marius, "but horses will not break a wall of infantrymen."

"Lancers? Mounted crossbowmen? Longbowmen can surely do

damage from a distance. The point is that Camjiata relies on superior firepower, and we can render his guns impotent in bursts. And then take advantage of their weakness."

The entire table might as well have been feeding him fruit with their own hands, the way they were seducing him with their respectful attention. The young woman who had made slighting comments about Phoenician baby-killers and whores offered him more wine. He glanced up with a smile that stabbed right through me, until his gaze flicked past her and I realized the smile was for me. The Two Gourds mansa raised a hand for silence.

Every person in the room turned to look at me. Six djeliw were present.

"So, young Andevai," said the old Two Gourds mansa. "Let us see what your wife can do."

Vai's smile vanished. People whispered as they cast glances at me. It took me a few moments to realize my expression must have matched my heart. I was no actress, to pretend to a bland, agreeable character that wishes nothing more than to jump through hoops like a trained dog. My gaze raked the table, for I was determined that these high-and-mighty men would not see me cringe or smile to please them.

It was a high-and-mighty gathering indeed! Six mansas were present: Four Moons, Two Gourds, Five Mirrors, and Viridor of White Bow House, as well as two others I identified by the tasseled whisks hanging from their robes. A Roman legate wearing the purple stripe of his rank was flanked by four fawning young tribunes. Lord Marius sat at the other end of the table beside an ornately dressed man who was surely the Parisi prince. At least ten other Celtic-born princely lords with their thick mustaches filled out the august assembly.

"She's just a girl," said the legate. "She doesn't even look like a Phoenician, if you ask me. But it would be like them to cuckoo a child into a nest of magisters, would it not?"

Lord Marius raised his glass of wine mockingly, as if toasting me with Amadou Barry's blood. "We dare not bring in a mirror, for fear she will cut a door and through it flee with the young man in tow. But let us see what else this strange creature can do."

"Eh? What manner of creature is she?" demanded the Parisi prince, lifting a pair of spectacles to his eyes to peruse me more clearly. "Bold

Hunter! My grandaunt was northern-born, up in the princedom of Carn. When I was but a little lad she used to frighten us with stories of black-haired beasts who had eyes the color of amber. They crept out of the ice and turned into lads and maidens to tempt the willing and then rip out their throats."

My hands curled into fists. My chin came up.

Vai said, coolly, "I cannot sit and listen to my wife being spoken of with disrespect. I will not tolerate it." He paused to survey the table. No one spoke. The legate coughed. Lord Marius set down his glass with the nod of a man who has just won a bet with himself.

Vai's gaze settled on me. The tension in his shoulders spoke more loudly than words. "Catherine?"

I was not a dog to perform tricks.

But I could not be the means by which he lost face in front of all these men.

So I wrapped the shadows around me, and vanished.

In the eruption of commentary and astounded exclamations, I padded over to the table, snagged Lord Marius's wineglass, and drained it. The wine rushed down my throat, pear essence kissed with a faint rind of peppery oranges. I flung the glass into a corner, where it shattered most pleasingly while I skated over to where Vai sat.

My lips brushed his ear as I muttered, "Don't push me too far."

Last I walked to the djeliw, who watched my perambulations with astonishment as our mansa watched them watch me. I composed my furious expression into something meant to resemble placid affability, for truly I was an amiable person who preferred to get along with everyone! The moment I unwound the shadows and reappeared, several of the men chuckled as if they guessed exactly my sentiments from the defiant set of my head.

"It explains how the girl escaped," said Lord Marius. "What of her cousin and brother?"

"There are more like her?" demanded the Parisi prince. "What fine spies such creatures will make!"

Vai kept his gaze on me to remind me to keep my lips closed. As if I would talk! I almost laughed as I realized he and the mansa had kept secrets from their allies: They had not told their allies that my cousin walked the dreams of dragons.

"A difficult woman to bind and chain, as you may imagine, but we managed it," said our mansa, as if binding and chaining me into his House had been his intention all along! "Lord Marius, I am sure you already have a scheme or two in mind with which to usefully employ the woman."

He caught my eye and gestured, flicking his fingers toward the door. Falling as I was into a red-hot fulmination, I strode out as proudly as I might. Let Andevai enjoy his little triumph! I was so angry I could not sit down even once I returned to our rooms. All I could bring myself to do was bounce the ball from wall to knee to wall to elbow, counting how many times I made the pass before I dropped it. At dusk I had to stop, by now sweaty and a little sore. I asked for a tray of food and a bath. I got what I asked for but not what I wanted.

Very late Vai came hurrying in to rush me back to the summer cottage.

"You were magnificent, love. They couldn't stop talking about you the rest of the day!" His smile glittered. "Some of them said they envied me—"

"I had far more freedom at Aunty's boardinghouse than I do here! It seems to me the women of Two Gourds House are too elegant and rarified to ever leave these walls, or perhaps it would just be considered shameful to do so. Certainly they scorn me too much to ask me to come along on their shopping trips and their tours of the famous landmarks of the famous city, of which need I remind you I have not seen a single paving stone nor a single vendor's umbrella."

"If they are treating you with disrespect, I will have a word with—"

"Yes! *You* will have a word. Everything I am here is due to my marriage to *you*. I might as well have allowed Prince Caonabo to arrest me! Whatever you may think, I am still being held like a prisoner as surety for *you*." I repeated the conversation I had overheard between the two mansas.

"Yes, yes, that is how they talk, that is how they see things. But they can be brought to change. What matters is that they know they need me, that I am the best. Do not forget that Camjiata is letting James Drake do as he wills. You cannot want that to continue, Catherine!"

"Of course I understand that James Drake has to be stopped! That is not my point. The locked room in the servants' wing was better than this because I had your mother and sisters to keep me company. I should have gone with them!"

"My sweet Catherine," he murmured, nuzzling me in just the way I liked best, "you know it makes all the difference to me to have you here. You have been so patient. I see how it chafes you."

"I dislike this coaxing manner, Andevai, with your wiles and caresses."

"We'll make a child."

Trembling, I shoved him to arm's length. "Is this the same man who swore we would bring no child into the world until we're free of clientage?"

"Yes, but—"

"Not to mention my sire."

"Yes, love, but—"

"I would be very careful what you say next."

He sighed.

"They won't even let me sew, except under their eye. As if they think I can effect an escape with a needle."

"My love," he murmured. This time I let him embrace me, because I was so tired of being alone all day that to feel the press of his hand on my back and the warmth of his chest against mine was the nectar I wished to feed on. "I promise you, we will go out tomorrow and promenade along the Sicauna River. We'll take coffee at one of the little cafés, as people do here."

Yet this night, finally, the kisses of a handsome man were not enough.

"If this is what it means to be wife of the mansa, I cannot live it. You would do better to marry the daughter of Two Gourds House and let her pour your wine!"

"Love, love, love, this is not what it will be once the war is over."

But it would. I knew it, and he did not want to know it.

Yet he was right that a war was being fought. The old order did not want to die, and why should it? The radicals wanted change, and why wouldn't they? Meanwhile Camjiata had a foot in each camp: His father and mother had both been born into the highest ranks, while his legal code would tear down the bed his noble forebears had long luxuriated in.

The bells of conflict rang down through the interwoven worlds. The dragons lost their hatchlings and began to die out, so they walked their dreams through the minds of mortal girls and by this means hatchlings survived, even if the girls did not. The courts drank mortal blood to strengthen themselves, and the salt turned them into ghouls, and thus, unable to change, as ghouls they fell into the mortal world and spread the salt plague that had killed so many.

So on and on, always the long struggle: The worlds are a maze with many paths.

"What about my sire?" I asked. "What are we to do when Hallows' Night comes, as it will?"

"I have been discussing Hallows' Night and troll mazes with the mansa—"

I shoved him to arm's length. "With the mansa!"

"Beatrice is the one who revealed to him that we know how to escape the Hunt. You can't wish people to die, Catherine! That's all I told him, love. None of your secrets, I promise you."

I could not scold him. I did not want people to die any more than he did. "Yet troll mazes won't help me," I muttered, letting him gather me against him.

He held me so close and so so sweetly. "My sweet Catherine, if we walk this road together, we will find a way through. I promise you, love. We will find a way."

When I kissed him, I could hold on to my patience for one more night. But I had to make something change.

36

At dawn a steward announced himself. Vai was commanded to accompany the mansa to the city of Senones to meet three Roman legions arriving from the east and discuss with them the difficulties of battling an army protected by a fire mage. He might be gone for weeks.

After he left, I wept hot tears of frustration. Then I dried my eyes.

In the indoor bedchamber, which we had never used, stood a writing desk equipped with paper, ink, and pens. I wrote an impassioned letter to Kofi because it was the only way I had to express the ferocity of my misgivings. Afterward I would have burned my bitter words, but I had no fire. Instead I concealed the folded paper inside the skull. For the longest time I stood at the open door of the suite, staring along the corridor. As long as my back was in sight, my attendants let me be. Now and again a servant passed on an errand. I could not quite comprehend how I had gotten here, wife to the heir of the mansa!

A young steward sauntered into view, carrying a tray on which lay a sealed letter. He mistook me for an attendant because of the simple colors and sensible cut of my clothes.

"Where is the woman who stewards here? I am instructed to give all correspondence that comes for the Four Moons heir to her first."

I made a pretty courtesy and flashed a flirting grin. "I shall take it in to her. She is attending on the heir's wife, who has a headache this morning for that the men rode away."

He leaned closer, with a confiding smile that I rather fancied. "Is it true, what they say?"

"What do they say?" I gave him a sly look to distract him as I slipped the letter off the tray.

"That she can vanish from plain sight and walk through mirrors. That she is a spirit woman the heir captured in the bush and brought back to be his wife to show off his power. That's why they can't marry him to any other women, because she would kill and eat them."

"It's all true!"

"What does she look like?"

"Nothing out of the ordinary. Haven't you ever seen her?" I heard footsteps behind me. "I'd best take this to the steward right away. You wouldn't want me to get in trouble, would you?"

"I could get you into the kind of trouble you'd like," he said with a grin.

I winked at him as I closed the door, then tucked the letter inside my jacket before anyone saw it. When they asked whom I had been talking to, I sniveled that a passing steward had told me the men had left already. With sobs I retreated to the summer cottage, the one place the djelimuso and steward would not follow. Gracious Melqart! What providence was this! The letter came from Chartji, and informed Vai that she and her three clerks had arrived in Lutetia and were putting up at an establishment called the Tavern with Two Doors just outside the city limits at the Arras Gate.

And her three clerks. Caith was one clerk. Who were the other two?

When Prince Caonabo arrested me, I had not allowed myself to be detained all mild and acquiescent, although who knows what I might have done had the man been cunning enough to shower me with ardent kisses and embraces, for clearly I was susceptible to such blandishments.

Instead I had leaped into action.

I conceived a violently imprudent plan.

I begged the steward to take me for a tour of the schoolrooms, since the heir and I hoped to bring into the world many well-behaved children. In one schoolroom I made myself useful with the older children by engaging them in a geography lesson in which they described to me in great detail the particulars of a map of Lutetia. When I returned to my rooms I kept the door to my suite open while I paged through books of fashion on a couch by the door. Every time I heard footsteps I took a turn around the sitting room that led past the door.

At mid-afternoon my labors were rewarded when the young steward ambled past, obviously on the lookout for me. Men did strut about life with a strong sense of their self-importance!

"Shh!" I whispered, "for they keep me trapped here. They don't want me to talk to people lest I say unkind things about the heir's wife."

"Have you unkind things to say of her?" he asked with keen interest as he ogled my chest. "I hear all kinds of smoke but have seen no fire."

"I could show you some fire," I said with a look meant to inflame his interest. "I've nothing to do but sit for hours in the garden. Not that the heir's wife needs watching by people like us."

"Is it true a djelimuso guards the suite at all hours, day and night?"

"It is. I can't hope to slip out as long as her eye is open! The frustrating part is that I could be gone for hours and she would never know, if I could just get out this door."

He was eager to show me what he could accomplish! We arranged for him to create a distraction in the morning at second bell, after which I would meet him at a place he named that I pretended to know the location of. He hadn't even asked my name, although by the evidence of his gaze he had become well acquainted with the shape of my breasts.

I hid Chartji's letter in the skull and retrieved the one to Kofi, and retreated to the summer cottage, where I threw tantrums and also actual objects any time anyone attempted to enter. By evening they simply waited outside for me to ring. At dawn I rang for broth and informed them I felt so ill I wanted only to sleep all day and must on no account be disturbed. Then I dressed in my boots, my riding skirt, and my repurposed cuirassier's jacket, which gave me the look of a humble but respectable woman. My cane and my locket gave me courage. The cacica I had to leave behind, because I saw no way to move her without the djelimuso's wondering why. Anyway, I had to leave Chartji's letter somewhere I could hope Vai would think to look for it.

What distraction the young steward concocted I did not know. As soon as I heard a commotion from the sitting room, I was up a tree and onto the wall and thence over the sloped roofs. Without djeliw following my every move it was easy for me to escape, as the mansa had known it would be.

With my newly acquired knowledge of Lutetia as a map in my 393 head, I enjoyed a refreshing walk down to the lovely Sicauna River and over a stone bridge and across the holy island dedicated to the Lady of the River with her diadem and boat. On such a fine sunny day many people walked the streets, but I sensed a mood of fear and anticipation. I strode along a wide boulevard leading to the northwest. The long facades of the buildings were broken by gates leading to interior courtyards. Flagstones shone, drenched by pools of light from the midday sun. Side avenues broke away to smaller temples, shops, and city manufactories powered not by steam but by hand. A long line of shuttered windows down one narrow lane bore the plain white stamp of goblinkind, but their workshops were closed down for the day. I saw no trolls at all, because no trolls were allowed into the central city by order of the Parisi prince.

After several miles I reached Arras Gate, built across an old defensive wall of earlier days. Folk stood in line at a toll station, arguing with the guards over the cost of import duties on the items they were carrying into the city. Wrapped in shadow I walked right through, no one the wiser. Outside the gate more buildings spread along the Arras Road, for the city was growing outward. To the left rose a wooded hill on whose height stood a holy sanctuary dedicated to one of the aspects of Mars the Soldier. Farther off to the left I glimpsed the smokestacks of a factory district. I asked directions to the Tavern with Two Doors.

On such a beautiful summer's day, trestle tables filled the tavern's outdoor courtyard. Men drank and ate and argued. A youth read aloud from a pamphlet for those who could not read.

" 'A Declaration of Rights and a Civil Code. Book One. Title One. Chapter One. Every person shall enjoy civil rights.' What do you think of that, eh? Every person!"

A lively argument arose among the men over who could be deemed a person. Did the word *person* include women? Inside, to my delight, I immediately spotted Rory seated in a corner next to a young man. They were sharing a mug of beer mostly, I thought, for the chance to dandle each other's fingers. I gently eased my shadows away so no one would be startled by my sudden appearance. Seeing me, Rory broke off. Excusing himself with an apologetic smile, he made his way to me. I followed him to the back, into a separate building made up of rooms where, for the first time, I saw trolls. In a sequestered courtyard clusters of trolls drank and ate. After so long, I had forgotten trolls saw my cane as a sword even in daylight.

"Roderic, what is that shiny blade?" called one red-and-yellow male, the question followed up by whistled inquiries from all around the courtyard. Feathered people turned to look with the bared teeth of trolls mimicking human emotions, in this case amusement and curiosity.

"My sister has come to visit," he replied, at ease in this flock. "Has Chartji flown off?"

Yes, she had, in company with the Honeyed Voice.

"The Honeyed Voice?" I asked as Rory hurried me out the back past a warren of lanes hung with mirrors and shards of glass whose flashing and spinning made me reel and gag. I felt like the very threads of being were unraveling.

"Those troll mazes are unpleasant, aren't they?" He steered us to a lane lined with shops whose windows had only glass, no mirrors. I leaned against a wall as nausea and headache did a frenetic dance that slowly receded. After a while, he went on. "The Honeyed Voice is what the feathered people call Bee. It's a play on words. She's a Bee and she gives speeches..."

"I know, Rory. I figured it out."

"What's got your hair up?" He peered at me. "You've had a fight with him! People do that, you know. After some talking and petting, it will all be set right again."

"We haven't had a fight."

His tone changed. "Cat, don't lie."

"We didn't have a fight. It's just the mansa got his claws into Vai. I have to rescue him, only he doesn't want to be rescued, he has everything he thinks he ever wanted. He can't see what kind of man he is going to become if he stays there. He thinks he can change them but they're changing him."

I burst into tears. Rory patted my back and fended off the impertinent queries of passersby by telling them his sister had had a row with her husband, nothing that wouldn't be fixed once he had had a manly talk with the rogue of a popinjay his sister had foolishly married all for being dazzled by the man's peacock feathers and melting eyes.

I could not help but laugh.

"That's better," he said.

"Where is everyone else?" I asked. "Chartji's letter said you were at the tavern."

"That's where we sleep. Today they're addressing a secret convocation of radicals. We'll go there."

He led me on a road that ran parallel to the old city walls. As we entered the interior courtyard of a large compound, I drew the shadows around me. People were hammering in workshops on the ground floor. Men sawed in the courtyard beside wagons piled with rope for haulage. The carpenters touched the brims of their red caps in a signal, and made no move to stop Rory. We descended a flight of stone steps into a basement lit by oil lamps and heavy with tobacco smoke, the scent of the Antilles. The fragrance made me lose hold of my threads, but no one took any notice of two more in the crowded cellar.

The smell of strong coffee wafted from a bar where men, and a few women, talked in the local cant at a speed I could not understand. The women wore loose, simply cut gowns, while the men wore neckerchiefs tied in exciting knots over jackets cut short in front and long in back.

At the back of this cavernous space, Kehinde Nayo Kuti was giving a demonstration of her jobber press. She wore a knee-length tunic over belled trousers in the Turanian style common in the south. It was practical garb for a traveler, and the brown fabric almost hid the many ink stains where she had unthinkingly wiped her fingers. Standing on a box, Bee acted as the professora's voice.

"The press can be taken apart and moved if the authorities raid. Besides that, when your prince demands another tax be levied on printers and pamphlets, think how hard it is to track it down. What you cannot chain, you cannot hold!"

"I'd like to hold you, sweetheart!" shouted some sad wit.

Bee pointed him out to laughter and applause. "If that is the best you can do in the way of courtship, Maester, then like this press I shall have to seek my words elsewhere. I have come to Lutetia to speak of justice and revolution, not to waste my time with men who are not serious about the great struggle we have undertaken."

"Cat Barahal!" Brennan Du slid in beside us to shake my hand.

"Chartji thought you might show up. Where is the cold mage?"

I sighed, for of all the things I had thought of, how to answer this question to anyone except Bee or Rory was not one of them.

Rory said, "He's a prisoner of his vanity."

"I beg your pardon? A prisoner of the banditry?" Brennan rubbed his ear. The roar in the chamber was astoundingly clamorous. Chartji and Caith flanked Bee, who was now wrangling with hecklers sure that women had no cause or right to speak in a public venue. "Come this way."

We moved into a low passage and emerged into an old storage room lit by two basement windows. Lines of afternoon light cast gold over a table strewn with pamphlets, blank sheets of foolscap, and pens and ink.

He slid a pamphlet out of a heap. "Your account of the revolutionary philosophy of the Expedition radicals has traveled across Europa while you have laid low. Many have read it. Have you been a prisoner or a spy?"

"Cat!" Bee appeared, trembling as she rushed to embrace me.

"Oh, Bee! I'm so glad you're here!" To my horror, I again burst into tears.

"Dearest! Has some terrible calamity befallen Andevai?"

Pleased with his cleverness, Rory repeated himself. "He's become a prisoner of his vanity."

Brennan chuckled. "Was he not that already? As the djeliw say, vanity is a mark of weakness, humility that of strength."

"The mansa made him his heir!" I cried.

Brennan whistled with real admiration. "When I suggested you spy in the mage House, I had no idea you would do so with such success!"

"Heir to Four Moons House?" demanded Bee. "So he will become the next mansa?"

I nodded, too choked to speak.

She patted my hand. "Blessed Tanit! No wonder you're crying! If there is one enticement Andevai could not resist, that would be it."

"It gets worse," I sniveled. "The mansa brought Vai's mother along to be prisoner with his sisters. Now with his elevation his mother is elevated, too! She was born a peddler's daughter and now she's the honored mother of the heir to Four Moons House!"

Brennan whistled again. "Bold Teutates! Remind me never to play chess with the mansa. That will have secured the young man's loyalty. You can't ask a man to take a course of action that will seem to him to be dishonoring his mother."

"Did you ask him to give up the heirship, Cat?" Bee asked. "Or did he cast you out so he could secure a more valuable bride?"

"Of course he didn't cast me out!" I crumpled a pamphlet in my hands. I hated the way my anger and distress surged like storm tides, ripping me this way and that until I could not even think straight for wanting to cry one moment and rage the next.

"Of course he didn't cast her out," said Rory with a disdainful sniff. "For one thing, his scent is still all over her, and pretty fresh. For another, he would think it would make him look bad, as if he's ashamed of Cat. If there's one thing he truly hates, it's the thought of looking bad or feeling demeaned in front of other people. No, there's one thing he hates worse. He hates people thinking he is ashamed of where he comes from, because a part of him is ashamed of it."

We all stared at him.

He explained with the patience of an elder to slow-witted children. "People often lie with their words, even if they don't mean to purposefully. But almost no people can lie with their bodies. Do you need me to go and scold him?"

I wiped tears off my cheeks. "No. It would just make him worse. They praise and fawn over him to his face and talk about his low origins behind his back. But they're scared of him, too, and so very impressed by how powerful he is."

Bee nodded, stroking my arm. "What now, Cat?"

I flipped through the pamphlets to give my hands something to do. The writings ranged from broadsheets in simple verse to Professora Nayo Kuti's lengthy tracts. "It was insupportable living in the mage House as the heir's wife with nothing to do or look forward to except—"

"You need not describe the whole," said Bee quickly.

"But I won't let the mage House have him. I love him too much to let them ruin him!"

"Only you could. Honestly, Cat, sometimes I don't know how you put up with him."

"No doubt I learned how to love annoying people by growing up with you!"

Rory snorted.

Without the least furrow of irritation, she smiled at Brennan in a gentle way that made her look as radiant as a kind goddess standing in a heavenly beam of light. "I suppose you did."

She glanced toward the archway as the two trolls and Kehinde came into the room. Chartji held aloft a candle lantern. Her taloned feet clacked as she walked in the oddly rhythmic glide trolls had. She bobbed to acknowledge me.

Kehinde came forward with hands extended to grasp mine. "Cat Barahal! I am so pleased to see you. May your heart be at peace." She looked at our expressions, and raised an eyebrow in inquiry. "What news do you bring?"

I drew myself up. "I've glimpsed the mage Houses and their princely and Roman allies from the inside. I'm now convinced the general is the only one who can overthrow their grip on power. But Vai will never support Camjiata as long as the general is allowing James Drake to use fire magic to fight his battles. Nor should he. So I am going to infiltrate Camjiata's army and kill James Drake."

Before anyone could respond to my bold and dramatic declaration, a shrill troll whistle sounded outside, followed by a cascade of human whistles. The rumble of voices from the chamber ceased so abruptly that for an instant I thought I had gone deaf.

"Here come the authorities!" said Brennan with a glint in his smile that got my heart pounding, and not in a romantic way. He looked like a person spoiling for a fight. "Kehinde, you and Bee go swiftly now. You, too, Cat."

"I am an accomplished swordswoman," said Bee.

"We need your voice most now," said Kehinde. "Come along."

To my surprise Bee meekly followed Kehinde and the trolls into the passage. The silence in the far room was replaced by the trampling of feet as people hurried to rescue the press.

Brennan shoved the table against the thick wall and climbed up on it to open one of the deep-set windows. "Cat! Go along after them now."

My stormy despair was overtaken by a desire to punch someone. I jumped up next to him. "Give me a leg up. I can fight dirty in ways you never imagined."

"Cat..."

I met his eye. "If you say because I am a woman, I am best away from the fight, I will lose all respect for you."

"Let her go first," said Rory. "You won't regret it."

With a shrug he made a basket with his hands. I shimmied through the window into a light well and up to the courtyard. A quick survey revealed many handy coils of rope on the wagons. Tying an end to a post, I uncoiled it across the paving stones to the far wall. When men wearing marshals' uniforms ran into the courtyard carrying muskets and flourishing halberds, I yanked on the rope with all my strength.

As I slammed back into the wall, the rope popped up tautly to waist height. None of them saw it coming, for they could not see me. The force of so many men pushing into the rope at the same time jerked me forward so hard I had to let go, but the men in front stumbled and the men behind bumped into them. Into this confusion I waded with my cane, whacking men in the back of the neck so they turned around to chastise their comrades. I grabbed muskets and halberds out of their hands and flung the weapons as far as I could. I trod on feet. Their boiled leather helmets made excellent balls to be tossed high, so they had to throw up their hands to protect themselves as the helmets crashed down. Flailing hands struck and pushed me. A burly man with stinking onion breath bumped hard into me, so I dropped to a crouch and he smacked heads with the man next to him. By sticking my cane between the legs of staggering men, I tripped four in a row before they thought to start kicking.

Laborers swarmed out of the building on all sides. I snatched up as many muskets and halberds as I could. Now mostly unarmed, and surrounded by men bearing hammers, adzes, and axes, the marshals shrank back into a defensive group.

Brennan sauntered into the gap between the two groups without the least evidence that he feared the muskets pointed at him. He rolled back his sleeves and put up his hands. "I challenge you all to put down your weapons and settle this as real men do, with our fists. Who will be first? It is sure not one man of you can outlast me."

Onion-breath man shoved past his fellows. "Let's see what ye have got."

They circled in the manner of men putting on a show in a boxing ring, but by the scowl on the marshal's face and the measuring gaze of Brennan, the fight was deadly serious. The marshal broke in to throw a blow that was easily parried by Brennan, who followed with a jab that landed square on the other man's nose. Blood gushed like a pungent iron brine. I thought it prudent to back away lest I betray myself. Other men bolted forward, and the courtyard dissolved into a mass of men slugging each other. I backed up to the cellar windows and dumped muskets and halberds into the window well. Rory watched the fight with a lazy smile.

"Aren't you going in?" I asked. "To prove you're a real man?"

"I'm not a man. I need prove nothing. If there's trouble, I'll pounce."

"That's not trouble?" The roil of the fight echoed against the walls.

"The marshals in Lutetia are underpaid and recruited from the plebeian class. They don't like to arrest men who share the same grievances they do. But they have no choice but to obey orders even though they chafe at them. Now they can say they fought."

Above, windows on the second story were thrown open. Bee stood framed in the opening.

"Enough! Those who oppress us feast on the blood we spill for them when we fight each other! Who is our true enemy? Our neighbor whose children cry for bread in the evening? Or the lord who throws the leavings from his heavily laden table to his pigs?"

As the fighting men paused to look up, women moved into the courtyard and thrust pamphlets into the hands of the marshals.

"What d'ye mean me to do with this?" shouted Onion Breath, shaking a pamphlet toward the upper windows. "D'ye think I can read?"

"If you cannot, then whose fault is that? The lord's children can all read. They who hold the lash do not want you to know you are not alone in speaking against its cruel bite! Why do you think they hate printing presses or any person whose voice spreads the news of a declaration of rights? Why do you think they fear a civil code whose laws will demolish the privileges of the few? Why do you think they send the likes of you to arrest printers and smash presses? Not for your sake! They aren't protecting *you*! Go on, then! Go, but remember that you are our brothers. Remember that we fight for you."

She stepped back into the gloom as Rory tugged on my wrist. Abandoning the weapons, we passed through a carpentry shop smelling of 401 sawdust and hurried by diverse passages into a hidden staircase and thus out onto another street. Brennan strode up with Bee. He had a scuffed chin and an abrasion on his right cheek. His trousers were ripped at the left knee.

"I'm getting slow," he said. "Invincible Andraste! How did you do that, Cat?"

Bee shook her head to indicate that whatever else she had told Brennan, my secrets had never passed her lips. "It's a Hassi Barahal secret," she said.

"Where are the others?" I asked as we set out.

"Taking down and moving the press," he said. "That was a spectacular diversion, Cat."

"My thanks." My heart was still pounding, and I had barely caught my breath, yet I felt alive as I had not for weeks now. Indeed, I was scarcely thinking of Vai constantly at all.

"Diversions are her specialty," said Bee with a laugh. "Dearest, I can't imagine how Andevai could ever imagine you would tolerate being closed within stultifying walls, whatever attentions he might think to assuage you with."

"Even I would get bored, no matter how good the petting was," said Rory.

By the time we reached the tavern I had worked up an impressive hunger. The Tavern with Two Doors was made up of two squares of buildings, one for human people and one for feathered people. Each had a central courtyard, linked by a shared wing. This central wing housed the kitchens, one for each courtyard, and other service rooms. Part of the ground floor, beneath the upper floor, lay open as a wide portico. Because it was summer, tables were set here, where rats from one side and trolls from the other could congregate as they wished. We took a table here. Men strolled up, a few to flirt with Bee but most to argue the serious business of radical philosophy. People spoke of rising up against the prince in order to open the city gates to Camjiata's army.

I ate my way through three platters of meats flavored with sauces, but more than that I relished the talk, the laughter, the freedom to say what I wished or to get up and take a turn around the trolls' courtyard had I the desire to do so, which I did more than once before the trolls went to bed at nightfall. Kehinde appeared late, having conveyed the components of the jobber press to its next hiding place. Rory slipped off to talk to the young man I had seen him with earlier.

I ate an entire tray of mouthwatering pastries while everyone else was debating the question of whether women could bear the burden of having the same rights as men, because if I had not kept my hands busy I would have punched every man who argued that women simply could not have any independent legal capacity separate from their fathers, husbands, or sons. I could have sat there all night, listening to Bee and Kehinde eviscerate them, with Brennan tossing in the occasional joking remark to assuage male vanity. We almost did sit there all night, talking under the gleam of lanterns because the Parisi prince, in concert with Two Gourds House, had forbidden the installation of gas lighting anywhere in the city or its outer districts.

The first birds chirruped a dawn song as we staggered to our rest. Brennan and Kehinde had taken a narrow room above the kitchens whose window looked over the trolls' courtyard. Here rooms were cheapest, since the trolls made many people uncomfortable. Chartji and Caith slept elsewhere.

A screen divided the room to create privacy. On the side where Kehinde and Bee slept was a bed just wide enough for two, supplemented by a narrow pallet, which Bee set on the floor as Kehinde took off her shoes by the light of a candle.

"Let you and Cat share the bed, Bee. I shall take the pallet for as long as Cat is with us."

"Are you sure, for we surely do not mind taking the pallet," Bee said with such solemnity that I gaped at her downcast gaze and folded hands. Tension bled between the two women, yet their polite respect toward each other seemed sincere.

"There are two of you. It is unreasonable of me to take the larger space." She glanced at the door as Brennan came in, looked our way, then vanished behind the screen. He whistled as he fussed around getting ready to sleep. A chair clacked as he shifted it. Ropes squeaked as he lay down. The tilt of Kehinde's head made me think she was blushing.

Bee slanted a portentous glance my way. "Cat and I will be glad to share the bed."

"Where is Rory?" I whispered as I settled onto the bed in my shift.

Kehinde chuckled. "He takes care of himself."

As Bee snuggled down between me and the wall, the professora pulled off her tunic and lay down in trousers and under-blouse.

I whispered. "Kehinde, if I may ask, I heard you were arrested by the prince here and had to return to Massilia. Isn't it risky for you to come back now?"

After a silence in which I thought I had perhaps offended her, she said, "The work must be done despite the risk. It is more important than one life." She blew out the candle.

Brennan coughed.

Bee and I lay side by side in the old familiar way, holding hands.

"After the war, we'll set up a little household together, you and me and Rory," she whispered. "Men can come and go if we approve it or wish it, dearest. We don't need them to live."

"Yes." My shattering despair subsided to a weary throb. "I can manage anything as long as we are together."

It was almost midday when Bee and I woke. Kehinde still slept, a hand gripping the end of one of her locks as if she had never let go of a child's habit. Brennan was gone.

We dressed and went out to wash our faces in a trough. The sun burnished the ebony of Bee's curls as she rubbed shadowed eyes. "Blessed Tanit! Cat, why did you let me drink so much?"

In late morning most of the tables were empty. We settled where we could look over the trolls' courtyard but also see into the courtyard of the other half of the inn. There we saw Rory laughing next to his friend. Bee tended her hangover with a mug of beer and a bowl of broth. I devoured a splendid spelt porridge garnished with butter and a creamy pear sauce.

"Whatever happened with Kemal?" I asked.

She swirled the dregs of the ale in the mug. "Once we reached Havery, I sent a letter to the New Academy. After some weeks I received a reply. He wrote all manner of pleasing words, but he reiterated that he cannot leave the hatchlings until he is certain of their safety. I cannot fault him for the sentiment, but I felt obliged to reply that I could not visit him in Noviomagus given the current unpleasantness wracking Europa. I have my work, too, you know! Speeches to declaim! People to scold into behaving better! Blessed Tanit! Perhaps after all this he has reconsidered his partiality for me now he has come into his full power."

I considered my empty spoon. "We are a sad pair."

"Dearest, what do you mean to do now?"

"Camjiata's skirmishers were last seen near the town of Cena. If I can find his army, I can sneak into his camp to kill Drake, and then return before Vai gets back from Senones and finds out I left. Then I'll convince him to leave the mage House and fight for the general."

"That's your plan? Do you think it will be easy to convince him to leave now that he's heir? With his monumental vanity, he'll believe he can change things from within. That the mansa made sure to bestow such an honor on Andevai's mother makes me respect the man's devious mind. Has Andevai been unkind to you? Is that what drove you away?"

"Not at all. If anything, he has been overly kind."

"That being so, you might have chosen a more prudent and less dramatic and public way of expressing your discontent."

"I did express my discontent! He said that my being there made 'all the difference,' to *him*."

She laughed. "I can see how that would have rubbed you the wrong way. Yet even you must see Andevai will take this defection very ill."

"I just had to get out of there."

Rory slipped onto the bench beside me, winkled the spoon from my hand, and started eating my porridge.

"Are you really willing to kill James Drake?" Bee asked.

"You have no idea how willing I am." My fingers clutched my cane so tightly that, had it been ordinary wood, I would have crushed it into splinters. "He means to kill Vai regardless, so I must do it to protect Vai. Even if I cannot live in the mage House and he cannot leave it and so we must be parted...at least I will know he lives and thrives in his chosen place."

Bee clapped one hand to her chest and the other, palm out, to her brow. "How affecting these maudlin ramblings are! I shall expire in their wake!"

Rory pressed a hand to my forehead. "Are you feverish, Cat?"

"It's not amusing!"

"What isn't amusing?" Brennan strolled up, looking fresh and handsome without a trace of hangover-sodden eyes. No wonder he was famous for his ability to hold his liquor! He glanced at Bee, then at Kehinde coming down the stairs from the upper floor with spectacles in hand as she squinted shortsightedly across the courtyard. After ordering porridge and ale, he sat next to me. Chartji and Caith joined us at the table. We exchanged morning greetings. Caith began picking through a heaping platter of nuts and dried berries, looking for the hazelnuts.

"Chartji, I'm wondering if you could see that this letter is dispatched to Expedition." I handed her the letter I had written to Kofi. "I know I have not a sestertius to my name, and that we must already be deeply in debt to the clutch—"

"I have an idea about that," said Bee.

"—but if you can send it with your regular dispatches to the Expedition office of Godwik and Clutch, they will know how to get it to this person, because he knows your aunt and uncle."

Chartji's crest flared with an emotion I could not interpret, but she took the sealed letter and tucked it inside her jacket. "It will be done. An interesting and important person he must be, this Kofi Osafo. The magister has already sent him six letters via my offices."

"Has he?" I asked, squinting as at a bright light. When was Vai writing to Kofi?

"I have long been in correspondence with Professora Alhamrai from the university in Expedition, whom you know," said Kehinde. "Recently we have been discussing the question of the ice shelves and whether they are shrinking or growing and how we might measure their extent. She has written about her theories of the properties of cold magic, which like all things"—here she spared such a jaundiced eye for Brennan that he laughed almost nervously, and she frowned as if she judged him a frivolous fellow—"can be explicated using the principles of science alone."

"Thus am I scolded," he said with a lightly mocking smile. "But what I want to know is how any fire mage can survive if he has not been accepted into the guild of blacksmiths. Everyone knows that a person born to the flame will die young in a fire of their own making."

I said, "James Drake survives by channeling the backlash of his fire magic into living people. An ordinary person will die if so used, but cold mages can absorb most backlash without harm."

Brennan whistled.

"A fascinating struggle between fire, which many natural historians believe releases energy, and this sort of freezing or locking of energy that it might be said the cold mages do," said Kehinde. "Where does the fire go when it flows into the cold mage?"

"We believe it disperses into the spirit world. The Coalition will fight by using the presence of cold mages to kill the combustion of Camjiata's superior weaponry. The general will fight by using Drake to throw the backlash into the cold mages, because when cold mages are acting as catch-fires, they can't kill combustion or work magic. Not to mention he will burn his enemy's houses, goods, and camps, and generally terrify the population."

Brennan considered a spoonful of porridge. "This is valuable information, Cat. If the mages nullify Camjiata's superior weaponry, then without this fire magic, the general may lose. The Invictus Legion is already here, working in concert with Lord Marius. My spies tell me three more legions are on the march from Rome to join the Coalition."

"Yes. Vai and the Four Moons mansa were sent to Senones to meet them. Camjiata's skirmishers have been spotted near the city of Cena."

"You are indeed an excellent spy, because I have not heard that news," said Brennan appreciatively. "But it doesn't change the fact that we can't risk harming the general's best weapon."

"Drake is an unscrupulous criminal! He kills people by burning them alive!"

"So does war," said Brennan. "So does revolution. So do the mage Houses and the princes with their unjust laws. Which deaths do you choose?"

"Justice can only ultimately be gained through law," said Kehinde. "But to get the law, it seems we must have the war."

"It seems wrong to me that people say terrible acts have to be tolerated because it serves our goals. If we can only win by allowing a man like James Drake to murder people indiscriminately and in such an awful way, then how are we different from the princely and mage Houses who rule by standing on the backs of those who serve them?"

Brennan offered me a courtly flourish. "Maestra, never believe the radical cause is without its own dilemmas and contradictions. We need Camjiata, and I believe he needs us."

"What happens when he doesn't need you any longer?" I demanded. "And what happens when Drake decides he no longer needs Camjiata? What do you think, Chartji?" I added, for all this time she had been listening with cocked head, picking at a bowl filled with nuts and sun-dried fruit but not popping more than one or two into her mouth.

She lifted her muzzle toward the courtyard of the feathered people. Because trolls went about their business during the day, the open expanse scattered with high tables and inclined perches lay mostly vacant. Only a few groups gossiped and negotiated in the corners, well away from each other.

The courtyard thereby provided an ample stage for the entrance of a man.

He wore a striking garment in the local style, quite different from his usual dash jackets. I was stunned by how extremely flattering it looked on what was, after all, an already well-formed figure. The unbuttoned front of the jacket was cut to the length of a waistcoat, displaying light-colored lawn trousers as well as a black waistcoat, while the back of the garment swept in two long tails to his knees. The black brocade of the fabric had a weave so tight that the cloth shone in the sunlight. To this muted ensemble he had added a neckerchief of the most shocking orange-and-gold fabric, simply tied, to give a splash of color.

He looked very very angry as he slapped gloves against a palm and scanned the courtyards. He had not yet seen us at our table in the shadow of the portico.

A curse rose from the kitchens as the stoves went out. Brennan slipped a hand under his coat as for a knife. Rory began to rise.

Chartji said, "Please sit down, Roderic. If fur flies, my brethren may grow heated."

Bee said, "I shall take care of *this*."

When he saw her emerge into the light, he strode to her as an arrow flies to its target.

"Andevai! I am overwhelmed with joy at seeing you safe and well after our long separation!"

"Where is she?" he demanded in a tone so grippingly arrogant that it took my breath away, and not in a pleasant way.

She bestowed an aggressive greeting kiss. "Now you are to say, 'How lovely to see you, Beatrice, and indeed it relieves my mind to know that you and Roderic survived your adventures unscathed after we were so rudely and violently parted on the river.'"

"I must assume you came to Lutetia with Chartji in answer to my letter, and have concocted some scheme to rip Catherine from me."

"To which I reply, 'My thanks for your good wishes, Andevai. It was a frightful journey, not an adventurous one at all. I was cold and hungry and damp. After we sold the boat to the most unpleasantly contemptuous man I have ever had the misfortune to meet if I do not include you when you are in this unreasonable mood, we had perforce to walk for twenty days over the muddiest paths and in the worst continual sleet I have ever experienced...'"

He was staring at her with such an expression of imperiousness being torn to shreds by her sarcastically cheerful tone that Brennan choked down a laugh, and Kehinde shushed him.

"...and I sickened!" she said, finally releasing his elbows. "I suffered the most grievous fever and cough for a month! 'Goodness, Beatrice,' you are to say now. 'How very glad I am that you survived this dreadful experience and took no lasting harm from these travails!'"

"Where is she?" he repeated. "I found the letter from Chartji hidden in the skull."

I could not bear it any longer. I got up and walked out into the courtyard.

"So," he said, without the least change of tone. "Gave you a single thought for me and my situation, Catherine? Did it not occur to you that the instant they discovered you gone they would send a messenger after us? Can you imagine how it looked for me in the company of the mansa"—his voice darkened and grew thick—"and his cursed nephew, and our exalted allies to be informed that my wife had absconded like a criminal? I had to turn tail like a dog and come riding back lest I be accused of being a conspirator! With the nephew to supervise my journey, no less! So the damage is done. Are you content now that you have made me look like a fool?"

My cheeks burned with the sting of humiliation.

Bee slapped him.

He took a step back, not in retreat but in surprise. Every troll in the courtyard slewed around to stare. Many shifted their weight forward, ready to lunge. He brushed at the outer corner of his right eye, where perhaps one of her nails had jabbed. A cold eddy of air swirled down over us.

"You will not speak to Cat that way! I don't care if you are her husband or the emperor of Rome. You will not! If you could think past your monstrous self-regard for one moment, you would pause to ask yourself why a woman who adores you as much as she does—although her devotion to you quite defies explanation—would take flight in such a precipitous way."

His lips pressed together, his hands clenched, and his chest actually thrust out as he assumed the stance of a belligerent man making ready to respond with every hoarded sharp scrap of anger.

Chartji glided past me and thrust out her taloned hand. "Well met, Andevai," she said. "I came at your request, as you see."

In the reflexive manner of a man who has had good manners drilled into him since childhood, he shook hands. Hers tightened over his, holding him so he could not let go. The cold air eased as if cut off.

She said, "Not here. It would be unwise. My brethren are accustomed to rat behavior, but some of these are young and not yet fully in control of their impulses. Rather—I might add in the capacity of your solicitor—like you, Magister."

His eyes flared. He jerked his hand out of her grip. The watching trolls stiffened, and even Chartji gave an aggressive bob of the head. Rory trotted out into the sun, unbuttoning his jacket, lips curled back.

"Kehinde, don't go out there," said Brennan, but she did, walking out into the sun with Brennan following right behind her to face Vai.

"Here is my answer, all of you ranged against me!" For once his undoubted beauty could not smooth away the distasteful contours of his conceit. "You have chosen your place then, Catherine! And I mine!"

He strode off toward the archway that led from the trolls' courtyard to the street beyond.

Goaded by a stab of pain both hot and desperate, I shouted after him. "Now we see what manner of man you have decided to become! Just like the ones who tormented you!"

He staggered to a halt in the shadow of the arched passage, catching himself with a fist on the wall. For a long, drawn-out silence no one moved, not him, not us, not the trolls.

Then, as if shaking awake from slumber, Andevai Diarisso Haranwy walked out to the street, out of my sight.

37

My heart plummeted out of my body. I groped for and leaned on Bee.

"Come sit down." Bee supported me back to the table. "You're shaking."

I was too numb for tears. Bee's arm did not comfort me.

Kehinde sat on my other side. She spoke in a low voice. "Cat, you need not honor a contract sealed without your consent. The same was done to me when I was but fifteen."

Brennan sat opposite, mouth twisted all awry. Chartji whistled softly. Rory still stood out in the courtyard, looking toward the archway.

The cold mage reappeared carrying the laced-up basket with the skull, as well as a leather bag. He crossed the courtyard as the watching trolls went back to their conversations. The light drenching his figure turned to shade as he came in under the portico. He set basket and bag on the table, then backed away to stand with arms crossed, staring into the distance. Bee simmered, looking ready to leap up and slap him again. Brennan studied him with a frown, while Kehinde pushed her spectacles up the bridge of her nose and watched me. Chartji waited beside the table. A few people moved past, staring at his expensive clothes and grim expression. He ignored everyone, yet I knew he was acutely aware of all of us. I was astonished he exposed himself to their censure.

He shifted, and we all started. Upon opening his mouth to speak, he closed it again.

After a moment he bowed his head and drew thumb and finger down the bridge of his nose. Finally he looked up. The tilt of his head and the rigid squareness of his shoulders revealed how hard he struggled to dig for words.

He let out a breath. "Might there be a private room where Catherine and I could talk?"

My cheeks were hot and my hands were cold, for I had not recovered from seeing him walk away, nor did I like the look of him bringing along the basket as if he meant to be rid of all reminders and encumbrances of me.

To my surprise Kehinde rose. Hers was not a large or boisterous figure, but when she wanted to, she commanded any space she was in. She bent her gaze on him, and because she was a woman older than he was, he listened, lifting his chin as if he knew he was about to take a hit.

"I do not know you, Magister. But if it were up to me, I would tell Cat she is well rid of a man who speaks to her in such a contemptuous way. Was it imprudent and disruptive of her to leave the mage House so precipitously? Perhaps. But I am thinking you would be better served to discover why you did not pay more attention to her grievances before it came to this."

His expression darkened with an angry flush, but to my astonishment he took in and released several ragged breaths without any hammer of magic. With an effort he spoke again, clipped and impatient. "What must I do to be allowed to have a few private words with my wife?"

Kehinde indicated the table. "While I consider, perhaps you would like something to eat or drink."

Vai clenched his hands to fists, sucked in air, and let it out. He moved to circle the table so he could sit by me, but Rory stepped in his path. The two men sized each other up. Rory smiled in a friendly but implacable way. Vai took in and released more harsh breaths as a curl of icy breeze tickled the air. At length he sat next to Brennan, and Rory settled in on his other side, boxing him in.

A server brought ale, bread, butter, and cheese. Everyone except Vai and me ate and drank. His tight jaw gave his mouth a sneer, but I knew he was battling embarrassment and feelings of humiliation, for he was certainly conscious of how badly he appeared. I could scarcely bear to look at him, for my emotions surged and ebbed and boiled in a bewildering confluence. Every time I did glance at him, it was to find him staring at me...glaring at me...beseeching me...I simply could no longer tell, and perhaps he did not quite know either.

Finally I could bear it no longer. I buttered a hank of bread and held it out. "Gracious Melqart, Vai! Could you please eat something!"

He rocked backward almost off the bench. But when the others looked at him, he took the bread and ate it and, after that, downed a mug of ale and then ate from a bowl of porridge that Rory insisted he share.

After this agony of a silent meal Kehinde rose. "I have a meeting to attend this afternoon. Magister, perhaps you would be so good as to accompany me and my companions. You might find our radical per-ambulations of interest. I must warn you that it would be best for you to make no use of cold magic, not in the neighborhood we are going to. But your fashionable clothes will make a suitably stylish impres-sion. If you do not wish to accompany me, you are free to leave."

"Catherine," he began hoarsely.

Brennan tucked a hand under Vai's elbow. "Magister, I think you need to listen to what Professora Nayo Kuti is saying."

"Is Catherine going with you?"

Bee grabbed my braid to let me know she would yank my head off if I said anything, for apparently I was not to be allowed to go. No doubt they feared Andevai would lure me into an out-of-the-way cor-ner and melt me with kisses, but I was made of sterner stuff than that!

Kehinde indicated the others. "Brennan and Bee will accompany me. Chartji as well. That will give you an opportunity to discuss your business with your solicitor, will it not?"

For the space of five full breaths he stared at me, willing me to speak. Under the table Bee pressed a foot down on top of mine. Trapped between her hand and her foot, I said nothing.

He shook his head as if shaking off drops of rain. "Very well. If that is what is required. There are some lads out on the street watching my horse. Shall I stable it here, or take it along?"

After it was agreed he ought to stable it, he went to make the arrangements. Rory and I carried the basket and leather bag up to the room.

Rory said, "They mean to leave me here so you won't be alone, Cat, 413 but I know how to handle Vai better than the others do. If you don't mind, I'll go with them."

"Maybe if we had handled him less and kicked him more, he might not so easily fall back into his unpleasant old habits."

"I don't know," mused Rory, "for I am sure he stopped himself from saying at least eleven cutting and cruel things just now. That he sat there and let them dictate to him shows he is listening, however little it may seem to someone who does not know him."

"How do you know people so well, Rory?"

He smiled. "People are easy to know. Human-people are emotional and hierarchical. Feathered-people are inquisitive and acquisitive."

I rested my head in my hands. "What are our kind of people?"

"I just enjoy being here." He patted my shoulder. "As for you, Cat, you are always struggling with all the different parts of you. You have your mother's loyalty and strength, and your stepfather's bold curiosity and love of stories. You have our sire's instincts, which is why you like to hunt and fight and be petted, but it's also why Vai can melt you with kisses when you really ought to be pushing him back a step so he can stop and think. I expect that in the mage House, the more he sensed you were uncomfortable and displeased with a situation he was increasingly attracted by—being heir—the more he exerted himself to please you in other ways."

"I suppose you're right."

"Of course I'm right!" He kissed my forehead.

Left alone, I apologized to the cacica as I lifted the skull out of the basket and made an offering of the last of the ale, when she ought to have been offered the first. The leather bag disgorged my wonderful riding clothes and boots, a sewing kit Vai had obviously obtained knowing I would want it, and my toiletries. The sight of these items wearied me beyond measure because they forced me to contemplate a life without Andevai. I lay down on the bed and promptly dozed off. Voices frayed in my dreams, only to dissolve into a remarkably erotic dream that woke me sweating.

The room was dim. Beyond, the tavern buzzed at full pitch. Knowing there were trolls about, I left my sword tucked under the mattress. I wrapped myself in shadows and crept downstairs. Twilight danced into evening. Lamps burned everywhere. I spotted Vai and the others as they walked in and washed up at the altar set out for ablutions and offerings. They settled at a table set up in an alcove at the far side of the trolls' courtyard, tucked next to the archway that led out to the street and thus as far from the kitchens as possible. A lamp set at Chartji's left arm lit the table. Something about trolls throttled Vai's cold magic around them, just as dragons had.

Vai had his back to me, so he did not see me pad up behind them. Such breeze as there was blew into my face, so Rory, sitting beside Vai, could not smell me. Vai was laughing at something Rory had just said. His sociable demeanor made him seem another man, the one I had gotten to know in Expedition, the one whose embraces I cherished, the one I loved.

"Show me the ice lenses again," said Kehinde with a pleasant smile she had certainly not displayed earlier. "I'm amazed Chartji brought them all the way from Havery packed in straw and moss and they did not melt."

He fished out three leather cords and pulled one off over his head, handing it to Kehinde. "This one is likely flawed, but the other two should work."

"Does the mansa know about the ice lenses?" Bee asked sharply.

He glanced down, shoulders tensing. Rory nudged Vai with his knee.

"No, the mansa does not know," said Vai stiffly.

"Are you going to tell him?" Bee pressed.

His chin came up, but remarkably his voice remained level. "Not yet. If I have to face James Drake, I will need the ice lens. And I plan to face him. All of you realize, don't you, that allowing Catherine to go after him is a death sentence for her?"

"Having seen Cat in a fight—" began Brennan.

"Catherine can certainly take care of herself in a fight. Or against an ocean full of sharks, for that matter. You simply do not comprehend the dangers of dealing with a fully fledged fire mage. Drake almost killed her once. Lord of All, Beatrice. You ought to know better! You saw how she was burned."

"It's true," Bee muttered.

Kehinde twirled the lens as she examined its icy gleam. "May I touch it, or will the warmth of my skin distort the lens?"

"That one is flawed, so it makes no matter if you touch it."

She ran a finger along its curved face. "How do you keep them from melting? I can speculate on several mechanisms, but I am no cold mage."

"I mean no offense by saying the secret belongs to those who remain silent."

"In fact," she replied with a touch of asperity as she handed it back to him, "Professora Alhamrai sent me a paper in which she detailed the manufacture and results of your experiments with ice lenses in detail."

He slipped it back underneath his clothes. My hands twitched, wishing to follow its path along his chest. "It is still not my place to speak of it. I just want all of you to see that I am not withholding crucial information from you. Is Catherine not to join us for our meal?"

"We may all wish to say a few things to you before we invite Cat to join us," said Kehinde.

"I certainly do," remarked Bee with an ominous smile.

"Yes, I'm well aware of your—" Vai broke off to look heavenward, as if the Lord of All might grant him the patience and calm he so sorely lacked. He splayed his hands on the table to brace himself. After sucking in several short breaths he took in a deep breath, let it out, and addressed Bee directly. His tone was as taut as a strung wire. "I acted in an insupportable manner. In fact, I was an ass. May Catherine join us now?"

"You are impressively persistent, I'll give you that," said Brennan. "Rory, go and ask—"

"I've not yet said everything I mean to say," interrupted Bee.

"Nor have I," said Kehinde. "What Catherine chooses is up to her. But I have something to say to you, Magister. If I had not seen you this afternoon in a far more convivial light, I would have called you irredeemable. It was an illuminating decision by Rory to take you to the carpenters' guild. You spoke well, and treated those humble men with respect. That gave me a different opinion of your character. You are a man of immense power and prestige. At your young age you are heir to one of the most powerful lineages in Europa. If you thereby feel this gives you the right, or perhaps more correctly the *need*, to treat others with contempt, then I believe you must examine your own self. And to speak so to a woman you claim to love...oh! When I was fifteen—"

Brennan got up to take a turn around the courtyard. Kehinde kept speaking, although her eyelids flickered as she forced herself not to watch him go.

"—my illustrious family married me to the son of an extremely wealthy man. He was at the time of the marriage somewhat older than Magister Diarisso, a man of the world with no patience for a quiet and sheltered girl who wanted only to please him. He still uses that tone to speak to me although we have been married for twenty years and I have gained a position of prestige through my scholarly work and writings. He now has two younger wives to fix his caustic nature on since I am so much abroad. I cannot but think ill of a man who feels it is his right and even his duty to treat other people with disdain."

His shoulders had been lifted and tight, but they eased as he absorbed the blow.

"I thank you for your honesty," he said in the tone of a man who has just been told his chest must be sliced open with a butcher's knife in order for a poisonous thorn to be extracted.

"What I want to know," said Bee, "is the whole of your intention in accepting the mansa's offer to make you heir. What could possibly have induced you to say yes when you know what the mage Houses are? Do you feel no shame that you courted Cat in part by expressing radical sentiments that quite go against everything the mage Houses stand for?"

Seeing that Bee was speaking, Brennan returned and sat down as Vai answered.

"What choices do people truly suppose I have? The perilous journey Catherine and I took from the ice to Sala in the dead of winter was salutary lesson enough, had you been with us! Why do you suppose mages have had to band together to live? How am I to manage without a mage House to protect me? I can't go back to Haranwy even if I wished to, for the village cannot survive if I am continually putting out their fires. No matter how much your kin love you, they must drive you out when your cold magic blooms. At best, you might hope for a little cottage with a hypocaust set away from the village in isolation, but most do not have the means or skill to build and maintain such a place properly. Although I can manage for several days in very cold temperatures without heat, Catherine saw what it does to me if I go too long without rest. Add to that the hatred and suspicion people feel toward cold mages. A man has to sleep."

He looked at them each in turn.

"As Catherine knows, I would be dead if not for her. She braved the spirit world to rescue me, as I knew she would." His back straightened as his head came up. The line of his neck had an elegant beauty visible only from the back, not that I was noticing such a thing at a time like this. "If the Master of the Wild Hunt could not keep us apart, then I don't see how you people can hope to."

"I think you are the one keeping the two of you apart," retorted Bee. "Don't change the subject. I am not yet satisfied with your answer."

But he now walked on ground where he felt confident. "What I am trying to say is that mage Houses exist for a reason. That they have abused their privileges is not the same thing as saying they ought to be abolished. Rather, they should be confronted and reformed. As for the rest, there is my mother to consider. I do not need to defend my actions in seeing her placed in a position of honor where no one can scorn or harm her and where she may receive the care she deserves. But I do see it is impossible for Catherine. She said long ago that she does not belong in Four Moons House, and it is true in ways I could not bring myself to accept when the mansa made me his heir. It will take much work and time for me to change the nature of the House enough that she can find a place alongside me. I thought I could easily make it palatable for now..." He pressed fingers to his eyes, then lowered them. "I was thinking more of my own triumph than her struggle. I let my pride go to my head, as I will no doubt do again someday—"

"Tomorrow," Bee muttered.

"—but I know it is my weakness."

"In truth, I think your vanity is your weakness, not your pride," added Bee. "The mansa pandered to your vanity by elevating you to become heir. That is how he captured you. In a way, he still has you trapped, for you speak of nothing now except how you will change the mage Houses and not how the mage House might change you."

"I think you have all made clear to me my faults," he retorted. "I need only apply to you, Beatrice, to be reminded of them!"

"You can be sure I will be ready to comply!"

418   "You're both right in part," remarked Rory, before the exchange

boiled over, "but your worst weakness, Vai, is that you are secretly a little ashamed of where you were born. If you were not, then nothing they say would matter. You are not comfortable in your skin."

Vai stared at Rory. A kind of shudder ran through his body, not so much physical, and yet as profound as at a blow that struck him to the heart. He shielded his face with a hand, hiding his expression, head propped on hand and elbow propped on table. I held my breath, yet not a touch of icy angry air sullied the humid evening heat.

Bee considered Vai with a thoughtful frown. Brennan was staring at his hands. Kehinde was nodding. What Chartji thought I could not guess.

Rory grinned around the table as if the somber mood had finally rubbed his fur the wrong way. "Is that not a clever way of phrasing it, coming from me? Comfortable in his skin?"

Brennan chuckled in the manner of a man desirous of any excuse to laugh.

Lowering his hand with a sigh, Vai looked at Chartji. "Have you anything to add to this litany of my faults, Chartji?"

"It is clearly a fascinating discussion for you rats," said Chartji, "but I am more interested in the case you wish me to bring to the law courts."

Brennan saw a man with a tray and waved him over. "I think we can now send Rory to ask Cat if she wishes to join us."

"No need to send anyone," said Vai in his smuggest tone. "She's been standing behind us the entire time."

Bee squinted into the darkness. "Cat? What a frightful spy you are, dearest!"

I waited until Brennan had spoken to the server and sent him off before unwinding the shadows.

"That is truly astounding," said Brennan with a startled smile.

Kehinde asked, "Has anyone ever studied you, Cat? There must be some explanation for how you can do that. Were you taught, or did you teach yourself?"

Vai rose to give me a place to sit next to him. He was staring at the ground, lashes shadowing his lovely eyes. When I hesitated he looked up, and I could not breathe. I saw exactly how it would go if he and I were left alone. I took a place next to Kehinde, facing him. Vai sat with   419 a resigned smile, but when a stout meal of mutton stew simmered in wine, pears poached in brandy, and fresh bread arrived, he ate just like anyone else and looked at me only ten or twelve times that I noticed, for every time I glanced at him he was watching me.

"If you apologize to him for leaving the mage House, I shall kick you," Bee said under her breath as I savored the moist meat, turnips, and carrots. Beneath the table the toe of her boot nudged my shin in warning.

"This seems to me a conundrum, Magister," said Kehinde. "Are you a radical or a cold mage?"

" 'He who tries to wear two hats will discover he does not have two heads.' That is what I have had to consider, is it not? I am a cold mage whether I wish to be or not. But why should I have to choose? It is not that mage Houses cannot exist in a just world, but that they must change. For example, the princely law courts are often used merely to stamp and seal the wishes of the prince and his noble kin. But that does not mean law and courts are not necessary, or cannot serve justice. Chartji and I have discussed how to use the law courts to challenge clientage."

Bee shook her head. "Every prince has his own law court. Furthermore, the mage Houses need not bow before princely law because they rule themselves and their lands as if they are princes. That does not even take into account the various different legal codes of the empire of Rome, the Iberian city-states, the Oyo kingdom that Kehinde comes from, and all the rest. Camjiata's legal code is meant to supersede all these individual local codes into a universal civil code that addresses specific natural rights."

"There is much to favor in the general's legal code," agreed Vai. "But when he dies, the princes and magisters who were forced to comply by force of arms will revert to their old ways. The princes who have already thrown their lot in with Camjiata will hope to avoid the legal implications of his civil code, thinking they can escape the provisions that shift their power and privilege most. Furthermore, the Iberian city-states that have banded together to support Camjiata's imperial enterprise will want a reward if he wins. When he dies, do you suppose the Iberians will go home so easily? They have hated the Romans for centuries—"

"For good reason," said Bee.

"—and may even draw all of Europa into a war between these two powers. How do you think your own people will fare, Beatrice?"

"I would suppose my own Kena'ani people are already working for Camjiata. The motherhouse of the Hassi Barahal family lies in Iberia, in the city of Gadir."

"That is my point. Even if Camjiata brings peace for a time, it will dissolve. Even if he puts his legal code in place across much of Europa, when he dies there will be a counter-revolt against that code."

"But the mark will be made," she protested. "People's expectations will have changed."

"We have a scheme to bring suits claiming that clientage goes against the natural right of every person and community to possess their own selves," said Chartji. "We will file suit in the courts of every prince, duke, and city-state. It will be remarkably interesting to see how each different case proceeds compared to the others, and what repercussions they have in each locality and then, in the larger arena, on each other."

Bee shook her head again. "Legal cases can take years or decades to proceed!"

"So can wars," said Chartji.

Vai nodded. "Change must come from all sides. Change is not a rope, a single line that you pull on. Change is a net. Or anyway, that is what Kofi always says."

He addressed his next words to me. "Maybe it is true I forgot my promise to Kofi a little because I was so dazzled by what the mansa offered me." He sat back to address the entire table. "But we all want the same things."

"The best strategy is to play them off each other," I said as I fiddled with the hem of my jacket, since I was too anxious to sit still. "They can't both end stronger than they have begun, because they desire only victory, and thus risk defeat. But if they are both weakened, that leaves opportunity for the humbler parties to rise."

Bee propped her chin on clasped hands. "That is why I stay with the radicals. Besides being a good orator, I can sometimes help people avoid arrest and know the safe places to hold meetings."

"I do support the radicals," said Vai, "and I can do so most fruitfully within the mage Houses. If Camjiata wins, he will need cold mages. I am therefore in a position to negotiate for how the Houses will cooperate with him afterward. If he loses, I can influence the mage councils when they are weakened and unstable because of the conflict. Either way, there will always be mage Houses. No matter how much you shake the boat, it will not turn over. We have to hold on to tradition but also allow it to change where it must."

"We have long wished to place a powerful agent within the mage Houses," said Brennan, "and this is honestly more even than we had hoped for."

"It might work," said Bee reluctantly.

Heart heavy, I looked down at my hands, for I knew Vai was right, that by training and temperament he belonged in the mage House, and I regretted it.

"May I speak to Catherine alone, please?" he asked, exactly as if he were a courting man requesting permission from my elders.

"Don't involve me in this," said Brennan. "I've already heard more than I feel I ought."

"It must be Catherine's choice, not ours to make for her," said Kehinde.

"I don't trust you with her," said Bee.

I frowned. "What do you think he's going to do? Kiss me?"

Rory laughed.

Bee rolled her eyes. "That's exactly what he's going to do. Instead of using reasoned words and rational arguments, the kind you would once have insisted on back when you were sensible and heartless, he will use kisses to seduce you back into his arms."

Ignoring her, Vai addressed me. "Seeing that the hour was late when we returned, I acquired a room for the night. We might speak privately there if you will, Catherine."

The axe blow of Bee's gaze struck me full on. "You who so proudly claimed at the academy that you did not fall in love with every handsome face you encountered! Now I look at you and despair!"

Vai's slyest smile crept light-foot onto his lips. "You can't possibly believe she could encounter a handsomer man. So by that logic, she is safe."

"Enough!" I got to my feet as Bee sputtered more from laughter than from indignation. "I will speak to you, Andevai, if only to spare 422 the others any more of this."

"Chartji," Vai added as he stood, "we need to be ready to take legal action as soon as an auspicious opening presents itself."

She whistled a few colorful notes. To my surprise he answered with a short melodic pattern. Her crest flared. Then she chuffed a laugh and flashed me a toothy grin. I made my good nights to the others, not that I felt at all flushed and self-conscious for leaving them in this way.

Vai had taken a chamber on the street side of the troll wing, a tiny room with a bed, a clothes rack, a dressing table and chair placed under the shuttered window, and barely enough room to turn around. The chamber was scrupulously clean, with fresh linen on the bed and plank floors still damp from being scrubbed. A basin, three pitchers of water, and a leather satchel rested on the table. A knock came on the door. Vai opened it to reveal Rory, who handed over the leather bag Vai had brought for me. Rory stepped into the little room to hug me, pressing his cheek to mine before letting go, then paused in the door to wish us a peaceful night.

Vai lifted an eyebrow as with a question. Rory rubbed a hand over his lips in a way that reminded me of a cat grooming with a paw, and then smiled and shut the door.

"I can't sleep on the other side of the tavern, for I would put out all the fires," Vai remarked as he set the bag under the clothes rack. "I had to ask them to take out the nests and arrange the room for rats." He untied his kerchief. "They all expect me to use my wiles and caresses, but as you know, Catherine, I have practice in denying myself what I most desire."

"Do you? At the mage House, I began to think what you most desired was the flattery and the attention of the other magisters and noblemen."

"Was I that unkind to you?"

"You weren't unkind. You were too kind. You were a little condescending. And you refused to see what was going on all around you."

He shrugged out of the cutaway jacket and tossed it with the kerchief on the bed. "You know I will not force you to stay in a place that seems to you a prison. I admit I could not hear your complaints because I was too overwhelmed by my victory. But Lord of All, love, you might not have chosen such words to shake me."

He meant the accusation I had thrown after him. "I spoke my worst fear, that you would become one of them."

With a frown he wedged the back of the chair under the latch and sat on it to wrestle off his boots. "I am one of them."

"You are not like your tormenters!" I sat on the bed, searching out the words I wanted to say without beating him over the head with them. "You are vain, my love. And you stand a little high upon your pride. I think Rory is right, that you are a tiny bit ashamed of where you come from and who your mother is, and then naturally because you are at heart a good son and a good man, you are ashamed of being ashamed."

He set the boots against the wall, not looking at me, but I knew Rory's words had made an impression on him. I also knew that as much as he struggled to control his worst impulses, he would never be a restful person to deal with. Rather like Bee, no matter what she thought about herself! Yet he had come back to face censure rather than walk away to a life he could easily lead without me.

"I do see what is going on among the mages, love, but that does not mean I will let it deter me. I never did before, and I will not now." He examined me in the most searching way. "I do see you cannot live within the mage Houses as they are currently run. Even if I asked you to, I see that you will not. What do you mean to do, Catherine?"

"Kill James Drake. Camjiata believes he controls Drake, but Drake must be using catch-fires. If Drake becomes as powerful as Queen Anacaona, do you believe he will behave as she did, with respect for the law and the ancestors? What will happen to the general's legal code then?"

He held my gaze. "You must promise me you will not challenge him unless there is absolutely no risk to you."

"Like stabbing him in the back?"

"You have no way to defend yourself if he uses you as a catch-fire!"

"Even fire mages have to sleep. Of course I will be prudent."

"It would be the first time," he muttered. "I would feel better if you took Rory with you to watch your back."

"I will. Vai, you must promise me you will not become the mage the mansa wants you to be."

"I will not become that man. No matter how it may seem, I have
424   had no change of heart. It always has been Kofi and the radicals of

Expedition I stand with, since the day I met him. Just as it has always and only been you for me, Catherine, from the moment I saw you. But above everything, you and I must trust each other."

Let kisses fall where they may: Desire may flourish or wither in the space of a breath. Trust is a rock that will withstand every storm.

I extended a hand. He took it between his. "I give you my trust, Vai."

"Always," he echoed. Releasing my hand, he rose to begin unbuttoning his waistcoat. "But next time, love, warn me beforehand so I can be prepared, or we can work out some better scheme."

The practiced way his fingers worked the rounded pearl buttons distracted me.

"Catherine? Had you something to say?"

"Oh! Yes. Why not tell the mansa I escaped so as to prove what a valuable spy I can be?"

"Why would they believe such a story?" He tossed his waistcoat on top of the jacket.

"They won't know for sure, will they? If the mansa truly means you to be his heir, then he must allow you to prove yourself. As an explanation, it may serve to put them on the defensive..."

As he pulled off his shirt, I forgot what I was going to say.

"Go on," he said.

At the dressing table he poured water into the basin and set in on his evening ablutions, washing his face and teeth and then using a damp cloth to wipe down his bare torso. In the midst of this he paused, wrinkling his brow as he pretended to be puzzled by my silence.

"Catherine? Had you more to say?"

A wave of aggravation swept me. Curse the man for being so attractive. "Andevai, those are gorgeous clothes and you look very handsome in them...or out of them...but if you do not hang them on the clothes rack they will get creased and rumpled."

He pulled me up off the bed and into his arms with such strength that my toes briefly left the ground. He was not minded to be subtle or coaxing or patient. I floated, the heady pleasure of his kiss like ambrosia, as it always was.

When we paused he spoke in a murmur against my cheek as his hands began to wander their familiar paths. "What makes you think I care?"

I slapped his hand. "Of course you care! Anyway, I can't bear to see such expensive clothes treated so carelessly. I shall do it, if you will not."

He sat us on the bed and undid the double row of buttons on my cuirassier's jacket. "Very well. Did you repair this, love? This is what you were wearing when you were shot. I would have thought it must have been cut off you."

"I did not want to throw away what they had almost ruined. It felt too much like defeat."

"It's beautiful work, making something new out of what was torn."

"They always think they are about to defeat us. For so long we have been at their mercy." I grinned. "But now we are going to fight back."

"Truly, now we can." He slipped me out of the jacket. "Only your bodice beneath! I see you have not forgotten the Expedition style of dressing, for I must say that you in a simple bodice and wrapped skirt waiting tables on a hot night is what I love best, however beautiful you look in your other clothes. Or out of them."

He undid the lacing on my bodice. The white pucker of scars on my shoulder he kissed as he began on the fastenings of my skirt.

I reveled in the caress of his lips on my neck and the playful wandering of his hands. "Vai, this is no time for me to risk becoming pregnant. Do you have...?"

"No need, love. Rory gave me the sign that you're not fertile right now."

I pulled out of his arms. "You and Rory have a *signal arranged*?"

"If you'd rather not, we shall stop here." By the crinkling at his eyes and the wry cut of his lips, he was laughing silently at me. "I can sleep on the floor."

"You will not be sleeping on the floor!"

"In truth, although I am sorry to have to say this to you, every night at Two Gourds House I returned ready to tell you everything that had happened. But you would drag me to the bed first and make it clear what you wanted before I even had a chance to talk. Naturally, given our exertions, I would fall asleep afterward. Then I was always called away early before we could converse at length."

"That's not how it happened!"

"It is!"

Blessed Tanit. Maybe it had been. "I was so very bored all day long."

His smile faded as he leaned forward to embrace me. "I did listen to what they said to me, love. I do hear you. I want you to know that, before we are parted."

"I know." I held him close, for the thought of tomorrow filled me with excitement at the challenge, and yet also with dread at leaving him and Bee.

"All will be well," he murmured, as if by sheer stubborn effort he could make it so.

I raised my lips to his and, after all, we forgot about the clothes until much later, at which point they were all rumpled and creased.

38

He was gone when I woke in the morning.

I hurriedly dressed and ran down to the courtyard to discover him in his rumpled clothes facing off with Bee across a table. A pot of coffee and her open sketchbook sat between them.

"Broken cups are little enough to go on," Bee was saying to him, tapping the sketch on the open page. It depicted a porcelain coffeepot and cups shattered into pieces around a tipped-over chair. Fortunately it was not the pot on our table.

I slipped onto the bench beside him, not sure of their mood because his eyebrows were raised and she wore a broody frown. His look acknowledging my arrival shared our night all over again. I smiled in answer.

Bee muttered under her breath, "Blessed Tanit, spare me," then, in a normal voice, "Do you really know what this is, Andevai?"

He looked at the sketch as his eyes narrowed. "I know exactly what it is. This is Gold Cup House at Lemovis. The Coalition army was retreating north out of Burdigala after we suffered a crushing defeat there. The Iberians were right behind us. The Coalition halted at Lemovis. The mage House called Gold Cup House lies at the edge of the town, on the river. The mansa and I went to them to warn them they should evacuate, because the mage House in Burdigala was burned to the ground during the battle, almost certainly by Drake. Even to that point, the mansa wasn't quite sure he believed me about fire magic. It's impossible to make people here in Europa understand, for all such magic has always been strictly contained and controlled by the blacksmiths."

"But wouldn't they notice when people died as catch-fires? When the mage House in Burdigala burned?" she asked.

"How do you distinguish a fire lit by a mage from one lit by tinder? In war, it is hard to believe in the deaths of catch-fires when dead people are everywhere. The mansa and I were having coffee with Gold Cup's mansa when Iberian skirmishers arrived in advance of Camjiata's main army. Drake specifically meant to strike at the mage House. He did not know the mansa and I were there. He threw his fire into Gold Cup's mansa, who was entirely unprepared to act as a catch-fire, and meanwhile set the whole cursed compound on fire. Children and elders trapped inside as if they were so much refuse!"

He looked away. Bee extended a hand to touch his arm, but she withdrew it and pressed her palm to her chest instead.

He shook himself. "That was when I discovered that to be a catch-fire is not just a passive thing, when the fire mage throws the backlash into you and you must endure it. In desperation, hoping to save the Gold Cup mansa's life, I found out it is possible to pull the backlash out of another person and into myself. Any cold mage can do it if they are strong enough. It was too late for the mansa of Gold Cup House, but working together the mansa and I were able to quench the fire. I am certain I almost got that cursed fire mage to burn himself up. Lord Marius had time to deploy his army on the best ground. It was a bloody battle, but against Camjiata, they say a draw is as good as a victory. Anyway, all that expensive porcelain shattered in just this arrangement when the old mansa toppled over. I remember it exactly."

"That's when the mansa named you heir, isn't it?" I said softly.

"Yes. That's when he finally believed me." He let out a breath. "Beatrice, I recognize the trust you have shown by sharing these sketches with me. I thank you."

"Most never mean anything to me. Yet the general could always find their meaning."

I shrugged. "So he claims. He could easily have guessed I would try to escape on a Phoenician vessel just as the tide turned that morning in Expedition. I suspect the sketches remind him of connections he then sews together. He doesn't need dreams for that."

"You're the last person who should be such a skeptic, Cat." She displayed a sketch of three hats: a half-crushed tricorn hat pinned by a badge in the shape of a lion's head, a fashionable shako like mine that was ornamented with peacock feathers, and a humble cloth cap with a shard of glass caught in its crumpled folds. "What can anyone possibly make of this?"

"The shako is what Camjiata's Amazons wear," said Vai. Under the table he hooked his foot around my ankle. "I thought the style would look well on Catherine. The lion's-head badge is the token of the Numantian League of Iberia, where Camjiata was born. The other is a farmer's cap."

"Yes, but what does it mean? Besides something to do with the war?" Bee refilled his cup and poured one for me. "Cat, dearest, do stand up and let me see those clothes. This isn't what you were wearing yesterday."

When I rose she examined my split skirt, jacket, and jaunty hat as Vai's somber expression lightened at her exclamation of delight.

"What a splendid outfit! I adore the shako, although I could never wear it. Goodness, Andevai, I shall have to ignore all your roostering about in the hope you will take me to a dressmaker and get me an entire new wardrobe, too. We are sister and brother now, are we not?"

He smiled. She smiled. A spark of connection flashed between them.

A server brought a bowl of porridge and a platter of bread as well as another pot of coffee. Rory plopped down, stifling a yawn, and waited for Bee to pour him coffee.

"Where are the others?" I asked as I dug into the porridge.

Bee said, "They have all left already for a meeting with the underground council of radical leaders. I'll follow after I have said goodbye to you, dearest."

Vai touched my hand. "We must go, love. I promised Lord Marius I would bring you to pour the wine at his midday dinner today."

"Did you?" demanded Bee. "Were all those fine speeches false coin, Andevai, just to make sure she would go back with you like a trophy on a rope?"

He met her gaze with a flicker of annoyance. "No. And you know they weren't, don't you? Maybe you just don't like that she is the center of people's attention for once, instead of you."

430   Rory looked up from his porridge. "I promise you, Cat, I will bite

their heads off if they do not behave, for it is a sunny day today and I am in too good a mood to have it ruined by their jealous posturing."

I laughed and, after a fraught pause, fortunately Bee and Vai did as well.

It was harder than I'd thought to leave Bee. Vai and Rory waited at the gate with the saddled horse and our gear.

"I wish I could come with you, dearest, as Rory can," she said.

"Camjiata will never let you go if he gets hold of you again, nor will the mansa. I do believe Kehinde and Brennan would let you walk away if you choose to do so."

"That is why I trust them." She bent a frown on me. "You must not let Vai bully you."

"He does not bully me."

"No, it's true, he doesn't. He fondles you with those sultry eyes. You're quite hopeless, Cat."

I took her hands. "Yes, but you do like him, don't you, Bee?"

"Gracious Melqart! What would you do if I said I did not?"

A quiver of fear made me cold, as if winter had kissed me.

"Oh, dearest!" She embraced me. "For your sake, I already love him. I suppose when we have a pleasant home with a hypocaust wing, I shall endure him well enough, and you and I shall have a private parlor with a stove where he is not allowed to enter." She laughed. "Cat! Your expression is quite confounded. He and I understand each other. The important thing is that he knows he has to maintain my good opinion, as he showed this morning. I respect his intellect and his rare and potent magic, which he has worked very hard to achieve. I do think he is a good man, and in ten years he may be bearable and in twenty he may even be likable."

"I suppose I deserved that for asking!" I said.

We both laughed, and I left her.

Rory, Vai, and I passed through Arras Gate, Vai leading the horse, and made our way down the boulevard toward the Lady's Island and the river.

"Nothing like family to keep you on your toes," remarked Rory.

Vai smiled in the irritating way he had when all his ill temper had dissolved as mist under the sun because he had gotten what he wanted. "Do you miss your family, Rory?"

"Me? Yes. But it wasn't to last, you know. Mother was already starting to look around for another mate. When she chose one, he would have driven me out, and I have no brothers to go a-roaming with. It's a lonely life to hunt alone. I like it here just fine. You're my brother now, Vai."

"So I am, Rory." Vai slipped a hand into the crook of Rory's elbow so they walked arm in arm. His easy, affectionate camaraderie with a man he trusted made me fall in love with him all over again.

They talked for a while of inconsequential things.

"You're quiet, love," Vai said at last, releasing Rory's arm and pulling me over next to him.

"Andevai, do you like Bee?"

Rory snorted. "That is a question I would tremble to answer were I you! For myself, I find her annoying, managing, and bossy. But I'm accustomed to such behavior from females."

Vai let go of my elbow and took my hand, just as if we were a courting couple in Expedition. "I love her like a sister. I realize her good opinion matters more to you than that of anyone else. She accepts that you love me. So she and I understand each other well enough. Why are you laughing, Catherine?"

I did not explain.

When we reached the forecourt of Two Gourds House, Vai was in a mood to throw his weight around. He demanded baths, food, horses, and a djeli to accompany us, as befitted his rank as heir. When I emerged refreshed, I discovered Rory in the entry hall lounging on a marble bench and surrounded by women. The highborn magisters who had scorned me in the women's quarters turned to me with an effusive friendliness that amused me. Would we return to Two Gourds House soon? Would my brother be staying with me? Was he married?

Naturally we had to wait for Vai, who appeared at length in fresh clothes. He rode alongside the djeli to converse on arcane matters of genealogy. Rory and I rode behind, with two grooms, two attendants, and two troopers.

"I must say, those women looked very bored," said Rory.

"I suppose they are. That's probably why they were so sour and unfriendly to me."

"I'll bet they would be up for some friskiness. You could let me loose there for a month and everyone would be much the happier for it."

I laughed. "I promise you, Rory, if we ever return there, I will certainly let you loose, just to enjoy the spectacle."

On the southern side of the river, the fields and pastures that lay beyond the city wall were crowded with the encampments of the Coalition army. An entire market had sprung up to serve the soldiers. I was glad to pass quickly through the market's sprawling, reeking, noisy clamor into the relative quiet of Lord Marius's command tent. The djeli walked in front, announcing our arrival with a song lauding Four Moons House and the exceptional nobility and formidable power of its mansa and the skilled magic and excellent cooking of its women. After this preface the djeli changed his tune. Singing with the very same melody Lucia Kante had drawn out of her fiddle, he detailed a brisk version of the battle of Lemovis in which Andevai's quick thinking and astonishing magic figured prominently.

Vai did not smile, but the man did develop a bit of a cocky swagger as we approached the waiting dignitaries. Not every man was announced with a song in his praise, although I wished the djeli did not insist on repeatedly referring to him in the Celtic way as "Andevai Hardd."

"Andevai the Handsome!" I murmured. "I shall have my work cut out for me, keeping your monstrous self-regard from swelling any larger than the bloated whale it already is."

He did not deign to look at me. "It's only conceit if it isn't true."

"Here are you, Andevai Hardd," said Lord Marius with a laugh, "just as you promised you would be. Apparently, I should not have doubted you, as some claimed I must."

He glanced into the crowd of men. The mansa of Four Moons House was not there, but his surly nephew glared, his lips curled in a triumphant sneer as he awaited Vai's downfall and humiliation. It was clear by the vulture-like expressions of the Roman legate and his tribunes that Vai had been the subject of discussion before we arrived.

We made our courtesies to the elders, the princes, the mansas, the Roman legate, and Lord Marius. Rory grazed down their ranks like a hungry saber-toothed cat through the succulent flanks of recently deceased cattle, being introduced, admiring their clothes and military adornments, making them laugh and putting them at their ease.

Vai addressed the company with a cool smile. "We had planned all

433

along to give a demonstration of how weak the defenses are at Two Gourds House and how thoroughly unprepared even the most skilled djeliw can be for one such as my wife. I did not realize she meant to act so soon, for as you must imagine a spirit woman captured from the bush can at times be a trifle wild and ungovernable."

The men chuckled, as Vai had meant them to. Their condescension was irritating, but it put them off the scent of his disgrace.

The mansa's nephew pushed forward. "You may all be intrigued by his success in holding on to such a freakish creature, but when a man's mother was born in a cart, he must be accustomed to living in the stable with the rest of the animals."

"Like all honorable men, I show respect to the mother who bore and raised me," said Vai with just the right touch of sternness. "As for your own envy, you'd have done better to apply yourself in the school-room instead of drinking, gambling, and whoring. Anyway, I don't see that you could have managed to win and keep such a wife even had you the courage and ambition to attempt the hunt."

"You were chosen to marry her only because the mansa did not want to waste a real man on a low marriage to a Phoenician girl who is merely a bastard with peculiar magic."

"You simply are incapable of comprehending the mansa's subtle mind." Vai nodded at Rory.

To my astonishment Rory stripped right there in front of every-one with an alacrity that needed no dreams of dragons to predict. When he was stark naked—and never the least ashamed to be so!—he smiled charmingly around the company and then looked at Vai. Given another nod, he changed in a smear of darkness from man to cat.

Of course there was a gratifying outcry as Rory prowled the tent's interior. He did look so lovely and magnificent, so sleek and powerful. The big cat padded up to the mansa's nephew and butted him so hard in the belly that the man tumbled onto his ass. No one laughed; they were all too cursed nervous.

Then the big cat turned around and sprayed him.

The harsh smell overwhelmed everything except the sudden silence. When Lord Marius burst out laughing, the rest felt free to join in. The mansa's nephew boiled up with knife drawn, full into the force of a

roar that shook the air and made every man stop laughing and cower.

All except Vai, who casually walked up to the cat and rested a hand on the beast's shoulder.

I approached Lord Marius. "My lord, I am truly sorry about Amadou Barry. Please remember that Bee did try to save him. I come before you to offer my services as a scout and spy."

He examined me, then nodded curtly. "You may pour the wine, Maestra Barahal."

Thus was my status restored. They were so enamored of their rank and privilege that they could not imagine I would reject it.

The men settled to places at the table. The mansa's nephew had to leave because he stank. Rory padded behind a screen and returned all dressed and smiling, to be offered a seat among the younger men, whom he quickly had eating out of his hand.

Lord Marius addressed the table. "Once the three legions out of Rome arrive, our Coalition will be too large a force for the general to defeat, whatever weaponry he carries in his arsenal. However, we suffer from a lack of reconnaissance. In the last months not a single scout has reported in."

The Roman legate gestured with his empty cup. "You cannot believe a woman spy can succeed where men have failed?"

"What have we to lose by trying?" asked Lord Marius. "It was a shepherd's wife who brought us news that Iberian skirmishers had been sighted near Cena."

The legate shook his head. "Camjiata's outriders can't have reached Cena so quickly. Such an ignorant woman most likely mistook our own skirmishers for Iberians. Women are not fit for war. More wine, Maestra."

As I poured, I smiled. "Do you think not, Your Excellency? I can easily sneak into the Iberian camp and out again without being seen."

He saluted me with his full cup. "A pretty young woman like you must always be seen and admired. The Iberians have stymied every attempt by the Coalition and our own imperial troops to spy. I cannot recommend you dress as an Amazon to infiltrate their camp because everyone knows the general merely entertains his troops with that battalion of prostitutes. No chaste, modest woman like yourself would wish to be associated with such unnatural creatures."

Vai tensed, surely preparing to defend my mother's honor. I shook

435

my head to warn him off replying, for I did not care one fig about the legate's opinion.

To my surprise Lord Marius retorted in a sharp tone, "You would not speak so if you had seen the Amazons smash the gate at the siege of Burdigala. One man will certainly out-grapple one woman, but train a battalion of women with soldierly discipline and superior rifles, and you will find them hard to break. I will never again speak slightingly of the Amazon Corps, let me assure you."

But just as I was feeling in charity with him, he turned to me, proffering a smile tinted with the prick of petty revenge. "I have a troop of skirmishers departing just now to scout south on the Cena Road. You can leave at once, Maestra. We will provide a kit for you."

Since I had brought my basket and cane, I could scarcely refuse. Maybe it was better to make the parting swift and sudden, for the pain of leaving first Bee and then Vai cut regardless.

We took a moment's privacy behind the screen. Vai clasped arms with Rory and released him. I thought he would kiss me, but instead he held my face in his hands as he whispered, "Return safely to me, my sweet Catherine."

I could not speak, for a throat-choking fear deadened my heart. Blind Fortune had us in her claws. Any terrible thing might happen.

We had to press on.

Rory and I left the tent at once to be given over into the care of a competent cavalry commander named Lord Gwyn, who was as white in complexion and hair as his name suggested.

Two main roads led south from Lutetia. To the east the Liyonum Road ran via Senones to the old city of Liyonum. The mansa had gone that way to meet the Roman army. Lord Gwyn and his troop rode down the central Cena Road past a fortified estate they called Red Mount, which overlooked the road and the prospect of the city walls a mile away. On golden fields, laborers were cutting hay. They measured our passing in silence.

We made camp for the night in a grove of trees.

I crept away to do my business in privacy, for the split skirt made riding easy but peeing difficult. As I was making my way back, I stumbled onto a footpath. Soft footfalls alerted me to the presence of someone else. A rushlight appeared, revealing a girl of perhaps sixteen years hurrying along with a sack slung over her back and her head down as she marked each fearful step.

I drew my shadows around me. That was why the soldiers did not see me when they stepped onto the path. "Here, now, lass, running away to meet a lover, are you?"

She bolted back, but a man stepped out on the path behind her as well. "What a pretty treat this is on a dark night!" he said in a tone I could not like.

She raised the feeble rushlight. "Don't come any closer! I'll burn you if you do!"

"With that little flame?" The threat brought gales of laughter.

"I'm a fire mage," she said stoutly, but her hand shook.

"Yes, we've all heard the rumor that the fire-stained can run to the general's army and make a new life there. You should have stayed home, lass, for we can't let you pass." They moved in on her.

I unwound the shadows. "Let her go on her way unmolested," I said.

Yet my appearance so startled her that she broke for the trees, and her mad dash so startled the soldiers that they jumped to attack. One grabbed her arm. She screamed and shoved the rushlight into his face. It blazed with a bright gout of fire that caught up into the leaves of the nearest tree. He shouted with pain and stumbled back.

Blessed Tanit! I knew I was too late even as I ran for her. She spun tumbling into the underbrush, keening and moaning and then abruptly silent. The rushlight guttered out. The flames in the branches died, but the smoky taste of her death lingered, for she was quite dead, killed by the backlash of her own untrained magic.

"Lord Gwyn sent us after you, Maestra," said one of the soldiers, grasping my arm. "You're not to leave camp ever, on Lord Marius's orders, unless the commander says so. Cursed little witch got what was coming to her, didn't she? Ragno's got a burn on his chin now."

"Let me go!"

He hesitated, grasp tightening, then looked past me. A black shape stalked the trees. It yawned to display saber teeth. The soldiers retreated hastily, and so did I, for there was nothing I could do for the dead girl.

She was dead because she had no catch-fire, no training, no chance   437 of a normal life. No wonder she had hoped to run away to the general's army.

Rory stayed in cat form all that night. At dawn he gifted me with a dead rabbit. In its own small way, the gesture was rather sweet, and seared over the campfire the meat was tasty.

Our troop moved south with skirmishers' haste, changing out horses, stopping at a village to commandeer sacks of grain from unhappy villagers before riding on. The soldiers treated me with propriety but their stares made me uncomfortable and Rory was in a constant state of half-leashed snarl. Lord Gwyn frequently halted to interview the locals. More than once he called a file of laborers out of the field and cracked questions over them as they stood with heads bowed, their surly anger like a cloud. They never had anything to say.

Another few miles south an old woman appeared, trudging with a bundle of reeds atop her head. She stopped stock-still, seeing the thirty soldiers and their horses. Then she saw the big cat.

"Salve, domine," she said with remarkable aplomb. "Lord of cats, what brings you here to this lonely community, riding with the prince's men?" With a wise smile she dropped her voice to a murmur. "Forty years too late if you chanced to wish to seduce me in your human body. For if you are as beautiful in your other form as in this one, I think I just might have let you."

Purring, Rory approached her cautiously and licked her hands. She smiled, then sobered as she eyed the soldiers and, with a frown, considered me alone among them.

"Do not fear us, old aunt," said Lord Gwyn. "Be on your way."

Rory escorted her past the troop and waited until she was out of sight before he loped after us as we rode on.

The blissful scent of summer lay everywhere. Ahead a tower and roofs marked the town of Castra. We clattered into town past well-tended buildings. People hurried inside and closed their doors. A small river ran through the middle of the town. After we crossed the bridge the soldiers led the horses to water. I walked downstream along the grassy bank, whacking at leaves. Birds warbled. An object spinning past on the silty green water caught my eye. I fished out a tricornered hat. One peak had been crushed. A badge in the shape of a lion's head was pinned on the felt.

With a shiver of misgiving I scanned the river. A white tassel flowed past, too far away to reach. A little farther downstream something had gotten caught in a bush that hung over the river: a sleeve trimmed with gold braid. I walked down and prodded at it.

An arm was still inside, although the hand had been blasted off, ragged bone shining. A dead man was caught in the branches. His face was bloated, his left eye was a gaping hole, and half his teeth were missing. Tendrils of black hair streamed out from his head, and he wore a white sash embroidered with the twin lions of Numantia.

I reeled back, gasping. Noble Ba'al! Death lay at hand, ugly and violent.

Yet my mind grasped the whole: Camjiata's army was somewhere upstream.

Lord Gwyn's shout carried from the bridge. "Can you cursed men not keep your eye on the girl?"

With no warning, volleys of rifle fire shook the air. Gouts of smoke rose all about the bridge as Lord Gwyn's skirmishers were attacked so suddenly that I stood in gaping confusion. Had the day not been peaceful just one breath ago, even the quiet corpse in its watery grave?

The battle raged in plumes of smoke, in the ragged cries of men hit and fallen, in the rumble of horses' hooves as survivors tried to escape the ambush. Rory raced up still in cat shape and shoved me with his head. Several men appeared on the other side of the river with rifles pointed right at me. They wore the same uniform as the dead man: Iberians! I pulled the shadows around me. Shot peppering behind us, Rory and I bolted through the dirt paths and fenced gardens of the outskirts of town. A cart track lay empty but for a solitary bird hunting for bugs. The shooting ceased. Crows flocked overhead, heading for the battleground.

We broke onto an empty pasture recently mown. Drying grass lay in raked strips along the uneven ground. A bird whistled in a lovely waterfall of song. Another bird chirruped four discordant notes. The skin of my neck prickled. Rory halted, ears forward. I slipped my cane from its loop.

We trotted across the pasture toward a towering shrub riddled with orange flowers. All was peaceful until a brightly plumaged body burst out of its branches, as tall as me, talons gleaming.

I leaped forward to whack the creature on the head. With a clicking stutter, it fell back as I fell back. We panted, at a momentary standstill, staring at each other.

A dancing spin of tiny mirrors and shards of polished metal flashed in my eyes. The feathered person stood clothed in a mimicry of a soldier's uniform weighted with shards of all the shiny things its kind loved. It flashed a bold yellow-and-red crest as it opened its muzzle to grin with predator's teeth, like a shark giving you a moment to accept that you've been honored by being chosen for its next meal.

Blessed Tanit protect me! Gracious Melqart give me strength! Noble Ba'al grant me wisdom!

It lunged for me.

Rory leaped. He smashed right into the troll, and they rolled, crashing through the brush. Orange petals spun in a cloud of color. I pulled shadows around me and ran after them. The troll snapped at Rory, who dodged aside to rake at the troll's flanks with his wicked claws. It stumbled. Its fluid whistle pierced the air, answered by a click and whistle. Blessed Tanit! Of course they never went anywhere alone.

As the troll whipped around to slash at Rory, I smacked it right over the eyes. Staggering back, it retreated with nostrils flaring, momentarily blinded.

A stab of reflected light cut across my face. Rory faded into the brush as two feathered people crept out of the trees about twenty paces apart, in hunting formation. The way they had of bobbing their heads as they swept the scene crawled a shiver down my skin. The blinded one whistled and clicked to them, blinking as it recovered. I held steady. Even in daylight and entirely exposed, my shadows hid me from them, and right now the wind was behind them so they could not smell me either.

They raised mirrors. Where these glances of light lanced across the field, they cut the threads of magic that bind the worlds. My shadows shredded into fraying ribbons whose ends I could not furl about myself. Whistling, the hunters stripped me of my concealment as they fanned out. One lashed its paddle of a tail as in a prelude to attack.

Yet the mirrors also cut right through the binding that made my sword appear as a cane in daylight. Freed from its net of shadow, the ghost hilt flowered into solidity. I grasped the hilt and drew my cold steel blade out of the spirit world and into the mortal world.

All three stopped dead in their tracks. Judging by their feathering and size, two were female and one male. They looked me over first with one eye, then the other, and then full on. My throat tingled, anticipating their bite.

"It's very shiny," I said, raising the blade as in salute. Their heads swayed as their gazes raptly followed the movement of the sword. "But don't think you can take me easily. The spirit of my mother is bound into this sword."

I turned and raced into the trees, thrashing through undergrowth in a rattle of noise, then stumbling unexpectedly onto a bushy verge along a major road. I was pretty sure we had found our way back to the main road to Cena, but I could not be sure. Rory nudged up beside me. He had a shallow graze on his right flank but nothing serious.

We crept forward through the grounds of a little roadside temple dedicated to the patron of travelers, Mercury Cissonius with his rooster and goat. Not a single priest attended the altar. The basin for ablutions had been overturned. Six corpses sprawled on the road, buzzing with flies. Their pockets had been turned out and their weapons and kit ransacked. I found Lord Gwyn, quite dead. Worst, one man's face was half ripped off as by the slashing bite of a big predator. A humble farmer's cloth cap lay on the ground, pierced by a shard of glass.

A thundering rumble rose and faded. A bird whistled in a waterfall of notes. Four trolls pushed out of the woods and onto the road. A fifth and sixth appeared on either side of the god's statue in the temple. We were surrounded.

No wonder no scouts or spies ever returned. Camjiata was using the feathered people as skirmishers to protect his lines and hide his army's movements. I braced myself for their attack as Rory hissed beside me.

A gust of wind rattled the branches. A drum rhythm paced through the woods. On its beat I heard a woman's voice call out a verse, answered by a chorus of women singing the response.

Man try to give yee money, what can he get?
He can't get nothing. Especially no kiss!

441

"Wait!" I said, brandishing my sword. "Look!"

They slewed their heads around. We all looked south to a bend in the road.

A column of soldiers marched into view, although they were almost dancing, so proud and mighty were they, and every single one a woman.

Four drummers led them while a fifth struck a bell, the drummers prancing and stepping on their way with every bit of flash and grin that any young man could muster. Their shakos were as jaunty as my own. All wore uniform jackets of dark green cloth piped with silver braid. Some wore trousers, while others preferred petticoat-less skirts tailored for striding. Most wore stout marching sandals laced along the length of the calf, brown legs and black legs and white legs flashing beneath skirts tied up to the knee. Four lancers walked in the first rank, tasseled spears held high, while the rest carried rifles and swords. A banner streamed on the wind: It depicted an antlered woman drawing a bow.

Amazons.

I took a step toward them before I knew I meant to. The rhythm beat right down into my heart. Was this not my inheritance as Tara Bell's daughter?

One of the djembe drums sang out a command. The other drums dropped to a waiting rhythm as the column halted in perfect precision. The woman holding the hand-bell caught sight of me, and she winked just as if she were flirting. Her smile had such a saucy cheer that I winked back.

A sergeant strode out to confer in a perfectly natural way with the trolls. She was short and stocky, Taino in looks but an Expeditioner in speech. After a discussion, the trolls gave a last and perhaps regretful look at my sword and bounded away into the trees.

The sergeant approached me, keeping her pistol leveled at the big cat. "What manner of traveler is yee, gal, for that shako give yee a bit of the look of an Amazon. Where came yee from? Yee cannot be local folk, for I never saw such a cat in these parts before this day."

"General Camjiata will give you a reward for bringing us to him."

She smiled. "Will he, now? Do yee mean to walk into headquarters

carrying naked steel?"

Reluctantly I sheathed my sword.

"*Cat!* Rory!" A tall gal streaked out of the column and slammed into Rory so hard that he staggered. She turned from him to embrace me. Tears glistened in her eyes. "What happened to yee? Did yee find Vai? I thought sure we should never see yee again!"

I gaped at her. "*Luce?* What are you doing here?"

Her joyful expression turned wary as she drew herself up defiantly. "Yee's not the only gal who can go adventuring. I enlisted with the general's army. I's an Amazon now."

"Trooper! Return to your place!"

"Wait, I beg you, Sergeant," I said. "This soldier can vouch for me and my . . . pet. She knew me in Expedition. I worked waiting tables at her grandmother's boardinghouse. Then I had to leave Expedition in order to rescue my husband. Which I did," I added with a glance at Luce.

"Yee don' say," said the sergeant with a narrowing of the eyes. "Is yee by any chance that maku what punched a shark?"

Luce laughed.

It isn't conceit if it's true.

"Why, yes. I am."

"Peradventure yee's come to join the Amazons, is yee?" She nodded at my cane. "Which yee cannot do if yee has a husband. Tch! No call to go wasting yee own self on a man, if yee ask me. Trooper, commandeer a cadre and escort her to headquarters, if yee reckon the cat is tame."

"Don' worry about the cat, Sergeant," said Luce, rubbing Rory's head as he purred most shamelessly. "He's easy to please."

The sergeant considered this display. With a shrug she whistled sharply. The drums rolled back into marching mode. We stepped off the road to allow the Amazons to pass. How they strutted with us for an audience, or maybe because they always did. I might have marched with them! But a different life had burst like an exploding cannon in my face, with its shrapnel of complications. Their life was not meant for me, and as they marched north out of my sight, a part of me regretted it.

39

Five gals peeled off from the column to gather beside Luce. They were strapping young women who looked as if they'd gotten bored of working in the factories or out on the farm and fancied adventure over marriage. I dug Rory's clothes out of my satchel and shook out a pagne as a screen. Behind the cotton cloth he changed and dressed, then stepped into view to the exclamations of the gals. He offered them his most promiscuous smiles.

"Rory, you can't just smile like that at strangers," I muttered.

"Why not? I saw you wink at that bell-playing woman!"

With a brilliant grin Luce took hold of his hand. "Here is Cat and Rory, the ones I have spoken so much of. We's to escort them to headquarters!"

She told us their names. The way the gals enthusiastically greeted us recalled me to the free and easy manners of Expedition gals, and how much I had enjoyed their friendship. We left the dead behind as crows descended to investigate.

Luce set a brisk pace as we walked along the verge, heading south. She had filled out, as tall as me now and with broader shoulders. With her black hair cropped short and a scar across one cheek, she had a piratical look that would have been at home on the airship with Nick Blade and the Hyena Queen. Carrying rifle and kit, she looked every bit the soldier, but I could not shake the girl from my mind. I could not stop myself from scolding her.

"How could you break your family's heart by running off?"

"Yee reckon yee get to have a heartsome beloved and run off to rescue him while the rest of us shall bide at home waiting? And meanwhile yee tell yee brother not to touch me so he say no to me while he go off with other folk? I's of age! Free to act as I wish! Especially after yee just left like that, just vanished, telling not a single person goodbye!"

"The opia *stole* Rory! I had to go after him!"

"'Tis always yee, Cat." She punched me so hard on the shoulder I staggered sideways as her comrades laughed. I was startled by how strong she was. "Yee punch sharks. Yee escape from Salt Island. Yee have a fine man to court yee despite the two-faced way yee treated him. Yee attract the notice of the commissioner of the wardens and of the infamous general, too! Young men came to drink at the boarding-house because yee was waiting tables and they all loved to flirt with yee, and women likewise, not that yee ever noticed Diantha's atten-tions in that way, did yee? Always, 'tis about yee! What was left for the likes of me? Yee know I love yee, Cat. Yee know I love me family. But I reckon I wasn' about to spend the rest of me life in me grandma's boardinghouse! Now I shall not!"

"Is this the sweetheart yee left behind?" asked one of the gals. To my surprise she indicated me.

"I'm Luce's sweetheart," cried Rory indignantly. "Aren't I, Luce?"

Luce sighed as at an old jest. Her comrades laughed.

"Rory," I said, "I believe that when a woman signs up to join the Amazon Corps, she swears an oath to engage in no sexual congress with a man for the term of her service."

"Oh!" He favored Luce with a sad smile that made her laugh with her old girlish delight, but a bolder, wiser look creased her smile now. "Well, then, Cat, that means you can't join the general's army, can you? For I'm certain you are not willing to give up—"

"Yes, yes, Rory. That's enough of that."

"If yee got Vai back, where is he, Cat?"

"He's being held prisoner by his mage House." I hated to lie to her, but I could not risk the truth. "That's why we've come. But tell me your story, Luce!"

The chance to tell her tale distracted her from my own. This grand and horrifying narrative beguiled me for several hours as we walked south. Files of infantry passed us in good order, mixed with cannon pulled by horses and the occasional baggage wagon. A column of   445

Expeditioners called out to the gals in a familiar way. A company of Taino soldiers marched in silence. Iberians strode along with a fierce demeanor, armed with rifles and their famous falcatas, the short swords that had driven back the first Roman invasion of Iberia two thousand years ago. Many tipped their caps to Luce and her cadre as a sign of respect.

We passed a lively column of pale Celts with lime-whitened short-spiked hair and their cousins and brothers of mixed and Mande blood wearing their dark hair in the same spiky style. "Here's to the heroines of Burdigala!" they called. "The drink's on us next time! And Rufus here wants his balls back!"

"We ate them already!" retorted one of the gals, to general shouts of laughter.

"Cooked or raw?" asked Rory, and they hooted and whistled in approval.

"What happened at Burdigala?" I asked.

"I must tell the tale in the order it happened so yee can comprehend the whole!" Luce said with a laugh, enjoying my rapt attention.

At a humble crossroads we turned east. Luce was finally telling me about the tumultuous siege of Burdigala. She had just related the thrilling episode of how Elephant Barca's skirmishers had arrived in the dark of night to take the Coalition from the rear—a source of crude joking among the gals that even made Rory blush—when we came into sight of the town of Stampae.

The town crawled with soldiers. What a flood of cannon and rifles and troops! A large encampment was coming down even though it was very late afternoon. Out beyond the camp lay freshly dug graves. Wounded soldiers leaning on crutches or with bandages wrapped around chests or heads waited stoically outside canvas tents marked with a caduceus.

Luce led us past an inn crowded with soldiers taking a drink or a piss, for the smell of urine penetrated everywhere. The town market hall had a marble façade and Roman-style pillars, while a low wall set off a dusty area where an outdoor market could be held. This expanse boiled with young women at exercises conducted with sticks the length of rifles.

Local men loitered at the fence. No one uttered a single teasing word or taunting call, although now and again a comment brushed up between them.

"Look at those shoulders! She must have wrestled bulls back on the farm!"

"Everyone knows women are a cursed sight meaner than men. I heard at Lemovis they plowed down a division of the crack Arverni militia, just crushed 'em. Cut their balls right off."

"We go around back," said Luce, rolling her eyes as her cadre hurried ahead. "If I shall have to hear one more idiot babbling about Amazons cutting off men's balls, I shall cut off his eggs just to prove 'tis no empty tale! I have heard that story a hundred times since I joined up! I wish they would just leave it be."

"It sounds very painful," observed Rory.

"'Tis not *true!*" she cried.

He frowned. "You don't love me like you used to, Luce. You used to purr at the sight of me."

She patted his arm. "That was a long time ago, Rory, and don' think yee kisses weren't delicious. But I've a sweetheart now, and anyway no time for men."

"How can anyone have no time for men?" he muttered, looking a bit peevish.

"Where is the general?" I asked.

"Why, this is the headquarters. The Amazon Corps is seconded to the command division. We's not regular army like the rest."

A woman dressed in the Amazon uniform and armed with sword and pistol emerged from the market hall with a brisk gait I recognized. Captain Tira changed course to intercept us. Luce and her cadre halted to salute.

"Washed up, did yee?" Captain Tira looked me up and down. She was a maku even by Europan standards, with sun-worn skin, hair as black as my own, and eyes that spoke of ancestors in far Cathay where, legend had it, a dragon emperor ruled. Maybe the stories were true! Whatever her origins, she was Camjiata's loyal soldier through and through. "Is the gal brought as a prisoner, or of she own wish?" she said to Luce.

"Of my own wish," I said.

"Yee shall come with me, then. Trooper, yee lot shall return to yee company. Dismissed."

Just like that, we were parted. Under Captain Tira's stern eye we dared not even embrace.

"Take care, Luce," I said, hoping my look spoke my heart.

"I shall find yee," she promised. They loped off, settling into a brisk jog.

The captain led us into the long, lofty market hall. By a tiled stove, the general sat in a chair receiving reports and visitors. Five clerks occupied a table, writing busily without looking up. A striking group they were: a Taino woman, a feathered person, an old Iberian man, a thin Celt, and a curly-haired Kena'ani scribe.

Seeing me, Camjiata rose in surprise. "Catherine Bell Barahal! One account had you eaten by wolves, while another said the opia had stolen you. Yet here you are, looking hale and hearty and in company with your mysterious brother. I am glad of it, for I would be sorry to know you were gone. But I see no cold mage, as I had thought to do. Nor is Beatrice with you." He examined me with a compassionate gaze that made me want to punch him. "Be sure you will always have a home with me if you are lost or bereaved or abandoned."

I had never met a man who could speak in such sentimental platitudes and yet have it sound so genuine and unforced. It was one of the most irritating things about him. Indeed, it irritated me so much that all the clever, cunning wiles I'd meant to weave fled straight out of my mind. "Do you have my father's journals? You stole them, just as you stole Bee's sketchbook!"

He dropped his gaze to the floor with a smile that made me instantly suspicious, as if he guessed the entirety of my plan. Then he looked up. "Have you come to demand them back? Or were you captured by my soldiers? What scheme have you in mind?"

"My husband has been taken prisoner by his own mage House. Rory and I escaped and have fled in the hope you will take us in and help us rescue him." As I spoke the words, I felt how false they sounded.

"What of Beatrice?"

"Her honeyed voice is raised on your behalf among the radicals."

"Raised on my behalf, but not in my presence. You would think she no longer trusts me with her dreams."

Never let it be said I could not think on my feet! "Her words prepare the way for you better than dreams!"

"It's true the Gallic towns and villages have proven more amenable than I had dared hope. I am sure it is due to the efforts of my radical allies agitating among the farmers and craftsmen and householders who will benefit the most once my legal code is proclaimed."

"To say laws are in place is not the same as having them enforced."

"Indeed, and thus our current conflict, no?" His Iberian lilt had gotten stronger.

"And another thing," I added. "Is Prince Haübey with you?"

"I would prefer to continue this conversation in a more private setting before—too late."

A frown darkened his face so quickly that as it smoothed into a neutral expression I wondered if I had mistaken it. I turned. Rory put a hand on my arm to hold me back as James Drake sauntered up the center of the hall.

"I couldn't believe what I just heard, and yet it is true. Cat Barahal! Washed up where she's not wanted."

He had a lovely woman on his arm. She wore a lemon-yellow gown trimmed with ribbons that looked fabulously well on her voluptuous figure, for she had the same sort of curves as Bee. Six soldiers wearing uniforms marked with the ship's mast of Armorica attended as an honor guard. Behind them swaggered four youths garbed in red dash jackets meant to look bold; two were girls, wearing skirts, reminding me of the girl who had died in the forest. Behind them shuffled six men weighted with heavy iron cuffs; they were uniformed in ugly jackets tailored out of a ghastly red-and-white fabric so ill cut that they made Drake look like quite the most fashionable man in the hall. Which of course he was, because he was wearing one of Vai's dash jackets, a gold damask that shone like flame. It was one of the garments Bee had been forced to leave behind when she'd fled the general's fleet in Sharagua.

I only realized I had taken a step forward when Rory yanked me to a halt.

In a murmur Camjiata said, "Not for that, Cat. Choose your blows wisely."

449

"That's an exceptionally lovely dash jacket, Drake," I said. "Too bad it doesn't fit you."

"This isn't the last thing that belongs to him I'll soon be slipping inside." He released his inamorata without a backward glance and had the gall to pace once around us, looking me over as if I were livestock for sale in the market. "You didn't appear at the standing inquiry in Expedition. So you were found guilty in absentia of the murder of the honored cacica. The sentence for murderers is life servitude in the cane fields or as a catch-fire."

A glamour of light pulsed as the unlit lamps along the walls flared. Folk murmured in awe and fear. They would have been even more frightened had they seen what I could see. A mist-like glamour writhed around Drake's body. Wisps like threads of spun light poured off him and created a lacework pattern through the lofty hall and into the six iron-cuffed men. One flinched, one cowered, one wept, and three stared with dull resentment. They all glowed as they channeled the backlash of his fire magic and poured it out of harm's way. In truth it was impressive to see how skillfully Drake parted the flood of his magic into six smaller streams, no one of them strong enough to overwhelm any single man.

My skin prickled. My heart beat faster.

"That's right, Cat," said Drake. "I now weave multiple fire banes as catch-fires. But I can still use you in the old-fashioned way, burning you up like kindling. No one will stop me because you're a condemned murderer. It would as easy for me to kill you as to take in my next breath."

The whisper of their magic stirred my blade. "I'm not unarmed."

Instead of stepping back prudently, he leaned closer. His unruly hair brushed my cheek as he whispered in my ear. "Neither am I. I'm training up an entire company of fire mages loyal only to me. Think of that before you taunt me. But if you kiss me, I'll consider allowing you to become my concubine instead of my catch-fire."

Rory snarled, causing Drake to startle back.

"You are too late, Drake. I have already been tried and acquitted by the Taino court of ancestors, in the spirit world." I swung the basket around and pulled out the skull.

Drake's nose wrinkled up. He brushed a finger along his clean-shaven chin, glanced at the pretty blonde, then looked back at me. "There is something very wrong with you, Cat. Put that skull away, if you please, for it does not impress or frighten me. Indeed, you do nothing but poke at people with your impertinent questions and your outrageous tales, and all to no purpose except to annoy."

He had never figured out that there was something odd about my answering questions with questions, not as Vai had immediately. Blessed Tanit! What an ass!

The thought made me smile mockingly, and of course my smile roused his temper.

"Enough! I am now wed to the daughter of the honored Armorican prince who is overlord of all the Veneti dukedoms. Such an honor is due me as a son of the Ordovici kings of old."

"The Ordovici kings of old? Of what are you trying to convince me, Drake?" I asked, for this boasting, defensive mood puzzled me. "That because you are highborn I ought to overlook your boorish behavior? You cannot think I regret the way we parted, or the choice I made."

He laughed nastily. "You'll soon be sorry you didn't take a princely crown when it was offered to you."

Camjiata stepped into the breach. "My steward has been at pains to signal that our dinner is ready to be served. Let us not delay the repast, for my command staff is waiting. Lord Drake, will you and Lady Angeline join us?"

She answered for Drake in a cultured, formal voice. "We would be pleased to join you, General."

She smiled soothingly at Drake—rather, I supposed, as Bee might say I sometimes smiled soothingly at Vai when he had climbed up onto his highest horse of intemperate disdain. Only, of course, Vai was no murderer. Was she a smart woman who had learned to manage him, or a frightened one eager to assuage his fits and starts? Her gaze flicked my way as she hooked fingers along his elbow.

"Come along, Cat," said Camjiata with an unusual hint of asperity. "I think you have made enough of a scene for the moment."

"Me?"

He steered me commandingly toward an interior door. In a side chamber, a table had been laid with settings. Eight people waited, expressions brightening with interest when they saw me and Rory, and 451 darkening when Drake and his bride—and the six catch-fires and the four young fire mages and the six soldiers—entered. Among the command staff I noted the one-eyed proprietor of the Speckled Iguana in Expedition, the man who had once fought alongside my mother at Alesia.

A woman stepped forward. She wore a sober brown skirt and jacket, fitted with a second cutaway sleeve on her left arm in the same green fabric and silver braid worn by the Amazon Corps. Her black skin was remarkably unlined considering her hair was half gone to silver.

"Proud Diana! You must be Tara Bell's child. Even with that hair and coloring, I would know you to be hers."

"Doctor Asante," Camjiata said, "I would like to introduce to you Catherine Bell Barahal."

She took my hands between hers and stared for the longest time in a way that made me dreadfully uncomfortable. Her dark eyes shone with unshed tears.

"You knew my mother?"

"I loved your mother very dearly, Catherine Bell Barahal. Besides that, I midwifed you into the world. Tara was weak from her terrible injuries. I trusted no one else to make sure she came through the ordeal alive. It was a frightful day." Her fingers tightened on mine. "Not that your life was ever at issue, for you came out squalling like so many cats fighting in an alley."

"You were there when I was born?" I repeated stupidly.

"Quite the noisiest newborn I have ever heard." She chuckled, then sobered. "I am glad to see you well, little cat, for I never heard of what became of you after Tara and Daniel fled."

"Yet now is not the time of speak of such things, Doctor," Camjiata murmured.

"Anyone would think you were trying not to anger Drake," I said in a low voice.

He casually stepped on my foot to silence me, then smilingly introduced me to his command staff, soldierly men with self-assured expressions. The one-eyed innkeeper was in reality the infamous Marshal Aualos, called by the Romans "the butcher of Zena." Captain Tira entered with a cadre of Amazons who arrayed themselves along the wall as the command staff took their places. Camjiata sat me at his left hand and Drake to his right. By the number of glances at the red-garbed youths and by Drake's smirking expression, I could tell the fire mage made everyone uncomfortable.

When wine was poured, Camjiata toasted the gathering.

"Here we have Captain Tara Bell's child, come to join our cause."

"And my bed," said Drake with a laugh. "Where is that cold mage, Cat? The one you claimed was dead, when in fact you spirited him away in order to keep him safe from me? Now you are come to spy for him."

"I came here to ask for help," I said. "He's being held prisoner."

"Which must explain why we have seen him riding with the Coalition forces. He quite spoiled my efforts to burn down the mage House in Lemovis. Do you think we're fools, Cat?"

Again, Camjiata's foot pressed on mine, unseen beneath the table.

It was a good thing he was seated between us.

"I think you are not in possession of all the facts," I retorted. "His family and indeed his home village is being held hostage for his behavior. He supports the general's legal code, but if he does not serve the mansa, they will all be put to death."

Drake's blue eyes sparked as a tendril of fire laced from him into one of the catch-fires. "If the general would release me to ride west, I would be happy to rid Four Moons House of its chain on Andevai Diarisso by burning the House to the ground. Then he need not be held hostage. Anyway, your excuses stink like lies. You can't possibly expect me to believe he was born into a rabble of unwashed, illiterate slaves. Or that he would risk his power and rank to help such people."

As he gloated, hoping to needle me into a burst of rash action, I watched the others. Marshal Aualos wore the blank mask of a man suppressing his feelings. Others—hardened soldiers!—looked nervous, as if they feared the whole chamber might roar into flames. Only Lady Angeline appeared unruffled. I admired the calm way she demolished her leek soup. I wondered if she, like Drake, found it so very unbelievable that a powerful cold mage could be born in a humble village.

Camjiata sighed. "Given that we have a war on, I thought we might discuss our plans. I believe that is the usual business of a command staff."

"In front of her?" Drake objected. "When she will certainly steal away into the night and spill every word she hears back to the mages?"

"The mages who tried to kill me, do you mean?" I retorted. "Truly, you have no idea of my history, to think I might ever wish to aid them!"

"I know something of your history, Maestra." Marshal Aualos broke in as if making a flanking movement to turn the tide of a skirmish. He had the breadth of a man gone stout with age but still packed with muscle, well prepared for soldiering. "Your mother was one of the best soldiers I ever served with. She was tall, like you, but heftier, very strong. Absolutely up to the mark in every way. But of course the Amazons always had to be better than the men just to prove they were fit for the task. Most folk in Europa say women ought not be engaged in war."

"If a war is being fought, surely women are engaged whether they wish to be or not. The only difference is whether they can defend themselves."

He smiled. "Spoken like your mother."

His words pleased me. "Thank you. As it happens, I read the words in my father's journals. The ones he wrote when he was collecting intelligence for his family in the service of the general's first war." I pressed my own boot atop Camjiata's rather harder than I needed to. He did not flinch.

"We may hope the daughter will prove as valuable as the father." Camjiata slid a glance at me that cut like a surgeon's scalpel. "As it happens, I left the journals at the Hassi Barahal house, in Gadir, with Daniel's next of kin. Yet some Hassi Barahals travel with the army, among my clerks and intelligencers. I'm sure my chief of intelligence will have some idea of how to make use of you."

Frowning, I stared at my plate. The moment of choice was upon me. Did I admire Camjiata's legal code more than I distrusted him? Did I stand with the radicals? Yes, I did.

I captured his gaze. "The Coalition army is camped outside Lutetia, under the command of Lord Marius of the Tarrant clan. A Roman army is marching north via Senones along the Liyonum Road, three legions in all plus a fourth already with the Coalition. Hard to see how you can defeat such an allied force."

"It is always hard to see victory if one does not have vision." His nod made me think he spoke in code, warning me, but he smiled impartially around the table. "My thanks, Cat. Your timely arrival and this intelligence gives us just the advantage we need at this juncture. Let us consider what this means. This army has the discipline and speed to reach Lutetia in two days' march. Our army is smaller than the combined alliance of Coalition and Romans. But if we reach Lutetia before the Romans do—something they won't expect we can manage—we can defeat the Coalition and immediately turn to face the Romans as they come up from the south. That gives us the advantage in both battles. Once we win Lutetia, I will proclaim the Declaration of Rights on the very steps of the prince's palace, where it was first proclaimed twenty-two years ago. My proclamation of a new and more expansive legal code will embolden many a prudent Gallic lord to abandon the Coalition and join our cause, just as it will rally the guilds and laborers and all those trapped by clientage to our side. Justice will be the reward gained by all."

"Now that I think of it," Drake said, "I haven't asked for any prize of war to this date, have I? All I want is the cold mage. I need him alive so he can acknowledge my long-awaited victory." He sipped at his wine with a musing smile. "People do feel envy when they must admit that another is better than they are. As your husband will soon discover."

Sadly, I laughed. I shouldn't have, but I did, nor did I trouble to hide my scorn. "Oh, he already knows he's better than you."

A thread of fire spun out of Drake and into me. Its heated touch made me gasp, half in fear and half with the cruel grasp of magic-borne lust. My fingers lost the strength to hold the utensils, which clattered onto the plate.

"Cat?" Rory pushed back his chair.

A second catch-fire shimmered, catching the backlash as one of the girls spun a candle flame above her cupped hand and took a threatening step toward Rory. He drew up short, to the girl's sarcastic laughter.

The girl hadn't Drake's finely honed control. Her catch-fire moaned, "It hurts."

"Stop it!" I shouted, leaping to my feet. My chair crashed to the floor behind me.

455

The sliced folds of roasted beef caught fire on my plate as heat scalded through me. I coughed, fumbling at my cane, for by the gods I would crack his head open before he killed me.

The heat ceased. The girl's dancing flame vanished. The catch-fire slumped to the floor, and not one person moved to help him. Yet I could not help but notice how Captain Tira had arrayed her soldiers, giving them clear shots at Drake and the four young fire mages. Lady Angeline cast me a look that would have murdered a lesser creature.

"Come now, Cat, don't make me angry." Drake brushed a strand of hair out of his eyes. "I just want you to watch when your husband begs me not to harm you because he's not strong enough to kill my fire. Or perhaps, better yet, when he's brought before me in shackles, and I ask you to choose between me killing him or you becoming my concubine for him to see."

I cast a disbelieving look at Camjiata, but he was watching Captain Tira in a fixed way that made me think he was ready to blink an order if need be. Melqart's Balls! Who was in charge here?

With curled lip, I addressed Drake. "Obviously to save his life I would do what I must."

"That would make you a whore."

"No, Drake. It would make you a coward. For this is the coward's way, to boastingly strut when there is no real threat to his own self." I turned my attention to the chamber at large, in disgust. "Have we played this scene for long enough? James Drake insults me, hoping to degrade me in your eyes, and I defend myself. Is there a hope for an end to this mockery? Or am I merely his latest victim...?"

I trailed off to let my thoughts catch up to my mouth. Fiery Shemesh! Vai had warned me to be prudent. But it was just so hard when Drake sat there lording it over them, him and his deadly fire magic and his young acolytes and their captive catch-fires. All of them could die. Captain Tira's pistol and sword were fast, but fire outraced steel.

So I smiled and laughed, stepped around Camjiata, and kissed Drake on the cheek as I had kissed my sire to take him off guard. He recoiled as if I had knifed him in the gut.

"You're so clever, all of you! I see what you're about. You don't trust me, me appearing so suddenly and with such a tale, so you have appointed Drake to carry out a cunning interrogation. But I assure you, everything I have told you is true. My husband's mother and sisters were dangled as hostages before him so he had no choice but to bow his head to the mansa's yoke. His radical sympathies have not changed."

I righted the chair, nodded at Rory, and sat down. My fingers trembled only a little as I considered the smoking ash of my beef. The mood in the chamber shifted from a knife's edge to blunt wariness.

"Bring the maestra a fresh plate," said Camjiata. "Please be aware, Drake, that Lutetia is the crucial battle of this entire campaign. This is no time to quibble over prizes as if we are boys playing a game of sticks in the river. I have promised you that when the time is right, we will turn our attention to the Ordovici Confederation, but I cannot do so if my army is defeated. Cat?" He examined me. "Are you well? You look pallid."

"When will the time be right?" muttered Drake under his breath. "How long must I wait to get back the throne and honor that are rightfully mine?"

"Ah, here is a fresh plate. I hope everything on it is to your liking, Cat."

It was an imperial portion of beef and a full half of roasted chicken. I knew better than to let anger and disgust harm my appetite. I dug in while the command staff discussed the speed with which the army could move, and how far from Lutetia's walls the hospital camp ought to be set up.

The meal's ending gladdened me, for escape from Drake's presence beckoned the way a street filled with the best fabric and tailoring shops calls to a fashionable woman with a limitless purse. Camjiata ushered me out of the room with a speed that took my breath away. Doctor Asante cut off Drake with a question that allowed us to get out the door, and the door shut behind us even before Rory could follow me. The general's fingers pinched so hard I almost yelped.

"Wait before you speak," he murmured.

He escorted me swiftly out of the hall and up a set of back stairs to a modestly furnished loft. Four young officers, one an Amazon, studied a table covered with maps. They acknowledged our entrance with salutes. He pressed me past them through an inner door into a long attic storeroom whose boxes and crates had been shoved back to leave room for bedrolls and gear. A window at the far end looked over the front of the market hall and the main square to an old stone castle tower rising above green trees.

Camjiata paused at a closed door that led into another room set in under the eaves. Hand on the latch, he paused. Long golden spears of late-afternoon sunlight lanced in through the window to illuminate his figure as in a portrait. As in a dream. His hair was pulled back and tied with an incongruously bright-green ribbon that matched the old-fashioned bottle-green dash jacket he wore, cuffs trimmed with lace.

He turned to address me with a serious look that quite disarmed me, for who would offer such a direct and confiding gaze to an enemy? His tone had an intimate color, as if despite everything he trusted me enough to speak his true mind.

"I need you to kill him. You're the only one who can."

40

This was what it meant to walk the dreams of dragons, for I had swum through this very moment when I had slept in the belly of the beast as we crossed the Great Smoke. That journey in the ocean of dreams had given me a brief taste of Bee's gift. I was too astounded to speak.

Footfalls hammered up the back steps.

"But not until we defeat the Coalition and their Roman allies," he went on, as if I had already agreed. "If we lose now, the mages, princes, and Romans will use their victory to crush the radicals and all dissent for another generation."

"You created a monster," I said.

"No, the monster created himself. Why do you think people hate and fear mages? Surely you can see their fears are not irrational. Still, young men are weapons that experienced men will wield. My weapon has proved more dangerous than I imagined. I doubt even Andevai Diarisso can stop him now."

"Are his fire mages loyal to you, or to him?"

His hesitation was so brief that I noticed it only because I was strung to a high pitch. He smiled crookedly. "You perceive my situation."

Drake strode into the attic from the other end. "Why did you rush away before I was done speaking to Cat? I want—"

"James!" His curt tone betrayed not a glimmer of disquiet. He might have been slapping down any underling. "Cat has business that will not be possible to manage once we're on the move."

He opened the door and ushered me into an attic room with a

sloped ceiling, four windows, a dozen lit lamps, and six people sitting at a table writing or reading dispatches.

A man I did not know glanced up. "Ah, General! We're just about done here. The Barahals have almost finished that cipher for your orders for Captain Barca."

The Barahals. There were two people in the room I had once thought I had known, before the day they had thrown me to the wolves.

Uncle Jonatan didn't even look up, so intent was he on a message he was turning into code. He had always been single-minded, more involved in his work than with his family, yet not a bad father for all that. His curly hair had entirely gone to silver since I had last seen him. The wrinkles in his forehead cut deep.

Aunt Tilly had paused to dip her quill in ink. Her face bore the beloved frown that meant she was considering how to stretch the turnips in the bin so no one in the house would go hungry. Her dark hair was pulled back in a bun and tucked under a scarf. Her merry, round face looked the same but for the dark circles under her eyes that spoke of hours of fretting. Yet she had always been able to dredge up a smile to hearten her children and ameliorate their disappointments, for just as Uncle Jonatan had remained engrossed in work, she had cared most about the well-being of those she loved.

Drake came up beside me in Vai's stolen clothes. How I hated him! He put a hand on my back in a proprietorial manner that made me tense, and him smile.

"Why would you bring a spy to spy on spies?" he demanded of the general. "I know she plans to betray us, but what you mean to gain by abetting her I cannot fathom."

Every head came up at the sound of his voice, just as deer startle when they catch the scent of a slavering wolf. His hand crept along the curve of my waist like a crawling poison. There I stood, caught between the man who had used my ignorance and fear to take advantage of me in a most intimate way, and the aunt and uncle who had raised me from childhood so they could sacrifice me to save their daughter.

Uncle Jonatan leaped to his feet. "Cat! Fiery Shemesh! Is Bee with you? Where is she?"

"Cat!" Aunt Tilly rose, grabbing onto the back of her chair for support as she swayed.

I was the one whose legs gave out. Camjiata neatly peeled me away from Drake's unwanted embrace and hauled me to a narrow bed placed along one wall. He set me down like a sack. I sat there numb, handless and footless, floating as if I no longer had body or will.

The other clerks hurriedly vacated the room. The click of the door closing behind them made me jump, as if all my skin were flayed and my heart laid out on the table to be carved into pieces by the knives of betrayal.

"I thought you loved me," I whispered. "All those years, I really thought you loved me."

Aunt Tilly's shame twisted her face, and I did not want to see it there.

Uncle Jonatan pressed a hand to my shoulder. "Cat, of course we loved you, it's just..."

"Don't touch me!" I shrieked, leaping up. Blindly tearing away from him, I slammed into the wall. Pain burst down my shoulder, and erupted in my heart. I sobbed until I thought my lungs would be ripped from my chest.

For there was no comfort. They had knowingly raised me and nurtured me and prepared me, so I could all willingly and innocently take their daughter's place as the sacrifice the family had to make to appease the angry mages.

"The mansa tried to kill me," I said hoarsely, not looking at them but rather at the burning lamps, the flame that consumes the oil that feeds it. "Would it have been a worthwhile sacrifice, if you had saved Bee knowing I was dead?"

"I explained this all to you already, Cat," said Uncle Jonatan. "But in the end, we lost Bee anyway, so we lost you both. We're just glad you're not dead."

"Only because of my own actions, and the decency of the man you forced me to marry! Did you never think you could have asked me to do it and I would have gone willingly? That I would have done anything to save Bee, at whatever cost to myself? How can any person embrace a child and then throw her away into the cold to die alone and abandoned? How can you live with yourself?"

461

I was shouting, hands clenched, tears streaming. How could all this rage and grief find an outlet? They could live with themselves: They had and they did! I pounded a fist into the wall over and over until the general caught my arm and held it, held me.

"Is Beatrice with you? Is she well?" Uncle asked.

A part of me wanted to claw his face by refusing to answer. But my mouth opened and I said, "She is well. Let her sisters be told so, for I know she misses them."

"Cat," said Aunt Tilly.

I shuddered to hear the voice that had soothed my childish hurts and warmed my orphaned heart with its affection.

Camjiata murmured, "Be brave like your mother."

So I looked up to meet Aunt Tilly's gaze.

Sorrow and shame had washed her skin to an ashy pallor, but she did not flinch from my accusing eyes. "Cat, I'm sorry for what happened that day. It took us by surprise. We did not know what else to do."

Her tender look scoured me, like an acidic bath thrown over my skin.

She did love me. She had loved me then.

And she had done it anyway.

I said, "At least the mansa never lied to me."

I turned my face into Camjiata's shoulder. I wanted to forget the terrible moment when she had given me a precious kiss on the forehead and, with that offering, released me to a fate whose end she could not guess except that the mages would be furious when they discovered the truth.

I wanted to forgive them so I did not have to live with this weight on my heart.

But all I could do was weep.

When I closed my eyes, a vision of my grandfather's malicious glare was chased by the light of flames as he spoke: *Begone. Begone. Begone.*

The door opened. I glanced up as Camjiata shook his head. Aunt and Uncle left the room. Aunt Tilly's face was streaked with tears. Rory stood in the attic looking ruffled and annoyed; behind him hovered a pair of young fire mages bouncing on their toes, as if they expected a fight.

"Why don't you kill them?" Drake asked, and in the wrinkling of his brow and the softening of his tone I read pity. "It would be fair recompense for what they did to you."

"Do you believe killing them will ease the pain or change anything," I cried, "except to orphan the children who depend on them?"

"You're so naïve, Cat. That they know the one they cast out has returned to destroy them will make the triumph all the more sweet." He glanced at the general.

"In due time, James," said Camjiata, "in due time, we will march to your old home. But not today."

"I have been patient."

"So you have," agreed the general so sincerely that I believed the general believed it.

Drake dusted his fingers together, tugging on the gloves that always concealed his hands, then turned and walked out. The general closed the door.

"This is where I sleep. You can rest here."

He set me on a bed, and I lay down because I hadn't the strength to stand.

Rory sat beside me and began rubbing my hands. A sort of blindness and deafness smothered me. I was a wounded animal panting in the shadows, too weak to lick my injuries.

Camjiata's voice rumbled softly. Rory replied. They conversed in a friendly manner as Rory's thumbs stroked back and forth along my palms until the tension eased from my hands. I surrendered to the waters of sleep, for it was better to drown than to suffer with the bloody scar that had been reopened.

Hungry wolves fed at my entrails. I ran from the Wild Hunt, but it was gaining, gaining, and my sire caught me in his icy claws. My severed head rolled down stone steps, bumping like a rubber ball used in batey. It tumbled off a cliff and plummeted into the Great Smoke. Leviathan purred.

Purred?

I woke in a dark chamber. Rory was stretched out beside me, snoring in that snuffling way he had. We were both still fully clothed. My sword, basket, and satchel rested at the foot of the bed. At the table Camjiata sat reading through a stack of dispatches by the light of an 463 oil lamp. The light shed gold on his face, but his eyes were pools of darkness.

I sat up.

Without looking up from his reading, he spoke in a low voice so as not to disturb Rory. "There is ale and bread on the side table. A basin, if you want to wash."

I slid off the bed. Rory did not stir, but something in his changed breathing made me think he had woken, as wild animals do at the least movement, but was pretending to be asleep to give us privacy. At the side table I washed my face in the basin, then sat opposite the general.

"Don't you sleep?" I asked.

"Cursed little. I concentrate best on dispatches at night, when no one disturbs me. A nap or two during the day suffices. How fare you, Cat?"

"Did you expect me to embrace them?"

"I thought it best to get the meeting out of the way. I can't say I expected your anger. Beatrice did not confide the full particulars to me."

"So you found a way to discover the full particulars by surprising me with the meeting."

He looked up with a wry smile. "Is that what you think of me, Cat?"

I could not fathom how I could like him, yet I did. "You want me to kill Drake. But how can I trust you? You betrayed me."

He glanced toward the door and nudged my foot under the table to signal me that people waited outside. "I did not betray you. You walked into Taino country of your own free will."

"That you can say that with a straight face and such sincerity is almost admirable! Everything I did was encouraged and machinated by you."

He smiled. "I've got some sack. It's an Iberian wine from the Sherez region near Gadir."

I felt the presence of a trap, a danger I wasn't aware of. Yet with the fall of night my sword had bloomed, even if to his eyes it still looked like a cane. The locket warmed my skin. My parents walked with me, so I nodded.

He fetched a bottle and two glasses. He poured, sipped from the glass as if to mock me for thinking he might mean to poison me, and handed it to me before pouring for himself. I shifted the glass to swirl the wine, then tasted. The liquor had a dark brown color and a strong, sweet taste that I did not like as much as rum's.

"I wish you hadn't given my father's journals to the family. I'll never get them back now."

He pushed aside the pile of dispatches. "If you go to Gadir, you can sue in court for *rei vindicatio*, the right to regain possession of something you already own. If you can stand up in court and swear that Daniel Hassi Barahal sired you and thus you are his next of kin."

My mouth had gone so dry that my voice emerged hoarse. "Daniel and Tara were married. That makes him my father."

"Yes. According to the law, the husband of a woman is the father of her children and thus has legal rights of guardianship over them. Whom was Tara protecting?"

I glared at him. "Tara was protecting *me*."

"I find it odd she would have believed that by dying she would protect you."

"She knew Daniel would protect me. I hope you don't find that odd."

"Indeed, I do not, for Daniel was exactly the sort of man who could raise another man's child as if it were his own and never love it less for all of that."

How he had me then! For I was seized by both overwhelming grief and passionate curiosity.

"What do you mean? What sort of man was he?"

He leaned closer, voice dropping to a murmur. "Ah, Cat, he was a better man than I am."

I sat back. "Are you mocking me?"

"No, I am not." I knew he meant it, although I could not have said why. "I am mocking myself. I have asked myself a thousand times since that day why she did not confide in me."

"The Amazon's oath she swore condemned her to death for becoming pregnant."

"She could have told me the truth. I would have found a way. But she felt only Daniel could rescue her, as if Tara had ever needed rescuing from anything except that hells-ridden, pestilent village she was born in. 465

That must be why she hid the pregnancy for so long, waiting for Daniel to come. Or perhaps she hoped that drill, or a battle, would cause her to miscarry and rid her of a thing she did not want."

"Do you know, General, I start to begin to like you again, and then you say something like that. My mother and father loved me."

"I do not dispute that they loved you. I've read his journals. There's a passage I recall in particular. 'Is some other man's bastard worth this to you?' So your Uncle Jonatan demanded of his brother Daniel. And Daniel writes, 'What happened on the ice does not matter. The child will be my child. I have promised Tara that, and even if I had not, it would make no difference, for my little cat is my sweet daughter, the delight of my life.' "

He examined me where I sat just outside the spill of light. "Why, Cat—are you crying?"

I wiped a tear from my cheek with the back of a hand. "There's no shame in grief. I lost my parents when I was six. I lost the love I would have had from them all the years from then to now. Think of what they lost! They lost the years they would have had to watch me grow up, to welcome more children, to treasure each other."

They were with me still, but it wasn't the same as if they were sitting across from me at a table in an attic room in a market town in the midst of a war.

"What happened on the ice?" he asked. "There is no journal for the crucial months, the ones during which you must have been conceived. It's missing, leaving only the mystery of you."

"The secret belongs to those who remain silent."

"A phrase I have heard before, from the lips of your husband. Think of this, Cat. If your aunt and uncle had not handed you over to the cold mages, you would never have married him. Destiny is a sharp goad. Never think otherwise."

"You think it destiny, and not just accident?"

" 'Where the hand of fortune branches, Tara Bell's child must choose.' We stand on the road washed by the tides of war, you and I. Is it accident that has brought us here? I believe it is not. I believe our fortunes are sealed before we are born."

He poured himself a second glass and topped up mine.

"Destiny and fortune are just words. I think you are ambitious,

General. Ambition is not the same as destiny. You only want to say it is."

He chuckled. "I like how you speak your mind, Cat. So few manage to be both honest and likable. That is one of your charms. Daniel had the same gift of speaking truth while making his listeners laugh. Do you want to know how I met them? Tara and Daniel, and Helene?"

A jolt like a blow from an axe split through my body. I managed to nod.

"I was a young captain in the army of the Numantian League. One of the princes who ruled the League had made a marriage alliance with a princely clan out of the city of Sala, one of the cities of the Wagadou Federation. The Wagadou Federation grew out of mostly Mande communities who had recently moved into the uninhabited lands northeast of the Rhenus River."

"Those lands weren't uninhabited. People lived there already."

He waved a hand with a casual dismissal. "Herders and trappers, living in the most appalling conditions. Best of all, the new territory was fertile ground for cold mages."

"Because of its proximity to the ice."

"Yes, so I understand, although naturally I know little of cold magic. The prince sent me to Sala to escort the noblewoman he was to marry back to Numantia. Instead we found ourselves embroiled in a war against the Atrebates and their allies. The war exploded all across the far north, into the boreal forest and the Barrens. The Celts who live right up against the Barrens are called the Belgae, a barbaric people. A few mage Houses had moved into that area fifty years earlier and civilized them. So we marched north and crossed the Boreal River."

He paused to drink.

I could not move, nor could I speak. I was frozen, as in ice.

"I met Daniel first, before either Tara or Helene. He was in the city of Sala, at the court of the ghana. He asked if he could travel north with our battalion because he wanted to explore the Barrens. Daniel was terribly entertaining. No man I've met before or since could keep a miserably cold and wet huddle of men around a guttering camp-fire laughing the way he could. He'd heard the Belgae were cannibals. Thought it might be best to investigate from a position of strength, if you will. With an army at his back."

"Were they cannibals?" I thought of my grandfather, crouching by his cauldron.

He smiled. "He asked in every village we came to if it was true the Belgae were cannibals. And they all said the same thing."

"What was that?"

"That they themselves weren't, but the neighboring village, the one they'd been having a feud with for years, was certainly known to eat human flesh."

I laughed.

He smiled, then sobered. "We fought a skirmish against those cursed Atrebates. Bad, marshy conditions, and low morale. Our cursed colonel turned tail and ran with his entire staff, those who were still alive. So I took over and managed an orderly retreat. We had to escape north because the Atrebates had blocked the road. We couldn't go overland because the ground was a mire. We ended up in a village next to a mage House, Crescent House."

I nodded. "Where your wife came from."

"Yes." His smile had a bittersweet quality. "And there she was."

"Helene?"

"Tara. She couldn't have been more than sixteen. I thought she was a boy at first, for she was dressed in men's clothing. She and her cousin and brother had been out hunting. They had come across remnants of the fighting and run back to warn the village with this mangy dog she kept for years and years—"

"She kept a *dog*?"

His gaze flashed up. I couldn't be sure if my outburst had surprised him or if he was gauging the import of my expression before he went on. "As it happened, the village was a client village to Crescent House. The elders insisted I pay my respects to the mansa at Crescent House and explain how I and my troops had come into their territory. Tara accompanied us to give a report on what she had seen. Daniel came, because you could never stop him from doing what he wanted. There we met Helene."

He poured himself another glass of sack, but I refused a third. The lamp cast gold and shadow over the table. And I thought to myself that maybe, just maybe, General Camjiata was a little lonely, a man who had lost the people he loved best.

He did not drink. He looked at me instead, his elbows braced on the table, his chin resting on his interlaced fingers. "You look so much like Tara."

I toyed with the glass, turning it around just for something to do. He leaned a little closer.

"Catherine Bell Barahal." A smile like regret wrinkled the corners of his eyes. "You should have been my daughter."

I inhaled sharply. There was no reply to that!

He added, "Had she married me instead of Daniel, you could have been my heir. We might still manage it."

"Your *heir*?"

"Like the didos of old, the queens of old Qart Hadast. Like Queen Anacaona. Is it so strange a thought? While it is true in these days most people in Europa would scoff at the thought of a woman ruling, that is purely due to local prejudice and current custom. You look surprised, Cat. You can't believe a woman cannot rule just as well as a man. You met the cacica. You were raised in a Kena'ani household."

"To rule as emperor is the wrong thing to wish for. We must work for Assemblies like the one in Expedition."

He chuckled. "Do you believe you can demand Assemblies in every city in Europa and have them established overnight?"

"No, of course one battle will not win the war." He had trapped me.

"It will take years, decades, more likely generations. Yet all might be accomplished swiftly if a single man could set it in place."

"And then what? Retire gracefully, leaving the happy subjects to rule themselves?"

He sipped at his glass.

"I don't believe you," I said.

"You want to believe me."

"I want to believe a lot of things! I want to believe my parents are alive and soon to be reunited with me. Is this what my mother feared? That you would claim me and pass me off as your own child? I won't be your heir, and I'm not your daughter."

In silence he studied me over the brim of his glass as if waiting for me to rethink my position and change my mind. But I was not to be trapped as Vai had been. I knew how to riposte.

"Did you love her?" I asked.

He drained the glass and set it down with a hard clunk. "You are not the only one to have lost those you held dear."

"I'm sorry they aren't with us now," I replied quickly, for his spike of anger startled me.

"This is why you and I will never be done, little cat, for we are all that remains of them."

"Maybe so. Anyway, as this war goes on, it seems we need each other."

I went to the side table to slice bread and smear dollops of cheese on top.

Many scribes and storytellers have recorded the history of the world, each colored by its author's own interpretation and illuminating only the part of the tale she feels is important or wishes to reveal. Stories tell us what we think we know about the world. Sometimes they share truth and knowledge, and sometimes they propagate lies and ignorance.

But words are only one road to change. The sword, which is not fighting but any form of action, is the other. Some cut a path that others may follow into the wilderness of possibility. The general saw not limits but unchained opportunity. I did not trust him, but I believed that, as Rory had once said, he said what he meant, and he meant what he said. At least in the moment he said it.

"What exactly is it you need me for, Cat?"

"Your legal code will release villages and clans from clientage. That's what I need." I offered him the plate. "Do you ever worry about your safety? Since I'm to be the instrument of your death."

"Will I die because of a deliberate action on your part against me? Might you be the tool someone else will use to destroy me? Or is your refusal to be my heir the death of my hopes to set in place a successor whose ideals will match my own and thus improve the destiny of humanity?"

I laughed. "Oh, that was well played, General. But the answer is still no."

He took several slices of bread off the plate. "You can't possibly believe that I believe you came to me because you have been seized by an overwhelming desire to join my army."

470   "We have a common enemy," I said in a low voice.

He glanced again toward the door, then smiled with a confiding look that drew an answering smile from me. Was I so starved for affection that I would rub up against any hand that offered a friendly pat?

"So we do. It is the only reason you are not weighted in chains and thrown into the river to drown. I mean that in the poetic sense, you understand."

"When you offered to make me your heir, did you mean that in the poetic sense as well?"

"Oh, no, Cat. I mean that with all seriousness."

"Even though you distrust my motives for coming here?"

"Were I to truly gain your loyalty, I would know it to be sincere and unshakable. Do not dismiss my offer out of hand."

Unlike with Vai and the mansa, nothing in the offer tempted me. "Should you gain your empire, it should then die with you. I will not be the means to prolong it. I stand with the radicals, General. Each day we add to our numbers. You are strong, but in the end, we will be stronger."

He lifted his glass as if in toast to my speech, then drank.

I drank with him, not in his honor but in honor of all those who fought. I could not help but see Bee and myself caught between the mansa and the general—just as, in another way, we were caught between courts and dragons. Vast forces battled, sweeping us up in their conflict. At first we had been ignorant pawns, able to run but never to stand. Alone we did not have the means or the strength to effect change.

But in the midst of the monstrous assembly that is slave to fortune, each solitary small figure who linked her hand to another built a chain of loyalty and trust.

We make ourselves into the net that we throw across the ocean.

41

Rory gave a copiously false yawn and rose to open the shutters. Roosters crowed. The creak of wheels and trample of feet and hooves drifted from the encampment as the army moved out.

"Where are we going today?" Rory asked as he plundered the remaining bread and cheese.

Aides and attendants clattered into the room to pack away the gear with impressive speed. The general personally escorted me to the latrines. Youths wearing the red jackets of fire mages hovered close all the while, like hawks waiting to dive on cautious rabbits. The truth was, I did fear their fire. Rory did not even try to flirt with them.

Faster than I had thought possible, the headquarters staff was on the road in a column of horses, carriages, and dust. We were led by a company of Amazons under the command of Captain Tira. A battalion of Iberian infantry marched behind. The baggage and hospital train would follow at the rear.

Rory chatted companionably with the young staff officers, but I stuck next to the general. I did not like the look of James Drake, wearing yet another of Vai's purloined dash jackets to spite me. What I least liked the look of was his squadron of thirty young fire mages. How many catch-fires he controlled I was not sure, for one of the carriages was locked, with caged persons inside, while a file of shackled catch-fires marched under guard of soldiers wearing Lady Angeline's badge.

We traveled hard all day on the main road, passing sections of the slow-moving baggage train. Columns of infantry marched away to either side, across fields, the army like locusts on the move. Messengers galloped up on spent horses with reports from the vanguard. In the town of Castra, where Lord Gwyn had died, we were met by cheering locals lining the road.

North of town we stopped to water and feed the horses. Soldiers ate stale bread and took naps. I walked upstream to wash my dusty face and hands.

Rory lay down on the grass and slid into a doze. I smiled to see his peaceful face lit by the sun. As for me, I was terribly hungry. The roofs of a farmstead rose nearby. I would have gone to beg food from them, but I had no money to pay for it and probably they had already had their granary emptied by a quartermaster.

"I wonder," I said to dozing Rory, "how a general who comes to liberate makes sure he isn't just seen as a thief."

He snorted awake, rising up on an elbow. I turned. Lady Angeline approached along the bank. Downstream, horses muddied the waters.

I made a pretty courtesy, for although as wife to the heir of Four Moons House I now ranked as her equal, I did not want anyone here to know of Vai's new status. "Your Highness."

Her gaze grazed along the length of Rory's body, and to my amusement she flushed when he winked at her. Unlike Drake, he did look good in Vai's clothes, even when they were rumpled from travel. She turned to me. "What am I to call you?"

"Maestra Barahal, as you wish, Your Highness. May I ask if you have been married long?"

"Let me make myself understood to you, Maestra. Do not make an enemy of me. I am the only child of the prince of Armorica, he who stands as overlord above the Veneti dukes."

"Ah." I surveyed her proud posture and confident stance. Her riding clothes suited her. Clearly she was a woman of taste, in most regards. "Yet if I am correct, by Gallic law you cannot rule in your own right because you are a woman. You must marry a man who will become son to your father and then prince in his place."

"You comprehend my situation astutely, Maestra. Unlike every other prince's son, James has no interest in ruling Armorica and will leave to me the inheritance I have earned."

I knew how to dig for information. "I suppose his ambitions are set on recovering his ancestral crown in the Ordovici Confederation." 473

"You think he is volatile and angry, but that is because you do not know the circumstances under which he was driven from his rightful place. In fact, he has a philosophical temperament, one that prefers to gaze at the stars and plumb the mysteries of the universe. When the time comes, he will be perfectly happy to leave the administration of both principalities to me."

"Goodness! I can understand that the chance to rule two principalities would be an inducement for a woman of your princely birth and ambition. Yet if the law were changed to allow the daughter to inherit equally to the son, such a dynastic marriage would not be necessary for you."

I had misunderstood her.

"The marriage suits me marvelously well."

"Ah. Well, then, a word of advice."

"Cat," said Rory, warningly.

I poked anyway. "Besides the bad fit, for the dash jackets are too loose and too tight in all the wrong places, the colors really do not benefit his complexion. Your attire is so exquisite in all ways that I cannot believe you have urged him to wear another man's clothes."

Her right eye half winked shut in a flicker of irritation. "He has promised to burn them all when the cold mage is dead." With that she returned to the main group. Drake came to meet her.

Rory got to his feet. "Cat, will you ever learn to keep your mouth shut?"

"Burn his lovely dash jackets! Think of the disrespect to the tailors who cut and sewed them!"

"Cat."

My volcanic ire subsided before it spilled over into gouts of red-hot stabbing. General Camjiata beckoned. On we rode through the long afternoon. Fortunately our pace was slow enough that at intervals Rory and I could dismount to walk instead of riding.

As twilight descended we entered the grounds of a lord's estate with a long artificial pond graced with fountains and a terraced set of clamshell-shaped lawns leading to a stately house. Troops stretched out on the grounds, having not even erected tents. They leaped to their feet with cheers as the general's entourage made its way to the

big house.

The general stood on the steps and raised a hand for silence.

"I came ashore in a rowboat from my exile," he cried. Back in the ranks, men called his words farther back yet, so all could hear. "You are the ones who had the courage and the vision to march! Let us not forget our ancient war with the Romans. Our grandparents did not forget! Our histories and songs do not forget! The bards remind us that from the northern shores of Africa all the way to the ice, we have all fought the Romans, sometimes alone, but on this day, together! We are the storm that will batter down the arrogance of our enemies! One sharp blow, and victory is ours!"

How they cheered, for his presence had a bonfire's glory. It warmed even me, although I knew better than to be smitten by a forceful man's vision of what could be if only he and I could come to an accommodation. Look how that had turned out, when Vai had courted me!

What had happened to the inhabitants of the lordly house I did not know, but a cadre of anxious servants set a hastily prepared meal before us in a once-magnificent dining room. Brass lamps were set out to replace richer fittings that had been looted. Young officers waited their turn to bring forward reports as the general and his staff ate through a leek soup, roasted mutton and turnips, pears stewed in wine, and several varieties of cheese.

"It will give me pleasure to burn this place down as we leave," said Drake, looking at me as he said it, for the man did need to boast constantly as he tried to intimidate me.

I held Drake's gaze as I speared a morsel of mutton, popped the meat into my mouth, and devoted my attention to enjoying its moist savor.

Camjiata glanced up from the dispatch lying at his left hand. "I am so relieved you enjoy your food, Cat. As for the house, it shall be spared for the hospital train. Lady Angeline, if you will remain behind to await the hospital, I know I can safely put you in charge of administering all. Your father asked me to make sure you stayed well back from the scene of battle, since you are pregnant."

Pregnant!

Drake's leering smirk turned to a lift of the chin as he contemplated this signal triumph. I opened my mouth to ask if it was truly Drake's, since all knew that fire mages were indifferently fertile. Rory's foot pressed down so hard on my toes that I yelped.

"What Cat means to say," Rory said as he kicked my shin for good measure, "is how delightful she finds the prospect of actually being allowed to sleep in a bed. Me, too. For I swear to you, I hurt all over." He waggled his eyebrows. "Especially my thighs, but not, alas, from any riding that would have pleased me."

The general chuckled, ignoring the blush of one of his younger officers. "You two will accompany me to the library, where I will spend the night. Perhaps there will be a chair for you to sleep in."

Several helpful orderlies dragged in a long couch on which Rory and I fit, curled up with our heads at each end and our feet commingling. I slept fretfully, for the general's lamp burned all night as messengers came and went. Very late, I woke needing the water closet.

"As soon as we have placed our line across the field," Camjiata was saying to a collection of officers, "we will commence bombardment with artillery."

A short, thin man dressed in the white sash of the Kena'ani sacred band—the famous Elephant Barca—spoke up just as I wrapped the shadows around me and crept for the door. "If the Roman army arrives while we're engaged with the Coalition, we'll be crushed between them."

"We will defeat the Coalition quickly, and pivot to hit the Romans while they're still trapped in columns, before they have time to deploy across the field. The key is to draw out and then capture or eliminate their cold mages."

A chill seized my heart. Had I made a terrible mistake in coming here, in leaving Vai behind? The thought took hold in my mind and would not let go. Anxiety muddled me, for although I found the water closet easily enough, I lost my way going back. Instead of returning to the library, I found myself at doors opening onto a stone terrace.

A solitary flame drew my eye. James Drake sat on a stool with five fire mages at his back, four catch-fires kneeling with heads bowed, and three people facing him like strangers brought before a prince.

"I will not lie to you," said James Drake in a kindly voice I scarcely recognized. "No fire mage is ever safe. If you wish to be safe, then learn from the blacksmiths how to lock away your fire and hope it never escapes."

"The blacksmiths would not have me!" said a stocky young man who stood with arms crossed belligerently.

"What of you?" Drake asked the younger of the two lads.

The youth was so thin he looked as if a breeze might blow him over. "We haven't the apprentice fee to pay to the guilds, me and my people."

"If I gave you that fee, would you choose a blacksmith's forge? For I will make you risk your life, right now, if you wish to join my company."

The lad stammered. "I wouldn't mind the blacksmith's guild. It's an honorable life. In a few years I could give my parents a cow. Men will pay a bride price to marry my sisters, if I'm a blacksmith. My parents can't afford to lose me. I'm the only son they have."

"Very well." Drake gestured. An attendant counted out coins into the lad's hand as the boy gaped at this largesse. "Our kind are sorely ill-used here in Europa, the lands of our birth. Go with my blessing. Make a good life for yourself."

As the lad hurried off into the night, Drake again bent his eye on the stocky young man. "Will you risk your life for a chance to join my company of mages?"

"I'm not afraid!"

"Better if you were. Fire knows no mercy. But very well. To weave fire, you must cast the backlash of the flame into another body. Otherwise it will burn you up from inside. I will raise an unlit candle. Put a spark to it. As you feel the answering burn from that combustion in your own flesh, throw it like a rope into the body of this catch-fire."

A candle and two lamps burned at Drake's feet. He blew them out. All sat in darkness lightened only by stars and a rising crescent moon.

"Be cautious," added Drake. "Even the lighting of one candle can kill a fire mage."

"I can light a candle!" boasted the young fellow.

With a snap the candle's wick flared. Then, as in echo, the two lamp wicks began burning with a bright golden flame.

"Throw the thread of fire into the catch-fire," said Drake. "Think of casting a line from a boat to the shore."

The youth staggered, clapping a hand to his chest, and dropped to his knees choking. His face got very red. The lamp flames flared with such brilliance that I blinked. Then he toppled over, mouth open, tongue black, and a trickle of blood coming out of his ears.

477

Drake waved forward an attendant. "Dispose of him."

Men dragged the body away as the others watched in silence.

"You never asked me," said the third supplicant, a girl about Luce's age.

Drake pulled off a glove. The skin was red and flaking, mottled with so many burn scars it was a wonder he could use his hands at all. He knelt and pinched out both flames. "I have nothing to ask you. The blacksmiths do not admit women to their guild. They teach them only how to lock away their fire. So either you will go home or you will try your luck."

"Do you mean us to die?" she asked boldly. Maybe the darkness gave her courage.

"No, not at all. If you have the knack of casting off the backlash, I will train you to hone that skill and nurture your fire. But even the best-trained fire mage can die. And you must be willing to see others die, for if you make one mistake with your catch-fires, as you will, their bodies will be served as this man's was."

"My bridges are burned. My home will be here, or in the spirit world."

She took in a sharp breath. The candle took flame. She sucked in a pained inhalation; I smelled a pinprick of ashy smoke. Light sparked in her eyes. Then a glowing thread spun out from her like an unwinding coil and streamed into the body of the nearest catch-fire. The man stiffened, arms rigid at his side, but the backlash was more trickle than roar.

The girl's lips parted, and her eyes widened. Her hands raised to press at her mouth. The candle's light danced along her pale skin. The rest of the world lay in shadow.

"Enough," said Drake. "You have a light touch, as women often do. If you wish to walk this road, you may enlist."

She dropped to her knees so abruptly I thought she was falling, but she was just stunned. The catch-fire relaxed as the backlash vanished. The candle burned on.

"Yes, that is my wish," said the girl through tears.

"Remain here then, and assist with the hospital tomorrow. Under no circumstances attempt even to light a candle, not until we have had time to train you in the preliminaries."

"Yes, my lord. Yes!" By the way she gazed raptly at him, I saw the cage he wove: He gave the fledgling fire mages a life otherwise denied them.

I fled to the library. It hurt to entertain the idea that Drake might be right about one thing.

Rory still slept. Camjiata sat alone at the desk, studying a map. He did not look up as I crept across the plush rug, for of course I was veiled in shadows.

"I can hear you moving about, Cat. Do you think I did not notice when you suddenly vanished? Dark Ataecina! Whence comes this shadow magic? Has the Hassi Barahal clan nurtured it close to their hearts all these years? Uniquely suited for a family of spies, don't you think? Or is it only you, Cat? Not cold, not fire, but a creature as yet unclassified by the scholars."

Fortunately, before I felt obliged to answer this salvo, all delivered in a cheerful tone, boots sounded in the corridor. I threw myself on the couch and pretended to be asleep as Drake walked in. The whiff of smoke made me choke.

"I have discovered another apt fire mage. Another girl."

"You seem to prefer the girls, James." Camjiata's tone seemed distracted, but I heard the edge cutting beneath his genial disinterest.

"Girls are more malleable. More grateful, for I give them a status and independence they cannot gain elsewise. Thus they are the most loyal of all. Most of them, anyway. Not this one." I felt the pressure of his gaze as he looked at me. I wanted to leap up and stab him, but Vai's cautions and my promise to the radical cause stayed my hand. "Women are so grievously shallow-minded. If the arrogant cold mage weren't so handsome and cocksure, she wouldn't love him half as well."

"Really, James, you must give up this unseemly obsession."

"I care nothing for her. Angeline is far more beautiful and an equal to me besides. But she will lead me to him."

"If you kill him, I will be seriously displeased with you."

Drake laughed. "And then what? Then what will you do?"

Tension stung like the snap of air before a thunderstorm breaks.

"Do you want to find out, James?"

Noble Ba'al, but I had to admire the general's self-assurance! Drake hesitated for so long I almost popped my head up just to enjoy the 479 expression that surely soured his face. Rory prodded me with his foot. I stayed curled up.

"Without my help, your partisans would never have been able to break you out of your island prison."

"I am aware of what I owe to you. But I am also aware of what you owe to me. You are a murderer, condemned by your own kinfolk in your own clan's court of law."

"They left me to burn after stealing my inheritance! Of course I acted to save myself!"

"Any justness in your actions does not change the fact that I brought you under my protection at considerable risk to my reputation."

"You promised me an army to take back what is mine."

"An army you shall have, once my victory is assured. How long do you think you will last without my support, James?"

"I am coming to question whether I need your support at all. My fire mages are loyal to me because they know I am the only one who will raise them up and defend them. They will never let any harm come to me. I used to think I needed your army, but now I wonder if all I need are powerful fire banes. Who would dare oppose me then?"

"A constant application of terror and grief is no way to rule." Footsteps sounded in the corridor. "Here are my officers. Have your people ready to ride within the half hour."

"I shall not be patient for much longer," muttered Drake.

The instant the sting of Drake's presence faded from the room, I kicked Rory's shins and got up. The staff officers nodded at me; they had accepted our presence among them with the alacrity of youthful disinterest. After all, they had a war to fight. We made a meal of bread and cheese, and I was glad to have it for I suspected that many of the soldiers got nothing. Before the sun's edge topped the horizon, the troops were moving north in their columns. The pops and cracks of gunfire signaled a skirmish far in the advance.

"This knife's edge must be walked cautiously," remarked Camjiata when he and I had a moment riding apart from the others. "You do understand, do not you, that if we lose this battle today, then all is lost?"

"Because the princes and mages will crack down so hard on dissent that it will be decades or generations before another radical movement has a chance to rise? Or because you'll have lost control of Drake? Never believe I am selfless enough to sacrifice my husband on the altar of your empire."

"Just buy me time, Cat. Do nothing rash." He glanced toward where Drake rode amid his company of mages, then back to me. "Had you been my daughter, you would have been loyal to me."

"Tara gave me the father she wanted me to have," I said softly, but he could not hear.

The rising sun bent its rays over the landscape. The road sloped upward along a gentle rise. Rumbling booms shook the air. A frantic blaring of trumpets, as with warning calls, was followed by the crackling of gunfire, which at length subsided into an uncanny quiet that made me more nervous than anything that had come before.

We turned off the main road and entered a village empty of every soul except the soldiers moving through. On a prominence men had felled three trees that blocked the view northeast over the battlefield. Clouds bunched up in the north, dark with unshed rain. Closer at hand a dense mist concealed the high ground and thus the entirety of the Coalition army. Camjiata surveyed the mist through a spyglass.

"James, the mist seems unnatural. I expected to see Lutetia's walls from here. Can you disperse it?"

"The mist is a fog created by cold magic. To create such an extent, across a full mile or more of ground, means many cold mages have coordinated their efforts."

"Can your fire magic not vanquish this cold fog, James? I'm surprised to hear it."

"I can do anything! But it's not worth risking fire mages so close to the lines. The sun will disperse it in time."

A smile teased Camjiata's lips, as if Drake's sullen defensiveness amused him, but I was sure I was the only one who noticed it. "Tell Marshal Aualos to order the artillery to begin a barrage into the mist. That will soften them and perhaps hasten the mist's dispersal as well."

Messengers came and went, one after the next. Sometimes they had to wait while Camjiata read dispatches and wrote replies for men ahead of them. Everything took so long as soldiers trudged into position and artillery was drawn in by horses. An hour passed, then another.

The battlefront expanded into the east, masses of men hidden by distance but also because the mist continued to hang low, not burning off even as the sun rose higher.

Finally the artillery began to fire in thundering blasts of sound. Smoke rose. I heard thumps, distant cries, the screams of horses. How must it feel to stand as death fell unseen out of the sky? How I hated this waiting! I was confident that Bee remained fairly safe in Lutetia, but where was Vai? How vulnerable was he?

Canyons of light appeared as cracks in the mist. Figures appeared and vanished like dreams of ghosts. With a rumble of hooves a troop of Coalition cavalry swept out of its misty concealment. Rifle fire from the Iberian line cracked as the infantry formed into squares to face the charge, but the horses did not crash into the square; instead, as the cavalry circled, all the rifles went silent. Out of this chaos of stillness and motion, crossbow bolts and longbow arrows flew with killing precision into the Iberian ranks. In the midst of the cavalry, despite the distance between us, I recognized Vai. I knew he would go with the first wave, put himself at risk in case the attack did not work.

Yet it did work. The desperate Iberians broke ranks to charge with their bayonets. As soon as the square's tight formation began to disintegrate, a second cavalry charge swept out of the shredding mist and smashed right into the Iberian infantry. The lines boiled into a mass of confusion.

"A new variation on an old tactic," remarked Camjiata to his staff. They were sweating. He was not. "Effective not just because the cold magic kills our rifles and cannon but particularly because their archers are superior to ours and naturally they have many more of them. James, if you place one fire mage in each square, can that mage then throw the backlash of their fire into the cold mages who are riding with the cavalry? Wouldn't that kill the cold mage's magic and leave the rifles free to fire?"

Drake brushed strands of red hair out of his eyes. The touch of his calfskin gloves left a smear of soot on his brow, but I did not mention it, for I did not like the way he looked at me. "Yes, it would, and it leaves the cold mages defenseless besides, for as long as they are acting as catch-fires, they are helpless. The best part is that the more powerful the cold mage, the more fire he can absorb and thus the more fire the fire mage can call. Ironic, isn't it?"

"Yet what can we most advantageously set on fire?" Camjiata mused. "The Coalition has many more cold mages than we do fire mages. Let your people set grass fires up the hill to keep the cold mages busy putting them out. I know you have been making some experiments with lending fire to artillery and rifles whose combustion has been killed by cold magic."

"All of this my mages can do," said Drake, but he seemed distracted as he scanned the field with a spyglass. Several of his wife's soldiers always stood between him and me.

The last of the mist spun away to reveal the Coalition army deployed on the higher ground, rank upon rank of infantry. Smoke rose in billows everywhere. I could just barely make out the dark line of Lutetia's walls in the distance. Thank Tanit the city was, for now, out of artillery range.

A staff officer had left several open bottles of wine on one of the tree stumps. I took a swallow straight from the bottle as I considered whether I should abandon Camjiata. I knew the general had to win, yet I was so afraid of what the fire mages might do. But what could I possibly do to safeguard Vai now that the battle had started? The cavalry company he had ridden down with had returned to the Coalition lines, and no doubt he had gone with them. I would never find him among the thousands and thousands of soldiers struggling in noise and smoke and blood.

Rory was pacing back and forth along the length of one of the fallen pines like a caged lion at the prowl. A crow sat on a branch, watching him. I hurried over and chased it off. He offered me an uncorked bottle from which he had been drinking.

I took a swig of a harsh sack, winced, and handed the bottle back to him. "This is awful."

Had he been in cat shape, his ears would have been flattened to his head. "This *is* awful! This isn't hunting. You creatures ought to settle your arguments in a better way. Couldn't one general challenge another for the right to stand with the pride? Who can possibly eat all that torn meat? If it were even tasty, which man-flesh is decidedly not!"

"How do you know what man-flesh tastes like?"

He stiffened, and for an instant I was sure he was going to snarl at me.

483

"Rory! Answer me!"

He took a step toward me, so threatening I raised my cane. Catching himself, he took a step back, but by the way his lips gapped to show a hint of teeth, I could see he was on the edge of biting or perhaps of telling me the truth. And I was suddenly very sure that I did not want to know the answer after all.

Artillery fire boomed over us. I ducked instinctively. "Never mind. It doesn't matter."

"There! Look!" a staff officer shouted to be heard above the deafening rattle and shot.

I ran back to the command group just in time to see yet another cavalry charge from out of the Coalition lines. Smoke rose from the guns in billows. The churn of ground between the two armies was speckled with fallen men, injured horses, and the detritus of lost weaponry. This time, as Coalition cavalry closed with the Iberians, fire broke out in the trampled grass around them. One rider in the middle ranks collapsed as if shot. A second rider toppled from his horse. As more men fell and horses tumbled, the cavalry sheared off and raced back toward their lines. A storm of bullets rained after their retreating backs.

The fire mages had gotten their range.

Yet even in the face of these devastating casualties, still another Coalition troop galloped down toward the artillery. Riders and horses fell before the barrage, but this time where fire broke out it was quenched. The artillery went dead. With shouts, the Coalition troops closed. Grass fires sparked up and died. Men fought hand to hand, swords and bayonets flashing.

A young officer wearing the white sash of the Kena'ani Sacred Band rode up on a lathered horse, pushing in front of another messenger. "General! Captain Barca sends his compliments and this message: The first outriders of the Roman column have been engaged about five miles south."

Camjiata glanced overhead to where the sun had almost reached the zenith. "We should have broken the Coalition army before now. Drake, why have your fire mages not crushed every cold mage on the field? You assured me that fire would easily defeat ice."

"There are so many cold mages, and they're working in concert in a way they did not before, not even at Lemovis."

"No doubt they can learn from experience as well as we can," remarked Camjiata as he took a spyglass from an orderly. "Matters grow urgent. Lord Marius need only hold his ground and not retreat until the Romans arrive, and then we will be crushed between anvil and hammer. Our frontal attacks are hurting them, but not fast enough."

He examined the sprawling field of battle in all its churning confusion, so many thousands of men that it seemed the earth crawled. "There. See how the Invictus Legion holds its ground. We have to turn their flank, for a frontal attack will not break them."

He angled the spyglass to the north. About half a mile away a fortified estate stood amid the green crowns of an orchard. I remembered passing the house and gardens with Lord Gwyn's skirmishers, who had told me it was called Red Mount. The compound had two walls, an outer wall that ringed the orchard and gardens and an inner wall that fortified the stone house. The flag of the Tarrant infantry, Lord Marius's own crack troops, flew from the main house.

A column of Iberian infantry had laid siege to the estate an hour earlier. As we watched, a skirmish raged. Fire scorched across the orchard. Defenders hiding in the trees raced for the inner wall to escape the flames, but even as they were running the flames were sucked right out, killed by cold magic. Crossbow bolts rained over the wall, pummeling the Iberian infantry as it tried to advance. The struggle within the walled orchard was not visible, nor from this distance could I hear the sounds of whatever desperate melee was taking place beneath the trees.

"How can it be we have not yet taken that estate?" demanded Camjiata of his staff. His temper flashed, as dark as storm clouds. "Can you not see that it anchors the western flank of the Coalition army? No wonder Lord Marius holds the field. He need not worry about this flank, and thus can keep his center strong and take heavy losses against our superior weaponry but smaller numbers. Drake, why have the fire mages you brag of been defeated yet again by cold magic?"

Drake had his own spyglass, which he turned toward the estate.

A second fire seared across the treetops. With a shout of triumph the Iberians swarmed forward. Yet once again the fire was sucked clean out of existence as quickly as if a god had inhaled it into immortal lungs.

Bolts and arrows from within the estate's inner wall poured down on the attackers, driving them back.

"There is your answer," said Drake. "There must be several powerful cold mages inside the walls of the estate. Some are absorbing the backlash while others are killing the fire."

"Then take care of this problem personally, James! Else I shall have cause to wonder if all your talk is nothing more than idle boasting. Probably it is the Diarisso cold mage, the one who is evidently stronger than you."

Drake threw the spyglass angrily to the ground and his blue eyes actually sparked, but then he controlled himself and, without another word, stalked off.

Camjiata watched him reach the horses before turning to his staff. "Captain Tira! Let the Amazons take the estate and hold it against all counterattacks until the Coalition army breaks or you are dead."

She nodded, as calm as if he had asked for tea. "It will be as you command, General."

I ran over to the fallen pine. Rory had passed out, dead drunk, his head pillowed on the satchel. I unslung the basket from my back and tucked it into Rory's embrace. The thought that Vai might be caught helpless within the compound as Drake poured fire through him while the general's forces advanced filled me with a frantic desperation. Luce was fighting, too! But Luce had made her choice, and I had to respect her decision.

I raced back to the general. "Let me go with the Amazons."

He stared as if I had sprouted snakes for hair and turned him to stone. "You truly fear your husband is the cold mage who defends the estate. You fear Drake *can* kill him."

"Drake said it himself. When they are being used as catch-fires, cold mages are helpless and vulnerable. I can help you. I can creep in unseen."

Anger did not knit his brow, but suspicion grew like a brewing storm. "Creep in and warn them? Is that your plan? If we do not take Red Mount, we will lose the battle. If we lose the battle, we lose the war. Do you understand me, Cat?"

For the radicals of this generation not to be stamped out and imprisoned and executed, Camjiata had to win. For Vai's village to be released from clientage now instead of decades from now, if ever, Camjiata had to win. For Bee to have a hope of living in peace, Camjiata had to win.

And if Camjiata lost, and the mage Houses and princes won, I would probably lose Vai to the mansa in the end.

"I understand what is at stake."

The ringing thunder of the artillery boomed around us, thrumming down into the belly of the world. Smoke gusted out of the wounded earth in murky clouds.

He studied me, and what he read in my expression I did not know. But he nodded. "Very well. Let the Coalition break, and the Roman army fall, and then you can have Drake and save your cold mage likewise. But not a moment before victory is mine." He glanced over to where Rory was huddled in the shadow of the tree. "I'll keep an eye on him for you. Strange. Why does he hate battle so? He did not strike me as a coward."

"He's no coward," I snapped. "He just has a heart, unlike you and me, General."

42

We marched to Red Mount. Luce was not in the company I was assigned to. The Iberian riflemen had hunkered down along the estate's outer wall. With caps set on the wall to draw enemy fire, they shot over it into the orchard. Drifting smoke spun into coils, concealing half the world. Soon I was sucking in lungsful of heat, chaff, and powder. I kept my gaze fixed on the feather in Captain Tira's shako, like a bird's wing in fog. A hand touched my back as for balance and a shoulder brushed mine as I waited, crushed within the close-packed ranks of my sisters.

We made our way in a crouch to the smashed gate. The constant hammer of noise pounded through my body. The Iberians were using planks and doors as shields behind which they pushed forward into the orchard. Scorched leaves crumbled underfoot. Spent bullets, musket balls, arrows, and crossbow bolts crunched under my boots. The peppering fire of rifles melded with the rhythm of drums.

I wrapped myself in shadow and smoke. Using a tree trunk as shelter I peered into the smoky fog of the orchard. Bodies littered the ground. The bloody and battered Iberians had stalled as a rain of arrows and the pop of musket fire trapped them in the ashy trees. One man cowered, huddled up like a broken child, sobbing.

Yet not five paces from him, a different man called laughingly to the Amazons, "These Tarrant bastards are saying no man can dislodge them. Let's see what you women can do!"

Amid the trees, a soldier was dragging himself along the ground with his arms. His uniform was so covered in ash and his face so smeared likewise that I could not tell whose side he was on. A white fox nipped at his heels, until I blinked and realized it was only smoke pooling on the ground. The soldier slumped forward, facedown. A flash of light about his form dazzled me. The smoky fox leaped, swallowed the light, and vanished. I shook myself, for I was seeing things that weren't there.

Through patches of smoke I surveyed the layout of the inner compound. There was a two-story fortified stone house with a tower, as well as a long stable and several sheds. The compound wall and the stable wall were cut with loopholes for defense.

A pattern emerged, once I looked for it.

I slipped out of my shadows to report to the captain, who was sheltering behind a broken door propped between two trees. "Captain Tira! All of their musket fire is coming from the western corner. That means the eastern gate and the house are where the cold mages stand."

"Of course it is," shouted the captain. It was hard to hear her even though I could have reached out to touch her. "Do you see that reflection of light in the tower window? It's a spyglass. They're directing their forces from up in the tower."

A body fell not ten strides from me. A cloud of wasps swirled over the corpse, but there were no wasps, only grit in my eyes.

A man ran up from the outer gate and crouched beside Captain Tira. I pulled the shadows around me just in time, as I realized it was Drake. He did not notice me. His lean face shone as pale as if he never got any sun, but I thought it was just that he was sweating. His blue eyes were so bright they gleamed like polished gems on the edge of burning.

"There are four cold mages," he shouted, already hoarse as he struggled to be heard above the din. "Three in the tower and one at the carriage gate. I will burn the carriage gate using the one at the gate as my catch-fire. I'll also set the roofs of the stables on fire. You'll have to move fast to break through once I do, or their arrows will kill you regardless."

"Why did your mages not set fire to the stables before this?" the captain asked.

"They're young and inexperienced," said Drake. "Also, there's a mage in the tower who is the strongest mage I've ever touched. He's the one we must defeat. His reach covers all but that one corner of the enclosure, where they've focused their muskets. Do you see?"

"Yes, I already know." Captain Tira smiled as to herself. "Very well, Drake. At your signal, we'll advance. You rid us of the cold mages, and we'll kill the officers."

She lifted a hand to give the command for forward, just as she nodded toward where she had last seen me. Thus was I given my orders: *Kill the officers.*

Drummers beat the roll of advance. A cadre of Amazons shielded Drake as the line pressed forward pace by pace through the trees into withering flights of arrows and the sting of musket balls. I could hear nothing but the shattering thunder of rifles around me. After an eternity we had made it halfway along the trees.

In my veil of shadows, the path I crept seemed to weave in and out of the interstices that bind the world. Threads stitch the world together. Every substance, solid or liquid or air, moves with the quivering resonance of a struck bell. I saw with altered eyes: Behind the closed carriage gates lay the bright well of a cold mage.

Rifles cracked in my ear. Beside me an Amazon collapsed, bleeding into the dirt. I flung myself down to use the fallen woman as a shield, but I had to roll away quickly when her body writhed and glowed. Drake was pouring the backlash of his magic into the wounded.

The carriage gates burst into fire so bright that its light speared into the sky. In answer a wash of ice slumped over all, and the flames died. I was close enough that my sword bloomed, so I twisted its hilt and drew the blade out of the spirit world.

Fresh fire tore into the roof of the stables as Drake poured the backlash into the mage at the gate. The magister flared like a candle, too weak to channel so much power, and his light snuffed out: He was dead. Within a fire blazing with doubled force, the carriage gate was consumed. This time, when the fire was killed by cold magic, the damage was already done, the gate demolished.

With a shout the Amazons pressed through the smoking ruins of the gate. The sound of a desperate melee rang on the air, groans and shouts and bayonets striking and the clatter and thunk of crossbows and the incessant fire of rifles. Just as I reached the gate, a hammer of cold killed every rifle in the orchard mid-fire and doused the flames on every roof. Still in shadow, I plunged through the charred planks and beams of the gate. The dead cold mage lay twisted in the wreckage, smoke pooling in his open mouth: He was not Vai.

I stared across a gravel-paved courtyard churned with smoke and bodies. A rifle cracked, and a man in Tarrant green who had taken cover in a stone arch went down as blood sprayed his head. A snarling cat as insubstantial as darkness clawed the bright spark of his soul out of his chest. A wolf sewn of mist leaped upon a woman who had a bayonet in her gut and swallowed her unmoored soul.

As the skirmish boiled across the courtyard, spirit hunters nipped at the fallen.

The Wild Hunt rides on Hallows' Eve, but its shadows linger all the year long: It is the Hunt that consumes the souls of the dying at the moment of death. There they prowled, my brothers and sisters, a glint of teeth in the smoke, a sliver of light on the wind. Because I stood with a foot anchored in each world, I could see the whole.

The Hunt does not take blood, only souls. For the Hunt itself is the gate through which the souls of the dead pass from the mortal world into the spirit world.

A bolt shot from the tower skimmed my hat's feather, jostling the cap off. Even invisible, I was not immune to death. No one in the mortal world is immune.

I ran for the stone house, dodging and ducking. I had to reach the tower before Drake did. The ribbon of his fire weaving spun up into the tower to splash into the well of the cold mage who sheltered there. Whoever that cold mage was, he was immensely powerful, able to absorb every bit of the backlash that Drake channeled into him. In a burst of heat, flames skimmed along the roof of the stables and sheds as Drake wakened more fire.

The stronger the cold mage, the better for Drake!

The door to the stone house was shut tight. Window slits gave cover for defensive shooting. A bolt loosed from within kissed my hair, just missing my ear. I slammed up against the wall of the house, now inside their range. How to get in?

The door burst into searing flames that chewed through it with such ferocity I had to retreat from its billowing heat. Men shouted inside, but not in panic. They sounded like soldiers sure of their strength and their good defensive position. In the courtyard and stables and orchard the battle raged on, a chaotic ferment of blood, noise, panic, and determination. Half the roofs in the compound were on fire.

A rising breath of cold magic warned me. I dropped to my knees.

Cold hammered down. Every soldier in the courtyard hit the ground as if felled by an axe blow. Where Drake was I did not know, but all the fires went out. The door of the stone house opened, half fallen off its hinges. Soldiers poured out. So intent were they on their foes that one stumbled over my back, knocking me sideways without even noticing I was a stone in their path. I dodged into the house as, behind me, the Amazons tried to rise before they got cut down.

I could not look back. I had my orders.

A Tarrant captain stood by an old-fashioned brick fireplace. He had a pistol in one hand and a sword in the other.

"The officers wear feathers in their caps. Aim for them," he said to his soldiers, who were standing calm and collected at the window slits leveling their crossbows.

I stuck him in the gut with my sword so hard up under the ribs that the point tapped brick behind as he gurgled. His eyes opened wide as his mouth formed soundless words, as a man might practice a polite introduction. A silent owl woven out of smoke swooped down and snapped up his soul.

If you are not to be killed, then you must kill. That is the law of the hunt.

I was halfway across the room to the stone stairs before any of the others noticed the captain's body sliding down the wall as he collapsed. As a sergeant came running I slashed my wicked sharp blade across the throat of the orderly behind him. No one noticed because they were all staring at the dead captain. I slipped past a pair of men guarding the steps and began my climb, dodging around men pressed to window slits, waiting to loose their bolts.

"Felt you a breeze—?"

"Bastards can't even hold the line against cursed beasts of women—!"

This foul-mouthed man I stabbed from the back and shoved so he tumbled down, his weight staggering those below him. How they

492

shouted in consternation, looking about for the spirit haunting them. Fool! Fool! Always letting my reckless lusts take hold of me.

That was how Andevai had courted me. I had seen what he was, arrogant and vain and determined to win once he entered any contest, and yet despite knowing he would see me as a challenge to be won, I still allowed myself to be dazzled by his physical beauty and his unrelenting admiration. He had seen my weakness, which was my desire for him, and so he had fed me one morsel at a time until I could no longer resist devouring the whole of what he offered. So be it. Maybe I was a fool, maybe I would one day get so angry at him that I would rip out his throat, but I cursed well was not going to let Drake or the mansa have him. He belonged to me.

The stairs led past an empty first-floor room and up to the top floor, which was a square room with four windows. On a table lay an unrolled map of the landscape over which the two armies struggled, with Red Mount marked by a bold red X. A man with lime-whitened spiky hair bent over the table, tapping a knife's point on the house in which we stood. The old mansa of Two Gourds House sat calmly in a chair. A middle-aged magister sat cross-legged on the floor, hands on knees, head bowed, panting as he collected himself. His face was reddened, blistered in places. He was not Vai.

"Let me take the next attack," said the old mansa. "You are weakening."

"No, no," gasped the other man. "You are the strongest, Mansa. As long as you remain strong, you can kill any fire they can raise and hammer them all to the ground."

The old mansa sighed, then beckoned to a pale youth even younger than Luce. "Take the secret way, child. Hurry. Deliver a message to Lord Marius that we must have reinforcements. We will hold, or we will die."

"I can help you by staying here, Mansa!" With his eager, innocent face, the lad reminded me of Luce before she had gone to war, the way she had been back in Expedition.

"No. This is not your battle. Go!"

I stepped aside to let the youth pass down the stairs because I could not bear to touch him any more than I could have hurt Luce. He looked so innocent. The middle-aged magister brightened as a new aura of fire's backlash wrapped his body. Fire broke out again across every roof in the compound except for the stone house's tile roof. Through the north-facing window I looked over a second courtyard, this one ringed by a barn and cowshed and with a brick well at the center. The lad came running out the back of the house, then hesitated and glanced up at the tower where the officer, standing all unaware next to me, looked down at him.

"Curse it! Go!" shouted the officer to the youth.

Two Amazons and an Iberian burst into the courtyard through an arched gateway that linked the two courtyards. The taller Amazon plunged toward the youth, striking with her sword. The lad parried, but the deficiencies of his sword craft reminded me of Vai: He was the pupil who learns fighting by rote and works on perfect imitations of the forms taught by the sword master. That did not make him an effective fighter.

Yet he had no need to be a masterful fighter. Just as I realized the lad was wielding cold steel, the backstroke of his blade caught the glove of the woman and cut just deep enough to draw blood. The tip of the cold steel blade writhed like a viper's tongue. The soldier swayed as the steel serpent drank her soul; she toppled.

Beside me the officer released a bolt that struck the Iberian in the back, sending him to a knee. The other Amazon dashed back to the clot of soldiers fighting hand to hand under the arch, dragging the Iberian with her.

The young cold mage climbed into the well and vanished.

"He's in the tunnel," said the officer.

A hailstorm battered over the estate, pounding so hard I could not hear anything except its drum on the roof. The catch-fire sagged forward as the channel of Drake's fire was cut off. A soldier caught him as he sagged sideways, too weak even to sit up. The other soldiers around me shot at the felled Iberians and Amazons below, taking their time, making each bolt count.

"An unlawful and dangerous power these fire mages wield," said the old mansa to the officer. He looked winded and weary, but his outrage was a cloak that shielded him. "Fortunate for us that the young Diarisso mage understood it before the rest of us did."

"Fortunate for us that the mansa of Four Moons House recognized the young man's worth, given his low origins," agreed the officer.

The old mansa smiled grimly. "True enough. More importantly, he knew exactly how to bridle the young man's rebellious spirit."

Perhaps the words angered me, just a little.

The old mansa looked right at me. "What shadow beast haunts this chamber? Beware!"

They turned on me, the five soldiers, the officer, the old mansa.

But I was the hunter's daughter. So I killed them, all of them, even the old man, because Camjiata had to win the battle today. I killed the blistered magister who had so courageously taken in all Drake's fire and was dying; ending his agony was a mercy.

When the Amazons broke through and poked their heads into the chamber, they found me crouched by the old mansa, wiping blood from my sword with hem of his boubou. Blood pooled around me. Cold steel cuts deep.

Their laughter hurt my ears. "Bellona bless! Our work's done for us already!

Rising, I wiped blood from my cheek with the back of a hand just as Drake appeared. He went straight to the mansa and nudged the old man's body with a foot in a most disrespectful manner.

"Stop that," I said. "Show respect to the elders."

He paused, taking me in from top to toe with a gaze made narrow by his deepening frown. "You pick a strange way to show respect. Think of what a powerful catch-fire he would have made. But I can't expect you to understand that."

He brushed past me. I could have bitten out his throat, but I crushed Camjiata's words close to my heart, hiding them from everyone else. Win the battle first, or the enemy will triumph. The old order has to go down if we mean to break the chains that shackle us.

At the north-facing window, Drake swore. "The other cold mage is escaped, curse it. Did anyone see him?"

I said nothing.

Boots stamped up the steps, and Captain Tira appeared. Her gaze swept the chamber. She said, "Excellent. Remove the bodies. This will serve as a good command post for the general. Cat Barahal. Are you injured?" She looked me up and down. "Wasn't that fabric green?"

The Amazons chortled. "Did a quick dye job, she did!"

Their laughter seemed discordant to me, although they found

themselves amusing enough with their voices pitched loud, for they, too, had been deafened by the constant thunder of gunfire. I wiped another thread of blood off my chin, flicked a wet drop out of my eye, and glanced around the tower chamber. A spray of blood cut a line across the map on the table. The officer lay slumped, his head caught on the back of the chair. The five soldiers sprawled at all angles across the room, throats slashed and bellies opened, their blood a spreading stain. Its smell rose like flies, stinging and noxious. A drop of blood seeping from the ceiling dripped onto my hand.

I staggered, bumped into a wall next to Drake, and sank to my knees.

He shoved me away. "Cruel Diana! You reek of blood! Get away from me."

Trembling, I could neither speak nor stand.

He rolled over the other magister and studied the two cold mages with a flat, emotionless expression. "With a strong enough cold mage, I can do anything," he murmured to himself, so quietly that I knew he did not mean for me to hear. "I don't need him. He's kept me caged all this time because he's afraid I will figure that out."

He stepped over to the table where Captain Tira was carefully wiping blood off the map and examined the topography, then snagged a spyglass that was lying across one corner.

"Where are you going, Lord Drake?" asked Captain Tira as he walked to the stairs. "The general is already calling the advance against the Coalition center. He'll need you soon enough."

"He does need me, doesn't he? Far more than I need him. I only need fire banes." The sting of his presence faded as he vanished down the stairs.

Captain Tira watched him go, but she said nothing and did nothing. I needed to follow him, but a heavy exhaustion pinned me down. A fog of oblivion hazed my vision. How long I knelt there, shaking, I did not know. The chamber was cleared of the dead. An orderly scattered buckets of dirt over the floor to absorb the blood. People left and arrived while I watched the wall go nowhere.

Captain Tira said, "She's been in a stupor since we took the tower, General."

"Send an orderly to find her something else to wear. Bloody Camulos! Give me a spyglass! Look at the Coalition center collapse! Captain Tira, I want the Amazon Corps to march to the eastern flank. Lieutenant! Ride this dispatch to Marshal Aualos. I want Lord Marius's retreating forces cut off from the city gates. I do not want any Coalition troops or any mages escaping into Lutetia. I want no street-by-street fighting. I want a clear, emphatic victory."

Artillery boomed in sheets of thunder. Drums and horns beat out the pace of the advance as Camjiata's army roared forward, rifles ablaze and smoke gusting in windy bursts.

Messengers came and went as the general directed the battle from the tower. The stone house echoed with the groans of wounded.

A man bumped into me, swearing as he dumped a pot of scalding coffee to splash on the floor.

The general said, "Get her out of the way!"

I opened my hands to find them coated in sticky, drying blood. Swells and ebbs of memory surged in my head: the way flesh parts like a sigh as the blade slices; the submissive acquiescence of the hunted when it accepts it has been marked for death. Blood was spattered all down the front of my clothes. I tried to shake myself free of the awful sight, only I could not get away from myself.

No one took the least notice of me stumbling down the steps. The stone house was crammed with wounded. The stink of blood and piss and excrement melded with the rumble of artillery and gunfire, although the sound was ebbing because the advance of Camjiata's army was pushing the battlefront away from our position. I staggered into the back court and to a trough filled with pink and slimy water. I stripped off my blood-sodden jacket and fumblingly managed the slippery buttons of the skirt. Then I dumped a bucket full of dirty water over me once, twice, three times until I was gasping and shivering and began, at last, to feel human.

In my bodice and drawers I decided I would have to hunt for clothes, for I could not bear to dress myself back in the blood of men I did not remember killing.

"Trooper! What in the seven hells are you doing here? Your Amazons marched out two hours ago!" A sergeant wearing the Armorican ship jabbed at me with his finger. "Dereliction! Guards! Arrest—!"

I grabbed his out-thrust wrist and twisted it until he yelped. "I am Camjiata's ward, not an Amazon. Leave me be!"

497

When I released his wrist, he retreated two steps. A tang of fearful respect charged his scent. "By the Black Bull! Are you the assassin they say killed twenty men in the first assault without receiving a scratch?"

I did not care to dignify this with an answer. "There's a tunnel in the well that leads out. Best you make haste to block it so no raiders can come through."

He backed away.

Through the open doors of the half-burned barn, I glimpsed a figure I knew. "Rory!"

I found him doing nurse's duty among the wounded, moistening faces, offering sips of water. He embraced me with a snarl of relief but pushed me away at once. "I'm very busy. I find I quite like tending the wounded, for I detest the hateful racket of the guns. If you go to the corner, you'll find some local women sorting through garments they've stripped from the dead."

The local women were a trio of old dames, one toothless, one deaf, and the third the very same old woman who had greeted Rory in his cat body as *dominus*. She did not recognize bedraggled me, but her weary eye measured me the same as if I had been her own niece.

"Gave a man some trouble to you? Are you harmed, girl?"

I wanted to laugh but the sound would not come. "No. No man harmed me."

I found a dead Amazon's uniform that fit me well enough with its sturdy wool jacket and cunningly sewn skirt that could be tied up to different lengths depending on what a woman needed on the march. The cloth was dirty but unbloodied, by which I assumed the woman who had worn it had died from a head wound. My cold steel had returned to a cane. Cupping the locket in my hand, I closed my eyes and breathed down the thread that bound me to Vai.

He was alive.

The barn really stank, not just with ash and blood and piss but with pain, which has a tang as hard as a claw. I found Rory holding the hand of an unconscious soldier. My brother's sweet smile calmed me, for the groans and whimpers and sobs rubbed like thorns against my heart.

I crouched beside him. "I have to go. Are you coming with me?"

"Shh. I like to hold the hands of the ones whose souls are passing

over."

Curious, I rested a hand on the unconscious man's cheek. When I closed my eyes and sank my thoughts as into a soundless ocean of smoke, I could first feel and then almost glimpse the delicately wavering glimmer of brightness that sparked through the man's body: the flickering brain, the subsiding heart. The settling darkness of death's tide hauled him out to sea. The soldier took in a shallow breath, and then not another. In the dark ocean of death, a shark glided past to snap up the man's soul and carry it to the other side.

Rory released the lifeless hand. "It brings them comfort to know they aren't alone when they depart. I love to hunt, Cat, but there's just something wrong with all this. It tastes bad." He closed the dead man's eyes and arranged the hands atop the chest. "You wouldn't rather stay here? There are so many who need aid and comfort."

"I have to find Drake."

With a sigh he rose. "I know better than to try to stop any female when she's determined to go out on the hunt. Very well."

"You stay here, Rory. I can see the noise and confusion trouble you."

"Vai told me to keep an eye on you."

"Is that what he told you? To keep me out of the fight?"

He laughed, a startling sound amid so much suffering. Yet not one head turned our way. No one cared if people laughed; it was better than crying. "You don't know him well if that's what you think he would say. He told me once that any person who knows the stories of hunters who captivate spirit women in the bush knows that a man does not try to cage or leash a spirit woman, because if he does, she will vanish back into the bush and nothing he can do will stop her. He asked me to walk beside you, Cat, as he would do if he were here. Goodness, you're being very snappish, and I must say that you stink of blood."

I shuddered, for there was a chasm in my heart blessedly veiled in darkness, and I did not want any light to shine down there.

"Calm, Cat. Calm." He stroked my arm. "I better come with you or you'll do something foolish. Probably you already have."

At the doors children were digging out precious bolts and bullets from the walls and collecting them in a sack. In the courtyard riders gathered. General Camjiata emerged from the stone house, writing on a scrap of paper. He handed paper to a messenger and pen to an aide, then saw me. With a nod he indicated I should accompany him.

"I have to find Drake," I said as I took the reins of a horse led up by an orderly.

"Cat, you'll never find him in this chaos. Stick with me, and he'll turn up. He always does."

"I'm not sure he will this time. I think he's gone rogue."

He did not answer, for we were already riding out of the estate. I had no grasp of the time, only that it was now late afternoon and the thrust of the battle had raged away to the southeast. The land was a sweep of trees, fields, and pasture. No doubt this bucolic landscape made a restful scene on ordinary days. Now it crawled with soldiers and was strewn with bodies, discarded weapons, and lost hats and tassels. Camjiata was right: Alone, I had no chance of finding Drake or Vai among so many tens of thousands.

Because the general had rolled up the Coalition's western flank, Lord Marius had fixed his efforts to the east in an attempt to keep open the Liyonum Road for the Romans as they marched up from the south. Even without the spyglass, it was easy to tell from a distance where cold mages were still fighting to kill the general's guns. Smoke would billow in clouds that hid whole sections of the field from view, then patches would clear with startling urgency as artillery and rifles ceased firing for a space. A wind was really picking up out of the east, and black clouds had piled up as if about to break down over the city.

Rory had his head down, hands over his ears. The noise just never let up.

"There they go!" said Camjiata, holding the spyglass to his eye.

Tents in the Coalition's encampment caught fire. A battle by magic chased through the field, fire rising, then dying, rising and dying and finally rising again, as in a game being played like cat and mouse. Fire mages were flushing out cold mages and tracking them down. Was Drake directing them? Was that where he was? A gray sleet moved in over the city but just before it reached the camp it died in a violent updraft of air. The encampment began to burn in earnest.

Meanwhile artillery was being shifted to the south and east. We followed it to a ridge, where the command unit halted. The hillside sloped down to a stream beyond which ran the Liyonum Road. The general intended to bombard the Romans as they marched in column along the road, thinking to rescue their allies.

500

A soot-stained messenger came pounding up. He wore the badge of the Iberian Lion Guard. "Dispatch from Marshal Aualos, General." He held up a folded paper.

Camjiata did not lower the spyglass, which was fixed on the burning encampment. Figures fled in all directions, many of whom surely were not soldiers. *People will die regardless.*

"Read it to me," he said.

"My lord Keita, we have cut off Lord Marius so he cannot reach the city gates. The Parisi prince is dead on the field. We have taken thousands prisoner. The citizens of Lutetia have barricaded the gates to their city. Of cold mages we have captured twenty-eight alive."

Twenty-eight cold mages taken prisoner! My icy heart flamed hot. Was Vai among them?

The general lowered the spyglass, handed it to me, and took the wrinkled paper to scrawl a note on it. "Tell the marshal that the cold mage Andevai Diarisso is to be sent directly to me."

"Marshal Aualos said to tell to your ears alone that the particular mage you seek is not among the prisoners."

I pressed a hand to my locket. It was still warm.

"I want the marshal to secure the encampment and the city gates. Harry any retreating Coalition units until they rout. I want Lord Marius captured, or dead if must be. When the Romans arrive, we will have them surrounded on three sides, with the river at their back."

We stood without water or shade for an hour or more as troops ponderously trudged past our position to meet the approaching Romans. Far to the south the crack and boom of rifle fire started up; about half an hour later the rumble of cannon woke a mile or more away. But for the sound, and the departure and arrival of messengers, our watch on the ridge passed uneventfully. I couldn't think for the constant noise. Rory tucked himself into the shade of a tree, where he leaned his head against the trunk and closed his eyes. Exhausted, I sank down beside him.

The pounding hammer filled every crevice of flesh, and blood, and air, and earth. I fell as off a cliff into a dream.

Winged as an eru, I flew above an ocean of smoke. All around clamored my brothers and sisters, each fashioned in their own shape, and all of us killers. Flashes of light like silvery minnows caught in the waves as the dying gave up life. My siblings dove into the waters to gulp up each soul.

The spirits of the dead walked through us, the hunter's children, from the mortal world into the spirit world.

I saw everything: A man rides away from his comrades on a desperate errand although they urge him to turn back. My eru's sight could not encompass the features by which a mortal person recognizes another: the flash of sweetness when he really smiled, the way his eyebrows rose when he was teasing me, the promise of his lips. I saw instead the fathomless well of a cold mage whose person is the conduit through which weave the energies that bind the worlds.

Vai.

Thunder jostled my sight, and I lost track of him. The current of battle swept me south. Camjiata had deployed his artillery parallel to the road. It pounded into the Roman columns caught marching at double time, trying to reach their Coalition allies. Every time the Romans tried to break out they were met with a fierce attack from the general's Iberian Lion Guard or his Amazon Corps. The Kena'ani skirmishers with their white sashes had moved miles down the column to hit the hapless rear guard, which was cut off from the front by the lumbering baggage train.

So small rats were, seen from the height. Their lives of no moment, not truly. So much death churns through the world that we look the other way lest we be overwhelmed by its weight. But I was my sire's daughter. I had no heart whose conscience burdened my wings.

Separated from its Coalition allies by the tide of the battle, the Invictus Legion retreated step-by-bloody-step south, hoping to meet and join up with its brother legions. However much I had disliked the legate, he held the ranks together under merciless fire. The remnant hunkered down at last within the walls of a lord's estate.

Farther south an eagle standard went down amid screams of angry victory shouted by jubilant Iberians. Pressed by an unrelenting stream of cannonade, the Romans broke and ran, all but the Ironclad Legion. Under the command of an unflappable young tribune, it worked its way along the river and, in a meeting of grim embraces, joined up with the Invictus.

Twilight reached its fingers out of the east as a front of cold air. The current of the past hauled me into the tower room where I had stalked hours ago.

The first two men have no warning. I am no cold mage, to kill with merely a cut, so I slice their throats open to bleed them out. Cold steel has a sharpness that tastes like finest wine. The others realize they are trapped in the room with a monster. They try to fight, even the old mansa of Two Gourds House tries to draw cold magic to stop me, so I incapacitate him next. The officer puts up the worst struggle, for he is a canny and experienced man who does not want to die. The pulse of his ebbing heart's blood booms in my ears.

"Cat! Wake up!" Rory was shaking me. Everything was all blurred and smeary. He embraced me so tightly I couldn't move. "Cat, you were having a nightmare."

Thunder shuddered through the earth. Drops of icy rain spattered onto my forehead. Instead of blood-soaked clothing, I wore an Amazon's uniform. Who was I? What had I become?

Rory pulled me to my feet. "We're moving out. Look at those clouds! No one wants to be up on this hill in a storm."

"The general is asking for you, Maestra," said a young officer. He ducked at a growl of thunder, for there really was a storm crashing in on the wings of twilight. "Hurry! The walls of Lutetia have caught fire."

The glow of flame lit the north as Camjiata's retinue moved out. A terrible fear ripped through me. The whole city would burn. Drake would burn it all, the mage House and every building inside the city walls, just to show he could do it. Bee was in there, and not just Bee but tens of thousands of ordinary people going about their lives.

Blessed Tanit protect them! I stared in horror as flames leaped along Lutetia's walls.

A blizzard of sleet swept in with the night, swift and brutal. Born out of cold magic, the storm slammed down and, just like that, extinguished the flames.

43

The sleet icing down over us could not cool my gloating smile. Now Drake would know who was stronger! Yes, he was a savagely powerful fire mage, but he lacked the wisdom and discipline that made a mage like Queen Anacaona so formidable.

Fiery Shemesh! I had completely forgotten about the head.

"Rory! Where is the cacica's skull? I left it with you!"

"Don't snap at me! I hid the basket and your satchel in the prickly branches of that felled pine. No one will find it, I assure you."

When I applied to the general he shook his head. "I'll escort you back to Red Mount myself, once we have settled this matter of the Romans. Two of the legions have dug themselves in for the night. If they prove recalcitrant, I shall need you to slip into their camp and kill their commanders."

I opened my mouth, but no words came out.

"Cat? Is this too much for you?" He bent his head, examining me. "While you slept, I received word that a number of mages escaped into Lutetia. You know I want your husband's cooperation. Help me now, and I will help you find him. Furthermore, I've heard no word of James, which as you may imagine concerns me."

"I think he's decided he doesn't need you anymore," I said, goading him.

Rather than reply he withdrew a pipe from his coat, considered its damp bowl, and tucked it back into the pocket. A messenger rode up with a dispatch, pulling his attention away from me. At length, as we rode about a mile south, the icy rain slackened and ceased. We came up to one of the Iberian infantry divisions, which had boxed in the two battered legions against the river.

At the general's arrival a cheer rose. Captain Tira marched up with a squadron of Amazons. Dirty, bloodied, exhausted, they danced forward to the pound of drums and the singing of their sisters. Luce her very own self presented a Roman eagle to the general. Her pride blazed. She had a bloodied nose, a cut on her left shoulder, and mud smeared in her short cropped hair as if she had wrestled an enemy onto the ground. I could scarcely recognize the girl who had befriended me with a cheerful grin at Aunty's boardinghouse. Then she saw me, and she laughed to see me and Rory still alive, but she did not break ranks to come to us. She had chosen her path. It no longer marched alongside ours.

The general made his way through the troops, greeting men, giving a private word to the worst-wounded. I trailed behind him, trying to wipe flakes of dried blood and the cling of weariness from my eyes. Because I was not paying attention, I scarcely noticed when Camjiata rode out onto the vacant ground between the two armies.

The two legions had anchored their defense on an old fortified estate very like that of Red Mount. This compound backed up against the Sicauna River. The walls and buildings had taken damage from artillery fire, but the legionnaires were tough, experienced men who had set up an effective perimeter. The general rode right into range and then closer yet. I was so astounded by his audacity that I followed, together with a pair of aides in braided uniforms and tricorn hats.

The general surveyed the night-shadowed Romans and a lit lamp. "Brothers! I salute you! You have fought nobly this day for the honor of the empire that gave birth to you. That empire gave birth to me as well, for my mother was born into the Aemilius clan. By the courage and valor with which you have fought I am brought to wonder what incompetent commanders have led you to this pass. For it is certain that now, shed of them, you find yourselves driven into a corner not of your making. Have your consuls done well by you? Were you not abandoned by the best of your legates, Amadou Barry? Let me tell you what you do not know. The emperor envied and feared Amadou Barry, so he rid himself of the man. He will deny it! But you will never find Amadou Barry's body."

Camjiata was no djeli, but he was doing a cursed beguiling job weaving a story that tugged at hearts and loins and drew the world in fresh colors for men worn out by battle.

"How do you know what happened to Amadou Barry?" I demanded in a low voice.

"I have never managed to insinuate a spy into a mage House, but getting informers into the household of Lord Marius was not difficult. Every word I spoke is true. The emperor sent Amadou Barry to Adurnam because he feared the young legate's popularity in Rome."

Noble Ba'al! That put a different smell on the rose!

The legate whose wine I had poured walked boldly out to confront the general. I pulled just enough shadow around me that he couldn't be bothered to notice me any more than the general's aides. "What do you want, General Keita? Our surrender? The Invictus do not surrender. Nor do our Ironclad brothers. Our honor forbids it."

Every word Camjiata spoke was pitched to carry as far as possible. "Of course I don't want your surrender. Your soldier's honor shines as brightly as ever. Yet Rome's honor has been tarnished in recent generations. You know it."

Soldiers murmured. They did know it.

"Selfish patricians long ago repudiated the ideals of the old republic. In recent years they have likewise turned hostile backs to the new river of change that beckons. I will restore Rome to the glory and influence that she deserves."

"You're an Iberian. Rome has always been your enemy."

"It is true that on my father's side I am of Iberian princely descent and also the son of the sons of the emperors of old Mali. But through my mother's blood I have a claim to Rome. Why should old enemies not become today's allies? What can Romans and Iberians not do, if they work together under strong leadership? Will you join me? The old emperor is weak. But I am not."

The legate considered the general's offer and, naturally, grasped for the promise of glory.

He raised an arm in salute. "Camjiata!"

Behind echoed first a ragged cheer, rising with each successive wave until its tide swept the legions. "For Rome!"

The general accepted their approbation with an unsmiling serious-ness appropriate for the auspicious occasion.

"Bastard," I muttered appreciatively. "Is this what you hoped for all along? To raise the Roman legions to fight for you as consuls used to do in the days of the old empire?"

"Rome has always been mine," he said. "That is my destiny. You will not be the one to take it from me, Cat."

"As long as Rome doesn't bother me, I won't bother Rome," I retorted, and he smiled.

I waited as he conferred with the legions' officers.

Then we rode the two miles or so back to Lutetia. Soldiers lit our way with lanterns as we drew up before a huge barricade that closed the Liyonum Gate into the city. Lanterns and torches blazed. Thou-sands of people stood on the walls and roofs, for it seemed half the citizenry of Lutetia had come to face the victor.

A young woman stood on a table, flanked by a blacksmith in guild robes and a djeli with blond hair swept up in lime-whitened spikes and gold earrings gleaming in the flame of the candle lantern he held. Half hidden among the crowd waited Brennan and Kehinde. Weaponry scavenged from the field was being hauled into the city.

Camjiata rode forward. His carelessly bold manner gave him a commanding presence. I alone followed. Bee marked me with a dark look that scolded me. Then, having dispensed with me, she pulled the shawl on her shoulder up over her hair and opened her arms in a matronly manner that mimicked the festival tableau called "Dame Fortuna Welcomes the Victors."

"The good citizens of Lutetia have given me leave to speak on their behalf, out of respect for the Lady of the River whose voice runs all through the city." Her voice had such resonance that, although she did not seem to be shouting, the sound carried deep into the evening. "We offer our thanks here today to you, General Camjiata. You have fought your battle outside our walls. In your wisdom you leave us to fight our battles inside them. This barricade we built from the furniture and pavilions of the prince's palace, which we have torn down as the first act of raising an assembly to rule in the place of a prince. We will follow the example of our brothers and sisters in the city of Expedition on the island of Kiskeya across the Atlantic Ocean and devise a means to rule ourselves. Your offering at the altar of our radical enterprise we accept gratefully."

"What offering is that?" he said, with a smile whose contours I could not interpret. Was he angry? Amused? Making ready to launch an attack into the city with his victory-soaked troops?

"You have generously shared your legal code as a model for the one that will be written here! Copies have been printed across Europa and now circulate on the streets of Lutetia."

"I am aware of the strenuous efforts of printers. May I not stand on the steps of the prince's palace and declaim the code? I did so twenty-two years ago on those very steps, only to have the law driven out by the hounds of greed who are ever whipped forward by princes and mages."

Bee smiled bounteously. "The people of Lutetia are grateful for your efforts. We think you have done enough."

"And wishful to see the backs of me and my army, is that what you are saying, Beatrice? Is this what you have seen in your dreams, that I will turn away when I and my army have won the victory that allows the citizens of Lutetia to overthrow their hated prince?"

She opened her hands, palms up. "Is this how you interpret my remarks, General? Can we ever see the truth when desire blinds us? Or do we call it truth because it is what we wish to see? If you try to enter the city, the citizens of Lutetia will resist. What you do now is up to you."

Judging by the crease of his forehead and the blade of his narrowed eyes, General Camjiata was not well pleased to be told to go fishing or go hang by a ragtag assembly of disorganized civilians whom his soldiers could easily crush. That the young woman he had groomed as his protégé had absconded to speak for them could not sit well either. But his was not a lightning temperament; he could swallow his temper and consider all the implications before he acted.

I muttered, "You would have done better to marry Bee when you had the chance, General."

He murmured in reply. "Well, Cat, so I see you have cherished a cunning plan deep against your heart all this time. I admit, I am impressed. I did not expect this."

He leaned forward, one hand on the reins and the other on his sword's hilt. At his back his soldiers shifted their arms. When victorious men see resistance from the defeated, they can become mean and impatient.

"I do have one question for the citizens of Lutetia. I have a report that cold mages were allowed to enter the city."

"The old mansa of Two Gourds House is dead, my lord general," said Bee. "The elders of the Assembly deemed it proper for his people to return him to his mage House so offerings can be made and songs sung over his body."

"It was not just one old man's corpse, but a whole troop of living ones. When folk claim to have rebelled against the old order, and yet assist the cold mages who have for so long worked hand in glove with the princes and lords to oppress them, I wonder if they are still only puppets acting in the service of my enemies."

"Do you think to bully us, General? Do you mean to stand ankle-deep in the blood of our men and women while you proclaim a legal code meant to bring justice and peace? If that is the war you intend to fight, then know you can kill us but never truly defeat us." Her voice dropped to a more intimate tone. "You know what manner of person I am, General. Do not make an enemy of me. We can still be allies."

He tipped back the edge of his tricornered hat as in mocking salute. "I see you learned from the Expeditioners how to take advantage of a conflict between two greater swords to allow the small knife its killing thrust. This has truly been a piece of drama worthy of you, Beatrice."

"My thanks," she replied with a mockingly pretty courtesy.

He raised his voice. "Citizens of Lutetia, let those of you who can hear my words repeat them to the many too far away to hear. Remember that I am a man who listens. When your revolution discovers itself in internal strife, as it inevitably will, you need only send a messenger. I shall be pleased to help you settle your city in a more orderly fashion. But on this night, obedient to your request, we will withdraw."

"What about Andevai?" I demanded as he reined his horse around. Grabbing his reins, I tugged him to a halt.

He raised a hand dismissively. "Why, Cat, I am marching on Rome to make her into what she ought to be. The offer we discussed remains open."

"You said you would help me find him!"

"I expect I am not the only one looking for your cold mage." As horns sounded the call for an orderly march, he bent close. "Drake is yours, Cat. I commend him to you. If you can find him, for I expect he has already left the field."

"Noble Ba'al! You goaded Drake to this point, didn't you? You used him and now you're discarding him. That's why you never stopped Drake and me from all our fighting in public. You plan to blame Drake's death on me, as my personal vengeance. His fire mages will turn their loyalty to you, never guessing you schemed his downfall all along."

"Surely you guessed I never trusted James Drake. As for you, Cat, I give loyalty where I receive it in return. You have made it clear your loyalties lie elsewhere."

I held his gaze with my own. "I could run you through right now."

He leaned so close I could have kissed his cheek as I might have my own father's. "But you won't. Not today."

He eased the reins out of my grip and rode away into the embrace of his army and his imperial dream.

I dismounted and ran forward as Bee hopped down off the table.

"Dearest!" she exclaimed, grabbing my hands. "I was so worried about you and Rory. Are you coming back now?"

I crushed her against me out of relief, but also so I could speak directly into her ear. "Was Vai one of the mages who fled into the city?"

"No. I'm sorry, Cat. I spoke myself to the mansa of Four Moons House, who was carried in among the wounded. He was with the Romans but got through the lines. He is very bitter about losing Andevai, for there was a strutting and unpleasant young mage with him who seemed unsuitably pleased that Andevai has gone missing. Then a young mansa named Viridor claimed that after the storm, Andevai rode away to find Lord Marius. It's all so confused. Dearest... oh, Cat."

"He's still alive," I said stubbornly.

"We'll find him."

As Camjiata's army withdrew to set up camp, men and women armed with muskets, axes, and looted swords settled in to guard the barricades through the night. Brennan and Kehinde shook my hand,

and Rory's, too, for after all, they had spent a lot more time with Rory even than I had.

"Brennan and I will remain for another month at least," said Kehinde. "We'll be assisting the locals as they draw up a charter for the governance of Lutetia. You can find us if you need us."

"May Fortune smile on you in your search," added Brennan.

Bee led the way with a lantern. We ventured through the shattered remains of the grand encampment that days ago had been the scene of so much life. A scorched vendor's cart lay tipped over, wheels broken. A dog nosed through the ashy remains of rounds of cheese. The shine of my candle's flame surprised a scurry of rats swarming a corpse, burrowing in through eyes and mouth. Thin children knelt beside a soldier, tugging a ring and a watch from the body.

Lights rose and fell as might tiny fire boats atop waves, marking the paths of men and women who also searched. We discovered a half-conscious man with a crushed foot and torn scalp. This nameless soldier Rory and I hauled awkwardly between us as he slipped in and out of awareness, calling for his mother. He was a Lutetian, no taller than me, and very young. I could not bear to leave him, and I was grateful when we found an old man driving a cart with wounded men in it bound for Red Mount. We sat on the tailgate and bumped along, helping the man gather in more wounded until the wagon was full.

On the Cena Road, men with lanterns were pulling corpses off the road to allow traffic through. Bee tied her shawl over her mouth and nose. "Doesn't the stench trouble you, Cat?"

"I don't have the leisure to be troubled." I hopped off the wagon and hailed an older man with an avuncular face. "What happened here, Uncle?"

"The Tarrant lord Marius and his troop made their last stand, is what happened. Too bad, for he fought well."

"Is the lord dead?"

"How should I know, lass? I heard he was chopped to pieces, and I heard he was wounded and carried off by the Iberians. This is no place for lasses on a night when men are drunk with blood and victory."

"I'm looking for my husband."

He sighed. "May the Three Mothers aid you in your search, then. Good fortune."

511

As he trudged away, I called after the wagon. "Rory! Bee! Bring the lantern. We'll know a cold mage is close if the flame dies."

"I can't smell anyone in this nasty stench," muttered Rory as he handed the lantern to Bee. "But maybe I can find him by his clothes."

"Blessed Tanit! How many dead there are!" Yet Bee gamely brandished the wrought-iron candle lantern over corpses laid in neat ranks like firewood. "Wouldn't it be easier to go to the manor house and find the cacica?"

A hundred paces away, soldiers were searching through a roadside ditch. "Ah! Curse it! The cursed sword bit me!"

"Here, stand aside, you prickless worm. Let me—Ah! Curse it! It burns!"

With drawn sword I ran to their lamps. "What have you there? Let me see."

"Oo! What pretty girl assaults us...?"

I bared my teeth at their insolent grimaces. Something in my demeanor made the men retreat. The sword lay grimed by dirt, but I knew it as Vai's cold steel instantly. I snatched it up with my right hand. Such a black tide of wild anger swept me that for a moment I went blind.

Rory shouldered up beside us. "Cat, best we move out of here before there is trouble."

"I'll cause trouble," I said, taking a step toward the men that made them hurry away.

Bee and Rory pulled me back and led me along the drive to Red Mount. Wounded men lay on the gravel of the two courtyards, packed like fish in a barrel. The awful stink blended with their cries and groans. Surgeons and healers worked by lamplight, assisted by soldiers and by elderly women bringing water for the injured. Mostly men just lay there, awaiting some distant hour when an exhausted doctor would finally take a quick glance at them.

"Cat, what about the cacica?" Bee repeated. "I tried to say this before, but you don't listen. If you can talk to her in a mirror, perhaps she can see the well of Andevai's power and lead you to him."

Blessed Tanit! Why hadn't I thought of that?

I swayed, leaning on Bee. "Rory, go and fetch our things. We'll meet by the well. Bee, you look through the sheds. I'm going to see if I can find Lord Marius. I give this sword into your hand, Bee, into your hand only, until we find Vai again."

Holding her breath she touched the hilt with a finger. When it did not spark or sting, she slipped it out of my hand. "Cold steel! Does this mean I need only draw blood to kill?"

"No. Only if you are a cold mage. But no weapon will shatter this one."

She tested its balance, then both she and Rory hurried off.

With shadows drawn tight around me, I crept into the stone house to see if I could find Lord Marius. He was still alive, lying on a couch in a sitting room with eight wounded officers. To my surprise Marshal Aualos was seated in a chair beside the couch, joking with Lord Marius as they shared a bottle of whiskey. Lord Marius's color was sallow, and his eyes glazed with pain, but he could still laugh as the Iberian officer told a lewd story about a man who had mistaken his wife for a sheep. Lord Marius's left arm had been mangled into a pulp.

Doctor Asante and her attendants entered. She spared only a glance for Marius's arm before she examined the other wounded officers. "Your arm will have to come off, Lord Marius. Marshal, please leave. I prefer to do my work without an audience." As the marshal and his aides left, she examined each man. "This one is dead. Take him out. Those two I cannot help and this one..."

Lord Marius had not the strength to heave himself up on his good arm but he watched her with a keen gaze. "Doctor, is there nothing you can do for my aide, young Butu? He's not sixteen. My cousin's son."

"My apologies, Lord Marius, but his belly has been opened. I have no way to heal such an injury. However, with some luck and a little cooperation, you may recover."

"But never fight again."

"Men battle with their minds far more than with swords. Do you mean to retreat to your country estate and never again involve yourself in politics?"

"Are you an Amazon, Doctor? Why else would a woman walk the battlefield?"

"I was an Amazon for many years, but now I am chief of the general's medical corps."

"He has placed a woman in charge?"

"I am a woman," she agreed with the raised eyebrows of a person who has heard the comment once too often to be amused by the necessity of explaining one more time. "I also am a doctor. If you have some objection to my expertise, I can send another person to tend to you."

"No, no." He chuckled although it hurt him. "I am sure you will treat me as tenderly as would my mother, were she still with us. The folk in our villages would come to her for lotions and compresses and such healing craft. I do not fear your touch. I am just surprised by the presence of women in the army. Women give life. It is not their place in the world to kill."

"Only to be killed? I do not like the sound of that conundrum, my lord. So I will ask you this: Does the she-wolf not hunt the same as her mate?" She spoke the words while staring straight at me, then crossed the room to the hearth where I stood out of the way. Setting her bag on a table, she pretended to look through it while speaking in a whisper. "What creature are you, that carries a spirit blade and waits in the shadows?"

"You're a fire mage," I breathed. "Only trolls and fire mages can see my sword when I'm hidden."

"Sharp Diana! It is you, little cat!"

"Why do you call me that?"

"It is what Daniel called you after I had washed you and placed you yowling in his arms. Know this, Catherine. He loved you the moment he saw you. We all did."

"What happened? Who are you?" I whispered. "What is your place in all this?"

She smiled affectionately, allowing me to glimpse pieces of a story Camjiata had never known and I had never suspected. "I loved your mother, and she loved me. But under the law you could only be claimed and protected by male guardianship, and we had to get Tara out of the prison quickly, for she was to be executed at dawn. Fortunately she loved Daniel also, and I trusted him. The general has promised me the new code will change the law so that women may stand equally in guardianship to men."

For the space of several breaths I had no words. But at length I murmured what abruptly seemed clear. "After Camjiata's defeat and capture, they were coming to find you, weren't they? When they died."

Truth is written in the face. Hers had measured suffering, others and her own, and she had kept walking to do the work she felt called to do even though she, too, had lost the ones she loved.

"Yet why are you here, child?" she asked gently. "I sense you are come in some desperation. You may always apply to me for aid, little cat."

My heart beat so hard. "Some day, Doctor, I pray we will have time to speak at length. But right now I'm looking for my husband."

She nodded. "The cold mage whom James Drake hates so very much."

"Doctor! Why do you mumble? What am I seeing there, a sword and a shadow..." In his grievously wounded state, Lord Marius had slipped partway into the threads that bind the worlds. "Camulos's Balls! It is Cat Barahal! Have you crept in to kill me? Is this what became of Amadou?"

Doctor Asante's two assistants were busy preparing the table for the surgery. I unwrapped the shadows and crossed to kneel beside the couch. "I told you the truth about Amadou Barry."

"He was ever a fool about that girl," he murmured, eyes rolling back at a stab of pain.

The doctor said, "We need to operate."

Desperate, I grasped Lord Marius's uninjured hand. "Please. I'm looking for my husband. I heard he was last seen going to aid some cold mages seconded to your battalion."

"Ah!" Was that a wince of physical agony, or had he seen a sight he dreaded to tell me of?

My heart pinched until I could not breathe and thought I might faint. "Tell me!"

"He never once drew his sword although I know cold steel in the hand of a cold mage need only draw blood to cut life from the body. His one concern was to kill fire, to save as many lives as he could. I think he must have spared twenty cold mages who would otherwise have been burned like torches by the enemy's fire mages. He could have escaped into Lutetia, but he came after us because there were three young cold mages seconded to my troop, and he knew they would be killed or enslaved." He winced. "He bore the brunt of magical attacks whose impact I could neither see nor understand. As we were surrounded and made our last stand, the truth is that he collapsed."

A tear seared my cheek. "Dead?"

"He was never hit by any physical weapon. More like he collapsed from exhaustion."

"Blessed Tanit!" I murmured. "Too much cold magic for too long with no rest."

"Then I was wounded," mumbled Lord Marius in a fevered recollection. "The red-haired fire mage took him. Threw his limp body over a horse and rode off with his company."

My heart stopped.

"Where?" I cried.

"I did not see…" He passed out.

"If I do not amputate the arm, he will die." Doctor Asante took my arm, then kissed me on the forehead, as a mother might. Finally she released me and turned to her patient.

In a daze I walked to the door. In the passageway I leaned against the wall. My legs had stopped working. Out of the sitting room issued the grinding scrape of a saw punctuated by the grunts and gasps of a man trying not to scream. Driven on as if lashed by a whip, I staggered back to the north courtyard and there sagged against the well in utter despair and confusion. Despite everything, I was so exhausted that I fell asleep.

Bee tugged me awake. "You can't believe who I found."

I bolted up. "Vai!"

"No. Juba!"

"Juba? Haübey!" The spark of hope dimmed, then flared. "Has Rory returned yet? What if he couldn't find the basket?"

"Calm down, dearest." She pressed her forehead against mine and bent her will to soothe my heart as her gaze pinned mine with bitter intensity. "Calm down."

She led me into the barn. Rory was sitting in a quiet corner, holding the hand of a dying man. He smiled, indicating the basket and satchel at his side. Bee grabbed them and made me follow her farther in.

Haübey worked by lamplight in a stall carpeted with straw. An oil lamp held by a Taino soldier made a shimmering splendor of the trickling streams of blood oozing across the chest of a wounded man. With a precise stitch Haübey was sewing up a frightful gash that ran from the man's shoulder to below his breastbone. Despite the urgency that nipped at my heels like wolves, I had the decency to wait.

The Taino prince Haübey, called Juba by Europans, resembled his brother Caonabo in every particular except that his black hair fell only to his shoulders rather than halfway down his back. His air of intensity sat in marked contrast to Caonabo's reserved demeanor. Also, Haübey had a fresh scar over his right eye. I had forgotten he was a healer. Although not a fire mage like his brother, he had been trained in a behique's knowledge even if he had not the full store of a behique's power.

Bee's gaze was fixed on Haübey as if judging where to aim her axe blow the best to split his head in two. "I haven't shown myself to him yet. I felt no fear in confronting the general, yet I hesitate now." Her fingers crushed my hand until I grunted in pain.

Finishing, he rose as he wiped blood off his hands. He nodded curtly, if absently, at me, then looked again. "The fire bane's lost woman! I had heard you walked with the general." His gaze tracked past me, and his eyes widened. "Beatrice!" He uttered her name so throbbingly that, had I not been heartless, exhausted, and desperately in search of my beloved, I should have blushed. "Why are you not in Sharagua with my brother?"

An incandescent anger transformed Bee's lovely features. "Did you plot it between you?"

He wiped his bloody forehead with the back of a hand. "I do not understand you."

"You understand me perfectly well. I have had a lot of time to think. Was Caonabo looking for a pretext to divorce me? One that all of you hoped would force me to return to Europa with the general? Would he have crafted some other reason for me to leave if this one had not come to hand? From the moment you discovered I walk the dreams of dragons, you've been plotting to use me, haven't you? You, your brother, your mother, your uncle: all of you. I thought you were better, that you cherished dreamers, but the Taino court connives no differently from the rest. You want cold mages for whatever war is brewing between you and your rivals. If the general won—with my help, of course!—he agreed to dismantle the mage Houses and give you first pick of the captive cold mages, didn't he?"

517

"First pick!" I exclaimed. "Was he intending all along to hand Vai over to you?"

Haübey took the lantern and dismissed his attendant, leaving us three alone with unconscious men. "You cannot think the Taino offer aid to the general in exchange for nothing?"

"He's trading you cold mages in return for your support?" I repeated stupidly.

"Why do you think I came to Europa in the first place two years ago?" Haübey asked. "Your wars and rivalries do not interest us. I came at the behest of my uncle to learn about cold mages. Instead I saw people living in unpleasant squalor. Children suffer hunger while others throw away food they cannot eat and will not share. People die of diseases any decently trained behique could cure. The streets run with filth, and there is no decent night lighting. The food is awful. And it's cold. But the music and drumming is good, and many of the women are beautiful." His gaze lifted to capture Bee's. He trembled as on the edge of a kiss.

She cut him with an angry frown. "Can it be that even to Caonabo I was nothing more than a tool to be used? Although I grant you that I was well handled and lovingly polished."

Haübey closed his hands to fists, although I could not be sure if it was her accusations or her insinuation of the intimacies she had shared with Caonabo, ones he had been denied, that upset him. "You see only the shadows that churn the Great Smoke, dreamer. You do not know what thoughts trouble a man."

Elsewhere a man groaned, begging for water. Rain began to fall with a steady drumming, and water dripped through the many scars in the burned roof to splash onto the wounded, who could not even cover themselves. In the stall next to us I heard Rory humming softly.

"Blessed Tanit!" Bee said. "How is it come to this, that I think only of my injured heart?"

I pulled the cacica's skull out of the basket. Startled, Haübey took a step away.

"Your Highness, at the request of your uncle and your brother, I deliver your mother's head to you. With this cemi, Prince Haübey, your kinsmen give you permission to return home. They want you back to lead the Taino army."

He stared, looking first confounded and then pleased. "So I am answered!"

"Just one thing first."

Digging into the satchel, I pulled out the sewing kit Vai had so thoughtfully given me. Of course it included a hand mirror, since I could not imagine that Vai could imagine existence without a mirror. I caught the skull in the reflection as I pulled the shadows around me. Haübey gasped gratifyingly when I vanished. Spun in my shadow, the skull shifted to the texture and weight of a living head and met my gaze in the mirror.

"Honored Cacica, my greetings," I said.

"My greetings, Niece. You have returned me to my son."

"So I have, honored one. As I promised."

She blinked to show her approval. "Your debt is paid, even if I cannot approve how my brother went about getting his way. We maintain righteousness because we hold to the law."

"The world changes," muttered Haübey. "The old ways no longer protect us. My uncle understands that, even if you did not, honored mother."

The cacica had not struck me as an impulsive, emotional woman, but judging by her glare, she and her impatient, headstrong son had more in common than I had thought. "Those who cast aside the law will wither like maize under drought. And so will the land!"

Haübey's brooding expression was sharpened by lips pressed so tight I wondered he did not cut himself. "I have something to say about how you treated Caonabo all those years, favoring me and neglecting him! I always resented it! He will make a noble cacique, even if you never thought so!"

This was really too much! I broke in. "The cacica is a wise and perspicacious woman! Do not speak to her so disrespectfully."

"How can Juba hear and speak to her when I cannot, except in the spirit world?" Bee asked.

The cacica turned her gaze from her son to me. "To the dreamer give my greetings, Niece. We who have ears can speak to our ancestors, that is why. A pity my brother connived with my sons to send her away. She was a proper influence. Yet what troubles you, Catherine Barahal? For I see a shadow in your heart."

"I beg your pardon for my abrupt manner. James Drake has stolen my husband. Can you tell me in which direction they have gone?"

"When a rot grows within the crop, it must be cut out quickly before it spreads its taint. Let me see." A thread spun away into the darkness of the mirror. She first whispered words that sounded like the drizzle of rain and the moan of wind, then spoke again in the language I could understand. "North they ride. Straight north."

North. Drake was going to use Vai to sow terror and death through his Ordovici homeland. Dread opened a gash in me through which all my fears poured. But I remembered my manners.

"My thanks to you, honored queen," I said, even if my voice shook. "Have you any other words you wish to say before I release you to your son?"

"Let my dead son know that I understand the tide has already washed this shore. What is done cannot be undone."

"As I am reminded when I look on you, honored one," I said politely.

"May the Good Great Spirit walk with you, Niece."

"*Taino-ti'*, honored queen. May the Good Great Spirit walk with you."

I lowered the mirror, tucked the skull into the basket, and offered it to Haübey. He took it gravely, but it was Bee he looked at.

"Come back with me, dreamer. You will live in a better place than this, honored among the Taino as a noblewoman. And if not for my sake, then for my brother's. I happen to know he feels true affection for you although he is not a man to say so."

"No." Her hand clasped mine firmly, even if her voice trembled. "My home is with Cat."

"We have to go," I said. And so we did, gathering Rory as we left.

"Where are the cold mages being held prisoner?" I asked an orderly, who directed me to a sergeant, who informed me they were being held in custody at the rear hospital. It was too far away; we didn't have time; we couldn't save everyone.

We walked north along the Cena Road to Lutetia. Bee's honey voice talked us through the barricade because they recognized her from her work with the radicals. How long ago it seemed that I had fled Two Gourds House and Vai had come to the inn looking for me. What if we had separated in anger, and had never spoken again?

"Cat, dearest, let me help you." Bee steadied me as I stumbled.

"I'm so glad you're here, Bee."

"I'll always be with you, dearest."

We reached the forecourt gates of Two Gourds House at daybreak. The compound was surrounded by armed citizenry, not hostile but definitely vigilant. In the forecourt mage troops stood guard. Their captain made us wait on the entry steps in the morning sun. The mansa of Four Moons House himself appeared with his djeli at his side and his repugnant nephew dogging his heels as if hoping for a scrap of meat. The mansa had sustained a gash on his chin. His left arm was in a sling. Yet he looked imposing in a formal indigo robe whose sleeves swept the ground as he strode down the forecourt steps and grasped my hand, speaking to me with his own voice.

"Catherine! Explain yourself!"

"I told you the village boy meant all along to betray us," broke in the nephew, in a sour tone. "He is probably dining with General Camjiata right now."

"People do not sit down to dinner in the morning," I snapped.

"Silence, boy!" said the mansa to his nephew before turning to me. "Catherine, please disabuse yourself of any belief that I am angry at Andevai. He saved many lives yesterday. If the tide of fire magic grew too strong for one of the others, Andevai would pull it into himself by the craft he learned from the Taino. He risked more than anyone else."

The nephew hunkered down as if enduring a rancid smell, his mouth shut for once.

"Was it Andevai's storm that quenched the fire that would have burned the city?" I asked.

The mansa's voice was hard, his manner impatient and proud. How like Vai he seemed, although I could not tell what emotions surged beneath the garment of his arrogance. "Andevai is not the only powerful cold mage. That was my storm, in concert with Mansa Viridor. But I must ask, was it all a ruse? Did you plan this victory with General Camjiata? I regret I could not recognize Andevai's worth until it was too late to bring him to trust me."

"You still don't understand him, Mansa. He respects you more than he will ever express to you. He was able to look past the scorn and contempt he endured and admire your strength and consistency in

521

your rule over Four Moons House. Not every mansa would have educated the village boy with the sons of the mage House. You didn't do what you ought to have done to stop their cruel bullying, but you did not force him to stand at the end of the line when he had earned the right to stand at the head. That is why he fought for the mage House as well as for the sake of his village. And, I admit, for his own pride, which as we both know is as vast as the heavens. Will you help me get him back?"

His gaze no longer frightened me because I understood him better now: He was a man who saw the world purely through the lens of his birth and his House.

"Where do you think he is?"

"James Drake has deserted General Camjiata's army and taken Vai prisoner. I believe Drake is going home to the Ordovici Confederation to get revenge on his family. Vai's cold magic makes Vai a powerful catch-fire. Imagine how powerful he will make Drake's fire magic."

Bee took hold of my hand. "Do you really suppose Drake can defeat Andevai? Were I a betting woman, I would put my money on Andevai."

"So would I, were it a duel between the two of them. But Drake has surely taken the most loyal of his fire mages with him to do his bidding. If I were Drake, I would have fire mages pouring backlash into Vai day and night to keep him incapacitated. Even Vai can't fight all of them. And he'll try to protect whatever other catch-fires Drake may have in his keeping."

The mansa gestured toward his steward. "I am not willing to sit idly by while Four Moons House is insulted in this egregious manner! But we have only a handful of horses left in this compound and they are either wounded or broken down from being overworked yesterday. I am told that General Camjiata has taken every able-bodied horse off the field. And since we magisters are trapped here, the citizens of Lutetia have no doubt rounded up the rest." He laughed in a manner that annoyed me. "There is your revolution for you. Trapped in our own House and yet not one word of thanks from the local citizens for the death and injury we took on ourselves that spared the city of Lutetia from being burned to the ground and ravaged. Rather, they treat us as if we are the ones who assaulted them and started this war!"

Bee glanced toward the compound gate. "I can negotiate with the citizens' council..."

A full-length mirror hung opposite the main doors in the entry hall.

"I have a better idea," I said. "But first, may we change out of these clothes and wash and eat something? Before we depart?"

Though in mourning, the residents of Two Gourds House treated us with every courtesy and were expeditious in bringing wash water and food. I did not inform them that I was the person who had killed their master. I didn't want Bee to know. I almost wept when a steward brought me the spruce-green skirt and resewn cuirassier's jacket, cleaned and ironed. I demanded provisions be brought. Back in the entrance hall the mansa and his attendants and soldiers had gotten into their riding clothes and uniforms, for they believed we would be traveling on horseback.

"If you will, Mansa, can you give me a tiny bit of cold magic?"

He raised an eyebrow interrogatively, but he obeyed with alacrity, plucking a spark of cold fire out of the air. My sword woke; I drew the blade into daylight. Folk did gasp and murmur, but the mansa frowned as he glanced toward the mirror and then back at me.

"Can you walk after him through the spirit world? Surely not, Catherine. You might vanish for weeks or months..." He trailed off.

In a silence weighted by every gaze following me, I approached the mirror. With so many cold mages in the entry hall, magic rippled in its depths. Rory's reflection shifted back and forth from cat to man. Bee stared fixedly, her dreaming eye alight on her forehead. As for me, my own reflection glared back at me. Was this the face Andevai had seen and fallen in love with the day I had walked down the stairs and he up them to where we had first met on the landing? Hard to imagine! I looked as if I meant to bite someone.

I would find him! And I would make James Drake pay!

I nicked my skin to draw blood, its smear bright on the blade. I thrust my sword into the mirror, up to the hilt. The cold steel cut a gateway between the mortal world and the spirit world. I parted the lips of the gate as I might part a curtain. A murky night hid the spirit world from my eyes. But I still had my voice.

"Let those who are bound to me as kin come to my aid!"

An icy wind kissed my nose. Like distant thunder my sire's voice laughed mockingly. A bee sting flamed as an ember on my hand, then faded. Wet noses prodded my arm and a rough tongue licked my face as the breath of cats warmed me. The creatures of the spirit world could not cross into the mortal world except on Hallows' Night...or in my wake, as Rory had.

"May blessings bring quiet sleep and plump deer to you and yours, Aunt," I said politely, "and let me assure you that your son is well and behaving himself as much as he can. But I seek my cousin eru and the one she travels with. If they will cross with me."

An eerie arc of day broke over the land. In its wake rolled a coach and four. The coachman drove right for my outstretched arm, and I grabbed at the harness and flung myself backward to draw them with me.

The coach rolled into the entry hall as people shouted and scattered. It kept on through the open front doors and glided a hand's span above the steps before settling to earth on the graveled forecourt. The horses stamped, a mist steaming off their pearlescent skin. The coachman tipped his hat to me. His blue eyes tightened with a smile that did not touch his lips. The footman jumped as lightly down from the back as if she had hidden wings. She flipped down the stairs and opened the door.

"What is your wish, Cousin?" the eru asked. In the eyes of everyone else she appeared as a man. Perhaps I just found her more comfortable to talk to as a woman.

"If you will convey us, I would be glad of it. Bee, Rory, get in."

The eru swung the bags of provisions up onto the roof.

"What means this, that those who served us now serve you?" The mansa looked ready to ignite.

"They do not serve me, nor did they ever serve you," I retorted. "But if you wish, Mansa, you can come with us. We could use a powerful cold mage."

"So it has come to this," he muttered. "I am being led by two girls."

His irritation brought a smile to my lips for the first time in days. I made an elegant courtesy. "Yet you must admit, Mansa, that my dearest cousin Bee and I are two exceedingly fine young women, with quite unexpected depths."

524   Only a man of his stature and birth could manage an expression

that so purely combined a censorious frown shaded by a wrinkle of amusement at his eyes, for as much as he disapproved of my bold way of speaking, it was equally obvious a part of him found it appealing.

"That is one way to describe it, Catherine. We have not the leisure for me to explain the other. My predecessor could not have imagined that the bargain Four Moons House forced onto the Hassi Barahal clan sixteen years ago would lead to this peculiar end."

But he wanted Vai back as much as I did, so he dismissed his djeli and gave orders to his nephew to follow with the surviving Four Moons soldiers and mages as soon as they could get horses. Then he got in.

The door was shut. The squinty gremlin eyes of the latch stared at me in what I thought might be surprise to find me back again. The coach jostled as the footman swung up onto the riding board in back. On the whip's snap we rolled, on our way at last.

44

Drake's trail led north in fire and ashes.

The first staging post lay in smoking ruins. Locals poking cautiously through the remains of a cottage, kitchen-house, and stable yard told us of fire and confusion none of them had been close enough to observe. The staging-post attendants were missing and the horses had all been stolen.

"A clever move on his part," remarked the mansa as he paced the scorched grounds of a third staging post, later that afternoon. "All the local militias are in disarray from the campaign. Had we not this magical conveyance, his actions would have slowed down our pursuit so greatly there would have been no chance we could catch him."

Seeing my distress, Bee ushered us back into the coach. As we headed into the gathering dusk, she talked to fill the silence. "Can the blacksmiths' guild not be recruited to help us?"

"What can they do?" he retorted. "They have devised their own means to control and channel the destructive chain of fire magic, but they cannot combat this. I am come to appreciate General Camjiata's devious mind. He raises a fire mage who can win his battles and discards him when he becomes too powerful, yet does so at no risk to himself. From what you've explained, Catherine, it seems to me the general pushed the man into embracing the worst of his anger without the man realizing he had been manipulated."

"Yes, it does seem that way."

I stared out the window at a rabbit racing across a meadow in fright for its life. A hawk stooped. With a gasp, I leaned to watch. In a flash of feathers the hawk thumped. Then we rocked around a corner and

I never saw whether the hawk had caught its prey or the rabbit had escaped.

"Of course you would recognize such a stratagem, since you possess the same sort of devious mind," said Bee. "For example, now we are thrown together as kinsfolk, allow me to commend you on your strikingly cunning ploy to elevate Andevai as your heir and thus bind him more tightly to the mage House. Considering everything I was told you said about him before, I would never have guessed you would do that."

He brushed a finger along the unscarred side of his chin as if deciding whether to dignify her barbed teasing with a reply. "It was no ploy. The young man is the most rare and potent cold mage of his generation in Four Moons House and possibly in all of Europa, although I must request you never repeat to him that I said so."

"Have no fear," Bee reassured him. "I, too, would prefer to avoid any chance his already bloated conceit might yet expand, difficult as it is to imagine it could get any vaster."

The mansa's smile flashed so unexpectedly that for an instant I wondered if a different person had fallen into the coach with us. "The confluence of such powerful cold magic with the sort of unusually good looks that bring so much consequential attention to his person has certainly fed a temperament already prone to vanity and pride."

Bee patted my hand, trying to get me to smile. "You see, Cat, this is where Andevai gets his pedantic way of speaking."

I sighed.

The mansa glanced from her to me and back to her. "Yet for all his faults, he displays a profound sense of responsibility, as well as a willingness to labor tirelessly for the benefit of the House. He has also the intelligence and discipline to look beyond his own desires to what may be best for the House. I am not blind. The world is changing, even if I cannot approve. Sadly, there are many who no longer seek my approval."

Bee offered him her most refulgent smile, an expression of considerable genius which she had worked for hours in front of a mirror to perfect. "As long as you respect and support my beloved cousin, and don't make her husband too miserable, I shall approve of you, Your Excellency."

He had the grace to laugh. "There is a great deal I thought I knew that I now discover I had not the least understanding of." He reached for the shutter on the door that opened into the spirit world. "Why this is never opened, for instance."

"Don't touch that!" Bee and I said at the same time.

Startled, he withdrew his hand. "What secret lies behind this closed door? For some years Four Moons House employed this very coachman and footman as servants. Then they vanished with you, Catherine, only to reappear again at your call."

A razor-toothed imp of mischief sank its fangs into my tongue. "The Master of the Wild Hunt has been spying on the mage Houses all along, seeking the most powerful among you to kill each year."

"Do you mean to explain to me how you know all this, Catherine? That Beatrice walks the dreams of dragons I know. Andevai has explained how troll mazes protect against the Wild Hunt. But I am still puzzled by what exactly you are, a secret my heir has not seen fit to share with me."

I no longer saw a reason to hide the truth. "What would you say if I told you my mother was a human woman and my sire the Master of the Wild Hunt?"

He sat back with a chuckle. "No wonder the boy can scarcely contain his vainglory when he speaks of you. I must say, Catherine, that gives me considerable relief, for it has been a goad on my pride that you escaped me three times."

I did not know what to say to that. I had not even shocked him!

We rocked along, wheels rumbling a steady rhythm. Bee made me eat cooked chicken and rolls and cheese. For half the night we rolled through forest, and eventually I slept, head resting on Bee's shoulder. I woke at dawn to the sight of Bee paging through her sketchbook under the thin light of a cloudy day. Both Rory and the mansa dozed, Rory with his hands curled up by his face and the mansa bolt upright, his big frame filling half the opposite bench and pressing Rory's slighter figure into the corner.

"Have you found anything new?" I asked, as if I could pull hope from her dreams.

"No." She handed the book to me. "For the last month, all I have dreamed of is fire, and I couldn't bear to draw all those flames for I swear to you I heard screams in them." She pinched a length of skirt between her finger and thumb. "I'm sorry. I shouldn't have told you."

Yet for all that I stared at every sketch, I could discern nothing to tell me how to save Vai. What if he and I weren't meant to meet ever again?

Mid-morning on the following day we stopped at a burned-out staging post to allow the coachman to tend his coach and horses. The mansa studied the coachman as the man watered the horses from a bucket whose lip never touched stream or well.

"No living horse can travel at such a steady pace without cease and not die," said the mansa. "What manner of creature are they?"

The coachman acknowledged the mansa's attention by flicking a forefinger against the rim of his cap, but did not deign to respond.

"The man mocks me," said the mansa, as if it were my fault.

I glanced up at him from under half-lowered eyelids, although I did not mean to be coy. "I would be cautious in assuming that he is man."

With a shake of his head he walked away.

Bee was still in the nearby woods doing her business. I approached the eru, who stood beside a stream watching the flash and subsidence of ripples.

"I want to thank you for coming at my call," I said.

Away from the others she wore her female aspect. "The law of kinship binds us. But there are other reasons to answer."

"Perhaps you can tell me what those might be," I said, careful not to ask a question.

"Perhaps my lips are chained."

"Perhaps the Master of the Wild Hunt chains you to his purpose."

Her gaze held a whisper of the wild fury of lofty winds where an eru might climb, when she is free to fly as she wishes. I could not see her third eye, but I knew it was there. "Perhaps I am not the only one who is chained. Chains reach deep and rise high, little cat. They may be anchored in the depths of the Great Smoke, or pull against us from the heights of the tallest peak. Do not mistake the servant for the master."

I thought of the courts atop the ziggurat feeding on the blood my sire brought them. Picking up a stone, I tossed it into the water. "I have been thinking about chains."

"Cat! Over here!" Rory knelt at the wall of a byre. "It's all dried now, but Vai pissed here."

I saw nothing except scuffed ground and what looked like half-formed letters scraped into the dirt and then obscured by footprints. "You can distinguish different people's urine?"

"Can't you? I shall never understand you Deadlands people. How do you distinguish who has been poking around where if you can't smell?"

"There's a thought I am grateful had never occurred to me before now."

A scrap of leather cord had been half shoved into a hole scraped under the byre's wall. I got hold of it and fished out the empty ring of an ice lens. The sight so congealed my legs that I sat down with a thump.

Rory pried my hand open to see what I was clutching. "He left this here on purpose, so we would know he is with Drake."

All along the road to Arras and then on to Audui, every isolated staging post had been burned. Worst, at one hostel the corpse of a magister had been stuffed headfirst down a well. When we pulled him out by the rope tied around his feet, the seeping blisters over every bit of his reddened skin told the story of how he had died.

"Over here." Rory beckoned from beyond the hostel's vegetable garden to an old and falling-down outhouse. He indicated a row of three stones and a pearl jacket button.

The mansa came up behind us. "Four stones for Four Moons House. The estate of Four Moons House lies on the Cantiacorum Pike. If they stay on this road, they will pass it. If Andevai attempts an escape there, he can hope for assistance."

"I don't think Vai will risk drawing Drake's anger down on the House, or on his village. And I'm certain he won't abandon the other mages." But I rubbed the dirt off the button and tucked it into my bodice.

The mansa insisted we break our headlong pace and spend one night at Audui's resplendent mage inn. In truth the amenities of a bath, a change of underclothes, the promise of a comfortable bed, and a decent supper improved my mood considerably. The steward in charge told us there had been a plague of fires tormenting the countryside, a freakish set of frightful blazes no one could explain although they had passed as quickly as they had come.

"How long ago?" I asked over a delicious meal of soup, roasted beef, yam pudding, fish in dill sauce, and apple dumplings.

"Just yesterday did all the reports come in, Maestra," said the steward in charge. "One of our own young grooms escaped a terrible fire yesterday at West Mile Post just four miles west of town."

"Can we talk to him?"

The lad was brought, white and trembling. He had a tendency to jump every time a door closed elsewhere in the inn, but Bee hastened forward to take hold of his hand as if he were a long-lost kinsman. No lad his age could resist her radiant glamour.

"You are the only one who can help us!" she exclaimed. "What was your name again?"

"They call me Rufus, Maestra, for my red hair."

"Tell us everything you saw, Rufus!"

"It was all fire, Maestra," the lad whispered in a hoarse voice. "But the man gave me a message." His gaze flashed toward me. "He said there would be a woman with black hair and golden eyes come after him. I was to speak to her when I saw her."

Had Vai managed to get a message to me? Hope surged.

"Go on," said Bee in her most encouraging tone.

The lad handled the words as cautiously as a knife. "He said, 'Nothing you can do will save him.'"

I recoiled as if struck.

Bee smiled. "Very good! Thank you for remembering. What did he look like, the man who spoke those words? Had he red hair and white skin, like yours?"

He nodded, gulping down a sob. "He did burn the whole compound, Maestra."

"Had they prisoners?" asked the mansa. "Any they treat differently from the rest?"

Concentration furrowed his brow. "Hard to count, I was that scared. But there was one they did hold away from all the others. Maybe he was sick, for he could barely walk. He was whistling a song, that one, and they did kick him to shut him up."

"What song?" I asked.

Like any Celt, he could remember a tune after hearing it once. He hummed the melody the djeli had sung when he had led Andevai to the meeting with the Romans, the one I had first heard in the spirit world on the fiddle of Lucia Kante.

The mansa handed the boy a coin. "You have done well."

We rose at dawn. At breakfast the mansa asked for coffee with a bowl of whipped and sweetened cream but I could not bear to touch it for it made me think of Vai so weak he could barely walk. Was he wounded? Beaten? Assaulted? Or was he simply exhausted to the edge of collapse? It would be just like Vai to believe he had to carry all the burden himself.

A headache throbbed behind my eyes as we set out. I was so sick of being in the coach.

As if catching my mood, the gremlin latch winked to life with a flickering sneer. "I have been very patient," the latch said in a thin whine that put the lie to the statement, "but all your cousin and that unpleasantly large and frowning cold mage do to pass the time is argue about this thing called politics and law which means nothing to me! Could you not tell me stories instead? Or at the least, let the cold mage draw some of those pictures in the air like the other one used to do. I'll tell you a secret if you do."

"Everyone claims to have a secret!" I said.

"Cat?" Bee bent to look at me. "You're very worn down, dearest, and now you're babbling. Perhaps you should try to sleep some more."

"I can't rest," I said, "but perhaps the mansa could explain to us how young magisters are taught the basic skill of illusion. It would make the time pass, would it not?"

To my surprise the gaze I fixed on the mansa, meant to be venturesome and coaxing and more likely appearing fractious and sour, softened his bearing. He had begun to treat Bee and me with the grave amusement shown by an exalted and wealthy uncle toward his impoverished but marginally respectable nieces, the ones who with better clothes and improved elocution might hope to make modest marriages to humble clerks. He drew the basic illusions every young magister was expected to master: a candle flame, a glinting gold ring, and a veil of mist that could be shaped into the shadows of living creatures. The slow play of shadow and light eased my mind and let me doze.

The next day we moved into a dense lowland scrub forest as the great valley of the lower Rhenus River opened before us. Now and again we caught glimpses of the wide river glittering to the west. We passed a toll station, which had been burned. Threads of smoke ghosting up from its embers told us that Drake's troop was not many hours ahead.

As night fell the mansa lit globes of cold fire to light our way. Scraps of cloud lightened the moon-scarred sky. Very late we halted in a lonely meadow amid the creak of insects and a night breeze winnowing the grass. The coachman preferred to water and care for the horses at night, and I was grateful for the chance to lie down on a blanket on the ground. An owl's white wings fluttered through the trees, and for an instant the weight of ice pressed down on me as if malevolent claws had reached across the worlds to throttle me. Then Bee put an arm around me and, comforted by her presence, I slept.

At dawn I woke to see a big furry flank draped alongside me. The big cat snored softly, until I punched him in the shoulder to wake him up.

"Rory! Where are your clothes? What are you doing?"

After he dressed and as we ate our provisions, he told his story. "I decided to scout. Drake's party is not even half a day ahead of us."

"I should have gone with you! I could have rescued Vai."

"No, you should not have gone. They have little mirrors hung up all about the camp, so they would have caught you."

"Like a troll maze! I wonder how Drake knew."

"Mirrors are no danger to me!" Rory smiled with the preening confidence of a male who accepts that he is lovely. "I scared their horses, so they lost more time because they had to round them up. Wasn't that clever?"

"Indeed." The mansa's puzzled frown would have amused me another time. Rory's shape change had taken him aback in a way the confession of my parentage had not.

"What about Vai?" I demanded.

"He was tied up and staked to a post. The other cold mages were tied up, but they looked like sheep to me, so fearful of the wolf they hadn't a bleat among them. I wasn't sure if Vai had seen me but then he began to talk. I must say, I wouldn't have used that tone of voice if I had been the one in captivity."

533

"What did he say?" asked Bee.

"He said, 'I'm surprised you can stand all these mirrors, Drake. They keep showing you how poorly you look in my clothes.' And Drake replied, 'I'll see how poorly you look as you beg me not to destroy your mage House.'"

"Gracious Melqart!" murmured Bee.

"Then I had to run, for their riflemen started shooting. I fear I gave us away."

The mansa said, "He already guesses we're following. Best we move quickly."

In another hour we reached a major curve in the road that opened onto a vista. The wide, flat valley at the confluence of the Rhenus River and the Temes shone in the sunlight. Horribly, all four ferry landings and the ferries were burning.

I shrieked out loud, out of sheer frustration. "How far is it to the next ferry? We'll have to go days out of our way!"

The mansa tapped my arm. "Enough, Catherine! Drake's people can't have had time to hunt down and burn every farmstead along the river. We can cross by rowboat. Four Moons land begins on the other side of the river, so we do not need the coach anymore. Many a path runs through backcountry to the main house. We may still reach the estate in time to assemble enough magisters on the main road to crush James Drake's flames."

Shaking with rage, I settled back into the seat as the mansa told the coachman his plan. Then the eru latched the shutters and closed the door, leaving us in darkness.

The mansa shaped a globe of cold fire. "Are we to be shut up like prisoners?"

A mouth glimmered on the latch. "I like it when he does that. Can he make more pictures?"

"Obviously we are promised secrets and then denied them!" I snapped, giving the latch a dark stare, although both Bee and the mansa did stare at me, for they could not hear the latch. Rory yawned, looking amused.

Two eyes like silvery stitches winked. "The other cold mage drew illusions of your face while you were sleeping, when he thought you weren't looking."

Oblivious to the latch's voice, the mansa went on. "Certainly these creatures have held their secrets close against themselves all this time. Servants ought not to act as if they are the masters. Such disrespect sows discord and disorder in the world."

"It's starting to get very stuffy in here," remarked Bee to the air.

"Is that what you call a secret?" I said, to the latch. "I already knew that!"

The mansa frowned. "I have indulged the two of you for many days now. But this is truly more than I can be expected to endure." He reached for the latch.

The gremlin's mouth stretched until its line ran the length of the latch, ready to bite.

For an instant I was tempted to let events play out on the unsuspecting mansa, but instead I set my hand on the latch so he could not. "Do not forget, Your Excellency, that the coach and eru serve another master."

"And you trust them?"

The latch licked my palm with its scratchy tongue, then said, muffled by my hand, "Can I help it if all I ever know about is what I see in here? I thought you were asleep and didn't know he had done that."

"I do trust them," I said, removing my hand and giving the latch a stern side-eye glance.

The mansa studied me with a thoughtful frown. "Very well. In this, you have the advantage of me."

Pressing my hands to my forehead, I breathed a soundless prayer to the blessed Tanit. "Blessed lady, let the righteous triumph and the wicked despair. Most of all, holy one, let me save his life and the lives of all those who do not deserve to suffer death at the hands of a man like James Drake. Not that any person deserves to suffer death in that wise, but you know what I mean."

I sat with face buried in hands for a long time, in a daze of such weary anxiety that I felt rocked as in a boat crossing a rushing river. When my sire had stolen Andevai on Hallows' Night, I had been more angry than fearful. My sire was not a creature of emotion. He was cruel in the way storms were cruel: They cared nothing for your vulnerability as they crashed through your life. If he wanted something, he had a reason for it that could be addressed.

535

But Drake's reasons had melted in the fire of his resentment, the sense that what he had lost could be regained only through the pain and humiliation of others. He had turned in on himself until he had become a mirror that did nothing but reflect his grievances back into his own face. That made him dangerous, but it also made him vulnerable.

The coach slowed to a halt. The door was opened from the outside, and the eru set down the steps so we could get out. Gritty ash burned in my eyes. Sobs and screams billowed with the smoke. We had come to a stop in a hamlet of inns, stables, shelters, and outbuildings. Every building in the village as well as two flat-bottomed ferries were on fire, a roaring blaze whose heat blasted our faces.

"Get down," said the mansa.

Bee had her head out of the coach, staring at local men who were beating at a fire as they tried to reach someone inside a house. They were so frantic they did not notice us.

"Sit down, Bee!" I dropped to my knees on the road.

The hammer of cold magic snuffed out every fire within sight, the flames sucked right out. The furnace heat turned in an eyeblink to the crackling of timbers buckling and the groan and smash of a wall toppling over. Every person in sight now lay on the ground. All except the eru. The mansa stared disbelievingly at the tall footman in his impeccable dress who appeared untouched by the impressive display. The eru offered a mocking servant's bow that made the mansa frown.

"Dearest," said Bee, clambering down, "are my eyes deceiving me, or have we crossed both rivers?"

Amazingly, we had reached the western bank.

Bee glanced up at the coachman, who sat upright and unruffled on the driver's bench. "And yet why not? For it seems your goblin makers have their own secret magic."

He removed his cap and slapped it against a hand to shake off ash. "Shall we go on? I am built for a steady, enduring pace rather than for speed. But we are not far behind them now."

The eru turned to me. "Cousin, is it your plan to come upon them on the road? For if we continue in this direction, I think it likely we shall do so."

"The fire mage has become quite powerful," I said. "Can you aid us with your magic, Cousin? For I must believe that you and the mansa, together, ought to be able to kill his fire."

"If Drake sees us coming up from behind, what is to stop him from simply killing Andevai?" Bee asked.

"Drake needs Vai. And Vai knows Drake needs him."

The mansa surveyed the village. The locals scrambled into the cold ruins, seeking survivors. "I do not like to think of what a company of fire mages led by a man with no conscience can do to Four Moons House if he chooses to practice his revenge there before he reaches his homeland."

A woman with a baby in her arms and a raw burn mark on her pale cheek shuffled forward to kneel before the mansa. "My lord mansa. What know you of this wicked spirit whose anger lashed out at us? You are come just in time. Otherwise we would have lost everything."

He pressed several sesterces into her hand. "No. I am come too late. I should have understood matters differently, and much sooner. Someone from the House will come to see what can be done with cleaning up and rebuilding. For now, you must do what you can."

Other supplicants began to approach, for it was obvious they knew who he was and did not fear to approach him in a respectful way. In their eyes he was a just master. He passed out coins to the survivors, emptying his purse in a rash manner that made Bee and me look at each other in disbelief. What if we needed that money later? To him it was trivial, something he expected to easily replace. He considered this generosity to be his duty. It was in this way, I supposed, that mages had built the edifice of their power over the generations.

On we traveled. Because we were traveling west, the door in the coach that opened into the spirit world faced the direction I most needed to look. So instead of looking ahead toward the graveled drive and the gatehouse to the estate, I could only stare through the other window as a drizzle clouded the north. Stands of birches flashed silver. Spruce darkened the slopes. In the distance a ring of round houses marked a village several miles off the road. The afternoon light turned to a hazy orange glow.

My nose twitched, and I sneezed.

"More smoke and more fire." Rory rubbed at eyes reddened by days of breathing ash.

The coach jolted to a halt.

The mansa flung open the door, then sucked in a harsh breath. "We are too late."

I scrambled out after him.

The turnpike from Audui to Cantiacorum was built atop the old Roman road in layers of crushed stone. South of the road a high stone wall demarcated the perimeter of the main estate of Four Moons House. A wide fan driveway fronted four arches, each ornamented with a phase of the moon. Between turnpike and wall lay a garden and the gatehouse supervised by the women magisters who tended the purification baths and gave or revoked permission for visitors to enter.

Ruin engulfed the gatehouse and the stables behind it. The carefully pruned hedges poured a greasy smoke into the air. Every tree was on fire. A dead woman sprawled on the steps, her face turned away from us and her bare back a grotesque fabric of savage burns.

When a magister powerful enough to rule as the head of a mage House is struck rigid with fury and he is standing not ten paces from you, you will be glad he is fighting on your side.

A powerfully cold wind rocked the coach. As the mansa started walking to the gatehouse, icy sleet began to fall. I drew my sword.

"How did they get past the gate?" I asked. "Is it not protected by a cold magic binding?"

"She who holds the keys to the gates must be alive to close or open them." His right hand clenched as he looked toward the body on the steps. He let out the hard exhalation of a man determined to get on with the painful task that has to be done.

"Was she your kinswoman?" I asked, for she had hair the same color as his.

"My sister," he said curtly. "Let Rory scout in his cat form. Go around to the back. I think they will not think to use a cat as a catch-fire. Go on."

Rory shed his clothes and turned from man to cat. He nudged my hands, licked Bee, yawned assertively at the mansa, and loped off. We got in the carriage.

The shadow of the arch passed over us as we entered the estate.

"Here is a riddle," the mansa said as we rolled down the wide avenue past black pine and a reed-choked pond. "Fire will burn as long as it has fuel and is not doused by water. If this man Drake uses Andevai as a catch-fire yet cannot fathom the well of Andevai's power, what then?"

"I told Vai once that the potency of his cold magic is the inverse of his modesty," I said.

"Cat, are you saying that by using Andevai as his catch-fire, Drake becomes as powerful as Andevai is vain?" Bee smiled at me with brows lifted in the way she had that provoked me to mischief. Her smile broke through the wall of relentless concentration I had raised around my fears. We broke into hysterical giggles.

The mansa stared as if to scold us but instead sat back with a stiff but honest smile. "I suppose a little levity cannot harm our cause. Anyway, it may well be an apt analogy that should give us pause, given what we know of Andevai's monstrously bloated conceit."

Bee snickered. I wiped tears from my eyes.

He set a fist on the window's rim and studied the orchard as we passed. The first time I had been driven this way, I had seen Kayleigh walking in the orchard among the field hands. Vai had halted our carriage to greet her. I had begun then to comprehend that the man I thought I saw was merely the clothes he showed to the world. What made him who he truly was ran far deeper. Just as it did in all of us.

The main house lay almost two miles from the road. Smoke boiled up above the trees, shimmering with heat.

"What better way to humiliate Vai than by destroying the House he has pledged to uphold and maintain?" I cried. "And likewise practice for the greater destruction he means to visit on his own home?"

"I fear you are right," said the mansa. He did not take his gaze from the smoke. "My surviving troops and magisters will be days behind us on the road. Beatrice, you must remain in the coach so you do not yourself need rescuing. Catherine, are you ready?"

Shared laughter had polished away the weight of my dread. I knew what I had to do.

"Mansa, the only way to kill James Drake is with cold steel."

"Andevai taught us how to pull the backlash off another and into ourselves, so I will keep the fire mages from using you as a catch-fire for long enough that you can reach him," he said without the least sign that he appreciated the irony of protecting me after he was the one 539 who had once demanded I be killed. "I will not let you burn. Best you scout first, however."

"Be safe, dearest." Bee grasped my hand, kissed my cheek, and let me go.

I pushed down the latch as we rumbled along the drive. As the door swung open I leaned out, feet in the coach and body braced on the door. The coach came to a halt just out of sight around the last curve of the drive from the House.

I hopped out. The coachman touched the brim of his cap in salute. The eru leaped onto the roof of the coach in a tremor of unseen wings. I wrapped the shadows around me and ran alone up to the House.

45

Four Moons House resembled a princely palace, with a broad fore-court, a grand portico reached by a series of stepped terraces, and an imposing building anchored by round rooms at either end and wings stretching behind to enclose interior gardens. A curtain-like shimmer of heat pushed smoke skyward from the back of the building. With cracks and bangs, windows, walls, and furniture shattered, broke, fell as the flames ate forward through the structure like a fiery leviathan devouring its helpless prey.

A troop of soldiers stood on the portico facing toward the House, their rifles trained on the doors to prevent anyone inside from ventur-ing out. Six young fire mages were ranged along the steps, each with a cold mage huddled in front being used as a catch-fire, although it seemed to my eye that they weren't trying to raise fire as much as sim-ply control the six magisters. Most likely there were other fire mages elsewhere around the estate. I had no idea how many had followed Drake and how many had been left behind with Camjiata's army.

About thirty people, mostly women, knelt on the highest terrace. White-haired elders and slender youths were treated with equal dis-respect. I recognized Serena among them, but I did not see Vai's mother or sisters.

Drake stood like a hero on the topmost step. Wrapped as I was within the threads of the worlds, I could easily see the geometry of his fire magic, the way he cast threads of backlash into all thirty of these mages. He had not the cacica's skilled and delicate touch. In her hands catch-fires were lit with a nimbus glow as the threads of their magic spun north to the far ice and through the spirit world and back again into the mortal world. These catch-fires blazed too brightly, flooded with more power than they could channel even though it was shared between them.

Only one mage still stood, braced upright by sheer force of will.

The well of Vai's power shone as radiant a blue as the sacred wells of the Antilles. Given so much fuel to burn, Drake's fire raged. He was pouring his fire into the palace and his backlash into the thirty cold mages. Even split among them it was obviously too much for them to handle, for many were too young or too ill or too elderly to sustain the heat. Vai was pulling streams of backlash out of them and into himself, to stop any one of them from flooding and thus dying.

That was how Drake was controlling Vai: Not by using him as a catch-fire but by forcing him to protect the people he felt responsible for. Of course the mansa had named him heir! The mansa had finally understood that once saddled with the burden, Vai would never lay it down.

I ran back to the coach, hopping up onto the sideboard.

"Mansa! Drake has trapped many of your people inside the house. If the fire isn't killed at once, they'll all die. But he's using all the remaining magisters as catch-fires. I don't know how you can possibly kill that much fire." I looked up at the eru, standing on top of the coach. "Cousin! Can you raise a storm?"

Cold wings opened as the eru bloomed into her true face. Her third eye blazed, blue ice. "Best hasten," she said in a ringing bell voice. "The fire grows."

Blades of sleet sliced the air as the coachman whipped the horses forward with a "Ha-roo! Ha-roo!"

As we swung around the corner, heat poured into my face and dark clouds surged overhead. The coach pulled up. The mansa climbed out and strode forward to face the man who was destroying his home. I leaped out after him, wreathed in my shadows, unseen.

Soldiers spun around to aim rifles at the coach, but every rifle clicked dead, for the mansa's cold magic killed their spark. Snow hissed across the burning building. The flames began to die.

With an ease that astounded me, Drake flung a thread of backlash into the mansa. At once the falling snow ceased, and the mansa staggered as a twisting skin of light surged around his body. He had no choice but to let the backlash pour through him, because if he did not allow it to kill his magic, it would kill him.

"Now, Cousin!" I called, closing the door of the coach to protect Bee.

Drake's eyes widened as he took in the sight of the eru standing atop the coach.

She spread her wings, their span like winter. Ice glittered along the manes and coats of the horses as she beat her wings to fan the storm. Cold cracked down over all, flames wavering beneath blasts of snow.

But fire beats back even winter. Drake threw such gouts of backlash into the cold mages that a child and then two elders toppled over. Vai frantically pulled more and more into himself, desperate to save the most vulnerable.

Flames leaped higher. The sheer frightening rush of fire stunned me. From deep inside the palace rose shouts and cries of such fear that they scoured my heart. I knew there were courtyards in which people could shelter, but I suddenly comprehended that none of it would be enough. Not even the eru's magic would be enough.

I had to kill Drake. Wrapped in shadow, I started toward the steps.

The mansa was lit by a silvery mantle of backlash that he shed continuously into the far distant ice. As I came up beside him he caught Vai's gaze across the gap between them. He nodded, and reached with his magic to pull all the backlash off Vai and into himself. The force of all that power smashed him to his knees. His body convulsed.

I dropped to my knees.

Momentarily free of backlash, Vai slipped an ice lens out of the neck of his jacket. In the Antilles the ice lens had allowed him to focus and amplify his weakened magic. His magic was not weak here. Its hammer slammed down so hard that my chin hit the dirt even though I was ready for it. The eru was flung to earth and the coach creaked, groaning. Even the coachman ducked his head.

Everyone was down, flattened, stunned. Everyone except Andevai. He was still standing. Even in torn, dirty, rumpled clothes, he looked magnificent.

The mansa was unconscious, scarcely breathing, a smoky odor swirling around his body. He could not help us. Still staggered by the sledgehammer blow, I pushed up, stumbled sideways, then forward, supporting myself on the tip of my sword.

"Catherine! Strike now!" I heard how weak Vai was by the hoarseness that burred his voice. He collapsed to one knee and barely caught himself on a hand. As Drake pushed himself up Vai lunged, grabbed Drake's ankle, and jerked the fire mage to a halt.

Drake laughed as he tugged his leg out of Vai's weakened grip. "I have played you all very well, have I not? For I have absorbed your strongest attack and still stand. You have nothing left."

Every cold mage lit with the backlash of Drake's fire magic. Horribly, so did the eru, for her magic, too, was caught in the funnel. She, too, became a conduit for his power. Only the coach and four remained impervious, and I breathed a prayer of thanks to the Blessed Tanit that I had insisted Bee remain inside.

Wild, bright fire flashed up from the wings and front of the House. The heat built like a furnace. So had Bee dreamed: Sheets of fire from which rose screams of fear and pain.

"Look for the glimmer of a blade, as I taught you," Drake shouted to his fire mages.

Fire magic spilled down the length of my sword, seeking a path into the spirit world that the cold steel could not give it, seeking me. I tossed it away before the sparks burned me. The moment it left my hand, it became visible to the soldiers.

A rifle went off, and a bullet ricocheted off the drive next to my feet. Another shot spat on the ground by my heels. A third shot sprayed gravel onto the sword. I jumped away from the sword, still in my shadows. Sheets of fire crackled up the walls of the House. One catch-fire, then another, and a third and a fourth and a fifth cried in agony as the backlash overwhelmed them. Vai and the eru had become rivers of light, shedding backlash in flood tides into the spirit world.

Drake soaked up the power and let it roar. Walls crashed in along the back of the House.

Another bullet hit close to my feet, the gravel it kicked up stinging my ankle. If I picked up my sword, Drake would have me. If I waited, all the cold mages and those trapped in the interior courtyard would die. The soldiers began to march toward the coach, firing at will. The coachman looked at me, for although he could not be hurt, there was likewise nothing he could do.

I raced back, flung open the door, and leaped into the interior of the coach.

Bee said, "Blessed Tanit, Cat! What terrible thing is happening?"

"Close your eyes!"

I opened the door into the spirit world and jumped out.

Night shrouded the world, the air as frozen as the icy water in which my sire had tried to drown me. But I was not daunted.

Holding on to the latch so I did not flounder away from the coach, I called. "Sire! Father! You are bound to me as kin. Come to my aid!"

A breath as of wings fluttered so close by my face that I flinched, but I did not retreat. Fingers of ice tightened over my arm, their touch engulfing me under the weight of an ice sheet. His three eyes gleamed in the darkness, and the third was a pulsing knot of blood.

"Beware of what you ask for, little cat. Do you understand there will be a price?"

"Yes. And I will pay it. Only me. No one else."

"Taken. What do you want?"

"Of your own self and will, you can only walk into the mortal world on Hallows' Night. But I am a spiritwalker. You can cross with me right now."

"At last you understand."

He laughed, and he sprang like a cat. He flowed like a viper. He struck like a raptor, the beat of unseen wings carrying me back through the coach. Bee sat as stiff as if she were encased in ice, but I had no time. I tumbled past her and to earth.

My sire was already standing on the gravel drive, as unruffled as you please. In his severe black jacket and trousers, and with his coldly handsome face, he looked like a man you never ever wanted to cross swords with because he would rather wait until you turned around and then stab you in back so he wouldn't have to go to the trouble of seeing the light drain out of your eyes.

"Intriguing," he said. "The cold mages pull heat and energy from the spirit world and lock it up in this world, thus stealing it from us, but this red-haired man is dispersing it through their bodies back into my realm. I would never have seen any of this if you had not escorted me through. I shall have to think about what this means."

"Father! He's going to kill all those people! Save them. Save Vai! I beg you."

"You are a slave to the chains that bind you to others. That makes you weak." His smile cut.

I licked a spot of blood off my lip. "No, it makes me strong."

The history of the world begins in ice, so the bards and djeliw claim, and it got so cold so fast I was pretty sure the world was going to end right under my feet. A gossamer undulation like wings of frost flared at his back, and the veins of his closed third eye smoked like night on his brow.

He raised a vast pressure of cold that began to choke down the fire. Drake's young fire mages collapsed first, crusted all over in a skin of ice. The soldiers cowered in fear, guns dead.

My ears throbbed. My eyes were sucked dry of moisture. My lips stung.

Drake saw us, for the shadows had been ripped right off me. I thought it must surely end quickly. What mortal could stand against the Master of the Wild Hunt?

But Drake blazed. The flood pouring through Andevai and the eru surged as an ocean tide around the fire mage. Like a volcano, Drake had become the flowing energy that consumes all in its path.

Soot spun in black tornadoes into the sky. Lightning sparked and flashed. The air above the palace grew so hot that a green aura of light appeared and twisted in the sky.

Ice and fire warred in perfect balance, neither able to retreat or to advance.

I ran forward to grab my sword. Drake did not notice. He dared not take his eye off the Master of the Wild Hunt, because no matter how powerful he and Andevai together were, fire mage and catch-fire, to falter even for an eyeblink would bring the ice crushing down.

I leaped up the steps, taking them two at a time. Just as I reached the top, Drake saw me coming. A thread of heat woke in my heart as he spun backlash into me with a fevered smile. Vai was blinded by the force of all that magic, and my sire was too far away to help me. It would take me only a few heartbeats to burn.

But I only needed one, for my sire had given me all the opening I needed.

I leaned into the thrust. Cold steel slid up under Drake's rib cage and pierced the beating fury of his heart. I ran him through up to the hilt.

His brow wrinkled as if he were puzzled by how close I stood.

I shoved, just one step more, to make sure I really had him. He rocked back. Caught on my blade, he could not pull away. His eyes flared and sparked in sheer stymied fury. He tried to speak, but although his mouth opened, no sound came out, only a trickle of blood.

There flashed in an instant through my mind a hundred triumphant retorts and gloating taunts, but in the end I realized I simply did not care enough to speak. With a grunt of pain, for my hand hurt from clenching so hard, I jerked the sword out of his body and turned the blade to cut his throat. Blood poured down his chest, ruining the dash jacket he had stolen from Vai. I stepped out of the way as he toppled face-first onto the stone stairs.

With a sound like a monstrous beast inhaling, the flames vanished as all the fires went out.

Drake was dead.

Dead.

I had to secure our precarious situation. The cold mages sprawled limp on the steps, but I had not the leisure to worry about them. The fire mages were frozen. The soldiers stared in horror at my sire. While it was true that a great deal of magic was billowing off him, to my eyes he looked like a perfectly ordinary man. And while his clothes certainly were severe for being sewn out of unrelenting black, they were not otherwise exceptional or astonishing. But the soldiers dropped their rifles and fell on their faces, begging for mercy.

A moment later several young fire mages and a few more soldiers came running around the side of the building, chased by a saber-toothed cat. They, too, surrendered in abject fear, but the instant the cat saw the Master of the Wild Hunt, he turned tail and ran.

I knelt beside Vai and bent to rest my cheek lightly against his lips. The whistling of his labored breathing calmed me. He was alive. Yet that was not his breath whistling. A teakettle hiss shivered the air.

Pinpricks of ice jabbed my skin. Crystals grew out across the scorched and blackened front of the building. Ice spread in curves and scallops, cones and six-sided lacework.

Years ago ice had devoured Crescent House.

Now ice was engulfing Four Moons House.

I could no more stop my sire than I could stop winter.

"Bee!" I cried, waving her forward from where she peered out the coach door. "Hurry!"

Without looking to see if she followed, I ran over the threshold into the building, looking neither to my left nor to my right. The path I had taken on the day the husband I had not wanted had brought me here remained fixed in my mind so clearly it took no effort for me to turn right, left, left, and then right to reach the long salon I recalled all too well. Its glass doors looked onto an interior garden enclosed by the wings of the House and a high stone wall behind.

The mural painted along the salon's walls, depicting the Diarisso ancestors guiding their kinsfolk and retainers and slaves along the hidden paths of the waterless desert to safety, had peeled and smeared and turned brown in patches where flames had begun to eat through the walls. Yet the strong-as-iron women and handsome men clothed in gold and orange strode undaunted, their chains of magical power and secret knowledge wreathing them like vines. The paint glittered with flashes of light as ice penetrated the walls. It made the mural seem to move, as if the ancestors were walking still into the future they had made for themselves out of the devastation of what they had been forced to leave behind.

The glass doors opening onto the garden had cracked and shattered from the heat. I wrapped the hem of my skirt around my hand and opened metal latches so hot they burned, then kicked down the framework of glass doors sagging on their hinges.

I could not count the number of people trapped in the garden. Some had been trying to lift others out over the back wall, but judging from the shouts beyond the wall and the scorched tops of trees, I guessed that several fire mages and soldiers had been stationed there to prevent anyone from escaping. Nearby a big cat roared.

I hated Drake all over again. What manner of man cared more for his own perverted sense of honor and pride than for people's lives?

Winter chased through the doors and kissed the air. Snowflakes drifted prettily through the chamber on a lazy wintry breeze. I shivered.

Bee did not need to be told what to do. How someone so small and lovely could bellow in quite that ear-shattering manner never failed to astound me. "Everyone! Listen! You will immediately follow me out the front doors. Now! If you stay behind, you will die."

Her honeyed voice had the rare gift of impelling people to obey without pausing to needlessly quibble. Nor were the people of Four Moons House fools: A fire-ravaged structure would soon collapse. We did not have time to explain the real danger.

More than a hundred people had taken shelter in the garden, many of them children, women, and elders. The djeli Bakary leaned on his cane, so stiff with age he had not been able to ride with the mansa to war. I waved Bee over to help him. The old steadied the young. The young assisted the old. I sought out Vai's mother and sisters, almost lost in the midst of the crowd as the flight began. Vai's mother was wracked by coughing.

"Bintou, help your mother. Wasa, that's a very fine new crutch you have. Don't let go of it. Yes, you can take the puppy, too. I'm going to carry you." Wasa's weight felt like nothing when I hoisted her into my arms. Fortunately the puppy was frightened enough that it did no more than whimper in her thin arms.

Other people led the way out. Bee stayed with Bakary and the slow-moving elders at the rear. The building creaked and moaned around us. Ice bloomed in feathered ridges. Thin blades of cloudy ice popped out from the walls.

"Move! Move!"

A booming roar shuddered through the fragile chambers as part of the building collapsed. The ice kept spreading. Glittering spires grew up from the floors. Clear branches snaked down from the broken ceilings.

We staggered out onto the portico and its terraced steps. The cold mages were beginning to shake themselves, to rise, to drag their unconscious and injured brethren away from the building. I helped Vai's mother and his sisters down to the gravel driveway, then ran back up the steps.

Serena lay in a pool of blood, doubled over in pain.

"Blessed Tanit!" I cried. "What injury have you taken? Let me help you away."

She grasped my hand with more strength than I would have expected. "No injury of the kind you mean. I fear this is a miscarriage. Where is my husband?"

The mansa was alive but unconscious and unresponsive. Blistering burns had bubbled up on his neck and arms. Ash rimed his mouth, a smear of blood caught at the corner. Serena knelt beside him and, with the tone of a woman used to command, called others to her.

Four Moons House was being inexorably trapped in ice. Amid the clamor of voices, an eerie grinding noise drowned all until the speech of humans was nothing more than the restless tickling of insects. Thick pillars of blue-green ice shot up alongside the doors, spearing all the way to the high roof above. Ice encased the great edifice, every span of it locked away in a transparent cage.

Within the disorganized spill of people along the lower terrace, I found Vai sprawled on the steps. It looked as if he had woken enough to start pulling himself away and then collapsed again. His eyes fluttered. A word formed on his lips but he hadn't the strength to get it out.

"Vai! Andevai! It's me. It's Catherine! Stay with me, my love. Don't leave me."

I looked for Bee and instead saw Rory, dressed only in trousers, padding toward me with an alarmed look on his face. He flung himself down on the other side of Vai, trembling with fear as he looked past me. Naturally I turned to see what frightened him so much.

Across the drive my sire dusted soot from his hands with a meticulous frown. He glanced at me across the gap between us and nodded to acknowledge the bargain we had agreed to. Then he gestured with his plain black cane as a lord does when he wants a servant to do something for him. The eru clambered up on the roof and tossed our luggage to the ground. My sire climbed into the coach. The latch winked as if reflecting light, or perhaps making a brassy gremlin scowl in my direction. My sire's hand covered the latch's face as he shut the door.

The eru furled her wings. The coachman tipped his cap at me.

"Ha-roo! Ha-roo!"

Wheels rumbled over the gravel drive as the horses first walked and then broke into a smooth carriage trot. The coach rolled away down the driveway. I waited for it to vanish into the spirit world, to cross the shadows and return my sire to his rightful home.

But it did not. It simply drove away back toward the main road, moving at a sedate pace as might a lordly man who has just paid a polite social call on a friendly neighbor.

I stared in consternation.

I had just let loose the Master of the Wild Hunt into the mortal world.

46

Rory tugged on my arm. "Is he gone, Cat? I know he saw me! I was afraid he would make me go with him."

"He's gone, Rory. You're safe."

"His children are never safe. No one is ever safe!"

"No, you're all safe," I said with certainty, and I hugged him.

Fortunately I did not have time to dwell on the bargain I had made. There was simply too much to do, with night falling over the displaced population of Four Moons House. Before anything else we sent runners to the nearby villages of Haranwy and Trecon. Then I cleaned the blood off my sword and hunted down the rest of Rory's clothes.

The icy sculpture of Four Moons House glittered as the moon rose. Moonlight coruscated through the many facets of the ice, splintering light across the terraces and driveway. In this eerie weave of shadow and bright, Bee and the stewards counted heads and sorted people by injury and need. The cold mages who had been Drake's prisoners were, like the mansa, injured and unconscious. Three were dead. The cold mages who had been at Four Moons House, like Serena, had absorbed some measure of backlash, but on the whole they had not been badly harmed, although all the pregnant women had gone into labor.

All the fire mages were dead. I pitied them, but I could not mourn.

Mostly I sat with Vai's head in my lap. No sign of injury marked him but he lay oblivious, the only movement the shallow rise and fall of his chest and the sluggish pulse at his throat. Wasa huddled next to me, petting the cowering puppy. Bintou fetched water for us from the well, and the cool liquid slowly eased her mother's coughing. I even got a little down Vai's throat. As the evening wore on I slipped in and out of a doze, glancing up now and again to search for Bee. She was always there, busy managing people. I just hadn't the strength.

In the middle of the night, wagons trundled up under the light of an almost-full moon and a clear sky. Andevai's half brother Duvai led the contingent from Haranwy. All were men, all armed with their hunter's bows, spears, scythes, and a few illegal rifles. I went to greet them.

"Peace to you, Andevai's brother, and to all who live in your compound," I said in the traditional way. "Do you have peace?"

"I am well, thanks to the mother who raised me," he replied, "and my family has peace also. And you, Cat Barahal?"

"I am well, thanks to my power as a woman."

He raised an eyebrow, as if something in my face made him take pause. Then he looked past me to the massif of ice that entombed Four Moons House.

"Will the village give these refugees shelter?" I asked. "On their behalf, and on my own, I ask for guest rights."

"That is our duty and obligation," he said. "We will do what we must."

"The mansa named Vai as heir."

"We heard the rumor." He glanced toward Vai's mother, who had not left Vai's side. The stubborn line of old resentment creased his brow. "An honor to his mother, indeed. He has made his choice between his two hats. This turn of events cannot have improved his conceit."

"I wouldn't be so sure about the hats. You must work honestly with him, Duvai. I think you will find him something changed. He is the village's ally, not its enemy, not its ruler."

"Is that what you think? You surely were determined to escape him the last time we met."

A flush warmed my cheeks. "I am something changed as well."

The resemblance between the two men was keen, although Duvai was lighter, having a mother who had been born in a Celtic village, and being therefore more mixed of feature and complexion. Ten years older, he had the surety of a man in his prime strength, fully aware of who he is and of his place in the world. Besides that, he was a hunter

553

who had braved the spirit world more than once and returned successfully.

"Are you something changed in the matter of my brother?" he said
with a chuckle that made me blush yet more. "I would not have taken
you for a woman to be bought by the offer of riches and rank, so I
must suppose he found another way to capture you."

"You are mistaken. No man can capture me. But he might have...
courted me."

His smirk resembled Vai's. "So my brother finally smiled at you,
did he?"

I had no answer to this, except to refrain from punching him.

"Grandmother made us promise never to fight each other. Out of
respect for her, and knowing she watches over us still, I will speak in
his favor. The elders of Haranwy have agreed to house as many of
these refugees as we can until a decision is reached. The rest can shelter at Trecon and other House villages."

The ice-bound House breathed like winter on our backs as we
walked away.

No one would ever live there again.

The mansa was brought to Grandmother's single-roomed house
with its tiny private courtyard. The room smelled of pine wreaths even
though no one had lived in it for some time. Vai was conveyed to the
room where his mother had lived for so many years with her children.
She directed him to be placed on a cot and asked for hot water to be
brought so he might be stripped of his grimy clothes and washed. This
task I asked to do, behind a screen for privacy. The furnishings in the
modest room were nothing compared to the luxurious riches in Two
Gourds House, but the modern circulating stove, the four-poster bed,
an oak table, and the rosewood wardrobe revealed the concern Vai had
taken both for his mother's comfort and for her status in the village.

He mumbled incoherent syllables. Settled in the bed, he tossed and
turned for the next three days, feverish one hour and shivering with
cold the next as I forced broth down his throat. Every now and then he
had lucid moments, during which I told him some of what had happened and fed him gruel. At length the worst of it eased, and he slept
like the dead.

At intervals I attended Bee, who sat for hours in the village's festival house acting as mediator. I admired her fair-minded intercessions between the demands of the Houseborn, many of whom had never set foot in so rustic a situation, and the complaints of the burdened villagers. Disputes were also sparked between the younger generation in the village, who agitated for resistance, saying this was their chance to throw off the yoke of clientage, and the elders, who refused to offend the ancestors and the gods by violating guest rights.

I just wanted to stab everyone when they started to argue. My foot got bruised from Bee stepping on it.

The mansa was dying. Everyone knew it but no one spoke of it. Rory had taken a violent liking to the old djeli, Bakary, and prowled around him seeking any pat of attention, which meant he spent most of his day in Grandmother's cottage listening to the old bard sing the story of the mansa's life and deeds, the tale of the Diarisso lineage, and the history of the world.

The history of the world begins with a seed. The seed is the kernel of what you are, but it is also the promise of what you can become.

On the fourth day a delegation arrived from Trecon, where the rest of the House refugees languished. The mansa's nephew had arrived with the mage House troop from Lutetia. Because the mansa had not regained consciousness, his nephew wanted to immediately convene the House council of elders to vote on the matter of the heirship.

I returned to Vai's mother's room to find Vai sitting on the edge of the bed clad in trousers and nothing else. With a hand braced on the wall he stood, trembling across his entire body as he steadied himself to take a step, another step, and a third. It was obvious he was headed for the screen behind which we washed and dressed and kept the chamber pot. He had not yet seen me.

He said in a strikingly peevish tone, "I will manage the business myself, Mama."

Twice I thought he would topple right over, but he got behind the screen without mishap.

I crossed to where his mother sat on a chair, knelt beside her, took her hand, and smiled up at her.

"He was never a patient invalid as a child," she remarked. "Fortunately he did not get sick often."

The girls were sitting at the table beside a window, perusing a book.

Wasa elbowed her sister. "Kayleigh used to say no one whined like Vai when he was sick."

"I heard that!" said Vai from behind the screen, not in a jocular tone.

Because I understood how much he hated feeling weak, I ventured behind the screen to find him sitting, head in hands, on the bench. A mirror and razor rested on the bench next to him. My footsteps brought his head up. His beard was unkempt, and his hair squashed on one side. His skin had an ashy sallowness and his eyes a gray weariness.

"I don't need help!" he snapped. "I can shave myself!"

"Nor have I the least desire to help you," I retorted. "I merely came to inform you that the mansa's nephew has arrived and is making an entirely predictable grab for the heir's seat."

"That would be a disaster for Four Moons House! Not to mention Haranwy and the other villages. It's not his right anyway, to make such a demand when the mansa has already spoken." He tried to stand but could not keep his feet under him. I had to catch him and ease him back down, for which he repaid me with a string of rude phrases directed not at me personally but at the uncaring world at large, which had not had the courtesy to allow him to heal faster.

"Stop it! Just pee and go back to sleep. Nothing will happen until you have recovered enough to face the elders."

He ran a hand along his beard, and I was sure he was thinking that he could not face the elders looking so scruffy. "What of the mansa? What news of him today?"

I shook my head. "No change. Magister Serena is recovering well, although she grieves over losing the pregnancy. You didn't tell me she's a diviner."

"You didn't ask."

I left him to it and went back to his mother. "I believe you are better suited than I to handle him when he is afflicted with this distemper."

She regarded me with an equanimity matched only by Vai's muttered cursing behind the screen. "Even as a child he had the habit of believing every sunny day would last forever to please him, and that clouds came as a personal affront."

"Catherine. Love."

That he used the endearment in his mother's hearing worried me. I went back to find him stretched out on the bench, an arm flung across his face. He had mottled bruising on his ribs from either the battle or his captivity, his wrists were reddened and scarred with rope burns, and he was thin from the privation of the last days. Benevolent Tanit! The man needed to eat!

"Lord of All," he murmured with disgust, "to think of how easily I was captured! I could not even break out of my captivity, nor prevent them from using me as a catch-fire for the entire cursed journey. When it came to the point, I could not even save the mansa. Now his useless nephew cocks about like a rooster crowing for attention, while I cannot stand."

Annoyance and pathos warred in my breast, and after a short struggle, annoyance punched pathos in the snout like the voracious shark it was.

"I will say this once, and not again. You were easily captured because you had collapsed in an exhausted faint after saving the lives of other mages and no doubt many other people on the day of the battle. As for being exploited as a catch-fire, that was an obvious decision on Drake's part for otherwise he could not have held you as prisoner. The problem is not that you are weak but that you are so unusually strong that Drake saw you as the means to effect his revenge. I may not fully agree with how the Taino treat catch-fires, but from what I saw they do regard them with respect. Drake stole the knowledge from them but not their care for the law and their respect for the balance that is needed to wield power responsibly. He was a thief, and a greedy, resentful, envious, selfish thief at that. Maybe his family stole his inheritance, or maybe they threw him out because they saw what a monster he was. I don't know. But in the end, Drake's frightening power came from the strength he took from you."

I paused to catch my breath. I had not realized how much anger I held against my heart for all the people who use others as nothing more than tools to build a house for themselves, who wrap chains around others and then claim they have the right and even the obligation to do so. Vexation overflowed like water over the brim of a full cup.

"To be perfectly honest, Andevai, it is nothing more than petulant vanity on your part to lie there after everything you have done 557 and querulously complain that it wasn't enough. Many thousands of people have died because of Camjiata's war and many more will die, and uncounted more have suffered because of the rule of unjust princes. You are just one person doing what you can. Even you cannot be catch-fire for all the injustice in the world!"

From the table, far enough away that they thought I couldn't hear, Bintou whispered to Wasa, "I can't believe she talks to him like that!"

"I'm going to learn to talk like that!" murmured Wasa. "I can't run about and hit people like Cat does, but I can become an orator like Cousin Bee. I'm going to become a hero and cause trouble all over everywhere!"

"Girls!" scolded their mother.

"So if you are done with your humble business about the pisspot, Husband, then go back to bed. You will get strong if you rest and meanwhile cease whipping yourself raw over the obvious fact that even your astoundingly monumental cold magic has its limits although clearly your vanity does not. Also, I will smack you if you keep whining like this, because I. Have. No. More. Patience. For. It."

He withdrew the arm that shielded his eyes. His tight jaw and frustrated sneer smoothed into loving concern as he examined me. "Catherine, are you well? Is something wrong, love? I am accustomed to you speaking your mind, but you sound sour and on edge. That's not like you."

In two months the Wild Hunt would ride up to my door and take me away, but I was not about to tell him that.

When I did not answer he sighed and, with a grimace, heaved himself up. "Yesterday I could not even sit up, so I am somewhat improved. I'll go back to bed and be patient a little longer."

"I doubt that," I muttered.

But he did go back to bed, stubbornly refusing my helping arm, and he ate every bit of the porridge his mother brought. Afterward he slept restfully.

I had a long talk about law and history with Bakary at the bedside of the mansa, where I found him whistling the spirit melody as he wove a song describing Andevai's magic and exploits. That night, as always, Bee slept on the far side of the bed while I took the middle between her and Vai. Rory was curled up in his cat form on the floor, with the puppy sleeping trustfully between his big paws. House children who had been sleeping in the village festival house lay crammed together on mats on the floor, exhausted from Rory letting them climb all over him. They had come to us because the mansa's nephew had taken over the festival house for his entourage without even asking the village elders for their permission.

Vai was dead asleep. I held Bee's hand, twisting and turning. "If the House council chooses the nephew, we'll be free. But we haven't a sesterce to our name, so I can't imagine what we'll do."

"I have an idea about that."

"Yet I fear for what will happen to the House in that case. I worry the nephew will take a petty revenge on Haranwy. Although I think regardless he'll have a village revolt on his hands. But if the council supports Vai...Bee, don't let Vai be trapped by the House."

"You're so tired you're fretting needlessly, Cat. This isn't like you."

"You won't leave me, will you? Never, not until the end?"

"Are you feeling well?" She pressed her lips to my forehead. "You're not feverish. Dearest, you must sleep. You mustn't get ill."

Sometimes the gods are merciful and will let you sleep instead of think.

In the morning, although still weak, Vai insisted on shaving and dressing and walking under his own power to his grandmother's house. There, by the bedside of the mansa and with his mother seated in a chair behind him, he requested permission of the House elders to stand before them. At once, and far less politely, the mansa's nephew challenged Vai's right even to stand there, much less claim to be heir. I did not know what to expect, but the months of war, the days of captivity, and perhaps even his slow recovery had planed down the edges and splinters that had always made Vai so quick to take offense when he felt his dignity and honor were being challenged.

This time he let the other man talk on and on, cajole and whine, even blame the destruction of the House on Vai as if Drake had never existed. The nephew complained at length about the lowborn origins of the village boy in such insulting terms that even though the House-born elders might well have scorned Vai's mother for being born in a cart with no lineage to her name, they still shuddered to see a dignified   559 mother mocked in public in front of her son. At length the nephew ran dry, and by this time everyone was certainly waiting for him to stop.

"Are you finished?" asked Vai. "Very well, then. With the permission of the elders of the House, I will answer."

They granted it.

"Your words speak for themselves. I would be ashamed to let such speech pass my lips. My mother knows I honor and respect her. That is all that needs to be said. As for the other, according to tradition, the mansa of a mage House is the man whose magic reaches the deepest. Can you stand before the elders of this council and tell them honestly that your magic is stronger than mine?"

Thus Vai defeated him.

Just then the mansa stirred, as though the voice of his heir had roused him. "Let it be Andevai," he whispered.

Andevai knelt beside him, taking his hand. "I am here, mansa. It shall be as you say."

The thread of the mansa's voice was barely audible. It clearly hurt him to speak, but he was determined to be heard. "Andevai, promise me on your mother's honor that you will stand as mansa and rebuild Four Moons House."

"I promise on my mother's honor."

His mother did not smile. She was not such a woman. But her pride was a light in the room.

As the council filed out, Rory slipped in. "I'll sit with you in attendance, with your permission," he said to Bakary and Serena. "He will pass soon to the other side."

Outside, Duvai confronted his brother. "What do you mean to do, Mansa?" he said mockingly.

Weary but unbowed, Vai frowned. "He yet lives. I am not mansa."

"The hunter has already crept into the shadows of the House. Death stalks that place."

I looked wildly around the open courtyard of the family's compound, but I did not see my sire in light or in shadow. Then a crow fluttered down to perch on the roof.

"Do you intend to stay here?" Duvai held a stout staff as tall as his head, tipped with a fringe of feathers and beads. He shifted it now from his left hand to his right, as if making ready for an attack. "You and your people are eating out our winter stores. You claim you mean to change things, but you're doing exactly what the mages have always done, living off our flesh."

Vai was tired enough that he allowed himself to lean on me as he met his brother's gaze without anger or malice. "What I mean to do, you will know when the mansa dies and I am free to act. But you may be sure that I intend to release every village from the clientage that binds it to Four Moons House. Until then, I ask you to remember what our father taught us."

"Our father told us that a hero is loved only on troubled days. Otherwise he causes too much disruption for the village to find him a comfortable presence. Is that what you meant to remind me of, Andevai?"

"Are those words meant for me because you think I am the hero? Because if they are, then you have directed them at the wrong person. Although I do not think of Catherine as disruptive. Just precipitous sometimes."

With a sigh Duvai handed his staff to his younger brother. No doubt Duvai felt it beneath the dignity of any man to have to lean on a woman, much less thank her for salvaging what she could out of a desperate situation.

Vai took the staff as if it were an offering of peace. "Brother, surely you do not forget that when I was a boy, I did nothing but follow after you."

"You were a terrible nuisance, always underfoot," agreed Duvai gravely.

I looked from one to the other, seeing the stamp of the father I had never met in their features but also in the way they both carried themselves as men. Strength can be used to harm, but it can also be used to build and to sustain. No doubt they had clashed in later years because they were so much alike. One had always known the place he meant to grow into. The other had hoped to follow, only to find himself completely uprooted and forced into unfriendly earth.

Vai rubbed the wood, approving the polish of the grain. "Father taught us that a man knows he is a man by the good he brings to his village."

Bakary appeared at the door of Grandmother's house. All the people loitering in the courtyard and at the gate to the family compound turned to look, every voice stilled.

The old djeli raised a hand skyward. "Mansa," he said, to Andevai.

Between one breath and the breath that was never taken, I found myself married to the mansa of Four Moons House. Not that anyone had asked if this was what I wanted!

The next day, in the ensuing gatherings and rituals, I crept away by the path I had taken when I had fled Haranwy almost two years ago. The open gate gave way to a track that led through gardens and pasture. A herd of fat sheep worked through the forage. I did not go far through the golden stalks of autumn. An orchard of apple, plum, and cherry had been harvested but for a few stragglers. An old stump made a good resting place. I sat for the longest time staring at the wind in the grass and the sway of branches, but everywhere I looked I saw my sire's shadow and felt the icy touch of his hand. The pulse of blood in my ears drowned me.

Where the hand of fortune branches, Tara Bell's child must choose.

I had made the only choice I could, not just once but many times. I had to save the ones I loved, for although I had grabbed for their hands, I hadn't been able to save my parents that terrible day. Maybe my sire had saved me. Maybe I had accidentally saved myself. All I remembered was how I had struggled to reach them.

It wasn't drowning I was truly afraid of. It was the moment my mother's hand had slipped away from mine as the current pulled her into the murky depths where my father had already sunk.

No more! I would not lose them! I would not!

So I had made the bargain with my sire. I wouldn't lose them, but they would lose me.

Bee's laughter floated like the memory of summer past and the promise of summer to come. She and Andevai appeared, arguing with the intensity of two people who agree on the fundamentals and are now clashing about what color the curtains should be. Rory trailed after them, distracted by the puppy racing around his heels and barking in excitement as it demanded he play.

"There you are, dearest!" Bee called. "Cat, you can't just run off like that. For one thing, it looks very disrespectful to the elders both of the village and of the mage House. Furthermore, something is bothering you, and I am going to bully you until you tell us what it is."

The puppy gnawed on my ankle while wriggling its hindquarters in ecstatic excitement.

"I know what you are thinking," said Vai.

"I don't believe you do," I said in my coolest voice, although in fact it was difficult to be morose when a puppy was chewing on my leg.

"I understand your concerns, Catherine." He flipped out the length of his dash jacket and sat beside me, shoving me with his hip to make room. "Beatrice and I already have a plan, although I agree we should have made it more clear to you. But you've been so distracted and tired and hard to talk to, love. You've not spoken a word about what happened to Drake, or why Four Moons House is now encased in ice just as if the Wild Hunt had devoured it. Just like Crescent House."

"It is an odd resemblance, is it not?" I agreed. "But the Master of the Wild Hunt can only enter the mortal world on Hallows' Night. Everyone knows that!"

He rubbed a finger along the trimmed magnificence of his beard. "That's true. Still, I did not know an eru had such power."

"Neither did I!" agreed Bee, with a suspicious look, but it was evident she had not the slightest memory of my sire's passage through the coach or what he had done.

"I did not know it either, but it appears to be an eru's work." It was no lie. The one who gave him birth had had an eru's form when he was disgorged. Rory looked a question at me, and I shook my head. He pulled his lips back as if to snarl at me, and I opened my eyes very aggressively, head jutted forward, until he backed off. Glimpsing his movement, the puppy gamboled after him.

"Is that all you have to say on the matter?" Vai demanded. "Because it seems no one witnessed every part of what happened except for you."

"I asked for their aid, for that is my right. I cut a path for them through the mirror. But they had no obligation to stay once Drake was dead."

At that moment I knew I would not tell them. They could not stop the Wild Hunt, nor could I allow them to follow me into the spirit world. If they knew what bargain I had made, the next two months would swamp them in misery and fear. It would be cruel to tell them. So I would keep silence and tell no one.

He took my hands in his. Bee set her arms akimbo and fixed him with an axe-blow glare. A wind teased through her curls, making them dance, like happiness. His breath brushed my ear.

"No kissing, Andevai!" said Bee. "You promised! You must present your argument in a reasoned and sensible manner."

He released my hands and stood. I had washed and mended his clothes while he was bedridden, but despite the skillful job I had done, they looked like clothes bought in the secondhand market, not like costly garments appropriate to a powerful magister whose status was every bit the equal of a prince's. Yet he looked so very fine. It wasn't the clothes that made him beautiful.

"Catherine, I know you have told me that you cannot live in Four Moons House. And you heard me promise the mansa on my mother's honor that I will rebuild Four Moons House. I am a cold mage, and I have to do it."

"I know, my love."

"Besides the promise to my mother, I have a responsibility to the House that educated me and to the mansa who raised me up. To every fledgling magister who may never get proper training, like the fire banes in Expedition. To my own family, to the village that birthed me, and also to the other villages chained by clientage to Four Moons House. To all villages so chained. All communities have a right to liberty, a right to the dignity and security of their own persons."

"After which," said Bee in a portentously deep voice, "he will cause all strife in the world to cease, every infant child to be born healthy, and all men to have the taste to dress fashionably and in colors that suit their complexions. What Andevai is working up to tell you, dearest, is that while he promised to rebuild Four Moons House, he cleverly did not specify *how* he would do so. Nor did the mansa ask. I keep trying to tell you about my plan, and you keep ignoring me."

I considered my folded hands, and then looked up at them. So bright they were in the afternoon sun. The wind fell cool across us, but the light cast a glorious, rich glow across the land. From here we could see a glint of the great river whose waters had so altered my life, although in truth it was the hunter who had acted that day for his own hidden reasons. He had driven me to this moment as hunters will, stalking their prey until they are cornered.

So be it. I still had life in me.

Rory scooped up the puppy and walked over to sit at my feet.

I smiled at them, whom I loved best in all the world. "What plan could you possibly have agreed on?"

47

Had I understood the monumental nature of their scheme, I might have taken a nap first.

To argue with elders who object to such a radical change of direction needs a honeyed voice and a stubborn persistence working in concert. The new mansa informed his people that no House could rise on the ruins of the old. The ice had caged it forever and, with it, the old chains by which Four Moons had long sustained itself. Those who did not wish to walk this new path with the mansa had the right to go elsewhere, to join whatever mage House would take them in. The deceased mansa's nephew and perhaps half of the survivors departed. I was surprised at how many stayed, including Serena and all of the House's djeliw. I couldn't blame the bards. Given the choice of the two men, I knew which one I would rather sing about.

The mansa called together the village councils and asked them to invoke *rei vindicatio*: A community belongs to itself. The ancient contracts were dissolved. Much of the farm and pastureland reverted to the villages, but enough remained for a home farm overseen by House stewards. Here those who wished to work the land would farm, with the surplus marked for the support of the new House.

To uproot and move seventy-one people from their accustomed life is no small undertaking. Remarkably, the September weather held fair for the two weeks' journey to the city of Havery. Everyone went a little hungry, and everyone except for the littlest, the eldest, and the infirm had to walk most of the way, but not one person died. There was only one serious fight, between two young men over a village girl from Trecon who had sneaked along with the kitchen staff to escape an unwanted marriage at home.

"Should we send her back?" Vai asked me that night.

We were camped next to a mage hostel along the turnpike that ran from Audui to Havery. Naturally the indoor places were given to the elders and the children, but Vai did demand the privilege of a private shelter. It was astonishing how a gal might come to appreciate a crude tent rigged of canvas in which she and her loved one could sleep alone every night on a mat on the hard ground with but a single blanket to cover them.

"The elders are split on the question and have asked if I or my wife wish to make our opinion known. We ought to respect the arrangements made by our elders. That is the way least disruptive to the harmonious peace of the community."

"Yes, because forcing a young woman into a marriage she does not wish for seems harmonious to me!"

"I can't suppose other women could possibly hope for the good fortune you had."

I pinched him in a sensitive spot, although that only made him laugh. "Thus you make my argument for me. It's one thing for the elders to interview compatible young people and see that they are introduced to each other in the hope that an interest will kindle between them. I understand they wish for family alliances that will benefit the community. But the young people must consent as well, otherwise it is just another form of clientage. Anyway, Vai, you are the last person who ought to argue against disrupting the harmonious peace of the old ways. I say let her stay with us. She can work off a fair price for her transport and food, and after that remain with the House or find her way into a situation she finds more pleasing." I rolled on top of him. "As I am about to do."

The elderly prince of Havery was a forward-thinking man who welcomed new technology, new faces, and new trade opportunities with the Amerikes, and who had introduced new laws by which an elected council shared the reins of ruling. As surprised as the man was when the young mansa, his elders' council, his lawyers, and his household presented themselves to request the prince's permission to establish a mage House in his city, he was astonished when Vai informed him that the House no longer held villages in clientage and would be setting up a carpentry yard to support itself.

"This is a radical step," the prince remarked as he bowed over Beatrice's hand, for it was evident they were already acquainted. "It appears the Honeyed Voice has sweetened yet another ear."

"In fact," said Vai, "it is her cousin, my wife, who coaxed me into bed with the radicals. Her, and my good friends from Expedition."

"You are welcome here," said the prince, to all of us. "My clan has long suffered, caught between the Parisi prince and the Veneti dukes with their Armorican overlord. That is why I have sought allies elsewhere." He nodded at Chartji and Godwik. They were not the only feathered people present at his court. "The presence of a mansa and his House will certainly give my rivals pause, especially now that the Iberian Monster's campaign has shaken up the entire continent."

"What news of the Iberian Monster?" I asked.

The old man indicated a stack of dispatches on a desk. "An interesting turn of events. He has rallied four Roman legions to his cause and declared his intention to depose the emperor and raise himself to that exalted place, after which he will reform the laws and some such palaver. Last we heard, he won a resounding victory near Nikaia. For the time being, that leaves us here in the Gallic Territories at a temporary peace. We shall see how long it lasts."

At the law offices of Godwik and Clutch, Chartji took us to a storage room. Here, by diverse means, had washed up most of the belongings we had lost hold of over the last months: Vai's carpentry tools and the other traveling gear he and I had abandoned when we had leaped into the Rhenus River; the chests left behind at Two Gourds House with all of Vai's dash jackets and the clothes he had had made for me; even, astoundingly, the chests Bee had been forced to leave with Camjiata, from which Drake had stolen some of Vai's clothing.

To my amazement, one of the chests contained all of my father's journals. The general had kindly sent these items on with a note that read:

It is never too late to change your mind.

Best of all, Bee unearthed the gold and fine linen Caonabo had asked her to deliver to Juba. The cloth shed a smoky flavor, dragon-like, from being packed in with tobacco leaves. "Haübey was meant to wear this finery on his return to Sharagua, but I have decided we need the money more than he does now he has been called back from exile. We can get an excellent price for the tobacco as well. It is no easy task to shelter, feed, and clothe almost one hundred people from nothing!"

The old Hassi Barahal compound where Aunt Tilly had been born had been boarded up in the wake of Camjiata's defeat sixteen years ago, when the household had dispersed either to Adurnam or to Gadir. With the proceeds from the sale of the gold, Four Moons House obtained the lease for this edifice, which backed up against a gentle tributary stream of the mighty Sicauna River in the northern quarter of town. In the next property over along the bank stood a run-down old villa with a hypocaust system in need of extensive repairs, owned by a Kena'ani shipping clan eager to make an ally of the mansa and his Kena'ani wife and her cousin by offering him use of the building as long as he made the necessary repairs and renovations at his own expense. With the weather rapidly growing colder, the able-bodied set to work to repair enough of the hypocaust system to shelter the cold mages through the coming winter, while the Barahal compound's buildings were cleaned for the rest of the household.

Five days after we arrived, with the heaviest of the cleaning behind us, Bee and I walked down to the harbor district to the law offices of Godwik and Clutch. I liked what I had seen of Havery, for the little port city had a free and easy flavor that reminded me of Expedition. A lively troll town expanded in the west, near a burgeoning factory district. Besides the usual port-city mix of people of every lineage, clan, ethnicity, guild, and profession, there were enclaves of merchants and artisans and sailors from Expedition, the Taino kingdom, and other Amerikan peoples as well.

"The prince has asked me if I will consider standing for the council when he calls for elections next year," Bee was saying, "and naturally I will, since many women may feel reluctant to put themselves forward. Someone must set a good example. But we must have a way to make a living as well. That's why the plan Andevai and I have concocted makes perfect sense. In a way, the mage House and the Godwik and Clutch consortium have become partners through your relationship with both of them. The best part is that you and I will finally get to do the work we were trained for."

I loved to watch her shine. She was a little like the puppy. She had gotten her teeth into an enterprise that matched her wit and her ambition.

"Trolls are excellent lawyers because they can pick through the fine points of the law. And they are clever scientists because the world fascinates them, and they're not really scared of anything except dragons. Also, they share everything within the clutch. The food on my plate is the food on your plate. That's why they have become such keen printers, spreading knowledge like seeds. But one thing troll printers and lawyers can't do is go places where they would be conspicuous for being trolls. Therefore, you and I—and Rory if he wants to—will act as their human agents. We will investigate things for them that they otherwise would have trouble knowing."

"We'll be spies," I said delightedly.

"If you must use that word, then I am content with it. Andevai says this is exactly the sort of scheme that will please you, Cat. Obviously it pleases me. I can scarcely wait to begin sneaking about and poking my nose into other people's business, just as we used to in the old days! I mean, when I am not making speeches in the Assembly. But he has been worried about you. He has stewards to take care of the day-to-day running of such a large household, for it is truly an unwieldy task best left to people trained from an early age to manage its complexities. He knows you don't belong in the mage House, nor does he expect you to serve it. He says you told him once that you wouldn't have minded being a warden in Expedition, and I can see how that would suit you. This is something like that, don't you think? You like our plan, don't you?"

I took her hand in mine. "Of course I do. It's a marvelous scheme. It's all splendid, what Andevai is doing, this new endeavor, everything!"

She pulled me to a stop under the feathery brown sign with orange letters that marked the door of the law offices of Godwik and Clutch. "Are you well, dearest?"

I clasped her hands tightly. "I'm at peace, Bee, except for one thing. You know I told you how I met your parents when I was with Cam-

jiata."

The storm clouds could not have moved in more swiftly, from clear sky to threatening rain. Her voice trembled. "I should have been there with you, Cat! You should not have to face all these terrible things alone!"

I had to look away from her then. My worn but thoroughly polished boots made a good alternative to her probing gaze. Vai did not like the way I polished my boots, so he had taken to doing it for me. "I just think that after all it would have been better if I had found it in my heart to forgive them. I felt so betrayed only because I loved them so much."

"They shouldn't have done it!"

"I know, but... it must have hurt them, too."

She heaved a dramatic sigh and was about to scold me when the door opened and Chartji poked her muzzle out. Her crest was flared in an odd pattern, some feathers flattened and some upright. She whistled a curt greeting, a bit off-key.

"Bee, a letter arrived for you this morning. Of course I did not open it, but it stinks of dragon and I would be grateful if you would remove it from the premises as quickly as possible."

With a shriek Bee released my hands and dashed inside.

Chartji bared her teeth at me. "Cousin, there is something about you that puzzles me. You rats are funny creatures, hard to understand, but I sense a shadow beneath your smile."

As the great general Hannibal Barca had famously said just before he and his queen, the Dido of Qart Hadast, defeated the Romans at Zama, *Either find a way, or make one.*

"I have a few questions about contracts I would like to ask you, Chartji. Is now a good time?"

On our walk home Bee could not contain herself. With the letter clutched in her hand, she stumbled frequently on the cobblestones as she read bits aloud to me. "'In the lore of my people, it is told that the women who walk the dreams of dragons may find among dragon-kind one mate to match them.' Isn't that romantical, Cat? He goes on. 'The obligations placed on me by my position as headmaster...' That's why he cannot leave yet. The hatchlings are still too young. They look like youths in size but they need constant care before they are ready to be left on their own. I wonder how many hatchlings the headmaster raised among people at the academy all those years without anyone being the wiser! Kemal begs me to never reveal their secret. He says that the lore of the dragons speaks of dark cruel times when the dragon-born were hunted and killed!"

"It seems to me, Bee, that you could go to Noviomagus for a month's visit. Then you might discover whether he is the, ah, mate to match you, which I rather doubt since you seem to still have feelings for Caonabo."

She sniffed imperiously. "According to tradition, Kena'ani women can take two husbands if it serves the clan: one husband from within the clan and one trade husband, an outsider, to seal an alliance."

"I can't figure which one you would call the trade husband and which one within the clan."

She ignored this perfectly legitimate question with an airy wave of her hand. "Anyway, when will I ever see Caonabo again? How can I ever afford even to go to Noviomagus? We can barely afford to feed everyone. The only reason we have managed all the renovation and repairs is that the household is doing all the work."

I swung her hand in mine. "That's true. But after Hallows' Night you must promise me you'll find a way to go. Just to see what happens. Do you promise me, Bee? Do you?"

"Gracious Melqart, Cat! If I protest that I do not want to, you'll know I am lying. And if I say yes, love will carry me across the distance like wings, I'll appear as giddy in love as you! Maybe after things are more sorted out here and the household is better established and everyone has a decent cot to sleep on . . . Prim Astarte! What I wouldn't give for decent plumbing!"

We discussed such mundane matters all the way home, and I cherished every word of it.

So it was that at midday on the last day of October, I finished darning a worn elbow on the last of Vai's dash jackets that needed repair, the much-abused but lovingly tended gold-and-red chained pattern he had worn the night of the areito and Hallows' Night and thus into the spirit world. As a fine elegant dash jacket suitable for court, it was utterly ruined, but I could read the course of our love across its mended injuries and still-shining threads and know it for the glorious

garment it was.

He had selected the sturdiest of his jackets to labor in, and they did get worn. I had worked hard to get all the mending done to my liking, sitting at an old secondhand table at the window in the corner room Vai had picked out for the mansa's study. At this table in the evenings, while I sewed and Bee drew or practiced declaiming and while visitors came and went, he wrote letters, planned lessons, practiced illusions, and had me read out loud to us from a recently published monograph by Professora Alhamrai regarding accounts of how shrinkage in the ice sheets correlated with the creep of hardy trees into the Barrens.

Besides the table and chairs, necessary for when the mansa wished to meet people, the spacious chamber was furnished with his clothes chests, the chest with my father's journals in it, a copper basin and pitcher on a stand, and the rolled-up mat on which he and I slept. Because Vai wasn't there, I heated the air with a little brazier. The hypocaust beneath the planks was blocked by old rubble and not yet cleared out because the dormitories had to be readied for winter first. Fortunately it had been an unusually mild autumn, with not a single snowfall.

"Cat!" Bee hurried in without knocking, as she always did when she knew Vai was elsewhere. "I just heard Andevai tell Serena that she must sell all his dash jackets. He wants them out of the house today, so he may begin the new year knowing he has sacrificed like everyone else."

"Gracious Melqart! I knew we had run low on funds for the kitchen, but I didn't know things had gotten this desperate!" I leaped up and, with Bee's help, hid my six favorite of his jackets in another chest, under the fur pelt blanket, together with the beautiful dressing robes.

Bee frowned and grabbed out of my hands the dash jacket sewn from the fabric of flowers bursting into fireworks. "I swear an oath to you, Cat, I just made up the pattern, I didn't dream it!"

I snatched the jacket out of her hands and folded it in paper just as the red coals in the brazier dulled to ash.

Magister Serena sailed into the room beside Vai's more clipped, impatient stride. Sadly they looked very handsome together, but I liked her enough that if someday such a suitable match were to be made because I was no longer there, I could bear the thought of it.

Vai smiled so sweetly at me that my heart melted all over again. "It   573 will take another month to get a substantial carpentry shop up and running," he was saying to one of the stewards, "and meanwhile we've had all these expenses to make the House livable. Take both chests. Sell everything. We must all begin the new year with an understanding of our changed circumstances. Don't argue with me, Catherine!"

"I said nothing! But besides the clothing you must have to wear every day, Andevai, I insist you set aside two elegant dash jackets for when you go to court or are invited to some lordly mansion for dinner. You cannot attend such functions wearing the clothes you work in. It would not reflect well on the House, would it?"

"Indeed it would not," said Serena in the manner of a woman who has lived all her life with the highest expectations of her rank and station. "The mansa of Four Moons House cannot appear looking as if he works as a common laborer."

Bee coughed. "Even if he does."

"In another year or two, everything will be different," I said placatingly. I had cleverly placed the two dash jackets I knew he would choose at the top of the chest: the fireworks and a damask whose orange and brown evoked colors popular among radical laborers. His decision to sell his beloved clothes had so agitated him that I was able to set those two and yet two more aside before the steward took away the chest.

Fortunately we then were called to the front of the house to eat our dinner of porridge, turnips, and a stew of fish, onion, and tomato. Afterward we helped settle the children and elders into the wagons that would convey everyone to troll town for the Hallows Festival. The household was going to spend the night and day within the maze of troll town, hidden from the Wild Hunt. The children were as excited as hornets.

Bee took my hands. "It seems unfair you cannot shelter in the troll maze as the rest of us do. I don't like to leave you alone." She bent a too-wary gaze on me, forehead all a-wrinkle. "Are you sure you're well, Cat? I swear to you there is a tone in your voice that makes me wonder if something is wrong."

I kissed her. "I do get to fretting on Hallows' Night about you, Bee. Even though I know you are safe in the troll maze, I can't help but worry. Don't be concerned for me. I promised Rory I would spend the night teaching him how to cheat at cards."

"Are you sure, Cat? I just feel there's something you're not telling me."

The Blessed Tanit was merciful. The wagons were ready to go, so I did not have to answer. I kissed her again as my heart broke and my smile never wavered. Off they went. I waved until I thought my arm would fall off.

"My sweet Catherine, you have avoided speaking to me all day." He stepped up behind me, slipping his arms around me.

"I thought you went with them!"

"Without a kiss? I think not. After all, love, I think perhaps I shall stay with you—"

"No!" My hard-won peace shattered. The boiling miasma of anger and terror and shame erupted like an engine that, after steaming along in such a delicate balance for so long, had at last overheated. "You have to go to troll town! He knows your blood! He threatened you!"

"Love, love, that's not what I meant. I will go to troll town and you will spend Hallows' Night and Day at the law offices, as we agreed. I just thought how accustomed I am becoming to falling asleep each night and waking up each morning with you in my arms. It seems hard to face a night alone. So with everyone gone and nothing to do for the rest of the afternoon..."

My pounding heart and ragged breathing slowly calmed. "Oh."

He chased me with kisses all the way back to the mansa's study.

Afterward we lay on the mat in the corner of the room in the corner of the quiet building, and he kissed me so tenderly I almost wept.

"I know your secret, love," he whispered against my ear.

My breath faltered. I pressed my face against his cheek, shuddering, for I had no idea how I was going to get through this now.

His smile brushed like love against my skin. "How many of my dash jackets did you hide?"

The air went out of me. I shut my eyes. "Only six besides the four I set aside already," I murmured hoarsely, as my mind whispered a prayer of thanks to the Blessed Tanit, protector of women. "We'd better go, Vai."

I dressed in the jacket I had made new out of what was torn. I buttoned on my spruce-green skirt that was so good for striding in, laced up my sturdy boots that had carried me through such a long journey,

575

and set on my head the jaunty Amazon's shako I had picked up on the battlefield from a fallen sister. I took only my locket and my sword. I twined my fingers intimately through his and savored the pleasure of walking hand in hand with him through the streets of Havery. A few people ran their final errands, but mostly the streets were empty as all made ready to shut their doors and light their candles against Hallows' Night.

"I do like it here," I said. "Although Aunty Djeneba's boarding-house is still my favorite place. You have some other scheme in mind, Vai. What is it?"

"We have two buildings," he said, "so why not two schoolrooms? It seems wrong to me that those poor young fire mages were killed precisely because James Drake offered them a future they could not otherwise have. Cold mages were treated in the Antilles something like fire mages are treated here, with scorn and suspicion. Surely mages can work together as equals. What is to stop us from establishing an academy in which we see what may come about if we act in concert rather than in antipathy?"

"People will fear the prospect of cold mages and fire mages acting in concert. They'll fear they will set themselves up as princes and lord it over all the people of the land."

"People do that anyway."

"I did feel sorry for those young fire mages. Imagine thinking that the best choice you have is to believe what James Drake is telling you! You'll have to answer people's fears, though. Naturally some magisters will abuse the knowledge and power they gain. I suppose that's what you talked about with the blacksmith in that little village when we were escaping down the river."

He smiled to let me know that no word of the conversation he had had with the blacksmith would pass his lips. "I also remember what the cacica told me. She said that the Taino believe every person is born with a kernel of power. Some waken it, and some never do. You were right to say that every child should have a chance to learn. Do you know, love, Beatrice and I are talking all the time about the things we want to do. All this work is going on for what she and I are hoping and planning for. But you never talk about what you're thinking about.

You must want something, Catherine. You can't be happy merely to go along with our schemes."

"I do want something." I smiled, for I loved him and Bee so much, and all the rest of them, too. "Just don't let Wasa get up to mischief. She has such a rascal spirit. I'll tell you the rest tomorrow night."

It was almost twilight as we reached the gates of troll town. The mirrors and shards of glass that surrounded the district flashed so agonizingly that I turned my back before the pain ripped through me. I kissed him and sent him on his way. The drums called him. They were already dancing, the strangest rhythm I had ever heard, for it was shot through with the whistling and clicking of trolls. It was a new song being born.

I smelled liquor, and the fresh fragrance of the traditional crossing buns filled with plum jam or yam custard. A rollicking party was already under way, as the sailors would have it.

Another sound rose out of the earth like mist and filtered down from the sky like rain: the horn calling the Wild Hunt to ride.

I ran the short distance to the harbor office of Godwik and Clutch, for I had promised Bee and Vai I would sit in a room with four mirrors until the danger had passed. Rory sulked on the stoop, seated on the stairs with a morose eye turned on me as I came up.

"I can't believe you never told them," he said. "Even Chartji left for troll town without knowing. How could you, Cat? And making me go along with it, too. It's not right."

"What good would it have done? You know them, Rory. They would have insisted on trying to hide me, or fighting the Wild Hunt, or something equally foolish and pointless. They would have spent the last two months so unhappy and grief-stricken and miserable. It's better this way."

"I'm not sure you have the right to choose for them."

The horn's cry rose a second time, gaining strength.

I sat next to him, holding his hand. "It's done now. Rory, this is your last chance to cross back over in your own body, for once I am gone you will only cross over by means of death. Do you want to return to the spirit world?"

He pressed his face into my shoulder, then shook himself, and tugged on my braid, and pushed me as a brother teases his sister. "No. My home is here now."

The third call licked the air like fire and breathed all the way into my bones. I heard the clip-clop of hooves and the scrape of wheels on cobblestones.

Rising, I pulled four letters from inside my jacket. "This is for Bee, this for Vai, this for Doctor Asante, and the last is for Aunt Tilly and Uncle Jonatan. You know what to say to Chartji. Now you'd better go before he sees you."

His lips were curled into the beginnings of a snarl as he snatched the letters out of my hand. "I'll see you off. Someone ought to."

Along the avenue, the lit Hallows' candles set in windows went out one by one. The coach rolled out of the gloom, the four horses gleaming like moonlight. The coachman tipped his hat in greeting. The eru leaped down from the back of the coach. Clouds scudded over the bright stars and thunder rumbled like the feet of the leashed Hunt troubling the sky as it waited to be released.

I glanced at the heavens, and then at the door as the eru opened it and bumped down the steps so I could climb in. She nodded, a spark of blue flashing on her forehead.

"I take it that a willing sacrifice need not be torn to pieces and have its head thrown down a well," I remarked as I entered the coach.

"No reason to do that unless they try to escape or fight back." My sire sat at his ease, one leg crossed elegantly. He looked past me at Rory, on the stoop. "Is that your brother? I do lose track, for there are so many of you."

The door closing cut off the view, but regardless my gaze had been caught by the large, gleaming object on the bench next to my sire. I had last seen the bronze cauldron in the temple of Carnonos watched over by my grandfather. The face of a horned man shone in the polished surface.

"Not a very good likeness, if you ask me," said my sire, noticing the direction of my gaze. "Imagine! He had the effrontery to pour water into it and watch me every Hallows' Night. I put a stop to that!"

"Did you kill him?"

"Kill him? Of course not! On Hallows' Night, the Hunt gathers up

the spirits of those fated to die in the coming year. We don't kill them.

You mortals kill each other, or you die of other causes. I only kill one mortal a year, and I do that because I am commanded to do so by my masters."

Strangely, the moment the coach arrived, all my fear had melted away like ice under heat. The coachman cracked his whip. I pulled the shutter back in time to wave at Rory as we rolled away down the street.

"Then what did you do in the mortal world all these weeks?" I demanded.

"Your mother piqued my curiosity. Tara had all sorts of interesting stories. She told me tales of what the mortal world is truly like, for of course I normally only catch a glimpse of it when I pass through." He ran a hand along the curve of the cauldron, tracing the figure meant to be him. Like a cat, he rather relished himself. "So besides wanting to get hold of this cauldron, I had a hankering, a curiosity if you will, to make one grand tour."

I laughed.

"Why does that amuse you? I do not understand your jests, little cat."

He was not like me or any human. When the river floods and drowns, it does not regret its victims. When a storm lays waste, it does not ponder the uses of power. Fire consumes and does not grieve. The ice gives no thought to what it crushes as it works its way over the land.

But I did not have to like him. "That my mother told you tales, that's all."

We turned the corner into a commercial district on the road leading out of town, lined with taverns and inns whose windows were ablaze with Hallows candles. These flames went out one by one as we rumbled along the cobblestones. The buzz of voluble conversation ceased, too, fading to an anxious silence that draped the street with its fear.

The luscious aroma of coffee drifted to my nose.

"Did you try coffee, Sire?"

"No." He sniffed. "Is that smell coffee? I wondered what that was but I didn't know how to go about getting it."

I stuck my head out the window. "Stop here! Sire, do you have any money?"

"Money? Oh! Yes, the stamped metal roundels."

He passed over a huge cloth bag so weighted with coins I had to set it on the floor, for it was too heavy for me to easily hold. I picked out a denarius by feel, hopped out, and dashed into a benighted coffee shop where men whispered in frightened voices about the suddenly extinguished lights. With so much confusion it was easy to place the denarius on the counter and take four full mugs back to the coach, one for each of us. I wanted to be wide-awake.

As the horses stamped we stood on the street and drank our coffee.

"My thanks," said the coachman.

"Sharp and nutty," said the eru, "with a taste of sun."

When I had drained my cup, I wiped a finger along the bottom and let the latch lick the last drops off my skin.

"Mmm," murmured the latch. "I like that!"

"What do you think?" I asked my sire.

An owl swooped down out of the night and landed atop the coach, golden eyes unblinking.

"I think it is time to go," he said. "The courts are waiting."

I looked him in the eye. His amber stare was just like mine. "It's what you made me for, is it not? To be the sacrifice."

A smile ghosted across his lips, then vanished as he glanced toward the owl and shook his head to remind me that the courts heard and saw everything he heard and saw, just as he could hear and see through the eyes of his Hunt. "All the others before you died. So are you trapped, little cat. You will never be free..."

His voice faded as on words left unsaid, for there were words he dared not say within the hearing of the owl because he was not the owl's master. The owl was spying on him.

But I could guess. *All the others before you died, because they failed. So you are trapped, because they could not understand and thus act. You will never be free unless I am also free.*

As a young man in the mage House, Vai had known in his heart all along that he might as a magister gain the power and glory granted him because of his magic, but he would not be free as long as his village was bound in clientage. A prince among slaves is still a slave. Freedom cuts in every direction. No one is truly free, if even one person lies in chains.

I knew what I had to do.

580   As the coach rolled on I unbraided my hair and combed it out

with my fingers. Let the courts be dazzled by its beauty! I pinched my cheeks to make sure they glowed, and moistened and bit my lips so they shone. My sire watched in silence, his expression a mask of ice.

Feeling bolder, I opened the shutters on both doors and gazed out over both the mortal world and the spirit world. On Hallows' Night, the coach traveled in both worlds at once.

The spirit world flashed past in changing aspects, all the possibilities that might ever have been and every gradient between: a world in which the mansa ruled, and one in which he suffered an early death in the hold of a ship, and one in which he owned a shop and sold white damask to women who would take it away and dye it into all the colors and patterns they could dream of.

In the mortal world we sped across the quiet waves of the Mediterranean Sea and past the spice-laden markets of Qart Hadast, the jewel of ports. The fields and trees of north Africa trailed away as bands of desert crept their fingers into the green. A long lonely stretch of golden rock and pale dunes passed beneath us until we reached a salt mine. The enterprising miners in the Malian Empire had broken through to an ancient gateway between the worlds and inadvertently unleashed the ghouls who craved the salt of mortal blood and being.

Wind blew grit into the interior of the coach. The land was so quiet where once people had lived and worked and thrived, where they would do so again. The coach rocked from side to side, bucketing as we descended into the pit. Salt links the worlds. Each gate swirls with energy, the power of transition and transformation. These threads bind us all.

The shutters slammed shut. I caught in a breath, the coach jolted to a stop, and all the air punched out of me. My entire body went numb.

My sire leaned forward until his face almost touched mine. "You must be what I made you to be, Daughter."

"Yes," I said, because I had finally understood what he wanted the day he had encased Four Moons House in ice. "After that, Sire, you will give up all claim to me and mine. For that matter, you will also give up any claim to bind any of your children who do not wish to be bound."

He extended a hand in the radical manner, and we shook to seal our bargain.

"By the way, may I have that big bag of coin?"

"Yes. I have no use for it."

The latch opened the door; the steps bumped down although the eru had not disembarked. That the eru acted as footman was a courtesy for mortal eyes, for the coach was as alive as I was.

My sire climbed out. I grappled with the bag of coins, slinging it over my back despite its distracting weight. No sensible young woman raised in an impoverished family walks away from a pot of gold, even if she may never get a chance to spend it.

I took in and released a breath for courage, and I went out after him. With a hand braced on the threshold of the coach door and my feet still on the steps, I paused to survey my ground as a general may do before a battle.

The palace of the courts lay before me, the realm of both shadow and light, as deep as the murkiest pit and as high as the brightest peak. What Vai had seen as a nest of starving ghouls determined to drain him of his blood, I had seen as a grand feast populated by elegantly clothed and peacock-feathered personages who had grown accustomed to their harvest. Hard to say which was true. Maybe they both were.

The Hunt surged in the air as a mass of boiling black cloud, my brothers and sisters. I saw crows and spotted hounds, smart-mouthed hyenas and silent vipers. A cloud of wasps and a spinning web of spiders jostled against women with lions' heads and men with the bodies of fish. Dire wolves prowled in their packs shoulder to shoulder with the tawny beauty of the big cats. Yet the hunters had been bound to serve not nature's course but the courts' desire.

The coach and horses were not touching the ground. I was pretty sure they could not.

I glanced back at the eru holding on at the back and ahead to the coachman sitting on the driver's bench at the front. The eru regarded me with all three eyes. "This is as far as we can take you, Cousin," she said.

I smiled. "Whatever happens, I want to thank you for the trust you've shown in me and the trust I've been able to give to you. Should things fall out in such a way that you discover leisure to do as you wish at some later date, my solicitor can be found at the law offices of Godwik and Clutch in the city of Havery, where you picked me up."

The coachman raised his whip in salute.

I jumped awkwardly down into the pit, shifted the heavy bag on my shoulders, and with my sword in hand walked forward after my sire. The pit had become a resplendent plaza crowded with hungry courtiers. They slipped and slid about so much I could not count them, but I began to think they were far fewer than I had first believed. They just took up so much room and never stopped grasping and moving. Eager to get their drop of the rich feast, they parted to make a path for us that led straight to the dais of glittering salt.

On the dais stood four chairs beaten out of gold and four stools carved from obsidian. As my sire approached, human-like presences solidified in the eight chairs: they who ruled as the day court and the night court, for the spirit world was washed by both light and dark. What manner of people they were I could not tell: Were they spirit creatures who had begun to lose the ability to change and had thus become more and more solid? Ancestors who craved a rigid sort of immortality? Elders who stood in relation to humans much as dragons did to the feathered people? I did not know, and right now I was not going to find out.

The courts awaited the sacrifice. Chains like whips lashed my sire to his knees before them. He knelt, but he did not bend his head; his lips were drawn back as if he wished to growl. The Hunt stirred with myriad hisses and chortles and howls and snarls.

"Give us what is ours." The voice of the courts thundered, many in one. "So you are required to do, because you are bound with the blood of the last feast, and because we bind you with the blood of this feast through the coming year."

They ignored me, so I walked past him and planted myself in front of the dais, facing up to their chairs.

"Peace to you," I said with my friendliest smile. "Does this night find you at peace?"

A vast and horrible silence smothered the world. Their golden eyes chained me with a will as heavy as eternity. I fell into the rip current of their gaze, into the breathing heart of the ice.

At their deepest levels, the worlds vibrate. A force flows through every part of existence. Cold mages can redirect this flow; fire mages energize and disperse it. As for what exists in the spirit world beyond

583

our ken, *courts* and *dragons* are just names we give to powers we do not comprehend and cannot escape.

Because I was my father's daughter I could make a story of it, a way to understand and put words to something far bigger than I was: In the worlds there is an ancient and unending duel between dragons and courts. In the Great Smoke, the mothers of dragons dragged innocent girls into the ocean of dreams, using mortal women to midwife their fragile hatchlings.

Thus the duel tipped to favor the dragons, and so the other side had fought back.

In the old village tales written down by my father in his journals, the Wild Hunt did not take blood. Death comes to all things in the mortal world, and the Wild Hunt rode on Hallows' Night to gather in the souls of those fated to die in the coming year.

Perhaps the cold mages had come to the attention of the courts because powerful cold magic caused changes in the flow and ebb of energy in the spirit world. Perhaps mages shone so brightly and their blood tasted so sweet that, once one had been taken to bind the Wild Hunt the very first time, the courts developed a taste for their blood and then a need for it and then a desperate craving. By drinking the blood of mortals they had in the end become what we called ghouls: creatures who devour the essence of others in order to live.

I did not have to devour the essence of others in order to live. I could live perfectly happily working in a humble office with my dear cousin, building up a respectable business that involved spying and sneaking, although obviously I would be first to volunteer to do the most dirty, adventurous, and strenuous work. I could sleep perfectly happily on a mat on the floor with the man I loved, even though obviously I would prefer to lie in a bed he had built for us, because it was more comfortable. I was eager to teach my brother to cheat at cards, to nurse Vai's mother through her weak spells and nurture Vai's sisters into women, to hope Luce survived the war, to get to know Doctor Asante, and to write about everything to Professora Alhamrai, and maybe even to return to Expedition someday to visit the people I had become so fond of. I wanted to introduce batey to Europa. That would be something, a ballcourt in every city and town!

The courts tried to hammer me flat under the crushing cold of the ice, they wanted me to be afraid, to give up, to give in. But I braced myself on my sword and warmed my hands on my locket. I answered the polite greeting they had not made, for they did not know how to reciprocate in the traditional way.

"I have no trouble, thanks to my power as a woman. I just want to clarify two things. There is one sacrifice each year. There cannot be another, and it is this sacrifice that binds the Wild Hunt and indeed all your servants for another year. So you all agree and accept me as the sacrifice?"

"We accept."

They were so hungry and impatient and greedy that they threw their chains off my sire and onto me. Their touch tore at my skin as a hundred sharp nails of ice, a net of barbs poised to puncture me and drink me dry.

"That being so, you take my mortal blood. Is that not right? Mortal blood seals the contract by which you first bound the Hunt and all your other servants?"

They answered by tightening the chains. A bloody seam opened on my breast right above my heart. So rich and sweet blood streams, alive with the salt of life and the spice of power. They suckled the air to suck me dry, to use the salt of my life to yet again chain those who served them.

Blessed Tanit! It hurt.

My soul was being torn from my body, all life and love and courage and strength pouring through the gash.

But I still had a tongue.

I still had breath.

I had a plan.

"My mortal blood I sacrifice. But only my mortal blood. You have no right or claim to my spirit blood, the blood I inherited from my sire. So if you have taken even a drop of my spirit blood, then the contract is broken."

48

The festive cacophony twirled on unceasing as I took in a breath and let it out, as I moistened my bone-dry lips. My legs and arms trembled, but I did not fall.

The throned presences leaned forward as if suckling on a suddenly dry teat. Stretched toward me a little more, as if puzzled. Then probed with talons and knife-bladed teeth. The sharp planes of their human-like visages wrinkled as they sniffed the air, as they tugged on the chains and, in increasing frustration, shook those chains to try to force the blood to flow.

But the chains no longer bound me because there was no possible way to separate my mortal blood from my spirit blood.

"I invoke *rei vindicatio*." My voice rang clear above the hissing whirl of the courts as the chains slithered off my body and wilted like withering vines on the ground. "Without my blood to seal the contract, we reclaim ownership of our own selves."

Insubstantial chains make no sound as they shatter.

What you hear are the defiant shouts as we rise.

My sire laughed with the howl of a man who has had to keep his contempt hidden for far too long. He sprouted eru's wings, unfurling them to their full majesty and making ready to fly. The Wild Hunt scattered with a boisterous roar, fleeing the courts.

"Sire!" I cried, although it was surely hard to hear me in the clamorous storm of its departure. "Sire! How do I get out of here? How do I get home?"

Like the ungrateful, manipulating creature he was, he flew away without a backward glance.

The plaza erupted in a blizzard of chaos. Daggers of ice burned my skin. The dais and its thrones dissolved in a shrieking wail whose punch was like a spear of thwarted greed and rage that drove me to my knees. Agony raked through my chest. But I could not faint. I could not falter.

The courts swelled like vast wings unfurling. Wave upon wave of furious beings pounded against me as storm waves thrash the shore. I drew my sword and frantically parried, deflecting their freezing bite and icy grip. But my strength was ebbing fast.

This was the one part of my plan I had been able to devise no answer for, the reason I feared I might not survive. I had thought to fight my way to the gate and through to the salt mine, where I might hope and pray to find enough water in the desert in order to live and travel a long road back to the ones I loved. But as the wrath of the courts rose like a flood tide around me, I realized I was going to drown before I could ever cut my way to the mortal world.

"Hsss! Hurry!"

A door swung open in the air above me. I shook off the bag of coins and heaved it into the coach, tossed my sword in after, and hooked an arm through the steps. Claws raked through my skirt and petticoats. Teeth fastened on my boot. I kicked until they fell back.

They were only gathering themselves for another, more ferocious assault. But the brief respite was all I needed to pull myself up, roll inside, and slam shut the door.

Gale winds tossed the coach up and down and sideways as it bucketed away from the palace. Where we went I did not know. I clung to my sword. The bag of coins slammed into my belly, winding me. Where the chains had bitten into me to take the first taste of my blood, my chest throbbed like fire. The pain of that wound deafened and blinded me and I just lay there panting in the hope that oblivion would claim me soon. All I could do was tighten my hand around my locket and pray that if I had just been infested with the salt plague, then the disease would consume me quickly and with less agony than this.

"Blessed Tanit," I murmured, "please bring me home."

My blood seeped onto the floor of the coach, moistening and melting into the coach's substance. Blood makes the gate.

I fell through.

The goddess caught me in her arms. She cradled me like a newborn, her brown face smiling down at me. Tears wet her cheeks. A crescent moon shone above her head to light the path for those who must walk into darkness.

"Choose, little cat. For you may have peace now if you wish it."

"I just want to go home."

Home is the people you care for, the ones who care for you in return.

Her kiss woke me back into the world. When I opened my eyes I found myself kneeling in a garden lush with pomegranates and ripe grapes and cascades of purple flowers. Before me rose a stone statue of the goddess wearing her lioness head, she who protects women but also gives them the strength to protect themselves.

The horns of a crescent moon sank into dawn. Pain pooled at my chest. Sticky blood oozed down my body to be swallowed by the damp soil. I blinked. A winter wind rattled through bare branches, for I now found myself huddled not in a summer garden but all alone and abandoned in an empty sanctuary. The air had a bitter, angry bite. Someone had stabbed me in the heart and then eaten out my head. I pitched forward onto my face.

A familiar and beloved voice spoke my name. "Catherine. My sweet Catherine, wake up."

A familiar and beloved hand took hold of mine. "Cat, wake up! What on earth got into her to wander off to Tanit's sanctuary when she ought to have been hiding inside like every other sensible person? I thought I was going to die of anguish when we got back and she was gone!"

"I should like to know what miscreant stabbed her in the chest. She's fortunate it is such a shallow wound."

"Look how her skirts are torn. I can't leave her for a single day without her getting into trouble!"

Warm lips brushed my forehead. "She's feverish. Let's get her home."

I dreamed I was turning into a pillar of salt, grain by grain. I was thirsty all the time, and hot, and uncomfortable, but there was always someone to wipe me down with a damp cool cloth or lift me up to spoon broth down my parched throat. I could not get enough salty

gruel to eat.

Sometimes Rory licked my face with his rough cat's tongue, rumbling softly as he guarded me in his cat shape. Sometimes Bee held my hand and sang to me, off-key, or combed out and rebraided my tangled hair. Sometimes Vai slept beside me in the bed he had built for us—although I had only slept in it once, I recalled its contours with intimate precision.

Obviously I was hallucinating, because I also saw Kayleigh sitting with her mother in attendance on my sickbed, and it was intriguing to watch how animated Vai's mother was with her eldest daughter compared to the stiff formality she offered her only son. For what seemed like hours Vai would sit on the bed gently stroking my hands or hair while talking softly to Kofi about the latest radical pamphlet by Professora Nayo Kuti or the setbacks the radical efforts had met with in the Veneti dukedoms under the hand of their overlord, the Armorican prince, and his pregnant daughter who would act as regent if she bore an infant son.

Kofi's laugh heartened me. "I reckon it is as well we happened to come when we did, for I thought sure I should have to tie yee to a chair lest yee burn down the entire building for the way yee lost yee head. Not that yee can burn things, fire bane! Peradventure yee shall have an easier life of it, Vai, if yee stop and think before yee panic."

"I did not panic!"

"You did," said Bee, for I just then realized she was sitting on the bed at my feet, her pencil scratching across a page.

"No more than you did, Beatrice!"

"Is this how it shall be, yee two always bickering?" demanded Kofi. "Because if it shall be this way, I can go back to a more restful domicile in Expedition and likewise not have to suffer this frightful cold."

"You only think this is cold because you've not yet experienced winter," muttered Vai so peevishly that Kofi laughed again, obviously teasing him, and I realized it was Kofi's willingness to joke with him that had likely won Vai's trust when the two men first met.

Bee broke in. "I think the worst was when we were searching and those men at the coffee shop said they had seen a young woman answering to Cat's description drinking coffee with the horned hunter god Carnonos on the street!"

"People will see anything in shadows when they're frightened," 589 said Vai, "but I admit it gave me a turn. For you know it's exactly the sort of thing she'd have thought she had to do, sacrifice herself to save us."

"It surely is, and it makes me so angry to imagine her even thinking of doing such a thing to us! Never telling us, sneaking off... well, she didn't, so all's well."

All's well, until you become a salter with sightless eyes, trapped inside a deathless crystal body with your own dying thoughts and a craving that will not go away.

I tossed and I turned, for the ground was rumbling and thumping beneath me. As in a restless dream a woman with feathers and shells in her hair entered the room. Her gentle hand traced my navel; her lips touched my forehead with a kiss that snaked through my body to kindle my blood. She spoke: "*She is clean.*"

Clean was all very well, but I needed to be able to talk!

Rory touched a finger to each of my eyes. "Cat, I swear, you talk constantly even in your sleep. It's safe to wake up. I never gave them the letters, so they don't know anything."

I opened my eyes. Rory sat in a chair next to me. I lay on the bed Vai had built for us, and strange it was to do so, for we had not had it with us before. A fabric-covered standing screen blocked my view of the rest of the room, its golden suns and silver moons smiling at me. By the quality of the light I guessed it to be mid-afternoon on a cloudy day. I heard the clatter and ring of utensils and cups as people ate at a nearby table.

"Why am I dreaming that Kofi and Kayleigh are here?" I demanded, although my voice came out as a hoarse whisper. "Have I been delirious?"

He rolled his eyes in an expression copied from Bee at her most aggravating. "That is one word for it. Kofi and Kayleigh and their baby and people arrived on Hallows' Day on a ship from Expedition. The Assembly in Expedition has sent Kofi to be ambassador to Europa, only no one really knew where he ought to go, so they sent him to Godwik and Clutch to get his bearings. Then Bee and Vai returned with the others at sunset on Hallows' Day. You can imagine what happened when they found you missing! It's fortunate we tracked you down as quickly as we did. I admit it was rather dramatic to find you just at sunrise in the goddess's temple. Are you better now?"

Venturesomely I swung my feet out from under the beaver-pelt blanket and set them on the plank floor, which radiated heat, for evidently the hypocaust had been repaired. I wore the nightgown I'd been given at White Bow House, and my chest had a poultice on it, wrapped into place by linen strips. "How long have I been sick?"

"Eight days."

According to report, if a human is bitten by a ghoul, the onset of the disease is so swift and implacable that the victim will become morbid in less than seven days. So the headmaster had read aloud to us the day Bee had argued with Bran Cof in his study.

Eight days! Well! This was encouraging! I stood, and my feet stayed under me. Holding on to Rory's arm, I shuffled to where I could see past the screen and into the room.

The scene of a family dinner just come to its end could not have been more charming even had Bee sketched it. Vai's mother was seated in the chair of honor, looking frail but aglow with happiness as she held the hand of her pregnant daughter, Kayleigh. Bintou and Wasa were fomenting mischief with a lad I was pretty sure was one of Kofi's young cousins, brought with him from Expedition. Old Bakary was seated next to Bee, and to my surprise Beatrice was paging through her sketchbook while the djeli made comments. Over at a lovely new desk Chartji, Caith, Godwik, and the Taino woman I had seen in my delirium bent over a schematic Kofi had unrolled. The *behica* was explaining about good plumbing, drinking water, and cholera.

Vai stood looking at it, too. He held a fat baby with chubby brown cheeks and a chortling laugh. I had just decided that I had to be dreaming when he turned his head and smiled at me, as if he'd known I was standing there. He gave a half-wink as if to say that I ought to notice how handsome he looked with a baby in his arms and didn't I want him to have one of his very own?

With a smile, I mouthed, *Soon but not yet.*

Then everyone else saw me, and their exclamations of delight and concern bent me like a reed under the onslaught of a winter gale. I retreated to the bed and sank down. Vai and Bee hurried in to sit on either side of me.

"Love, how are you?"

"I'm hungry! I could eat a whole side of beef and have room for turnips besides!"

"We were so worried," said Bee, wringing my hands until I grimaced and said, "Ouch!"

Vai brushed strands of hair off my brow. "Why on earth did you go to Tanit's sanctuary on Hallows' Night without telling anyone? We thought you had been taken by the Wild Hunt!"

"I don't remember that part very well," I said truthfully. "But I do remember that you asked me if I had anything I wanted to do. I want to build batey courts in Europa so we can have our own batey leagues and tournaments. Isn't that a good idea? And in a few years we can go to the desert and destroy any of the ghouls that were caught on the other side of the gate. Without blood, no more will ever fall into the mortal world. If the last of them are hunted down, there is a chance the salt plague can be eradicated. Wouldn't that be something?"

Bee pressed the back of a hand to my forehead. "Is she still feverish?"

"No, that's exactly the sort of adventure I would expect her to undertake." Vai flicked a finger along my cheek. "However, there is one thing we've all been waiting for you to explain, Catherine."

Rory had been leaning against the wall, arms crossed. He sighed as might a long-festering boil when it is at last punctured. "You may as well tell the truth, Cat. When you called the coach and four and the eru into this world to help you hunt down and kill James Drake, you had to make a bargain with them that you would allow them to live in your household for as long as they wished." He opened his eyes wide and raised his eyebrows, head jutted forward aggressively, in warning.

Blinking was all I could manage. "Oh."

Vai said, "You can imagine our surprise when we brought you home from Tanit's temple and found the coach, the horses, a heavy bag of gold coins, and the two of them in the stable."

Bee leaned into my shoulder. "In the hay, indulging in a most ardent embrace. I thought it was sweet, although Andevai did not find it as amusing."

"Did you not, my love?" I asked.

"We found them a room," he said. I hadn't known the man could blush like that!

"Do they bide here still?"

"They do," said Vai, "and in truth, it is convenient to have them, for we could not otherwise afford to house a coach, much less stable four horses. I just find it a little odd."

They both stared at me with the expressions of people who suspect the worst but feel you are not quite yet up to being accused of perfidy.

In the end it wasn't just that I could wind shadows about me and sneak around where people didn't want me to go. It was that I understood the importance of misdirection.

"Now that we have a coach and four, you can go to Noviomagus, Bee. We can go as soon as I'm stronger. Perhaps Chartji has some business for us to take care of there as well, so we can combine work and love! I am sure there are radicals to meet with, too, for it seemed to me that the prince and mage House in Noviomagus had not the least interest in listening to the radical cause."

"That would be delightful," cried Bee, blushing.

"Yes, for the first hour, until you fall simpering into Venus's coils and I am left to mope about Noviomagus on my own, although that kindly steward I met at Five Mirrors House might be sympathetic to my sad plight."

Vai frowned. "What manner of reckless mischief you can get up to on your own or together I don't even like to think. Not that it's any of my business, mind you, for I am sure you can do as you please," he added as Bee opened her mouth to expostulate.

"You ought to be cautious, though, Bee," I added thoughtfully. "Maybe you did dream of that fabric before Vai found it, and you just didn't realize it. I know dragon dreamers are barren when they mate with men, but Kemal isn't a man even when he's in man form."

"Cat!" Blushing, she clutched her sketchbook to her breast.

Vai was still vexing himself over my mention of the kindly steward. "I need to negotiate with the mansa of Five Mirrors House regardless on another matter. Viridor can meet me there. He and I have begun a correspondence regarding new pedagogical methods. I'll send a dispatch to alert them. Kofi needs to see something of Europa, and I wish to introduce him around."

So it was that twelve days later, with a light fall of snow dusting the ground, I set off to escort my cousin to meet a dragon with whom she had the intention of becoming romantically involved.

Bee was so charmingly nervous that she kept running back into the house for things she was sure she had forgotten. The coachman stood at the horses' heads, chatting with Kofi. In company the eru had proven to be much more reserved than the relaxed coachman, so she waited by the door with one eye on the sky, as if making sure a blizzard was not about to drop in.

Shivering, I climbed in to warm myself with heated bricks tucked inside my fur cloak. I had just received two letters. One was from Doctor Asante, written in the manner of a close kinswoman desirous of getting to know better a beloved child from whom she had been long separated. I had read it ten times already. The other was a letter from Kehinde via Chartji, explaining that a printer had been jailed by the prince of Colonia and asking if I might lend my skills to a mission to rescue the man before he was executed for sedition. Colonia wasn't far from Noviomagus. I could probably manage it by myself.

"You're looking thoughtful, love. What are you considering doing that I don't want to hear about until it's over?" Vai arranged himself on the seat opposite with care, as if he believed a many days' journey in the coach would not wrinkle his clothing simply because he did not wish it.

I smiled, for Rory and I had, between us and the coachman and eru, covered our tracks. "I can't help but be reminded of the evening you and I met and married all in the space of an hour. Do you know, Vai, you're so awfully handsome I suppose I might have been able to fall in love with you that first evening when you took me away from my aunt and uncle's house, if only you hadn't been so awful in every other way."

He relaxed, stretching out his feet to tangle with mine. "My grandmother warned me it is rash and reckless for a man and woman to join their affections in marriage just for the sake of physical attraction. Marriage is meant to be arranged by the elders so no trouble comes of it. Falling in love with my good looks would have been a terrible mistake. If an understandable one."

"I certainly had no chance to fall in love with your humble demeanor. Since I doubt you have one."

He glanced at me through half-lidded eyes in the coy way he had when he had drawn out just the sort of teasing joke he loved me to make. Rory stuck his head in, gave me a kiss, embraced Vai in a brotherly farewell, and bounded away into the house far too eagerly.

"I was surprised when Rory decided to stay behind," I remarked.

"You see, I did forget it!" cried Bee as she clambered in, plopped down next to me, and set a basket on my lap. "Sweet yam pastries, crescent rolls, rice and peas that Kayleigh made for Kofi, and a jar of Serena's yam pudding. Rory has made me a bet that he will seduce her before we return."

"Good fortune with that," Vai said. "Serena is not interested in dalliance."

"How would you know?" I demanded.

He flashed a smile, silently laughing at me. "She's angling for a prestigious marriage with a very promising magister from Five Mirrors House. There are two powerful candidates to be heir, and the mansa there wants to move one out of the way so there is no trouble."

Bee batted her eyelashes as her most dangerously honeyed smile lit her face. "If that is the case, don't you worry about bringing such a powerful magister into Four Moons House?"

He looked at her blankly. "No. Why would I?"

Kofi stuck his head in. "I shall ride up front to see the countryside. Fair wild, I call this!"

"I want to hold on in back with the eru," I said.

"No!" Bee and Vai spoke at the same time, as Kofi shut the door.

"You are so recently recovered, dearest," said Bee. "It really is outside of enough that you are making such a long journey so soon."

"It was your idea!"

"It was your idea!" retorted Bee primly. "I only agreed because it is time *I* got to have an adventure!"

"Because giving radical speeches and slamming down rude hecklers as soldiers march to arrest you is not an adventure? Wrestling an overloaded rowboat for hundreds of miles down the Rhenus River with only a lazy cat for company is not an adventure? Sleeping with the most famously handsome radical in Europa—"

"What?" said Vai. "Bee and Brennan Du...what?"

"—is not an adventure? Not to mention the part where you marry 595 a prince of the Taino, or are asked to run for a seat on the first elected council in Europa."

Bee sighed happily, paging through her sketchbook with the dreamy blush of an addled schoolgirl. "Yes! Who knows what will happen next?"

The latch's sliver eyes and wire mouth glittered as its sour little voice woke. "I won't know. No one tells me anything."

In the sudden hush that throttled the ones I loved best in all the world, the coachman snapped his whip and cried, "Ha-roo! Ha-roo!" The eru leaped onto the back of the coach, and we rolled out onto the street, wheels rumbling on stone.

Bee put her nose down by the latch, which matched her glare for glare.

In a low voice Vai said, "I thought you were just making that up to entertain us, like you do."

"What do I ever make up, I should like to ask? Andevai! You do believe I punched a shark, don't you?"

"Yes, love, I believe you punched a shark just like I believe you drank coffee with the Master of the Wild Hunt on the streets of Havery on Hallows' Night."

Bee sat up. Her eye turned on me as her expression bloomed into the full flower of indignant suspicion. "But she did punch a shark. James Drake was on the beach and saw it happen. He told the general and me all about it."

They looked at each other, sharing an unspoken thought, and then they looked at me.

In the depths of the ice, wreathed in ice, sleeps the Wild Hunt, and when it wakes, all tremble in fear. In the depths of the black abyss there drifts in a watery stupor the leviathan whose lashing tail can smash ships into splinters and drive the sundered hulks under the waves. In the depths of the smoke lies coiled in slumber the Mother of All Dragons. If she stirs, waking, the world changes. So we are told.

But none of that seemed at all frightening compared with the prospect of Bee and Andevai united in exasperation and anger, against me.

Me!

I thought about how many days it was going to take us to reach

Noviomagus and how many hours of that time they were going to spend scolding and haranguing me as only they could.

"Everyone knows all the good parts except me," groused the latch. "For instance, where are we now and where are we going? Why? How did we get here?"

There is more than one way to skin a cat. Or at least, if you're the cat, to stay unskinned by rebuking tongues and accusing eyes for just a little longer.

"Fortunately, it's a very expansive story and one I can tell you if you don't mind hearing every piece of it all. At length."

"Catherine, I believe you owe us some manner of explanation!"

"Cat, what have you been hiding from us? *What did you do?*"

"I don't mind, no matter how long it takes!" said the latch, with the nearest thing to a real smile I had ever seen on its dour face. "Do you have any of that coffee stuff? That was very tasty."

"We can get coffee along the way like we did before. Let me see. There's a great deal you don't know, so it's best if I start at the beginning."

First I peeked into the basket to see that there was indeed a jar of Serena's most excellent yam pudding tucked to one side. Then I settled myself more comfortably on the seat and smiled at my beloved if fulminating cousin and my handsome if reproachful husband. Finally I winked at the latch that had just saved me.

The latch winked shyly back, like a child caught out on its first budding infatuation.

Never let it be said I could not talk my way out of any trouble that I could not punch.

"The history of the world begins in ice, and it will end in ice."

extras

orbit

meet the author

April Quintanilla

KATE ELLIOTT has been writing stories since she was nine years old, which has led her to believe either that she is a little crazy or that writing, like breathing, keeps her alive. Her previous series are the Crossroads Trilogy (starting with *Spirit Gate*), The Crown of Stars septology (starting with *King's Dragon*), the Novels of the Jaran, and a collaboration with Melanie Rawn and Jennifer Roberson called *The Golden Key*. She likes to play sports more than she likes to watch them; right now, her sport of choice is outrigger canoe paddling. She has been married for a really long time. She and her spouse have three children, as well as a miniature schnauzer (aka the Schnazghul). Her spouse has a much more interesting job than she does, with the added benefit that they had to move to Hawaii for his work. Thus the outrigger canoes.

Find out more about the author at www.kateelliott.com. You can also find extras there, including short fiction set in the Spiritwalker universe.

introducing

If you enjoyed
COLD STEEL,
look out for

THE IRON WYRM AFFAIR
A Bannon and Clare Novel
by Lilith Saintcrow

*Emma Bannon, forensic sorceress in the service of the Empire,
has a mission: to protect Archibald Clare, a failed, unregistered
mentath. His skills of deduction are legendary, and her own
sorcery is not inconsiderable. It doesn't help much that they
barely tolerate each other, or that Bannon's Shield, Mikal,
might just be a traitor himself. Or that the conspiracy killing
registered mentaths and sorcerers alike will just as likely kill
them as seduce them into treachery toward their Queen.*

*In an alternate London where illogical magic has turned
the industrial revolution on its head, Bannon and Clare now
face hostility, treason, cannon fire, black sorcery, and
the problem of reliably finding hansom cabs.*

The game is afoot.

Emma Bannon, Sorceress Prime and servant to Britannia's current incarnation, mentally ran through every foul word that would never cross the lips of a lady. She timed them to the clockhorse's steady jogtrot, and her awareness dilated. The simmering cauldron of the streets was just as it always was; there was no breath of ill intent.

Of course, there had not been earlier, either, when she had been a quarter-hour too late to save the *other* unregistered mentath. It was only one of the many things about this situation seemingly designed to try her often considerable patience.

Mikal would be taking the rooftop road, running while she sat at ease in a hired carriage. It was the knowledge that while he did so he could forget some things that eased her conscience, though not completely.

Still, he was a Shield. He would not consent to share a carriage with her unless he was certain of her safety. And there was not room enough to manoeuvre in a two-person conveyance, should he require it.

She was heartily sick of hired carts. Her own carriages were *far* more comfortable, but this matter required discretion. Having it shouted to the heavens that she was alert to the pattern under these occurrences might not precisely frighten her opponents, but it would become more difficult to attack them from an unexpected quarter. Which was, she had to admit, her preferred method.

Even a Prime can benefit from guile, Llew had often remarked. And of course, she would think of him. She seemed constitutionally incapable of leaving well enough alone, and *that* irritated her as well.

Beside her, Clare dozed. He was a very thin man, with a long, mournful face; his gloves were darned but his waistcoat was of fine cloth, though it had seen better days. His eyes were blue, and they glittered feverishly under half-closed lids. An unregistered mentath would find it difficult to secure proper employment, and by the looks of his quarters, Clare had been suffering from boredom for several weeks, desperately seeking a series of experiments to exercise his active brain.

Mentath was like sorcerous talent. If not trained, and *used*, it turned on its bearer.

At least he had found time to shave, and he had brought two bags. One, no doubt, held linens. God alone knew what was in the second. Perhaps she should apply deduction to the problem, as if she did not have several others crowding her attention at the moment.

Chief among said problems were the murderers, who had so far eluded her efforts. Queen Victrix was young, and just recently freed from the confines of her domineering mother's sway. Her new Consort, Alberich, was a moderating influence—but he did not have enough power at Court just yet to be an effective shield for Britannia's incarnation.

The ruling spirit was old, and wise, but Her vessels...well, they were not indestructible.

And that, Emma told herself sternly, *is as far as we shall go with such a train of thought*. She found herself rubbing the sardonyx on her left middle finger, polishing it with her opposite thumb. Even through her thin gloves, the stone prickled hotly. Her posture did not change, but her awareness contracted. She felt for the source of the disturbance, flashing through and discarding a number of fine invisible threads.

Blast and bother. Other words, less polite, rose as well. Her pulse and respiration did not change, but she tasted a faint tang of adrenaline before sorcerous training clamped tight on such functions to free her from some of flesh's more...distracting...reactions.

"I say, whatever is the matter?" Archibald Clare's blue eyes were wide open now, and he looked interested. Almost, dare she think it, intrigued. It did nothing for his long, almost ugly features. His cloth was serviceable, though hardly elegant—one could infer that a mentath had other priorities than fashion, even if he had an eye for quality and the means to purchase such. But at least he was cleaner than he had been, and had arrived in the hansom in nine and a half minutes precisely. Now they were on Sarpesson Street, threading through amusement-seekers and those whom a little rain would not deter from their nightly appointments.

The disturbance peaked, and a not-quite-seen starburst of gunpowder igniting flashed through the ordered lattices of her consciousness.

The clockhorse screamed as his reins were jerked, and the hansom yawed alarmingly. Archibald Clare's hand dashed for the door handle, but Emma was already moving. Her arms closed around the tall, fragile man, and she shouted a Word that exploded the cab away from them both. Shards and splinters, driven outwards, peppered the street surface. The glass of the cab's tiny windows broke with a high, sweet tinkle, grinding into crystalline dust.

Shouts. Screams. Pounding footsteps. Emma struggled upright, shaking her skirts with numb hands. The horse had gone avast, rearing and plunging, throwing tiny metal slivers and dribs of oil as well as stray crackling sparks of sorcery, but the traces were tangled and it stood little chance of running loose. The driver was gone, and she snapped a quick glance at the overhanging rooftops before the unhealthy canine shapes resolved out of thinning rain, slinking low as gaslamp gleam painted their slick, heaving sides.

Sootdogs. Oh, how unpleasant. The one that had leapt on the hansom's roof had most likely taken the driver, and Emma cursed aloud now as it landed with a thump, its shining hide running with vapour.

"*Most* unusual!" Archibald Clare yelled. He had gained his feet as well, and his eyes were alight now. The mournfulness had vanished. He had also produced a queerly barrelled pistol, which would be of *no* use against the dog-shaped sorcerous things now gathering. "*Quite* diverting!"

The star sapphire on her right third finger warmed. A globe-shield shimmered into being, and to the roil of smouldering wood, gunpowder and fear was added another scent: the smoke-gloss of sorcery. One of the sootdogs leapt, crashing into the shield, and the shock sent Emma to her knees, holding grimly. Both her hands were outstretched now, and her tongue occupied in chanting.

Sarpesson Street was neither deserted nor crowded at this late hour. The people gathering to watch the outcome of a hansom crash pushed against those onlookers alert enough to note that something entirely different was occurring, and the resultant chaos was merely noise to be shunted aside as her concentration narrowed.

Where is Mikal?

She had no time to wonder further. The sootdogs hunched and wove closer, snarling. Their packed-cinder sides heaved and black tongues lolled between obsidian-chip teeth; they could strip a large adult male to bone in under a minute. There were the onlookers to think of as well, and Clare behind and to her right, laughing as he sighted down the odd little pistol's chunky nose. Only he was not pointing it at the dogs, thank God. He was aiming for the rooftop.

You idiot. The chant filled her mouth. She could spare no words to tell him not to fire, that Mikal was—

The lead dog crashed against the shield. Emma's body jerked

as the impact tore through her, but she held steady, the sapphire now a ringing blue flame. Her voice rose, a clear contralto, and she assayed the difficult rill of notes that would split her focus and make another Major Work possible.

That was part of what made a Prime—the ability to concentrate completely on multiple channellings of ætheric force. One's capacity could not be infinite, just like the charge of force carried and renewed every Tideturn.

But one did not need infinite capacity. *One needs only slightly more capacity than the problem at hand calls for*, as her third-form Sophological Studies professor had often intoned.

Mikal arrived.

His dark green coat fluttered as he landed in the midst of the dogs, a Shield's fury glimmering to Sight, bright spatters and spangles invisible to normal vision. The sorcery-made things cringed, snapping; his blades tore through their insubstantial hides. The charmsilver laid along the knives' flats, as well as the will to strike, would be of far more use than Mr Clare's pistol.

Which spoke, behind her, the ball tearing through the shield from a direction the protection wasn't meant to hold. The fabric of the shield collapsed, and Emma had just enough time to deflect the backlash, tearing a hole in the brick-faced fabric of the street and exploding the clockhorse into gobbets of metal and rags of flesh, before one of the dogs turned with stomach-churning speed and launched itself at her—and the man she had been charged to protect.

She shrieked another Word through the chant's descant, her hand snapping out again, fingers contorted in a gesture definitely *not* acceptable in polite company. The ray of ætheric force smashed through brick dust, destroying even more of the road's surface, and crunched into the sootdog.

Emma bolted to her feet, snapping her hand back, and the

line of force followed as the dog crumpled, whining and shattering into fragments. She could not hold the forcewhip for very long, but if more of the dogs came—

The last one died under Mikal's flashing knives. He muttered something in his native tongue, whirled on his heel, and stalked toward his Prima. That normally meant the battle was finished.

Yet Emma's mind was not eased. She half turned, chant dying on her lips and her gaze roving, searching. Heard the mutter of the crowd, dangerously frightened. Sorcerous force pulsed and bled from her fingers, a fountain of crimson sparks popping against the rainy air. For a moment the mood of the crowd threatened to distract her, but she closed it away and concentrated, seeking the source of the disturbance.

Sorcerous traces glowed, faint and fading, as the man who had fired the initial shot—most likely to mark them for the dogs—fled. He had some sort of defence laid on him, meant to keep him from a sorcerer's notice.

Perhaps from a sorcerer, but not from a Prime. Not from me, oh no. The dead see all. Her Discipline was of the Black, and it was moments like these when she would be glad of its practicality—if she could spare the attention.

Time spun outwards, dilating, as she followed him over rooftops and down into a stinking alley, refuse piled high on each side, running with the taste of fear and blood in his mouth. Something had injured him.

Mikal? But then why did he not kill the man—

The world jolted underneath her, a stunning blow to her shoulder, a great spiked roil of pain through her chest. Mikal screamed, but she was breathless. Sorcerous force spilled free, uncontained, and other screams rose.

She could possibly injure someone.

Emma came back to herself, clutching at her shoulder. Hot blood welled between her fingers, and the green silk would be ruined. Not to mention her gloves.

At least they had shot her, and not the mentath.

Oh, damn. The pain crested again, became a giant animal with its teeth in her flesh.

Mikal caught her. His mouth moved soundlessly, and Emma sought with desperate fury to contain the force thundering through her. Backlash could cause yet more damage, to the street and to onlookers, if she let it loose.

A Prime's uncontrolled force was nothing to be trifled with.

It was the traditional function of a Shield to handle such overflow, but if he had only wounded the fellow on the roof she could not trust that he was not part of—

"*Let it GO!*" Mikal roared, and the ætheric bonds between them flamed into painful life. She fought it, seeking to contain what she could, and her skull exploded with pain.

She knew no more.